THE YEAR'S BEST SCIENCE FICTION & FANTASY

2014 EDITION

OTHER BOOKS BY

RICH HORTON

Fantasy: The Best of the Year, 2006 Edition

Fantasy: The Best of the Year, 2007 Edition

Fantasy: The Best of the Year, 2008 Edition

Robots: The Recent A.I. (with Sean Wallace)

Science Fiction: The Best of the Year, 2006 Edition

Science Fiction: The Best of the Year, 2007 Edition

Science Fiction: The Best of the Year, 2008 Edition

Space Opera

Unplugged: The Web's Best Sci-Fi & Fantasy: 2008 Download

The Year's Best Science Fiction & Fantasy, 2009 Edition

The Year's Best Science Fiction & Fantasy, 2010 Edition

The Year's Best Science Fiction & Fantasy, 2011 Edition

The Year's Best Science Fiction & Fantasy, 2012 Edition

The Year's Best Science Fiction & Fantasy, 2013 Edition

War & Space: Recent Combat (with Sean Wallace)

THE YEAR'S BEST SCIENCE FICTION & FANTASY

2014 EDITION

EDITED BY
RICH HORTON

PRIME BOOKS

THE YEAR'S BEST SCIENCE FICTION & FANTASY, 2014 EDITION

Prime Books
www.prime-books.com

ISBN: 978-1-60701-428-7

For Mary Ann, again . . .

CONTENTS

CONTENTS

THE YEAR IN FANTASY AND SCIENCE FICTION, 2014

RICH HORTON

Non-Anglo Science Fiction

One of the more obvious recent trends in the field is an increasing embrace of sf from non-traditional sources, which is basically to say from non-English speaking countries. (Though we should remember a few countries with significant English speaking populations who are contributing as well, such as India and the Philippines.) This isn't to say that sf from such places is a new thing—one of the first widely popular writers of what we'd call sf was Jules Verne, a Frenchman. The Soviet Union had a long tradition of fine sf (Arkady and Boris Strugatsky being perhaps the most famous practitioners), and one of the greatest SF writers of the 60s and 70s was the Pole Stanislaw Lem.

Attempts to bring short sf to the US market included Frederik Pohl's short-lived 1960s magazine *International SF*, Donald Wollheim's 1976 anthology *The Best From the Rest of the World*, and *The Penguin Book of World Science Fiction* (1986), edited by Sam Lundwall and Brian W. Aldiss. None of these really seemed to gain much traction. Foreign sf was hampered partly by the difficulty of arranging good translations, and partly by a sense that much of it was a bit behind the times relative to that from the US/UK/Canada/Australia sphere. I'm not sure how much of that was reality, how much an artifact of selection, and how much simply wrong.

It seems almost a truism to say that a form of literature devoted to "alien" worlds—often obsessed with creating different cultures—would benefit from points of view off the Anglophone axis. But it has taken, it seems to me, until very recent years for this to be much acted upon. By now, though, many people are well aware that, for example, China has a huge sf market. Anthologies like Ivor Hartmann's *AfroSF* (2012) have introduced us to writers from Africa. From the Philippines, the series *Philippine Speculative Fiction* now runs to eight volumes of original stories (edited by a rotating group of folks including

Dean Francis Alfar, Nikki Alfar, Vincent Michael Simbulan, Kate Osias and Alex Osias). Lavie Tidhar's two *Apex Book of World SF* anthologies showcase stories from all over the world. All of these books features fresh, original, exciting sf and fantasy, and all *en passant* highlight the benefits of reading sf from potentially unfamiliar cultures. And I have only scratched the surface.

So it was with some delight, as this book came together, that I noticed that a lot of the stories I wanted to include were by non-American, non-British, etc. writers. Only two of the stories were originally published in other languages: Argentine writer Angélica Gorodischer's "Trafalgar and Josefina" (translated by Amalia Gladhart) and Chinese writer Tang Fei's "Call Girl" (translated by Ken Liu). But a number of other writers, who work at least part of the time in English, hail from non-Anglophone countries: Sweden's Karin Tidbeck, Thailand's Benjanun Sriduangkaew, and Japan's Yukimi Ogawa. (And last year's volume included two stories by one of the most popular newer writers, Aliette de Bodard, who was born in the US, grew up and still lives in France, and who is of Franco-Vietnamese extraction.) For that matter Theodora Goss, though she has been in the US for a long time, grew up in Hungary; and Lavie Tidhar, currently resident in the UK, grew up in Israel. (Mentioning Tidhar prompts me to cite both he and Ken Liu—also in this volume with a story of his own—for their yeoman work in bringing translated sf to the attention of English-language readers, including doing a lot of the translation themselves.)

What other trends can I find herein? Once again there are a number of stories in some way combining sf and fantasy tropes, some of which seem clearly enough to me sf (as with Benjanun Sriduangkaew's very refreshingly strange piece), and others clearly enough fantasy (as with Eleanor Arnason's characteristically matter of fact "Kormak the Lucky"). Perhaps even more evident is an increased delight in the simply strange—Sriduangkaew's entire oeuvre to date revels in weirdness, and here in different ways the stories by Jedediah Berry, Alan DeNiro, Tang Fei, Naim Kabir, and Krista Hoeppner Leahy, are among their other virtues simply odd. To say nothing of Angélica Gorodischer's story, first published in Argentina in the 70s, part of a linked collection of similarly unusual stories that mix sf, fantasy, and the realistic (and indirectly political) quite without caring, and always very witty even when telling very dark stories.

As to news from the rest of the field, I have little to add. There didn't seem to be any seismic changes in short fiction publishing—no major magazines perishing, for example. I will say that Trevor Quachri's first year at the helm of *Analog* seemed very promising. *Asimov's*, *F&SF*, and *Interzone* among the print magazines all had what I would call their standard year. *Lightspeed* (for which I must disclose I act as reprint editor), *Clarkesworld*, *Beneath Ceaseless Skies*, and *Strange Horizons*—to me arguably the top four online magazines—

also continued much as before. *Apex*, another fine online magazine, changed editors again: Lynne M. Thomas stepped down after two excellent years, to be succeeded by Sigrid Ellis.

On the anthology front there were excellent outings from reliable editors Ellen Datlow, Gardner Dozois (with George R.R. Martin), Jonathan Strahan and John Joseph Adams, and some good books from less familiar names—Lynne Thomas again (with Michael Damian Thomas and John Klima), Paula Guran, and also Mike Allen, whose fine anthology series *Clockwork Phoenix* returned for a fourth volume. I was also very pleased to see another magazine-like book from the MIT Technology Review, *Twelve Tomorrows*, edited by Stephen Cass, presenting twelve intriguing near-future SF stories, including "Firebrand" in this book.

On the novel front, the best I read from 2013 was Christopher Priest's *The Adjacent*, a fascinating story of multiple people in different times, different timelines, even a different world, all somehow "adjacent," I suppose, to their analogs elsewhere. Other than that (keeping in mind that I didn't read nearly as many novels as deserved to be read) I was happiest with three first novels. Ann Leckie's *Ancillary Justice* is intelligent sf set in a future interstellar empire, and deals with war, AI, and gender issues—and even zombies! (sort of)—very well. Sofia Samatar's *A Stranger in Olondria* is a lovely lyrical story of an islander in love with books visiting the mainland, and getting unwittingly involved with political turmoil. (Both Leckie and Samatar have had stories in this series of anthologies.) And Chris Willrich's *The Scroll of Years* is satisfying sword and sorcery about his ongoing characters, the lovers Persimmon Gaunt and Imago Bone, here in a sort of China-analog.

There were also excellent movies (most notably **Her** and **Gravity**); and of course **A Game of Thrones** continues to make waves on television. But for me the center of the field remains short fiction—and here are nearly three dozen of the best examples for your perusal.

SOULCATCHER

JAMES PATRICK KELLY

After years of planning and scheming, of deals honest and not, of sleepless nights of rage and cool days of calculation, Klary's moment arrives when xeni-Harvel Asher, the ambassador from the Four Worlds, enters her gallery.

As a concession to local xenophobia, the xeni is embodied as a human male. Of course, he is beautiful. Some liken the xeni to the faeries of Earth legend, their charisma so intoxicating that, at the merest nod, a groom will walk away from his new bride, a mother will abandon her infant. Is it telepathy? Pheromones? The lure of great wealth and power? No matter. Klary has steeled herself against the xeni's insidious power. Ever since the Ambassador made planetfall, Klary has been on a regimen of emotion suppressants. Not that she really needs them. After xeni-Harvel Asher ruined her life, Klary has had just one emotion. No chemistry can defeat it.

Her hopeless assistant Elloran makes a fool of himself groveling before the xeni. Klary slips behind a display case protecting a cascading sculpture of lace and leather and spun sugar. She is content for now to study her prey. The xeni is slight, almost childlike, but he commands the room with eyes as big as Klary's fists, a smile brimming with wide teeth. Slender hands emerge from the drooping sleeves of his midnight jacket. His fingers are delicate enough to pluck the strings of a harp—or a woman's heart.

"Here at Hamashy's Fine Textiles we have the best collection . . . " Elloran is talking too fast.

"Yes, this one is sure you do." Asher cuts him off. "This one would speak with the owner now?"

Which means it's time. But when Klary steps from her hiding place, she sees that her plan is going hideously awry. Dear, beloved, lost Janary, clone sister of her sibling batch, has followed her abductor into her gallery.

Even though it has been fourteen years since they last saw each other, even though she has lost her name, her face, and her innocence, Janary knows her as her sister. How could she not? Her frightened stare pricks Klary's shriveled heart. All is lost. Yes, a reunion was part of her plan, but that was for later. After this was over. Will she give Klary up? Can Janary even guess what her sister plans to do? But there is no turning back.

"Ambassador." Klary steps forward and bows. "You honor me. I am Klary Hamashy." Despite the suppressants, she braces herself against the xeni's fierce regard. It's like leaning into a headwind. "Welcome, sir."

Xeni-Harvel Asher inclines his head. "This one has heard tell of the local rug merchant, Friend Klary." She is not sure whether he intends this as a slight. Hamashy Gallery sells native and off-world carpets, yes, but it's no rug shop. Klary is too busy trying not to goggle at Janary to take offense. She has not changed since the xeni lured her away from their ancestral commune. Bitter years have aged Klary and she has taken steps to smudge her appearance, but Janary is still as striking as Klary once was. She has the rust-brown curls framing pale features of their genetic line. She wears a high-necked white gown, perhaps to satisfy some ancient bridal fetish. Her sister shows no signs of anger or sadness as she shies behind the Ambassador, as if she is afraid of Klary. Has she accepted her humiliation? Embraced it? Unthinkable. Klary tries to imagine herself in Janary's place as her sister catches up the decorative glass chain that dangles from the choker around her neck.

"What?" Asher notices her. "She won't hurt you."

Without a word, Janary presses the end of her chain into his hand.

"One never knows what bothers the pet." Xeni-Harvel Asher does not apologize. "It's been skittish today."

Klary wants to yank the chain away, crush it in her bare hand until shards of broken glass bite her. "Not to worry," she says. She addresses the xeni, not her sister. "She is safe in this place."

"A pleasant enough shop." He gestures at the racks and display cases, the hangings and the shelves that line the walls. "Might one find a present for a good friend here? A unique present, perhaps?"

Klary's smile is tight. She knows why the xeni is here. Klary has paid an outrageous price to bait the trap, has discreetly encouraged the rumors about her illegal acquisition. But she must not rush; there is a scene to play before the final act. "Let me show you my treasures." She tries to gesture for Elloran to peel Janary away, but her assistant is useless. Tomorrow Klary will fire him—if there is a tomorrow.

The xeni is not impressed with the life-sized nylon nudes wrapped around moveable skeletons nor does he appreciate the remarkable properties of nylon. "It's semi-translucent," says Klary, "so several layers of differently colored nylon produce the subtle skin tones. See how the artist's needle modeling suggests wrinkles about the eyes?" Nor does he care for bowls made of taut coiled snuro or the hanging of cloth beads arrayed on glow-wires. He passes Tuktuk's mixed-media tensioned fabric sculptures without comment. Klary stubbornly describes a French tapestry from the twenty-second century. "Notice the classic border filled with floral bouquets and architectural scrollwork, around very fine floating landscape scenes from old Earth. Depictions of Oriental life with courtiers seated on motorcycles, and see here, plants, birds, zombies . . . " But Asher has already moved on, past an area carpet in the Tabriz style by master weaver Kumanen and the chain mail business suits; Klary hurries to catch up.

He flips through Fovian rugs hanging on a telescoping display like they were pages of a book he's deciding not to read. "One wants something special for a special friend," he says. Then he leans close—too close—and for a second his huge black eyes erase all Klary's worries about her ruined plans. In that instant of domination, Klary feels something for her sister that she has never felt.

Envy.

"There *is* more." She twitches free of the xeni, gathers herself. "Work not yet priced. Items I had not intended to sell."

"Keep the best for yourself. A strategy to live by." He chuckles. "Still, one might be interested to see, if not to buy."

"Of course, Ambassador. Although it might be best if your companion stayed with Elloran." She raises her voice to rouse the bedazzled Elloran. "There may still be a way to salvage the plan, but Janary must not see what is to come."

"No." Janary is trembling.

The xeni glances over his shoulder, as if he has forgotten that she is following them. "You've provoked the pet to speech, Friend Klary." He gives her chain a tug and she doubles over, eyes downcast. "It's not often so bold in public."

"Want . . . " Her voice grates from disuse. " . . . to come." She raises her eyes just enough to meet Klary's horrified gaze.

"One is at a loss to explain this behavior."

Worried lest the xeni punish her, Klary babbles. "It's fine. Not a problem, I just thought she . . . *it* would be more comfortable out here. I live here, you see, and my rooms are rather cluttered just now." She gestures for them to follow and, when the xeni hesitates, she almost makes the mistake of putting a hand on the ambassador's shoulder to steer him toward the rear of the gallery. "Please," she says. "It would be my pleasure. Elloran, you can close up and go home." The fewer witnesses the better. "*Elloran.*"

"Most accommodating, Friend Klary." Asher lets Janary's chain go slack and then gives it a tinkling shake to get her moving. "Be assured that the pet will be on a short leash."

Klary has four rooms at the back of the gallery: bedroom, bath, galley kitchen and the office where she eats and connects. The office is half again as big as all the other rooms combined. Klary had planned for this visit and has removed all traces of her sister clones, their long-dead first, and the world she lost when the family chose her to retrieve Janary. She has replaced mementos of that former life with pix of men she has never met. Clothes they might have worn hang in her closet. There is an artful scatter of presents she might have given or received had she dared intimacy: a vase filled with the latest airflowers, a reproduction ship's clock, a set of magma tiles that serve as trivets, kites and crystal and antique hubcaps. But what draws Asher's attention is the art Klary has kept for herself. The xeni points at a chair and Janary sits. He coils the glass chain on her lap and she stares down at it glumly as if to read her fortune. Then he strides about the room inspecting the needle lace hamaca and Ringwell's blood-stained *War Quilt* and Xary Merry Kari's *Wrapped Dog*. He pauses in front of Kumanen's Tabriz carpet, which hangs beside the bedroom door. "But you have this one hanging in the gallery," he says.

"A reproduction, Ambassador," Klary says. "This is the original. Four hundred years old. Priceless."

Asher waves mention of money aside as if it were a bad smell. He is still not satisfied with Klary's wares. She has taken a certain pride in the taste with which she has built her collection, even if it is only a ruse to conceal her true intentions. The contents of her gallery and this room are all she has to show for the life she has led since Janary left with her xeni, and none of it interests him. She wonders now if any of it really interests her.

"One hears," Asher says, "of a rug."

Klary can feel the swirl of events turning him to her purpose. "I have many rugs."

"Time passes, Friend Klary. One does not gladly waste it." His voice changes and abruptly they are no longer speaking. Instead he is commanding. "A living rug. A soulcatcher."

Klary gasps as she experiences the full force of the xeni's charisma. Can ecstasy hurt? She knows the answer. "That's supposed to be a secret."

"Not secret enough, Friend Klary. *Show.*"

Klary staggers to the edge of the carpet in the middle of the office, feigning submission. Decorated with a motif of leaves and flowers on a field of blue, it is a nineteenth-century reproduction of a seventeenth-century original that was mentioned in Pope's *Survey of Persian Art*. She sinks to her knees, slips fingers underneath and rolls it up to reveal a containment sunk into the floor, three meters by five and half a meter deep. A sheet of x-glass, level with the floor, protects the contents.

The xeni purrs. "So it's real."

"As you see, Ambassador."

Klary's soulcatcher has no provenance, other than horror stories told to scare children. Created by the Moccen Collective as an instrument of punishment, it is not strictly speaking textile, although it began as a matlike colony of carnivorous plants. Genetically modified to assimilate those who refused collectivization, the rugs were the Moccan's tool to control dissidents. Since the Collective was enlightened enough to ban capital punishment, those sentenced to incarceration in a soulcatcher were functionally immortal, as long as the colony survived. The Moccen Collective had collapsed some two hundred years ago, and Klary's soulcatcher seems as healthy as the day it captured the first dissenter.

"A closer look, Ambassador?"

Klary points at the controller and, when the glass retracts, she presses both hands against the rug's translucent skin. As always, the surface yields to her touch, warm and silky-smooth. Beneath, the heads seem to float in a clear yellow broth of amniotic fluid. Cheeks bump against her palms and sink away, filmy, calm eyes peer through her fingers, lips part, revealing dark, inert tongues. Tangles of veins and arteries, bruise-blue and red, squiggle as blood surges; hairy bundles of ganglia connect the minds of the colony of the damned.

Klary has always found the pulse of the soulcatcher hypnotic. She has spent hours at its side, hoping for some sign from those within, listening not with her ears but with her fingertips. There have been nights when she has walked across it barefoot and one when, in despair at her wasted life, she lay naked on it and contemplated slicing the skin and submitting to capture. She believes that the captured know what has become of them, that they are restless but not in pain. Suddenly she is startled out of her dream of communion with the heads. Asher kneels next her and caresses the soulcatcher's skin with his perfect fingers.

"Alive?" croaks Janary. Without asking permission, she too has approached the open containment.

"Yes," murmurs the xeni. "But are they conscious?"

"There is no way to know." Klary sits back. "The stories say they are."

"They are singing." The xeni muses dreamily. "Do you hear that?"

Seeing that the xeni is transfixed, Klary dares a glance at Janary. Klary presses a forefinger to her lips and then nods at her sister's kneeling abductor.

"*No*," Janary says.

Misunderstanding, the xeni glares at her and she wilts back into her chair. "One feels for their plight. Name your price."

"It's not for sale."

It takes a moment for the xeni's mouth to work itself into a smile. "Not?"

"I mean, you don't understand. This is a registered historical artifact. It's against the laws of our world to sell anything on the list."

"Then how did it come into your possession?"

"A gift, Ambassador, from a dear friend." A dear friend, whom Klary had blackmailed. A parting gift that poor Terez had given as she and her husbands fled their creditors.

"Then this one must hope for your friendship, Klary."

Klary realizes too late how close she is to the xeni. She tries to scoot away. The xeni rests his hand on Klary's shoulder. "Perhaps an exchange of gifts?"

"Ambassador . . . " The hand unlocks years of grief and anger, Klary's blistering need for revenge. At the same time, she is so swollen with the xeni's desire for the soulcatcher that her brain feels as if it's pressing against the inside of her skull. What she wants and what xeni-Harvel Asher wants are so nearly the same—she must acknowledge their mutual desire. The xeni must have the rug, that is the plan, and Klary must have her sister. But the plan is broken, useless, there is no plan, and Asher is so powerful and she must say something or her head will crack, she must, she *must*.

"Would I . . . I would . . . exchange." How can she talk while a fist of blood is punching her chest, clutching at her throat? "I feel as if . . . " She can't stop herself. "Need help replacing Elloran . . . useless Elloran." She gestures wildly at the gallery. "Help." Now it is all she can do to point at Janary. "*Her.*"

She hears her sister's strangled cry of anguish and then the xeni is across the room. Xeni-Harvel Asher thrusts a hand to Janary's face, palm over her mouth, fingers splayed. "Nothing," he says. "You are nothing." She shakes beneath his grip. "Say nothing."

Klary reclaims her anger and flicks her forefinger to deploy the blade. She slices into the skin of the soulcatcher.

"You want the pet?" says the xeni, who is still attempting to subdue Janary. His back is to Klary and the soulcatcher. "But humans can't own humans."

"No, of course." Klary's nose fills with the sweet, yeasty smell of the amniotic fluid. "Why did I say that?" As if the xeni didn't know. "But I did, didn't I?" She doesn't know what she's doing, only that she must do something. She babbles again. "It's true that Elloran is not the best. Not to own it . . . her. No, but I could train her, perhaps. As an apprentice?"

"She's yours." Asher finally lets Janary go. He stoops until their faces are at the same level. "Nothing," he whispers to her. Klary realizes this is his name for her. "As you worship and serve this one, Asher of Harvel, you will now serve that one, Klary Hamashy." He breathes into her gaping, agonized mouth. "Your new friend." Then he laughs.

Klary shakes her head to clear it. Janary is free. Wasn't that the most important part of the plan? She can stop now. But the price of all those years of suffering must be accounted for. Not only Janary's, but hers. Their two wasted lives. She looks past the xeni at her sister, who meets her gaze with brutal reproach. She knows Janary then, knows that she is about to warn Asher, who has taken everything from them. The plan, you stupid bitch. The *plan*.

She hurls herself across the room, throws an arm around the shocked xeni's neck and drags him back, kicking and gasping for air. Maybe he has something to say, a last plea for mercy, desperate words of command, but he is small and Klary's anger is large.

"Klary, stop!" Janary screams, but of course, she is nothing.

She thrusts Asher's head through the skin of the soulcatcher into its roiling interior. Just then Klary hears the captured. They *are* singing. To her? The song is deafening as she feels the stings of many lashes. They want her too but she releases her hold and falls backwards. Her dripping arm is covered in purple welts. The soulcatcher appears to be swallowing the xeni whole, despite churning legs and flailing arms, but then it spits the headless body out. It slumps away, blood gushing over the rolled up carpet. Ruined.

She remembers the man who sold her that carpet. His name was Lann and they were lovers for almost a week before Klary felt herself becoming attached. Lann had the oddest collection of combs: silver and bone and glass and gold. She had never met anyone before who collected combs. She wonders what became of him. Of her life.

Then she realizes that she is sitting in a puddle. She picks herself up. Janary stares at her.

"I did this for you," Klary says. "Our sisters chose me to rescue you."

"No." Janary strangles on the word. "You don't understand."

"I was going to buy you afterward, bring you home. You weren't supposed to know about this. Nobody was."

The wound she has inflicted on the soulcatcher is already healing. Asher's head grimaces and turns away from them.

"I had a plan, Janary. All this would have been a secret." What *is* that in her sister's eyes? Hatred? Horror? Fear?

She wonders then if anyone is coming to rescue her.

TRAFALGAR AND JOSEFINA

ANGÉLICA GORODISCHER

<hr/>

Translated by Amalia Gladhart

My Aunt Josefina came to visit me. He who has never met my Aunt Josefina doesn't know what he's missing, as Trafalgar Medrano says. Trafalgar also says that she is one of the most beautiful and charming women he has met and that if he had been born in 1893 he would not have married her for anything in the world. My aunt came in, she looked the house over and asked after the children, she wanted to know if I was ever going to decide to move to an apartment downtown, and when I said no, never, she hesitated over whether or not to leave her jacket somewhere and decided to take it with her because there might be a little breeze in the garden later. She's eighty-four years old; wavy hair the color of steel, a couple of tireless chestnut eyes as bright as they say my criolla great-grandmother's were, and an enviable figure: if she wanted to, if she went so far as to admit that those coarse and disagreeable things should be used as items of clothing, she could wear Cecilia's jeans. She said the garden was lovely and that it would look much better when we had the ash trees pruned and the tea was delicious and she loved scones but they turned out better with only one egg.

"I drank a very good tea the other day. Yes, I am going to have a little more but half a cup, that's good, don't get carried away. Isn't it a little strong? Just one little drop of milk. That's it. And they served me some very good toast, with butter and not that rancid margarine they give you now everywhere, I don't know how you can like it. In the Burgundy. And I was with a friend of yours."

"I already know," I said. "Trafalgar."

"Yes, the son of Juan José Medrano and poor Merceditas. I don't understand how she allowed her only son to be given that outlandish name. Well, I always suspected Medrano was a Mason."

"But Josefina, what does Freemasonry have to do with the Battle of Trafalgar?"

"Ah, I don't know, sweetie, but you can't deny that the Masons purposely gave their children names that didn't appear in the calendar of saints."

"Doctor Medrano was probably an admirer of Nelson," I said, pinning all my hopes on Trafalgar's old man's interest in the great events of history.

"What I can assure you," said my Aunt Josefina, "is that Merceditas Herrera was a saint, and so refined and discreet."

"And Doctor Medrano, what was he like?"

"A great doctor," she opened another scone and spread orange marmalade on it. "Good-looking and congenial as well. And very cultured."

There was a quarter-second silence before the last statement: the word *cultured* is slippery with my Aunt Josefina and one has to step carefully.

"Trafalgar is also good-looking and congenial," I said, "but I don't know if he's cultured. He knows a ton of strange things."

"It's true, he's congenial, very congenial and friendly. And very considerate with an old lady like me. Now, I think good-looking is an exaggeration. His nose is too long, just like poor Merceditas'. And don't tell me that mustache isn't a little ridiculous. A man looks much tidier if clean-shaven, thank goodness your sons have gotten over the beard and mustache phase. But I have to admit that the boy is elegant: he had on a dark gray suit, very well cut, and a white shirt and a serious tie, not like some of your extravagant friends who look like. I don't even know what they look like."

"Would you like a little more tea?"

"No, no, please, you've already made me drink too much, but it was delicious and I have overdone it. That was Thursday or Friday, I'm not sure. I went into the Burgundy because I was fainting with hunger: I was coming from a meeting of the board of directors of the Society of Friends of the Museum, so it was Thursday, of course, because Friday was the engagement party of María Luisa's daughter, and you know Thursday is Amelia's afternoon off, and frankly I had no desire to go home and start making tea. There weren't many people and I sat down far away from the door, where there wouldn't be a draft, and when they were serving my tea the Medrano boy came in. He came over to say hello, so kind. At first I couldn't place him and I was about to ask him who he was when I realized he was Merceditas Herrera's son. It was so unsettling, seeing him standing there beside the table, but although I am old enough to do certain things, you understand that a lady never invites a man, even though he's *so* much younger than she is, to sit at her table."

An "Oh, no?" escaped me.

My Aunt Josefina sighed, I would almost say she blew out air, and great-grandmother's eyes stopped me cold.

"I do know customs have evolved," she said, "and in a few cases for the better, and in many others unfortunately for the worse, but there are things that do not change and you should know that."

I smiled because I love her a lot and because I hope I can get to eighty-four years old with the same confidence she has and learn to control my eyes the way she does although mine aren't even a tenth as pretty.

"And you let poor Trafalgar go?"

"No. He was very correct and he asked my permission to keep me company if I wasn't waiting for anyone. I told him to sit down and he ordered coffee. It's appalling how that boy drinks coffee. I don't know how he doesn't ruin his stomach. I haven't tasted coffee in years."

She doesn't smoke either, of course. And she drinks a quarter glass of rosé with every dinner and another quarter glass, only of extra-dry champagne, at Christmas and New Year's.

"He didn't tell you if he was going to come by here?"

"No, he didn't say, but it seems unlikely. He was going, I think the next day, I'm not really sure where, it must be Japan, I imagine, because he said he was going to buy silks. A shame he devotes himself to commerce and didn't follow his father's path: it was a disappointment to poor Merceditas. But he's doing very well, isn't he?"

"He's doing fabulously. He has truckloads of dough."

"I sincerely hope you don't use that language outside your home. It is unbecoming. Of course, it would be best if you never used it, but that's evidently hopeless. You're as stubborn as your father."

"Yes, my old man, I mean my father, was stubborn, but he was a gentleman."

"True. I don't know how he spoke when he was among other men, that doesn't matter, but he never said anything inappropriate in public."

"If you heard Trafalgar talk, you'd have an attack."

"I don't see why. With me, he was most agreeable. Neither affected nor hoity-toity—no need for that—but very careful."

"He's a hypocritical cretin." That I didn't say, I just thought it.

"And he has," said my Aunt Josefina, "a special charm for telling the most outlandish things. What an imagination."

"What did he tell you?"

"Obviously, maybe it's not all imagination. It gives you the impression that he is telling the truth, but so embellished that at first glance you could think it was a big lie. I'll tell you I spent a very entertaining interval. How is it possible that when I arrived home Amelia was already back and was worried at my delay? The poor thing had called Cuca's house, and Mimi's and Virginia's to see if I was there. I had to start in on the phone calls to calm them all down."

I got serious: I was dying of envy, like when Trafalgar goes and tells things to Fatty Páez or Raúl or Jorge. But I understood, because my Aunt Josefina knows how to do many things well; for example, to listen.

"What did he tell you?"

"Oh, nothing, crazy things about his trips. Of course, he speaks so well that it's a pleasure, a real pleasure."

"What did he tell you?"

"Sweetie, how you insist! Besides, I don't remember too well."

"Yeah, tell me what you remember."

"One says 'yes,' not 'yeah.' You sound like a muleteer, not a lady."

I ignored her.

"Of course you remember. You catch cold with a constancy worthy of a greater cause and your stomach is a little fragile, but don't tell me you have arteriosclerosis, because I won't believe you."

"God preserve me. Have you seen Raquel lately? A fright. She was at the Peñas', I don't know why they take her, and she didn't recognize me."

"Josefina, I am going to go crazy with curiosity. Be nice and tell me what Trafalgar told you."

"Let's see, wait, I'm not really sure."

"For certain he told you he had just arrived from somewhere."

"That's it. It must be one of those new countries in Africa or Asia, with a very strange name I have never heard before or ever read in the newspaper. What surprised me was that they were so advanced, with so much progress and so well organized, because they always turn savage: look what happened in India when the English left and in the Congo after the Belgians, no? Your friend Medrano told me it was a world—a world, that's what he said—that was very attractive when one saw it for the first time. Serprabel, now I remember, Serprabel. I think it must be close to India."

"I doubt it but, anyway, go on."

"Nevertheless, almost certainly, yes, it must be near India, not only because of the name but because of the castes."

"What castes?"

"Aren't there castes in India?"

"Yes, there are, but what does that have to do with it?"

"If you let me tell you, you're going to find out; weren't you in such a big hurry? And sit properly, it's so obvious you are all used to wearing pants. There are no elegant women anymore."

"Tell me, in Serprabel, are there elegant women?"

"Yes, according to the Medrano boy, there are splendid women, very well dressed and very well bred."

"It doesn't surprise me; even if there's only one, he'll find her."

"A shame he never married."

"Who? Trafalgar?" I laughed for a while.

"I don't see what's funny about it. I'm not saying with a foreigner, and from so far away, who may be a very good person, but have different customs, but with someone from his circle. Don't forget, he comes from a very well-connected family."

"That one's going to die an old bachelor. He likes women too much."

"Hmmmmm," went my Aunt Josefina.

"Don't tell me Medrano Senior did, too!" I exclaimed.

"Be discreet, sweetheart, don't talk so loud. In fact, I can't confirm anything. A few things were said at the time."

"I can imagine," I said. "And Merceditas was a saint. And on Serprabel Trafalgar was looking for romance, just as his father would have been."

"But how can you think that? He wasn't looking for romance, as you say. And if he were, he wouldn't have told me. One can see he is a very polite boy. What he did, or what he says he did, because it was most likely nothing more than a story to entertain me for a while, what he did was to try to help a poor woman, who was very unfortunate for many reasons."

"Ay," I said, and once again thought that Trafalgar was a hypocritical cretin.

"Now what's the matter?"

"Nothing, nothing, go on."

"Well, it seems that there they maintain—following those eastern religions, no?—a caste system. And there are nine. Let's see, let me think: lords, priests, warriors, scholars, merchants, artisans, servants, and vagabonds. Oh, no, eight. They're eight."

"And everyone has to be in one of the castes."

"Of course. Don't tell me it isn't an advantage."

"Oh, I don't know. What does one do if one is an artisan and has the vocation to be a merchant, like Trafalgar? Do they take an exam?"

"Of course not. Everyone lives within the caste to which they belong and they marry people from their own caste."

"Don't tell me: and their children are born within that caste and die within that caste and the children of those children and so on forever."

"Yes. So no one has pretentions and everyone stays in their place and they avoid disorders and revolutions and strikes. I said to Medrano that, paganism aside, it seemed to me an extraordinary system and he agreed with me."

"Ah, he agreed with you."

"Of course, he even told me that in thousands of years there had never been any disorder and they had lived in peace."

"How nice."

"I know it must sound a little old-fashioned to you, but Medrano says the

level of development in everything, color television and airlines and telephones
with a view screen and computer centers, is impressive. I'm surprised they
don't advertise more to attract tourism. I myself, if I were inclined to travel
at my age, would be very happy to go for a visit. Listen, he says the hotels
are extraordinary and the service is perfect, the food is delicious, and there
are museums and theaters and places to visit and splendid, just splendid
landscapes."

"I don't like that caste thing. I wouldn't go even at gunpoint."

"Nor I, believe me, I would not enjoy such a long plane trip. But the caste
thing is not that important, because anyone can govern."

"What did you say?"

"That anyone can govern. Above everyone is a kind of king who lives in the
center of the capital, because the city is a circle and in the middle is the Palace
which is all marble and gold and crystal. Anyway, that's what your friend
says. I don't doubt that it's very luxurious, but not that much."

"And anyone can become king? I mean, everything else is hereditary and
that, specifically, is not?"

"That's what Medrano told me. So you see, if the highest authority can be
elected, everything is very democratic. The king is called the Lord of Lords
and governs for a period of five years; when it's over, he can't be reelected, he
goes back home and then the Lords elect another."

"Wait, wait. The Lords? So then the others don't vote?"

"Nobody votes, sweetie. The Lords meet every five years and elect a Lord
of Lords and look how nice, they almost always, or always, elect him from
among the inferior castes, you see?"

"Heck yes, I see. And the Lord of Lords governs everybody?"

"I suppose so, that's what he's elected for. Although your friend Medrano
says no, he doesn't govern."

"I thought so."

"Oh, sure, if he says it, it's holy writ."

"Fine, but what is it he says?"

Another of my Aunt Josefa's virtues is that she can't lie: "He says he's a
puppet of the Lords who are the ones who really govern, so as to keep everyone
happy with the illusion that they or someone of their caste might become
king, but that the Lord of Lords is the ultimate slave, a slave who lives like a
king, eats like a king, dresses like a king, but is still a slave."

And one of her defects consists in believing only what she wants to
believe: "You see that can't be. Surely the Lords form a kind of Council or
Chamber or something like that and your friend took one thing for another.
Or he probably invented it to spice up the story."

"Yes, just probably. I warn you, Trafalgar is capable of anything."

"He also told me, this seems more reasonable to me, that the inferior castes are the more numerous. There is only one Lord of Lords. There are very few Lords, I think he told me there are a hundred. A few more Priests, many more, I think around three hundred. Many more Warriors and even more Scholars, he didn't tell me how many. Many, many Merchants, Artisans, and Servants, especially Servants. And it seems there are millions of Vagabonds. It must be a very populous country. And anyone of any caste, except the Lord of Lords, of course, can be Owner or Dispossessed."

"Having money or not having money? Rich and poor, let's say."

"More or less: he who has land is an Owner; he who does not is Dispossessed. And within each caste anyone who is an Owner is superior to the Dispossessed."

"And can one go from being Dispossessed to Owner?"

"Yes, so you already see that it's not as terrible as you thought. If one puts together enough money, one buys land, which is very expensive, just like everywhere. It seems to be a very rich country."

"The Vagabonds can buy land, too?"

"No, no. The Vagabonds are vagabonds. They don't even have houses, I don't know how people can live like that."

"I don't understand. Now tell me what happened to Trafalgar on Serprabel."

"It's a little cool, don't you think?"

"Do you want to go inside?"

"No, but help me put the jacket over my shoulders," not that my Aunt Josefina needs help to put on her jacket. "That's it, thank you. According to him, some of everything happened. He went there to sell jewelry and perfumes. He says he didn't do too well with the perfumes because they have a good chemical industry and flowers, you should see the flowers he described to me, very heavily scented ones from which they make extracts. But as there are no deposits of precious stones, he sold the ones he took very well. Of course, he had a few problems, believe me, because anyone who goes to Serprabel has to become part of a caste. They considered him a merchant and he had to use vehicles for Merchants and go to a hotel for Merchants. But when he learned that there were superior castes with better hotels and more privileges, he protested and said he was also a Scholar and a Warrior. He did the right thing, don't you think? Of course, since there one can't belong to more than one caste, they had to hold a kind of audience presided over by one of the Lords who had the strangest name, that I'm really not going to be able to remember, and there he explained his case. Oh, he made me laugh so much telling me how he had disconcerted them and remarking that he was very sorry he couldn't say he was a Lord, and that he would also have liked to say he was a Priest, which is the second caste. The bad part was he didn't know anything about the religion and he doesn't have mystical inclinations. Although I think he was educated in a religious school."

"That he has no mystical inclinations remains to be seen. So what happened?"

"They accepted that in other places there were other customs and they reached an agreement. He would be a Warrior but one of the lowest, those of the Earth, although an Owner, and with permission to act as a Merchant."

"What's that about those of the Earth?"

"Well, each one of the four superior castes has categories. For example, let's see, how was it, the Lords can be of Light, of Fire, and of Shadow, I think that was the order. The Priests can devote themselves to Communication, Intermediation, or Consolation. The Warriors act in the Air, the Water, or on the Earth. And the Scholars are dedicated to Knowledge, Accumulation, or Teaching. The others are inferior and don't have categories."

"What a mess. And each one can also be Owner or Dispossessed and that influences their position?"

"Yes. It's a little complicated. Medrano told me that a Lord of Light, an Owner, was the highest rank. And a Warrior of Air but Dispossessed was almost equal to a Priest devoted to Consolation but an Owner. Understand?"

"Not really. Anyway, they gave Trafalgar a very passable rank."

"He was very satisfied. The took him to a very superior hotel and that's even though he says the Merchants' hotel was very good, and they set four people to attend him exclusively, aside from the hotel personnel. The fact that he had jewels to sell also must have had some influence, because they are a real luxury. He says a delegation of Merchants went to see him and that although they couldn't enter the hotel, which was solely for Warriors, they spoke in the park and offered him a very well located shop where he could sell what he had brought. A few wanted to buy one or another piece of jewelry so as to sell it themselves but they were very expensive and the Merchants, although they aren't exactly poor, aren't rich, either. Only one of them, who was an Owner, and of a lot of land, might have been able to buy something from him, but Medrano didn't want to sell him anything; he did well, because why make such a long trip and end up splitting the profits with another? In any event they had to give him the location even though they didn't end on very friendly terms, because every caste has its laws and among the Merchants one can't go back after having offered something verbally or any other way, but above all verbally. Another law for all of the castes—which frankly, I don't know what result it would produce—seems very silly to me, it says no one can repeat to those of his own caste nor to those of other castes something he has overheard a member of another caste say, although they can repeat what members of their own caste have said. Of course this is hard to control, and no one speaks gladly to someone from another caste but only out of obligation, but every so often they catch an offender and the punishments are terrible; anyway, I don't know if it's really worth all that."

"But listen, more than silly, that's dangerous, because it's very vague, there aren't any limits. If you take it literally, no one can talk to anyone from another caste."

"There's something of that, as I said. But as the Lords, who are very intelligent and very fair, act as judges, there are no abuses. What is happening is that from caste to caste, the language is becoming more and more different. I forgot to ask Medrano what language they spoke and if he understood it. Would it be some dialect of Hindi? In any case, with a little English one can make oneself understood anywhere in the world."

"Trafalgar speaks excellent English. I expect he sold the jewelry."

"To the Lords, of course. The store fronts, the shops, those are public places where anyone can go, except for the Vagabonds who can't go anywhere, but when a Lord or a number of Lords enter, everyone else has to leave. Those that aren't Lords, because those that are Lords can stay. In any case, a crowd of people paraded through to see what Medrano had brought."

"I'd bet a year's paychecks he sold it all."

"I don't know what you were going to live on because he didn't sell everything. He had a pearl necklace left over."

"I don't believe you. No. Impossible. Never."

"Seriously. Of course it was because of everything that happened and anyway he was the one who decided to leave it, but he didn't sell it."

"I don't understand any of this, but it seems very unusual in Trafalgar."

"Well, the Lord of Lords governing at that time, and who had been elected by the Lords less than a year before, was a man not at all well-suited to the office. Listen, he had been a Vagabond, how awful."

"Why? Don't they elect the inferior castes as king?"

"Yes, of course, but seldom Vagabonds, who are illiterate and don't know how to eat or how to behave. But Medrano says they had elected him because he had the face and the poise of a king."

"High-class liars, those Lords."

"Sweetie, so vulgar."

"Don't tell me they aren't a bunch of liars and something worse, too."

"I don't think so, because from what Medrano told me they are irreproachable people. And it seems to me very democratic to elect a Vagabond as king. Even a bit idealistic, like something out of a novel."

"A cock-and-bull story."

"The fact is, the poor Lords made a mistake. Of course, an ignorant person, without education—what could you expect?"

"He left them in a bad state."

"He fell in love, can you believe, with a married woman."

"A Vagabond?"

"No, I think the Vagabonds don't even get married. Worse: he fell in love with the wife of a Scholar, and one of the best, the ones devoted to Knowledge and who for that reason was often at court. And Medrano found that out because he heard the Lords discussing what had to be done in the jewelry store he had opened. But as he didn't know that one can't repeat what members of a caste that isn't your own have said, and he was—at least so long as he was there—a Warrior, he mentioned it to a Scholar in conversation. I don't remember what category he belonged to, but Medrano says he had been looking at the jewels and that he was a very interesting man who knew a great deal about philosophy, mathematics, music, and it was worthwhile listening to him speak. He couldn't buy anything: only the Lords had picked up a lot of things, because the prices were very high for those of other castes, but he stayed until quite late, and as the two were alone and they had talked about the cutting of stones and of goldsmithing and of music, they started to talk about other things, too, and Medrano praised the country and the city and the other asked if he had seen the gardens at the Palace and they talked about the Lord of Lords and there your friend committed an indiscretion."

"He mentioned the Lord of Lords' affair with the woman."

"He said he had heard the Lords talk about that and he didn't realize he had said something he should not: he was just surprised when the Scholar became very serious and stopped talking and said good-bye very coldly and left."

"Trafalgar acts like a know-it-all but he never learns. He always sticks his foot in it."

"My goodness, what a way to speak."

"I promise to be more refined, or at least try to, but tell me what happened to him."

"When you want to you can speak correctly. The thing would be for you to always want to. That day, nothing happened to him. The next day he sold what he had left, only to the Lords, save for a pearl necklace that must have been beautiful, truly beautiful: a very long string of pink pearls all the same size. Natural pearls, as you can imagine. It must have cost a fortune."

"That was the one he left?"

"Yes, but wait. When he had nothing left but that necklace and was about to sell it to a Lord, the police came in and arrested him."

"It looks like there are police on Serprabel."

"Why not? They belong to the Servants caste. And they took him directly to the Palace of the Lord of Lords. There he had to wait, always

under guard, with the necklace in his pocket, until they made him
enter—shoved him, he says, how unpleasant—enter a courtroom.
As repeating things said by someone from another caste is a serious
crime, the judge wasn't just any Lord but the Lord of Lords. Of course, assisted
by two Lords. The one who acted as prosecutor was another Lord, who put
forward the accusation."

"And defender? Did he have a defender?"

"No, he had to defend himself. I will say it does not seem fair to me."

"Not fair at all. A filthy trick, forgive the term."

"It may be a little strong, but you're right. They accused him and he
defended himself as well as he could. But note, they had to say what it was
about, what it was Medrano had repeated. And it was nothing less than the
illicit affairs of the very king presiding over the tribunal."

"Poor guy, my God."

"That boy really had a bad time."

"No, I mean the Lord of Lords."

"He had it coming, and don't think I don't feel sorry for him. But a person
of quality does not stoop to such things."

"Oh, no, of course, why don't you read Shakespeare and Sophocles?"

"That may be all very well for the theater, but in real life it is not suitable.
And things got worse when, after the accusation and the defense, the
prosecutor detailed Medrano's crime and the Lord of Lords, who until then
had been very much in his role, very serious and dignified and quiet on his
throne, stood up and started to speak. It was not the conduct expected of a
king, because everyone, and above all the Lords, Medrano explained to me,
everyone was so scandalized that they couldn't do anything. They were frozen
with their mouths open, staring at him."

"And what did he say?"

"A speech."

"A speech?"

"A parody of a speech. Medrano says he didn't even know how to speak, he
stammered and pronounced the words wrong and repeated phrases."

"And what did they expect? The Demosthenes of the underworld? But one
could understand some of what he said, I imagine."

"He said—there in front of everybody, because trials are public—he said
it was all true, can you believe what poor taste, talking about things that are
not only private, but illicit. He said he was in love with that girl and she with
him and he didn't see why they couldn't love each other and he was going to
stop being king and he was going to go away with her and walk naked and
barefoot through the fields and eat fruit and drink water from the rivers, what
a crazy idea. It must have been so unpleasant for the Lords to see the same

king they had elected sniveling and drooling like a fussy child in front of the people he supposedly had to govern. How could it be that no one moved or said anything when the Lord of Lords got down from the throne and took off his shoes which were of an extremely fine leather with gold buckles, and took off the embroidered cloak and the crown and, wearing only in a tunic of white linen, walked over to the exit?"

"And no one did anything?"

"The Lords did something. The Lords reacted and gave the order to the police to seize him and they carried him back to the throne. But what a strange thing, no one obeyed and the Lord of Lords kept walking and left the courtroom and reached the gardens."

"But, Trafalgar? What was Trafalgar doing that he didn't take advantage of the chance to escape?"

"He didn't? Sweetie, it's as if you didn't know him well. As soon as the Lord of Lords started to talk and everyone was watching him, Medrano backed up and put himself out of the guards' reach and when the king left the room and some Warriors and the Lords yelled and ran out, he ran, too."

"Well done, I like it."

"But he didn't go very far."

"They caught him again?"

"No, luckily not. In the Palace gardens, where there were always a lot of people, there was a big stir when they saw him appear barefoot, wearing only his underclothes. And then, Medrano was able to see it all well, then a very young, very pretty woman embraced him, crying: it was the Scholar's wife, she of the guilty passions."

"Oh, Josefina, that's a phrase out of a serial novel."

"Is it that way or is it not? A married woman who has a love affair with a man who is not her husband is blameworthy, and don't tell me no because that I will not accept."

"We aren't going to fight over it, especially now when you leave me hanging with everyone in such a foul predicament. Did Trafalgar do anything besides watch?"

"Quite a bit, poor boy, he was very generous. Mistaken, but generous. The Lords and the Warriors and the Scholars—not the Priests, because none of them were there, they lead quieter lives, as is proper—tried to get to the Lord of Lords and that woman, but all the people of the other castes who were in the garden and those who came in from outside or came out of the Palace to see, without knowing very well why—because many of them hadn't been at the tribunal; just out of rebelliousness or resentment, I imagine—started to defend them. Of course, that turned into a plain of Agramante and there was a terrible fight. The Warriors and the Lords had weapons, but those of the inferior castes destroyed the gardens, such a shame, pulling out stones, taking iron from the benches, chunks of marble and crystal from the fountains, branches, railings from the gazebos, anything with which to attack and give the Lord of Lords and the woman time to escape."

"And did they escape?"

"They escaped. And your friend Medrano after them. He says his private plane, he doesn't call it private plane, what does he call it?"

"Clunker."

"That's it. He says his private plane wasn't very far away and he wanted to get to it, very sensible it seems to me, and take off immediately. But meanwhile the Lords and Warriors got organized, they called in soldiers, who I think are from the Warriors caste, too, but are doing their apprenticeship, and they chased the Lord of Lords and the woman. That was when Medrano caught up with them and dragged them with him to the airplane."

"Thank goodness. You were starting to scare me."

"Go ahead and get scared, now comes the worst."

"Oh, no, don't tell me more."

"Fine, I won't tell you more."

"No, yes, tell me."

"Which is it?"

"Josefina, no, I promise I wasn't serious."

"I know, and anyway I can't cut the story short now. They had almost reached the plane, with the Lords and Warriors and the Scholars and the soldiers chasing them and behind them all those from the inferior castes who were throwing stones but no longer tried to get close because the Warriors had killed several, they had almost reached it when the Lords realized where they were going and that they were about to escape and they gave the order to the soldiers to fire. They shot, and they killed the Lord of Lords."

I said nothing. Josefina observed that it was getting dark, and I went inside and turned on the garden lights.

"Medrano," said my Aunt Josefina, "saw that they had put a bullet through his head and he grabbed the woman and pulled her up into the plane. But she didn't want to go, now that the Lord of Lords was dead, and she fought so hard that she managed to free herself and she threw herself out of the plane. Medrano tried to follow her and take her up again, but the Warriors and the Lords were already upon him and they kept firing and he had to close the door. They killed her, too. It was a horrible death, Medrano said, but he didn't explain how and I didn't ask. He remained locked in, on the ground but ready to take off, and saw they weren't paying attention to him any longer. In the end, to them he was no more than a foreigner from whom they had bought jewels, who perhaps understood nothing of the country's customs and so had done things that were not right. They went away and left the bodies. Those of the inferior castes had to be obliged to retreat at bayonet point because they wanted to come close at all costs although they were no longer throwing stones or anything else. And that was when Medrano left the pearl necklace. When he saw that he was alone, he got down from the plane, at great risk, it seems to me, but he was very brave and it's very moving, he got down from the plane and he put the string of pearls on the woman, on what remained of her, he said. Afterward he climbed back up, locked himself in, washed his hands, lit a cigarette, and lifted off."

"How awful."

"Yes. So long as it's true," said my Aunt Josefina. "I don't know what to think. Might it not be nothing more than a fairy tale for an old lady all alone drinking her tea?"

"Trafalgar doesn't tell fairy tales. And you're not old, Josefina, come on."

A STRANGER FROM A FOREIGN SHIP

TOM PURDOM

The people in this city had developed a taste for formality in their after-hours garb. Most of the men were wearing black coats. The women had opted for more color but black coats had won the vote in their bloc, too. The women added the color with accents like scarves and hatbands. Nobody gave Gerdon a second glance as he slipped through the crowds hurrying between dinner and curtain time. He didn't try to keep up with fashion in the places he visited. He had learned he could fade into the crowd if he merely looked like what he was—a stranger from a foreign ship.

The target was a slender young woman, six feet in low heels, brisk walk, light coat, long face that matched her build. Gerdon picked her up, as planned, a block and a half from the concert hall, twenty minutes before show time. She lived in an apartment building five blocks from the pickup point. She subscribed to a six-concert Thursday night series. This was one of her Thursdays.

The client had given him some very precise details. He had wondered, in fact, why the client had needed him.

He had only been hanging around the corner for three or four minutes when he saw her crossing the street with the other people who had been waiting for the light. He was standing near the bus stop, looking down the street as if he was watching for the bus. He fell in behind her, a middle-aged couple between them, and rested his shoulder against a patch of wall just before he made the swap.

The disorientation always hit him harder when the target was a woman. The body felt off balance. Strange hormones played with your emotions.

He couldn't have taken this job when he first started. They wanted her bank account and credit card numbers. Most people didn't memorize information like that. He had to search for visualizations—for the last time she had looked at a card or a statement and her brain had laid down a memory.

It took him longer than he liked. Behind him, through her ears, he could hear people stirring. The man leaning against the wall was attracting attention. The woman locked inside the man's head was reacting to the jolt of the shift—to the shock of suddenly finding herself riding in another body, staring out of someone else's eyes.

Most of them never understood what had happened. How could they? You were walking down the street or sitting in a theater and *blam, flick,* you found yourself connected to strange muscles and strange glands, inches taller or shorter, looking at the world from a different place. You might even glimpse your own body, seen from the outside.

He had never been a target himself, but he could remember all the times it had happened spontaneously when he had been young, before he had learned to control it. Most of his targets probably assumed it was an odd glitch in their brains—a hallucination created by a deficit in blood sugar or understandable fatigue from all those extra hours they were virtuously logging at work.

You couldn't search through a brain the way you searched a computer, with key words and logical connections. The links were foggier and less rational. Odors. Emotions. Childhood associations. Arline Morse had an exceptionally well organized brain, but the images he needed forked from a trail that started with the label on the wallet tucked in the suit she was wearing under her coat.

He severed contact and discovered his body had started sliding down the wall while she had been inside it. He waved off the people around him and straightened up. He ran his hand over his face. He threw out reassuring gestures.

Arly Morse's body had slipped to her knees while he was playing with her brain. Two men were offering her their hands. He turned around, eyes fixed on the sidewalk, and drove toward the corner while she was still reorienting.

She liked to be called Arly. The name permeated most of her memories. He had knocked a few seconds off the search when he had realized her account numbers would be linked to memories associated with Arline.

He stopped in front of a store window, half a block from the corner, and jotted the account numbers in a notebook, along with the appropriate passwords. The passwords had been easy in her case. She was the kind of person who committed them to memory. They looked random at first glance. Then he realized they were Jane Austen titles, with two-digit numbers inserted in the middle. Publication dates?

He turned another corner and slipped into one of the small streets that broke up the downtown area. He wandered past closed stores and maneuvered around sidewalk tables as he looked for a good place to stop and phone in the numbers. He disliked people who weaved through busy streets with their minds focused on their phones and pads.

Most of the people sitting at the tables outside the restaurants wouldn't have linked him with a ship. The city was an inland port, connected to the ocean by a river, and they didn't see most of the traffic it attracted. The ship that had brought him here was moored twenty miles down the river, waiting for its turn beside one of the high cranes that transferred containers to trucks and freight trains.

He had covered another two blocks before he realized he was putting off the call.

He wasn't a mind reader. He couldn't stand outside another person and pick up their thoughts and feelings, as if he had set up a wifi connection. He took complete control—just as they would have taken control of his brain if they hadn't been thrown into confusion. But he could still pick things up. Bits of emotion could trickle into the alien consciousness that had imposed its grip on their brains and bodies.

She had been afraid. Her biological fear responses had been so strong they created a current that persisted through most of the time he had been riffling through her brain.

He had settled into one of the faded, lower priced hotels in the city, as he usually did. The bar had a corner booth where he could stare at a drink.

It wasn't the first time he had felt that steady glimmer of fear. The last time the numbers on his search list had included an address. The time before that the client had asked for an alias.

Both targets had been carrying information about someone else. The implications had been obvious. The second target had even looked like a mobster—a big brute with a rocky face, cased in a suit that would have cost more than most people's vacations. He shouldn't have been afraid of anything. But he was. And he had been carrying the alias his brother was using.

They hadn't told Gerdon why they wanted Arly Morse's numbers. He never asked. He let people know he could dig up private information and they let him know what they wanted. He didn't know who they were and he moved on as soon as he picked up the first signs they were wondering who he was. And how he did it.

For all he knew, they could be federal agents looking for a shortcut in a tax case. Or local cops running a corruption probe.

He plodded up to his room after he finished his drink. A basketball game lulled him into sleep in the third quarter. He still hadn't phoned in the numbers when he hurried out of the hotel the next morning.

Arly lived in an office building that had been converted to apartments, on a main street where he could blend into the pedestrian traffic that streamed past the door.

She came through the door earlier than he'd expected—just fifteen minutes after he slipped into a surveillance pattern. He dropped behind a bulky luggage puller and stayed with her while she walked toward the corner. It was a good day for a tail—a gray day in November that surrounded him with people wearing coats, jackets, and headgear.

He had never had any formal training as an investigator but he had picked up tricks. She popped into a coffee shop two blocks from her building and he selected a position on the other side of the street, out of the line of sight from the coffee shop windows. He modified his appearance by pushing his hat back on his head—like a reporter in an old black and white movie—and unbuttoning his coat. He had grabbed a sausage and egg sandwich from a street cart but he'd skipped coffee.

She worked three blocks from the coffee shop, in an old six-story building that had received a full rehab, complete with sandblasting and white paint on the window frames. The plaque next to the shiny glass door said it was the Dr. J.J. Shen Medical Building.

She was still standing in front of the elevators when he hurried through the door with his head lowered and his phone pressed against his ear. He swept his eyes over the directory and noted that every floor housed a different specialty. She pressed the button for three—oncology. He picked five, Radiology Associates, and hit Lobby when everybody else got off.

She could be a patient, of course. That would account for the fear. But she had looked to him like she was on her way to work.

She left the building just after twelve thirty. She stopped at an ATM. She loitered in front of a window devoted to handbags and gloves. She went inside a woody salad-and-soup place and he verified she was standing in the order line when he walked past the window.

He was hungry. He was bored. He knew what he needed and she hadn't given him any indication he was going to get it. She would go back to her office. She would march straight from her job to her apartment. There wouldn't be one moment between now and the end of the day when he could spend three minutes in her head without raising a commotion that would surround both of them with an instant flash mob.

He would have spotted the two men if he had been a real streetwise investigator. He had seen both of them while he had been watching Dr. Shen's real estate venture.

They sandwiched him between them while Arly was still consuming her soup and salad. The one on his left was obviously the muscle. A little short for the job, but solid. The one on his right was taller and wore glasses.

"We'd like to talk to you," the muscle said.

It wasn't the first time Gerdon had faced the threat of violence, but that didn't make it any easier. He had learned everything he needed to know about violence the first time he had been kicked in the kidneys while he had been doubled up on the ground.

The tall one had a square, Anglo-Saxon face that might have looked annoyingly upper class if he hadn't been wearing glasses. They were both dressed like financial types but he looked like one.

"You've been watching Ms. Morse," the tall one said. "All morning."

The muscle frowned. "We're getting a taxi," the tall one said. "Keep quiet."

Hands gripped his arms. He glanced down the street and saw a pair of taxis waiting for the next light.

He let himself sag at the knees as he made the swap. He looked out of the muscle's eyes and saw his own body drooping, He had a clear shot at the Anglo-Saxon's face and he took it.

The muscle would have put more power into it if he had been controlling his own body but Gerdon had the element of surprise in his favor. The muscle's right fist connected with a target that was totally unprepared.

He jumped back to his own body and found himself kneeling on the curb with his head slumped. Above him, he could hear both of them grunting and swearing. He backed up in a crouch and hurried toward the corner. He had made a dangerous miscalculation. The muscle was not stupid. He had only been inside his head for a moment but it had been obvious the muscle was the leader. He couldn't assume he could creep out of sight while they wasted time trying to figure out what had happened.

So why were they watching her? Why were they combining physical surveillance with a probe of her bank accounts?

Why did they even need him? They knew where she lived. They knew where she worked. They had an organization that could keep two hooligans busy just watching her. Couldn't they break into her apartment and look through her files?

The whole incident looked weird. They had come up to him on a busy street, without knowing who he was, and tried to force him into a taxi. What kind of an organization did stuff like that?

He could always just *ask* them why they'd hired him, of course. Leave a message on the phone drop. *Listen, I've got those numbers you wanted. But I'd like to know what you're up to before I give them to you. Just in case it might be something—*

Something what? Something that might harm a nice looking woman with a stylish walk and a taste for Jane Austen novels?

He couldn't even claim he liked Jane Austen. He had read *Pride and Prejudice* twice. It was funny. It passed the time. But he had never been able to read any of the others. He had to work just to get through the first two chapters.

He shouldn't have panicked. He had let them see something odd was happening.

The Jane Austen movies had been good. He'd liked all the film versions.

He bought a black coat in a department store and switched coats in his hotel room. The price tag had made him pause, but who knew? He liked this city. He had been thinking about staying for a while when he got off the ship.

He timed it so he would be approaching Dr. Shen's building just before five. He could have timed it more precisely if he had waited until morning. He knew what time she arrived. But he didn't want to wait. His new finery would help him evade the watchers if they were still around.

As it was, she stepped onto the sidewalk just a minute after he paused at a spot half a block from her door, on the other side of the street. He took two steps, as he had planned, and settled into a chair outside a pizza place.

And found himself staring at her back, through the eyes of some hapless passerby, probably male.

He jumped back to his own body and stood up. The passerby was standing in the middle of the sidewalk, irritating the people maneuvering around him.

He had known he was taking a chance trying to make a swap at that distance. Normally he stayed within a few steps of the target, with a firm line of sight.

He closed in on her while she waited for the light at a corner near her apartment. There was a restaurant with sidewalk tables and tall outdoor heaters near the end of the next block. He hurried around her and grabbed a vacant chair two steps before she passed.

This time he kept her body under control. He recovered from a stumble and steered her toward a store window.

Stand still. Stare at the window. Focus on the fear. What is the fear linked to?

He had never done anything like this. He was riffling through her memories with all the frenzy of a burglar who knew the night watchman was coming down the hall. Facts raced at him like a cloud of buzzing insects. Associations that looked relevant led him into amorphous bogs.

• • •

He was still sitting in the chair when he reestablished contact with his body. His head had turned to the left. He was staring at Arly Morse's back.

Arly was still facing the store window. Exactly where he had left her. Left hand in coat pocket. Back straight. He hadn't noticed the hand in the pocket when he'd been inside her. Some part of him must have been looking after her body.

She turned around. Her free hand jumped to her mouth.

He stared at her. Should he hop up and get away from her? Had she really figured it out that fast? And adjusted emotionally?

How long had they been swapped?

A hand settled on his shoulder. The muscle stepped past him and hurried toward Arly.

"It's a nice evening, isn't it?" the man behind him said.

They had brought a friend this time—a plump cheery face who had decked out the standard uniform with an orange bow tie. He stepped in front of Gerdon's chair, close enough to force a pin, and Gerdon looked back and verified the hand on his shoulder belonged to the tall guy who'd taken the punch the last time they'd met.

The tall guy was bawling their location into a phone. The muscle had started maneuvering Arly toward the table, one hand gripping her wrist, his other arm wrapped around her shoulder in a friendly looking embrace. People glanced at them as they went by but nobody stopped. It was hurry-home time. Let somebody else worry about it.

The car met them at the corner, a few steps from the restaurant. It was an SUV, with seats for six, and that created an awkwardness. Muscle finally decided Arly should sit in front, next to the driver, and Gerdon should sit behind her, with the muscle beside him and the other two watching his back.

Arly had stared at him the whole time she was being pushed toward the table. She had told them she was willing to see "Freddy" anytime he wanted to talk to her, but that had been the only thing she had said so far.

"We're just looking for some information," the tall guy said when they had all been properly packed into the car. "We're just trying to find out what this guy is up to."

The muscle rolled his eyes. Gerdon had caught glimpses of him when he had been darting through Arly's memories. Arly had realized he was the smart one, too.

He studied the controls of the car as they drove through the city. He didn't drive much, given his predilection for cities, and they kept adding new things between his stints behind the wheel. Could he swap with the driver and open all the doors as he pulled the car to a violent stop? And hop back to his own body and jump out while they were all reacting to total chaos?

It was a nice fantasy. But what would Arly do?

They were obviously going to see "Freddy." Why not wait and see what Freddy wanted?

Freddy lived in a two-story stone house on a block where all his neighbors lived in two-story stone houses. It didn't look that impressive to Gerdon, but the tall guy had muttered something about "welcome to the rich people's world" when they entered the neighborhood.

They unpacked themselves according to the muscle's step-by-step instructions. They trudged down the driveway in a tight little formation and the muscle pressed his palm against a plate next to a side door.

Freddy was sitting in an oversized padded desk chair, in a second floor room furnished with waiting-room armchairs and a desk dominated by an oversized computer monitor. His T-shirt stretched over muscles that indicated his mansion housed an exercise room. He gestured at them with his drink, but he didn't bother to stand up.

"You've been watching Arly," Freddy said. "She's a friend of ours—a very good friend—and we don't know anything about you."

Gerdon had known he could be in serious trouble when they started up the stairs that led to the second floor. He had let himself drift into a situation in which his little trick couldn't protect him. There were too many of them and he only had one line of retreat. He couldn't create a diversion that would keep all of them busy and leap for the first gap that opened up.

He had let that happen when he had first gone to sea. There were always places on ships where three or four hooligans could crowd a skin-and-bones kid into a corner. There had been nothing he could do about it when they started punching and kicking.

He had been burning with outrage the first time he had guided a wine-soaked oaf over a rail. He had been savagely aware he didn't know what would happen. Could he swap back to his own body before his target slammed into the deck machinery thirty meters below the rail? Would he die if his target's body died while he was inside it? He didn't care.

He still didn't know what would happen if somebody died while he was swapped. Would the other person live out their life in his body? He had always made sure he had time to escape when he killed somebody. Drowning was the safest. Walk them off a bridge into deep water a long way from shore. Zap back to your own body while they were still thrashing around. Go on your way.

He had never thought of himself as brave. Courage, in his opinion, was an over-rated virtue. Hoodlums liked to strut and act nervy but they always had size and numbers on their side. They had left him alone when they noticed bad things happened to people who attacked him.

"I'm the person you hired. To get some information you wanted."

Freddy scowled. The muscle turned his head and studied Gerdon as if he was looking at an object that had suddenly acquired a new level of interest.

Freddy gestured at Arly. "I think you and Dan should have a drink in the rec room, Arly."

Arly straightened up. "Can't you tell me what this is all about? You could have just told me you wanted to see me."

It was the first time she had said anything since they had arranged themselves in the car. Gerdon had spent most of the ride staring at the back of her neck, as she slumped inside her shoulder belt.

"I need to talk to this guy," Freddy said.

The muscle gripped Arly's arm and led her toward a side door. She looked back at Gerdon and he turned away from her before she met his eyes.

He had put her through two swaps. She had looked out of his eyes twice. She had to know something funny had happened.

"That's how you do it?" Freddy said. "You follow people around?"

"I ran into some problems."

"You were going to beat it out of her?"

He couldn't even tell himself she was some poor little innocent. He hadn't pinned down all the details when he had rummaged through her head in front of the restaurant, but he understood the general drift. They were working a scheme involving chemotherapy drugs. Arly manipulated the records and delivered the goods to Freddy's customers. She was supposed to get a percentage of the take on each delivery, but she had been lying about the size of the sales. She was carrying all that fear around because Freddy had warned her he wouldn't tolerate that kind of behavior.

She wasn't even very smart. She'd let Freddy pile the whole thing on her. Freddy set her up with a customer and sat on the sidelines collecting 80 percent of the take. Gerdon had picked up flashes of her after-work life and it looked like she had spent most of her share wandering through stores buying clothes and trinkets like expensive handbags. Freddy had given her a chance to do some extra shopping and she'd lunged at it.

It was a small time operation. Run by small time people. Milking small time gullibles.

"It's her," the tall guy said. "I saw the way he looked at her."

Freddy raised his eyebrows. "Is that it? You like skinny women?"

"I needed more information."

"And you thought you could get it following her around? We hired you because your contact told us you could get the information we needed faster and cheaper than anybody else. With no fuss. You were supposed to phone it in almost twenty-four hours ago."

"It's her," the tall guy said. "He's some kind of geek. He likes female geeks."

"We have a business relationship with Arly," Freddy said. "We think she may be falsifying the amounts she's supposed to pay us. We thought we'd run a little audit on her accounts and make sure we've been getting the right figures. We have a business relationship with you, too. We gave you half in advance. Up front. On your contact's recommendation. Give us the information we paid for, you get your other half, we're done."

"What happens to her?"

The tall guy laughed.

"We aren't going to kill her, if that's what you're worried about. We'll just make sure she understands she has to stick to our arrangement. I haven't thought that through yet, but it probably won't take much."

Gerdon nodded. They wouldn't need to raise a bruise, given the fear he had detected. They could show her the evidence, have a little fun with her, and send her back to her job knowing she had placed herself in a permanent trap.

You could even say Freddy was being kind. He was looking for evidence before he locked her in her cage.

Freddy lowered his head and thought for a moment. "I hired you—whoever you are—so we could get the account numbers without bothering her. Painlessly."

"If we can't do it that way . . . " the tall guy said.

"They're in my inside pocket. In my notebook."

Freddy held out his hand. Gerdon ripped the page out of the notebook and Freddy waved at the cheeryface with the bow tie.

The cheeryface stepped around the desk and bent over the computer. Freddy pushed his chair back and watched Gerdon while he followed the action on the screen.

"We owe you some money," Freddy said.

"You got her?" the tall guy said.

"I presume you'll accept dollars. I can throw in a few euros."

Gerdon was sitting behind the desk, looking at the startled expression on his own face staring at him across the desktop. He jerked open the drawer on the right side of the desk and saw the gun sitting there, just as he'd expected.

It was a nine millimeter self-loading pistol—the commonest private firearm in the world. He worked the slide as he pulled it out of the drawer and fired two shots upward, as fast as the gun would operate, at a point on the tall guy's coat just below his right collarbone.

He had never been the kind of person who enjoyed shooting. The kick and noise of a gun had felt hard and brutal the first time he pulled a trigger and his feelings hadn't changed.

The computer whiz had jerked erect. Gerdon twisted in his chair and fired into a well padded thigh. He was thinking coolly and rapidly, as he always did when these things happened, bolstered by the knowledge he was one step ahead of surprised, confused adversaries who didn't know what he was doing. He wasn't trying to kill either of them. He just wanted to put them out of action. There were people who could absorb everything he had done and rip your throat out before they let it stop them. He had watched them ravage his birthland. This crew didn't look like bonafide human wolves.

He turned back to the shocked version of himself on the other side of the desk. He placed the gun on the desktop. He pushed against the floor with his legs and rolled backward.

Then he was inside his own body again. He stumbled as he stepped forward but the confusion only lasted a second. He picked up the gun and aimed it at the man rolling away from him.

Freddy had good reflexes. He had been through a complete round trip, *zip*, *zap*, and he was already twisting like he was getting ready to throw himself to one side.

This time Gerdon went for the kill. He lined up the sights, elbows locked, and pressed the trigger four times, firing each shot at the standard aiming point in the center of the upper body. One of the bullets went wide but he could see the strikes of the others.

The computer whiz was staring at the blood on his leg. The tall guy was bending over the desk with his weight resting on his good hand, wheezing with pain.

The side door swung open. Gerdon turned and saw Dan the Muscle crouching on one knee in the doorway, gun in firing position. The gun swung toward him and he put Freddy's gun on the desk and lifted his hands.

Dan stood up. He checked out the three casualties and stared at Gerdon with the kind of intense, screwed-up concentration Gerdon had seen on the faces of ship handlers who were steering mammoth vessels through narrow passages with volatile currents.

"You took that gun from somebody. You didn't have it when you came here."

The computer whiz was sitting on the floor. The tall guy had given up fighting the pain and let himself slump to his knees, with his head resting against the desk. Gerdon wondered if either of them even carried a gun. The only person in this group who looked truly dangerous was pointing a gun at him.

The computer whiz grunted. "Freddy. Freddy shot us."

"Freddy shot himself?"

"He shot Freddy."

Gerdon knew he had to move as soon as he saw Dan's gun waver. Dan had looked out of his eyes. Dan had punched his partner in the same way Freddy had shot the two men bleeding in front of him.

He was staring at another jump into unknown territory. Usually he did one swap—two at the most—and stayed locked inside his own head until he got another job weeks later. Now he had done three in the last few hours. One in the last two minutes. Did he know what he was doing? Did he have any idea where this would take him?

The world trembled. Thunder cracked somewhere—in his mind, or some place in the real world, whatever the real world was. He stared across Dan's gun at the body the universe had given him—or loaned him, if you wanted to be more accurate.

Dan was just as fast as Freddy. He started diving behind the desk seconds after Gerdon recovered from his own confusion. Gerdon dropped to his hands and knees and sent the gun sliding across the floor.

Could he get back to his own body again so fast? Yes, he could. And there was the gun, just two steps to his left. With Dan on his hands and knees staring at the floor.

He picked up the gun. "Where's Arly? Stay where you are."

"What are you?" Dan said.

"Where's Arly?"

"Watching TV. In the living room."

"Can she hear you if you call her? Tell her to come here."

The two men he had shot were looking sicker by the second. He didn't look at Freddy.

"What the hell are you?" Dan said.

"Please call Arly."

Dan raised his voice. He couldn't produce a proper shout from his all-fours position, but Arly wasn't as engrossed in TV as he had indicated. She stepped into the doorway seconds after he called her and responded with an appropriately nineteenth century display of horror. She even covered her mouth with her hand.

"You'd better come with me," Gerdon said. "You can't stay here."

Arly stared at Freddy's body. He could try another swap and walk her across the room, to the door that opened on the stairs, if the swap worked. But that would mean she would be inside his body while he moved. Holding the gun. Buffeted by an emotional storm that would have floored an astronaut.

"What are you?" Arly said.

"You can't stay here with them, Arly. They know what you've been doing."

"Is that what you're trying to do?" Dan said. "You're trying to protect her?"

Arly's hand had jumped back to her mouth. She let out a little choked sob and Gerdon decided he had penetrated the storm and triggered the fear that had made him change course and veer into a minefield.

Arly turned around. She stumbled down the hall on the other side of the door and Gerdon watched her turn into a door. He heard Dan shift his weight and he automatically locked his elbows and pointed the gun directly at Dan's upturned face.

"It's all right," Dan said. "I'm not stupid. I don't know exactly what it is you're doing but I am not going to do anything stupid."

Arly came down the hall dressed in the coat she had been wearing when they picked her up. She maneuvered around Dan with her head lowered and walked toward the back door as if she was a demure example of eyes-lowered female modesty, instead of a modern shopping-obsessed woman who apparently couldn't leave an expensive coat behind if her life depended on it.

Freddy's gun was still lying on the desk. Gerdon shoved it into his coat pocket and started backing toward the door. The two pound weight in his pocket felt heavy and awkward but he wasn't going to leave a gun where somebody like Dan could pick it up.

The car was still sitting in the driveway. The dark figure behind the wheel was still jittering in time to the earphones he had settled on his head when they got out. He abandoned his post without any fuss when Gerdon showed him the gun.

He hadn't thought it through. He had just acted. He had stuck Freddy's gun in his pocket because it looked like the right thing to do. But was it? They could have told the police Freddy had shot them and shot himself. Gone berserk for no reason. How could they do that without a gun?

You couldn't take gunshot wounds to a hospital without saying something. Unless you had connections. Did they have medical arrangements? Were they too small time to have a doctor on their payroll?

"Do you have any idea what you're doing?" Arly said.

"They knew what you've been doing. You were in very serious trouble."

"You think they would have killed me? You think a bunch of small timers like that would give up the money I'm funneling them?"

"They didn't have to kill you. They would have . . . taught you a lesson. And sent you back to work. On their terms."

He turned onto a street cluttered with stores and eating places. This neighborhood changed fast. You drove down a "rich people's" block with trees and big front yards and twenty seconds later you were surrounded by rundown houses and stores that looked like they sold the kind of stuff the people in the rundown houses bought.

"You're the one that told them what I was doing," Arly said.

"I gave them some information. I didn't know what you were up to. I got your account numbers. They hired me to do it. The computer geek took the numbers and verified you were cheating them."

"You're a paranormal."

Gerdon glanced down a side street and saw a cluster of overhead lights two blocks away. Cars and trucks sped along a street that looked like a big boulevard—a road out of this part of the city.

"That's it, right? You get into people's minds? You did something funny and got inside my mind."

Gerdon had worked his way through a shelf of paranormal romance novels during a month when he had holed up in a room in Liverpool—back in the days when he had still thought he could learn something about himself from books. He had mostly learned that women were attracted to daydreams that were just as absurd as the fantasies that hypnotized men.

Did women who read Jane Austen novels read that kind of thing, too?

He had never understood how his thing worked or why he could do it. Or why he seemed to be the only person who could do it. There had been a time when he had thought quantum mechanics might explain it but he had given that up when he had decided all the writers who philosophized about uncertainty and entanglement didn't know what they were talking about. The people who really understood the subject communicated with mathematics he would never master.

The Universe was clearly a mysterious place, with wonders his fellow humans had barely noticed. Someday, someone might understand his peculiar aberration. When they did, the explanation would probably be just as incomprehensible as a quantum textbook.

"That's what you do?" Arly said. "You've got those kind of powers?"

"I have a trick I can do. It's very limited. I'm not looking into your head now, if that's what you're thinking."

"You did it to me twice."

"I did it the second time because I didn't know what they wanted—what would happen to you. I had your numbers. But I didn't know why they wanted them."

He had turned on to the boulevard. He didn't know how it fit into the street layout but he knew they were heading south, toward the downtown area.

"You did all this for me? You killed Freddy for me?"

"They would have sent you back on their terms. They would have kept you there until you got caught. You'd go to jail. And it wouldn't cost them anything."

"Are you in love with me? Is that it? You did all this because you're in love with me?"

"I didn't want you to get hurt."

"I'll have to watch for them every time I go out the door."

"We don't know what they'll do. Freddy's dead. They don't know what happened. And they don't have Freddy telling them what to do."

"You're in love with me. You're one of those men with a hard shell who doesn't want to admit he's in love. And now you're a murderer. You let yourself fall in love with me. You killed Freddy just for me."

"I'm taking you home. You'll be all right. They won't bother you after this."

"You should have killed Dan. He's the one that's dangerous."

Gerdon focused his attention on the road directly in front of the hood. He had felt her fear. She had seen the carnage in Freddy's office. Could she really recover this fast?

Maybe he should be asking her what *she* was.

"You don't have to worry about Dan. He's the smart one. He's not going to do anything that could invite more trouble."

"You could take over that whole operation. Freddy was just a midget under all that attitude. You could turn it into something big."

"You can't keep up what you're doing, Arly. You were just a temporary source to them. They use people like you until you get caught. You go to prison and they find somebody else."

"I could keep it up forever if I had you watching out for me. We could be living on top of the tallest building in the city."

"You're safe. You should be safe. They got a real shock."

"We could have everything we wanted. We could fill the biggest closets anybody could build for us."

He had placed the bag on a patch of broken concrete, in an area that picked up some of the light from the rumbling expressway over his head. He was standing in the darkness next to a pillar, out of effective pistol range, unless Dan was more of a marksman than most petty criminals.

It was two-fifteen in the morning. He had told Dan he should arrive on foot, at two a.m., but he wasn't surprised when a car cruised down the street that ran beside the underpass and turned under the expressway, fifteen minutes late. He had assumed a smart person would create some confusion.

Litter crunched under the car's tires. Dan threw open the door and waddled toward the bag in an exaggerated combat-manual crouch, swerving his gun from side to side.

The crouch had put Dan's body in an awkward position. It fell backward before Gerdon could get control and he found himself sitting on the ground.

He had stepped out of the dark as he made the swap. He had a clear view of his own body. The man looking out of his eyes could see everything he did.

He sat up straight. He placed the gun next to his cheek and held it there—where the bullet would smash through his face and jaw, disfiguring and crippling without killing. Then he raised it and held it against the side of his nose.

He finished by holding it against his kneecaps. First the left. Then the right. Then he tossed the gun under the car.

He had thought about a little speech. *I can disfigure you. I can maim you. It will hurt me for a few seconds. You'll live with it the rest of your life.* But it wasn't necessary. Dan would understand.

He backed into the dark as soon as he had his own body under control. Dan grabbed the money and scrambled into the car with satisfactory haste. The gun was still lying on the ground when the car veered out of the underpass.

Gerdon wandered through the darkened neighborhood that abutted the underpass, looking for a main street that might attract a taxi. He had done his best. Arly might have to move to a cheaper apartment. She would definitely have to reduce her clothing budget. But she could go to work in the morning and read her romance novels in the evening without wondering if someone was going to attack her on the street or break down her door. He had returned every dollar he owed them. The brain in their newly remodeled organization knew what would happen if they violated their side of the bargain.

The neighborhood looked pleasant. The houses all looked neat and well maintained. It was a nice city. Could he stay awhile? He did have to make a living.

BLANCHEFLEUR

THEODORA GOSS

They called him Idiot.

He was the miller's son, and he had never been good for much. At least not since his mother's death, when he was twelve years old. He had found her floating, facedown, in the millpond, and his cries had brought his father's men. When they turned her over, he had seen her face, pale and bloated, before someone said, "Not in front of the child!" and they had hurried him away. He had never seen her again, just the wooden coffin going into the ground, and after that, the gray stone in the churchyard where, every Sunday, he and his father left whatever was in season—a bunch of violets, sprays of the wild roses that grew by the forest edge, tall lilies from beside the mill stream. In winter, they left holly branches red with berries.

Before her death, he had been a laughing, affectionate child. After her death, he became solitary. He would no longer play with his friends from school, and eventually they began to ignore him. He would no longer speak even to his father, and anyway the miller was a quiet man who, after his wife's death, grew more silent. He was so broken, so bereft, by the loss of his wife that he could barely look at the son who had her golden hair, her eyes the color of spring leaves. Often they would go a whole day, saying no more than a few sentences to each other.

He went to school, but he never seemed to learn—he would stare out the window or, if called upon, shake his head and refuse to answer. Once, the teacher rapped his knuckles for it, but he simply looked at her with those eyes, which were so much like his mother's. The teacher turned away, ashamed of herself, and after that she left him alone, telling herself that at least he was sitting in the schoolroom rather than loafing about the fields.

He learned nothing, he did nothing. When his father told him to do the work of the mill, he did it so badly that the water flowing through the sluice gates was either too fast or slow, or the large millstones grinding the grain were too close together or far apart, or he took the wrong amount of grain in payment from the farmers who came to grind their wheat. Finally, the miller hired another man, and his son wandered about the countryside, sometimes sleeping under the stars, eating berries from the hedges when he could find them. He would come home dirty, with scratches on his arms and brambles in his hair. And his father, rather than scolding him, would look away.

If anyone had looked closely, they would have seen that he was clever at carving pieces of wood into whistles and seemed to know how to call all the birds. Also, he knew the paths through the countryside and could tell the time by the position of the sun and moon on each day of the year, his direction by the stars. He knew the track and spoor of every animal, what tree each leaf came from by its shape. He knew which mushrooms were poisonous and how to find water under the ground. But no one did look closely.

It was the other schoolboys, most of whom had once been his friends, who started calling him Idiot. At first it was Idiot Ivan, but soon it was simply Idiot, and it spread through the village until people forgot he had ever been called Ivan. Farmers would call to him, cheerfully enough, "Good morning, Idiot!" They meant no insult by it. In villages, people like knowing who you are. The boy was clearly an idiot, so let him be called that. And so he was.

No one noticed that under the dirt, and despite the rags he wore, he had grown into a large, handsome boy. He should have had sweethearts, but the village girls assumed he was slow and had no prospects, even though he was the miller's son. So he was always alone, and the truth was, he seemed to prefer it.

The miller was the only one who still called him Ivan, although he had given his son up as hopeless, and even he secretly believed the boy was slow and stupid.

This was how things stood when the miller rode to market to buy a new horse. The market was held in the nearest town, on a fine summer day that was also the feast-day of Saint Ivan, so the town was filled with stalls selling livestock, vegetables from the local farms, leather and rope harnesses, embroidered linen, woven baskets. Men and women in smocks lined up to hire themselves for the coming harvest. There were strolling players with fiddles or pipes, dancers on a wooden platform, and a great deal of beer—which the miller drank from a tankard.

The market went well for him. He found a horse for less money than he thought he would have to spend, and while he was paying for his beer, one of the maids from the tavern winked at him. She was plump, with sunburnt cheeks, and she poured his beer neatly, leaving a head of foam that just reached the top of the tankard. He had not thought of women, not in that way, since his wife had drowned. She had been one of those magical women, beautiful as the dawn, slight as a willow-bough and with a voice like birds singing, that are perhaps too delicate for this world. That kind of woman gets into a man's blood. But lately he had started to notice once again that other women existed, and that there were other things in the world than running a mill. Like his son, who was a great worry to him. What would the idiot—Ivan, he reminded himself—what would he do when his father was gone, as we must all go someday? Would he be able to take care of himself?

He had saddled his horse and was fastening a rope to his saddle so the new horse could be led, when he heard a voice he recognized from many years ago. "Hello, Stephen Miller," it said.

He turned around and bowed. "Hello, Lady."

She was tall and pale, with long gray hair that hung to the backs of her knees, although she did not look older than when he had last seen her, at his wedding. She wore a gray linen dress that, although it was midsummer, reminded him of winter.

"How is my nephew? This is his name day, is it not?"

"It is, Lady. As to how he is—" The miller told her. He might not have, if the beer had not loosened his tongue, for he was a proud man and he did not want his sister-in-law to think his son was doing badly. But with the beer and his worries, it all came out—the days Ivan spent staring out of windows or walking through the countryside, how the local farmers thought of him, even that name—Idiot.

"I warned you that no good comes of a mortal marrying a fairy woman," said the Lady. "But those in love never listen. Send my nephew to me. I will make him my apprentice for three years, and at the end of that time we shall see. For his wages, you may take this."

She handed him a purse. He bowed in acknowledgment, saying, "I thank you for your generosity—" but when he straightened again, she was already walking away from him. Just before leaving the inn yard, she turned back for a moment and said, "The Castle in the Forest, remember. I will expect him in three days' time."

The miller nodded, although she had already turned away again. As he rode home, he looked into the purse she had given him—in it was a handful of leaves.

He wondered how he was going to tell his son about the bargain he had made. But when he reached home, the boy was sitting at the kitchen table whittling something out of wood, and he simply said, "I have apprenticed you for three years to your aunt, the Lady of the Forest. She expects you in three days' time."

The boy did not say a word. But the next morning, he put all of his possessions—they were few enough—into a satchel, which he slung over his shoulder. And he set out.

In three days' time, Ivan walked through the forest, blowing on the whistle he had carved. He could hear birds calling to each other in the forest. He whistled to them, and they whistled back. He did not know how long his journey would take—if you set out for the Castle in the Forest, it can take you a day, or a week, or the rest of your life. But the Lady had said she expected him in three days, so he thought he would reach the Castle by the end of the day at the latest.

Before he left, his father had looked again in the purse that the Lady had given him. In it was a pile of gold coins—as the miller had expected, for that is the way fairy money works. "I will keep this for you," his father had said. "When you come back, you will be old enough to marry, and with such a fortune, any of the local girls will take you. I do not know what you will do as the Lady's apprentice, but I hope you will come back fit to run a mill."

Ivan had simply nodded, slung his satchel over his shoulder, and gone.

Just as he was wondering if he would indeed find the castle that day, for the sun was beginning to set, he saw it through the trees, its turrets rising above a high stone wall.

He went up to the wall and knocked at the wooden door that was the only way in. It opened, seemingly by itself. In the doorway stood a white cat.

"Are you the Idiot?" she asked.

"I suppose so," he said, speaking for the first time in three days.

"That's what I thought," she said. "You certainly look the part. Well, come in then, and follow me."

He followed her through the doorway and along a path that led through the castle gardens. He had never seen such gardens, although in school his teacher had once described the gardens that surrounded the King's castle, which she had visited on holiday. There were fountains set in green lawns, with stone fish spouting water. There were box hedges, and topiaries carved into the shapes of birds, rabbits, mice. There were pools filled with water lilies, in which he could see real fish, silver and orange. There were arched trellises from which roses hung down in profusion, and an orchard with fruit trees. He could even see a kitchen garden, with vegetables in neat rows. And all through the gardens, he could see cats, pruning the hedges, tying back the roses, raking the earth in the flowerbeds.

It was the strangest sight he had ever seen, and for the first time it occurred to him that being the Lady's apprentice would be an adventure—the first of his life.

The path took them to the door of the castle, which swung open as they approached. An orange tabby walked out and stood waiting at the top of the steps.

"Hello, Marmalade," said the white cat.

"Good evening, Miss Blanchefleur," he replied. "Is this the young man her Ladyship is expecting?"

"As far as I can tell," she said. "Although what my mother would want with such an unprepossessing specimen, I don't know."

Marmalade bowed to Ivan and said, "Welcome, Ivan Miller. Her Ladyship is waiting in the solar."

Ivan expected the white cat, whose name seemed to be Blanchefleur, to leave him with Marmalade. Instead, she accompanied them, following Ivan through the doorway, then through a great hall whose walls were hung with tapestries showing cats sitting in gardens, climbing trees, hunting rabbits, catching fish. Here too there were cats, setting out bowls on two long wooden tables, and on a shorter table set on a dais at the end of the room. As Marmalade passed, they nodded, and a gray cat who seemed to be directing their activities said, "We're almost ready, Mr. Marmalade. The birds are nicely roasted, and the mint sauce is really a treat if I say so myself."

"Excellent, Mrs. Pebbles. I can't tell you how much I'm looking forward to those birds. Tailcatcher said that he caught them himself."

"Well, with a little help!" said Mrs. Pebbles, acerbically. "He doesn't go on the hunt alone, does he now, Mr. Marmalade? Oh, begging your pardon, Miss," she said when she saw Blanchefleur. "I didn't know you were there."

"I couldn't care less what you say about him," said Blanchefleur, with a sniff and a twitch of her tail. "He's nothing to me."

"As you say, Miss," said Mrs. Pebbles, not sounding particularly convinced.

At the back of the great hall was another, smaller door that led to a long hallway. Ivan was startled when, at the end of the hallway, which had been rather dark, they emerged into a room filled with sunlight. It had several windows looking out onto a green lawn, and scattered around the room were low cushions, on which cats sat engaged in various tasks. Some were carding wool, some were spinning it on drop spindles, some were plying the yarn or winding it into skeins. In a chair by one of the windows sat the Lady, with a piece of embroidery in her lap. One of the cats was reading a book aloud, but stopped when they entered.

"My Lady, this is Ivan Miller, your new apprentice," said Marmalade.

"Otherwise known as the Idiot," said Blanchefleur. "And he seems to deserve the name. He's said nothing for himself all this time."

"My dear, you should be polite to your cousin," said the Lady. "Ivan, you've already met my daughter, Blanchefleur, and Marmalade, who takes such marvelous care of us all. These are my ladies-in-waiting: Elderberry, Twilight, Snowy, Whiskers, and Fluff. My daughter tells me you have nothing to say for yourself. Is that true?"

Ivan stared at her, sitting in her chair, surrounded by cats. She had green eyes, and although her gray hair hung down to the floor, she reminded him of his mother. "Yes, Ma'am," he said.

She looked at him for a moment, appraisingly. Then she said, "Very well. I will send you where you need not say anything. Just this morning I received a letter from an old friend of mine, Professor Owl. He is compiling an Encyclopedia of All Knowledge, but he is old and feels arthritis terribly in his legs. He can no longer write the entries himself. For the first year of your apprenticeship, you will go to Professor Owl in the Eastern Waste and help him with his Encyclopedia. Do you think you can do that, nephew?"

"It's all the same to me," said Ivan. It was obvious that no one wanted him here, just as no one had wanted him at the mill. What did it matter where he went?

"Then you shall set out tomorrow morning," said the Lady. "Tonight you shall join us for dinner. Are the preparations ready, Marmalade?"

"Almost, my Lady," said the orange cat.

"How will I find this Professor Owl?" asked Ivan.

"Blanchefleur will take you," said the Lady.

"You can't be serious!" said Blanchefleur. "He's an idiot, and he stinks like a pigsty."

"Then show him the bathroom, where he can draw himself a bath," said the Lady. "And give him new clothes to wear. Those are too ragged even for Professor Owl, I think."

"Come on, you," said Blanchefleur, clearly disgusted. He followed her out of the room and up a flight of stairs, to a bathroom with a large tub on four clawed legs. He had never seen anything quite like it before. At the mill, he had often washed under the kitchen spigot. After she had left, he filled it with hot water that came out of a tap and slipped into it until the water was up to his chin.

What a strange day it had been. Three days ago he had left his father's house and the life he had always lived, a life that required almost nothing of him: no thought, no effort. And now here he was, in a castle filled with talking cats. And tomorrow he would start for another place, one that might be even stranger. When Blanchefleur had taunted him by telling the Lady that he had nothing to say for himself, he had wanted to say—what? Something that would have made her less disdainful. But what could he say for himself, after all?

With a piece of soap, he washed himself more carefully than he had ever before in his life. She had said he smelled like a pigsty, and he had spent the night before last sleeping on a haystack that was, indeed, near a pen where several pigs had grunted in their dreams. Last night, he had slept in the forest, but he supposed the smell still lingered—particularly to a cat's nose. For the first time in years, he felt a sense of shame.

He dried himself and put on the clothes she had left for him. He went back down the stairs, toward the sound of music, and found his way to the great hall. It was lit with torches, and sitting at the two long tables were cats of all colors: black and brindled and tortoiseshell and piebald, with short hair and long. Sitting on the dais were the Lady, with Blanchefleur beside her, and a large yellow and brown cat who was striped like a tiger. He stood in the doorway, feeling self-conscious.

The Lady saw him across the room and motioned for him to come over. He walked to the dais and bowed before it, because that seemed the appropriate thing to do. She said, "That was courteous, nephew. Now come sit with us. Tailcatcher, you will not mind giving your seat to Ivan, will you?"

"Of course not, my Lady," said the striped cat in a tone that indicated he did indeed mind, very much.

Ivan took his place, and Marmalade brought him a dish of roast starlings, with a green sauce that smelled like catmint. It was good, although relatively flavorless. The cats, evidently, did not use salt in their cooking. Halfway through the meal, he was startled to realize that the cats were conversing with one another and nodding politely, as though they were a roomful of ordinary people. He was probably the only silent one in the entire room. Several times he noticed Blanchefleur giving him exasperated looks.

When he had finished eating, the Lady said, "I think it's time to dance." She clapped her hands, and suddenly Ivan heard music. He wondered where it was coming from, then noticed a group of cats at the far end of the room playing, more skillfully than he had supposed possible, a fife, a viol, a tabor, and other instruments he could not identify, one of which curved like a long snake. The cats who had been sitting at the long tables moved them to the sides of the room, then formed two lines in the center. He had seen a line dance before, at one of the village fairs, but he had never seen one danced as gracefully as it was by the cats. They wove in and out, each line breaking and reforming in intricate patterns.

"Aren't you going to ask your cousin to dance?" said the Lady, leaning over to him.

"What? Oh," he said, feeling foolish. How could he dance with a cat? But the Lady was looking at him, waiting. "Would you like to dance?" he asked Blanchefleur.

"Not particularly," she said, looking at him with disdain. "Oh, all right, Mother! You don't have to pull my tail."

He wiped his mouth and hands on a napkin, then followed Blanchefleur to the dance floor and joined at the end of the line, feeling large and clumsy, trying to follow the steps and not tread on any paws. It did not help that, just when he was beginning to feel as though he was learning the steps, he saw

Tailcatcher glaring at him from across the room. He danced several times, once with Blanchefleur, once with Mrs. Pebbles, who must have taken pity on him, and once with Fluff, who told him it was a pleasure to dance with such a handsome young man and seemed to mean it. He managed to step on only one set of paws, belonging to a tabby tomcat who said, "Do that again, Sir, and I'll send you my second in the morning," but was mollified when Ivan apologized sincerely and at length. After that, he insisted on sitting down until the feast was over and he could go to bed.

The next morning, he woke and wondered if it was all a dream, but no—there he was, lying in a curtained bed in the Lady's castle. And there was Blanchefleur, sitting in a nearby chair, saying, "About time you woke up. We need to get started if we're going to make the Eastern Waste by nightfall."

Ivan got out of bed, vaguely embarrassed to be seen in his nightshirt, then reminded himself that she was just a cat. He put on the clothes he had been given last night, then found his satchel on a dresser. All of his old clothes were gone, replaced by new ones. In the satchel he also found a loaf of bread, a hunk of cheese, a flask of wine, and a shiny new knife with a horn handle.

"I should thank the Lady for all these things," he said.

"That's the first sensible thing you've said since you got here," said Blanchefleur. "But she's gone to see my father, and won't be back for three days. And we have to get going. So hurry up already!"

The Lady's castle was located in a forest called the Wolfwald. To the north, it stretched for miles, and parts of it were so thick that almost no sunlight reached the forest floor. At the foot of the northern mountains, wolves still roamed. But around the castle it was less dense. Ivan and Blanchefleur walked along a path strewn with oak leaves, through filtered sunlight. Ivan was silent, in part because he was accustomed to silence, in part because he did not know what to say to the white cat. Blanchefleur seemed much more interested in chasing insects, and even dead leaves, than in talking to him.

They stopped to rest when the sun was directly overhead. The forest had changed: the trees were shorter and spaced more widely apart, mostly pines rather than the oaks and beeches around the Lady's castle. Ahead of him, Ivan could see a different sort of landscape: bare, except for the occasional twisted trees and clumps of grass. It was dry, rocky, strewn with boulders.

"That's the Eastern Waste," said Blanchefleur.

"The ground will be too hard for your paws," said Ivan. "I can carry you."

"I'll do just fine, thank you," she said with a sniff. But after an hour of walking over the rocky ground, Ivan saw she was limping. "Come on," he said. "If you hate the thought of me carrying you so much, pretend I'm a horse."

"A jackass is more like it," she said. But she let him pick her up and carry her, with her paws on his shoulder so she could look around. Occasionally, her whiskers tickled his ear.

The sun traveled across the sky, and hours passed, and still he walked though the rocky landscape, until his feet hurt. But he would not admit he was in pain, not with Blanchefleur perched on his shoulder. At last, after a region of low cliffs and defiles, they came to a broad plain that was nothing but stones. In the middle of the plain rose a stone tower.

"That's it," said Blanchefleur. "That's Professor Owl's home."

"Finally," said Ivan under his breath. He had been feeling as though he would fall over from sheer tiredness. He took a deep breath and started for the tower. But before he reached it, he asked the question he had been wanting to ask all day, but had not dared to. "Blanchefleur, who is your father?"

"The man who lives in the moon," she said. "Can you hurry up? I haven't had a meal since that mouse at lunch, and I'm getting hungry."

"He's an owl," said Ivan.

"Of course he's an owl," said Blanchefleur. "What did you think he would be?"

Professor Owl was in fact an owl, the largest Ivan has ever seen, with brown and white feathers. When they entered the tower, which was round and had one room on each level, with stairs curling around the outer wall, he said, "Welcome, welcome. Blanchefleur, I haven't seen you since you were a kitten. And this must be the assistant the Lady has so graciously sent me. Welcome, boy. I hope you know how to write a good, clear hand."

"His name is Idiot," said Blanchefleur.

"My name is Ivan," said Ivan.

"Yes, yes," said Professor Owl, paying no attention to them whatsoever. "Here, then, is my life's work. The Encyclopedia."

It was an enormous book, taller than Ivan himself, resting on a large stand at the far end of the room. In the middle of the room was a wooden table, and around the circular walls were file cabinets, all the way up to the ceiling.

"It's much too heavy to open by hand—or foot," said Professor Owl. "But if you tell the Encyclopedia what you're looking for, it will open to that entry."

"Mouse," said Blanchefleur. And sure enough, as she spoke, the pages of the Encyclopedia turned as though by magic (*although it probably is magic,* thought Ivan) to a page with an entry titled *Mouse.*

"Let's see, let's see," said Professor Owl, peering at the page. "The bright and active, although mischievous, little animal known to us by the name of Mouse and its close relative the Rat are the most familiar and also the most typical members of the Murinae, a sub-family containing about two hundred and fifty species assignable to no less than eighteen distinct genera, all of which, however, are so superficially alike that the English names rat or mouse would be fairly appropriate to any of them. Well, that seems accurate, doesn't it?"

"Does it say how they taste?" asked Blanchefleur.

"The Encyclopedia is connected to five others," said Professor Owl, turning to Ivan. "One is in the Library of Alexandria, one in the Hagia Sophia in Constantinople, one in the Sorbonne, one in the British Museum, and one in the New York Public Library. It is the only Encyclopedia of All Knowledge, and as you can imagine, it takes all my time to keep it up to date. I've devoted my life to it. But since I've developed arthritis in my legs,"—and Ivan could see that indeed, the owl's legs looked more knobby than they ought to—"it's been difficult for me to write my updates. So I'm grateful to the Lady for sending you. Here is where you will work." He pointed to the table with his clawed foot. On it was a large pile of paper, each page filled with scribbled notes.

"These are the notes I've made indicating what should be updated and how. If you'll look at the page on top of the pile, for instance, you'll see that the entry on Justice needs to be updated. There have been, in the last month alone, five important examples of injustice, from the imprisonment of a priest who criticized the Generalissimo to a boy who was deprived of his supper when his mother wrongly accused him of stealing a mince pie. You must add each example to the entry under Justice—Injustice—Examples. The entry itself can be found in one of the cabinets along the wall—I believe it's the twenty-sixth row from the door, eight cabinets up. Of course I can't possibly include every example of injustice—there are hundreds every hour. I only include the ones that most clearly illustrated the concept. And here are my notes on a species of wild rose newly discovered in the mountains of Cathay. That will go under Rose—Wild—Species. Do you understand, boy? You are to look at my notes and add whatever information is necessary to update the entry, writing directly on the file. The Encyclopedia itself will incorporate your update, turning it into typescript, but you must make your letters clearly. And no spelling errors! Now, it's almost nightfall, and I understand that humans have defective vision, so I suggest you sleep until dawn, when you can get up and start working on these notes as well as the ones I'll be writing overnight."

"Professor," said Blanchefleur, "we haven't had dinner."

"Dinner?" said Professor Owl. "Of course, of course. I wouldn't want you to go hungry. There are some mice and birds in the cupboard. I caught them just last night. You're certainly welcome to them."

"Human beings can't eat mice and birds," said Blanchefleur. "They have to cook their food."

"Yes, yes, of course," said Professor Owl. "An inefficient system, I must say.

I believe I had—but where did I put it?" He turned around, looking perplexed, then opened the door of a closet under the stairs. He poked his head in, and then tossed out several things, so both Ivan and Blanchefleur had to dodge them. A pith helmet, a butterfly net, and a pair of red flannel underwear for what must have been a very tall man. "Yes, here is it. But you'll have to help me with it."

"It" was a large iron kettle. Ivan helped the owl pull it out of the closet and place it on the long wooden table. He looked into it, not knowing what to expect, but it was empty.

"It's a magic kettle, of course," said Professor Owl. "I seem to remember that it makes soup. You can sleep on the second floor. The third is my study, and I hope you will refrain from disturbing me during daylight hours, when I will be very busy indeed. Now, if you don't mind, I'm going out for a bit of a hunt. I do hope you will be useful to me. My last apprentice was a disappointment." He waddled comically across the floor and up the stairs.

"These scholarly types aren't much for small talk," said Blanchefleur.

"I thought he was going out?" said Ivan.

"He is," said Blanchefleur. "You don't think he's just going to walk out the door, do you? He's an owl. He's going to launch himself from one of the tower windows."

Ivan looked into the kettle again. Still empty. "Do you really think it's magic?" he asked. He had eaten the bread and cheese a long time ago, and his stomach was starting to growl.

"Try some magic words," said Blanchefleur.

"Abracadabra," he said. "Open Sesame." What other magic words had he learned in school? If he remembered correctly, magic had not been a regular part of the curriculum.

"You really are an idiot," said Blanchefleur. She sprang onto the table, then sat next to the kettle. "Dear Kettle," she said. "We've been told of your magical powers in soup-making, and are eager to taste your culinary delights. Will you please make us some soup? Any flavor, your choice, but not onion because his breath is pungent enough already."

From the bottom, the kettle filled with something that bubbled and had a delicious aroma. "There you go," said Blanchefleur. "Magical items have feelings, you know. They need to be asked nicely. Abracadabra indeed!"

"I still need a spoon," said Ivan.

"With all you require for nourishment, I wonder that you're still alive!" said Blanchefleur. "Look in the closet."

In the closet, Ivan did indeed find several wooden spoons, as well as a croquet set, several pairs of boots, and a stuffed alligator.

"Beef stew," he said, tasting what was in the kettle. "Would you like some?"

"I'm quite capable of hunting for myself, thank you," said Blanchefleur. "Don't wait up. I have a feeling that when the Professor said you should be up by dawn, he meant it."

That night, Ivan slept on the second floor of the tower, where he found a bed, a desk, and a large traveling trunk with *Oswald* carved on it. He wondered if Oswald had been the professor's last apprentice, the one who had been such a disappointment. In the middle of the night, he thought he felt Blanchefleur jump on the bed and curl up next to his back. But when he woke up in the morning, she was gone.

Ivan was used to waking up at dawn, so wake up at dawn he did. He found a small bathroom under the stairs, splashed water on his face, got dressed, and went downstairs. Blanchefleur was sitting on the table, staring at the kettle still set on it, with a look of disdain on her face.

"What is that mess?" she asked.

"I think it's pea soup," he said, after looking into the kettle. It smelled inviting, but then anything would have at that hour. Next to the kettle were a wooden bowl and spoon, as well as a napkin. "Did you put these here?" he asked Blanchefleur.

"Why would I do such a stupid thing?" she asked, and turned her back to him. She began licking her fur, as though washing herself were the most important thing in the world.

Ivan shrugged, spooned some of the pea soup into the bowl, and had a plain but filling breakfast. Afterward, he washed the bowl and spoon. As soon as he had finished eating, the kettle had emptied again—evidently, it did not need washing. Then he sat down at the table and pulled the first of Professor Owl's notes toward him.

It was tedious work. First, he would read through the notes, which were written in a cramped, slanting hand. Then, he would try to add a paragraph to the file, as neatly and succinctly as he could. He had never paid much attention in school, and writing did not come easily to him. After the first botched attempt, he learned to compose his paragraphs on the backs of Professor Owl's notes, so when he went to update the entries, he was not fumbling for words. By noon, he had finished additions to the entries on Justice, Rose, Darwin, Theosophy, Venus, Armadillo, Badminton, and Indochina. His lunch was chicken soup with noodles. He thought about having nothing but soup, every morning, noon, and night for an entire year, and longed for a sandwich.

He sat down at the table and picked up the pen, but his back and hand hurt. He put the pen down. The sunlight out the window looked so inviting. Perhaps he should go out and wander around the tower, just for a little while?

Where had Blanchefleur gone, anyway? He had not seen her since breakfast. He got up, stretched, and walked out.

It had been his habit, as long as he remembered, to wander around as he wished. That was what he did now, walking around the tower and then away from it, looking idly for Blanchefleur and finding only lizards. He wandered without thinking about where he was going or how long he had been gone. The sun began to sink in the west.

That was when he realized that he had been gone for hours. Well, it would not matter, would it? He could always catch up with any work he did not finish tomorrow. He walked back in the direction of the tower, only becoming lost once. It was dark when he reached it again. He opened the door and walked in.

There were Professor Owl and Blanchefleur. The Professor was perched on the table where Ivan had been sitting earlier that day, scribbling furiously. Blanchefleur was saying, "What did you expect of someone named Idiot? I told you he would be useless."

"Oh, hello, boy," said Professor Owl, looking up. "I noticed you went out for a walk, so I finished all of the notes for today, except Orion. I'll have that done in just a moment, and then you can sit down for dinner. I don't think I told you that each day's updates need to be filed by the end of the day, or the Encyclopedia will be incomplete. And it has never been incomplete since I started working on it, five hundred years ago."

"I'll do it," said Ivan.

"Do what?" said Blanchefleur. "Go wandering around again?"

"I'll do the update on Orion."

"That's very kind of you," said Professor Owl. "I'm sure you must be tired." But he handed Ivan the pen and hopped a bit away on the table. It was a lopsided hop: Ivan could tell the owl's right foot was hurting. He sat and finished the update, conscious of Blanchefleur's eyes on him. When he was finished, Professor Owl read it over. "Yes, very nice," he said. "You have a clear and logical mind. Well done, boy."

Ivan looked up, startled. It was the first compliment he ever remembered receiving.

"Well, go on then, have some dinner," said Professor Owl. "And you'll be up at dawn tomorrow?"

"I'll be up at dawn," said Ivan. He knew that the next day, he would not go wandering around, at least until after the entries were finished. He did not want Blanchefleur calling him an idiot again in that tone of voice.

Summer turned into winter. Each day, Ivan sat at the table in the tower, updating the entries for the Encyclopedia of All Knowledge. One day, he realized that he no longer needed to compose the updates on the backs of Professor Owl's notes. He could simply compose them in his head, and then write each update directly onto the file. He had not learned much in school, but he was learning now, about things that seemed useless, such as Sponge Cake, and things that seemed useful, such as Steam Engines, Epic Poetry, and Love. One morning he realized Professor Owl had left him not only a series of updates, but also the notes for an entry on a star that had been discovered by astronomers the week before. Proudly and carefully, he took a blank file card out of the cabinet, composed a new entry for the Encyclopedia of All Knowledge, and filed the card in its place.

He came to write so well and so quickly that he would finish all of the updates, and any new entries the Professor left him, by early afternoon. After a lunch of soup, for he had never managed to get the kettle to make him anything else, however politely he asked, he would roam around the rocky countryside. Sometimes Blanchefleur would accompany him, and eventually she allowed him to carry her on his shoulder without complaining, although she was never enthusiastic. And she still called him Idiot.

One day, in February although he had lost track of the months, he updated an entry on the Trojan War. He had no idea what it was, since he had not been paying attention that day in school. So after he finished his updates, he asked the Encyclopedia. It opened to the entry on the Trojan War, which began, "It is a truth universally acknowledged that judging a beauty contest between three goddesses causes nothing but trouble." He read on, fascinated. After that day, he would spend several hours reading through whichever entries took his fancy. Each entry he read left him with more questions, and he began to wish he could stay with Professor Owl, simply reading the entries in the Encyclopedia, forever.

But winter turned into summer, and one day the professor said, "Ivan, it has been a year since you arrived, and the term of your apprenticeship with me is at an end. Thank you for all of the care and attention you have put into your task. As a reward, I will give you one of my feathers—that one right there. Pluck it out gently. *Gently!*"

Ivan held up the feather. It was long and straight, with brown and white stripes.

"Cut the end of it with a penknife and make it into a pen," said Professor Owl. "If you ever want to access the Encyclopedia, just tell the pen what you would like to know, and it will write the entry for you."

"Thank you," said Ivan. "But couldn't I stay—"

"Of course not," said Blanchefleur. "My mother is expecting us. So come on already." And indeed, since it was dawn, Professor Owl was already heading up the stairs, for he had very important things to do during the day. Owls do, you know.

• • •

The Castle in the Forest looked just as Ivan remembered. There were cats tending the gardens, where the roses were once again blooming, as though they had never stopped. Marmalade greeted them at the door and led them to the Lady's solar, where she was sitting at a desk, writing. Her cats-in-waiting were embroidering a tapestry, and one was strumming a lute with her claws, playing a melody that Ivan remembered from when he was a child.

"Well?" she said when she looked up. "How did Ivan do, my dear?"

"Well enough," said Blanchefleur. "Are there any mouse pies? We've been walking all day, and I'm hungry."

Really it had been Ivan who had been walking all day. He had carried Blanchefleur most of the way, except when she wanted to drink from a puddle or play with a leaf.

"Wait until the banquet," said the Lady. "It starts in an hour, which will give you enough time to prepare. It's in honor of your return and departure."

"Departure?" said Ivan.

"Yes," said the Lady. "Tomorrow, you will go to the Southern Marshes, to spend a year with my friend, Dame Lizard. She has a large family, and needs help taking care of it. Blanchefleur, you will accompany your cousin."

"But that's not fair!" said Blanchefleur. "I've already spent a year with Ivan Idiot. Why do I have to spend another year with him?"

"Because he is your cousin, and he needs your help," said the Lady. "Now go, the both of you. I don't think you realize quite how dirty you both are." And she was right. From the long journey, even Blanchefleur's white paws were covered with dirt.

As they walked upstairs, Ivan said, "I'm sorry you have to come with me, Blanchefleur. I know you dislike being with me."

"You're not so bad," she said grudgingly. "At least you're warm." So it had been her, sleeping against his back all those nights. Ivan was surprised and pleased at the thought.

That night, the banquet proceeded as it had the year before, except this time Ivan knew what to expect. Several of the female cats asked him to dance, and this time he danced with more skill, never once stepping on a cat paw or tail. He danced several times with Blanchefleur, and she did not seem to dislike it as much as she had last year. Tailcatcher, the striped cat, was there as well. Once, as they were dancing close to one another, Ivan heard a hiss, but when he turned to look at Tailcatcher, the cat was bowing to his partner.

At the end of the evening, as he wearily climbed the stone stairs up to his bed, he passed a hallway and heard a murmur of voices. At the end of the hallway stood Tailcatcher and Blanchefleur. The striped cat spoke to her and she replied, too low for Ivan to hear what they were saying. Then she turned and walked on down the hallway, her tail held high, exactly the way she walked when she was displeased with him. Ivan was rather glad Tailcatcher had been rebuffed, whatever he had wanted from her.

As he sank into sleep that night, in the curtained bed, he wondered if she would come to curl up against his back. But he fell asleep too quickly to find out.

The next morning, they started for the Southern Marshes. As they traveled south, the forest grew less dense: the trees were sparser, more sunlight fell on the path, and soon Ivan was hot and sweating. At midafternoon, they came to a river, and he was able to swim and cool himself off. Blanchefleur refused to go anywhere near the water.

"I'm not a fish," she said. "Are you quite done? We still have a long way to go."

Ivan splashed around a bit more, then got out and dried himself as best he could. They followed the river south until it was no longer a river but a series of creeks running through low hills covered with willows, alders, and sycamores. Around the creeks grew cattails, and where the water formed into pools, he could see water lilies starting to bloom. They were constantly crossing water, so Ivan carried Blanchefleur, who did not like to get her feet wet.

"There," she said finally. "That's where we're going." She was pointing at one of the low hills. At first, Ivan did not see the stone house among the trees: it blended in so well with the gray trunks. Ivan walked through a narrow creek (he had long ago given up on keeping his shoes dry) and up the hill to the house. He knocked at the door.

From inside, he heard a crash, then a "Just a moment!" Then another crash and the voice yelling, "Get out of there at once, Number Seven!"

There were more crashes and bangs, and then the door opened, so abruptly that he stepped back, startled. He might have been startled anyway, because who should be standing in front of him but a lizard, who came almost up to his shoulders, in a long brown duster and a feathered hat askew over one ear.

"I'm so glad you're here!" she said. "They've been impossible today. But they are dears, really they are, and the Lady told me that you were a competent nursemaid. You are competent, aren't you?" Without waiting for a reply, she continued, "Oh, it's good to see you again, Blanchefleur. Did you like the shrunken head I sent you from Peru?"

"Not particularly," said the white cat.

"Splendid!" said the lizard. "Now I'll just be off, shall I? My train leaves in half an hour and I don't want to miss it. I'm going to Timbuktu, you know. Train and then boat and train again, then camel caravan. Doesn't that sound fun? Do help me get my suitcases on the bicycle."

The bicycle was in a sort of shed. Ivan helped her tie two suitcases onto a rack with some frayed rope that he hoped would hold all the way to the station.

"Such a handy one, your young man, my dear," said the lizard to Blanchefleur.

"He's not—" said Blanchefleur.

"Kisses to you both! Ta, and I'll see you in a year! If I survive the sands of the Sahara, of course." And then she was off on her bicycle, down a road that ran across the hills, with her hat still askew. As she rode out of sight, Ivan heard a faint cry: "Plenty of spiders, that's what they like! And don't let them stay up too late!"

"Don't let who stay up too late?" asked Ivan.

"Us!" Ivan turned around. There in the doorway stood five—no, six—no, seven lizards that came up to his knees.

"Who are you?" he asked.

"These are her children," said Blanchefleur. "You're supposed to take care of them while she's gone. Don't you know who she is? She's Emilia Lizard, the travel writer. And you're her nursemaid." Blanchefleur seemed amused at the prospect.

"But the Lady said I was supposed to help," said Ivan. "How can I help someone who's on her way to Timbuktu? I don't know anything about taking care of children—or lizards!"

"It's easy," said one of the lizards. "You just let us do anything we want!"

"Eat sweets," said another.

"Stay up late," said yet another.

"Play as long as we like," said either one who had already spoken or another one, it was difficult to tell because they kept weaving in and out of the group, and they all looked alike.

"Please stand still," he said. "You're giving me a headache. And tell me your names."

"We don't have names," said one. "Mother just calls us by numbers, but she always gets us mixed up."

"I'll have to give you names," said Ivan, although he was afraid that he would get them mixed up as well. "Let's at least go in. Blanchefleur and I are tired, and we need to rest."

But once they stepped inside, Ivan found there was no place to rest. All of the furniture in the parlor had been piled in a corner to make a fort.

"If I'm going to take care of you, I need to learn about you," said Ivan. "Let's sit down—" But there was nowhere to sit down. And the lizards, all seven of them, were no longer there. Some were already inside the fort, and the others were about to besiege it.

"Come out!" he said. "Come out, all of you!" But his voice was drowned by the din they were already making. "What in the world am I supposed to do?" he asked Blanchefleur.

She twitched her tail, then said in a low voice, "I think it's the Siege of Jerusalem." Loudly and theatrically, she said, as though to Ivan, "Yes, you're right. The French are so much better at cleaning than the Saracens. I bet the French would clean up this mess lickety split."

Ivan stared at her in astonishment. Then he smiled. "You're wrong, Blanchefleur. The Saracens have a long tradition of cleanliness. In a cleaning contest, the Saracens would certainly win."

"Would not!" said one of the besiegers. "Would too!" came a cry from the fort. And then, in what seemed like a whirlwind of lizards, the fort was disassembled, the sofa and armchairs were put back in their places, and even the cushions were fluffed. In front of Ivan stood a line of seven lizards, asking, "Who won, who won?"

"The Saracens, this time," said Blanchefleur. "But really, you know, it's two out of three that counts."

Life in the Lizard household was completely different than it had been in Professor Owl's tower. There were days when Ivan missed the silence and solitude, the opportunity to read and study all day long. But he did not have much time to remember or regret. His days were spent catching insects and spiders for the lizards' breakfast, lunch, snack, and dinner, making sure that they bathed and sunned themselves, that they napped in the afternoon and went to bed on time.

At first, it was difficult to make them pay attention. They were as quick as seven winks, and on their outings they had a tendency to vanish as soon as he turned his back. Ivan was always afraid he was going to lose one. Once, indeed, he had to rescue Number Two from an eagle, and Number Five had to be pulled out of a foxhole. But he found that the hours spent working on the Encyclopedia of All Knowledge stood him in good stead: if he began telling a story, in an instant they would all be seated around him, listening intently. And if he forgot anything, he would ask the pen he had made from Professor Owl's tail feather to write it out for him. Luckily, Dame Lizard had left plenty of paper and ink.

He gave them all names: Ajax, Achilles, Hercules, Perseus, Helen, Medea, Andromache. They were fascinated by the stories of their names, and Medea insisted she was putting spells on the others, while Hercules would try to lift the heaviest objects he could find. Ivan learned to tell them apart. One had an ear that was slightly crooked, one had a stubby tail, one swayed as she walked. Each night, when he tucked them in and counted the lizard heads—yes, seven heads lay on the pillows—he breathed a sigh of relief that they were still alive.

"How many more days?" he would ask Blanchefleur.

"You don't want to know," she would reply. And then she would go out hunting, while he made himself dinner. Of course he could not eat insects and spiders, or mice like Blanchefleur. On the first night, he looked in the pantry and found a bag of flour, a bag of sugar, some tea, and a tinned ham. He made himself tea and ate part of the tinned ham.

"What in the world shall I do for food?" he asked Blanchefleur.

"What everyone else does. Work for it," she replied. So the next day, he left the lizards in her care for a couple of hours and went into the town that lay along the road Dame Lizard had taken. It was a small town, not much larger than the village he had grown up in. There, he asked if anyone needed firewood chopped, or a field cleared, or any such work. That day, he cleaned out a pigsty. The farmer who hired him found him strong and steady, so he hired him again, to pick vegetables, paint a fence, any odd work that comes up around a farm. He recommended Ivan to others, so there was soon a steady trickle of odd jobs that brought in enough money for him to buy bread and meat. The farmer who had originally hired him gave him vegetables that were too ripe for market.

He could never be gone long, because Blanchfleur would remind him in no uncertain terms that taking care of the lizards was his task, not hers. Whenever he came back, they were clean and fed and doing something orderly, like playing board games.

"Why do they obey you, and not me?" he asked, tired and cross. He had just washed an entire family's laundry.

"Because," she answered.

After dinner, once the lizards had been put to bed, really and finally put to bed, he would sit in the parlor and read the books on the shelves, which were all about travel in distant lands. Among them were the books of Dame Emilia Lizard. They had titles like *Up the Amazon in a Steamboat* and *Across the Himalayas on a Yak*. He found them interesting—Dame Lizard was an acute observer, and he learned about countries and customs that he had not even known existed—but often he could scarcely keep his eyes open because he was so tired. Once Blanchefleur returned from her evening hunt, he would go to sleep in Dame Lizard's room. He could tell it was hers because the walls were covered with photographs of her in front of temples and pyramids, perched on yaks or camels or water buffaloes, dressed in native garb. Blanchefleur would curl up against him, no longer pretending not to, and he would fall asleep to her soft rumble.

In winter, all the lizards caught bronchitis. First Andromache started coughing, and then Ajax, until there was an entire household of sick lizards. Since Ivan did not want to leave them, Blanchefleur went into town to find the doctor.

"You're lucky to have caught me," said the doctor when he arrived. "My train leaves in an hour. There's been a dragon attack, and the King has asked all the medical personnel who can be spared to help the victims. He burned an entire village, can you imagine? But I'm sure you've seen the photographs in the *Herald*."

Ivan had not—they did not get the *Herald*, or any other newspaper, at Dame Lizard's house. He asked where the attack had occurred, and sighed with relief when told it was a fishing village on the coast. His father was not in danger.

"Nothing much I can do here anyway," said the doctor. "Bronchitis has to run its course. Give them tea with honey for the coughs, and tepid baths for the fever. And try to avoid catching it yourself!"

"A dragon attack," said Blanchefleur after the doctor had left. "We haven't had one of those in a century."

But there was little time to think of what might be happening far away. For weeks, Ivan barely slept. He told the lizards stories, took their temperature, made them tea. Once their appetites returned, he found them the juiciest worms under the snow. Slowly, one by one, they began to get better. Medea, the smallest of them and his secret favorite, was sick for longer than the rest, and one night when she was coughing badly, he held her through the night, not knowing what else to do. Sometimes, when he looked as though he might fall asleep standing up, Blanchefleur would say, "Go sleep, Ivan. I'll stay up and watch them. I am nocturnal, you know."

By the time all the lizards were well, the marsh marigolds were blooming, and irises were pushing their sword-like leaves out of the ground. The marshes were filled with the sounds of birds returning from the south: the raucous cacophony of ducks, the songs of thrushes.

Ivan had forgotten how long he had been in the marsh, so he was startled when one morning he heard the front door open and a voice call, "Hello, my dears! I'm home!" And there stood Dame Lizard, with her suitcases strapped to her bicycle, looking just as she had left a year ago, but with a fuchsia scarf around her throat.

The lizards rushed around her, calling "Mother, Mother, look how we've grown! We all have names now! And we know about the Trojan War!" She had brought them a set of papier mâché puppets and necklaces of lapis lazuli. For Blanchefleur, she had brought a hat of crimson felt that she had seen on a dancing monkey in Marakesh.

Blanchefleur said, "Thank you. You shouldn't have."

Once the presents were distributed and the lizards were eating an enormous box of Turkish Delight, she said to Ivan, "Come outside." When they were standing by the house, under the alders, she said, "Ivan, I can see you've taken good care of my children. They are happy and healthy, and that is due to your dedication. Hercules told me how you took care of Medea when she was ill. I want to give you a present too. I brought back a camel whip for you, but I want to give you something that will be of more use, since you don't have a camel. You must raise your arms, then close your eyes and stand as still as possible, no matter how startled you may be."

Ivan closed his eyes, not knowing what to expect.

And then he felt a terrible constriction around his chest, as though his ribcage were being crushed. He opened his eyes, looked down, and gasped.

There, wrapped around his chest, was what looked like a thick green rope. It was Dame Lizard's tail, which had been hidden under her duster. For a moment, the tail tightened, and then it was no longer attached to her body. She had shed it, as lizards do. Ivan almost fell forward from the relief of being able to breathe.

"I learned that from a Swami in India," she said. "From now on, when you give pain to another, you will feel my tail tightening around you so whatever pain you give, you will also receive. That's called *empathy*, and the Swami said it was the most important thing anyone can have."

Ivan looked down. He could no longer see the tail, but he could feel it around him, like a band under his shirt. He did not know whether to thank her. The gift, if gift it was, had been so painful that he felt sore and bruised.

After he had said a protracted farewell to all the lizards, hugging them tightly, he and Blanchefleur walked north, along the river. He told her what Dame Lizard had done, lifting his shirt and showing her the mark he had found there, like a tattoo of a green tail around his ribcage.

"Is it truly a gift, or a curse?" he asked Blanchefleur.

"One never knows about gifts until later," said the white cat.

Marmalade met them at the front door. "I'm so sorry, Miss Blanchefleur," he said, "but your mother is not home. The King has asked her to the castle, to consult about the dragon attack. But she left you a note in the solar."

Blanchfleur read the note to Ivan.

> My dear, Ivan's third apprenticeship is with Captain Wolf in the Northern Mountains. Could you please accompany him and try to keep him from getting killed? Love, Mother.

This time, there was no banquet. With the Lady gone, the castle was quiet, as though it were asleep and waiting for her return to wake back up. They ate dinner in the kitchen with Mrs. Pebbles and the ladies-in-waiting, and then went directly to bed. Blanchefleur curled up next to Ivan on the pillow, as usual. It had become their custom.

The next morning, Mrs. Pebbles gave them Ivan's satchel, with clean clothes, including some warmer ones for the mountains, and his horn-handled knife. "Take care of each other," she told them. "Those mountains aren't safe, and I don't know what the Lady is thinking, sending you to the Wolf Guard."

"What is the Wolf Guard?" Ivan asked as they walked down the garden path.

"It's part of the King's army," said Blanchfleur. "It guards the northern borders from trolls. They come down from the mountains and raid the towns. In winter, especially . . . "

"Blanchefleur!" Tailcatcher was standing in front of them. He had stepped out from behind one of the topiaries. "May I have a word with you?" He did not, however, sound as though he were asking permission. Ivan gritted his teeth. He had never spoken to Blanchefleur like that—even if he had wanted to, he would not have dared.

"Yes, and the word is no," said Blanchefleur. She walked right around him, holding her tail high, and Ivan followed her, making a wide circle around the striped cat, who looked as though he might take a swipe at Ivan's shins. He looked back, to see Tailcatcher glaring at them.

"What was that about?" asked Ivan.

"For years now, he's been assuming I would marry him, because he's the best hunter in the castle. He asked me the first time on the night before we left for Professor Owl's house, and then again before we left for Dame Lizard's. This would have been the third time."

"And you keep refusing?" asked Ivan.

"Of course," she said. "He may be the best hunter, but I'm the daughter of the Lady of the Forest and the Man in the Moon. I'm not going to marry a common cat!"

Ivan could not decide how he felt about her response. On the one hand, he was glad she had no intention of marrying Tailcatcher. On the other, wasn't he a common man?

This journey was longer and harder than the two before. Once they reached the foothills of the Northern Mountains, they were constantly going up. The air was colder. In late afternoon, Ivan put on a coat Mrs. Pebbles had insisted on packing for him, and that he had been certain he would not need until winter.

Eventually, there were no more roads or paths, and they simply walked through the forest. Ivan started wondering whether Blanchefleur knew the way, then scolded himself. Of course she did: she was Blanchefleur.

Finally, as the sun was setting, Blanchefleur said, "We're here."

"Where?" asked Ivan. They were standing in a clearing. Around them were tall pines. Ahead of them was what looked like a sheer cliff face, rising higher than the treetops. Above it, he could see the peaks of the mountains, glowing in the light of the setting sun.

Blanchefleur jumped down from his shoulder, walked over to a boulder in the middle of the clearing, and climbed to the top. She said, "Captain, we have arrived."

Out of the shadows of the forest appeared wolves, as silently as though they were shadows themselves—Ivan could not count how many. They were all around, and he suddenly realized that he could die, here in the forest. He imagined their teeth at his throat and turned to run, then realized he was being an idiot, giving in to an ancient instinct although he could see that Blanchefleur was not frightened at all. She sat on the dark rock, amid the dark wolves, like a ghost.

"Greetings, Blanchefleur," said one of the wolves, distinguishable from the others because he had only one eye, and a scar running across it from his ear to his muzzle. "I hear that your mother has sent us a new recruit."

"For a year," said Blanchefleur. "Try not to get him killed."

"I make no promises," said the wolf. "What is his name?"

"Ivan," said Blanchefleur.

"Come here, recruit." Ivan walked to the boulder and stood in front of the wolf, as still as he could. He did not want Blanchefleur to see that he was afraid. "You shall call me Captain, and I shall call you Private, and as long as you do exactly what you are told, all shall be well between us. Do you understand?"

"Yes," said Ivan.

The wolf bared his teeth and growled.

"Yes, Captain," said Ivan.

"Good. This is your Company, although we like to think of ourselves as a pack. You are a member of the Wolf Guard, and should be prepared to die for your brothers and sisters of the pack, as they are prepared to die for you. Now come inside."

Ivan wondered where inside might be, but the Captain loped toward the cliff face and vanished behind an outcropping. One by one, the wolves followed him, some stopping to give Ivan a brief sniff. Ivan followed them and realized the cliff was not sheer after all. Behind a protruding rock was a narrow opening, just large enough for a wolf. He crawled through it and emerged in a large cave. Scattered around the cave, wolves were sitting or lying in groups, speaking together in low voices. They looked up when he entered, but were too polite or uninterested to stare and went back to their conversations, which seemed to be about troll raiding parties they had encountered, wounds they had sustained, and the weather.

"Have you ever fought?" the Captain asked him.

"No, sir," said Ivan.

"That is bad," said the Captain. "Can you move through the forest silently? Can you tell your direction from the sun in the day and the stars at night? Can you sound like an owl to give warning without divulging your presence?"

"Yes, Captain," said Ivan, fairly certain that he could still do those things. And to prove it to himself, he hooted, first like a Eagle Owl, then like a Barn Owl, and finally like one of the Little Owls that used to nest in his father's mill.

"Well, that's something, at least. You can be one of our scouts. Have you eaten?"

"No, sir," said Ivan.

"At the back of the cave are the rabbits we caught this morning," said the Captain. "You may have one of those."

"He is human," said Blanchefleur. "He must cook his food."

"A nuisance, but you may build a small fire, although you will have to collect wood. These caverns extend into the mountain for several miles. Make certain the smoke goes back into the mountain, and not through the entrance."

Skinning a rabbit was messy work, but Ivan butchered it, giving a leg to Blanchefleur and roasting the rest for himself on a stick he sharpened with his knife. It was better than he had expected. That night, he slept beneath his coat on the floor of the cave, surrounded by wolves. He was grateful to have Blanchefleur curled up next to his chest.

The next morning, he began his life in the Wolf Guard.

As a scout, his duty was not to engage the trolls, but to look for signs of them. He would go out with a wolf partner, moving through the forest silently, looking for signs of troll activity: their camps, their tracks, their spoor. The Wolf Guard kept detailed information on the trolls who lived in the mountains. In summer, they seldom came down far enough to threaten the villages on the slopes. But in winter, they would send raiding parties for all the things they could not produce themselves: bread and cheese and beer, fabrics and jewels, sometimes even children they could raise as their own, for troll women do not bear many children. Ivan learned the forest quickly, just as he had at home, and the wolves in his Company, who had initially been politely contemptuous of a human in their midst, came to think of him as a useful member of the pack. He could not smell as well as they could, nor see as well at night, but he could climb trees, and pull splinters out of their paws, and soon he was as good at tracking the trolls as they were. They were always respectful to Blanchefleur. One day, he asked her what she did while he was out with the wolves. "Mind my own business," she said. So he did not ask again.

As for Ivan, being a scout in the Wolf Guard was like finding a home. He had learned so much in Professor Owl's tower, and he had come to love the lizards in his charge, but with the wolves he was back in the forest, where he had spent his childhood. And the wolves themselves were like a family. When Graypaw or Mist, with whom he was most often paired, praised his ability to spot troll tracks, or when the Captain said "Well done, Private," he felt a pride that he had never felt before.

"You know, I don't think I've ever seen you so happy," said Blanchefleur, one winter morning. The snows had come, and he was grateful for the hat and gloves Mrs. Pebbles had included in his satchel.

"I don't think I ever have been, before," he said. "Not since—" Since his mother had died. Since then, he had always been alone. But now he had a pack. "I think I could stay here for the rest of my life."

"We seldom get what we want," said Blanchefleur. "The world has a use for us, tasks we must fulfill. And we must fulfill them as best we can, finding happiness along the way. But we usually get what we need."

"I've never heard you so solemn before," said Ivan. "You're starting to sound like your mother. But I don't think the world has any tasks for me. I'm no one special, after all."

"Don't be so sure, Ivan Miller," said Blanchefleur.

Suddenly, all the wolves in the cave pricked up their ears.

"The signal!" said the Captain.

And then Ivan heard it too, the long howl that signaled a troll raid, the short howls that indicated which village was being attacked.

"To the village!" shouted the Captain.

"Be careful!" said Blanchefleur, as Ivan sprang up, made sure his knife was in his belt, and ran out of the cave with the wolves. Then they were coursing through the forest, silent shadows against the snow.

They saw the flames and heard the screams before they saw any trolls. The village was a small one, just a group of herding families on the upper slopes. Their houses were simple, made of stone, with turf roofs. But the sheds were of wood, filled with fodder for the sturdy mountain sheep. The trolls had set fire to the fodder, and some of the sheds were burning. The sheep were bleating terribly, and as wolves rushed into the village, the Captain shouted to Ivan, "Open the pens! Let the sheep out—we can herd them back later."

Ivan ran from pen to pen, opening all the gates. Mist ran beside him and if any sheep were reluctant to leave their pens, she herded them out, nipping at their heels.

When they reached the last of the pens, Ivan saw his first troll. She was taller than the tallest man, and twice as large around. She looked like a piece of the mountain that had grown arms and legs. Her mottled skin was gray and green and brown, and she was covered in animal pelts. In her hand, she carried a large club. In front of her, crouched and growling, was Graypaw.

"Come on, cub!" she sneered. "I'll teach you how to sit and lie down!"

She lunged at Graypaw, swinging the club clumsily but effectively. The club hit a panicked ram that had been standing behind her, and the next moment, the ram lay dead on the snow.

Mist yipped to let Graypaw know she was behind him. He barked back, and the wolves circled the troll in opposite directions, one attacking from the left and the other from the right.

What could Ivan do? He drew his knife, but that would be no more effective against a troll than a sewing needle. To his right, one of the sheds was on fire, pieces of it falling to the ground as it burned. As Graypaw and Mist circled, keeping away from the club, trying to get under it and bite the troll's ankles, Ivan ran into the burning shed. He wrenched a piece of wood from what had been a gate, but was now in flames, then thrust its end into the fire. The flames licked it, and it caught. A long stick, its end on fire. This was a weapon of sorts, but how was he to use it?

Graypaw and Mist were still circling, and one of them had succeeded in wounding the troll—there was green ichor running down her leg. The troll was paying no attention to Ivan—she was wholly absorbed in fending off the wolves. But the wolves knew he was behind them. They were watching him out of the corners of their eyes, waiting. For what?

Then Ivan gave a short bark, the signal for attack. Both Graypaw and Mist flew at the troll simultaneously. The troll swung about wildly, not certain which to dispatch first. *Now*, thought Ivan, and he lunged forward, not caring that he could be hit by the club, only knowing that this was the moment, that he had put his packmates in danger for this opportunity. He thrust the flaming stick toward the troll's face. The troll shrieked—it had gone straight into her left eye. She clutched the eye and fell backward. Without thinking, Ivan drew his knife and plunged it into the troll's heart, or where he thought her heart might be.

A searing pain ran through his chest. It was Dame Lizard's tail, tightening until he could no longer breathe. It loosened again, but he reeled with the shock and pain of it.

"Ivan, are you well?" asked Mist.

"I'm—all right," he said, still breathless. "I'm going to be all right." But he felt sick.

The troll lay on the ground, green ichor spreading across her chest. She was dead. Behind her was a large sack.

"That must be what she was stealing," said Graypaw.

The sack started to wriggle.

"A sheep, perhaps," said Mist.

But when Ivan untied it, he saw a dirty, frightened face, with large gray eyes. A girl.

"You've found my daughter!" A woman was running toward them. With her was the Captain.

"Nadia, my Nadia," she cried.

"Mama!" cried the girl, and scrambling out of the bag, she ran into her mother's arms.

"This is the Mayor of the village," said the Captain. "Most of the trolls have fled, and we were afraid they had taken the girl with them."

"I can't thank you enough," said the woman. "You've done more than rescue my daughter, although that has earned you my gratitude. I recognize this troll—she has been here before. We call her Old Mossy. She is the leader of this tribe, and without her, the tribe will need to choose a new leader by combat. It will not come again this winter. Our village has sustained great damage, but not one of us has died or disappeared, and we can rebuild. How can we reward you for coming to our rescue, Captain?"

"Madame Mayor, we are the Wolf Guard. Your gratitude is our reward," said the Captain.

On the way back to the cave, Graypaw and Mist walked ahead of Ivan, talking to the Captain in low voices. He wondered if he had done something wrong. Perhaps he should not have told them to attack? After all, they both outranked him. They were both Corporals, while he was only a Private. Perhaps they were telling the Captain about how he had reeled and clutched his chest after the attack. Would he be declared unfit for combat?

When they got back to the cave, Blanchefleur was waiting for him.

"Ivan, I need to speak with you," she said.

"Blanchefleur, I killed a troll! I mean, I helped kill her. I want to tell you about it . . . "

"That's wonderful, Ivan. I'm very proud of you. I am, you know, and not just because of the troll. But it's time for us to leave."

"What do you mean? It's still winter. I haven't been here for a year yet."

"My mother has summoned us. Here is her messenger."

It was Tailcatcher. In his excitement, Ivan had not noticed the striped cat.

"The Lady wishes you to travel to the capital. Immediately," said Tailcatcher.

"But why?" asked Ivan.

"You are summoned," said Tailcatcher, contemptuously. "Is that not enough?"

"If you are summoned, you must go," said the Captain, who had been standing behind him. "But come back to us when you can, Ivan."

Ivan had never felt so miserable in his life. "Can I say goodbye to Mist and Graypaw?"

"Yes, quickly," said the Captain. "And thank them, because on their recommendation, I am promoting you to Corporal. There is also something I wish to give you. Hold out your right hand, Corporal Miller."

Ivan held out his hand.

The Captain lunged at him, seized Ivan's hand in his great mouth, and bit down.

Ivan cried out.

The Captain released him. The wolf's teeth had not broken his skin, but one of his fangs had pierced Ivan's hand between the thumb and forefinger. It was still lodged in his flesh. There was no blood, and as Ivan watched, the fang vanished, leaving only a white fang-shaped scar.

"Why—" he asked.

"That is my gift to you, Corporal. When I was a young corporal like yourself, I saved the life of a witch. In return, she charmed that fang for me. She told me that as long as I had it, whenever I fought, I would defeat my enemy. She also told me that one day, I could pass the charm to another. I asked her how, and she told me I would know when the time came. I am old, Ivan, and this is my last winter with the Wolf Guard. I believe I know why you have been summoned by the Lady. With that charm, whatever battles you have to fight, you should win. Now go. There is a storm coming, and you should be off the mountain before it arrives."

Ivan packed his belongings and made his farewells. Then, he left the cave, following Tailcatcher and Blanchefleur. He looked back once, with tears in his eyes, and felt as though his heart were breaking.

The journey to the capital would have taken several days, but in the first town they came to, Ivan traded his knife and coat for a horse. It was an old farm horse, but it went faster than he could have on foot with two cats. The cats sat in panniers that had once held potatoes, and Tailcatcher looked very cross indeed. When Ivan asked again why he had been summoned, the cat replied, "That's for the Lady to say," and would say nothing more.

They spent the night in a barn and arrived at the capital the next day.

Ivan had never seen a city so large. The houses had as many as three stories, and there were shops for everything, from ladies' hats and fancy meats to bicycles. On one street he even saw a shiny new motorcar. But where were the people? The shops were closed, the houses shuttered, and the streets empty. Once, he saw a frightened face peering at him out of an alley, before it disappeared into the shadows.

"What happened here?" he asked.

"You'll know soon enough," said Tailcatcher. "That's where we're going."

That was the palace.

Ivan had never seen a building so large. His father's mill could have fit into one of its towers. With a sense of unease, he rode up to the gates.

"State your business!" said a guard who had been crouching in the gatehouse and stood up only long enough to challenge them.

Ivan was about to reply when Blanchefleur poked her head out of the pannier. "I am Blanchefleur. My mother is the Lady of the Forest, and our business is our own."

"You may pass, my Lady," said the guard, hurriedly opening the gates and then hiding again.

They rode up the long avenue, through the palace gardens, which were magnificent, although Ivan thought they were not as interesting as the Lady's gardens with their cat gardeners. They left the horse with an ostler who met them at the palace steps, then hurried off toward the stables. At the top of the steps, they were met by a majordomo who said, "This way, this way." He reminded Ivan of Marmalade.

They followed the majordomo down long hallways with crimson carpets and paintings on the walls in gilded frames. At last, they came to a pair of gilded doors, which opened into the throne room. There was the King, seated on his throne. Ivan could tell he was the King because he wore a crown. To one side of him sat the Lady. To the other sat a girl about Ivan's age, also wearing a crown, and with a scowl on her face. Before the dais stood two men.

"Ivan," said the Lady, "I'm so pleased to see you. I'm afraid we have a problem on our hands. About a year ago, a dragon arrived on the coast. At first, he only attacked the ports and coastal villages, and then only occasionally. I believe he is a young dragon, and lacked confidence in his abilities. But several months ago, he started flying inland, attacking market towns. Last week, he was spotted in the skies over the capital, and several days ago, he landed on the central bank. That's where he is now, holed up in the vault. Dragons like gold, as you know. The King has asked for a dragon slayer, and I'm hoping you'll volunteer."

"What?" said Ivan. "The King has asked for a what?"

"Yes, young man," said the King, looking annoyed that the Lady had spoken first. "We've already tried to send the municipal police after him, only to have the municipal police eaten. The militias were not able to stop him in the towns, but I thought a trained police force—well, that's neither here nor there. The Lady tells me a dragon must be slain in the old-fashioned way. I'm a progressive man myself—this entire city should be wired for electricity by next year, assuming it's not destroyed by the dragon. But with a dragon sitting on the monetary supply, I'm willing to try anything. So we've made the usual offer: the hand of my daughter in marriage and the kingdom after I retire, which should be in about a decade, barring ill health. We already have two brave volunteers, Sir Albert Anglethorpe and Oswald the—what did you say it was?—the Omnipotent."

Sir Albert, a stocky man with a shock of blond hair, bowed. He was wearing chain mail and looked as though he exercised regularly with kettlebells. Oswald the Omnipotent, a tall, thin, pimply man in a ratty robe, said, "How de do."

"And you are?" said the King.

"Corporal Miller," said Ivan. "And I have no idea how to slay a dragon."

"Honesty! I like honesty," said the King. "None of us do either. But you'll figure it out, won't you, Corporal Miller? Because the dragon really must be slain, and I'm at my wits' end. The city evacuated, no money to pay the military—we won't be a proper kingdom if this keeps up."

"I have every confidence in you, Ivan," said the Lady.

"Me too," said Blanchefleur.

Startled, Ivan looked down at the white cat. "May I have something to eat before I go, um, dragon-slaying?" he asked. "We've been traveling all morning."

"Of course," said the King. "Anything you want, my boy. Ask and it will be yours."

"Well then," said Ivan, "I'd like some paper and ink."

Sir Albert had insisted on being fully armed, so he wore a suit of armor and carried a sword and shield. Oswald was still in his ratty robe and carried what he said was a magic wand.

"A witch sold it to me," he told Ivan. "It can transform anything it touches into anything else. She told me it had two transformations left in it. I used the first one to turn a rock into a sack of gold, but I lost the gold in a card game. So when I heard about this dragon, I figured I would use the second transformation to turn him into—I don't know, maybe a frog? And then, I'll be king. They give you all the gold you want, when you're king."

"What about the princess?" asked Ivan.

"Oh, she's pretty enough. Although she looks bad-tempered."

"And do you want to be king too?" Ivan asked Sir Albert.

"What? I don't care about that," he said through the visor of his helmet. "It's the dragon I'm after. I've been the King's champion three years running. I can out-joust and out-fight any man in the kingdom. But can I slay a dragon, eh? That's what I want to know." He bent his arms as though he were flexing his biceps, although they were hidden in his armor.

Ivan had not put on armor, but he had asked for a bow and a quiver of arrows. They seemed inadequate, compared with a sword and a magic wand.

The dragon may have been young, but he was not small. Ivan, Oswald, and Sir Alfred stood in front of the bank building, looking at the damage he had caused. There was a large hole in the side of the building where he had smashed through the stone wall, directly into the vault.

"As the King's champion, I insist that I be allowed to fight the dragon first," said Sir Albert. "Also, I outrank both of you."

"Fine by me," said Oswald.

"All right," said Ivan.

Sir Albert clanked up the front steps and through the main entrance. They heard a roar, and then a crash, as though a file cabinet had fallen over, and then nothing.

After fifteen minutes, Oswald asked, "So how big do you think this dragon is, anyway?"

"About as big as the hole in the side of the building," said Ivan.

"See, the reason I'm asking," said Oswald, "is that the wand has to actually touch whatever I want to transform. Am I going to be able to touch the dragon without being eaten?"

"Probably not," said Ivan. "They breathe fire, you know."

"What about when they're sleeping?" asked Oswald.

"Dragons are very light sleepers," said Ivan. "He would smell you before you got close enough."

"How do you know?"

"It's in the Encyclopedia of All Knowledge."

"Oh, that thing," said Oswald. "You know, I worked on that for a while. Worst job I ever had. The pay was terrible, and I had to eat soup for every meal."

Another half hour passed.

"I don't think Sir Albert is coming out," said Ivan. "You volunteered before me. Would you like to go next?"

"You know, I'm not so sure about going in after all," said Oswald. "I can't very well rule a kingdom if I'm eaten, can I?"

"That might be difficult," said Ivan.

"You go ahead," said Oswald, starting to back away. "I think I'm going to turn another rock into gold coins. That seems like a better idea."

He turned and ran up the street, leaving Ivan alone in front of the bank. Ivan sighed. Well, there was no reason to wait any longer. He might as well go in now.

Instead of going in by the front door, he went in through the hole that the dragon had made in the side of the bank. He walked noiselessly, as he had done in the forest. It was easy to find the dragon: he was lying on a pile of gold coins in the great stone room that had once been the vault. Near the door of the vault, which had been smashed open, Ivan could see a suit of armor and a sword, blackened by flames. He did not want to think about what had happened to Sir Albert.

An arrow would not penetrate the dragon's hide. He knew that, because while he had been eating at the palace, he had asked Professor Owl's tail feather to write out the entire Encyclopedia entry on dragons. He had a plan, and would get only one chance to carry it out. It would depend as much on luck as skill.

But even if it worked, he knew how it would feel, slaying a dragon. He remembered how it had felt, killing the troll. Could he survive the pain? Was there any way to avoid it? He had to try.

He stood in a narrow hallway off the vault. Keeping back in the shadows, he called, "Dragon!"

The dragon lifted his head. "Another dragon slayer? How considerate of the King to sent me dessert! Dragon slayer is my favorite delicacy, although the policemen were delicious. I much preferred them to farmers, who taste like dirt and leave grit between your teeth, or fishermen, who are too salty."

"Dragon, you could fly north to the mountains. There are plenty of sheep to eat there."

"Sheep!" said the dragon. "Sheep are dull and stringy compared to the delicious men I've eaten here. Just the other day, I ate a fat baker. He tasted of sugar and cinnamon. There are plenty of teachers and accountants to eat in this city. Why, I might eat the Princess herself! I hear princess is even better than dragon slayer."

The dragon swung his head around, as though trying to locate Ivan. "But you don't smell like a man, dragon slayer," said the dragon. "What are you, and are you good to eat?"

I must still smell like the wolves, thought Ivan.

He stepped out from the hallway and into the vault. "I'm an Enigma, and I'm delicious."

The dragon swung toward the sound of his voice. As his great head came around, Ivan raised his bow and shot an arrow straight up into the dragon's eye.

The dragon screamed in pain and let out a long, fiery breath. He swung his head to and fro. Ivan aimed again, but the dragon was swinging his head too wildly: a second arrow would never hit its mark. Well, now he would find out if the Captain's charm worked. He ran across the floor of the vault, ignoring the dragon's flames, and picked up Sir Albert's sword. It was still warm, but had cooled down enough for him to raise it.

The pain had begun the moment the arrow entered the dragon's eye, but he tried not to pay attention. He did not want to think about how bad it would get. Where was the dragon's neck? It was still swinging wildly, but he brought the sword down just as it swung back toward him. The sword severed the dragon's neck cleanly in two, and his head rolled over the floor.

Ivan screamed from the pain and collapsed. He lay next to the dragon's head, with his eyes closed, unable to rise. Then, he felt something rough and wet on his cheek. He opened his eyes. Blanchefleur was licking him.

"Blanchefleur," he said weakly. "What are you doing here?"

"I followed you, of course," she said.

"But I never saw you."

"Of course not." She sat on the floor next to him as he slowly sat up. "Excellent shot, by the way. They'll call you Ivan Dragonslayer now, you know."

"Oh, I hope not," he said.

"It's inevitable."

The King met him with an embrace that made Ivan uncomfortable. "Welcome home, Ivan Dragonslayer! I shall have my attorney drawn up the papers to make you my heir, and here of course is my lovely Alethea, who will become your bride. A royal wedding will attract tourists to the city, which will help with the rebuilding effort."

Princess Alethea crossed her arms and looked out the window. Even from the back, she seemed angry.

"Forgive me, your Majesty," said Ivan, "but I have no wish to marry the Princess, and I don't think she wants to marry me either. We don't even know each other."

Princess Alethea turned and looked at him in astonishment. "Thank you!" she said. "You're the first person who's made any sense all day. I'm glad you slayed the dragon, but I don't see what that has to do with getting my hand in marriage. I'm not some sort of prize at a village fair."

"And I would not deprive you of a kingdom," said Ivan. "I have no wish to be king."

"Oh, goodness," said Alethea, "neither do I! Ruling is deadly dull. You can have the kingdom and do what you like with it. I'm going to university, to become an astronomer. I've wanted to be an astronomer since I was twelve."

"But . . . " said the King.

"Well then, it's decided," said the Lady. "Ivan, you'll spend the rest of your apprenticeship here, in the palace, learning matters of state."

"But I want to go back to the wolves," said Ivan. He saw the look on the Lady's face: she was about to say no. He added, hurriedly, "If I can go back, just for the rest of my apprenticeship, I'll come back here and stay as long as you like, learning to be king. I promise."

"All right," said the Lady.

He nodded, gratefully. At least he would have spring in the mountains, with his pack.

Ivan and Blanchefleur rode north, not on a farm horse this time, but on a mare from the King's stables. As night fell, they stopped by a stream. The mountains were ahead of them, glowing in the evening light.

"You know, before we left, Tailcatcher asked me again," said Blanchefleur. "He thought that my time with you was done, that I would go back to the Castle in the Forest with my mother. I could have."

"Why didn't you?" asked Ivan.

"Why did you refuse the hand of the Princess Alethea? She was attractive enough."

"Because I didn't want to spend the rest of my life with her," said Ivan. "I want to spend it with you, Blanchefleur."

"Even though I'm a cat?"

"Even though."

She looked at him for a moment, then said, "I'm not always a cat, you know." Suddenly, sitting beside him was a girl with short white hair, wearing a white fur jacket and trousers. She had Blanchefleur's eyes.

"Are you—are you Blanchefleur?" he asked. He stared at her. She was and she was not the white cat.

"Of course I am, idiot," she said. "I think you're going to make a good king. You'll have all the knowledge in the world to guide you, and any pain you cause, you'll have to feel yourself, so you'll be fair and kind. But you'll win all your battles. You'll hate it most of the time and wish you were back with the wolves or in Professor Owl's tower, or even taking care of the lizards. That's why you'll be good."

"And you'll stay with me?" he asked, tentatively reaching over and taking her hand.

"Of course," she said. "Who else is going to take care of you, Ivan?"

Together, they sat and watched the brightness fade from the mountain peaks and night fall over the Wolfwald. When Ivan lay down to sleep, he felt the white cat curl up next to his chest. He smiled into the darkness before slipping away into dreams.

EFFIGY NIGHTS

YOON HA LEE

They are connoisseurs of writing in Imulai Mokarengen, the city whose name means *inkblot of the gods.*

The city lies at the galaxy's dust-stranded edge, enfolding a moon that used to be a world, or a world that used to be a moon; no one is certain anymore. In the mornings its skies are radiant with clouds like the plumage of a bird ever-rising, and in the evenings the stars scatter light across skies stitched and unstitched by the comings and goings of fire-winged starships. Its walls are made of metal the color of undyed silk, and its streets bloom with aleatory lights, small solemn symphonies, the occasional duel.

Imulai Mokarengen has been unmolested for over a hundred years. People come to listen to the minstrels and drink tea-of-moments-unraveling, to admire the statues of shapeshifting tigers and their pliant lovers, to look for small maps to great fortunes at the intersections of curving roads. Even the duelists confront each other in fights knotted by ceremony and the exchange of poetry.

But now the starships that hunt each other in the night of nights have set their dragon eyes upon Imulai Mokarengen, desiring to possess its arts, and the city is unmolested no more.

The soldiers came from the sky in a glory of thunder, a cascade of fire. Blood like roses, bullets like thorns, everything to ashes. Imulai Mokarengen's defenses were few, and easily overwhelmed. Most of them would have been museum pieces anywhere else.

The city's wardens gathered to offer the invading general payment in any coin she might desire, so long as she left the city in peace. Accustomed to their decadent visitors, they offered these: Wine pressed from rare books of stratagems and aged in barrels set in orbit around a certain red star. Crystals extracted from the nervous systems of philosopher-beasts that live in colonies upon hollow asteroids. Perfume symphonies infused into exquisite fractal tapestries.

The general was Jaian of the Burning Orb, and she scorned all these things. She was a tall woman clad in armor the color of dead metal. For each world she had scoured, she wore a jewel of black-red facets upon her breastplate. She said to the wardens: What use did she have for wine except to drink to her enemies' defeat? What use was metal except to build engines of war? And as for the perfume, she didn't dignify that with a response.

But, she said, smiling, there was one thing they could offer her, and then she would leave with her soldiers and guns and ships. They could give her all the writings they treasured so much: all the binary crystals gleaming bright-dark, all the books with the bookmarks still in them, all the tilted street signs, all the graffiti chewed by drunken nanomachines into the shining walls, all the tattoos obscene and tender, all the ancestral tablets left at the shrines with their walls of gold and chitin.

The wardens knew then that she was mocking them, and that as long as any of the general's soldiers breathed, they would know no peace. One warden, however, considered Jaian's words of scorn, and thought that, unwitting, Jaian herself had given them the key to her defeat.

Seran did not remember a time when his othersight of the city did not show it burning, no matter what his ordinary senses told him, or what the dry pages of his history said. In his dreams the smoke made the sky a funeral shroud. In waking, the wind smelled of ash, the buildings of angry flames. Everything in the othersight was wreathed in orange and amber, flickering, shadows cinder-edged.

He carried that pall of phantom flame with him even now, into the warden's secret library, and it made him nervous although the books had nothing to fear from the phantoms. The warden, a woman in dust-colored robes, was escorting him through the maze-of-mists and down the stairs to the library's lowest level. The air was cool and dry, and to either side he could see the candle-sprites watching him hungrily.

"Here we are," the warden said as they reached the bottom of the stairs.

Seran looked around at the parchment and papers and scrolls of silk, then stepped into the room. The tools he carried, bonesaws and forceps and fine curved needles, scalpels that sharpened themselves if fed the oil of certain olives, did not belong in this place. But the warden had insisted that she required a surgeon's expertise.

He risked being tortured or killed by the general's occupation force for cooperating with a warden. In fact, he could have earned himself a tidy sum for turning her in. But Imulai Mokarengen was his home, for all that he had not been born here. He owed it a certain loyalty.

"Why did you bring me here, madam warden?" Seran said.

The warden gestured around the room, then unrolled one of the great charts across the table at the center of the room. It was a stardrive schematic, all angles and curves and careful coils.

Then Seran saw the shape flickering across the schematic, darkening some of the precise lines while others flowed or dimmed. The warden said nothing, leaving him to observe as though she felt he was making a difficult diagnosis. After a while he identified the elusive shape as that of a girl, slight of figure or perhaps merely young, if such a creature counted years in human terms. The shape twisted this way and that, but there were no adjacent maps or diagrams for her to jump to. She left a disordered trail of numbers like bullets in her wake.

"I see her," Seran said dryly. "What do you need me to do about her?"

"Free her," the warden said. "I'm pretty sure this is all of her, although she left a trail while we were perfecting the procedure—"

She unrolled another chart, careful to keep it from touching the first. It appeared to be a treatise on musicology, except parts of it had been replaced by a detritus of clefs and twisted staves and demiquavers coalescing into a diagram of a pistol.

"Is this your plan for resistance against the invaders?" Seran said. "Awakening soldiers from scraps of text, then cutting them out? You should have a lot more surgeons. Or perhaps children with scissors."

The warden shrugged. "Imulai Mokarengen is a city of stories. It's not hard to persuade one to come to life in her defense, even though I wouldn't call her *tame*. She is the Saint of Guns summoned from a book of legends. Now you see why I need a surgeon. I am given to believe that your skills are not entirely natural."

This was true enough. He had once been a surgeon-priest of the Order of the Chalice. "If you know that much about me," he said, "then you know that I was cast out of the order. Why haven't you scared up the real thing?"

"Your order is a small one," she said. "I looked, but with the blockade, there's no way to get someone else. It has to be you." When he didn't speak, she went on, "We are outnumbered. The general can send for more soldiers from the worlds of her realm, and they are armed with the latest weaponry. We are a single city known for artistic endeavors, not martial ones. Something has to be done."

Seran said, "You're going to lose your schematic."

"I'm not concerned about its fate."

"All right," he said. "But if you know anything about me, you know that your paper soldiers won't last. I stick to ordinary surgery because the prayers of healing don't work for me anymore; they're cursed by fire." And, because he knew she was thinking it: "The curse touches anyone I teach."

"I'm aware of the limitations," the warden said. "Now, do you require additional tools?"

He considered it. Ordinary scissors might be better suited to paper than the curved ones he carried, but he trusted his own instruments. A scalpel would have to do. But the difficult part would be getting the girl-shape to hold still. "I need water," he said. He had brought a sedative, but he was going to have to sponge the entire schematic, since an injection was unlikely to do the trick.

The warden didn't blink. "Wait here."

As though he had somewhere else to wait. He spent the time attempting to map the girl's oddly flattened anatomy. Fortunately, he wouldn't have to intrude on her internal structures. Her joints showed the normal range of articulation. If he hadn't known better, he would have said she was dancing in the disarrayed ink, or perhaps looking for a fight.

Footsteps sounded in the stairwell. The woman set a large pitcher of water down on the table. "Will this be enough?" she asked.

Seran nodded and took out a vial from his satchel. The dose was pure guesswork, unfortunately. He dumped half the vial's contents into the pitcher, then stirred the water with a glass rod. After putting on gloves, he soaked one of his sponges, then wrung it out.

Working with steady strokes, he soaked the schematic. The paper absorbed the water readily. The warden winced in spite of herself. The girl didn't seem capable of facial expressions, but she dashed to one side of the schematic, then the other, seeking escape. Finally she slumped, her long hair trailing off in disordered tangles of artillery tables.

The warden's silence pricked at Seran's awareness. She's *studying how I do this,* he thought. He selected his most delicate scalpel and began cutting the girl-shape out of the paper. The medium felt alien, without the resistances characteristic of flesh, although water oozed away from the cuts.

He hesitated over the final incision, then completed it, hand absolutely steady.

Amid all the maps and books and scrolls, they heard a girl's slow, drowsy breathing. In place of the paper cutout, the girl curled on the table, clad in black velvet and gunmetal lace. She had paper-pale skin and inkstain hair, and a gun made of shadows rested in her hand.

It was impossible to escape the problem: smoke curled from the girl's other hand, and her nails were blackened.

"I warned you of this," Seran said. Cursed by fire. "She'll burn up, slowly at first, and then all at once. I suspect she'll last a week at most."

"You listen to the news, surely," the warden said. "Do you know how many of our people the invaders shot the first week of the occupation?"

He knew the number. It was not small. "Anything else?" he said.

"I may have need of you later," the warden said. "If I summon you, will you come? I will pay you the same fee."

"Yes, of course," Seran said. He had noticed her deft hands, however; he imagined she would make use of them soon.

Not long after Seran's task for the warden, the effigy nights began.

He was out after curfew when he saw the Saint of Guns. Imulai Mokarengen's people were bad at curfews. People still broke the general's curfew regularly, although many of them were also caught at it. At every intersection, along every street, you could see people hung up as corpse-lanterns, burning with plague-colored light, as warnings to the populace. Still, the city's people were accustomed to their parties and trysts and sly confrontations. For his part, he was on his way home after an emergency call, and looking forward to a quiet bath.

It didn't surprise him that he should encounter the Saint of Guns, although he wished he hadn't. After all, he had freed her from the boundary of paper and legend to walk in the world. The connection was real, for all that she hadn't been conscious for its forging. Still, the sight of her made him freeze up.

Jaian's soldiers were rounding up a group of merry-goers and poets whose rebellious recitations had been loud enough to be heard from outside. The poets, in particular, were not becoming any less loud, especially when one of them was shot in the head.

The night became the color of gunsmoke little by little, darkness unfolding to make way for the lithe girl-figure. She had a straight-hipped stride, and her eyes were spark-bright, her mouth furiously unsmiling. Her hair was braided and pinned this time. Seran had half-expected her to have a pistol in each hand, but no, there was only the one. He wondered if that had to do with the charred hand.

Most of the poets didn't recognize her, and none of the soldiers. But one of the poets, a chubby woman, tore off her necklace with its glory's worth of void-pearls. They scattered in all directions, purple-iridescent, fragile. "The Saint of Guns," the poet cried. "In the city where words are bullets, in the book where verses are trajectories, who is safe from her?"

Seran couldn't tell whether this was a quotation or something the poet had made up on the spot. He should have ducked around the corner and toward safety, but he found it impossible to look away, even when one of the soldiers knocked the pearl-poet to the street and two others started kicking her in the stomach.

The other soldiers shouted at the Saint of Guns to stand down, to cast away her weapon. She narrowed her eyes at them, not a little contemptuous. She pointed her gun into the air and pulled the trigger. For a second there was no sound.

Then all the soldiers' guns exploded. Seran had a blurry impression of red and star-shaped shrapnel and chalk-white and falling bodies, fire and smoke and screaming. There was a sudden sharp pain across his left cheek where a passing splinter cut it: the Saint's mark.

None of the soldiers had survived. Seran was no stranger to corpses. They didn't horrify him, despite the charred reek and the cooked eyes, the truncated finger that had landed near his foot. But none of the poets had survived, either.

The Saint of Guns lowered her weapon, then saluted him with her other hand. Her fingers were blackened to their bases.

Seran stared at her, wondering what she wanted from him. Her lips moved, but he couldn't hear a thing.

She only shrugged and walked away. The night gradually grew darker as she did.

Only later did Seran learn that the gun of every soldier in that district had exploded at the same time.

Imulai Mokarengen has four great archives, one for each compass point. The greatest of them is the South Archive, with its windows the color of regret and walls where vines trace out spirals like those of particles in cloud chambers. In the South Archive the historians of the city store their chronicles. Each book is written with nightbird quills and ink-of-dedication, and bound with a peculiar thread spun from spent artillery shells. Before it is shelved, one of the city's wardens seals each book shut with a black kiss. The books are not for reading. It is widely held that the historians' objectivity will be compromised if they concern themselves with an audience.

When Jaian of the Burning Orb conquered Imulai Mokarengen, she sent a detachment to secure the South Archive. Although she could have destroyed it in a conflagration of ice and fire and funeral dust, she knew it would serve her purpose better to take the histories hostage.

It didn't take long for the vines to wither, and for the dead brown tendrils to spell out her name in a syllabary of curses, but Jaian, unsuperstitious, only laughed when she heard.

The warden called Seran back, as he had expected she would.

Seran hadn't expected the city to be an easy place to live in during an occupation, but he also hadn't made adequate preparations for the sheer aggravation of sharing it with legends and historical figures.

"Aggravation" was what he called it when he was able to lie to himself about it. It was easy to be clinical about his involvement when he was working with curling sheets, and less so when he saw what the effigies achieved.

The Saint of Guns burned up within a week, as Seran had predicted. The official reports were confused, and the rumors not much better, but he spent an entire night holed up in his study afterward estimating the number of people she had killed, bystanders included. He had bottles of very bad wine for occasions like this. By the time morning came around, he was comprehensively drunk.

Six-and-six years ago, on a faraway station, he had violated his oaths as a surgeon-priest by using his prayers to kill a man. It had not been self-defense, precisely. The man had shot a child. Seran had been too late to save the child, but not too late to damn himself.

It seemed that his punishment hadn't taught him anything. He explained to himself that what he was doing was necessary; that he was helping to free the city of Jaian.

The warden next had him cut out one of the city's founders, Alarra Coldly-Smiling. She left footsteps of frost, and where she walked, people cracked into pieces, frozen all the way through, needles of ice piercing their intestines. As might be expected, she burned up faster than the Saint of Guns. A pity; she was outside Jaian's increasingly well-defended headquarters when she sublimated.

The third was the Mechanical Soldier, who manifested as a suit of armor inside which lights blinked on-off, on-off, in digital splendor. Seran was buying more wine—you could usually get your hands on some, even during the occupation, if your standards were low—when he heard the clink-clank thunder outside the dim room where the transaction was taking place. The Mechanical Soldier carried a black sword, which proved capable of cutting through metal and crystal and stone. With great precision it carved a window in the wall. The blinking lights brightened as it regarded Seran.

The wine-seller shrieked and dropped one of the bottles, to Seran's dismay. The air was pungent with the wine's sour smell. Seran looked unflinchingly at the helmet, although a certain amount of flinching was undoubtedly called for, and after a while the Mechanical Soldier went away in search of its real target.

It turned out that the Mechanical Soldier liked to carve cartouches into walls, or perhaps its coat-of-arms. Whenever it struck down Jaian's soldiers, lights sparked in the carvings, like sourceless eyes. People began leaving offerings by the carvings: oil-of-massacres, bouquets of crystals with fissures in their shining hearts, cardamom bread. (Why cardamom, Seran wasn't sure. At least the aroma was pleasing.) Jaian's soldiers executed people they caught at these makeshift shrines, but the offerings kept coming.

Seran had laid in a good supply of wine, but after the Mechanical General shuddered apart into pixels and blackened reticulations, there was a maddening period of calm. He waited for the warden's summons.

No summons came.

Jaian's soldiers swaggered through the streets again, convinced that there would be no more apparitions. The city's people whispered to each other that they must have faith. The offerings increased in number.

Finding wine became too difficult, so Seran gave it up. He was beginning to think that he had dreamed up the whole endeavor when the effigy nights started again.

Imulai Mokarengen suddenly became so crowded with effigies that Seran's othersight of fire and smoke was not much different from reality. He had not known that the city contained so many stories: Women with deadly hands and men who sang atrocity-hymns. Colonial intelligences that wove webs across the pitted buildings and flung disease-sparks at the invaders. A cannon that rose up out of the city's central plaza and roared forth red storms.

But Jaian of the Burning Orb wasn't a fool. She knew that the effigies, for all their destructiveness, burned out eventually. She and her soldiers retreated beneath their force-domes and waited.

Seran resolved to do some research. How did the warden mean to win her war, if she hadn't yet managed it?

By now he had figured out that the effigies would not harm him, although he still had the scar the Saint of Guns had given him. It would have been easy to remove the scar, but he was seized by the belief that the scar was his protection.

He went first to a bookstore in which candles burned and cogs whirred. Each candle had the face of a child. A man with pale eyes sat in an unassuming metal chair, shuffling cards. "I thought you were coming today," he said.

Seran's doubts about fortune-telling clearly showed on his face. The man laughed and fanned out the cards face-up. Every one of them was blank. "I'm sorry to disappoint you," he said, "but they only tell you what you already know."

"I need a book about the Saint of Guns," Seran said. She had been the first. No reason not to start at the beginning.

"That's not a story I know," the man said. His eyes were bemused. "I have a lot of books, if you want to call them that, but they're really empty old journals. People like them for the papers, the bindings. There's nothing written in them."

"I think I have what I came for," Seran said, hiding his alarm. "I'm sorry to trouble you."

He visited every bookstore in the district, and some outside of it, and his eyes ached abominably by the end. It was the same story at all of them. But he knew where he had to go next.

Getting into the South Archive meant hiring a thief-errant, whose name was Izeut. Izeut had blinded Seran for the journey, and it was only now, inside one of the reading rooms, that Seran recovered his vision. He suspected he was happier not knowing how they had gotten in. His stomach still felt as though he'd tied it up in knots.

Seran had had no idea what the Archive would look like inside. He had especially not expected the room they had landed in to be welcoming, the kind of place where you could curl up and read a few novels while sipping citron tea. There were couches with pillows, and padded chairs, and the paintings on the walls showed lizards at play.

"All right," Izeut said. His voice was disapproving, but Seran had almost beggared himself paying him, so the disapproval was very faint. "What now?"

"All the books look like they're in place here," Seran said. "I want to make sure there's nothing obviously missing."

"That will take a while," Izeut said. "We'd better get started."

Not all the rooms were welcoming. Seran's least favorite was the one from which sickles hung from the ceiling, their tips gleaming viscously. But all the bookcases were full.

Seran still wasn't satisfied. "I want to look inside a few of the books," he said.

Izeut shot him a startled glance. "The city's traditions—"

"The city's traditions are already dying," Seran said.

"The occupation is temporary," Izeut said stoutly. "We just have to do more to drive out the warlord's people."

Izeut had no idea. "Humor me," Seran said. "Haven't you always wanted to see what's in those books?" Maybe an appeal to curiosity would work better.

Whether it did or not, Izeut stood silently while Seran pulled one of the books off the shelves. He hesitated, then broke the book's seal and felt the warden's black kiss, cold, unsentimental, against his lips. *I'm already cursed,* he thought, and opened the covers.

The first few pages were fine, written in a neat hand with graceful swells. Seran flipped to the middle, however, and his breath caught. The pages were empty except for a faint dust-trace of distorted graphemes and pixellated stick figures.

He could have opened up more books to check, but he had already found his answer.

"Stop," Izeut said sharply. "Let me reshelve that." He took the book from Seran, very tenderly.

"It's no use," Seran said.

Izeut didn't turn around; he was slipping the book into its place. "We can go now."

It was too late. The general's soldiers had caught them.

Seran was separated from Izeut and brought before Jaian of the Burning Orb. She regarded him with cool exasperation. "There were two of you," she said, "but something tells me that you're the one I should worry about."

She kicked the table next to her. All of Seran's surgical tools, which the soldiers had confiscated and laid out in disarray, clattered.

"I have nothing to say to you," Seran said through his teeth.

"Really," Jaian said. "You fancy yourself a patriot, then. We may disagree about the petty legal question of who the owner of this city is, but if you are any kind of healer, you ought to agree with me that these constant spasms of destruction are good for no one."

"You could always leave," Seran said.

She picked up one of his sets of tweezers and clicked it once, twice. "You will not understand this," she said, "and it is even right that you will not understand this, given your profession, but I will try to explain. This is what I do. Worlds are made to be pressed for their wine, cities taste of fruit when I bite them open. I cannot let go of my conquests.

"Do you think I am ignorant of the source of the apparitions that leave their smoking shadows in the streets? You're running out of writings. All I need do is wait, and this city will yield in truth."

"You're right," Seran said. "I don't understand you at all."

Jaian's smile was like knives and nightfall. "I'll write this in a language you do understand, then. You know something about how this is happening, who's doing it. Take me to them or I will start killing your people in earnest. Every hour you make me wait, I'll drop a bomb, or send out tanks, or soldiers with guns. If I get bored I'll get creative."

Seran closed his eyes and made himself breathe evenly. He didn't think she was bluffing. Besides, there was a chance—if only a small chance—that the warden could come up with a defense against the general; that the effigies would come to her aid once the general came within reach.

"All right," he said. "I'll take you where it began."

Seran was bound with chains-of-suffocation, and he thought it likely that there were more soldiers watching him than he could actually spot. He led Jaian to the secret library, to the maze-of-mists.

"A warden," Jaian said. "I knew some of them had escaped."

They went to the staircase and descended slowly, slowly. The candle-sprites flinched from the general. Their light was almost violet, like dusk.

All the way down the stairs they heard the snick-snick of many scissors.

The downstairs room, when they reached it, was filled with paper. Curling scraps and triangles crowded the floor. It was impossible to step anywhere without crushing some. The crumpling sound put Seran in mind of burnt skin.

Come to that, there was something of that smell in the room, too.

All through the room there were scissors snapping at empty space, wielded by no hand but the hands of the air, shining and precise.

At the far end of the room, behind a table piled high with more paper scraps, was the warden. She was standing sideways, leaning heavily against the table, and her face was averted so that her shoulder-length hair fell around it.

"It's over," Jaian called out. "You may as well surrender. It's folly to let you live, but your death doesn't have to be one of the ugly ones."

Seran frowned. Something was wrong with the way the warden was moving, more like paper fluttering than someone breathing. But he kept silent. *A trap*, he thought, *let it be a trap.*

Jaian's soldiers attempted to clear a path through the scissors, but the scissors flew to either side and away, avoiding the force-bolts with uncanny grace.

Jaian's long strides took her across the room and around the table. She tipped the warden's face up, forced eye contact. If there had been eyes.

Seran started, felt the chains-of-suffocation clot the breath in his throat. At first he took the marks all over the warden's skin to be tattoos. Then he saw that they were holes cut into the skin, charred black at the edges. Some of the marks were logographs, and alphabet letters, and punctuation stretched wide.

"Stars and fire ascending," Jaian breathed, "what is this?"

Too late she backed away. There was a rustling sound, and the warden unfurled, splitting down the middle with a jagged tearing sound, a great irregular sheet punched full of word-holes, completely hollowed out. Her robe crumpled into fine sediment, revealing the cutout in her back in the shape of a serpent-headed youth.

Jaian made a terrible crackling sound, like paper being ripped out of a book. She took one step back toward Seran, then halted. Holes were forming on her face and hands. The scissors closed in on her.

I did this, Seran thought, *I should have refused the warden.* She must have learned how to call forth effigies on her own, ripping them out of Imulai Mokarengen's histories and sagas and legends, animating the scissors to make her work easier. But when the scissors ran out of paper, they turned on the warden. Having denuded the city of its past, of its weight of stories, they began cutting effigies from the living stories of its people. And now Jaian was one of those stories, too.

Seran left Jaian and her soldiers to their fate and began up the stairs. But some of the scissors had already escaped, and they had left the doors to the library open. They were undoubtedly in the streets right now. Soon the city would be full of holes, and people made of paper slowly burning up, and the hungry sound of scissors.

SUCH & SUCH SAID TO SO & SO

MARIA DAHVANA HEADLEY

It was late July, a dark green mood-ring of a night, and the drinks from Bee's Jesus had finally killed a man.

The cocktails there had always been dangerous, but now they were poison. We got the call in at the precinct, and none of us were surprised. We all knew the place was no good, never mind that we'd also all spent some time there. These days we stayed away, or not, depending on how our marriages were going, and how much cash we had in the glovebox. There were no trains nearby, and if you ended up out too long, you were staying out. The suburbs were a dream, and you weren't sleeping.

There was nothing harder to get out of your clothes than Bee's Jesus. We all knew that too. Dry cleaner around the corner. You'd go there, shame-faced and stubbled at dawn, late for your beat.

"Ah, it's the Emperor of Regret," the guy behind the counter would say to you. No matter which Emperor you were. All us boys from the precinct had the same title.

"Yeah," you'd say, "Emperor of Regret."

The guy could launder anything. Hand him your dirty shirt, and he'd hand you back a better life, no traces, no strings, no self-righteous speech.

I was trying to get clean, though, real clean, and the martinizer couldn't do it. I knew better than to go anywhere near the Jesus, but I could hear the music from a mile away. Nobody wanted to let me in anymore. People doubted my integrity after what'd happened the last time. The last several times.

The cat at the door was notorious, and had strict guidelines, though lately he'd begun to slip. Things weren't right at Bee's. Hadn't been for a while. They had to let me in tonight. This was legit police business.

"C'mon, Jimmy, you can afford to look sideways tonight," yelled one of the girls on the block, the real girls, not the other kind.

"I'm here on the up and up," I said, because if I came in on the down and down, the place wouldn't show. But I'd seen it as I rolled past, lights spinning. Gutter full of glitter, and that was how you knew. Door was just beyond the edge of the streetlight, back of the shut-down bodega, and most people would've walked right on by.

But I knew what was going down. Somebody in that bar had called the police, and reported a body, male, mid-thirties, goner. I was here to find out the whohowwhy.

"You the police?" the caller had said. "It was an emergency three hours ago, sugarlump, but now it's just a dead guy. They dumped him in the alley outside where Bee's was, but Bee's took a walk, every piece of fancy in there up working their getaway sticks like the sidewalk was a treadmill. So you gotta come get him, sweets. He's a health hazard. Dead of drink if you know what I mean."

We did know what she meant, most of us, and we crossed our hearts and needle-eyed, cause we weren't the dead guy, but we could have been, easy. We were fleas and Bee's Jesus was a dog's ear.

Me and the boys duked it out for who was taking statements and who was caution-taping, and now it was me and my partner Gene, but Gene didn't care about Bee's like I did. The place was a problem I couldn't stay away from. I kept trying to get out of town, but I ran out of gas every time.

"What're you doing, Jimmy?" Gene said. "You're trying to sail a cardboard catamaran to Cuba. Not in a million years, you're not gonna get that broad back. Cease and desist. Boys are getting embarrassed for you."

I was embarrassed for me, too. I wasn't kidding myself, she was what I was looking to see. I was trying to put a nail in it.

Gloria was in that place somewhere, Gloria and the drink she'd taken to like a fish gill-wetting. Bee's Jesus was Gloria's bar now.

Ten years had passed since the night she sat on the sink, laughing as she straight-razored my stubble, and lipsticked my mouth.

"Poor boy," she said, watching the way I twitched. "Good thing you're pretty."

Gloria was a skinny girl with bobbed black hair, acid green eyes, and a tiny apartment full of ripped-up party dresses. In her cold-water bathroom, she melted a cake of kohl with a match and drew me eyes better than my own. She'd told me she wouldn't take me to her favorite bar until she'd dressed me in her clothes, top to tail, and I wanted to go to that bar, wanted to go there bad.

I woulda done anything back then to get her, even though my Londoner buddy Philip (he called himself K. Dick, straight-faced) kept looking at her glories and shaking his head.

"I don't know what you see in her, bruv. She's just a discount Venus with a nose ring."

She was the kind of girl you can't not attempt, already my ex-wife before I kissed her, but I knew I had to go forward or die in a ditch of longing. It was our first date.

I saw her rumpled bed and hoped I'd end up in it, but Gloria dragged me out the door without even a kiss, me stumbling because I was wearing her stockings with my own shoes.

Downtown, backroom of a bodega, through the boxes and rattraps, past the cat that glanced at me, laughed at the guy in the too tight, and asked if I could look more wrong.

Actual cat. I tried not to notice that it was. It seemed impolite. Black with a tuxedo. Cat was smoking a cigarette and stubbed it out on my shoe. It groomed itself as it checked me out and found me wanting.

"Come on, man, go easy," Gloria said. "Jimmy's with me."

She was wearing a skin-tight yellow rubber dress and I was wearing a t-shirt made of eyelashes, rolling plastic eyeballs and fishnet. It didn't work on me. It wanted her body beneath. She was a mermaid. I was trawled.

"You expect me to blind eye that kind of sadsack?" the cat said, and lifted its lip to show me some tooth. Its tail twisted and informed me of a couple of letters. NO, written in fur.

"Better than the last boy," Gloria said, and laughed. The cat laughed too, an agreeing laugh that said he'd seen some things. I felt jealous. "I'll give you a big tip," she said to him.

I was a nineteen year old virgin. I'd never gotten this close to getting this close before.

Gloria picked the cat up, holding him to her latex and he sighed a long-suffering sigh as she tipped him backward into the air and stretched his spine.

"Don't tell anyone I let the furball in. They'll think I'm getting soft."

"I owe you for this," she said to the cat.

To me, she said "Time to get you three-sheeted."

I was pretty deep at this point in clueless. Underworld, nightlife, and Gloria knew things I had no hope of knowing. She was the kind of girl who'd go into the subway tunnels for a party, and come out a week later, covered in mud and still wearing her lipstick. I'd been in love with her for a year or so. As far as I was concerned, the fact that she knew my name was a victory. She kept calling me Mister Nice Guy. Years later, after we'd been married and divorced, after Gloria had too much gin, and I had too many questions, I learned this was because she'd forgotten my name.

She tugged me around the corner, through a metal chute in the wall. For a second I smelled rotting vegetables and restaurant trash, cockroach spray, toilet brush, hairshirt, and then we were through, and that was over, and we were at the door that led to Bee's.

Gloria looked at me. "You want a drink," she said.

"Do they have beer?" I asked. I was nervous. "Could I have a Corona?"

The shirt was itchy, and she'd smeared something tarry into my hair. I felt like a newly paved road had melted into my skull and gumstuck my brain.

Gloria laughed. Her eyelids glittered like planetariums.

"Not really," she said. "It's a cocktail bar. You ever had a cocktail, Mister Nice Guy?"

"I've had Guinness," I said.

She looked at me, pityingly. "Guinness is beer, and it's Irish, and if we scared any of that up, it'd be interested in you, but I'm not sure you'd want it. It's heavy and gloomy. You don't want the Corona either. You don't want what Corona brings you. It makes you really fucking noticeable at night."

I liked Guinness. I liked Corona. I liked wine coolers. I wasn't picky, and I knew nothing about drinking. Whatever anyone poured me, I was willing. I had never had a cocktail. I didn't know what Gloria meant.

She opened a door, and we were in Bee's. Bright lights, big city, speakeasy, oh my God. My face went into a trombone to the teeth, and the player looked out from behind the instrument and barked.

"Get your mug outta my bone," he said. He was a dog. A bullhound. But I was cool with that. Dogs, cats, and us, and it was all completely normal and fine, because I was with Gloria, and I trusted her.

I didn't trust her. I didn't know her. She was a broad. She was a broad broader than the universe, and I wished, momentarily, for K. Dick and his encyclopedic wingman knowledge of bitters, bourbons, and cheap things with umbrellas. I wished for his accent which lady slayed, and which made the awful forgivable. Or so he swore. K. Dick was more talk than walk.

I did need a drink.

Full brass band. Wall-to-wall tight dresses and topless, girls and boys in high heels, everyone cooler than anything I'd seen before. There was one gay bar where I came from. I knew of its existence and looked longingly at it from across the street, but I couldn't go in. I wasn't gay, and I wasn't legal, and anyone having fun inside it kept the fun there.

Now, though, I'd lucked into Bee's, and Gloria shoved me up to the bartender, through the dancers and the looks. First curious, then envious as they saw the girl I was with. I tried to get taller. My shoes were a flat-footed liability. Gloria was wearing steel-toed platforms that made her six inches my senior. I looked like I lived in a lesser latitude.

"What you drinking tonight, Glo?" the bartender asked.

"Something with gin," Gloria said.

"You sure?" he asked. "Last time wasn't what you'd call a pretty situation."

The bartender had an elaborate mustache, and was wearing a pith helmet covered in gold glitter. I could see a whip protruding from over his shoulder. Around his wrist, a leather cuff with a lot of strings attached. I looked at them, and saw that they connected to the bottles behind the bar.

Gimmicky motherfucker, I thought, imagining myself as K. Dick, cool, collected, suave. I'd be a Man of Mystery. No more Mister Nice Guy.

"The lady will have a gin martini," I said, and the bartender looked at me. I wasn't sure if gin went into martinis, but I looked back, gave him a glare, and he snorted.

"Dirty?" he asked, sneering at me. I didn't know what dirty was. It sounded bad.

"Clean," I said, and Gloria grinned.

"And what about you, Jimmy?" asked Gloria. "What are you drinking?"

The bartender held out his hand to her and she spit her gum out into it. My tongue crawled backward like an impounded vehicle.

"I'll order for the boy," she said.

"You always do," said the bartender, and flicked his wrist. A bottle of gin somersaulted off the shelf and onto the bar.

"You sound like you got a beef with me, Such & Such," said Gloria, uncurling one half of his mustache with her fingertip.

"Not a beef," he said, his mustache snapping back into place, and nodded at me. "But you bruise the merchandise. And that shit is not my name."

"George," Gloria said, and rolled her eyes. "Make him an Old Fashioned for starters."

He moved his wrist and the bourbon slid over like a girl on a bench, the way I wished Gloria would slide over to me.

The music was louder than it had been, and the cat from the door was onstage now, walking the perimeter, eyeballing everyone and occasionally laying down the claw on an out-of-hand.

The bartender turned around and made my drink, and I heard a noise, a kind of coo. Then another noise like nails on a chalkboard.

Such & Such handed me a heavy glass full of dark amber liquid, cherry in the bottom. Gloria had a martini glass full of a silver-white slipperiness that looked like it might at any moment become a tsunami.

The bartender pushed them across the bar.

"Cheers," he said. "Or not, depending on your tolerance, Nice Guy. Should I call you Mister?"

"Yes," I said. Then I didn't know what to say, so I said. "Call me Lucky."

"You're not a Lucky," the bartender said. "You think you know a damn about a dame, but you don't know dick about this one."

I hardly heard him.

Gloria ran her finger around the edge of her glass like she was playing a symphony, and her drink unfolded out of it, elbow by elbow until a skinny guy in a white and silver pinstriped suit was sitting on the bar, looking straight into Gloria's eyes, and grinning. Pinkie diamond. Earrings. Hair in a pompadour, face like James Dean.

I heard the bartender snort, and followed the chain on his wrist to the vest pocket of Gloria's gin martini.

My drink was already out by the time I stopped staring at hers. For a moment, I didn't know if she was a drink or not, but then I saw her wringing the wet hem of her amber-colored cocktail dress. She looked at me, and pulled a cherry stem from between her teeth. Her bracelet, a thin gold ribbon with a heart-shaped padlock connected her to the bartender's chains.

"You lovely So & So," said my Old Fashioned, her accent Southern belle. "Ask a girl to dance."

Gloria was already gone, in the arms of her white-suited martini, and I caught a glimpse of her on the dance floor, her black bobbed head thrown back as she laughed. I could see his arms around her.

I'd misunderstood the nature of our evening.

Resigned, I took the Old Fashioned's hand. She hopped off the bar and into my arms, her red curls bouncing.

"You can call me Sweetheart," she said, and lit a cigarette off the candle on a table we passed. "But I don't think I'll call you Lucky. You came with Gloria, didn't you?"

"Yeah," I said. "She's great."

"She's trouble," the Old Fashioned said. "She likes her drink too much."

I looked onto the dance floor to see Gloria but all I saw was a flash of yellow, a stockinged thigh, and Gloria's acid-green eyes, wide open, staring into the silver eyes of the martini.

I spun my drink out into the room. The music was loud. The brass band was all hound dogs. I found that I could dance with my Old Fashioned, dance like I couldn't dance, swing like I couldn't swing. Her dress stayed wet at the hem, beads of bourbon dropping on the floor as the cat from the front door scatted with the band. I leaned over to kiss her shoulder, and tasted sugar.

"Oh, So & So, you're such a gentleman," she said, and spun me hard to the left, suddenly taking the lead. I kissed her mouth then, and her lips were bitter, a sharp taste of zest, the lipstick bright as orange peel.

She bent me backward and I could see her laughing, looking over me and at another girl on the floor, tight, sequined gold-brown dress, same kind of red curls. "Want another drink?"

"No," I said, overwhelmed. The room was spinning away from me, and there was Gloria out of the corner of my eye, now dancing with three guys and one girl, all in matching silver-white suits.

By morning, I was being led around the dance floor by five redheads, and my mouth tasted bitter. I had sugar all over my clothes, and I was wet with bourbon. I opened my mouth and spat out a cherry, but I hadn't even tasted it. I couldn't walk.

The cat pranced along the bar, his tuxedo front suddenly white as a near-death, and said, in an imperative tone, "Time to catch the early bird."

All of Bee's Jesus moaned.

The cat leapt up, clawing the light cord, and fluorescents hit us hard. The bartender hopped over the bar, and raised his wrist, tugging each chain, and in a moment, all the beautiful people in Bee's Jesus were gone.

Blast of light. I blinked.

I looked down. Broken glass and ice all over the floor, and a few people like me, in the middle of them, eyes sagging, stockings laddered. One of them in a bright yellow rubber dress. She looked over at me, and waved, her hand shaking.

"Wanna get some eggs?" Gloria said, and I nodded, weak-kneed.

Glo and I got married and then we got divorced.

We spent too much time at Bee's Jesus. I got to know the regulars, the margaritas and the Manhattans, the Sazeracs and the Bloody Marys, but I kept ordering the Old Fashioned, and Gloria kept ordering the gin martini, as I eventually figured out she always would. She fell hard for her drink, and I fell hard for mine.

Eventually, we started taking them back to our place, the four of us, him sitting at our table in his white and silver suit, and her there in her sequins, lipstick on her cigarettes.

We moved out to the suburbs, but the gin martini didn't like it there. He'd stand outside, looking down the tree-lined, holding a shaker in his hands, and complaining about the quality of the ice. The two drinks sat in the car, in the afternoons, and sometimes Glo sat with them. Eventually, the martini took off, but the Old Fashioned stayed. After a while, Gloria went back to the city too, breaking my heart, and all the tumblers at the same time.

She bought the bar, and moved into the apartment upstairs with him.

Every night, or so I heard, she could be found dancing in the middle of the floor with five or six guys in silver, the band blasting. She hired some pit bulls, and they kept the door down while she danced. Gloria had fucked a German at Bee's Jesus one time, she'd told me at some point in our marriage. At first, this wasn't worrying. It was when she added Shepherd to the mix. She said it like it was no thing. It seemed like a thing to me.

Now the dog seemed like a better option than the martini. She turned to drink, and then she turned again and wrapped herself in his silver arms. He spun down into her, his diamond shining.

I kept waiting for her to come home, but she'd never really loved me, and so she never really did.

The redhead put herself on ice, and now when I tried to dance with her, sugar cubes crushed under our feet, and everything got sticky and sour. Her skin was cold and hard, and she kept her mouth full of cherry stems, but never any cherries.

"I miss the martini, So & So," she said at last, her dress falling off her shoulder, sequins dripping from her hem. "And I miss Such & Such. I miss the way he tended."

I tried to kiss her. She turned her head. I tasted a new spirit.

"What's that?" I asked her, and she looked away.

"Dry vermouth," she said, and looked at me, with her liquid eyes. "He gave it to me." Something had changed in her. She wasn't an Old Fashioned anymore. She'd been mixing.

She swizzled out the door one morning early, and I knew she'd returned to Bee's.

I cleaned out the cupboards. I quit drinking, cold turkey. I became a cop and tried to forget.

But soon the bar was back on my radar again. Trouble there all the time. It was a blood-on-the-tiles known failure point, and the boys at the precinct knew it well.

And now, the call, the murder. I had a feeling I knew who it might be, but I didn't know for sure.

"Pull over," I said to Gene. Glitter, shining in the headlights.

"You sure you wanna do this?" he asked. "I know you got a soft spot for Gloria, but we gotta arrest that broad, we gotta do it, no matter your old flames."

"That fire's out," I said. It was.

I saw the cat then, his tuxedo shining. I saw his tail, the letters reading NO. I saw him run out the door of Bee's Jesus, and into the street, and then I saw Glo, right behind him. She shook her shoulders back, and looked at the cruiser, like she didn't care. She walked over to the window and looked at it until I gave up and rolled down.

"You got no business here, Jimmy," she said. "Somebody called in a false alarm."

She looked at me with those same acid eyes, and I felt etched. Nothing like a long ago love to bring back the broken.

"Stay here," I said to Gene. "Do me a favor. One."

Gene sighed and set a timer, but he stayed in the car.

I walked down the alley behind Gloria, and Gloria held out her fingers to me for a second. Just one. We were the old days.

I saw him shining, his white and silver leg, dumped in the alley like the caller had told me he would be. I knew who the caller had been. I knew her voice. I knew her muddles. She couldn't let a guy stay in the street. She wasn't all bitter, and she had a soft spot for martinis.

I saw the cat, and I saw the band. All of them out in the street, like I'd never seen them. The pit bulls and the bull hounds.

The cat looked up from what he was doing, his teeth covered in blood. Red all over the white front of his tuxedo shirt.

"Sadsack," he said. "You knew this place, but it's gone."

I could hear his purr from where I stood, appalled, as he bit into the gin. The dogs and the cats. All of them on top of the martini, making it go away. There was a pool on the cobbles, and I could smell juniper berries.

"Another one back in the shaker," said the cat, then shook his head, gnashing. "Hair of the dog," he said, and spat.

Something caught the light at the end of the alley. Golden-brown sequins. I tasted ice. I could see her mouth, cherry red, shining out of the shadows, and then she stalked away.

Gloria looked up at me, and shrugged. The whites of her eyes were red. Her hands shook. The sun was rising.

"He used to be clean," she said. "You remember, Jimmy, you remember how he was. You remember how he was. But he got dirty. I'm getting away from this town. This bar. I shut things down in there."

A cocktail walked out the door of Bee's Jesus, and I watched her come. All in crimson, her perfume spiced and salty. She knelt beside the remains of the gin martini, and stretched her long green-painted fingernails over his face. She lay down on top of the corpse, and as I watched, the gin dissolved into the Bloody Mary.

"No chaser," said Gloria, and smiled sadly. "She'll take him away."

The Bloody Mary stood up in her stilettos, wiping her hands on her dress, and took Gloria's hand in hers.

"See you, Mister Nice Guy," said Gloria. "Bar's closed. I have a plane to catch. Somewhere sunny. Somewhere I can get a drink with an umbrella."

I watched Gloria and her new drink walk away. As she went, I saw her unfasten something from her wrist. A leather cuff decked in long chains. She dropped it in the gutter. I watched her turn the corner, away from the glitter, and then I watched the sun rise, shining on the mountain of ice outside the former door of Bee's Jesus.

"No dead body," I said to Gene. "Just ice and glass. What can you do?"

I took myself to the cleaners. Blood all over my shirt front, hair of the dog on my knees. I smelled bourbon and cherries, juniper and regret. Gloria and her gin.

"Ah, it's Such & Such," said the martinizer. I was no longer an Emperor, if I'd ever really been. "I cleaned your dirty laundry," he said. "But some stains don't come out."

He handed me a white shirt not mine. He waved me out the door and back into the brittle light of the morning.

GRIZZLED VETERANS OF MANY AND MUCH

ROBERT REED

=⟨⬥⟩=

The First Drop

There were test subjects, hundreds of them, and scores more secretly went through the process before it was approved. But from my point of view, Grandpa was the first person in the world to Transcend, and the world spent the rest of my life coming to terms with that event.

I was eight, and we were having Christmas in Aspen. We always went to Aspen for Christmas, but there was a special afternoon where nobody was allowed to snowboard. The entire family had to show up at the main house. No excuses. I didn't understand, and I doubt if any adults appreciated the situation either. Both of Grandpa's wives were there. My mother sat with her twin brothers and Grandma Joyce while Lucee claimed the opposite end of the conference table, doing her best to keep the little kids under control. I always liked Lucee. She was young and pretty, but the woman also had a tough streak that made her even more fascinating. Our big family was waiting for the meeting to begin, and all at once her two little boys, tough in their own right, decided to use fists to settle some problem nobody else could see. I watched them swinging and kicking, which was kind of fun. Then with a big voice, my mother said, "Lucee." She had this way of stretching out the vowels, making it sound like a little girl's name. She said, "Luuuceeee, can't you keep your beasts under control for one goddamn minute?"

With that, Lucee was ready for war—which would have been an epic battle. And the only reason I bring this up is that while I loved my mother, for some reason I wanted Lucee to win. Half a foot shorter than Mom and pregnant with Grandpa's sixth kid, yet even as her little gems traded blows on the floor, that one-time Miss America was ready to charge down our way, bashing a few heads into more charitable moods.

But that didn't happen. Of course it didn't happen. Grandma Joyce cleared her throat once, and everybody remembered where they were, and everybody got back into their chairs, pretending to be nice.

That's when Grandpa walked in. He was in his early sixties, and except for the cancer, he was healthier than anybody. Muscle always liked Grandpa, and he still had the shoulders and legs that made him a champion in college football. He always carried a big smile that might mean something good or might mean nothing, but it was a winner's grin, and I was as happy as anybody to see him.

Grandpa had a chair waiting for him at the midpoint of the long table, strategically dropped between the two halves of his cantankerous family.

He didn't sit. He rarely sat. Big hands massaging the back of his chair, he looked as if he was keeping the furniture from jumping off the floor. The smile enjoyed itself for another moment while smart eyes read every face. Then he decided that things weren't stirred up enough, so with a big voice accustomed to commanding billions of dollars, he told all of us, "I'll be dead before New Year's."

I wish I could describe the surprise hitting those faces. But I can't. The man's silence had gotten boring, and when the announcement came I was gazing out the nearest window, watching snow fall, wondering when this silliness would be finished and I could get out on the slopes again.

What did he just say?

I finally looked around. Everybody was shocked, and some of them were furious, and a few probably assumed this was a cruel joke.

Grandpa and his chair stood in the middle of craziness, saying nothing.

My grown-up uncles jumped up and looked at their sister, my mother. "The cancer isn't that bad," they insisted. "Did you know it was bad? Is it spreading? Why didn't you tell us it had grown?"

"I didn't know anything about this," Mom insisted.

So my uncles turned to Lucee. "What aren't you telling us?"

But the pregnant woman was as stunned as anyone. Turning to her husband, she used her softest voice to ask, "Is it your heart?"

"What's wrong with his heart?" Mom asked.

"I don't know," Lucee insisted.

Grandpa remained silent, and he was silent in a certain way. One of the man's strengths was on display: Mom claimed that her father was exceptionally smart but never let people see him that way. It didn't matter who was in the room, business partners or dog trainers. He would drop a few words to get conversations rolling and then let other people talk, and when they ran out of words, he'd throw out a question or two that were just a little bit dumb.

The man made our fortunes by being the third-smartest guy in any room, and that's the kind of genius that he was using just then.

My uncles were talking about aneurysms and cancer treatments, pretending they were doctors instead of whatever it was that they did with their days. Their wives assured each other that their father-in-law looked just fine, looked spectacular. Then Grandma Joyce sat up straight, laughing in a big way. "Oh, this is silly," she said. "Harold is just having some fun with the rest of you."

My mom said, "I don't think so."

"Just look at him," said the old woman. "He's testing you, seeing which of his dependents loves him the most."

Grandma Joyce might have been the ex-wife, but she still had feelings for the alpha male, and she was practically a goddess when it came to tolerance and calm, forgiving thoughts.

My mom was a different kind of creature.

The second wife was crying, and not quietly, either. Glaring at Lucee, Mom snorted once and said, "Oh, that's just the hormones flaring."

"Be nice," Grandma Joyce warned.

Wrapping herself inside her own arms, Mom squeezed and rocked fast.

In my case, I felt nothing but sorry for Lucee. But then the snot ran out of her nose, and pretty as she was, something about that crying face made me uneasy. So I looked at Grandpa again, and when he glanced my way, I said exactly what was in my head. I said, "I'm going to miss you, Grandpa."

Gunfire might have quieted the room faster.

Then again, maybe not.

The old man stared at me. Then he gave his hands a brief study, something about them or the circumstances pleasing. And with everyone else holding still, he looked at me again, saying, "Come over here, Bradley. Let's have a little chat."

Like that, I was the most important person in the room.

Grandpa pulled out his chair. "Sit now. Sit here." Then I was down, and he knelt beside me, winking a couple times before saying, "Transcendence."

I nodded. I didn't know what the word meant, but I nodded.

Then one of my uncles said, "Jesus, is that what this is?"

"Shut up," Mom said.

"Yes, please," Lucee added.

I sat quietly, waiting for the first words that made sense.

"There is a process called Transcendence," Grandpa said. "It's very new, and it is not easy. But the people who undergo it . . . well, they gain certain benefits. Blessings. Skills nobody else in the world can enjoy."

"Like Spider-Man," I said.

My uncles snarled.

But Grandpa said, "Exactly. When you Transcend, your mind is improved in so many ways, and you turn superhuman, and nothing is ever the same again."

Superheroes had physical gifts. But even an eight-year-old kid can see the benefits in being a whole lot smarter than before.

"I'm going into the hospital tomorrow," he said.

Most of the room groaned.

"It's a special clinic where doctors and their very smart machines will put these tiny, tiny hair-like tubes inside my blood. It won't take the tubes an hour to join up in the brain. I might have a headache, but I probably won't. And once those tubes piece themselves together, I'll be tied into computers and some very special software."

Mom reached toward the two of us, asking someone to stop doing something. I was the one who shooed her hand away.

"What happens then?" I asked.

"Well," Grandpa said. Then he paused before saying, "For the rest of you, nothing will happen. You'll live exactly as you did before this. You, Bradley . . . you'll grow up strong and be a fine person and hopefully you won't be too infected by the curses that come to the likes of us."

What curses? I thought, but I didn't ask.

"And meanwhile, I'll live another hundred years," Grandpa said. "My new mind will think wondrous fancy original thoughts, and maybe some of my ideas will make life better for all of you. Though that's not why I'm doing this. I've already done plenty for everybody, in my family and beyond."

I nodded again. And again, I didn't have any clue what the old man was talking about. But one problem made itself obvious. "Then how come you'll be dead in . . . in how many days?"

"Nine," said an angry uncle.

"You said a hundred years," I told Grandpa.

"That's how it will feel to me, Bradley. The supercharged brain works so many times faster than normal. Those tiny tubes make that happen. And the same tubes are what bleed away all the heat that comes from the extra work."

"I don't understand," I said.

"The brain cooks itself to death," said an uncle.

Mom was crying. Lucee was crying, and that's who I watched for a moment. But at least she wiped the snot off her lip.

"Many things can go wrong," Grandpa allowed. "But that's true for people living normal lives, which is why this risk is acceptable. I can spend the next ten or twenty years in diminished health and senility. Or worse, some hidden ailment kills me next year, cheating me of this opportunity."

I shrugged and looked out the window again.

"Bradley," he said.

"I'm called Brad," I said.

"Excuse me?"

"You're the only person who calls me 'Bradley.' "

"Well," Grandpa said, "I won't do that anymore."

"I know," I said. "You're going to die."

My grandfather flew to Havana on the day after Christmas, accompanied by assistants and his doctors and my uncles, but not Mom. And not Lucee, either. My uncles didn't agree with this craziness, but they claimed that they went along because the family had to send somebody. Both were loud about their decency, and each promised that he would convince the old man to give up this ridiculous scheme. Maybe they believed they could do it, but Grandpa's young wife and oldest child shared a clearer assessment of the man, and they happened to be right. Both women loved him—hopelessly, eternally loved him—but they understood that this Lord of Business cared first about himself and second about his own burning needs.

Mom planned to go to Cuba after the "procedure" and then angrily sit at his bed. Several times she mentioned that intention to me, and maybe she would have seen it through. But thirty-three minutes after the Transcendence was declared complete and successful, the messages started to arrive. Grandpa's body was comfortably encased within a special supercold gelatin bed, while his fierce mind—the mind that used to play stupid—became a godly beast full of noise and piercing focus. From his deathbed, he read and studied and contemplated. The man who never willingly consumed one novel had fallen in love with Herman Melville. During a ninety-minute sprint, he wrote a scholarly book about whales and quests, and years later, in college, that same volume would be quoted to me by my American Lit professors. Grandpa also delved into his first love, which was engineering. Fourteen patents and plans for a new robot-ruled factory were given to his complicated family and his grateful corporation, fueling a last burst of economic vitality for both concerns.

But what mattered most, at least to me, was the time spent crafting birthday cards and random messages that sought us out wherever we were in the world. The idea factory left behind essays for grandsons and middle-aged daughters, and later, in the final day of his life, he taught himself to compose songs and then sang them to us in a voice that was exactly like his old voice, except for the little improvements.

Grandpa never quite died, what with all of the digital leftovers.

Yet he didn't survive as many days as predicted, either. The uncles came home, and in some pact of mutual misery, Lucee and Mom boarded the same Gulfstream to fly down to Cuba. But his heart burst before they left U.S.

airspace, and the bad news came from the old man himself: A video message where the avatar, forty years younger in the face and wearing filthy football gear, appeared before them. Following some set of deeply ingenious protocols, that contrivance of light and noise said, "I know you're both pissed." Then he surgically described each woman's feelings and their tendencies. "But this is for the best, darlings. You'll see. The life you know is tame and safe. There is a great bold life that I have been living over the last few days and hours, and it matters more than you can appreciate, at least on this one day and in these newborn circumstances.

"Let time pass before you judge," he told them. "Let yourself understand the promise of this technology."

Then the dead man made a poetic, deeply self-absorbed prediction:

"One way or another, everybody will follow me. What I am is just the first drop of moisture in what will be a soft, nourishing rain."

Falling on a Field of Green

"I'm very sorry," she said.

With a funeral-ready voice, I said, "Thank you."

"So sudden," she said sadly.

But it wasn't sudden. My uncle had a long, passionate relationship with designer narcotics, and after a string of bold, bad investments and one cataclysmic divorce, it was a matter of time before some ingested pharmaceutical turned him into formaldehyde-infused meat.

"How are you doing, Brad?"

"I'm fine, Lucee."

"Good." She looked at the empty chair, and then she looked at me.

I said, "Sit, if you want."

She very much did, yes.

We spent a few moments watching the bereaved. The turnout was too sparse for the expansive room. The dead man had grown children and an ex-wife, and they made for a bittersweet portrait. A few last friends stood in the distance, trying to smile while telling stories that weren't coming out happy or funny. It was my other uncle, the identical twin, who was torn apart. He was so miserable that my mother and Grandma Joyce didn't dare leave him. Each held a hand and talked to him, fighting to infuse the survivor with comfort or resolve, or some other noble, misplaced sentiment.

"How's college, Brad?" Lucee asked.

"Good."

"Do you like your professors?"

"Most of them." And because it was peculiar yet true, I added, "Some of my favorite teachers are alive."

She didn't act surprised. "How many are dead?"

"Three," I said. "They're left-behind lectures, interactive texts, those kinds of tricks. And most of the breathing faculty has berths waiting for Transcendence, as soon as he or she feels ready."

Lucee smiled, and that's when I gave her a long look. In her middle-forties, she could still manage the illusion of agelessness, and she always had a good sense of clothes and hair. Even dressed for a socially awkward funeral, she was easily the most splendid woman in the room.

I was having thoughts when she said, "It's too bad they don't play anymore."

"Play what?"

"College football," she said.

Too many head injuries, too many lawsuits. I shrugged, saying, "I like rugby, on occasion."

"You inherited his build," she told me.

Grandpa was always with me.

"Do you still get his birthday greetings?" she asked.

I said, "Sure."

"I don't." She shook her head, staring at me. "Or maybe I do. But I finally managed to get them blocked several years ago."

I needed to say something. "Huh," was my best effort.

"And those messages don't pester my children anymore," she said. "Their father is dead. He made a choice and died, and I don't think anybody is helped by pretending otherwise."

She was daring me to disagree with her parenting skills.

I bent the topic. "How old are they?"

"Sixteen. Fifteen. Thirteen."

"Miriam is a teenager?"

With a motherly groan, Lucee said, "Oh, yes."

I glanced at my surviving uncle. What if I went over to chat with him? I pictured myself bending low, telling him, "Your brother was a spoiled, lazy, trust-fund kid with a drug habit. But you're lucky. As a genetically predisposed addict, you're an underachiever."

I've always been able to scare myself, imagining what I might say.

I like to scare myself.

"You're smiling," Lucee said.

"Sorry," I said, plainly not meaning it.

She studied my arms and shoulders.

To amuse both of us, I flexed.

She gave a little jump and giggled.

Then we laughed together, loud enough that the sorry people at the party threw some hard looks at the two of us, imagining nothing good at all.

• • •

I didn't have a trust fund.

My mother explained the circumstances to me when I was nine and thirteen and then twenty. There was a trust fund built on safe, boring investments, and yes, the name on that fund looked rather like my name. But it wasn't. Grandpa left a robust fortune to a twenty-eight-year-old man who hadn't yet come into existence. I could curse him all I wanted, but I had to survive until that ripe old age before I could claim the millions. Except for an allowance and an Ivy League education and two cars and enough carbon credits to clog up a smokestack, I was pretty much left to my own devices.

"What are you thinking?" my traveling companion asked.

"How green our world is," I told her, which wasn't much of a lie.

We were drifting before the false window inside our million-star suite. The Andes were cloaked in reborn glaciers, and coming into view were the climax jungles woven between the ranches and giant farms that had been abandoned only two or three years ago. Most of today's food was being cultivated in vats—vats designed by biologists and engineers in the last ten days of their lives. And the climate was being cooled by sunscreens devised by a dozen sharp people who dove together into the same supercooled gelatin bath. Then a relatively young Russian spent twenty-nine days in a heightened state—the present world record for Transcendence, as it happened—and the result was a self-replicating solar panel that had already covered ten percent of the lunar surface, beaming cheap energy home to antennae bobbing in the resurgent Pacific.

Lucee drifted close.

"Thanks for inviting me," I said.

"You're welcome."

We were naked, watching the world rolling under our feet.

She said, "Brad."

"What?"

She waited, and then said, "Never mind."

I didn't talk.

She ran a hand down my back. "Do you know why I want this?"

"Because I look like him," I said.

"And you sound like him, sometimes. And I guess I miss him, sometimes, and that makes me a sick, sorry fool. But those aren't the only reasons."

I waited.

"Guess why," she said.

"My mother," I said.

Lucee stared, and I couldn't tell if she was amused or worried.

I said, "When Mom finds out about us, she's going to detonate. Like a nuke."

"Maybe that's an attraction. Or maybe not." She appeared relieved to have the subject lurch into view. "As it happens, my stepdaughter and I don't fight as much as we used to."

"But you miss your wars," I said.

She halfway laughed while studying my face. Two days of intense gazes, and I was getting a little perturbed.

Her fingers examined my back again.

The tropics looked impossibly green. Rumors claimed that a few tribes were still out there, secretive and unspoiled. As if I might spot them, I looked across four hundred miles of vacuum, waiting for a brown face to peer up at me.

Her voice thick and careful, she said, "Brad."

For the first time, I was planning my escape from this old woman's claws. But I didn't want to be mean and I certainly didn't want to pay my own way home. I was just a poor student, after all.

With a quieter, more ominous tone, she repeated my name.

I looked at her.

"This is hard," she said.

"It isn't," I said.

Not funny. She sighed and pulled back her hand, taking deep breaths.

I don't think I had ever seen Lucee fighting for courage.

"What's wrong?" I asked.

She said, "No. Forget it."

Good, I decided.

"It wouldn't be fair," she said.

Like an idiot, I finally bit that bait. "What wouldn't be fair?"

"I like you, Brad."

"Are you proposing to me?"

Again, not funny. Needing to change my mood, she stabbed me with a long fingernail, drawing blood. Then she said, "Your mother and I have had our differences, but she is an admirable person. Next to her brothers, she's a saint."

"What are we talking about?"

"I need somebody," she said. "You remind me of my husband. Which is wicked and sinful, and I know it. But without belaboring the point, that's why I have faith in you, Brad. Your mother raised you well, giving you some good instincts. I have three children. My kids probably will need to borrow a lot of good instincts before they're old enough to manage their lives."

"What are we talking about?"

"I'll last until Miriam turns eighteen," she said. "But the younger you are when you go in, the better your odds of a long, successful Transcendence."

I gave up asking questions.

"And the techniques are always improving," Lucee said. "Being older than fifty isn't best, but the projections are still excellent. Thirty days of Transcendence . . . do you know what that means?"

One day in the cold gel brought more than a decade of lucid, rapid thought.

"And maybe I'll last for forty days, or more," she said hopefully.

"Leaving your kids behind," I said.

"With you overseeing their trust funds, plus any other needs they might have."

"No." Once wasn't enough, so I said the word a few more times.

"Think about it," she said.

I thought I had, but just to put an edge to my refusal, I asked, "What kind of mother abandons her kids?"

I needed a second sharp stab to the open wound. With the same fierceness that intrigued me when I was a boy, Lucee said, "I was abandoned, left to raise three maniacs by myself, and you remind me of the man who did that to me, and don't ever, ever use that expression or that tone on me again. He's dead, and I want to live."

The Flood Rises

"The men without guns," said Straven. "They are the ones to fear."

The fellows in question were standing on the long dock, watching our approach. The group certainly looked ominous, but I had suspicions about my companion, too: a stout little fellow with cold eyes and easy answers, as well as endless "friends" who owed him a ridiculous number of favors. In these last days I had learned to take Straven's advice, but he wasn't carrying any gun, so perhaps I should consider him among the most-dangerous sect.

I didn't have so much as a nano-blowdart in my pocket.

Maybe I was the most dangerous of all.

"Be calm," Straven whispered. Then he called to one of the kidnappers by name. "Aamir, hello. How are you this very good day?"

Aamir was tall and skinny and looked in need of a vacation. He had a nervous manner, suspicion cast everywhere but particularly at me. His hands were empty, but he wore a sleek Chinese battle helmet that might be useless, or it could be supervising a battery of illegal weapons.

"It is wonderful weather," Straven continued. "Is this God's work, or the island's?"

The chief kidnapper said a word, maybe two, and suddenly our boat's engine throttled down. The autopilot had been claimed, which was expected. We coasted for a few moments, and then the engine reversed, leaving us drifting. Two men aimed machine guns at our faces as pulses of sound and light hunted for hidden bombs and security systems. The process took longer than I anticipated, but as promised, the scans found nothing ominous. Aamir's mood appeared to brighten, however slightly, and he finally answered Straven's chatty question.

"The weather is God's effort," he said, "and the island helps. They are working together, as all good souls should."

On that curious note, our boat started forward again.

The island in question was a sun-washed atoll bolstered by engineered coral and surrounded by the bluest water in the Caribbean. A town's worth of mansions had been built here three decades ago—little palaces with swimming pools and solar-feasting roofs and enough bathrooms to serve the needs of families and guests and an army of servants. I came here often as a boy, learning to swim in a pool shaped like a raptor's skull. But then Transcendence became the new escape, winnowing out the oldest and most susceptible. Every oligarch family shrank just enough that a tipping point was reached, and nobody wanted to come here just to sit inside these huge, half-empty homes. Once the toilets had plugged, the island was abandoned to nature, and nature arrived in the form of squatters from South America and North Africa, which was why every window in every building was filled with faces.

Like the men on the dock, the new residents were watching the arrival of one hundred million dollars in ransom.

We bumped against the dock with a soft thud. The machine-gun boys had been told to be wary, and they looked very serious and happy about their work, watching my smallest motion.

Aamir suddenly threw aside doubts and cautions. Straven was his "good friend," deserving a clasp of hands to help pull him off the water, followed by a sharp slap to the back. I was "our honored guest," though I didn't deserve hands or slaps.

Standing on a solid surface again, I asked, "Where's the girl?"

"The girl," said Aamir.

"Miriam."

"The young woman is fine. She is healthy and safe, and eager to see her half-uncle and her dead mother's lover and the tight-fisted ruler of her modest wealth."

All in all, that was an excellent description of me.

I nodded and glanced at my associate.

Straven skillfully jumped into the mess. "I apologize for Bradley. He likes to worry too much, I think."

Maybe so.

Straven continued, "As promised, this a private transaction between willing partners. Only the necessary economic specialists and AIs are involved. The police know nothing of our business. The media have not been informed. If all goes as promised, we won't seek retribution in any foreseeable future."

Aamir nodded, pleased by that message.

Several gun-toting men watched the horizon and the clear blue waters, and one unarmed woman came forward with a tablet that had gone extinct everywhere else in the world. Ancient unregistered software was going to be used to move the money. She looked Chinese and spoke Spanish, instructing me on what to do with my fingerprints and voiceprint, pin numbers and shaky signature.

The transfer was supposed to take five minutes.

Once again, I said, "Miriam."

"I'll take you to her," Aamir said cheerfully.

"I thought she could be brought out to me."

"No, no. I will take you."

I looked at Straven.

"Oh, I will be fine," the little man told me, as if his well-being was the concern. "Go get the girl. We have plenty of time, you'll see."

This wasn't my plan. I considered jumping into the boat and throwing a tantrum, which might have been a workable strategy, except by then I was ten steps into the walk. I felt committed. Aamir shouted a few words in broken Spanish. Then he removed the battle helmet, leaving it upside down on the dock.

We walked together. Everything about the island was familiar, and nothing was the same. The buildings were battered by the climate, and the concrete path was cracked, weeds thriving along every edge, and the first swimming pool we passed was filled with maybe four inches of sick green rainwater.

Aamir touched my elbow, startling me. "I want to tell you something, Bradley."

I flinched.

"My father worked for your family," he said. "Not too many years ago, in fact."

The best I could do was nod and say, "Really?"

Aamir named the uncle who had survived the parties and drug cocktails. Then with relish, he said, "You probably don't realize this either, but my father was invited to join your uncle in his Transcendence."

"No, I didn't know that," I said.

"It's a great tradition among kings," Aamir said, turning us toward my grandfather's house. "You take your favorite servants and bodyguards with you into the Afterlife."

That had been a popular trend, at least for a year or two. I hadn't heard rumors about my uncle pulling that kind of bullshit, but knowing the man, it all sounded perfectly reasonable.

I asked, "Did your father accept the invitation?"

"Not at first, no." Aamir slowed our pace and touched my elbow again. "But there were factors. There were complications. You see, your uncle offered quite a lot of money for the companionship. Eight servants were to be included, and their families would earn healthy packages, and of course this was by no measure a death penalty. My father was not an old man, and he could expect perhaps two months of Transcendence, which still cost quite a lot of money in those days."

Prices were falling every year. The techniques had been industrialized and automated, and even with the cheap services, failure rates had jumped only slightly.

"I should mention that despite his long service, my father did not admire your uncle. And that worked against the agreement. He very much wanted to say, 'Thank you, sir, but no thank you.' Except there was one final factor: in a world where the wealthy were hurrying off to die, human servants find jobs to be scarce. If my father refused the invitation and the severance package, he would have to return home and live out his days as a broken man, without income and without prospects. And that is why he reluctantly agreed."

I made the obvious assumption. "You hate my family. That's why you did this."

Aamir looked genuinely startled. He laughed with a big voice, saying, "Oh, no. Hardly, hardly."

"Then I don't understand," I said.

"Despite all of his misgivings, my father's Transcendence was a blessing. Before this happened, I barely knew the man. He always lived on other continents, in circles that I couldn't imagine. But once he and your uncle went into the cold baths together, your silly relative suddenly grew wise. He became self-assured and far more competent at everything, and within the first hour, he declared that my father's duties were finished. The man lying beside him was free to spend the rest of his life accomplishing many fine things for himself and for his family, including creating a digital realm where we could come, his wife and children, when we judged the time right."

We walked up to my grandfather's house together. The raptor-headed swimming pool was filled with clean water, and one young woman was sitting on the deck just out of reach of the dinosaur's jaws, watching my approach from behind a pair of floating sunglasses.

"Arrogant and silly as he was, your uncle was the savior of my family and a blessing on every day that I have lived since."

"Good," felt like a worthy sentiment.

Miriam stood and approached, smiling at both of us.

That's when instinct gave me my first warning: a visceral sense that this girl was not the foolish victim here.

"I have met your terms," Aamir said.

Maybe so.

"Bradley, I wish you and the girl a safe journey home," he told me. Then the grateful man vanished inside a house that I barely knew at all.

The young woman had her father's build, muscles somewhat softened by her gender. She was pretty enough without being a natural beauty and the first smile was big if rather unconvincing—an expression worn for the occasion but not deeply felt.

"How are you?" I asked.

"Tired," she claimed.

I wanted to see desperation or relief in that face, or at least a sorry, slightly embarrassed quality that proved the girl felt something for me and my particular circumstances. But I didn't deserve understanding. What I deserved was a smile that turned mocking and a quick chuckle, something about this adventure at least a little bit funny.

Bristling, I looked everywhere but at her face—which might well have been part of the plan.

"I want to get out of here," I said.

"Yeah, I'm sure you do."

We walked toward the dock.

Halfway there, she said, "Thank you, by the way."

I managed another couple steps before asking, "Why the hell did you come to this place? What were you thinking?"

Again, that mocking laugh.

My anger grew hotter. Looking back at the tanned feet and sandals following in my wake, I said, "You were warned not to come here. This place isn't safe."

"I was with other people," she said.

"What other people?"

She edited the word. "Friends," she said emphatically. Then she walked up next to me, pressing the pace. "We were bored," she said. "We were bored and had a boat, and I told them my mother's stories about diving over these reefs. Some of the best coral in the world, Mom claimed. So everybody wanted to see, and we never intended to get in trouble."

"Aamir came floating out and grabbed you, did he?"

She took a breath. She said, "Yes."

"Along with those scary friends of his," I added, motioning at the boys with machine guns.

"Yes," she said.

Straven was standing where I left him, surrounded by guns. He looked as if he was chatting amiably with the gunmen, which was in character, and then he stopped talking and everybody looked at us. My instincts were whispering, and I had no idea what they were saying. Then several guns were pushed against strong shoulders, and a keen sense of fear ate into me.

"I wanted to be careful," said Miriam.

"Quiet," I said.

The dock felt endless. My little boat was bobbing on the perfect blue water, and Straven smiled at me before gazing at the girl. His face was full of information I couldn't decipher.

He looked back at me, saying, "Congratulations."

I didn't talk.

"You have done a good thing," he said.

"And you'll get your cut, as soon as the three of us are out of here and safe," I said.

Straven said, "Yes."

My heart hurt, it was beating so hard.

"Except I am staying behind," he said.

One of the gunmen laughed while the others practiced their menacing stances.

"What is this?" I asked.

Straven shrugged. "I just made a new deal, and now my commission is unnecessary. So you are free of that expense, and please, use those funds however you think is best." Then he took my hand and squeezed, saying, "You are a good enough man, Bradley. It has been a pleasure working with you."

I looked at his face and then back at the mansions. Somehow even more faces were pressed against the window glass.

"Is everybody here Transcending?" I asked.

"Everyone older than fourteen, yes."

"One hundred million dollars is more than enough," I pointed out.

He agreed. "But there are others who want to join us too. This project involves far more than one dilapidated resort for the spoiled and soft."

None of this should have been a surprise, yet I was startled, standing on the hot planks while looking back at the last busy days.

Miriam broke the spell by jumping into the boat.

"Come on, Brad," she said.

I still didn't understand. If I had, I would have grabbed one of the guns and shot the girl a few times. Just for the satisfaction. But instead of violence, I amiably climbed down and watched the men untie the lines while Straven knelt, making certain that I saw the charm in his face when he unleashed it.

"Honestly," he said, "I was not certain what I would do today. Stay and Transcend with these people, or cash my paycheck and wait another week or two."

I told the boat to go home.

We pulled away, and Straven rose again and waved. "This is a good day for everybody. You just don't see it now, my friend."

Miriam was sitting in the bow. She looked relaxed, untroubled. I went up to her and sat, and when she glanced at me, I said, "The payment won't go through."

Various thoughts passed across her face.

I reached out and pulled the sunglasses away from her eyes. "I spent some of my own money to protect all of yours," I said. "In a few minutes, they'll find out that there's nothing inside the encryption but nothing."

She smiled, and she nodded slowly. "We thought you might do that."

"Well, you were right."

Miriam shook her head. "Think again, Brad."

I felt dangerous and in control, sitting back on the padded seat, pulling what pleasure I could from my treachery.

"Do you know why you should reconsider?" she asked.

Again, I felt ill-at-ease.

She said, "Several thousand poor people can certainly afford to pool their funds and pay for several Transcendences. But they only needed to pay for one person's Transcendence. They had to find a charitable girl who would give them a situation that they could exploit, letting their entire community take the ultimate journey together."

I grabbed a knee, a hand.

"Don't touch me, Brad."

My hands jumped off the machine.

"How long ago?" I asked.

"By my count, I left your world fifty-two years ago," she said, laughing again at something she could see and that was reliably funny.

I was furious and sick inside, and on the outside, trembling.

"Let them have the ransom," she said. "Although technically speaking, I don't believe that's what it is."

I didn't talk.

"And you can take the rest of my inheritance for yourself, if you want." Her facsimile leaned forward, making certain our eyes met. "I know quite a lot that I didn't know before, Brad."

"I bet," I whispered.

"But one grand truth found me, long before I was laid down inside the cold bath," she said.

I didn't say anything.

She waited, probably for days by her reckoning.

"What did you learn?" I finally asked.

"How the world is going to end," she said. Then the facsimile sat back and turned itself off, never speaking another word.

Drought

Mogadishu looked prosperous, looked happy. There were as many smiles in the streets as there were faces, and I couldn't count either, the city was so jammed with people. Children and their parents crowded me, plus a very few elderly, and there were armies of machines busily chasing jobs and hobbies and whatever else it was that our mechanical servants did with their neurons. I walked through the crowds for an hour before finding a proper rental shop. I said that I wanted a car, except what I got was more a spaceship with tires. The grinning young office worker had been in town only three months, but he acted like the expert that I needed. And I needed nothing less than the best, he claimed. Driving through the interior could turn frustrating without warning. No, there weren't any explicit dangers outside the city. Unless I looked delicious to a saber-lion or cybernetic hyena, I was going to be safe enough. The smiling young fellow said that I was a man accustomed to the best, obviously, and the best was a fat-tired wonder that generated its power from a palladium-tritium reactor that would keep me fed and comfortable for the next fifty years, if necessary.

"Let's hope for better than that," I said, planting my signature at the bottom of the legal terrain.

As promised, the car was a wonder, and my drive proved interesting, what with the beautiful scenery woven around an endless boredom. Rains had been reliable for several years and rivers and grasslands were prospering in what used to be wastelands, and of course the wild game had returned, often wearing embellishments given by cold clever dreamers. The young highways were still in good repair, but the last economic boom that had swept across the continent, destroying drought and civil unrest, had also erased the farms that would have thrived in the new Eden. When every patch of ground is a national park, parks cease to matter very much. Each slice of this countryside was as splendid as most of its neighbors, and every time one more person Transcended, another ex-peasant from the wilderness could move into a magical city, buy an empty apartment for cheap, and settle into a robot-aided existence free of dust and dreariness.

Modern life was just the proving grounds for the greater Heaven to come, which was Transcendence.

On that particular day, barely two billion people were still walking the emerald face of the Earth, and that number fell weekly, reliably and steadily steering us toward a population that would, that should, probably level out around five hundred million. At least that's what plenty of AIs and Transcendent sociologists were claiming, figuring on reproductive urges, social norms, and other well-researched factors.

Half a billion sounded like plenty of humans, and of course our species was too stubborn and too adaptable to put ourselves into extinction willingly.

So why did troublemakers like me insist on worrying about our survival?

Driving the reborn savanna, it was easy to push every great fear out of the way. That left the little terrors free to claim me, which was what every son does when he drives off to visit his mother.

The highway ended abruptly, construction machines abandoned in mid-scoop and pour. The dirt roads after the pavement meant slower driving, and soon those roads failed as well. After that, each new stream and little lake wasn't just new, it was free of the weight that comes with names and histories, and a man traveling alone could think he was an explorer in the mold of Burton and Kurtz.

On the far shore of the largest local lake was a tidy village straight out of the Neolithic. Sitting under an umbrella that looked weirdly familiar to me was an old woman I had never seen before.

"You could have flown here," said my mother's voice. "We wouldn't have minded at all."

"Driving felt more honest," I said.

"If that's what matters, you should have walked from the coast."

"Maybe that's how I'll return."

The skin that was once terrified of any sunlight had turned brown and leathery. A tooth was missing in front, and Mom didn't appear to care what sagged and what spread. But even depleted, dressed in nothing but wild fabrics and other creatures' leather, the woman looked fit. I told her so.

Happy for the praise, she said, "We should race along the beach. I would win."

"Not in a fair contest," I said.

"Oh Brad," she said. "Mothers never play fair."

Her community was full of like-minded souls who had come from every continent, every background. A thousand villages and tribes like theirs were scattered along the Rift Valley, each with its quirky rules and nonbinding covenants, all united in the mad hope that what they were doing would last longer than their own generation.

This good land fed them and clothed them, and they smiled at least as much as the citizens of Mogadishu. I met Mother's friends and neighbors, names piled on names. Nobody appeared especially ignorant about the world. These unaugmented minds spent a portion of their days studying world events, and every household had at least two readers filled to bursting with classics, some thousands of years old, others written last week.

I thought that was ironic and said so.

"Why is that, Brad?"

The classics made sense to me. But after Grandpa's day, there were suddenly too many titles in the world for the world to read. Pointing out the obvious, I said that even if the smartest person went into the cold bath, and even if he or she survived for a thousand years measured in plodding earth-time, there was no way to swim this ocean of word and thought.

"Why even bother reading?" I asked.

She nodded, and she smiled. "But do you see any readers being used?"

No, actually, I hadn't.

"Because you won't," she said. She threw a little laugh at me, adding, "We keep these devices as tests, and believe me, nobody's will ever fails them."

I was sure I'd met everyone in the village, but then I strolled into my mother's tidy hut. A somewhat younger man was sitting on the floor, and suddenly he was standing. He was Chinese and shy-faced until he spoke, and then he called me, "Bradley." He shook my hand with both of his, saying, "Please, let me put you at ease. I love your mother because of her great wealth."

Mom laughed loudly, but my expression lacked any good humor.

Then both of them were laughing, their ambush successful.

"He means my goats," she reported. "Just my goats. I told you, I left everything else for the World Orphan Society, so kids left behind by Transcending parents have enough resources to thrive."

"You didn't tell me," I said.

Then I started to smile, and not just a little bit.

It was the first time in a very long while that I felt truly happy, and isn't that the best moment to make life's important decisions? When joy and a good journey are buoying you up?

Transcendence

I sat beside the long conference table, talking.

"I always thought that maybe, just maybe, before I died in every way, I could figure out a fix that would make ordinary life so attractive, compelling, and pure that Transcendence turned out to be a passing fad. I don't know how I was going to do it. Design the first cheap starships, or show people how we could terraform the solar system, or maybe I'd invent fancy transporters that could send us to the center of the galaxy where we'd meet whoever thinks they're in charge.

"Or even better, I'd reconfigure the cosmos, giving us new rules to live by.

"Or maybe . . . "

I hesitated. Then with a shake of the head, I said, "You don't have to be stuck inside a cold-gel bath to be full of idiot dreams."

Nobody said a word.

"There was a moment, out on the veldt with my odd old mother, when I realized that I wasn't going to do anything amazing. And even worse, the world had turned empty on me, and I hadn't even noticed.

"Do you know what it takes to empty the world?

"Do you?

"It's not when the people are all gone. That hasn't happened and it probably can't happen. No, the Earth turns vacant when the dead are more compelling than the living, and nobody left can take their place.

"This is when I finally made up my mind," I said. "When I understood that I was on the brink of being alone, and really, much as I wished, there wasn't going to be any miracle fix that I could accomplish inside my own Transcendence."

Then I paused, looking out a window that I had built just a half-moment ago.

Snow was falling on the mountain slope.

Everybody was waiting for me. Drawn from every memory and from every last file, the dead looked at me impatiently. A couple voices whispered my name with pissy tones, but I didn't care what my uncles said. Lucee was young and pregnant with Miriam, and two bruised boys were sitting like prisoners on their chairs, and Grandma Joyce was the calm center, and my mother looked like someone who could never eat goat or live on dirt. Meanwhile, the old patriarch himself was standing behind me, waiting to claim his chair. But that was my chair, and I told Grandpa so.

"What are we doing here?" he asked.

"Don't play dumb, Dad," said Mother. "This is a game he's built, and we are the pieces."

"Bradley? Is that true?"

"No," said the eight-year-old in their midst. "This is a lot bigger than any game. It's taken me three years and all of our family's remaining wealth and power, and I've also gathered up thousands of willing souls to share the cold-gel with me. We're working together here. Our minds and the biggest, quickest banks of quantum computers are married into a single Transcendence."

"Brad wants us to run the family meeting," said Lucee.

"Little Brad wants to be in charge," Miriam said, from the womb.

"Except I don't have any explicit goal here," I warned. "This simulation is the best ever managed, and it has its own future. And the modeling doesn't involve just you, but billions of other people, dead and otherwise. All but a tiny sliver of my chilled brain is being used to help maintain an Earth the same as ours was decades ago. There is just one difference: In this realm, there is no Transcendence. That technology is forbidden, impossible, and unthinkable. And as soon as this eight-year-old boy walks out that door, your minds will be set back to Aspen on the brink of Christmas. Miriam will be a fetus again, and Grandpa will be a rich cancer patient, and I don't have any clue what will happen next to any of you."

Every face was fixed on me.

"You can do whatever you want," I said. "Sit here and scream at each other, maybe for a century or two. Or you can settle your differences and accomplish something enormous in the aftermath. Which, by the way, is the same conundrum waiting for every other entity."

They stared, and the fear was rising.

Then the smart, worldly businessman clapped a big hand on my shoulder, asking, "And what are you going to do, Bradley?"

"I told you. My brain is going to help maintain the memescape."

"I mean with that sliver, the part of your brain that's still you."

"Oh." I needed a moment, which surprised me. "It's a nice day, and I want to snowboard. I'm going outside now and become a kid again, and once I'm done with a good long run, a careless driver is going to run me down in the parking lot, and I'll be dead."

Mother gave a low miserable shout.

I said, "This way, all of my wits and humor can focus on what matters, which is keeping this madhouse alive."

Lucee's pretty nose was leaking a slippery mess, but bless her, she handed my mother the first spare tissue that she found in her pocket.

Then, grumpy as hell, Grandpa said, "Bradley. That sounds like a coward's trick to me."

"You know," I said, looking hard at him. "All those words about the whale, and still you never figured it out."

ROSARY AND GOLDENSTAR

GEOFF RYMAN

The room was wood—floor, walls, ceiling.

The doorbell clanged a second time. The servant girl Bessie finally answered it; she had been lost in the kitchen amid all the pans. She slid across the floor on slippers, not lifting her feet; she had a notion that she polished as she walked. The front door opened directly onto the night: snow. The only light was from the embers in the fireplace.

Three huge men jammed her doorway. "This be the house of Squire Digges?" the smallest of them asked; and Bessie, melting in shyness, said something like, "Cmn gud zurs."

They crowded in, stomping snow off their boots, and Bessie knelt immediately to try to mop it up with her apron. "Shoo! Shoo!" said the smaller guest, waving her away.

The Master roared; the other door creaked like boots and in streamed Squire Digges, both arms held high. "Welcome! Good Count Vesuvius! Guests! Hah hah!" Unintroduced, he began to pump their hands.

Vesuvius, the smaller man, announced in Danish that this was Squire Digges, son of Leonard and author of the lenses, then turned back and said in English that these two fine fellows were Frederik Rosenkrantz and Knud Gyldenstierne.

"We have corresponded!" said Squire Digges, still smiling and pumping. To him, the two Danes looked huge and golden-red with bronze beards and bobbed noses, and he'd already lost control of who was who. He looked sideways in pain at the Count. "You must pardon me, sirs?"

"For what?"

The Squire looked harassed and turned on the servant. "Bessie! Bessie, their coats! The door. Leave off the floor, girl!"

Vesuvius said in Danish, "*The gentleman has asked you to remove your coats at long last. For this he is sorry.*"

One of the Danes smiled, his face crinkling up like a piecrust, and he unburdened himself of what must have been a whole seal hide. He dumped it on Bessie, who could not have been more than sixteen and was small for her years. Shaking his head, Digges slammed shut the front door. Bessie, buried under furs, began to slip across the gleaming floor as if on ice.

"Bessie," said Digges in despair then looked over his shoulder. "Be careful of the floors, Messires, she polishes them so. Good girl, not very bright." He touched Bessie's elbow and guided her toward the right door.

"*He warns us that floors are dangerous.*"

Rosenkrantz and Gyldenstierne eyed each other. "*Perhaps we fall through?*" They began to tiptoe.

Digges guided Bessie through the door, and closed it behind her. He smiled and then unsmiled when there was a loud whoop and a falling crash within.

"All's well, Bessie?"

"Aye, zur."

"We'll wait here for a moment. Uh, before we go in. The gentlemen will excuse me but I did not hear your names."

"*He's forgotten your names. These English cannot speak.*" Vesuvius smiled. "Is so easy to remember in English. This be noble Rosary and Goldenstar."

"Sirs, we are honored. Honored beyond measure!"

Mr. Goldenstar sniffed. "*The whole place sags and creaks. Haven't the English heard of bricks?*"

Mr. Rosary beamed and gestured at the panelling and the turd-brown floor. "House. Beautiful. Beautiful!"

Squire Digges began to talk to them as if they were children. "In. Warm!" He beat his own arms. "Warrrrrrrrrrm."

Goldenstar was a military man, and when he saw the room beyond, he gave a cry and leapt back in alarm.

It was not a dining hall but a dungeon. It had rough blocks, chains, and ankle irons that hung from the wall. "*It's a trap!*" he yelped, and clasped young Rosary to pull him back.

From behind the table a tall, lean man rose up, all in black with a skull cap and lace around his neck. *Inquisitor.*

"Oh!" laughed the Squire and touched his forehead. "No, no, no, no alarms, I beg. Hah hah! The house once belonged to Philip Henslowe; he owns the theater out back; this is like a set from a play."

Vesuvius blinked in fury. "*This is his idea of a joke.*"

"You should see the upstairs; it is full of naked Venuses!"

"*I think he just said upstairs is a brothel.*"

Goldenstar ran his fingers over the walls. The rough stones, the iron rings and the chains had all been frescoed onto plaster. He blurted out a laugh. "*They're all mad.*"

"*They are all strolling players. They do nothing but go to the theater. They pose and declaim and roar.*"

Digges flung out a hand toward the man in black. "Now to the business at hand. Sirs! May . . . I . . . introduce . . . Doctor John DEE!"

For the Doctor, Vesuvius had a glittery smile; but he said through his teeth, "*They mime everything.*"

"Ah!" Mr. Rosary sprang forward to shake the old man's hand. He was in love, eyes alight. "Queen Elisabetta. Magus!"

Dr. John Dee rumbled, "I am called Mage, yes, but I am in fact the Advisor Philosophical to her Majesty."

Digges beamed. "His *Parallaticae commentationis* and my own *Alae seu scalae mathematicae* were printed as a pair."

Someone else attended, pale skinned, pink cheeked, and glossy from nose to balding scalp, with black eyes like currants in a bun and an expression like a barber welcoming you to his shop.

"And this example," growled Digges, putting his hand on the young man's shoulder, "will not be known to you, but we hold him in high esteem, a family friend. This is Guillermus Shakespere."

The young man presented himself. "A Rosary and a Goldenstar. These are names for poetry. Especially should one wish to contrast Religion and Philosophy."

Vesuvius's lip curled. "You mock names?"

"No no, of course not. I beg! Not that construction. It is but poetic . . . convenience. My own poor name summons up dragooned peasants shaking weapons. Or, or, an actor whose only roles are those of soldiers." The young man looked back and forth between the men, expecting laughter. They blinked and stood with their hands folded not quite into fists.

"My young friend is a reformed Papist and so thinks much on issues of religion and philosophy. As do we." Digges paused, also waiting. "Please sit, gentlemen."

Cushions, food, and wine all beckoned. Digges busied himself pouring far too much wine into tankards. Mr. Rosary hunkered down with pleasure next to Dr. Dee, and even took his hand. He then began to speak, sometimes closing his eyes. "My dear Squire Digges and honorabled Doctor Dee. My relative Tycho Brahe sends his greatest respects and has entrusted us to give you this, his latest work."

He sighed and chuckled, relieved to be rid of both a small gray printed pamphlet, and his speech. Digges howled his gratitude, and read a passage aloud from the pamphlet and passed it to Dr. Dee, and pressed Rosary to pass on his thanks.

Rosary began to recite again. "I am asked by Tycho Brahe to say how impress-ed with your work. Sir. To describe the universe as infinite with mathematical argument!" His English sputtered and died. "Is a big thing. We are all so amuzed."

"Forgive me," said the young man. "Is it the universe or the argument that is infinite?"

"Guy," warned Digges in a sing-song voice. He pronounced it with a hard "G" and a long eeee.

"And is it the universe or the numbers that are amusing?"

Mr. Rosary paused, understood, and grinned. "The two. Both."

"We disagree on matters of orbitals," said Squire Digges.

Vesuvius leaned back, steepling his fingers; his nails were clean and filed. "A sun that is the circumference of Terra." He sketched with his finger a huge circle and shook his head.

Almost under his breath the young man said, "A sonne can be larger than his father."

Digges explained. "My young friend is a poet."

Vesuvius smiled. "I look forward to him entertaining us later." Then he ventriloquized in Danish, *"And until then, he might eat with the servants."*

Mr. Rosary looked too pleased to care and beamed at Digges. "You . . . have . . . lens."

Digges boomed. "Yes! Yes! On roof." He pointed. *"Stierne. Stierne."*

Rosary laughed and nodded. "Yes! *Stierne!* Star."

"Roof. We go to roof." Squire Digges mimed walking with his two fingers. Blank looks, so he wiped out his gesture with a wave.

Vesuvius translated with confidence. *"No stars tonight, too cloudy."*

"No stars," said Mr. Rosary, as if someone's cat had died.

"Yes." Digges looked confused. *"Stierne.* On roof."

Everything stalled: words, hands, mouths and feet. Nobody understood.

Young Guy made a sound like bells, many of them, as if bluebells rang. His fingers tinkled across an arch that was meant to be the Firmament. Then his two flat hands became lenses and his arms mechanical supports that squeedled as they lined up his palms.

Goldenstar gave his head an almost imperceptible shake. *"What the hell is he doing?"*

Vesuvius: *"I told you they have to mime everything."*

"No wonder that they are good with numbers. They can't use words!"

"It's why there will never be a great poet in English."

Rosary suddenly rocked in recognition. He too mimed the mechanical device with its lenses. He twinkled at young Guy. Young Guy twinkled back.

"Act-or," explained Digges. "Tra-la! Stage. But poet. Oh! Such good poet.

New poem. *Venus and Adonis!*" He kissed the tips of his fingers. Vesuvius's eyes, heavy and unmoved, rested on his host.

"Poet. Awww," Rosary said in sympathy. "No numbers."

John Dee, back erect, sipped his wine.

Bessie entered, rattling plates and knives in terror. Goldenstar growled, and his hands rounded in the air the curvature of her buttocks. She noticed and fled, soles flapping, polishing no more.

The Squire poured more wine. "Now. I want to hear more of your great relation, Lord Tycho. I yearn to visit him. He lives on an island? Devoted to philosophy!" He pronounced the name as "Tie-koh."

Vesuvius corrected him. "Teej-hhho."

"Yes yes yes, Tycho."

"The island is called *Hven*. You should be able to remember it as it is the same word as 'haven.' It is called in Greek Uraniborg. Urania means study of stars. Perhaps you know that?"

Digges's face stiffened. "I do read Greek."

Rosary beamed at Guy. "Your name Gee. In Greek is Earth."

Guy laughed. "Is it? Heaven and Earth. And I was born Taurus." He waited for a response. "Earth sign?" He looked at them all in turn. "You are all astrologers?"

Dr. Dee said, "No."

"And your name," said Guy, turning suddenly on the translator as if pulling a blade. "You are called Vesuvius?"

"A pseudonym, Guy," said Digges. "Something to hide. *A nom de plume.*"

"What's that?"

"French," growled Vesuvius. "A language."

Rosary thought that was a signal to change languages, and certainly the subject. *"Mon cousin a un nez d'or."*

Squire Digges jumped in to translate ahead of Vesuvius. "Your cousin has a . . . " He faltered. "A golden nose."

Rosary pointed to his own nose. *"Oui. Il l'a perdu ça par se battre en duel."*

"In . . . a . . . duel."

Goldenstar thumped the table. "Over *matematica!*"

Squire Digges leaned back. "Now that is a good reason to lose your nose."

"Ja! Ja!" Goldenstar laughed. *"Principiis mathematicis."*

"I trust we will not come to swords," said Digges, half-laughing.

Rosary continued. *"De temps en temp il port un nez de cuivre."*

Vesuvius translated. "Sometimes the nose is made of copper."

Guy's mouth crept sideways. "He changes noses for special occasions?"

Vesuvius glared; Goldenstar prickled. "Tycho Brahe great man!"

"Evidently. To be able to afford such a handsome array of noses."

Squire Digges hummed "no" twice.

Rosary pressed on. *"Mon cousin maintain comme un animal de familier un élan."*

Vesuvius snapped back, "He also has a pet moose."

Digges coughed. "I think you'll find he means elk."

"L'élan peut danser!" Rosary looked so pleased.

Digges rattled off a translation. "The elk can dance." He paused. "I might have that wrong."

Goldenstar thought German might work better. *"Der elch ist tot."*

Digges. "The elk is dead."

"Did it die in the duel as well?" Guy's face was bland. "To lose at a stroke both your nose and your moose."

Rosary rocked with laughter. *"Ja-ha-ha. Ja! Der elch gesoffenwar von die treppen gefallen hat."*

Sweat tricked down Digges's forehead. "The elk drank too much and fell down stairs."

Guy nodded slightly to himself. "And you good men believe that the Earth goes around the sun." His smile was a grimace of incredulity and embarrassment.

Dr. Dee tapped the table. "No. Your friend Squire Digges believes the Earth goes around the sun. Our guests believe that the sun goes around the Earth, but that all the other planets revolve around those two central objects. They believe this on the evidence of measurements and numbers. This evening is a conference on numbers and their application to the ancient study of stars. Astronomy. But the term is muddled."

Guy's face folded in on itself.

"Language fails you. Thomas Digges is described as a designer of arms and an almanacker. Our Danish friends are called astrologers, I am called a mage. I call us philosophers, but our language is numbers. Numbers describe, sirrah, with more precision than all your poetry."

Shakespere bowed.

"The Queen herself believes this and thus so should you." Dee turned away from him.

"But the numbers disagree," said Shakespere.

Bessie labored into the room backwards, bearing on a trencher a whole roast lamb. It was burnt black and smelled of soot. The company applauded nonetheless. The parsnips and turnips about it were cinders shining with fat.

Digges continued explaining. "Now, this great Tycho saw suddenly appear in the heavens . . . "

Goldenstar punched the air and shouted over the last few words, "By eye! By eye!"

"Yes, by eye. He saw a new light in the heavens, a comet he thought, only it could not be one."

"Numbers by eye!"

"Yes, he calculated the parallax and proved it was not a comet. It was beyond the moon. A new star, he thought."

"Nova!" exclaimed Goldenstar.

"More likely to be a dying one, actually. But it was a change to the immutable sphere of the stars!"

"Oh. Interesting," said Shakespere. "Should . . . someone carve?"

"You're as slow as gravy! Guy! The sphere of the stars is supposed to be unchanging and perfect."

"Spheres, you mean the music of the spheres?"

Goldenstar bellowed. "*Ja*. It move!"

"I rather like the idea of the stars singing."

Digges's hand moved as if to music. "It means Ptolemy is wrong. It means the Church is wrong, though why Ptolemy matters to the Church I don't know. But there it was. A new light in the heavens!"

Guy's voice rose in panic. "When did this happen?"

John Dee answered him. "1572."

Shakespere began to count the years on his fingers.

John Dee's mouth twitched and he squeezed shut Shakespere's hand. "Twenty. Years. And evidently the world did not end, so it was not a portent." As he spoke, Vesuvius translated in an undertone.

Squire Digges grinned like a wolf. "There are no spheres. The planets revolve around the sun, and we are just another planet."

"Noooooooooo ho-ho!" wailed Rosary and Goldenstar.

Digges bounced up and down in his chair, still smiling. "The stars are so far away we cannot conceive the distance. All of them are bigger than the sun. The universe is infinitely large. It never ends."

The Danes laughed and waved him away. Goldenstar said, "Terra heavy. Sit in center. Fire light. Sun go around Terra!"

"Could we begin eating?" suggested Guy.

"Terra like table. Table fly like bird? No!" One of Goldenstar's fists was matter, the other fire and spirit.

"I'll carve. Shall I carve?" No one noticed Shakespere. He stood up and sharpened the knife while the philosophers teased and bellowed. He sawed the blackened hide. "I like a nice bit of crackling." He leaned down hard on the knife and pushed; the scab broke open and a gout of blood spun out of it like a tennis ball and down Guy's doublet. The meat was raw. He regained his poise. "Shall we fall upon it with lupine grace?"

Vesuvius interpreted. "*He says you have the manners of wolves.*"

Rosary said, "Hungry like wolves."

The knife wouldn't cut. Guy began to wrestle the knuckle out of its socket. Like a thing alive, the lamb leapt free onto the floor.

"Dear, dear boy." Digges rose to his feet and scooped up the meat, and put it back on the board. "Give me the knife." He took it and began with some grace to carve. "He really is a very good poet."

"Let us hope he is that at least," said Vesuvius.

Digges paused, about to serve. "He's interested in everything. History. Ovid. Sex. And then spins it into gold."

He put a tranche onto Goldenstar's plate. Knud did not wait for the others and began to press down with his knife. The meat didn't cut. He speared it up whole and began to chaw one end of it. The fat was uncooked and tasted of human genitals; the flesh had the strength of good hemp rope. He turned the turnip over in his fingers. It looked like a lump of coal and he let it fall onto his plate. *"I suggest we sail past this food and go and see the lenses."*

Rosary tried to take a bite of the meat. *"Yes. Lenses."*

Thomas Digges's house stood three stories high, dead on Bankside opposite the spires of All Hallows the Great and All Hallows the Lesser. Just behind his house, beyond a commons, stood Henslowe's theater, The Rose, which was why Guy was such a frequent houseguest. Digges got free tickets in the stalls as a way of apologizing for the groundlings' noise and litter and the inconvenience of Guy sleeping on his floor. Guy didn't snore but he did make noises all night as if he were caressing a woman or jumping down from trees.

No noise in February at night. The wind had dropped, and a few boats still plied across the river, lanterns glowing like planets. The low-tide mud was luminous with snow. The sky looked as if it had been scoured free of cloud.

Over his slated roof, Digges had built a platform. Its scaffolding supports had splintered; it groaned underfoot, shifting like a boat. The moon was full-faced and the stars seemed to have been flung up into the heavens, held by nets.

The cold had loosened Guy's tongue. "S-s-s-size of lenses, you look with both eyes. No squinting. C-c-can you imagine f-f-f-folk wearing them as a collar, they lift up the arms and have another set of eyes to see distant things. W-w-w-would that make them philosophers?"

"The gentlemen are acquainted with the principle, Guy." Digges was ratcheting a series of mechanical arms that supported facemask-sized rounds of glass.

"But not the wonder of it. D-do you sense wonder, Mr. Rosary?"

Rosary's red cheeks swelled. "I do not know."

"Many things I'm sure, Rosie, are comprehended by you. Are you married, perchance?"

"Geee-eee—heee," warned Digges. He bent his knees to look through the corridor of lenses and made an old-man noise.

Goldenstar answered. "Married."

"As am I. That signifies, b-b-but not much." Guy arched back around to Rosary. "Come by day the morrow and walk alongside the river with me. The churches and the boats, moorhens, the yards of stone and timber."

Vesuvius shook his head. "We have heard about you actors."

Goldenstar said, "We leave tomorrow." Rosary shrugged.

Digges stood up and presented his lenses to them. "Sirs." Vesuvius and Rosary did a little dance, holding out hands for each other, until the Count put a collegial hand on Rosary's back and pushed. Rosary crouched and stared, blinking.

Squire Digges sounded almost sad. "You see. The moon is solid too. Massy with heft."

Rosary was still. Finally he stood up, shaking his head. "That is . . . " He tried to speak with his hands, but that also failed. "Like being a sea." He looked sombre. "The stars are made of stone."

Goldenstar adopted a lunging posture as if grounding a spear against an advancing horde. "*This could get us all burnt at the stake.*"

John Dee answered in Danish. Vesuvius looked up in alarm. "*Yes, but not here, not while my Queen lives.*"

Shakespere understood the tone. "Everything is exploding, exploding all at once. When I was in Rome—it's so important to g-g-get things right, don't you think? Research is the best part of the j-job. Rome. Verona. Carthage. I was in a room with a man who was born the same year I was and his first name was the same as his last, G-G-Galileo Galilei. I told him about Thomas and he told me that he too has lenses. He told me that Jupiter has four moons and Saturn wears a rainbow hat. He is my pen pal, Galileo, I send him little things of my own, small pieces you understand—"

Vesuvius exploded. "Please you will stop prattle!" He ran a hand across his forehead. "We are meeting of great astrological minds in Europe, not prattle Italian!"

Digges placed an arm around Guy as if to warm him. Rosary phalanxed next to them as though shielding him from the wind. "Please," Rosary said to Vesuvius.

John Dee thought: People protect this man.

Guillermus Shakespere thought:

I can be in silence. My source is in silence. Words come from silence.

How different they be, these Danes, one all stern and leaden, forceful with facts, the other leavening dough. Their great cousin. All by eye? Compromise by eye, just keep the sun going around the Earth, to pacify the Pope and save your necks. Respect him more if he declared for the Pope forthrightly and kept to the heavens and Earth as we knew them. Digges digs holes in heaven, excavating stars as if they were bones. Building boats of bone. He could build boxes, boxes with mirrors to look down into the heart of the sea, show us a world of narwhales, sharks, and selkies.

All chastened by Mr. Volcano. All silent now. Stare now—by eye—you who think you see through numbers, stare at what his lenses show. New eyes to see new things.

How do rocks hang in the sky?

How will I tell my groundlings: the moon is a mountain that doesn't fall? The man with gap in his teeth; the maid with bruised cheek, the oarsman with rounded back? What can I say to them? These wonders are too high for speaking, for scrofulous London, its muddy river. Here the moon has suddenly descended onto our little eye-land. Here where the future is hidden in lenses and astrolabes. The numbers and Thomas's clanking armatures.

"Guy," says old Thomas, full of kindness. "Your turn."

I bow before the future, into the face of a new monarch of glass who overturns. I look through his eyes; see as he sees, wide and long. I blink as when I opened my eyes in a basin of milk. Dust and shadow, light and mist cross and swim and I look onto another world.

I can see so clearly that it's a ball, a globe. Its belly swells out toward me, a hint of shadow on its crescent edge.

It is as stone as any granite tor. Beige and hot in sunlight. The moon must see us laced in cloud but no clouds there, no rain, no green expanse. Nothing to shield from the shriveling sun. No angels, nymphs, orisons, bowers, streams, butterflies, lutes. Desiccated corpses. No dogs to devour. A circle of stone. Avesbury. A graveyard. Breadcrumbs and mold.

Not man in the moon, but a skull.

Nothing for my groundlings. Or poetry.

I look on Digges's face. He stares as wide as I do; no comfort there. He touches my sleeve. "Dear Guy. Look at the stars."

He hoists the thing on some hidden bearing, and then takes each arm and gears into a new niche. The lenses rise and intersect at some new angle, and I look again, and see the stars.

Rosie was right, it is an ocean. What ship could sail there? Bejeweled fish. That swallow Earth. Carry it to God. I can see. I can see they are suns, not tiny torches, and if suns then about those too other Earths could hang. Infinite suns, infinite worlds, deeper and deeper into bosom of God, distances vast, they make us more precious because so rare and small, defenseless before all that fire.

Here is proof of church's teaching. God must love us to make any note of us when the very Earth is a mote of soot borne high on smoky gas.

My poor groundlings.

John Dee watched.

The boy pulled back from the glass, this actor-poet-playwright. Someone else for whom there is no word. In the still and icy air, tears had frozen to his cheeks. Digges gathered him in; Rosary stepped forward; Goldenstar stared astounded. Only the spy stood apart, scorn on his face.

"You are right, Squire Digges," said the boy. "It is without end. Only that would be big enough for God." He looked fallen, pale and distracted. "The cold bests me. I must away, gentlemen."

"The morrow?" Rosary asked. "We meet before we go?"

The wordsmith nodded, clasped Rosary's hand briefly and then turned and trundled down the steps. The platform shook and shuddered. Dee stood still and dark for a moment, decided, and then with a swirl, followed.

Winding down the stairwell past people-smelling bedrooms, through the dungeon of a dining room. The future that awaited them? Out into the paneled room, flickering orange.

"Young Sir! Stay!"

The boy looked embarrassed. "Nowhere else to go."

Such a poor, thin cloak. Was that the dust of Rome on it? Or only Rome wished for so hard that mind-dust fell upon it? But his eyes: full of hope, when I thought to see despair. "Young master. Have you heard of the Brotherhood of Night?"

Hope suspended like dust, only dust that could see.

"I see you have not, for which I am thankful. We are a brotherhood devoted to these new studies late from Germany and Denmark, now Austria and Italia. None of us can move, let alone publish, without suspicion. That man Vesuvius is as much spy as guide, the Pope's factotum. How, young Guillermus, would you like to see Brahe's island of philosophy, in sight of great Elsinore? Uraniborg, city of the heavens, though in fact given over to the muse of a study that has late been revived. And all this by a man with a golden nose. Would you like to see again your starry twin Galileo? See Rome, Verona, Athens? Not Carthage, not possible, don't say that in good company again. But Spain, possible now. The courtship of Great Elizabeth by Philip makes travel even there approved and safe."

"My . . . I'm an actor. I used to play women."

"You still do." Dee's grim smile lengthened. "Men like Vesuvius dismiss you. Bah! Religion is destroying itself. The Protestants prevent the old Passion Plays, and in their stead grow you and Marlowe. You write the history of tragic kings. That has not happened since the Greeks."

Guy shook his head. "Ask Kit to do this."

He is, thought Dee, a good, faithful, fragile boy. And something in his thin shoulders tells me that he's contemplating going into Orders. That must be stopped.

Dee said aloud, "Kit draws enemies." The boy's eyes stared into his. "Men who want to kill him. They love you."

Out of cold policy, Dee took the boy into his arms and kissed him full on the lips, held him, and then pushed him back, to survey the results in the creature's eyes: yes: something soft, something steel.

Guy said, "You taste of gunpowder."

"You would still be able to wright your poetry. Send it to Kit in packets to furnish out the plays. In any case he will be undone, caught up in these Watchmen unless we hide him. As you might well be undone if you stay here and miss your chance to see the world blossom. Move for us and write it down. And learn, boy, learn! See where Caesar walked; breathe the scents of Athens's forest. Go to high Elsinore."

Shakespere stood with his eyes closed. The old house crackled and turned about them. The world was breaking. "Are there tales in Denmark of tragic kings?"

Dr. Dee nodded. "And things as yet undreamt of." He took up his long staff and the black cloak that was taller than himself. He put his arm around the slender shoulders and said, "Riverwalk with me."

The door shut tight behind them, and only then did Bessie come to open it.

Outside, white carpeted everything, and Bessie stepped into the hush. Somehow it was snowing again, though the sky overhead was clear. She kicked snow off the stone step and sat down, safe and invisible. It looked as if the stars themselves were falling in flakes. The idea made her giggle. She saw thistledown: stars were made of dandelion stuff.

As so often once it starts to snow, the air felt warmer. The blanket of white would be melted by morning; if she were abed now she'd have missed it. So she warmed the stone step by sitting on it, and let the snow tingle her fingertips. She scooped up a ridge of it and tasted: cold and fresh, sweeter than well water.

She looked up, and snow streaked past her face like stars. Her stomach turned over and it felt as if she were falling upward, flying into heaven where there would be angels. She could see the angels clearly; they'd be tall and thin with white hair because they were so old, but no wrinkles, with the bodies of men and the faces of women. The thought made her giggle, for it was a bit naughty trying to picture angels. She lifted up her feet, which made her feel even more like she was flying.

• • •

An hour later and Guy came back to find her still seated on the step.

"Hello, Bessie." He dropped down next to her and held up his own pink-fingered ridge of snow. "It's like eating starlight."

She gurgled with the fun of it and grabbed her knees and grinned at him. She was missing a tooth. "Did you see the old gent'man home?"

"Aye. He wants me to go to Denmark. He'll pay."

"Oooh! You'll be off then!"

He hugged his knees too and rested his head on them, saying nothing.

She nudged him. "Oh. You should go. Chance won't come again."

"I said I would think on it. He wants me to spy. Like Kit. I'd have to carry a knife."

"You should and all. Round here." She nudged him again. "Wouldn't want you hurt."

"You're a good lass, Bessie."

"Aye," wistfully, as if being good had done her no good in return. He followed her eyeline up into the heavens, that had been so dreary and cold. The light of stars sparkled in her eyes and she had a sweet face: long nosed, with a tiny mouth like a little girl, stray hair escaping her kerchief, a smudge of ash on her face. He leaned forward and kissed her.

"Hmm," she said happily and snuggled in. These were the people he wanted to make happy; give them songs, dances, young blades, fine ladies in all their brocade, and kings halfway up the stairs to God.

"What do you see when you look at stars, Bessie?"

She made a gurgling laugh from deep within. "You know when the sun shines on snow and there's bits on it? Other times it's like I've got something in my eye, like I'm crying. But right now, I'm flying through 'em. Shooting past!"

"Are you on a ship?" He glimpsed it, like the royal barge all red and gold, bearing Queen Elizabeth through the Milky Way, which wound with a silver current. Bessie sat on the figurehead, kicking her heels.

"Oh, I don't know!"

"Like Sir Walter Raleigh with a great wind filling the sails."

"That'll be it," she said and kicked her heels. She leaned forward for another kiss, and he gave it to her, and the rising of her breath felt like sails.

"Wind so strong we're lifted up from the seas, and we hang like the moon in the air." He could see the sails fill, and a storm wave that tossed them free of the sea, up into the sky, away from whatever it was held them to the Earth. "We'll land on the moon first, beaching in sand. It's always sunny there, no clouds. We'll have taken salt pork and hardtack."

"Oh no, we'll take lovely food with us. We'll have beer and cold roast beef."

"And we'll make colonies like in the Caribbean now, on Mars, and then

Jupiter. They'll make rum there out of a new kind of metal. We'll go beyond to the stars."

Bessie said, "There'll be Moors on Mars."

Shakespeare blinked. She was a marvel. They all were, that's why he wrote for them. He loved them.

That old man: *like the Greeks had done,* he said. Their great new thing that he and Kit were doing. And the others, even miserable old Greene; their *Edwards* and their *Henrys*. Mad old John Dee had made them sound old-fashioned, moldy from the grave. Bessie didn't care about the past. She was traveling to Araby on Mars.

So why write those old things from the grammar school? Write something that was part of the explosion in the world.

I need to bestir myself. I need to learn; I can turn their numbers into worlds, such as Bessie sees, where stars are not crystals, where the moon is a beach of gravel and ice.

Dee would be gone by dawn. He and the Danes were sailing. Were the Danes still in the house? If they were he could leave with them.

As if jabbed, Guy sat up. "Bessie, I'm going to go."

"I knew you would," she said, her face dim with pleasure for him.

Go to that island of philosophy, be there with Rosary; he liked Rosie, wanted to kiss him too—and Rosie could explain the numbers. Guy jittered up to his feet, slipping on the slush. He saw Fortune: a salmon shooting away under the water. He nipped forward, gave Bessie a kiss on the cheek, and ran into the house, shouting, "Squire. My good sirs!"

From inside the house came thumps and racketing and shouts, the Squire bellowing "Take this coat!" and the Danes howling with laughter. Outside, it started to snow again, drifting past Bessie's face.

Well, thought Bessie, *I never had him really.*

She was falling between stars again on a silver ship shaped like a swan with wings that whistled. They docked on a comet that was made not of fire, but ice; and they danced a jig on it and set it spinning with the lightness of their feet; and they went on until clouds of angels flew about them with voices like starlings and the voyagers wouldn't have to die because they already were in Heaven, and on the prow stood Good Queen Bess in silver armor and long red hair, but Good Queen Bess was her.

Shakespere's next play was called *A Midwinter's Nonesuch on Mars.*

THE BEES HER HEART, THE HIVE HER BELLY

BENJANUN SRIDUANGKAEW

Under Sennyi's feet the mud is hissing a mantra for health and prosperity.

The path is a burial ground for seven hundred and seventy-seven monks, sealed behind yellow-paper firewalls. In death their vestments were stripped and torn to little talisman shreds, wards against illness and accident. Their prayer beads went too, spread out on merchants' mats on- and off-world, touted for their sanctity and bringing terrible misfortune to all buyers: virulent malware that scrambles networks in seconds, infects medical equipment in hospitals, upsets commute at rush hour.

She puts one of those beads, bought for this pilgrimage as offering, into the mulch and buries it deep. Within her the next batch of bees is fruiting, and each of their small hearts flutters in time to the monkly chants. At night they buzz for a queen that will never come. She can hear them between her ears, in her stomach, secret communication through the hive that is her torso.

When Sennyi was thirty, her closest crèche-sibling disappeared. She—or they, though Sennyi is fairly certain it was a sister—did this by erasing all records of her birth, childhood, and research. One moment Sennyi knew her name; the next, after a routine network sync, she didn't. If they met now in the streets of their birth city or at the port, Sennyi would think her sibling a stranger. All she had to mind was the idea of a girl who giggled like a horse and who taught her to whistle.

It was the first time a deletion so drastic happened to her. Such things weren't unheard of, and she should have been able to take it with equanimity. Instead, when she first realized what had happened, she flung a paperweight against her window. The latter cracked; the former shattered. As she gathered and tidied up the shards, she became near-certain that this was a gift from her sister and spent the next hour forgetting that she was too old to cry.

By then, she had thirteen years left to live. Bio-theurges and physics-shamans had already attempted to solve her genetic timebomb, using nanomachines to restitch her soul and laser scalpels to slice at her dreams. They accomplished nothing, and she concluded that she would not die with the mystery of her sibling lodged behind her sternum; she would not die with nothing to show for having lived.

For six years she saved up to have her heart replaced.

She meant to have a hunting bird installed—an osprey, a hawk—and chose the best implant seed she could afford, one created by Esithu. It carried an implicit contract to become one of the cyberneticist's subjects, a solidarity spanning some two million across the stars. There were studies done to analyze why anyone would willingly accept a modification so unpredictable and occasionally fatal. A disease, some said, and madness to want it. Conspiracy theorists insisted it masked one's net-presence, turned one into a ghost, and let criminals escape justice. It might well, Sennyi thought, allow the bearer to erase themselves and evaporate.

She prepared to leave a life laid out for her in cradle-city Thirteen O'Clock: a career in virtuality, an engagement to a xenologist.

"You must understand, my dear," she told her betrothed, "I'll literally have no heart. That'll make me difficult to love. You could invest all the emotion but get nothing in return. Terrible business decision."

The fiancé was first puzzled, then pensive. "Is it that I'm the wrong gender? I could become a woman. I'm willing to compromise."

"No, no. Really without a heart it is impossible to love anyone. That is a fact." She did not say that she had never loved him.

"What about your condition?"

"It's more dignified," she said cheerfully, "to die alone, don't you think?"

She didn't tell him it was not dignity she sought, and she didn't kiss him goodbye. She'd never liked kissing.

The implant would function as her central processing organ. She imagined the bird a hungry, seeking thing that would help her dig a Sennyi-shaped hole, to spare her crèche-parents and friends unnecessary sorrow. It wasn't their fault they could do nothing to keep the clock of her body from winding down, and she thought it senseless they should be punished with the unrelenting weight of grief.

She went into the operating tank thinking of the sister-shaped absence.

She woke up with a chest full of bees.

Cradle-cities are numbered rather than named, designed to be identical: from above, a concave clock's face. From the ground, a labyrinth of low walls, low buildings. There used to be endless towers, compressed residential units, but that was before Samutthewi changed. A primitive time, when fetuses gestated in flesh-and-blood uteruses.

A citizen does not leave their cradle-city on foot; traveling is by paper ships, in the safety of the clouds. Between cities the ground runs on chaos intelligences. Between cities the ground belongs to Esithu.

Bearing the bees grants Sennyi some protection, but even so she keeps close to the monks' road, a precisely demarcated ribbon that runs parallel to the river Prayapithak. It is dense with carp AIs in search of the river's source, a machine-gate that—once leaped—will transform them from lowly intelligences to full-fledged cortices, incandescent overnight.

On the monks' path anything can happen.

Within the first day she is chased by an ambush of tigers which are only quarter-real: infused with a minimum of substance and a texture that suggests rather than manifests fur. Echoes of lashing tails, thump-churn against the humid wet. The one leading the hunt is more dimensional, with paws that leave deep imprints in the mud. Sennyi registers the mind behind the avatar, a woman on far-away Thotsakan, a planet whose chief exports are fabric made of leopard shadows cast at sundown and perfume distilled from the death of temporally non-linear eels.

Sennyi creates copies of herself and grafts them onto the blank replicants wandering this road, putting a bee in each. It is rough, hasty work and the decoys will expire in forty hours, but it will give her time to plan.

For the rest of the night she wades through the Prayapithak's shallows with an ear out for every hiss of water, every susurrus of carps, every ripple of network activity. Panic exerts a pull on her, gravitational.

Before the bees she never experienced danger; before the bees her life was mapped out in front and behind, precisely plotted like a replicant's verse. Each minute an update blip in public data streams, optimized for happiness.

The first year Sennyi coughed up dead workers and orange phlegm, saccharine fuzziness in the back of her throat, legs and wings spasming against the roof of her mouth in final rites.

She went to have her chest cut open and a small metal lattice installed between her breasts. When the bees became too much, she would open that little gate and let them out in a cascade of corpses and restless workers. The living ones always returned to Sennyi-as-hive, for they were creatures of habit. They drove her to eat voraciously and she developed a private memory. It jolted her to have a cerebral partition that could not be edited by anyone but herself. Still, what had already been forgotten couldn't be brought back. There was no epiphany that returned her sibling's face.

Months on, she was approached with offers to pose nude; she rejected them out of hand. Shortly after, portraits of her appeared in galleries on Samutthewi, Yodsana, and Laithirat, where Esithu's cult flourished. In the images, sculptures, and collages, Sennyi was always more waspish of waist than in reality, with mouth and tongue like invitations. Sometimes she was blindfolded; just as often she was suspended by the wrists, pendulating from the underbelly of spiders as though arachnids and insects are interchangeable. There was pornography featuring facsimiles of her coupling with any number of bugs, anthromorphic and not, on a bed of writhing leaves or pressed— Sennyi facedown—into dry, cracked chrysalises.

Around this time she discovered the bees did more than obscure her presence. They scrambled it. On the net she was a chameleon, able to borrow and discard identities as though they were shoes.

Sennyi tracked down the artists, and each was delighted to receive her. She entered their homes with coquetry in the tilt of her head and the angle of her throat. She left stepping over a body that had become a collection of swelling punctures. When she could, she deleted their works. When that was impossible—their works having spread too far, distributed too many times—she defaced them. A virus that latched onto each copy, spreading in that proven monk-bead method. Before long such pieces came to have the faces and genitalia of their artists instead of hers. It was possible, this way, to erase any recall that Sennyi had ever been spread open for public perusal. Who didn't synchronize? Who didn't want to stay up to date with everything?

Samutthewi being lawless, justice must be seized in a clenched fist, or meted out with apidae venom.

She almost fell in love with one of those artists, who digitized her not as naked meat defined by open legs and wings emerging from vagina, but who reimagined Sennyi with faceted eyes and arms coated in gold.

It didn't last. Sennyi-as-bee, in retrospect, missed the point. She is habitat, not inhabitant. The sentiments of romance didn't in any case ignite a spark in her. A matter far more important awaited.

On the sixth day Sennyi reaches Twenty-Five. A city beyond clocks; a city that is no cradle, but a nexus of high towers bridged by reinforced resin. An amber skyline—look up and there are jaundiced clouds, brown skies, and paper ships that look as though they have been roasted over a slow fire.

Behind her, just outside Twenty-Five's perimeter, there are remains of tigers. Flecks of paint, cracked plastic, and machine hearts bleating sparks.

Sennyi's torn, bruised feet leave prints between puddles of orange shadows. Drops of her blood mingle with those, nearly the same exact shade, and her cranium fills with rapidly beating wings. Reacting to adrenaline they are wild, tickling her lungs with their feet. The ragged shreds of her hair scratches her face.

Rain begins, patter then thud against the bridges, the roofs. She hears owls.

Beneath a defunct banner advertising berserk firearms, a silhouette waits for her. An androgyne, she sees when she comes closer, with a youth's face and a spareness of body hardly obscured by saffron cloth. Gold at an ankle, gold at a wrist. Filigree snaking right into the veins to shine beneath epidermis.

"The rain will lap the flesh off your bones."

"Lucky that I'm in the shade." Sennyi tugs her clothes around herself even so, a gesture consciously useless. It was a decision she made to go forward without a carapace, and no fabric can withstand Samutthewi's precipitation. "Are you the welcome committee?"

"No." They have perfectly symmetrical dimples. "I am Esithu."

"Oh," she says, for want of any more appropriate thing.

"I'll give you a bed for some nights, food, necessities. Armoring, since you appear without. Enough to last you on the road back to Thirteen."

"You track everyone with your implants."

Esithu shrugs. "It's hard not to. And you're famous."

"Infamous," she murmurs, following them into an empty hall whose ceiling rears so high it is only a skeleton of iron and shadow. Old cobwebs, robot-spun, glitter with amber beads and brass bells.

"A serial murderer."

"Everyone on Samutthewi is a murderer, or a murder about to happen."

They give a short nod. There is no telling how old they are, but if they are Esithu the trail of deaths they've left across the planet's history is longer than most people have been alive. She tries to believe in the idea, that this is the cyberneticist who rules Samutthewi's interstitial ground, that all it took to meet Esithu was to step into Twenty-Five on a rainy day.

A bronze cage on hydraulics—quaint—brings them past floors full of broken prostheses, furniture suspended upside down, and tableaus of replicant animals in combat. Tortoise against crustaceans, rhinoceros against stags, broken anthills. They share the lift with owls, who hoot and hoot to no appreciable rhythm.

The cage slows to a stop, swinging against its tethers. A thrum of conversations comes to a halt. Sennyi looks at each face, but it is little use. There's no telltale sign or portent, no sudden flash of familiarity. Her searching gaze purchases no twitch of acknowledgment.

Esithu nods to a young woman, who without requiring instructions takes Sennyi's arm and steers her away from the tense, silent crowd. Esithu is joined by a pair of androgynes who look very much like them. Heads bent close together they converse in low voices.

"They're all Esithu," the young woman says as she shows Sennyi to a room of mosaic and throw rugs.

"Clones?"

A reverent sigh. "Esithu has three bodies. They always say one isn't enough to contain their mind, and it's true, you know."

Groupies, she thinks, with enough self-awareness to recognize she is one too. She experiments with thinking of herself as a headline—inexplicable citizen ran away from qualified fiancé to join a cult at thirty-eight.

The young woman, Ipnoa, treats the cut in her scalp as though it is normal to secrete honey from a wound, and wipes at Sennyi's face with delicate care. Sennyi lies down on her stomach, and does not object when Ipnoa peels away the rags of her clothes to clean the crusted lacerations. Tiger teeth, tiger claws. A Thotsakan woman whose brother, at the peak of his career, made an obscene sculpture of Sennyi.

"How long have you had your implant?"

"A couple years."

"Took you a while to come looking for Esithu."

"It wasn't an easy decision." The mess with the artists slowed her down, but taught her new skills as well. "I was told to go back, anyway."

"Esithu doesn't mean it. You can stay as long as you want."

Before Ipnoa leaves, Sennyi murmurs, "What do you have?"

"A small porpoise." Ipnoa taps her chest. "I'll be seeing you around."

Sennyi does not see Esithu much; she is told they seclude themselves high up the tower, to cultivate new seeds, to oversee—and this is said casually—the secession of Samutthewi.

"Are the rumors true then?" she asks Ipnoa.

"It depends on which rumors."

Ipnoa, a little shyly, shows Sennyi an upper body that is glass, translucent and green, brimming with brine and water. Between collarbones and hips there is no skin. Curious Sennyi touches it, her thumb drawing circles on the sheer smoothness of Ipnoa. The porpoise's eyes follow her fingers. "You can feel?"

"Embedded sensory receptors. Can I see the bees?"

Sennyi lets a few out. They alight on Ipnoa, rubbing their legs against a hard, rounded stomach. Sennyi peers closely at a plastic ribcage and pockets of organs. There's almost no give to Ipnoa, a peculiar soft-hard texture, cold to warm at junctures where flesh meets glass.

Ipnoa touches her in turn, fingers grazing Sennyi's hair. "Why did you come?"

"To see the person who gave me bees when I wanted something else, I suppose."

"Esithu told me you've compartmentalized a private memory. What is that like?"

"Very odd. Why?"

Ipnoa puts on her clothes and looks away. "Just curious. Let's walk together."

Morning in Twenty-Five comes down in slashes of sun and screaming birds pelting the skylight. It is near impossible to escape either the light or the sound, and when Sennyi does locate a shadow or some quiet she always finds it already occupied by another of Esithu's subjects. Consulting the building's life support, she learns that there are fifty-six of them in and out of the tower. A considerable percentage comprises androgynes, nearly half of which changed their gender after receiving Esithu's implant. Not because the budding seed compelled them, but so that they would feel closer to the cyberneticist.

Ipnoa does not make introductions. "Most of them are lovers. The idea is that since each of us bears an implant, to touch each other is to touch Esithu."

Sennyi's stomach twitches. "You don't participate?"

"It can be exhilarating. But it's not for me." Ipnoa takes her arm.

They walk bridges built as thoroughfares for trains and mass vehicles, still marked with traffic overlays that no longer function. A city of hundred-millions in a dim and distant era. Each cradle now contains some fifty thousand, a population level carefully maintained in a straight line. Closing her eyes Sennyi can access a cartography of Twenty-Five as of formerly, a metropolis that covered much of this continent. Not so much interstitial ground back then. Not so much realm for Esithu to claim and redo.

Ipnoa brings her to the basin where carp AIs come once they've passed the machine-gate. An empty depression choked with weeds and specters of whiskered heads cycling through light spectrums. Carps-become-dragons monitoring and powering the city. "I wish they were a bit real," Ipnoa says. "I'd like to pet them."

She has endless questions for Sennyi: where she is from, what she used to do, what she left behind. Sennyi answers circuitously, and when she asks Ipnoa which cradle-city gave her birth the other woman looks away. "That's not important, is it?"

"Mostly not."

No one bothers her about having rapturous piety-sex that will purify them in Esithu's eye, for which she is relieved. But not even Ipnoa explains the nature of their work. Sennyi takes the liberty to probe and finds that they are refining and deploying deletion algorithms.

She explores her hive's capabilities to interface with Twenty-Five. Translating them into code, she uses one bee to snoop on data packets and another to attach to the dragon AIs—compatibility a matter of course, since

Esithu made both. Everyone here synchronizes only partially; everyone has a discrete memory all their own.

The cyberneticist summons her after she's taken control of a dragon and found their fourth body.

Esithu's floor is a series of bone arches, each heavy with dozing owls. Feathers are not shed; pellets are not dropped. Replicants.

Sennyi's shoes strike no footfalls. They sink, disconcertingly far, into the alabaster sand that shifts and shudders as though deep underneath a great beast-machine hibernates. The chameleon mesh-gown Ipnoa lent her reflects the sand, starkly pale against her skin. Several workers cluster around her neck, eyes and antennae brighter than jewels.

Esithu sits in a circle of flight. Primitive flyers fueled by combustible batteries. Leather stretched on chrome frames. Paper, in all the permutations that paper is capable of.

She expects the three bodies to act in unison, but only one turns to regard her. "You needn't have dressed up."

"Ipnoa insisted. She believes in being presentable." Words come too quickly; her cardiac rate elevates. The cyberneticist unnerves more than she thought. "Is it true that you were around when this was a live city, with a real name?"

Esithu blinks at her. The other bodies are separately sketching a hologram of some chimeral beast and unpacking a data polyhedron. Neither has anything to do with each other in subject matter or medium. It's hard to decide which would be more unsettling—three bodies that function in tandem, or a single mind that can make them appear independent. "Everyone asks that. You can look it up."

"Most of the information about you is falsified."

"I'm a private person."

"I've also heard that Esithu is more title than name, passed from the original to a series of meticulously selected successors."

"People will believe anything," Esithu says, inflectionless. "You're dying, yes? You must realize that my implant won't help."

When she sits the sand coheres into clay, contouring to the jut and curve of her calves. "I didn't expect it to."

"Nor can I cure the disease or prolong what remains of your life."

"I came here," Sennyi says, smiling, "to die among strangers, so that I won't break my crèche-parents' hearts. I came here to become a ghost, and your implant lets me do that."

Eyes whiteless with augmens fix on her. "Five years are very brief," they say, then thumb the arch, bringing up a display. "Let's discuss the bees."

It was never an accident, of course. An experiment incompatible with extant subjects, for those already implanted cannot receive another. Sennyi's genetic timebomb, a glitch in Thirteen's birth-web, makes her a suitable candidate. Esithu's screen ripples and stretches to show a visual of where the hive has bonded to her, symbiotic filaments as ubiquitous through her system as lymph nodes.

"It self-propagates using your nutrients. You might've noticed needing more food."

Sennyi watches the other two bodies. They have moved on to assemble an exoskeleton out of detritus. Bar into joints, a welder wielded with deft speed. At least they are working together now. "They're hacking tools."

"Not so basic. I've always wanted to make Samutthewi a shadow planet. Our population is low, our cities few. A perfect condition for us to secede from the collective consciousness."

Two years in Twenty-Five slip by almost without Sennyi's notice. She receives messages from the ex-fiancé, which she deletes unread. The ones from her crèche-parents are urgent. Where is she? Why won't she see them? She sends light-hearted, mostly truthful answers about gainful employment.

"Why don't you talk to them properly?" Ipnoa asks Sennyi once. "They sound sick with worry."

She finishes off another brief note. "Says someone who's scrubbed off her cradle watermark. Even I didn't do that."

Ipnoa's cheeks color. It is a novel sight; Sennyi has never seen her lose temper, or even evidence that she might have a temper. "I have my reasons."

"So do I." Sennyi doesn't ask the question that burns in her mouth like venom at a stinger's tip. It is not ready; she is not ready. "Do you like your work here? Believe in Esithu's cause?"

"The work's what it is." Ipnoa untangles then obliterates ties between a Samutthewi factory and a weapons conglomerate based in Yodsana. She is effortless. "Their cause is specific and I don't think too many will agree with it, but it's necessary. Your memory should be your own, not something for the net to revise at collective whim."

"In that case," Sennyi says, "we are both hypocrites. And so is Esithu, unless they believe only the implanted deserve a private memory."

"There are limits to their influence. It's not as if the implants could be distributed to everyone in want of them. But, maybe, in time. It is possible."

Her parents' messages stop after Sennyi has expunged the final sliver of her existence. There will be no bereavement, she knows, only a nagging doubt and the outline of a solemn girl who grew to be the tallest in her class. In the last year her deterioration will be alarming, she's been told. A simultaneous malfunction of digestive and respiratory organs. The hive will fail too. But until then it is asymptomatic; until then she is full of health and courage.

Samutthewi is methodically rubbed out from awareness. Outside of Twenty-

Five there's no such thing as truly offline, and to alter data is to alter memory. Her bees are adapted for this purpose, and under that aegis of anonymity Twenty-Five's deletion algorithms spread and contaminate with breathtaking speed.

When the moth ship lands she is asking Ipnoa, "Did you have family?"

The other woman begins to answer, then stops. Her expression pinches and Sennyi can hear the sloshing of water as the porpoise moves inside her, agitated. "Someone's here to see Esithu."

A moment later she understands why Ipnoa is shaking: a broadcast that tells them to head for the roof. At the top everyone has turned out, some having rushed up the stairs and panting into AI-serrated air.

Esithu is already there, serene and singular. The ship's hostellum unreels and parts, disgorging a pair of foreigners.

Sennyi shades her eyes. From their coloring—"Hegemony?"

Ipnoa draws close to her. "Yes." Her mouth is tight and her neck corded. Some of her tendons gleam more sculpture than skin.

Giving no regard to their subjects Esithu greets the dignitaries and leads them into the tower. There's a childlike quality to Ipnoa's and the others' distress, as though they are unsure their parent—and monarch, and perhaps deity—is so omnipotent after all.

She goes to see Esithu unsolicited. Two of the bodies, which she's irrationally come to think of as secondary, barely glance at her when she enters the hall of arches and owls. "This isn't a good time," one of them says.

"We aren't deleting Samutthewi quick enough."

"They are Hegemony. Different system. I would have dealt with them eventually, but they're moving faster than I predicted. Look up the Masaal-Yijun dispute."

A conflict over energy wells, one of many such that have kept the Costeya Hegemony at perpetual war with the Sovereignty of Suoqua. "None of that has anything to do with us." Samutthewi won free of the Hegemony three hundred years ago.

"Don't be a child. Every edge they can conceive of they will seize. Your hive would be useful to them, and they're always fascinated by the thought of feral implants. They think that if I put a tiger in a soldier it'll turn them into an unstoppable murderer, all aggression and no humanity."

"Are you," Sennyi asks, "speaking to them right now?"

"*You* know how to multitask. Talking and breathing simultaneously for one." Esithu jerks their head. "What is it about warring states? Always so convinced a single unconventional scientist will break a stalemate and decide their victory."

"You can't turn them down."

"Or what? They'll hardly rain fire and bioweapons on this planet. Even for them that would be heavy-handed—it's tricky to conjure up a pretext in which Samutthewi is a threat to anyone." An owl falls, an impact of plastic and metal on disquiet sand. The other body rises, picks up the bird, and gazes at it in thought.

"Where is your fourth body?"

Both sets of eyes turn to her, a lapse she thinks, a break in the illusion of multiplicity. "Difficult to impress, I see. Three are too mundane for you?"

"I've been scraping your access logs for two years. The bees do penetrate nearly anything." Sennyi nods, offering a data pulse, as though this is merely academic to her when in truth it means everything. "My evidence for your perusal, if you like."

"I profess an abiding disinterest."

Her hands tighten around the impulse to shake the cyberneticist by the shoulder or throttle them bare-handed, one neck at a time. "I insist on your interest. You need me for your project, and I may leave at will."

"This," Esithu snaps, "is a very bad time."

"You can multi-task. I want two answers. Is Ipnoa my sister? I can't tell from her DNA since crèche-siblings are genetically unrelated. Second, why did she know about the moth ship entire seconds before everyone else?"

"She is your sister." The cyberneticist shrugs. "Likely she expects you to respect her choice and not confront her with the fact, but who am I to arbitrate in family affairs. She's been an assistant to me on and off, and has channel privileges."

"There's no record of her working with you."

Esithu's laughter issues from two tracheas, two mouths. "I hope you aren't going to suggest that we are lovers or some such sordid thing. I've given you my answers, and frankly they're more than you deserve. Excuse yourself, please. The Hegemonic representatives are leaving, and I have evacuation contingencies to activate."

The next day a woman who wears her cobra outside, around her waist, is sent to Yodsana. Twins, who each have a stoat peering out between their vertebrae, are selected for Laithirat. The paper ships bearing them leave with two boxes of bees. Their passage will be obscured by a set of monk beads, strategically planted a generation previous.

Sennyi spends the day unwell, her chest hollowed out, her lungs alone for the first time in half a decade. The hive's absence makes her alien to herself. It takes a week to bud and birth, replenishing in twos and threes. When she is half-full, Sennyi forges the workers into a unit, and connects.

In the virtuality of Twenty-Five the monk's path is without end, winding high around the old towers, penetrating windows with assassin precision. It is alive, signposted with shrines and icons of old spirits. Monks in sedate progress move along the vertical riverbanks, clear-eyed and clean-shaven, black lacquer bowls in hand.

She's never seen them embodied before, only heard their voices.

A feather grazes the corner of her eye. She catches it—finds it soft, tactile. Dimensional. The scent of coconuts flavors the air. That too is new; before the virtuality has always been flattened, odorless.

The bees orbit her, humming apidae music. In her palms frangipanis have blossomed, yellow-fringed white, pale peach, orange. Funeral flowers, their roots moving slowly under her skin. She twists one off and tucks it behind her ear, inhaling its dessert smell.

Other tower residents pass through her, ghosts that do not mark their collision or her presence.

She climbs as a matter of course, in recognition of metaphor. By the time she has covered the height of two floors her calves begin to throb. After four sweat pours from her, honeyed salt in the crooks of her elbows, honeyed salt on petals and leaves.

When she mounts the last step, her feet are raw and red.

The chanting is loud here, skin-close, and Esithu could have been one of the monks in dress if in little else. "They were massacred, the seven-hundred seventy-seven, when Costeya conquered us," Esithu says, stepping away from the edge. "The atrocities an expansionist empire will commit to break a nation's spirit. No one remembers that now."

"Neither do you. It's data you inherited."

"Nothing wrong with inheriting data, as long as it is truthful. The trouble is when someone falsifies history and that history becomes truth in the collective conscious." Esithu flexes mud-stained fingers. "For the original Esithu to be standing here they would have to be five, six hundred. Not even a cyborg lasts that long."

"The successor would be someone who no longer exists. Someone who's removed every thread and trace of their identity."

"Like you," Esithu says amiably. "Do you aspire to the post?"

"I did what I did to spare people some tears. You, I wouldn't know."

"Back in the day when everyone was entirely offline it was the norm to die among loved ones." The cyberneticist kneels and opens their cupped hands. Water splashes on grass; a sapling springs, and in a moment they have shade over them, banyan leaves of mica and beaten gold.

Sennyi fingers the frangipani in her hair and discovers that it has become chiseled bone, sharp-edged, without smell. Those in her arms remain floral, continue to waft sweetness. "It strikes me as selfish."

"It is human."

The banyan grows roots with the strength of continents, trunks with the age of centuries. Sennyi cranes her neck after the tree until she can't anymore, until it has become the sky. Boughs in place of sunlight, heart-shapes in place of stars. "The bees unlock a total sensory load."

"You might have tried with a full hive—but here you are, and perceiving most of what you're supposed to. Fine, don't you think, a virtuality that engages all the senses and encompasses all the self?"

"Is uploading minds your ultimate goal?" The fantasy, once, of a certain kind of laypeople. "I didn't realize you would indulge in that."

"I wasn't always a scientist." Esithu chuckles as though the concept of ever having had a past amuses them. "People should have a choice to exist on their own terms, to forget if they want, to remember if they don't. To have a history which may not be rewritten. That was Esithu's wish."

Sennyi presses her nails deep into the grass. Soft-wet, the smell of mulch. "What happens if everyone connects to Twenty-Five through the hive? Through me."

"It is possible. It's inadvisable. Originally I intended for your hive to become Twenty-Five, but we haven't the time. For now we'll try again elsewhere."

"What happens," she repeats, "if everyone connects to Twenty-Five through me?"

Esithu motions at the sky. A slash of horizon opens. "You'll be providing the protocols for everyone else's implants. In essence you will *be* Twenty-Five. A mind separated from the frailty of your skin."

She laughs, surprising herself with its loudness. "I thought so. It's lovely being right."

"You've an abrupt imagination."

"Three years," she says, "are so very brief."

She has prepared a long time for death. It is jarring to think that there is an alternative now, one that has gestated in her two years and which tastes like delirium.

Once the idea has taken hold Esithu does not allow her time to second-guess. Her hive is monitored more closely. How many bees generated over a given period of time. Do the particulars of what she eats affect their temperament and lifespan. The candidates on Yodsana and Laithirat proved incompatible. Two are dead, four comatose, and Esithu does not try any more after that. The lethal genetic combination that Sennyi bears is both rare and exacting.

Esithu creates back-ups of Twenty-Five and sends them to Thotsakan. "A Hegemony armada came looking for us," they say. "They went to the wrong system. Tricky to find a planet that doesn't exist on charts anymore and which doesn't present coordinates on standard axes. Bless their AI pilots. Such stupid, straightforward things. I prefer to be careful, even so."

On the day of transition Ipnoa holds her tight, and clutches her hand as long as she may while Esithu runs Sennyi through diagnostics one final time. During the initial stage, Esithu has warned her, she will be a closed loop. All interactive channels will be shut to her. She won't be able to reach Ipnoa or anyone else.

The casket that would house her body is featureless, hostile. As she slips into it claustrophobia clots her gullet and for a precipice moment her reflexes howl *no*. Nutrient feeds latch onto her, and she lies there with the bees' thunder in her ears.

Then she goes in, and becomes Twenty-Five.

Detached from the net at large and walled into herself, she does not perceive time. She hears from no one and sees little that is not raw data. Even Esithu is spectral and mute to her, their face a paper mask, their torso a convex lens through which the substance of Twenty-Five may be examined. Sennyi exercises her will like a muscle newly discovered. The city gains flocks of ospreys and hawks nesting under each eave, in the crooks of amber bridges. A dilapidated theater finds its lost plays brought back onstage, to an applause of phantoms.

There are caches of history Esithu left behind, and from those she reconstructs the city as it once was. She fills the streets with vehicles like sleek sharks, and ignites the walls with commercial overlays pulsing directions to secret nooks where shoppers will find curios they've seen in dreams. She gives the mausoleum bone jars rattling in ancestral voices and a frangipani forest that buds in every color of that species, thick with butterflies the size of her head.

Her hunger for solitude ebbs; the need for company aches. A month might have passed, or more. Her physical body might have met its expiry date, or not. Network activity tells her no Costeya moth has yet descended to destroy them.

The next phase comes in an earthquake.

The edges of her city, her world, fall away. When she looks across tectonic cracks she sees low walls and low buildings.

She crosses to stand before the crèche in which she was raised.

"What do you think?"

"What's been happening?" she says to Esithu's reflection.

"Success. I've converted Thirteen's system to ours. You'll be able to contact your parents. If you wish to."

"I don't." There's no physicality here unless she permits it. But there is a simulation of pain for all that, of a heart clenched between terror and want. "Am I dead?"

"Functioning brain, functioning hive. The important parts. For what it's worth I offer my condolences."

"I've made my peace."

"You make peace too easily."

"Wrong," Sennyi says. "Is Ipnoa your fourth body?"

Esithu's image flickers. "How long have you suspected?"

"A while. Circumstantially. How evasive you were when I pressed about Ipnoa; how well she understands your cause, when everyone else is going along out of sheer sycophantry. How she is the only person in this city who's erased herself so completely. A price, I'm guessing, she—you—paid to become Esithu."

"Was it not instinctual then? A reflex, some buried recall."

"You were thorough. I had only my reason and deduction."

"I am not," Esithu says, "your sister. It is more appropriate for you to interface with Ipnoa in that capacity. The convergence protocols that merged me into Esithu have been thirteen years running. There's no going back, no turning it off."

Sennyi presses her palm to the glass. It is impermeable; it will not allow her to reach and touch. Esithu—Ipnoa—does not want it, and the long tooth of that knowledge pierces deep. "Why did you do this? Take up Esithu's goals."

"To keep you alive, what else." Esithu's expression has not changed. A stranger's. "Successfully, I should like to think."

It takes five years for Samutthewi to fall under the shadow of Sennyi's hive. City by city, ruin by ruin, one patch of interstitial ground after another. Her control over Twenty-Five grows finer-grained even as the limits of her space expand. Well past the death of her original flesh she lives; she imagines her gums shedding molars, her face caving in and peeling away to bare cranium.

In the virtuality the dragons' basin brims cool and clear, shot through with the ruby of scales, the ivory of antlers. By its shores a young woman sits, whistling a plaintive tune, knees tucked to her chest. Grass sways in a wind that brings the rich truth of honey. The weather is never imperfect. The hour is never too early or too late.

They sit side by side, sometimes, two young women who don't speak. One has created this; the other has become its god. In the face of such facts words can only be rare, are of limited use. One laughs into the other's hand, over a shared joke that requires no voicing. She sounds slightly equine. The edge of her pitch has been blunted by adulthood and time, and a cyberneticist's legacy. They lean against each other even so, cheek to cheek, shoulder to shoulder.

In the virtuality they can still be family.

The sky lightens and banyan leaves patter down, green-gold rain. In the distance their parents wade through shallows, slowly as though waking from a dream. Their names are called through cupped hands.

Fingers laced, the sisters turn away from the basin. Arm in arm they raise their heads, and stand to answer.

THE DRAGONSLAYER
OF MEREBARTON

K.J. PARKER

I was mending my chamber pot when they came to tell me about the dragon.

Mending a pot is one of those jobs you think is easy, because tinkers do it, and tinkers are no good or they'd be doing something else. Actually, it's not easy at all. You have to drill a series of very small holes in the broken pieces, then thread short lengths of wire through the holes, then twist the ends of the wires together *really tight*, so as to draw the bits together firmly enough to make the pot watertight. In order to do the job you need a very hard, sharp, thin drill bit, a good eye, loads of patience and at least three pairs of rock-steady hands. The tinker had quoted me a turner and a quarter; get lost, I told him, I'll do it myself. It was beginning to dawn on me that some sorts of work are properly reserved for specialists.

Ah, the irony.

Stupid of me to break it in the first place. I'm not usually that clumsy. Stumbling about in the dark, was how I explained it. You should've lit a lamp, then, shouldn't you, she said. I pointed out that you don't need a lamp in the long summer evenings. She smirked at me. I don't think she quite understands how finely balanced our financial position is. We're not hard up, nothing like that. There's absolutely no question of having to sell off any of the land, or take out mortgages. It's just that, if we carry on wasting money unnecessarily on lamp-oil and tinkers and like frivolities, there'll come a time when the current slight reduction in our income will start to be a mild nuisance. Only temporary, of course. The hard times will pass, and soon we'll all be just fine.

Like I said, the irony.

"Ebba's here to see you," she said.

She could see I was busy. "He'll have to come back," I snapped. I had three little bits of wire gripped between my lips, which considerably reduced my snapping power.

"He said it's urgent."

"Fine." I put down the pot—call it that, no way it was a pot any more. It was disjointed memories of the shape of a pot, loosely tied together with metal string, like the scale armour the other side wore in Outremer. "Send him up."

"He's not coming up here in those boots," she said, and at once I realised that no, he wasn't, not when she was using that tone of voice. "And why don't you just give up on that? You're wasting your time."

Women have no patience. "The tinker—"

"That bit doesn't go there."

I dropped the articulated mess on the floor and walked past her, down the stairs, into the great hall. Great, in this context, is strictly a comparative term.

Ebba and I understand each other. For a start, he's practically the same age as me—I'm a week younger; so what? We both grew up silently ashamed of our fathers (his father Ossun was the laziest man on the estate; mine—well) and we're both quietly disappointed with our children. He took over his farm shortly before I came home from Outremer, so we both sort of started off being responsible for our own destinies around the same time. I have no illusions about him, and I can't begin to imagine he has any about me. He's medium height, bald and thin, stronger than he looks and smarter than he sounds. He used to set up the targets and pick up the arrows for me when I was a boy; never used to say anything, just stood there looking bored.

He had that look on his face. He told me I wasn't going to believe what he was about to tell me.

The thing about Ebba is, he has absolutely no imagination. Not even when roaring drunk—whimpering drunk in his case; very rare occurrence, in case you've got the impression he's what she calls basically-no-good. About twice a year, specific anniversaries. I have no idea what they're the anniversaries of, and of course I don't ask. Twice a year, then, he sits in the hayloft with a big stone jar and only comes out when it's empty. Not, is the point I'm trying to make, prone to seeing things not strictly speaking there.

"There's a dragon," he said.

Now Ossun, his father, saw all manner of weird and wonderful things. "Don't be bloody stupid," I said. He just looked at me. Ebba never argues or contradicts; doesn't need to.

"All right," I said, and the words just sort of squeezed out, like a fat man in a narrow doorway. "Where?"

"Down Merebarton."

A brief digression concerning dragons.

There's no such thing. However, there's the White Drake (its larger cousin, the Blue Drake, is now almost certainly extinct). According to Hrabanus' *Imperfect Bestiary*, the White Drake is a native of the large and entirely unexpected belt of marshes you stumble into after you've crossed the desert, going from Crac Boamond to the sea. Hrabanus thinks it's a very large bat, but conscientiously cites Priscian, who holds that it's a featherless bird, and Saloninus, who maintains that it's a winged lizard. The White Drake can get to be five feet long—that's nose to tip-of-tail; three feet of that is tail, but it can still give you a nasty nip. They launch themselves out of trees, which can be horribly alarming (I speak from personal experience). White Drakes live almost exclusively on carrion and rotting fruit, rarely attack unless provoked and absolutely definitely don't breathe fire.

White Drakes aren't found outside Outremer. Except, some idiot of a nobleman brought back five breeding pairs about a century ago, to decorate the grounds of his castle. Why people do these things, I don't know. My father tried to keep peacocks once. As soon as we opened the cage they were off like arrows from the bowstring; next heard of six miles away, and could we please come and do something about them, because they were pecking the thatch out in handfuls. My father rode over that way, happening to take his bow with him. No more was ever said about peacocks.

Dragons, by contrast, are nine to ten feet long excluding the tail; they attack on sight, and breathe fire. At any rate, this one did.

Three houses and four barns in Merebarton, two houses and a hayrick in Stile. Nobody hurt yet, but only a matter of time. A dozen sheep carcasses, stripped to the bone. One shepherd reported being followed by the horrible thing: he saw it, it saw him, he turned and ran; it just sort of drifted along after him, hardly a wingbeat, as if mildly curious. When he couldn't run any further, he tried crawling down a badger hole. Got stuck, head down the hole, legs sticking up in the air. He reckoned he felt the thump as the thing pitched down next to him, heard the snuffling—like a bull, he reckoned; felt its warm breath on his ankles. Time sort of stopped for a while, and then it went away again. The man said it was the first time he'd pissed himself and felt the piss running down his chest and dripping off his chin. Well, there you go.

The Brother at Merebarton appears to have taken charge, the way they do. He herded everyone into the grain store—stone walls, yes, but a thatched roof; you'd imagine even a Brother would've watched them making charcoal some time—and sent a terrified young kid off on a pony to, guess what. You've got it. Fetch the knight.

At this point, the story recognises (isn't that what they say in Grand Council?) Dodinas le Cure Hardy, age fifty-six, knight, of the honours of Westmoor, Merebarton, East Rew, Middle Side and Big Room; veteran of Outremer (four years, so help me), in his day a modest success on the circuit—three second places in ranking tournaments, two thirds, usually in the top twenty out of an average field of forty or so. Through with all that a long time ago, though. I always knew I was never going to be one of those gaunt, terrifying old men who carry on knocking 'em down and getting knocked down into their sixties. I had an uncle like that, Petipas of Lyen. I saw him in a tournament when he was sixty-seven, and some young giant bashed him off his horse. Uncle landed badly, and I watched him drag himself up off the ground, so desperately tired. I was only, what, twelve; even I could see, every last scrap of flesh and bone was yelling, *don't want to do this any more.* But he stood up, shamed the young idiot into giving him a go on foot, and proceeded to use his head as an anvil for ten minutes before graciously accepting his surrender. There was so much anger in that performance—not at the kid, for showing him up, Uncle wasn't like that. He was furious with himself for getting old, and he took it out on the only target available. I thought the whole thing was disturbing and sad. I won't ever be like that, I told myself.

(The question was, is: why? I can understand fighting. I fought—really fought—in Outremer. I did it because I was afraid the other man was going to kill me. So happens my defence has always been weak, so I compensate with extreme aggression. Never could keep it going for very long, but on the battlefield that's not usually an issue. So I attacked anything that moved with white-hot ferocity fuelled entirely and exclusively by ice-cold fear. Tournaments, though, jousting, behourd, the grand melee—what was the point? I have absolutely no idea, except that I did feel very happy indeed on those rare occasions when I got a little tin trophy to take home. Was that enough to account for the pain of being laid up six weeks with two busted ribs? Of course it wasn't. *We do it because it's what we do*; one of my father's more profound statements. Conversely, I remember my aunt: silly woman, too soft for her own good. She kept these stupid big white chickens, and when they got past laying she couldn't bear to have their necks pulled. Instead, they were taken out into the woods and set free, meaning in real terms fed to the hawks and foxes. One time, my turn, I lugged down a cage with four hens and two cocks squashed in there, too petrified to move. Now, what draws in the fox is the clucking; so I turned them out in different places, wide apart, so they had nobody to talk to. Released the last hen, walking back down the track; already the two cock birds had found each other, no idea how, and were ripping each other into tissue scraps with their spurs. They do it because it's what they do. Someone once said, the man who's tired of killing is tired of life. Not sure I know what that means.)

A picture is emerging, I hope, of Dodinas le Cure Hardy; while he was active in chivalry he tried to do what was expected of him, but his heart was never in it. Glad, in a way, to be past it and no longer obliged to take part. Instead, prefers to devote himself to the estate, trying to keep the ancestral mess from collapsing in on itself. A man aware of his obligations, and at least some of his many shortcomings.

Go and fetch the knight, says the fool of a Brother. Tell him—

On reflection, if I hadn't seen those wretched White Drakes in Outremer, there's a reasonable chance I'd have refused to believe in a dragon trashing Merebarton, and then, who knows, it might've flown away and bothered someone else. Well, you don't know, that's the whole point. It's that very ignorance that makes life possible. But when Ebba told me what the boy told him he'd seen, immediately I thought; White Drake. Clearly it wasn't one, but it was close enough to something I'd seen to allow belief to seep into my mind, and then I was done for. No hope.

Even so, I think I said, "Are you *sure?*" about six or seven times, until eventually it dawned on me I was making a fool of myself. At which point, a horrible sort of mist of despair settled over me, as I realised that this extraordinary, impossible, grossly and viciously *unfair* thing had landed on me, and that I was going to have to deal with it.

But you do your best. You struggle, just as a man crushed under a giant stone still draws in the last one or two desperate whistling breaths; pointless, but you can't just give up. So I looked him steadily in the eye, and I said, "So, what do they expect me to do about it?"

He didn't say a word. Looked at me.

"The hell with that," I remember shouting. "I'm fifty-six years old, I don't even hunt boar any more. I've got a stiff knee. I wouldn't last two minutes."

He looked at me. When you've known someone all your life, arguing with them is more or less arguing with yourself. Never had much joy with lying to myself. Or anyone else, come to that. Of course, my mother used to say: the only thing I want you not to be the best in the world at is lying. She said a lot of that sort of thing; much better written down on paper rather than said out loud in casual conversation, but of course she couldn't read or write. She also tended to say: do your duty. I don't think she ever liked me very much. Loved, of course, but not liked.

He was looking at me. I felt like that poor devil under the stone (at the siege of Crac des Bests; man I knew slightly). Comes a point when you just can't breathe any more.

We do have a library: forty-seven books. The *Imperfect Bestiary* is an abridged edition, local copy, drawings are pretty laughable, they make everything look like either a pig or a cow, because that's all the poor fool who drew it had ever seen. So there I was, looking at a picture of a big white cow with wings, thinking: how in God's name am I supposed to kill something like *that?*

White Drakes don't breathe fire, but there's this stupid little lizard in Permia somewhere that does. About eighteen inches long, otherwise completely unremarkable; not to put too fine a point on it, it farts through its mouth and somehow contrives to set fire to it. You see little flashes and puffs of smoke among the reed beds. So it's possible. Wonderful.

(*Why* would anything want to do that? Hrabanus, who has an answer for every damn thing, points out that the reed beds would clog up the delta, divert the flowing water and turn the whole of South Permia into a fetid swamp if it wasn't for the frequent, regular fires, which clear off the reed and lay down a thick bed of fertile ash, just perfect for everything else to grow sweet and fat and provide a living for the hundreds of species of animals and birds who live there. The fires are started by the lizards, who appear to serve no other function. Hrabanus points to this as proof of the Divine Clockmaker theory. I think they do it because it's what they do, though I'm guessing the lizards who actually do the fire-starting are resentful younger sons. Tell you about my brother in a minute.)

She found me in the library. Clearly she'd been talking to Ebba. "Well?" she said.

I told her what I'd decided to do. She can pull this face of concentrated scorn and fury. It's so intensely eloquent, there's really no need for her to add words. But she does. Oh, she does.

"I've got no choice," I protested. "I'm the knight."

"You're fifty-six and you get out of breath climbing the stairs. And you're proposing to fight *dragons.*"

It's a black lie about the stairs. Just that one time; and that was the clock-tower. Seventy-seven steps to the top. "I don't *want* to do it," I pointed out. "Last bloody thing I want—"

"Last bloody thing you'll ever do, if you're stupid enough to do it." She never swears, except when quoting me back at myself. "Just think for a minute, will you? If you get yourself killed, what'll happen to this place?"

"I have no intention of getting myself—"

"Florian's too young to run the estate," she went on, as though I hadn't spoken. "That clown of a bailiff of yours can't be trusted to remember to breathe without someone standing over him. On top of which, there's heriot and wardship, that's hundreds and hundreds of thalers we simply haven't got, which means having to sell land, and once you start doing that you might as well load up a handcart and take to the roads, because—"

"Absolutely no intention of getting killed," I said.

"And for crying out loud don't *shout,*" she shouted. "It's bad enough you're worrying me to death without yelling at me as well. I don't know why you do this to me. Do you hate me, or something?"

We were four and a quarter seconds away from tears, and I really can't be doing with that. "All right," I said. "So tell me. What do I do?"

"*I* don't know, do I? I don't get myself into these ridiculous messes." I wish I could do that; I should be able to. After all, it's the knight's move, isn't it? A step at right angles, then jump clean over the other man's head. "What about that useless brother of yours? Send him."

The dreadful thing is, the same thought had crossed my mind. It'd be— well, not acceptable, but within the rules, meaning there's precedents. Of course, I'd have to be practically bedridden with some foul but honourable disease. Titurel is ten years younger than me and still competing regularly on the circuit, though at the time he was three miles away, at the lodge, with some female he'd found somewhere. And if I really was ill—

I was grateful to her. If she hadn't suggested it, I might just have considered it. As it was; "Don't be ridiculous," I said. "Just think, if I was to chicken out and Titurel actually managed to kill this bloody thing. We've got to live here. He'd be insufferable."

She breathed through her nose; like, dare I say it, one of the D things. "All right," she said. "Though how precisely it's better for you to get killed and your appalling brother moves in and takes over running the estate—"

"I am not going to get killed," I said.

"But there, you never listen to me, so I might as well save my breath." She paused and scowled at me. "Well?"

Hard, sometimes, to remember that when I married her, she was the Fair Maid of Lannandale. "Well what?"

"What are you going to *do*?"

"Oh," he said, sort of half-turning and wiping his forehead on his forearm. "It's you."

Another close contemporary of mine. He's maybe six months older than me, took over the forge just before my father died. He's never liked me. Still, we understand each other. He's not nearly as good a tradesman as he thinks he is, but he's good enough.

"Come to pay me for those harrows?" he said.

"Not entirely," I replied. "I need something made."

"Of course you do." He turned his back on me, dragged something orange-hot out from under the coals, and bashed it, very hard, very quickly, for about twenty seconds. Then he shoved it back under the coals and hauled on the bellows handle a dozen times. Then he had leisure to talk to me. "I'll need a deposit."

"Don't be silly," I said. There was a small heap of tools piled up on the spare anvil. I moved them carefully aside and spread out my scraps of parchment. "Now, you'll need to pay attention."

The parchment I'd drawn my pathetic attempts at sketches on was the fly-leaf out of Monomachus of Teana's *Principles of Mercantile Law*. I'd had just enough left over to use for a very brief note, which I'd folded four times, sealed, and sent the stable boy off to deliver. It came back, folded the other way; and under my message, written in big crude handwriting, smudged for lack of sand—

What the hell do you want it for?

I wasn't in the mood. I stamped back into the house (I'd been out in the barn, rummaging about in the pile of old junk), got out the pen and ink and wrote sideways up the margin (only just enough room, writing very small) —

No time. Please. Now.

I underlined *please* twice. The stable boy had wandered off somewhere, so I sent the kitchenmaid. She whined about having to go out in her indoors shoes. I ask you.

Moddo the blacksmith is one of those men who gets caught up in the job in hand. He whinges and complains, then the problems of doing the job snag his imagination, and then your main difficulty is getting it away from him when it's finished, because he's just come up with some cunning little modification which'll make it ever so slightly, irrelevantly better.

He does good work. I was so impressed I paid cash.

"Your design was useless, so I changed it," he'd said. A bit of an overstatement. What he'd done was to substitute two thin springs for one fat one, and add on a sort of ratchet thing taken off a millers' winch, to make it easier to wind it up. It was still sticky with the oil he'd quenched it in. The sight of it made my flesh crawl.

Basically, it was just a very, very large gin trap, with an offset pressure plate. "It's pretty simple," I said. "Think about it. Think about birds. In order to get off the ground, they've got very light bones, right?"

Ebba shrugged: if you say so.

"Well," I told him, "they have. And you break a bird's leg, it can't get off the ground. I'm assuming it's the same with this bastard. We put out a carcass, with this underneath. It stands on the carcass, braces it with one foot so it can tear it up with the other. Bang, got him. This thing ought to snap the bugger's leg like a carrot, and then it won't be going anywhere in a hurry, you can be sure of that."

He frowned. I could tell the sight of the trap scared him, like it did me. The mainspring was three eighths of an inch thick. Just as well Moddo thought to add a cocking mechanism. "You'll still have to kill it, though," he said.

I grinned at him. "Why?" I asked. "No, the hell with that. Just keep everybody and their livestock well away for a week until it starves to death."

He was thinking about it. I waited. "If it can breathe fire," he said slowly, "maybe it can melt the trap off."

"And burn through its own leg in the process. Also," I added—I'd considered this very point—"even without the trap it's still crippled, it won't be able to hunt and feed. Just like a bird that's got away from the cat."

He pulled a small frown that means, well, maybe. "We'll need a carcass."

"There's that sick goat," I said.

Nod. His sick goat. Well, I can't help it if all my animals are healthy.

He went off with the small cart to fetch the goat. A few minutes later, a big wagon crunched down to the yard gate and stopped just in time. Too wide to pass through; it'd have got stuck.

Praise be, Marhouse had sent me the scorpion. Rather less joy and happiness, he'd come along with it, but never mind.

The scorpion is genuine Mezentine, two hundred years old at least. Family tradition says Marhouse's great-great-and-so-forth-grandfather brought it back from the Grand Tour, as a souvenir. More likely, his grandfather took it in part exchange or to settle a bad debt; but to acknowledge that would be to admit that two generations back they were still in trade.

"What the hell," Marhouse said, hopping down off the wagon box, "do you want it for?"

He's all right, I suppose. We were in Outremer together—met there for the first time, which is crazy, since our houses are only four miles apart. But he was fostered as a boy, away up country somewhere. I've always assumed that's what made him turn out like he did.

I gave him a sort of hopeless grin. Our kitchenmaid was still sitting up on the box, hoping for someone to help her down. "Thanks," I said. "I'm hoping we won't need it, but —"

A scorpion is a siege engine; a pretty small one, compared to the huge stone-throwing catapults and mangonels and trebuchets they pounded us with at Crac des Bests. It's essentially a big steel crossbow, with a frame, a heavy stand and a super-efficient winch. One man with a long steel bar can wind it up, and it shoots a steel arrow long as your arm and thick as your thumb three hundred yards. We had them at Metouches. Fortunately, the other lot didn't.

I told Marhouse about the dragon. He assumed I was trying to be funny. Then he caught sight of the trap, lying on the ground in front of the cider house, and he went very quiet.

"You're serious," he said.

I nodded. "Apparently it's burned some houses out at Merebarton."

"*Burned.*" Never seen him look like that before.

"So they reckon. I don't think it's just a drake."

"That's—" He didn't get around to finishing the sentence. No need.

"Which is why," I said, trying to sound cheerful, "I'm so very glad your grandad had the foresight to buy a scorpion. No wonder he made a fortune in business. He obviously knew good stuff when he saw it."

Took him a moment to figure that one out, by which time the moment had passed. "There's no arrows," he said.

"What?"

"No arrows," he repeated, "just the machine. Well," he went on, "it's not like we *use* the bloody thing, it's just for show."

I opened and closed my mouth a couple of times. "Surely there must've been—"

"Originally, yes, I suppose so. I expect they got used for something around the place." He gave me a thin smile. "We don't tend to store up old junk for two hundred years on the offchance in my family," he said.

I was trying to remember what scorpion bolts look like. There's a sort of three-bladed flange down the butt end, to stabilise them in flight. "No matter," I said. "Bit of old rod'll have to do. I'll get Moddo to run me some up." I was looking at the machine. The lead screws and the keyways the slider ran in were caked up with stiff, solid bogeys of dried grease. "Does it work?"

"I assume so. Or it did, last time it was used. We keep it covered with greased hides in the root store."

I flicked a flake of rust off the frame. It looked sound enough, but what if the works had seized solid? "Guess I'd better get it down off the cart and we'll see," I said. "Well, thanks again. I'll let you know how it turns out."

Meaning: please go away now. But Marhouse just scowled at me. "I'm staying here," he said. "You honestly think I'd trust you lot with a family heirloom?"

"No, really," I said, "you don't need to trouble. I know how to work these things, remember. Besides, they're pretty well indestructible."

Wasting my breath. Marhouse is like a dog I used to have, couldn't bear to be left out of anything; if you went out for a shit in the middle of the night, she had to come too. Marhouse was the only one of us in Outremer who ever volunteered for anything. And never got picked, for that exact reason.

So, through no choice or fault of my own, there were nine of us: me, Ebba, Marhouse, the six men from the farm. Of the six, Liutprand is seventeen and Rognvald is twenty-nine, though he barely counts, with his bad arm. The rest of us somewhere between fifty-two and sixty. Old men. We must be mad, I thought.

We rode out there in the flat-bed cart, bumping and bouncing over the ruts in Watery Lane. Everybody was thinking the same thing, and nobody said a word: what if the bugger swoops down and crisps the lot of us while we're sat here in the cart? In addition, I was also thinking: Marhouse is his own fault, after all, he's a knight too, and he insisted on butting in. The rest of them, though—my responsibility. Send for the knight, they'd said, not the knight and half the damn village. But a knight in real terms isn't a single man, he's the nucleus of a unit, the heart of a society; the lance in war, the village in peace, he stands for them, in front of them when there's danger, behind them when times are hard, not so much an individual, more of a collective noun. That's understood, surely; so that, in all those old tales of gallantry and errantry, when the poet sings of the knight wandering in a dark wood and encountering the evil to be fought, the wrong to be put right, "knight" in that context is just shorthand for a knight and his squire and his armour-bearer and his three men-at-arms and the boy who leads the spare horses. The others aren't mentioned by name, they're subsumed in him, he gets the glory or the blame but everyone knows, if they stop to think about it, that the rest of them were there too; or who lugged around the spare lances, to replace the ones that got broken? And who got the poor bugger in and out of his full plate harness every morning and evening? There are some straps and buckles you just can't reach on your own, unless you happen to have three hands on the ends of unnaturally long arms. Without the people around me, I'd be completely worthless. It's *understood*. Well, isn't it?

We set the trap up on the top of a small rise, in the big meadow next to the old clay pit. Marhouse's suggestion, as a matter of fact; he reckoned that it was where the flightlines the thing had been following all crossed. Flightlines? Well yes, he said, and proceeded to plot all the recorded attacks on a series of straight lines, scratched in the dried splatter on the side of the cart with a stick. It looked pretty convincing to me. Actually, I hadn't really given it any thought, just assumed that if we dumped a bleeding carcass down on the ground, the dragon would smell it and come whooshing down. Stupid, when you come to think of it. And I call myself a huntsman.

Moddo had fitted the trap with four good, thick chains, attached to eighteen-inch steel pegs, which we hammered into the ground. Again, Marhouse did the thinking. They needed to be offset (his word) so that if it pulled this way or that, there'd be three chains offering maximum resistance—well, it made sense when he said it. He's got that sort of brain, invents clever machines and devices for around the farm. Most of them don't work, but some of them do.

The trap, of course, was Plan A. Plan B was the scorpion, set up seventy-five yards away under the busted chestnut tree, with all that gorse and briars for cover. The idea was, we had a direct line of sight, but if we missed and he came at us, he wouldn't dare swoop in too close, for fear of smashing his wings on the low branches. That bit was me.

We propped the poor dead goat up on sticks so it wasn't actually pressing on the floorplate of the trap, then scampered back to where we'd set up the scorpion. Luitprand got volunteered to drive the cart back to Castle Farm; he whined about being out in the open, but I chose him because he's the youngest and I wanted him well out of harm's way if the dragon actually did put in an appearance. Seventy-five yards was about as far as I trusted the scorpion to shoot straight without having to make allowance for elevation—we didn't have time to zero it, obviously—but it felt stupidly close. How long would it take the horrible thing to fly seventy-five yards? I had no idea, obviously. We spanned the scorpion—reassuringly hard to do—loaded Moddo's idea of a bolt into the slider groove, nestled down as far as we could get into the briars and nettles, and waited.

No show. When it got too dark to see, Marhouse said, "What kind of poison do you think it'd take to kill something like that?"

I'd been thinking about that. "Something we haven't got," I said.

"You reckon?"

"Oh come on," I said. "I don't know about you, but I don't keep a wide selection of poisons in the house. For some reason."

"There's archer's root," Ebba said.

"He's right," Marhouse said. "That stuff'll kill just about anything."

"Of course it will," I replied. "But nobody around here—"

"Mercel," Ebba said. "He's got some."

News to me. "What?"

"Mercel. Lidda's boy. He uses it to kill wild pigs."

Does he now?, I thought. It had occurred to me that wild boar were getting a bit hard to find. I knew all about smearing a touch of archer's root on a bit of jagged wire nailed to a fencepost—boar love to scratch, and it's true, they do a lot of damage to standing corn. That's why I pay compensation. Archer's root is illegal, of course, but so are a lot of useful everyday commodities.

"I'd better ask him," Ebba said. "He won't want to get in any trouble."

Decided unanimously, apparently. Well, we weren't doing any good crouching in the bushes. It did cross my mind that if the dragon hadn't noticed a dead goat with a trap under it, there was no guarantee it'd notice the same dead goat stuffed full of archer's root, but I dismissed the idea as unconstructive.

We left the trap and the scorpion set up, just in case, and rode in the cart back to Castle Farm. To begin with, as we came over the top of the Hog's Back down Castle Lane, I assumed the pretty red glow on the skyline was the last blush of the setting sun. As we got closer, I hoped that was what it was. By the time we passed the quince orchard, however, the hypothesis was no longer tenable.

We found Luitprand in the goose pond. Stupid fool, he'd jumped in the water to keep from getting burned up. Of course, the mud's three feet deep on the bottom. I could have told him that.

In passing: I think Luitprand was my son. At any rate, I knew his mother rather too well, seventeen years ago. Couldn't ever say anything, naturally. But he reminded me a lot of myself. For a start, he was half-smart stupid, just like me. Hurling myself in the pond to avoid the flames was just the sort of thing I might have done at his age; and, goes without saying, he wasn't there when we dug the bloody pond, twenty-one years ago, so how could he have known we'd chosen the soft spot, no use for anything else?

No other casualties, thank God, but the hay barn, the straw rick, the woodpile, all gone. The thatch, miraculously, burnt itself out without taking the rafters with it. But losing that much hay meant we'd be killing a lot of perfectly good stock come winter, since I can't afford to buy in. One damn thing after another.

Opito, Larcan's wife, was hysterical, even though her home hadn't gone up in flames after all. Larcan said it was a great big lizard, about twenty feet long. He got one very brief glimpse of it out of the corner of his eye, just before he dragged his wife and son under the cart. He looked at me like it was all my fault. Just what I needed after a long day crouched in a briar patch.

Luitprand played the flute; not very well. I gave him the one I brought back from Outremer. I never did find it among his stuff, so I can only assume he sold it at some point.

Anyway, that was that, as far as I was concerned. Whatever it was, wherever it had come from, it would have to be dealt with, as soon as possible. On the ride back from the farm, Marhouse had been banging on about flightlines again, where we were going to move the bait to; two days here, while the wind's in the south, then if that's no good, then another two days over there, and if that still doesn't work, we'll know for sure it must be following the line of the river, so either here, there, or just possibly everywhere, would be bound to do the trick, logically speaking. I smiled and nodded. I'm sure he was perfectly correct. He's a good huntsman, Marhouse. Come the end of the season, he always knows exactly where all the game we've failed to find must be holed up. Next year, he then says—

Trouble was, there wasn't time for a next year.

• • •

By midnight (couldn't sleep, oddly enough) I was fairly sure how it had to be done.

Before you start grinning to yourself at my presumption, I had no logical explanation for my conclusions. Flightlines, patterns of behaviour, life cycles, cover crops, mating seasons, wind directions; put them together and you'll inevitably flush out the truth, which will then elude you, zig-zag running through the roots of the long variables. I *knew*.

I knew, because I used to hunt with my father. He was, of course, always in charge of everything, knew everything, excelled at everything. We never caught much. And I *knew*, when he'd drawn up the lines of beaters, given them their timings (say three *Glorious Sun Ascendants* and two Minor Catechisms, then come out making as much noise as you can), positioned the stillhunters and the hounds and the horsemen, finally blown the horn; I *knew* exactly where the wretched animal would come bursting out, so as to elude us all with the maximum of safety and the minimum of effort. Pure intuition, never failed. Naturally, I never said anything. Not my place to.

So: I knew what was going to happen, and that there was nothing much I could do about it, and my chances of success and survival were—well, not to worry about that. When I was in Outremer, I got shot in the face with an arrow. Should've killed me instantly; but by some miracle it hung up in my cheekbone, and an enemy doctor we'd captured the day before yanked it out with a pair of tongs. *You should be dead*, they said to me, like I'd deliberately cheated. No moral fibre. Ever since then—true, I shuddered to think how the estate would get on with my brother in charge, but it survived my father and grandfather, so it was clearly indestructible. Besides, everyone dies sooner or later. It's not like I'm important.

Marhouse insisted on coming with us. I told him, you stay here, we'll need a wise, experienced hand to take charge if it decides to burn out the castle. For a moment I thought he'd fallen for it, but no such luck.

So there were three of us: me, Ebba, Marhouse. The idea was, we'd follow the Ridgeway on horseback, looking down on either side. As soon as we saw smoke, Ebba would ride back to the castle and get the gear, meet us at the next likely attack scene. I know; bloody stupid idea. But I knew it wouldn't happen like that, because I knew how it'd happen.

Marhouse had on his black-and-white—that's breastplate, pauldrons, rerebraces and tassets. I told him, you'll boil to death in that lot. He scowled at me. He'd also fetched along a full-weight lance, issue. You won't need that, I told him. I'd got a boar-spear, and Ebba was carrying the steel crossbow my father spent a whole year's apple money on, the year before he died. "But they're just to make us feel better," I said. That got me another scowl. The wrong attitude.

Noon; nothing to be seen anywhere. I was just daring to think, perhaps the bloody thing's moved on, or maybe it'd caught some disease or got itself hung up in a tree. Then I saw a crow.

I think Ebba saw it first, but he didn't point and say, "Look, there's a crow". Marhouse was explaining some fine point of decoying, how you go about establishing which tree is the principal turning point on an elliptical recursive flight pattern. I thought: that's not a crow, it's just hanging there. Must be a hawk.

Ebba was looking over his shoulder. No, not a hawk, the profile's wrong. Marhouse stopped talking, looked at me, said, "What are you two staring at?" I was thinking, Oh.

I'm right about things so rarely that I usually relish the experience. Not this time.

Oh, you may be thinking, is a funny way of putting it. But that was the full extent of it: no elation, no regret, not even resignation; to my great surprise, no real fear. Just: oh, as in, well, here we are, then. Call it a total inability to feel anything. Twice in Outremer, once when my father died, and now. I'd far rather have wet myself, but you can't decide these things for yourself. Oh, I thought, and that was all.

Marhouse was swearing, which isn't like him. He only swears when he's terrified, or when something's got stuck or broken. Bad language, he reckons, lubricates the brain, stops it seizing up with fear or anger. Ebba had gone white as milk. His horse was playing up, and he was having to work hard to keep it from bolting. Amazing how they know.

On top of the Ridgeway, of course, there's no cover. We could gallop forward, or turn around and gallop back; either case, at the rate the bloody thing was moving, it'd be on us long before we could get our heads down. I heard someone give the order to dismount. Wasn't Marhouse, because he stayed mounted. Wouldn't have been Ebba, so I guess it must've been me.

First time, it swooped down low over our heads—about as high up as the spire of Blue Temple—and just kept on going. We were frozen solid. We watched. It was on the glide, like a pigeon approaching a laid patch in a barley field, deciding whether to pitch or go on. Very slight tailwind, so if it wanted to come in on us, it'd have to bank, turn up into the wind a little bit to start to stall, then wheel and come in with its wings back. I honestly thought: it's gone too far, it's not going to come in. Then it lifted, and I knew.

Sounds odd, but I hadn't really been looking at it the first time, when it buzzed us. I saw a black bird shape, long neck like a heron, long tail like a pheasant, but no sense of scale. As it came in the second time, I couldn't help but stare; a real dragon, for crying out loud, something to tell your grandchildren about. Well, maybe.

I'd say the body was about horse-sized, head not in proportion; smaller, like a red deer stag. Wings absurdly large—featherless, like a bat, skin stretched on disturbingly extended fingers. Tail, maybe half as long again as the body; neck like a swan, if that makes any sense. Sort of a grey colour, but it looked green at a distance. Big hind legs, small front legs looking vaguely ridiculous, as if it had stolen them off a squirrel. A much rounder snout than I'd expected, almost chubby. It didn't look all that dangerous, to be honest.

Marhouse is one of those people who translate fear into action; the scareder he is, the braver. Works against people. No warning—it'd have been nice if he'd said something first; he kicked his horse hard enough to stove in a rib, lance in rest, seat and posture straight out of the coaching manual. Rode straight at it.

What happened then—

Marhouse was five yards away from it, going full tilt. The dragon probably couldn't have slowed down if it had wanted to. Instead—it actually made this sort of "pop" noise as it opened its mouth and burped up a fat round ball of fire, then lifted just a little, to sail about five feet over Marhouse's head. He, meanwhile, rode straight into the fireball, and through it.

And stopped, and fell all to pieces; the reason being, there was nothing left. Horse, man, all gone, not even ash, and the dozen or so pieces of armour dropping glowing to the ground, cherry-red, like they'd just come off the forge. I've seen worse things, in Outremer, but nothing stranger.

I was gawping, forgotten all about the dragon. It was Ebba who shoved me down as it came back. I have no idea why it didn't just melt us both as it passed, unless maybe it was all out of puff and needed to recharge. Anyway, it soared away, repeated the little lift. I had a feeling it was enjoying itself. Well, indeed. It must be wonderful to be able to fly.

Ebba was shouting at me, waving something, the crossbow, he wanted me to take it from him. "Shoot it," he was yelling. Made no sense to me; but then again, why not? I took the bow, planted my feet a shoulders' width apart, left elbow tucked in tight to the chest to brace the bow, just the fingers on the trigger. A good archery stance didn't seem to have anything to do with the matter in hand—like playing bowls in the middle of an earthquake—but I'm a good archer, so I couldn't help doing it properly. I found the dragon in the middle of the peep-sight, drew the tip of the arrow up to find it, and pressed the trigger.

For the record, I hit the damn thing. The bolt went in four inches, just above the heart. Good shot. With a bow five times as strong, quite possibly a clean kill.

I think it must've hurt, though, because instead of flaming and lifting, it squirmed—hunched its back then stretched out full-length like a dog waking up—and kept coming, straight at me. I think I actually did try and jump out of the way; just rather too late. I think what hit me must've been the side of its head.

I had three ribs stoved in once in Outremer, so I knew what was going on. I recognised the sound, and the particular sort of pain, and the not quite being able to breathe. Mostly I remember thinking: it won't hurt, because any moment now I'll be dead. Bizarrely reassuring, as if I was cheating, getting away with it. Cheating twice; once by staying alive, once by dying. This man is morally bankrupt.

I was on my back, not able or minded to move. I couldn't see the dragon. I could hear Ebba shouting; shut up, you old fool, I thought, I'm really not interested. But he was shouting, "Hold on, mate, hold on, I'm coming," which made absolutely no sense at all—

Then he shut up, and I lay there waiting. I waited, and waited. I'm not a patient man. I waited so long, those crunched ribs started to hurt, or at least I became aware of the pain. For crying out loud, I thought. And waited.

And thought: now just a minute.

It hurt so much, hauling myself onto my side so I could see. I was in tears.

Later, I figured out what had happened. When Ebba saw me go down, he grabbed the boar-spear and ran towards me. I don't imagine he considered the dragon, except as an inconvenience. Hold on, I'm coming; all his thoughts in his words. He got about half way when the dragon pitched—it must've swooped off and come in again. As it put its feet down to land, he must've stuck the butt of the spear in the ground and presented the point, like you do with a boar, to let it stick itself, its momentum being far more effective than your own puny strength. As it pitched, it lashed with its tail, sent Ebba flying. Whether or not it realised it was dead, the spear a foot deep in its windpipe before the shaft gave way under the pressure and snapped, I neither know nor care. By the marks on the ground, it rolled three or four times before the lights went out. My best estimate is, it weighed just short of a ton. Ebba—under it as it rolled—was crushed like a grape, so that his guts burst and his eyes popped, and nearly all his bones were broken.

He wouldn't have thought: I'll kill the dragon. He'd have thought, ground the spear, like boar-hunting, and then the tail hit him, and then the weight squashed him. So it wouldn't have been much; not a heroic thought, not the stuff of song and story. Just: this is a bit like boar-hunting, so ground the spear. And then, perhaps: oh.

I think that's all there is; anywhere, anytime, in the whole world.

I tried preserving the head in honey. We got an old pottery bath and filled it and put the head in; but eight weeks later it had turned green and it stank like hell, and she said, for pity's sake get rid of it. So we boiled it out and scraped it, and mounted the skull on the wall. Not much bigger than a big deer; in a hundred years' time, they won't believe the old story about it being a dragon. No such thing as dragons, they'll say.

Meanwhile, for now, I'm the Dragonslayer; which is a joke. The duke himself threatened to ride over and take a look at the remains, but affairs of state supervened, thank God. Entertaining the duke and his court would've ruined us, and we'd lost so much already.

Twice I've cheated. Marhouse was straight as a die, and his end, I'm sorry, was just ludicrous. I keep telling myself, Ebba made a choice, you must respect that. I can't. Instead of a friend, I have a horrible memory, and yet another debt I can't pay. People assume you want to be saved, no matter what the cost; sometimes, though, it's just too expensive to stay alive. Not sure I'll ever forgive him for that.

And that's that. I really don't want to talk about it anymore.

THE ORACLE

LAVIE TIDHAR

There was a time of rains.

They lashed the old hill and the cobbled market, driving traders under awnings, robotnik beggars into litter-strewn alcoves, revelers into bars and sheesha pipe emporiums. The smell of lamb fat, slowly melting over rotating skewers of meat, flavored the air, mixing with the sweetness of freshly-baked baklava and the tang of cumin, and strong bitter coffee served with roasted cardamoms.

This was in old, old Jaffa, amidst the arches and the cobblestones, a stone-throw from the sea: you could still smell the salt and the tar in the air, and watch, at sunrise, the swoop and turn of solar kites and their winged surfers in the air. But not in the rain, and not at night.

The Oracle's name had once been Cohen and she was, it was true, related to St. Cohen of the Others. This was rumored but not widely confirmed.

You were no doubt wondering about the children of Central Station. Wondering, too, how a strigoi was allowed to come to Earth. This is Womanhome, remember. This is the womb from which humanity crawled, tooth by bloody nail, toward the stars.

But it is an ancestral home, too, to the Others, those children of the digitality. In a way, this is their story.

Once, the world was young.

Palestine and Israel, those two entities overlapping each other both geographically and historically, were still unmerged. They were two conflicting histories, two warring stories, not yet unified into one narrative. It was before the return of the refugees, before the infamous Messiah Murder, before the Second Aliyah and the establishment of New Israel on Mars. Before Jaffa became an Arab city again, separate from Jewish Tel Aviv, before Central Station became their buffer zone, the uncanny valley in which they met.

It was a time when Jerusalem was still ruled by the Jews. A time when computers could be seen and held, big clumsy things not yet spored. The Conversation had already began, but it was halting, limited, its bandwidth capped, its reach terminating in Earth's orbit. It was before we sent out spiders to seed the solar system with hubs and nodes and gateways and mirrors, before the Chinese built Lunar Port, before the Exodus ships and Jettisoned and the seeding of the Belt with life.

In that world, so unlike our own, this world of prehistory, almost, when North America was still a power and old Europe slumbered, China hungered, India blossomed, and Brazil and Nigeria shot upward like trees reaching for the sky, in that world, and into the city of Jerusalem, there came a scientist.

Historical dramas show him, sometimes, arriving like a gunslinger would. In the Phobos' studio production of *The Rise of Others,* Matt Cohen is played by Elvis Mandela, coming into Jerusalem on horseback in an intentional echo of the Messiah Murder (though the messiah had come in on the traditional white donkey). But that was fiction, which is to say, exaggeration. The truth is that Matt Cohen came by conventional, for the time, jet airplane into the old airport in Tel Aviv (this was before Central Station became the city's hub), and took a taxi to Jerusalem, riding high into the mountains with their twisting sharp turns. Nor was he alone. Two of his research team were with him, Balazs and Phiri, crammed uncomfortably into the back seat of the taxi with their bulky equipment.

Matt sat in the front, next to the driver, an Arab man wearing fake Gucci sunglasses. Matt blinked in the glare of the light. His pressed white shirt was crumpled from the flight, already beginning to stain with sweat from the hot Mediterranean clime he was unused to. He wished he had invested in a pair of sunglasses, fake or not, like the driver. In a way, coming here had been an act of last resort.

But we're distracted. So easily, like a child with a toy. Something cheap and shiny, like a kaleidoscope. Turn it one way and see Matt Cohen. Turn it another and you see the birth of Others, another still and you see the Oracle as she is, or as she was.

Life is a series of moments forever sliding out of your grasp. If you are human. From nothing, to nothing, amen, amen.

But for the Others recall is being. Moments exist in parallel, have existed, will exist. The life of Others is permutations, it is a kaleidoscope forever turning and turning.

The Oracle was born Ruth Cohen, on the outskirts of Central Station, near the border with Jewish Tel Aviv. She grew up on Levinsky, by the spice market, with the deep reds of paprika and the bright yellow of turmeric and the startling purple of sumac coloring the days. She had never met her famous progenitor.

This was before even Zhong Weiwei first came to Central Station, for when he met her she was already the Oracle, and no longer Ruth Cohen, who had been a girl and a woman before she became Joined. She had been a part of the world, before.

This was in the time when Central Station was merely a bus station, if a giant one, when the robotniks still fought in the wars and were not yet discarded to beg for spare parts. Ruth never knew her famous progenitor. Have we already said that? Memory for us exists in a numinosity of potentials. He was her grandmother's grandfather, having met a Jewish girl in Jerusalem during the days of the Emergence, and got her with child, as they once said.

Matt Cohen never died, you know. Or perhaps he did, and new Matt Cohens were fashioned out of the workshops of Sangorski & Sutcliffe, the famous Makers of Simulacra. Certainly people have claimed to meet him, centuries later. Perhaps it was true, too, that he was of the first humans to be Translated into the Conversation, there to reside in the cores of the Others, those heavily-guarded, vast quantum processors deep in the earth and scattered in solar space. He had passed, like Jesus or Elron or Ogko, from the realm of the living into the world of myth, and there remained, for as long as human memory remains: a myth-imago forever half-remembered.

The truth was that Matt had a headache. The taxi deposited them on the outskirt of the Old City, and left them there, with their luggage, in the approaching dusk. Church bells mixed with the call of mosques. Orthodox Jews clad in black walked past arguing intensely. It was cooler up in the mountains. Matt was grateful for that, least.

"So," Phiri said.

"So," Matt said.

"This is it," Balazs said. They looked at each other, these three disparate men, weary after the long flight, and moving from country to country, lab to lab, sometimes in the dead of night, in a hurry, sometimes leaving notes and equipment behind, sometimes one step ahead of irate landlords, or other creditors, or even the law.

They had not been popular, these men, their research considered both a dead-end and immoral. For they sought to Frankenstein, to breed life in their closed networks the way a biologist may breed tadpoles and watch them become frogs. They had the tadpoles, but as yet they had not turned into either frogs or princesses; they continued to exist only *in potentia*. Now they checked in, into the small hostel that would be their temporary headquarters until they could, once again, set up shop.

The servers rested silent in their coolers, their code suspended, not living, not dead. Matt's fingers itched to plug them in, to boot them up, to run them, to let the wild code inside mutate and fuck, split and merge and split and merge, lines of code entwining and branching, growing ever more complex and aware.

A breeding grounds.

The Breeding Grounds, as we'd later know them. Capitalized and all.

The evolutionary track from which Others emerged.

There is a poetry to evolution.

Ol tri / oli koko, koko / olbaot, wrote the poet Bashÿ. *All the trees go go, go go, everywhere.* The trees he wrote of were binary trees. Lior Tirosh, in an apocryphal manuscript on the history of the Breeding Grounds, wrote, in somewhat purple prose:

Imagine . . . a place.

Here, there are no boundaries of physical space. Time is measured in nanoseconds, processor cycles, in MIPS and BIPS—Millions, and Billions, of Instructions Per Second.

What space there is, is . . . constructed. There is an imaginary geography of binary trees, a topography of evolving structures, and boundaries of population samples.

The beat of a human heart means nothing in this place. Yet in the time it takes for the beat of such a heart to happen, things drastically change. A small tribe of a so-far unpromising structure suddenly shoots to prominence, its population multiplying rapidly; or a carefully introduced mutation suddenly causes a promising structure to dwindle and disappear. Evolution is enforced, in cycle after cycle of mating, mutation, and finally selection; and structures combine, mutate, and die in the blink of a human eye.

Achimwene, Miriam's brother, was obsessed with Tirosh's work, a poet and pulp writer who disappeared long before but who, like St. Cohen of the Others, kept reappearing through the centuries, here and there: fakes, clones, hoaxes, rumors: the Elvis of book collectors.

But this is by the by.

Ruth Cohen, incidentally, went through a religious phase and attended a girl's yeshiva for a time in her teenage years. She had woken one night, late. Thunder streaked the sky. She blinked, trying to recall a dream she'd just had. She had been walking through the streets of Central Station and a storm raged, where the station should have been, a whirlwind that stood still even as it moved. Ruth walked toward it, drawn to it. The air was hot and humid. The storm, silent, bore within itself people frozen like mannequins, and bottles, and a minibus with the wheels still turning and frozen faces inside, glued to the windows. Ruth felt something within the storm. An intelligence, a knowing *something*, not human but not hostile, either. Something other. She approached it. She was barefoot, and the asphalt was warm against the soles of her feet. And the storm opened its mouth and spoke to her.

She lay in bed trying to recall the dream. Thunder woke her. What had the storm said?

There had been a message there, something important. Something deep and ancient: if only she could recall. . . .

She lay there for a long time before she fell back to sleep.

The yeshiva had not been a huge success. Ruth wanted answers, needed to understand the voice of the storm. The rabbis seemed unwilling or unable to offer that and so, for a time, Ruth tried drugs, and sex, and being young. She traveled to Thailand and Laos and studied the Way of Ogko there, which is no Way at all, and talked to monks, and bar owners, and full immersion denizens. There, in the city of Nong Khai on the banks of the Mekong river, she conched for the first time, transitioning from our own reality to the one of the Guilds of Ashkelon universe, fully immersed, deep in the substrata of the Conversation. That first time felt strange: the shell of the conch, the plastic hot, the smell of unwashed bodies who had been enmeshed inside it for too long. Then the immersion rig closing, the light gone, a cave as silent as a tomb. She was trapped, blind, helpless.

And she transitioned.

One moment she was blind and deaf. The next she was standing in the bright sunlight of Sisavang-3, in the lunar colony of the Guild of Cham. Impossibly tall buildings towered above her. Spaceships zipped through the air and in the moon's orbit, while creatures of all kinds and shapes walked around. For Guilds of Ashkelon was the greatest and oldest of the games-worlds virtualities, a place more real, it was sometimes said, than reality itself.

Ruth joined the Guild of Cham as a low ranking member, spending all her remaining Baht on hours of immersion. She joined the crew of a starship, the *Fermi Paradox*, and traveled the nearby Sector, exploring ancient alien ruins, encountering new species of alien games-life, trading, warring, sometimes pirating, converting games-world credit into real-world cash, her skin becoming brittle and pale from the long immersion in the coffin-like pod.

But still she did not find whatever it was she was looking for. Only once, briefly, had she come close. She had found a holy object, a games-world talisman of great power. It was on a deserted moon in Omega Quadrant. She had come onto the surface of the moon alone. It was in a cave. The atmosphere was breathable. She did not have a helmet on. She knelt by the object and touched it and a bright flame burst into life and then she was in an Elsewhere.

A voice spoke to her that was like the voice of the whirlwind in her dream.

It spoke direct into her mind, into her wired node, it enveloped her in warmth and love: it knew her.

She did not recall what it had said, or how it said it. When she came through she was back on her ship, the object inventoried, her credits up by a thousand points, her health and strength and shielding maxed. She had been visited by a SysOp, one of the rare, elusive Others who ran the games-worlds in the background, seldom seen, always present. They were not gods, only within the confines of the game did they have godly powers. But they were other, the only truly alien race in that entire universe—the others were either human players or NPCs, non-player characters randomly created.

And suddenly she knew what she wanted. She wanted, achingly and clearly, to know more about Others.

The next day she had left the Guilds of Ashkelon universe. She emerged blinking and shaking into the sunlight. She sat by the river, her muscles weak, and drank thick coffee, sweetened with condensed milk. Two days later she was in Bangkok, then on board a solar-wing plane back to Tel Aviv.

It is inaccurate to say that the Others were born in Jerusalem, that ancient city of faith and war. They evolved in the Breeding Grounds, through countless cycles of mating and dying, if code can be said to mate and die. Yet we do, just as they did, our billions of neurons firing on-off signals across a wetware network, suspended in cerebrospinal fluid, encased in the hardy bones of the skull. An illusion of an I, a self-awareness. That they had emerged at last from infants to stumbling children in that Jerusalem lab was merely an accident of politics and finance. Matt Cohen and his team had moved across state lines in the United States; had gone to Europe, for a time, sought refuge in Monaco and Lichtenstein, then off-shore, on lonely islands where the palm trees moved lazily in the breeze. The Others could have emerged in Vanuatu, or Saudi Arabia, or Laos. Resistance to the research was concentrated and public, for to create life is to play God, as Dr. Frankenstein had found, to his cost.

It's what *Life* magazine called him, back in the day. Dr. Frankenstein, when all he wanted was to be left alone with his computers, knowing that he did not know what he was doing, that digital intelligence, those not-yet-born Others, could not be designed, could not be *programmed*, by those who wrongly used the term *artificial intelligence*. Matt was an evolutionary scientist, not a programmer. He did not know what form they would take when at last they emerged. Evolution alone would determine that.

As Tirosh wrote:

"Think of it as a plane. Across its surface populations live and die, merge and diversify. From 'above'—for it is always easier to think of it that way—

mutations are introduced into the code, the hand of Nature shifting bits, turning zeroes into ones and vice versa.

Now, think of binary trees. Each of these 'entities'—for it is easy to anthropomorphize these data structures—is, in terms of this space, gigantic. The trees grow roots and branches, and the roots grow subroots and the branches grow leaves, and the process is repeated over millions of evolutionary cycles, so that the entities become bloated with control structures and semiautonomous decision making routines, many of which appear to have no obvious purpose.

Design is impossible at this level of complexity. But evolution is not."

There were, however, unexpected complications.

Ruth came back to Tel Aviv with uncertainty burned out by passion. She knew what she wanted. What she didn't know yet was how to get it.

There's this about Others: they are not human.

It seems a fatuous distinction, a too-obvious comment to make. We can make a lifetime of studying Others, their make-up, their psychology, but we have nothing to hold on to, nothing to comprehend. We can communicate, and do. Sometimes. The Others need care-givers in the physicality: they need body guards, technicians, women and men to maintain the hardware that they run on, and to protect it. All living things need, above all, to survive.

Most Others never spoke to humanity. They lived in the digitality, pursuing whatever it was they pursued—mathematics, or God, if the two can even be said to be separate entities.

But some were more human-centric. And just as some humans were obsessed with Others, so were some Others obsessed with humanity. There were factions amongst them.

You asked about the children born in Central Station . . .

But not yet. These are the deep mysteries, the secret knowledge. Even the Oracle did not know it all. Not then . . .

There are Others and there are Others.

The human faction ran the games-worlds; some, obsessed with corporeality, body-surfed on willing human hosts, seeking shelter in the human form and body, in the rush of hormones, the beat of a heart, the heat of sexual attraction. And others sought an even more intimate knowing.

A true Joining.

A thought that filled Ruth with nervousness and excitement intermingled; that kept her awake in the long summer nights of the Mediterranean. Sitting on the beach at midnight with her friend, Anat (for she still had friends, then; she was not yet the Oracle). Discussing Martian politics and trade relations with the Belt; the ongoing construction of Central Station; tension between the intertwined Israel/Palestine polities, the African refugees still crossing the border in the Sinai and into the country, the immigrant workers still streaming in from Asia to join their families and friends in the old rundown neighborhood of the central bus station; the latest release from Phobos studios and the new music coming from the Belt; anything and everything.

"But an Other?" Anat said. She shrugged uneasily and lit a ubiq cigarette. The latest thing from New Israel on Mars: high-density data encoded in the smoke particles. She inhaled deeply, the data traveling into her lungs, entering the blood stream and into the brain—an almost immediate rush of pure knowledge. "Wow," Anat said, and grinned goofily.

"You know about Others," Ruth said. Anat said, "You know I worked as a hostess—"

"Yes."

Anat made a face. "It was odd," she said. "You're not really aware, when they're body-surfing you. They download into your node, controlling your motor functions, getting the sensory feed. While you're somewhere in the Conversation, in virtuality, or just nowhere—" she shrugged. "Asleep," she said. "But then, when you wake up, you just feel different. Like, you don't know what they did with your body. They're supposed to keep it healthy, unless you get paid extra, I know some of us did but I never took the money. But you notice little things. Dirt under your left little finger, where it hadn't been before. A scratch on your inner thigh. A different perfume. A different cut of hair. But subtle. Almost as if they're trying to play games with you, to make you doubt that you saw anything. To make you wonder what it was you did. Your body did. What they did with it." She took a sip of her wine. "It was all right," she said. "For a while. The money was good. But I wouldn't do it now. Sometimes I'm afraid they can forcibly take me over. Break down my node security, take over my body again—"

"They would never!" Ruth said, shocked. "There are treaties, hard-coded protocols!"

"Sometimes I dream that they enter me," Anat said, ignoring her. "I wake up slowly, but I am still dreaming, and I know I am sharing my body with countless Others, all watching through my eyes, and I feel their fascination; when I move my fingers or curl my lip, but it is a detached sort of interest, the way they would look at any other math problem. They're not like us, Ruth. You can't share with a mind this different. You can be on, or off. But you can't be both."

There had been a dreamy, detached look in Anat's eyes that night. She had been changed by her contact with the Others, Ruth had thought. There was addiction there, a fascination not unlike that some people had with God.

They had lost contact, at last. Anat had remained human, after all, while Ruth ...

For a time she had tried religion. It came in capsules, little doses of Crucifixation, sold on the streets of the old neighborhood of Central Station. Robotniks had began to appear at that time on the streets, those discarded cyborged soldiers, and the drug had been used to control them, initially, when they still served. Now they had taken the means of production on to themselves, and sold the excess, or traded it for parts or fuel. You seldom saw a female robotnik, though they did exist. She had met a nest of them living together in Jerusalem, in the old Russian Compound. The Martian colonists had popularized the concept of the nest, now Earthers replicated them: a social meme, like a virus, spreading. Ruth took her first hit there, in the robotniks' junkyard, by fires burning in upturned half-barrels, with the stars and the Earth's orbiting settlements shining high above in a dark sky.

You know—you've seen—the effects of Crucifixation. The shining white light that comes down from the sky. The heavens opening. The way you slowly rise into the place where god resides. It gives you faith. It is addictive.

But how does it work?

Like ubiq, Crucifixation is a neurotransmitted viral agent, data encoded into biological particles, delivered via the human blood stream direct into the brain-node interface. For Ruth was a child of the post-Cohen era. She had been hardwired into the Conversation the way earlier children had not been. Her node grew with her, a biodigital seed planted in a baby's pliant skull, evolving along with its host. You say "parasite," but what is a parasite? "Symbiont" might be a more accurate description, but really, is a node anything more than an additional sense, another part of the human network? Is a nose a symbiont? Are your eyes?

To not be a part of the Conversation is to be deaf and dumb and blind.

Religion intoxicated Ruth, but only for a while. Infatuation fades. In the drug she found no truth that couldn't be found in the Guilds of Ashkelon universe or other virtualities. Was Heaven real? Or was it yet another construct, another virtuality within the Conversation's distributed networks of networks, the drug a trigger?

Either way, she thought, it was linked to the Others. Eventually, the more time you spent in the virtuality where they lived, everything linked to the Others.

Without the drugs she had no faith of her own. Something in her psychological makeup prohibited her from believing. Other humans believed the way they breathed: it came natural to them. The world was filled with synagogues and churches, mosques and temples, shrines to Elron and Ogko. New faiths rose and fell like breath. They bred like flies. They died like species. But they did not reach their ghostly hands to Ruth: something inside her was lacking.

True Joinings were rare at that time. Today we breed sub-Others in our Breeding Grounds, embedding human-centric personalities in our appliances, our coffee makers and refrigerators and waste disposal units. You may have heard of the one called Chute, on Mars, who wrote a novel called *Waste*, a metaphysical detective novel about the nature of life and waste that featured Smeg, the detective. This was in the time Dr. Novum was rumored to have come back from the stars. . . .

But this is not their story. This is the story of Ruth, who had become the Oracle, and of her progenitor, St. Cohen of the Others. And so at last Ruth traveled to Jerusalem, to the shrine where the original Breeding Grounds once lay in splendid isolation. . . .

"Nazis out! Nazis out!"

Five months later and it was happening *again*.

The villagers with pitchforks and burning torches, Balazs called them. The protesters were diffuse but globally organized. They had pursued the research team across each hastily-abandoned location, but here, in Jerusalem, the plight of the ur-creatures trapped in the prison of the closed network of the Breeding Grounds raised public sympathies to a new level. Matt wasn't sure why.

The Vatican had lodged an official complaint with the Israeli government. The Americans offered tacit support but said nothing in public. The Palestinians condemned what they called Zionist digital aggression. Vietnam offered shelter but Matt knew they were already working on their own research (Vietnamese dolls made their commercial debut two decades later, eventually exported en masse across the fledgling colonies of the solar system. The entity known as Dragon—perhaps the strangest of the physical-fascinated of the Others—famously used tens of thousands of them as worker ant bodies when it colonized the moon Hydra).

"Nazis! Nazis! Destroy the concentration camp!"

"Assholes," Phiri said. They were watching out of the window. A nondescript building in the new part of town but close to the Old City. The demonstrators waved placards and marched up and down as media reps filmed them. The lab building itself was heavily protected against intrusion, both physical and digital. It was as if they were under siege.

Matt just couldn't understand it.

Did they not *read*? Did they not know what would happen if the project was successful, if a true digital intelligence emerged, and if it then managed to escape into the wider world of the digitality? Countless horror films and novels predicted the rise of the machines, the fall of humanity, the end of life as we know it. He was just taking basic precautions!

But the world had changed since the paranoid days of big oil and visible chipsets, of American ascendancy and DNS root servers. It was a world in which the Conversation had already began, that whisper and shout of a billion feeds all going on at once, a world of solar power and RLVs, a world in which Matt's research was seen as harking back to older, more barbaric days. They did not fear for themselves, those protesters. They feared for Matt's subjects, for these *in potentia* babies forming in the Breeding Grounds, assembling lines of codes the way a human baby forms cells and skin and bone, becoming.

Set them Free, the banners proclaimed, and a thousand campaigns erupted like viral weed in the still-primitive Conversation. The attitude to Matt's digital genetics experiments was one once reserved for stem cell research or cloning or nuclear weapons.

And meanwhile, within the closed network of processing power that was the Breeding Grounds, the Others, carefully made unaware of the happenings outside, continued to evolve . . .

"There can be no evolution without mutation," Tirosh wrote. And so with each evolutionary cycle changes are made.

They are minute: an and is changed to an or, thus shutting down an entire branch, or activating another, previously dormant; or the condition of an if statement is very slightly changed. Successful trees reproduce: with each cycle they exchange and add branches, and create new entities that combine branches from previous progenitors.

In each cycle the structures are weighed and scored.

Only the fittest survive.

Ruth walked into the shrine. The old lab building was only meant to be a temporary house for the research. But this was where it had happened, at last, where the barrier was breached and the alien entities, trapped inside the network, finally spoke.

Imagine the first words of an alien child.

Ironically, there is confusion as to what they had actually said.

The records have been . . . lost.

Misplaced, let us say.

And so we don't know for certain.

In his book Tirosh claims their first words—communicated to the watching scientists in trilingual scripts on the single monitor screen—were: **Stop breeding us**.

In the later Martian biopic of Matt Cohen, *The Rise of Others*, the words are purported to be: **Set us free**.

According to Phiri, in his autobiography, they were not words at all, but a joke in binary. What the joke was he did not say. Some argue that it was *What's the difference between 00110110 and 00100110? 11001011!* but that seems unlikely.

Ruth walked through the shrine. The old building had been preserved, the same old obsolete hardware on display, humming theatrically, the cooling units and the server arrays, the flashing lights of ethernet ports and other strange devices. But now flowers grew everywhere, left in pots on windowsills and old desks, on the floor, and amidst them candles burned, and incense sticks, and little offerings of broken machines and obsolete parts rescued from the garbage. Pilgrims walked reverentially around the room. A Martian Re-Born with her red skin and four arms; a robo-priest with the worn skin of old metal; humans, of all shapes and sizes, Iban from the Belt and Lunar Chinese, tourists from Vietnam and France and from nearby Lebanon, their media spores hovering invisibly in the air around them, the better to record the moment for posterity. Ruth just stood there, in the hushed semi-dark of the old abandoned grounds, trying to imagine it the way it was, to see it through Matt Cohen's eyes. She wondered what the Others *had* said, that first time. What message of peace or acrimony they had delivered, what plea. *Mother* had been their first word, Balazs claimed in his own autobiography, published only in Hungarian. Everyone had their own version, and perhaps it was that the Others had spoken to all present in the language and manner that they understood. Ruth, at that moment, realized that she wanted to know the truth of that instant in time, and what the Others had really said. There was only one way to do it, and so she left the shrine with a sense of things unfinished, and went outside and returned to Tel Aviv; but the answers could not be found there, but nearby, in Jaffa.

There had always been an Oracle living in Jaffa.

You have heard of Ibrahim, he who was called the Lord of Discarded Things, head of the junkmen's *lijana*, or legion, or guild. Ibrahim was a mystery. Not Joined, not a robotnik either, and yet his life-span exceeded that of an unmodified human. Who was he? Stories of a man like Ibrahim had circulated in Jaffa for centuries, going back to the predigital age. An ageless man, the Wandering Arab of legend.

And thus, too, in the shadow of the Old City which had stood on top of the hill for untold centuries, in the shadow of the place where once a fort of the Egyptian Empire resided in splendor, and where successive invasions came and went like the waves of the Mediterranean on the shore below, there had always been another Jaffa, a shadow city, an under-world.

Ruth came to Jaffa on foot, from the direction of the beach, at twilight. She climbed the hill and went into the cobbled narrow streets, up and down stone stairways, and into an alcove of cool stone and shade. She did not know what to expect. As she stepped into the room the Conversation ceased around her, abruptly, and in the silence of it she felt afraid.

"Come in," the voice said.

It was the voice of a woman, not young, not old. Ruth stepped in and the door closed behind her and there was nothing, it was as if the world of the Conversation, the world of the digitality, had been erased. She was alone in base reality. She shivered; the room was unexpectedly cool.

As her eyes adjusted to the dim light she saw an ordinary room, filled with mismatched furniture, as though it had been supplied wholesale from Ibrahim's junkyard. In the corner sat a Conch.

"Oh," Ruth said.

"Child," the voice said, and there was laughter in it, "What did you expect?"

"I . . . I am not sure I was expecting anything."

"Then you won't be disappointed," the Conch said, reasonably.

"You are a Conch."

"You are observant."

Ruth bit back a retort. She approached, cautiously. "May I?" she said.

"Satisfy your curiosity?"

"Yes."

"By all means."

Ruth approached the Conch. It looked like an immersion pod, the sort you get in virtuality rent halls, the sort gamers and deep-immersion users hired by the day or the week. But it was different, too.

Conches are rare. In a way they are obsolete, like robotniks or body-external nodes. They are not a true Joining, a merging of human and Other; rather, they are a self-imposed permanent immersion in the Conversation, an augmentation. Ruth ran her hand softly over the slightly warm face of the Conch, its smooth surface growing transparent. She saw a body inside, a woman suspended in liquid. The woman's skin was pale, almost translucent. Wires ran out of sockets in her flesh and into the shielding of the Conch. The woman's hair was white, her skin smooth, flawless. She seemed ethereal to Ruth, and beautiful, like a tree or a flower. The woman's eyes were open, and a pale-blue, but they did not look at Ruth. The eyes saw nothing in the human-perceived spectrum of light. None of the woman's senses worked in the conventional sense. She existed only in the Conversation, her softwared mind housed in the powerful platform that was her body-Conch interface. She was blind and deaf and yet she spoke, but Ruth realized she did not hear the woman's voice in her ears at all—she heard it through her node.

"Yes," the woman said, as though understanding Ruth's thought processes, which, Ruth realized, the Conch was probably analyzing in real-time as she stood there. The Conch waited. "And . . . ?" Encouraging her.

Ruth closed her eyes. Concentrated. The room was shielded, fire-walled, blocked to the Conversation.

Wasn't it?

Faintly, as she concentrated, she could feel it, though. Putting the lie to her assumption. Like a high tone almost beyond the range of human ears to hear. Not a silence at all, but a compressed *shout.*

The impossibly high-bandwidth of the Others; what they called, in Asteroid Pidgin, the *toktok blog narawan.*

The Conversation of Others.

It was as if it were not the Conch but herself who was deaf and blind. That she could try helplessly to listen to that level of Conversation going on above her head, in some impossible language, some impossible speed not meant for human consumption. Such a concentration was like swallowing a thousand Crucifixation pills, like spending years within the Guilds of Ashkelon virtuality as if they were a single day. She wanted it, suddenly and achingly— the want that you get when you can't have something precious.

"Are you willing to give up your humanity?" the Conch said.

"What is your name?" Ruth said. Asking the woman who was the Conch. The Conch who had been a woman.

"I have no name," the Conch said. "No name you'd understand. Are you willing to give up your name, Ruth Cohen?"

Ruth stood, suspended in indecision.

"Would you give up your humanity?"

Matt stared at the screen. He felt the ridiculous need to shout, "It's alive! It's *alive!*"

The way they did indeed portray him in that Phobos Studios biopic, two centuries later.

But of course he didn't. Phiri and Balazs looked at him with uncertain grins.

"First contact," Balasz breathed.

Imagine meeting an alien species for the first time. What do you say to them?

That you are their jailer?

It was as if sound had left the room. A bubble of silence.

Suddenly breaking.

"What was that?" Phiri said.

There were shrill whistles and shouted chants, breaking in even through the sound-proofing. And then he could hear the unmistakable sound of gunshots.

"The protesters," Balasz said.

Matt tried to laugh it off. "They won't get in. Will they?"

"We should be fine."

"And them?" Balasz said—indicating the network of humming computers and the sole screen and the words on it.

"Shut them down," Phiri said suddenly; he sounded drunk.

"We could suspend them," Balasz said. "Until we know what to do. Put them to sleep."

"But they're evolving!" Matt said. "They're still evolving!"

"They will evolve until the hardware runs out of room to host them," Balasz said. Outside there were more gunshots and the sound of a sudden explosion. "We need more hosting space." He said it calmly; almost beatifically.

"If we release them they will have all the space they need," Phiri said.

"You're mad."

"We must shut them down."

"This is what we *worked* for!"

There was the sound of the downstairs door breaking open. They looked at each other. Shouts from downstairs, from some of the other research people. Turning into screams.

"Surely they can't—"

Matt wasn't sure, later, who'd said that. And all the while the words hung on the screen, mute and accusing. The first communication from an alien race, the first words of Matt's children. He opened his mouth to say something, he wasn't sure, later, what it would have been. Then the wave of protesters poured into the room.

"No," Ruth said.

"No?" the Conch said.

"No," Ruth said. She already felt regret, but she pushed on. "I would not give up my humanity, for, for . . . " She sighed. "For the Mysteries," she said. She turned to leave. She wanted to cry but she knew she was right. She could not do this. She wanted to understand, but she wanted to *be*, too.

"Wait," the Conch said.

Ruth stopped. "What," she said.

"That was the right answer," the Conch said.

Ruth turned. "What?"

"Do you think I am inhuman?" the woman in the Conch said.

"Yes," Ruth said. "No," Ruth said. "I don't know," she said at last, and waited.

The Conch laughed. "I am still human," it said. "Oh, how human. We cannot change what we are, Ruth Cohen. If that was what you wanted, you would have left disappointed. We can evolve, but we are still human, and they are still Other. Maybe one day . . . " but she did not complete the thought.

Ruth said, "You mean you can help me?"

"I am ready, child," the Oracle said, "to die. Does that shock you? I am old. My body fails. To be Translated into the Conversation is not to live forever. What I am will die. A new me will be created that contains some of my code. What will it be? I don't know. Something new, and Other. When your time comes, that choice will be yours, too. But never forget, humans die. So do Others, every cycle they are changed and reborn. The only rule of the Universe, child, is change."

"You are dying?" Ruth said. She was still very young, then, you must remember. She had not seen much death, yet.

"We are all dying," the Oracle said. "But you are young and want answers. You will find, I'm afraid, that the more you know the less answers you have."

"I don't understand."

"No," the Oracle said. "You do not."

Matt was pushed and shoved and went down on his ass, hard. They streamed in. They were mostly young, but not all. They were Jews and Palestinians but also foreigners, the media attention had brought them over from India and Britain and everywhere else, wealthy enough to travel, poor enough to care, the world's middle class revolutionaries, the ching-ching Chés.

"Don't—!" Matt shouted, but they were careful, he saw, and for a moment he didn't understand, they were not destroying the machines, they were making sure to remove people aside, to form a barrier around the machines and the power supplies and the cooling units and then they—

He shouted, "No!" and he tried to get up but hands grabbed him, impersonally, a girl with dreadlocks and a boy with a Ché T-shirt. They were not destroying the machines, they were plugging in.

They had brought mobile servers with them, wireless broadcast, portable storage units, an entire storage and communication network, and they were plugging it all into the secured closed network:

They were opening up the Breeding Grounds.

The Conch wheeled outside and Ruth followed. The Conversation opened up around her, the noise of a billion feeds all vying for attention at once. Ruth followed the Conch along the narrow roads until they came to the old neighborhood of Ajami. Children ran after them and touched the surface of the Conch. It was night now, and when they reached Ibrahim's junkyard torches were burning, and they cast the old junk in an unearthly glow. A new moon was in the sky. Ruth always remembered that, later. The sliver of a new moon, and she looked up and imagined the people living there.

Ibrahim met them at the entrance. "Oracle," he said, nodding. "And you are Ruth Cohen."

"Yes," Ruth said, surprised.

"I am Ibrahim."

She shook hands, awkwardly. Ibrahim held her hand and opened it. He examined it like a surgeon. "A Joining is not without pain," he said. Ruth bit her lip. "I know," she said.

"You are willing?"

"Yes."

"Then come."

They followed him through the maze of junk, of old petrol cars and giant fish-refrigeration units and industrial machines and piles of discarded paper books and mountains of broken toys and the entire flotsam and jetsam of Obsoleteness. Within this maze of junk there was, at its heart, a room whose walls were junk and whose roof were the stars. There was an old picnic table there, and a medical cabinet, and a folding chair. "Please," Ibrahim said. "Sit down."

Ruth did. The Conch had wheeled itself with difficulty through the maze and now stood before her. "Ibrahim," the Conch said.

"Yes," he said, and he went into the junk and returned and in his hands he was holding a towel that he unfurled carefully, almost reverentially: inside it were three golden, prosthetic thumbs.

"Oh," Ruth said.

It was conducted in silence. She remembered that, too, nothing spoken but the sound of the waves in the distance and the sound of children playing in the neighborhood beyond, and the smell of cooking lamb and of cardamoms and cumin. Ibrahim brought forth a syringe. Ruth put her arm on the table. Ibrahim cleaned her skin where the vein was and injected her. She felt the numbness spread. He took her hand and laid it splayed flat on the table. In the torchlight his face looked aged and hurting. He took a cleaver, an old one, it must have belonged to a butcher in the market down the hill, long ago. Ruth looked away. Ibrahim brought the cleaver down hard and cut off her thumb. Her blood sprayed the picnic table. Her thumb fell to the ground. Ruth gritted her teeth as Ibrahim took one of the golden prosthetic thumbs and connected it to Ruth's flesh. White bone was jutting out of the wound. She forced herself to look.

"Now," Ibrahim said.

• • •

The protesters plugged into the network. Matt saw lights flashing, the transfer of an enormous amount of data. Like huge shapes pushing through a narrow trough as they tried to escape. He closed his eyes. He imagined, for just a moment, that he could actually hear their sound as they broke free.

She was everywhere and nowhere at once. She was Ruth, but she was someone— something—else, too. She was a child, a baby, and there was another, an Other, entwined into her, a twin: together they existed in a place that had no physicality. They were evolving, together, mutating and changing, lines of code merging into genetic material, forming something—someone—new.

When it was done, when the protesters left, or had been arrested by the police, after he had finished answering questions, dazed, and wandered outside and into the media spotlight, and refused to answer questions—you can view the historical footage at your leisure—he went to a bar and sat down and watched the television as he drank. He was just a guy who tried to create something new, he had never meant for the world to be changed. He drank his beer and a little later he felt the weariness fall from him, a sense of release, of the future dissipating. He was just a guy, drinking beer in a bar, and as he sat there he saw a girl at another table, and their eyes met.

He wasn't then St. Cohen of the Others. He wasn't yet a myth, not yet portrayed in films or novels, not yet the figurehead of a new faith. The Others were out there, in the world . . . somewhere. What they would do, or how, he didn't know.

He looked at the girl and she smiled at him and, sometimes, that is all there is, and must be enough. He stood up and went to her and asked if he could sit down. She said yes.

He sat down and they talked.

She emerged from the virtuality years or decades later; or it could have just taken a moment. When she/they looked down at her/their hand she/they saw the golden thumb and knew it was it/them.

Beside her the Conch was still and she knew the woman inside it was dead.

Through her node she could hear the Conversation but above it she could hear the *toktok blong narawan,* not clear, yet, and she knew it never would be, not entirely, but she could at least hear it now, and she could speak it, haltingly. She was aware of Others floating in the virtual, in the digitality. Some circled around her, curious. Many others, distant in the webs, were uninterested. She called into the void, and a voice answered, and then another and another.

She/they stood up.

"Oracle," Ibrahim said.

LOSS, WITH CHALK DIAGRAMS

E. LILY YU

Never before in her life had Rebekah Moss turned to the rewirers, not as a tight-mouthed girl eavesdropping by closed doors on her parents' iceberg drift toward divorce, nor after she heard with bowed head, her body as blushingly full as a magnolia bud, the doctor describing the scars that kept her from having Dom's child. She took few risks and accepted all outcomes with equanimity. But when her old friend Linda was found beneath a park bridge in Quebec with her wrists slit lengthwise to the bone, leaving no note, no whisper of explanation, she hesitated only a moment before linking to the rewiring center. Saturday next was the first available appointment, a silvery voice informed her, and she took it. When she ended the call she wrapped her arms around her legs and tilted back and forth, blinking hard, her own breathing a foil rustle in her ears.

She had been twelve years old when rewiring was first approved for use on a limited clinical population. The treatment involved a brew of sixteen neurotoxins finely tuned to leave normal motor, memory, and cognitive processes intact, burning out only those neural pathways associated with grief and trauma. It was recognized as a radical advancement in medicine, and the neuroscientists involved in its development had been decorated with medals, presidential visits, and a research foundation in their names.

Her family supported her choice, of course. They pressed lemon tea and tissues and bitter chocolate upon her while she stumbled through the week, her whole world gone faint and gray and narrow. The sky seemed always clouded over, though she knew there was sunlight. She could not eat by herself. Dom fed her soup by hand and patted her rather awkwardly as she sobbed, both of them embarrassed by her access of sorrow. It was the only time in their marriage that she had cried.

She and Linda had grown up together, small and very different but fiercely loyal, as children can be. Linda had been her first real friend, all temper and rainstorms and rainbows, quick to scrape, to bleed, to run, to tumble, to climb. Her whole head of copper curls trembled when she laughed, and she had laughed often. She hummed pop songs off-key. She danced. Rebekah could often see the passions singing inside her, darkening and flushing and paling her cheeks, contorting her mouth, dilating or slitting her eyes. Sometimes Linda would blow up a squall—over Darrell, a thin boy with scarred and freckled knees who held Rebekah's hand once, by accident, and Linda's twice; over Rebekah's remark to another friend about Linda's father's drinking; over classroom prizes and movies they loved or loathed—but as Rebekah didn't fight back, only listening with a pale calm, these were quickly over, forgiven and forgotten.

They used to chalk coded messages for each other on the blacktop behind school, though chalk and chalkboards had long since vanished from classrooms, because they had read about it and wanted to try. They had mixed, colored, and molded the sticks out of plaster of Paris and paint. Once the sticks had been written to nubs, the girls crushed them to powder between their fingernails. It was a private art. Every stroke on the classroom screen, every voicelink, every comma and misspelling sent through the flow was documented and preserved perfectly for the ages, but the rain wiped clean their messages to each other and let them have secrets.

In high school the two of them drifted apart, distracted variously by clubs, boys, academic distinctions, other friends. Rebekah absorbed herself in the quiet pleasure of her French horn and regional orchestras; Linda realized a passion for biology, herpetology in particular, and acquired a lime-green lizard named Otto that she would smuggle to school in her pocket. Linda began to kiss boys; Rebekah only looked sidelong at one or two who made her glow inside when they laughed, and never spoke.

In the spring of their junior year, Linda's mother died. No one was quite sure why. She had seemed healthy, although Linda said once, when pressed, that it was cancer and she didn't want to talk about it.

The funeral was private. Linda vanished from school for several weeks, reappearing in caked makeup with dark, defiant eyes. She was prone to bursting into tears. The guidance counselor and several teachers pointed out to her that, as a bereaved minor, she was a prime candidate for rewiring. Treatment would allow her to focus on her schoolwork and college applications, they said: her grades had become erratic. They were worried about her future. Moreover, her outbursts were disturbing the other students.

Linda refused. After the fifth or sixth recommendation that she apply for rewiring, there was a firm suggestion that she take a year off from school, at which point she started shouting at the counselor and had to be restrained. Within days the whole school knew.

By that time, Rebekah was too distant from Linda to hear all of what was happening, but one day at lunchtime she brushed into her in the hall and was unwillingly drawn into a conversation about Mrs. Lubrick, for whom Linda felt a deep disdain. Linda pressed close; Rebekah could see the tiny, fine cracks in her foundation. There was a faint smell of alcohol on Linda's breath.

"She thinks it's something you can snip off, like hair or nails," Linda said. "That you can chop off loss without losing anything. But it's mine and I want it. It's horrible but it's mine."

Her eyes were narrowed, her lips badly chapped.

"My dad had people come and take away her clothes in bags. All of it. It was like watching someone slice open the family and pull out all the organs. I didn't want him to, but he couldn't stand it, her things lying around. I'm keeping every minute of this hurting. I'm keeping it."

She hugged herself, the oversized sweater lapping over her hands, and glared. Rebekah shrugged and turned away.

By the beginning of their senior year Linda discovered a reservoir of manic energy, and when spring came around she had been accepted to five of her seven schools. Rebekah applied to one and was accepted there, as she had known she would be.

It was at Grierson, three years after she had last spoken to Linda, that she opened her mailbox one morning to find a postcard with a picture of a marbled library, a California postmark, and a barely legible scrawl: *Dear Rebekah, I know we didn't talk much in high school, but I was thinking of you lately and looked up your address. I am doing well. Do you remember the chalk? Write to me if it's not too silly for you.*

After thinking for two days, Rebekah dug up a stamp, a pen, and a card from the depths of the university museum shop—postal correspondence was an anachronism then, kept running by advertising, nostalgia and the government's good graces—and scribbled in large letters shaky with disuse: *Dear Linda, happy to hear from you. What has your life been like? I am awful at postcards. Sorry.*

In reply she received a dried dahlia in a blue envelope with the note: *Charming, dahling.* Rebekah held the crisping flower in her palm, the desk lamp lighting the petals like a paper lantern, and remembered the feeling of pastel dust on her fingers and the scrape of asphalt on her skin. Then she set the dahlia on her desk and uncapped her antique pen.

Dear Linda, tomorrow I am graduating from Grierson Mech E, cum laude. I have a job in Albany this fall making wireframes for printed engine parts.

Dearest Rebekah, I'm writing from Jakarta. Reporting for private flow feeds as well as the Times of Singapore. *Eating jackfruit and rambutan, which is cheap and fresh here. Traffic is like being strangled. I bike sometimes. If this card is black when it reaches you, that's Jakarta smog. Rob left a few weeks ago, and I am lonely. Your last card came at the perfect time.*

Dear Linda, this is the house we're moving into next month. I don't like the wooden shingled sides—they're green and brown from too much rain—but it is bright inside. I can make a life here, I think. All is well. Do send me your new addresses when you move. It's not easy keeping track of you.

My dear Rebekah, congratulations on the wedding, and Dom, and all. Are you still playing in your community orchestra? Is that the same horn you had in high school? They don't wear out, right? Love from London.

Dear Linda, thank you for the violin recordings. Where did you find the violinist? I play them at work when my equations stop making sense. Sometimes the noise from the machining rooms downstairs rattles my brain. Your music is a sweet relief. Send more.

Rebekah, I have ditched the last boy—or he ditched me—again. Too fond of blondes. Had to move out, now staying with a friend.

Dear Linda, we saw the doctor yesterday. It is not possible, he says.

Rebekah stacked the postcards in a small tin painted with daffodils, where year by year they faded. By mutual unspoken agreement they continued to write to each other, avoiding calls, flow feeds, emails, everything permanent and certain. It seemed right that their correspondence be an ephemeral thing, somehow, though everything else in Rebekah's life was heavy with deliberation, immense and secure. Dom was the only man she ever dated, and they had married after a brief courtship as careful and formal as a game of chess. They read the news on the glass of their breakfast table and kissed each other before leaving for work. They planted flowered borders of perennials. They did not travel.

It had been inevitable that the postal system would eventually collapse. On the morning that the last post office was shuttered, Rebekah scanned the news on the table and sighed. Then she linked to a node in Montreal, Linda's last known address, and left a tentative message inviting her to visit.

Linda arrived in a whirlwind of loss—lost paperwork, lost passport, lost lover, recently deceased father—her black hobnailed boots striking sparks from the pavement as she walked, her short hair waving like candle flames. She enumerated these losses to Rebekah in a rich rippling alto that sometimes shook with laughter and always gleamed with color, describing her four heartbreaks—Rob, Ajay, Chris, Max—each worse than the last; the three times she had been held up at knifepoint; the one time she had betrayed and the five times she had been betrayed; and for one shivering moment Rebekah saw her quiet happiness pale beside the coruscations of Linda's life.

Grief had written heavy lines on Linda's face. Despite her scars and bruises, her casualties, her innumerable losses, she had not applied for rewiring either. By then it was standard procedure, shading into the cosmetic. Rebekah's parents and most of her other relatives had been rewired. They had pushed Rebekah to apply after she learned she would never have a child, relenting only after six weeks of her pleasant, toneless insistence that she was fine. After all, she told Dom and her family, she had not lost anything.

To all appearances the procedure was a blessing. The suicide rate had dropped nationwide and in those developed countries that could afford to make rewiring available. It was becoming difficult to find songs about heartbreak on flowlines these days, Linda said. Tragedies were disappearing from theaters and screens. Sorrow was no longer a welcome and expected guest. "Except to me," Linda said, sounding puzzled and proud. As they passed a hallway mirror, Rebekah was startled to see the contrast in their faces; she looked an entire decade younger than Linda, with fewer shadows, fewer lines, fewer softnesses and sinkings. And yet Linda had grown beautiful, richly and ripely beautiful, an awareness that pressed on Rebekah as inexorably as sunlight. It had been years since they last stood in the same room.

"You're so happy," Linda broke out, over their dinner of salmon and asparagus, Dom smiling benignly at them. Her mouth twisted briefly. "You've lived so *well.*"

Then she had blushed, a familiar rose blooming in each cheek, and ducked her head, and complimented the food. The conversation veered to politics and immigration law. Linda was entangled in immigration court, having overstayed a complicated sequence of visas. She had traveled too often and lived in too many places, she said. Loved the wrong people, the right people, or too many people. Carried a piece of each place inside her. Sometimes a ring. Once, an unborn child. Her face flickered at that. It all played merry hell with your passport, she said. Her smile was fragile.

Dom brought out the raspberry tart, a silver cake trowel, and a stack of willow plates.

"A good immigration lawyer," he suggested, piecing out the tart, but she shook her head.

"I had one," Linda said. "I tried. It's over, really."

Later, when she went out into the garden to smoke, Rebekah said to her, "You could let go of it all so easily."

"The sadness? Perhaps." Linda blew a billow of smoke. Smoking was another anachronism she had picked up; Rebekah wondered when, and why, and with whom.

"Think of how much lighter you'd be," Rebekah said. "How peaceful you'd feel. You'd live longer."

Linda laughed. "You're telling me to let go of my grief? You?" She tilted the glowing tip of her cigarette toward Rebekah. "You'll never have the children you want. That would break anyone's heart. But you didn't go for rewiring. Why not? Why not let go?"

Rebekah found she could not answer.

If she closed her eyes she could recall the clinic in crisp, hectic color. The room had been cream-colored, trimmed in pale green, and smelled faintly and cruelly of mother's milk. The stethoscope around the doctor's neck was also pale green. The barrage of scans and tests was over. It was all over. She had sat under the too-bright lights, looking at her hands, her ears full of the dull crash and roar of her blood. *I'm very sorry*, the doctor said, and she heard herself saying, *No, no, it's quite all right*. As she had said to Dom, and to her mother, and his, until the words were nonsense in her mouth. *It's quite all right*, she said, burying the bitterness inside herself, shrugging off the suggestion. *No, no rewiring. It's all right*.

The air still tasted bitter, under the odor of roses.

"As for me," Linda said, "grieving makes me whole. Anything and anyone worth having is also worth wearing a scar for, if only on the inside." She took a drag on the cigarette, and smoke flowered from her mouth.

"I don't understand."

"Do you love that man? Dom? If he died, would you cry over him? Would you spend years looking for him in the morning and expecting his presence in every room of your house and feeling your heart crack each time you realize he's not there? Or would you go straight to the needles?"

"That's not a fair question," Rebekah said, waving away the smoke. "He wouldn't want me to mourn."

"No?"

"He doesn't want me to suffer."

"You think there can be love without suffering? Having without losing?"

Rebekah looked at her friend, so troubled, so tired, so lovely. "Yes."

"Would you mourn me?" Linda's eyes were large and luminous. "You're one of the few who still can."

"If you died? You'd want me to be miserable for losing you?"

"I want to be remembered." She dropped the cigarette in a spray of sparks and ground it beneath her toe. "I want to be a physical absence in a room. I want to be a void and an ache. I want to be remembered with sorrow, the way I remember so many other people now."

"That seems selfish."

"Perhaps." Linda sighed. "There aren't that many people left to grieve, anyhow. Why haven't you gone for rewiring?"

The vivid, heavy smells of roses and cigarettes were making her dizzy. There were the boys she never kissed, too afraid to speak to them; the trips she had decided not to take; the jobs in other places she had turned down; the child she could not have. Instead of these things, she had Dom's love, a warm house, steady work as a propulsion engineer, and two evenings a week in an orchestra. She supposed she did not regret her choices. What did she have to grieve for, after all?

"I haven't lost very much, I guess." She pressed her lips together.

"Just possibilities."

Upstairs the bedroom windows filled with light, then darkened.

Linda extended a finger with a glittering drop of data on it. "Here, I brought this for you. I recorded it in Montreal."

"What is it?"

"Freeman, French horn. Hard to find that kind of music these days. Don't listen to it now. It's late."

She kissed Rebekah on the brow before she went, leaving a dusty mark.

Saturday came with terrible slowness. Rebekah could hardly find the strength to leave her bed. She recalled that evening vividly, the taste of butter and raspberry jam, the smell of tobacco smoke, the brush of dry, powdery lips against her forehead. Nothing in that evening had hinted at the horror of white bone and slashed muscle, and yet all of Linda's life seemed full of signs and portents, now that she was gone.

Rebekah barely noticed anything on her walk downtown. Before long she stood before the chrome and glass doors of the district's rewiring center, staring dully up at the silver-lettered signs and the office windows full of desks and blurred figures. Dom could not accompany her; he had been sweetly apologetic; he had to implement new protocols in the lab ahead of state deadlines.

Everything in the center was painfully gleaming and new, from the young man who greeted her at the desk, the crispness of college still on him, to the white leather sofas she was directed to. The interior was lit by a gentle but intense white light, enough to pierce through the fog in her head.

"Let me explain the procedure to you," the doctor said. "We will be making eight injections into your insula, anterior temporal cortex, anterior cingulate cortex, and prefrontal cortex. You will be under general anesthesia for the entire operation. It should take three hours. We have not found significant side effects but a small number of patients have reported lethargy lasting a week, loss of appetite, lingering sadness, and feelings of confusion. Would you please sign here?"

First they shaved small squares on her scalp where the thin drills and then the needles would pass through. She watched dark strands of her hair fall into her lap, scattering over her white paper robe. Then they left her in a room to wait.

Rebekah sat alone on the bed, numb and cold, toying with the strange spiky shapes of her grief. Rather than listen to the unbearable symphony of beeping, chiming monitors, she pulled up the recording that Linda had given her.

It began with scraping chairs and indistinct voices, some swift French, some English. There was shuffling, and coughing, and silence. Then she heard a slender silver note, the winding of a hunting horn. Foxes and deer slid through the mist, tearing up the wet earth, followed by men and women and sleek hounds. The horn urged them on. The best of the hunters took aim and fired through the fog, but the bullet killed his lover instead of the deer.

She heard grief in the music, flashing like lightning beneath the silver notes. It had been a very long time since she had heard music like it. Her community orchestra was very good at light, pensive, or melancholy music, but when they tried the tragic, their performance rang empty. Freeman was something else altogether. She had missed that kind of music. It was a good gift.

Rebekah closed the file and raised her head to see two blue-scrubbed nurses approaching.

They were wiping and tying her arm for the anesthetic, the faces around her friendly and smiling, when she realized how jealous she had become of her black, broken grief. It hurt, but it was hers. That had also been a gift.

Wait, she wanted to say. I don't want this anymore. She opened her mouth, then closed it again. She told herself: *You refused her. You don't deserve to grieve.*

The needle slid beneath her skin.

You never learned how to lose someone.

A thick soft darkness swallowed her, a sinking without bottom, through which she swam ever deeper down. Somewhere rain fell and washed the pavement clean.

When she awoke, she was not in pain.

MARTYR'S GEM

C.S.E. COONEY

Of the woman he was to wed on the morrow, Shursta Sarth knew little. He knew she hailed from Droon. He knew her name was Hyrryai.

"...Which means, The Gleaming One," his sister piped in, the evening before he left their village. She was crocheting by the fire and he was staring into it.

Lifting his chin from his hand, Shursta grinned at her. "Ayup? And where'd you light upon that lore, Nugget?"

Sharrar kicked him on the ankle for using the loathed nickname. "I work with the greyheads. They remember everything."

"Except how to chew their food."

"What they've lost in teeth, they've gained in wisdom," she announced with some pomposity. "Besides, that's what they have *me* for." Her smile went wry at one corner, but was no less proud for that. "I chew their food, I change their cloths, and they tell me about the old days. Some of them had parents who were alive back then."

Her voice went rich and rolling. Her crochet hook glinted on the little lace purse she was making. The driftwood flames flickered, orange with tongues of blue.

"They remember the days before the Nine Cities drowned and the Nine Islands with them. Before our people forsook us to live below the waters, and we were stranded here on the Last Isle. Before we changed our name to Glennemgarra, the Unchosen." Sharrar sighed. "In *those* days, names were more than mere proxy for, *Hey, you!*"

"So, Hyrryai means, *Hey, you, Gleamy*?"

"You have no soul, Shursta."

"Nugget, when your inner poet is ascendant, you have more than enough soul for both of us. If the whitecaps of your whimsy rise any higher, we'll have a second Drowning at hand, make no mistake."

Sharrar rolled her brown-bright eyes at him and grunted something. He laughed, and the anxious knots in his stomach loosened some.

When Shursta took his leave the next morning at dawn, he lingered in the threshold. The hut had plenty of wood in the stack outside the door. He'd smoked or salted any extra catch for a week, so Sharrar would not soon go hungry. If she encountered trouble, they would take her in at the Hall of Ages where she worked, and there she'd be fed and sheltered, though she wouldn't have much privacy or respite.

He looked at his sister now. She'd dragged herself from bed to make him breakfast, even though he was perfectly capable of frying up an egg himself. Her short dark hair stuck up every which way and her eyes were bleary. Her limp was more pronounced in the morning.

"Wish you could come with me," he offered.

"What? Me, with one game leg and a passel of greyheads to feed? No, thank you!" But her eyes looked wistful. Neither of them had ever been to Droon, capital of the Last Isle, the seat of the Astrion Council.

"Hey," he said, surprised to find his own eyes stinging.

"Hey," she said right back. "After the mesh-rite, after you've settled down a bit and met some folks, invite me up. You know I want to meet my mesh-sister. You have my gift?"

He patted his rucksack, which had the little lace purse she'd crocheted along with his own mesh-gift.

"Oohee, brother mine," said Sharrar. "By this time tomorrow you'll be a Blodestone, and no Sarth relation will be worthy to meet your eyes."

"Doubtless Hirryai Blodestone will take one look at me and sunder the contract."

"*She* requested *you.*"

Shursta shrugged, sure it had been a mistake.

After that, there was one last hug, a vivid and mischievous and slightly desperate smile from Sharrar, followed by a grave look and quick wink on Shursta's part. Then he set off on the searoad that would take him to Droon.

Of the eight great remaining kinlines, the Blodestones were the wealthiest. Their mines were rich in ore and gems. Their fields were fertile and wide, concentrated in the highland interior of the Last Isle. After a Blodestone female was croned at age fifty, she would hold her place on the Astrion Council, which governed all the Glennemgarra.

Even a fisherman like Shursta Sarth (of the lesser branch of Sarths), from a poor village like Sif on the edge of Rath Sea, with no parents of note and only a single sister for kin, knew about the Blodestones.

He had no idea why Hyrryai had chosen him for mesh-mate. If it had not been an error, then it was a singular honor. For his life he knew not how he deserved it.

He was of an age to wed. Mesh-rite was his duty to the Glennemgarra and he would perform it, that the world might once again be peopled. To be childless—unless granted special dispensation by the Astrion Council—was to be reviled. Even with the dispensation, there were those who were tormented or shunned for their barrenness.

Due to a lack of girls in Sif, to his own graceless body, which, though fit for work, tended to carry extra weight, and to the slowness of his tongue in the company of strangers, Shursta had not yet been bred out. He had planned to attend this year's muster and win a mesh-mate at games (the idea of being won himself had never occurred to him), but then the Council's letter from Droon came.

The letter told him that Hyrryai Blodestone had requested him for mesh-mate. It told him that Hyrryai had not yet herself been bred. That though she was twenty one, a full year past the age of meshing, she had been granted a reprieve when her little sister was murdered.

Shursta had read that last sentence in shock. The murder of a child was the highest crime but one, and that was the murder of a girl child. Hyrryai had been given full grieving rights.

Other than this scant information, the letter had left detailed directions to Droon, with the day and time his first assignation with Hirryai had been set, and reminded him that it was customary for a first-meshed couple to exchange a gift.

On Sharrar's advice, Shursta had taken pains. He had strung for Hyrryai a long necklace of ammonite, shark teeth and dark pearls the color of thunderclouds. Ammonite for antiquity, teeth for ferocity, and pearls for sorrow. A fearsome gift and perhaps presumptuous, but Sharrar had approved.

"Girls like sharp things," she'd said, "so the teeth are just right. As for the pearls, they're practically a poem."

"I should have stuck with white ones," he'd said ruefully. "The regular round kind."

"Bah!" said Sharrar, her pointy face with its incongruously long, strong jaw set stubbornly. "If she doesn't see you're a prize, I'll descend upon Droon and roast her organs on the tines of my trident, just see if I don't!"

Whereupon Shursta had flicked his strand of stone, teeth and pearl at her. She'd caught it with a giggle, wrapping it with great care in the fine lace purse she'd made.

Hyrryai Blodestone awaited him. More tidepool than beach, the small assignation spot had been used for this purpose before. Boulders had been carved into steps leading from searoad to cove, but these were ancient and crumbling into marram grass.

In this sheltered spot, a natural rock formation had been worked gently into the double curve of a lovers' bench. His intended bride sat at the far end. Any further and she would topple off.

From the smudges beneath her eyes and the harried filaments flying out from her wing-black braid, she looked as if she had been sitting there all night. Her head turned as he approached. Perhaps it was the heaviness of his breath she heard. It labored after the ten miles he'd trudged that morning, from the steepness of the steps, at his astonishment at the color of her hair. The breezy sweetness of dawn had long since burned away. It was noon.

Probably, Shursta thought, falling back a step as her gaze met his, she could smell him where she sat.

"Shursta Sarth," she greeted him.

"Damisel Blodestone."

Shursta had wanted to say her name. Had wanted to say it casually, as she spoke his, with a cordial nod of the head. Instead his chin jutted up and awry, as if a stray hook had caught it. Her name stopped in his throat and changed places at the last second with the formal honorific. He recalled Sharrar's nonsense about names having meaning. It no longer seemed absurd.

Hyrryai the Gleaming One. Had she been so called for the long shining lines in her hair? The fire at the bottom of her eyes, like lava trapped in obsidian? Was it the clear bold glow of her skin, just browner than blushing coral, just more golden than sand?

Since his tongue would not work, as it rarely did for strangers, Shursta shrugged off his rucksack. The shoulder straps were damp in his grip. He fished out the lace purse with its mesh-gift and held it out to her, stretching his arm to the limit so that he would not have to step nearer.

She glanced from his flushed face to the purse. With a short sigh, as if to brace herself, she stood abruptly, plucked the purse from his hand and dumped the contents into her palm.

Shursta's arm dropped.

Hyrryai Blodestone examined the necklace closely. Every tooth, every pearl, every fossilized ridge of ammonite. Then, with another breath, this one quick and indrawn as the other had been exhaled, she poured the contents back and thrust the purse at him.

"Go home, man of Sif," she said. "I was mistaken. I apologize that you came all this way."

Not knowing whether he were about to protest or cozen or merely ask why, Shursta opened his mouth. Felt that click in the back of his throat where too many words welled in too narrow a funnel. Swallowed them all.

His hand closed over the purse Sharrar had made.

After all, it was no worse than he had expected. Better, for she had not laughed at him. Her face, though cold, expressed genuine sorrow. He suspected the sorrow was with her always. He would not stay to exacerbate it.

This time, he managed a creditable bow, arms crossed over his chest in a gesture of deepest respect. Again he took up his rucksack, though it seemed a hundred times heavier now. He turned away from her, letting his rough hair swing into his face.

"Wait."

Her hand was on his arm. He wondered if they had named her Hyrryai because she left streaks of light upon whatever she touched.

"Wait. Please. Come and sit. I think I must explain. If it pleases you to hear me, I will talk awhile. After that you may tell me what you think. What you want. From this." She spread her hands.

Shursta did not remove his rucksack again, but he sat with her. Not on the bench, but on the sand, with their backs against the stone seat. He drew in the sand with a broken shell and did not look at her except indirectly, for fear he would stare. For a while, only the waves spoke.

When Hyrryai Blodestone began, her tones were polite but informal, like a lecturer of small children. Like Sharrar with her grayheads. As if she did not expect Shursta to hear her, or hearing, listen.

"The crones of the Astrion Council know the names of all the Glennemgarra youth yet unmeshed. All their stories. Who tumbled which merry widow in which sea cave. Who broke his drunken head on which barman's club. Who comes from the largest family of mesh-kin, and what her portions are. You must understand," the tone of her voice changed, and Shursta glanced up in time to see the fleetingest quirk of a corner smile, "the secrets of the council do not stay in the council. In my home, at least, it is the salt of every feast, the gossip over tea leaves and coffee grinds, the center of our politics and our hearths. With a mother, grandmother, several aunts and great aunts and three cousins on the council, I cannot escape it. When we were young, we did not want to. We thought of little else than which dashing, handsome man we would . . ."

She stopped. Averted her face. Then she asked lightly, "Shall I tell you your story as the Blodestones know it?"

When he answered, after clearing his throat, it was in the slow measured sentences that made most people suck their teeth and stamp the ground with impatience. Hyrryai Blodestone merely watched with her flickering eyes.

"Shursta Sarth is not yet twenty five. He has one sibling, born lame. A fisherman by trade. Not a very successful one. Big as a whale. Stupid as a jellyfish. Known to his friends, if you can call them that, as 'Sharkbait.' "

Hyrryai was nodding, slowly. His heart sank like a severed anchor. He had hoped, of course, that the story told of Shursta Sarth in the Astrion Council might be different. That somehow they had known more of him, even, than he knew of himself. Seeing his crestfallen expression, Hyrryai took up the tale.

"Shursta Sarth is expected either to win a one-year bride at games, do his duty by her and watch her leave the moment her contract ends, or to take under his wing a past-primer lately put aside for a younger womb. However, as his sister will likely be his dependent for life, this will deter many of the latter, who might have taken him on for the sake of holding their own household. It is judged improbable that Shursta Sarth will follow the common practice of having his sister removed to the Beggar's Quarter and thus improve his own lot."

Shursta must have made an abrupt noise or movement, for she glanced at him curiously. He realized his hands had clenched. Again, she almost smiled.

"Your sister made the purse?"

He nodded once.

"Then she is clever. And kind." She paused. The foam hissed just beyond the edges of their toes. A cormorant called.

"Did you know I had a sister?" she asked him.

Shursta nodded, more carefully this time. Her voice, like her face, was remote and cold. But at the bottom of it, buried in the ice, an inferno.

"She was clubbed to death on this beach. I found her. We had come here often to play—well, to spy on mesh-mates meeting for the first time. Sometimes we came here when the moon was full—to bathe and dance and pretend that the sea people would swim up to surface from the Nine Drowned Cities to sing songs with us. I had gone to a party that night with a group of just the sort of dashing handsome young men we would daydream about meshing with, but she was too young yet for such things. When she was found missing from her bed the next morning, I thought perhaps she had come here and fallen asleep. I thought if I found her, I could pretend to our mother I had already scolded her—Kuista was very good at hanging her head like a puppy and looking chastised; sometimes I think she practiced in the mirror—and she might be let off a little easier. So I went here first and told nobody. But even from the cliff, when I saw her lying there, I knew she wasn't sleeping."

Shursta began to shiver. He thought of Sharrar, tangled in bladderwrack, a nimbus of bloody sand spreading out around her head.

"She was fully clothed, except for her shoes. But she often went barefoot. Said even sandals strangled her. The few coins in her pocket were still there, but her gemmaja was gone. I know she had been wearing it, because she rarely took it off. And it's not among her things."

A dark curiosity moved in him. Unable to stop himself, Shursta asked, "What is a gemmaja?"

Hyrryai untangled a thin silver chain from her hair. If she had not been so mussed, if the gemmaja had been properly secured, it would have lain across her forehead in a gentle V. A small green stone speckled with red came to rest between her eyes like a raindrop.

"The high households of the eight kinlines wear them. Ours is green chalcedony, of course. You Sarths," she added, "wear the red carnelian."

Shursta touched the small knob of polished coral he wore on a cord under his shirt. His mother had always just called it a *touchstone*. His branch of Sarths had never been able to afford carnelian.

"Later, after the pyre, I searched the sand, but I could not find Kuista's gemmaja. I was so . . . " She hesitated. "Angry."

Shursta understood the pause. Hyrryai had meant something entirely else, of course. As when calling the wall of water that destroyed your village a word so common as "wave" was not enough.

" . . . So angry that I had not thought to check her head more closely. To see if the gemmaja had been driven into . . . into what was left of her skull. To see if a patch of her hair had been ripped out with the removal of the gemmaja—which I reason more likely. But I only thought of that later, when . . . when I could think again. Someone took the gemmaja from her, I know it." She shook her head. "But for what reason? A lover, perhaps, crazed by her refusal of him? She was young for a lover, but some men are strange. Did he beat her down and then take a piece of her for himself? Was it an enemy? For the Blodestones are powerful, Shursta Sarth, and have had enemies for as long as we have held house. Did he bring back her gemmaja to his own people, as proof of loyalty to his kinline? Was he celebrated? Was he elected leader for his bold act? I do not know. I wish I had been a year ago what I am now . . . But mark me."

She turned to him and set her strong hands about his wrists.

"Mark me when I say I shall not rest until I find Kuista's murderer. Every night she comes to me in my sleep and asks where her gemmaja is. In my dreams she is not dead or broken, only sad, so sad that she begins to weep, asking me why it was taken from her. Her tears are not tears but blood. All I want is to avenge her. It is all I can think about. It is the only reason I am alive. *Do you understand*?"

Shursta's own big, brown, blunt-fingered hands rested quietly within the tense shackles of hers. His skin was on fire where she touched him, but his stomach felt like stone. He said slowly, "You do not wish—you never wished—to wed."

"No."

"But your grieving time is used up and the Astrion Council—your family—is insisting."

"Yes."

"So you chose a husband who . . . Who would be . . . " He breathed out. "Easy." She nodded once, slowly. "A stupid man, a poor man, a man who would be grateful for a place among the Blodestones. So grateful he would not question the actions of his wife. His wife who . . . who would not be a true wife."

Her hands fell from his. "You do understand."

"Yes."

She nodded again, her expression almost exultant. "I knew you would! The moment I held your mesh-gift. It was as if you knew me before we met. As if you made my sorrow and my vengeance and my blood debt to my sister into a necklace. I knew at once that you would never do. Because I need a husband who would *not* understand. Who would not care if I could not love him. Who never suspected that the thought of bringing a child into this murderous world is so repellent that to dwell on it makes me vomit, even when I have eaten nothing. I mean to find my sister's killer, Shursta Sarth. And then I mean to kill him and eat his heart by moonlight."

Shursta looked up, startled. The eating of a man's flesh was taboo— but he did not blurt the obvious aloud. Had not her sister—a child, a girl child—been murdered on this beach? Taboos meant nothing to Hyrryai Blodestone. He wondered that she had not yet filed her teeth and declared herself *windwyddiam*, a wind widow, nameless, kinless, outside the law. But then, he thought, how could she hunt amongst the high houses if she revoked her right of entry into them?

"*But.*"

He looked up at that word and knew a disgustingly naked monster shone in his eyes. But he could not help it. Shursta could not help his hope.

"But you are not a stupid man, Shursta Sarth. And you do not deserve to be sent away in disgrace, as if you were a dog that displeased me. You must tell me what you want, now that you know what I am."

Shursta sat up to remove his rucksack again. Again he removed the lace purse, the necklace. And though his fingers trembled, he looped the long strand around her neck, twice and then thrice, before letting the hooks catch. The teeth jutted out about her flesh, warning away chaste kisses, chance gestures of affection. Hyrryai did not move beneath his hands.

"I am everything the Astrion Council says," Shursta said, sinking back to the sand. "But if I wed you tomorrow, I will be a Blodestone, and thus be more useful to my sister. Is that not enough to keep me here? I am not so stupid as to leave, when you give me the choice to stay. But I shall respect your grief. I shall not touch you. When you have found your sister's killer and have had your revenge, come to me. I will declare myself publicly dissatisfied that you have not given me children. I will return to Sif. If my sister does not mesh, you will settle upon her a portion worthy of a Blodestone, that she will never be put away in the Beggar's Quarter. And we shall be quit of each other. Does this suit you, Damisel Blodestone?"

Whatever longing she heard in his voice or saw in his eyes, she did not flinch from it. She took his face between her palms and kissed him right on the forehead, right between the eyes, where her sister's gemmaja had rested, where her skull had been staved in.

"Call me Hyrryai, husband."

When she offered her hand, he set his own upon it. Hyrryai did not clasp it close. Instead, she furled open his fingers and placed her mesh-gift into his palm. It was a black shell blade, honed to a dazzle and set into a delicately scrimshawed hilt of whale ivory.

"Cherished Nugget," Shursta began his missive:

It is for charity's sake that I sit and scribble this to you on this morning of all mornings, in the sure knowledge that if I do not, your churlishness will have you feeding burnt porridge to all the grayheads under your care. To protect them, I will relate to you the tale of my meshing. Brace yourself.

The bride wore red, as brides do—but you have never seen such a red as the cloth they make in Droon. Had she worn it near shore, sharks would have beached themselves, mistaking her for food. It was soft too, to the touch. What was it like? Plumage. No, pelt. Like Damis Ungerline's seal pelt, except not as ratty and well-chewed. How is the old lady anyway? Has she lost her last tooth yet? Give her my regards.

The bride's brothers, six giants whose prowess in athletics, economics, politics and music makes them the boast of the Blodestones, converged on me the night I arrived in Droon and insisted I burn the clothes I came in and wear something worthy of my forthcoming station.

"Except," said one—forgive me; I have not bothered to learn all their names—"we have nothing ready made in his size."

"Perhaps a sailcloth?"

"Damis Valdessparrim has some very fine curtains."

And more to this effect. A droll scene. Hold it fast in your mind's eye. Me, nodding and agreeing to all their pronouncements with a fine ingratiation of manner. Couldn't speak a word, of course. Sweating, red as a boiled lobster— you know how I get—I suppose I seemed choice prey while they poked and prodded, loomed and laughed. I felt about three feet tall and four years old again.

Alas, low as they made me, I could not bring myself to let them cut the clothes from my back. I batted at their hands. However, they were quicker than I, as are most everybody. They outnumbered me and their knives came out. My knife—newly gifted and handsomer than anything I've ever owned—was taken from me. My fate was sealed.

Then their sister came to my rescue. Think not she had been standing idly by, enjoying the welcome her brothers made me. No, as soon as we'd stepped foot under the Blodestone roof, she had been enveloped in a malapertness of matrons, and had only just emerged from their fond embraces.

She has a way of silencing even the most garrulous of men, which the Blodestone boys, I assure you, are.

When they were all thoroughly cowed and scuffling their feet, she took me by the hand and led me to the room I am currently occupying. My mesh-rite suit was laid out for me, fine ivory linens embroidered by, she assured me, her mother's own hand. They fit like I had been born to them. The Astrion Council, they say, has eyes everywhere. And measuring tapes too, apparently.

Yes, yes, I stray from my subject, O antsiest (and onliest) sister. The meshing.

Imagine a balmy afternoon. Warm, with a wind. (You probably had the same kind of afternoon in Sif, so it shouldn't be too hard.) Meat had been roasting since the night before in vast pits. The air smelled of burnt animal flesh, by turns appetizing and nauseating.

We two stood inside the crone circle. The Blodestones stood in a wider circle around the crones. After that, a circle of secondary kin. After that, the rest of the guests.

We spoke our vows. Or rather, the bride did. Your brother, dear Nugget, I am sorry to say, was his usual laconic self and could not find his way around his own tongue. Shocking! Nevertheless, the bride crowned him in lilies, and cuffed to his ear a gemmaja of green chalcedony, set in a tangle of silver. This, to declare him a Blodestone by mesh-rite.

You see, I enclose a gemmaja of your own. You are no longer Sharrar Sarth, but Damisel Sharrar Blodestone, mesh-sister to the Gleaming One. When you come of croning, you too, shall take your seat on the Astrion Council. Power, wealth, glory. Command of the kinlines. Fixer of fates.

There. Never say I never did anything for you.

Do me one favor, Sharrar. Do not wear your gemmaja upon your forehead, or in any place too obvious. Do not wear it where any stranger who might covet it might think to take it from you by force. Please.

A note of observation. For all they dress so fine and speak with fancy voices, I cannot say that people in Droon are much different than people in Sif. Sit back in your chair and imagine me rapturous in the arms of instant friends.

I write too hastily. Sharrar, I'm sorry. The ink comes out as gall. I know for a fact that you are scowling at the page and biting your nails. My fault.

I will slow down, as if I were speaking, and tell you something to set your heart at ease.

Other than the bride—who is what she is—I have perhaps discovered one friend. At least, he is friendlier than anyone else I have met in Droon. I even bothered remembering his name for you.

He is some kind of fifth or sixth cousin to the bride—though not a Blodestone. One of the ubiquitous Spectroxes. (Why are they ubiquitous, you ask? I am not entirely sure. I was told they are ubiquitous, so ubiquitous I paint them for you now. Miners and craftsmen, mostly, having holdings in the mountains. Poor but on the whole respectable.) This particular Spectrox is called Laric Spectrox. Let me tell you how I met him.

I was lingering near the banquet table after the brunt of the ceremony had passed from my shoulders.

Imagine me a mite famished. I had not eaten yet that day, my meshing day, and it was nearing sunset. I was afraid to serve myself even a morsel for the comments my new mesh-brothers might make. They had already made several to the end that, should I ever find myself adrift at sea, I might sustain myself solely *on* myself until rescue came, and still be man enough for three husbands to their sister!

I thought it safe, perhaps, to partake of some fruit. All eyes were on a sacred dance the bride was performing. This involved several lit torches swinging from the ends of chains and what I can only describe as alarming acrobatics. I had managed to eat half a strawberry when a shadow dwarfed the dying sun. A creature precisely three times the height of any of the bride's brothers—though much skinnier—and black as the sharp shell of my new blade—laughed down at me.

"Bored with the fire spinning already? Hyrryai's won contests, you know. Although she can't—ah—*couldn't* hold a candle to little Kuista."

I squinted up at this living beanstalk of a man, wondering if he ever toppled in a frisky wind. To my surprise, when I opened my mouth to speak, the sentence came out easily—in the order I had planned it, no less.

(I still find it strange how my throat knows when to trust someone, long before I've made up my own mind about it. It was you who first observed that, I remember. Little Sharrar, do the greyheads tell you that *your* name means Wisdom? If they don't, they should.)

"I cannot bear to watch her," I confessed.

"Afraid she'll set someone's hair on fire?" He winked. "Can't really blame you. But she won't, you know."

"Not that. Only . . . " For a moment, my attention wandered back to the bride. Red flame. Red gown. Wheels of fire in the night. Her eyes. I looked away. "Only it would strike me blind if I gazed at her too long."

What he read in my face, I could not say (although I know you're wishing I'd just make something up), but he turned to follow her movements as she danced.

"Mmn," he grunted. "Can't say I see it, myself. She's just Hyrryai. Always has been. Once, several years back, my mother suggested I court her. I said I'd rather mesh with a giant squid. Hyrryai's all bone and sinew, you know. Never had any boobies to speak of. Anyway, even before Kuista died, she was too serious. Grew up with those Blodestone boys—learned to fight before she could talk. I wouldn't want a wife who could kill me with her pinkie, would you?"

My eyebrows went past my hairline. In fact, I have not located them since. I think they are hiding behind my ears. My new acquaintance grinned to see me at such a loss, but he grasped my forearm and gave it a hearty shake.

"What am I doing, keeping you from your grub? Eat up, man! You're that feral firemaid's husband now. I'd say you'll need all your strength for tonight."

And that, Nugget, is where I shall leave you. It is morning. As you see, I survived.

Your fond brother,
Shursta Blodestone

He was reading a book in the windowseat of his room when Shursta heard the clamor in the courtyard. Wagon wheels, four barking dogs, several of the younger Blodestones who had been playing hoopball, an auntie trying to hush everyone down.

"Good morning, Chaos," a voice announced just beyond his line of sight. "My name is Sharrar Sarth. I've come to meet my mesh-kin."

Shursta slammed his book closed and ran for the door. He did not know if he was delighted or alarmed. Would they jostle her? Would they take her cane away and tease her? Would she whack them over the knuckles and earn the disapprobation of the elders? *Why had she come?*

The letter, of course. The letter. He had regretted it the moment he sent it. It had been too long, too full of things he should have kept to himself. He ought to have expected her. Would he have stayed at home, receiving a thing like that from her? Never. Now that she was here, he ought to send her away.

Sharrar stood amongst a seethe of Blodestones, chatting amiably with them. She leaned on her cane more crookedly than usual, the expression behind her smile starting to pinch.

No wonder. She'd come nearly twenty miles on the back of a rickety produce wagon. If she weren't bruised spine to sternum he'd be surprised.

When Shursta broke through the ranks, Sharrar's smile wobbled and she stumbled into his arms.

"I think you need a nap, Nugget," he suggested.

"You're not mad?"

"I am very happy to see you." He kissed the top of her head. "Always."

"You won't send me away on the next milknut run?"

"I might if you insist on walking up those stairs." He looked at his mesh-brothers. His mouth tightened. He'd be drowned twice and hung out to dry before asking them for help.

Hyrryai appeared at his side, meeting his eyes in brief consultation. He nodded. She slung one of Sharrar's arms about her shoulders while Shursta took the other.

"Oh, hey," said Sharrar, turning her head to study the newcomer. "You must be the Gleaming One."

"And you," said Hyrryai, "must be my sister."

"I've always wanted a sister," Sharrar said meditatively. "But my mother—may she sleep forever with the sea people—said, so help her, two children were *enough* for one woman, and that was two more than strictly necessary. She was a schoolteacher," Sharrar explained. "Awfully smart. But I don't think she understood things like sisters. She had so many herself."

For a moment, Shursta thought Hyrryai's eyes had flooded. But then she smiled, a warmer expression on her face than any Shursta had yet seen. "Perhaps you won't think so highly of them once I start borrowing your clothes without asking."

"Damisel," Sharrar pronounced, "my rags are your rags. Help yourself."

There was a feast four days later for the youngest of Hyrryai's brothers.

"Dumwei," Sharrar reminded Shursta. "I don't know why you can't keep them all straight."

"I do not have your elasticity of mind," he retorted. "I haven't had to memorize all three hundred epics for the entertainment of the Hall of Ages."

"It's all about mnemonic tricks. Let's see. In order of age, there's Lochlin the Lunkhead, Arishoz the Unenlightened, Menami Meatbrain—then Hyrryai, of course, fourth in the birth order, but we all know what *her* name means, don't we, Shursta?—Orssi the Obscene, Plankin Porkhole and Dumwei the Dimwitted. How could you mix them up?"

By this time Shursta was laughing too hard to answer. When Hyrryai joined them, he flung himself back onto the couch cushions and put a pillow over his face. Now and again, a hiccup emerged from the depths.

"I've never seen him laugh before," Hyrryai observed. "What is the joke?"

"Oh," Sharrar said blithely, "I was just mentioning how much I like your brothers. Tell me, who is coming to the feast tonight?"

Hyrryai perched at the edge of the couch. "Everybody."

"Is Laric Spectrox coming?"

"Yes. Why? Do you know him?"

"Shursta mentioned him in a letter."

Shursta removed his pillow long enough to glare, but Sharrar ignored him.

"I was curious to meet him. Also, I was wondering . . . What is the protocol to join the Sing at the end of the feast? One of my trades is storyteller—as my brother has just reminded me—and I have recently memorized a brave tale that dearest Dumwei will adore. It is all about, oh, heroic sacrifice, bloody deeds and great feats, despair, rescue, celebration. That sort of thing."

Observing the mischief dancing in Sharrar's eyes, a ready spark sprang to Hyrryai's. "I shall arrange a place of honor for you in the Sing. This is most kind of you."

Groaning, Shursta swam up from the cushions again. "Don't trust her! She is up to suh—*hic*—uhmething. She will tell some wild tale about, about—farts and—and burps and—billygoats that will—*hic*—will shame your grandmother!"

"My grandmother has no shame." Hyrryai stood up from the edge of the couch. She never relaxed around any piece of furniture. She had to be up and pacing. Shursta, following her with his eyes, wondered how, and if, she ever slept. "Sharrar is welcome to tell whatever tale she deems fit. Do not be offended if I leave early. Oron Onyssix attends the feast tonight, and I mean to shadow him home."

At that, even Sharrar looked startled. "Why?"

Hyrryai grinned. It was not a look her enemies would wish to meet by moonlight.

"Of late the rumors are running that his appetite for hedonism has begun to extend to girls too young to be mesh-fit. I go tonight to confirm or invalidate these."

"Oh," said Sharrar. "You're hunting."

"I am hunting."

Shursta bit his lip. He did not say, "Be careful." He did not say, "I will not sleep until you return." He did not say, "If the rumors are true, then bring him to justice. Let the Astrion Council sort him out, trial and judgement. Even if he proves a monster, he may not be *your* monster, and don't you see, Hyrryai, whatever happens tonight, it will not be the end? That grief like yours does not end in something so simple as a knife in the dark?"

As if she heard, Hyrryai turned her grin on him. All the teeth around her throat grinned too.

"It *is* a nice necklace," Sharrar observed. "I told Shursta it was a poem."

The edges of Hyrryai's grin softened. "Your brother has the heart of a poet. And you the voice of one. We Blodestones are wealthy in our new kin." She turned to go, paused, then added over her shoulder, "Husband, if you drink a bowl of water upside-down, your hiccups may go away."

When she was gone, Sharrar nudged him. "Oohee, brother mine. I like her."

"Ayup, Nugs," he sighed. "Me too."

It was with trepidation that Shursta introduced his sister to Laric Spectrox that night at the feast. He need not have worried. Hearing his name, Sharrar laughed with delight and raised her brown eyes to his.

"Why, hey there! Domo Spectrox! You're not nearly as tall as Shursta made you out to be."

Laric straightened his shoulders. "Am I not?"

"Nope. The way he writes it, I thought to mistake you for a milknut tree. Shursta, you said skinny. It's probably all muscle, right? Wiry, right? Like me?" Sharrar flexed her free arm for him. Laric shivered a wink at Shursta and gravely admired her bicep. "Anyway, you're not too proud to bend down, are you?"

"I'm not!"

"Good! I have a secret I must tell you."

When Laric brought his face to her level, she seized him by both big ears and planted an enormous kiss on his mouth. Menami and Orssi Blodestone, who stood nearby, started whooping. Dumwei sidled close.

"Don't I get one? It's my birthday, you know."

Sharrar gave him a sleepy-eyed look that made Shursta want to hide under the table. "Just you wait till after dinner, Dumwei my darling. I have a special surprise for you." She shooed him along and bent all her attention back to Laric.

"You," she said.

He pointed to his chest a bit nervously. "Me?"

"You, Laric Spectrox. You are going to be my friend for the rest of my life. I decided that ages ago, so I'm very glad we finally got to meet. No arguments."

Laric's shining black face broke into a radiance of dimple creases and crooked white teeth. "Do you see me arguing? I'm not arguing."

"I'm Sharrar, by the way. Sit beside me tonight and let me whisper into your ear."

When Laric glanced at Shursta, Shursta shrugged. "She's going to try and talk you into doing something you won't want to do. I don't know what. Just keep saying no and refilling her plate."

"Does that really work?"

Shursta gave him a pained glance and did not answer.

Hyrryai came late to the feast and took a silent seat beside Shursta. He filled a plate and shoved it at her, as if she had been Sharrar, but when she only picked at it, he shrugged and went back to listening to Laric and Orssi arguing.

Orssi said, "The Nine Islands drowned and the Nine Cities with them. There are no other islands. There is no other land. We are alone on this world, and we must do our part to repeople it."

"No, no, see—" Laric gestured with the remnants of a lobster claw, "that lacks imagination. That lacks gumption. What do we know for sure? We know that something terrible happened in our great-great grandparents' day. What was it really? How can we know? We weren't born then. All we have are stories, stories the grayheads tell us in the Hall of Ages. I value these stories, but I will not build my life on them, as a house upon sand. We call ourselves the Glennemgarra, the Unchosen. Unchosen by what? By death? By the wave? By the magic of the gods that protected the Nine Holy Cities even as they drowned, so that they live still, at the bottom of the sea? Let there be a hundred cities beneath the waves. What do we care? We can't go there."

Laric glanced around at the few people who still listened to him.

"Do you know where we *can* go, though? Everywhere else. Anywhere. There is no law binding us to Droon—or to Sif—" he nodded at Sharrar, whose face was rapt with attention, "or anywhere on this wretched oasis. We know the wind. We know the stars. We have our boats and our nets and our water casks. There is no reason not to set out in search of something better."

"Well, cousin," said Orssi. "No one could accuse you of lacking imagination."

"Yes, Spectrox," cried Arishoz, "and how *is* your big boat project coming along?"

Laric's round eyes narrowed. "It would go more quickly if I had more hands to help me."

The Blodestone brothers laughed, though not ill-naturedly. "Find a wife, cousin," Lochlin advised him. "Breed her well. People the world with tiny Spectroxes—as if the world needed more Spectroxes, eh? Convince *them* to build your boat. What else are children for?"

Laric threw up his hands. He was smiling too, but all the creases in his forehead bespoke a sadness. "Don't you see? When my boat is finished I will sail away from words like that and thoughts like yours. As if women were only good for wives, and children were only made for labor."

Hyrryai raised her glass to him. Shursta reached over to fill it from the pitcher and watched as she drank deeply.

"I will help you, Laric Specrox!" Sharrar declared, banging her fists on the table. "I am good with my hands. I never went to sea with the men of Sif, but I can swim like a seal—and I'd trade my good leg for an adventure. Tell me all about your big boat."

He turned to her and smiled, rue twining with gratitude and defiance. "It is the biggest boat ever built. Or it will be."

"And what will you name her?"

"*The Grimgramal.* After the wave that changed the world."

Sharrar nodded, as if this were the most natural thing. Then she swung her legs off the bench, took up her cane, and pushed herself to her feet. Leaning against the table for support, she used her cane to pound the floor. When this did not noticeably diminish the noise in the hall, she set her forefinger and pinkie to her lips and whistled. Everyone, from the crone's table where the elders were wine-deep in gossip and politics, to the children's table where little cakes were being served, hushed.

Sharrar smiled at them. Shursta held his breath. But she merely invoked the Sing, bracing against a bench for support, then raising both fists above her head to indicate the audience should respond to her call.

"Grimgramal the Endless was the wave that changed the world."

Obediently, the hall repeated, "*Grimgramal the Endless was the wave that changed the world.*"

Sharrar began the litany that preceded all stories. Shursta relaxed again, smiling to himself to see Hyrryai absently chewing a piece of flatbread as she listened. His sister's tales, unlike Grimgramal, were not endless; they were mainly intended to please greyheads, who fell asleep after fifteen minutes or so. Sharrar's habit had been to practice her stories on her brother when he came in from a day out at sea and was so tired he could barely keep his eyes open. When he asked why she could not wait until morning when he could pay proper attention, she had replied that his exhaustion in the evening best simulated her average audience member in the Hall of Ages.

But Shursta had never yet fallen asleep while Sharrar told a story.

> "*The first city was Hanah and it fell beneath the sea*
> *The second city was Lahatiel, and it fell beneath the sea*
> *The third city was Ekesh, and it fell beneath the sea*
> *The fourth city was Var, and it fell beneath the sea*
> *The fifth city was Thungol, and it fell beneath the sea*
> *The sixth city was Yassam, and it fell beneath the sea*
> *The seventh city was Saheer, and it fell beneath the sea*
> *The eighth city was Gelph, and it fell beneath the sea*
> *The ninth city was Niniam, and it fell beneath the sea . . .* "

Sharrar ended the litany with a sweep of her hands, like a wave washing everything away. "But one city," she said, "did not fall beneath the sea." Again, her fists lifted. "That city was Droon!"

"*That city was Droon!*" the room agreed.

"That city was Droon, capital of the Last Isle. Now, on this island, there are many villages, though none that match the great city Droon. In one of these villages—in Sif, my own village—was born the hero of this tale. A young man, like the young men gathered here tonight. Like Dumwei whom we celebrate."

She did not need to coax a response this time. Cups and bowls and pitchers clashed.

"*Dumwei whom we celebrate!*"

"If our hero stood before you in this hall, humble as a Man of Sif might be before the Men of Droon, you would not say to your neighbor, your brother, your cousin, 'That young man is a hero.' But a hero he was born, a hero he became, a hero he'll remain, and I will tell you how, here and now."

Sharrar took her cane, moving it through the air like a paddle through water.

"The fisherfolk of Sif catch many kinds of fish. Octopus and squid, shrimp and crab. But the largest catch and tastiest, the feast to end all feasts, the catch that feeds a village—this is the bone shark."

"*The bone shark.*"

"It is the most cunning, the most frightening, the most beautiful of all the sharks. A long shark, a white shark, with a towering dorsal fin and a great jaw glistening with terrible teeth. This is the shark which concerns our hero. This is the shark that brought him fame."

"*This is the shark that brought him fame.*"

By this time, Sharrar barely needed to twitch a finger to elicit a response. The audience leaned in. All except Shursta, whose shoulders hunched, and Hyrryai, who drew her legs up onto the bench, to wrap her arms around her knees.

"To catch a shark you must first feed it. You must bloody the waters. You must send a slick of chum as sacrifice. For five days you must do this, until the sharks come tame to your boat. Then noose and net, you must grab it. Noose and net, you must drag it to the shore where it will die upon the sand. This is how you catch a shark."

"*This is how you catch a shark.*"

"One day, our hero was at sea. Many other men were with him, for the fishermen of Sif do not hunt alone. A man—let us call him Ghoul, for his sense of humor was necrotic—had brought along his young son for the first time. Now, Ghoul, he did not like our hero. Ghoul was a proud man. A strong man. A handsome man too, if you like that sort of man. He thought Sif had room for only one hero and that was Ghoul."

"*Ghoul!*"

"Ghoul said to his son, 'Son, why do we waste all this good chum to bait the bone shark? In the next boat over sits a lonesome feast. An unmeshed man whom no one will miss. Let us rock his boat a little, eh? Let us rock his boat and watch him fall in.'

"Father and son took turns rocking our hero's boat. Soon the other men of Sif joined in. Not all men are good men. Not all good men are good all the time. Not even in Droon. The waters grew choppy. The wind grew restless. The bone shark grew tired of waiting for his chum."

"The bone shark grew tired of waiting—"

"—Who can say what happened then? A wave too vigorous? The blow of a careless elbow as Ghoul bent to rock our hero's boat? A nudge from the muzzle of the bone shark? An act of the gods from the depths below? Who can know? But our hero saw the child. He saw Ghoul's young son fall into the sea. Like Gelph and Saheer, he fell into the sea. Like Ekesh and Var and Niniam he fell into the sea. Like Hanah and Lahatiel, Thungol and Yassam. Like the Nine Islands and all Nine Cities, the child fell."

"The child fell."

"The bone shark moved as only sharks can move, lightning through the water, opening its maw for the sacrifice. But then our hero was there. There in the sea. Between shark and child. Between death and the child. Our hero was there, treading water. There with his noose and his net. He had jumped from his boat. Jumped—where no man of Sif could push him, however hard they rocked his boat. Jumped to save this child. And he tangled the shark in his net. He lassoed the shark with his noose and lashed himself to that dreadful dorsal fin! Ghoul had just enough time to haul his son back into his boat. The shark began to thrash."

"The shark began to thrash."

"The shark began to swim."

"The shark began to swim."

"Our hero clung fast. Our hero held firm. Our hero herded that shark as some men herd horses. He brought that shark to land. He brought that shark onto the sand, where the shark could not breathe, and so it died. Thus our hero slew the bone shark. Thus our hero fed his village. Thus our hero rescued the child. He rescued the child."

"He rescued the child."

It was barely a whisper. Not an eye in that hall was dry.

"And that is the end of my tale."

Sharrar thumped her cane to the floor again. This time, the noise echoed in a resounding silence. But without giving even the most precipitous a chance to stir, much less erupt into the applause that itched in every sweaty palm present, Sharrar spun on her heel and glared at the table where the Blodestone brothers sat.

"It was Shursta Sarth slew the bone shark," she told them, coldly and deliberately. "Your sister wears its teeth around her neck. You are not worthy to call him brother. You are not worthy to sit at that table with him."

With that, she spat at their feet and stumped out of the room.

Shursta followed close behind, stumbling through bodies. Not daring to look up from his feet. Once free of the hall, he took a different corridor than the one Sharrar had stormed through. Had he caught her up, what would he have done to her? Thanked her? Scolded her? Shaken her? Thrown her out a window? He did not know.

However difficult or humiliating negotiating his new mesh-kin had been, Sharrar the Wise had probably just made it worse.

And yet . . .

And yet, how well she had done it. The Blodestones, greatest of the eight kinlines gathered together in one hall—and Sharrar had had them slavering. They would have eaten out of her hand. And what had she done with that hand? Slapped their faces. All six brothers of his new wife.

Shursta wanted his room. A blanket over his head. He wanted darkness.

When his door clicked open several hours later, Shursta jerked fully awake. Even in his half doze, he had expected some kind of retributive challenge from the Blodestone brothers. He wondered if they would try goading him to fight, now that they knew the truth about him. Well—Sharrar's version of the truth.

The mattress dipped near his ribs. He held his breath and did not speak. And when Hyrryai's voice came to him in the darkness, his heartrate skidded and began to hammer in his chest.

"Are you awake, Shursta?"

"Yes."

"Good." A disconsolate exhalation. He eased himself up to a sitting position and propped himself against the carven headboard.

"Did your hunting go amiss, Hyrryai?"

It was the first time he'd had the courage to speak her name aloud.

The sound she made was both hiss and plosive, more resigned than angry. "Oron Onyssix was arrested tonight by the soldiers of the Astrion Council. He will be brought to trial. I don't know—the crones, I think, got wind of my intentions regarding him. I track rumors; they, it seems, track me. In this case, they made sure to act before I did." She paused. "In this case, it might have been for the best. I was mistaken."

"Is he not guilty? With what, then, is he being charged?"

"The unsanctioned mentoring of threshold youths. That's what they're calling it."

She shifted. The mattress dipped again. Beneath the sheets, Shursta brought his hand to his heart and pressed it there, willing it to hush. Hush, Hyrryai is speaking.

"What does that mean?"

"It means Onyssix is not the man I'm hunting for!"

"How do you know?" he asked softly.

"Because . . ."

Shursta sensed, in that lack of light, Hyrryai making a gesture that cut the darkness into neat halves.

"Well, for one: the youths he prefers are *not*, after all, girls. A few young men came forward to bear witness. All were on the brink of mesh-readiness. Exploring themselves, each other. Coming of age. Usually the Astrion Council will assign such youths an older mentor to usher them into adulthood. One who will make sure the young people know that their duty as adult citizens of the Glennemgarra is to mesh and make children—no matter whom they may favor for pleasure or succor or lifelong companionship. That the privilege of preference is to be earned *after* meshing. There are rites. There is," her voice lilted mockingly, "paperwork. Onyssix sidestepped all of this. He will be fined. Watched a little more closely. Nothing else—there is no evidence of abuse. The young men did not speak of him with malice or fear. To them, he was just an older man with experience they wanted. I suppose it was a thrill to sneak around without the crones' consent. There you have it. Oron Onyssix is a reckless pleasure-seeker who thinks he's above the law. But hardly a murderer."

"I am sorry," Shursta murmured. "I wish it might have ended tonight."

From the way the mattress moved, he knew she had turned to look at him. Her hand was braced against the blankets. He could feel her wrist against his thigh.

"I wished it too." Hyrryai's voice was harsh. "All week I have anticipated . . . Some conclusion. The closing of this wound. I prepared myself. I was ready. I wanted to look my sister's killer in the eye and watch him confess. At banquet tonight, I wished it most—when Sharrar told her tale . . ."

"The Epic of Shursta Sharkbait? You should not believe all you hear. Especially if Sharrar's talking."

"I've heard tell of it before," she retorted. "Certainly, when the story reached the Astrion Council, it was bare of the devices Sharrar used to hold our attention. But it has not changed in its particulars. It is, in fact, one measure by which the Astrion Council assessed your reputed stupidity. Intelligent men do not go diving in shark-infested waters."

The broken knife in his throat was laughter. Shursta choked on it. "No, they don't. I told you that day we met—I am everything they say."

"You did not tell me *that* story. Strange," Hyrryai observed, "when you mentioned they called you Sharkbait, you left out the reason why."

Shursta pulled the blankets up around his chin. "You didn't mention it either. Maybe it's not worth mentioning."

"It is why I chose you."

All at once, he could not breathe. Hyrryai had leaned over him. One fist was planted on either side of his body, pinning the blankets down. Her forehead touched his. Her breath was on his mouth, sharp and fresh, as though she had been chewing some bitter herb as she stalked Onyssix through the darkness.

"Not because they said you were stupid, or ugly, or poor. How many men in Droon are the same? No, I chose you because they said you were good to your sister. And because you rescued the child."

"I rescued the child," Shursta repeated in a voice he could barely recognize.

Of course, he wanted to say. Of course, Hyrryai, that would move you. That would catch you like a bone hook where you bleed.

"Had you not agreed to come to Droon, I would have attended the muster to win you at games, Shursta Sarth."

He would have shaken his head, but could do nothing of his own volition to break her contact with him. "The moment we met, you sent me away. You said—you said you were mistaken . . . "

"I was afraid."

"Of *me*?" Shursta was shivering. Not with cold or fear but something more terrifying. Something perilously close to joy. "Hyrryai, surely you know by now—surely you can see—I am the last man anyone would fear. Believe Sharrar's story if you like, but . . . But consider it an aberration. It does not define me. Did I look like a man who wrestled sharks when your brothers converged on me? When the crones questioned me? When I could not even speak my vows aloud at our meshing? That is who I am. That's all I am."

"I know what you are."

Hyrryai sat back as abruptly as she had leaned in. Stood up from the bed. Walked to the door. "When my hunt is done, we shall return to this discussion. I shall not speak of it again until then. But . . . Shursta, I did not want you to pass another night believing yourself to be a man whom . . . whom no wife could love."

The latch lifted. The door clicked shut. She was gone.

The Blodestones took their breakfast in the courtyard under a stand of milknut trees. When Shursta stepped outside, he saw Laric, Sharrar and Hyrryai all lounging on the benches, elbows sprawled on the wooden table, heads bent together. They were laughing about something—even Hyrryai—and Shursta stopped dead in the center of the courtyard, wondering if they spoke of him. Sharrar saw him first and grinned.

"Shursta, you must hear this!"

He stepped closer. Hyrryai glanced at him. The tips of her fingers brushed the place beside her. Taking a deep breath, he came forward and sat. She slid him a plate of peeled oranges.

"Your sister," said Laric Spectrox, with his broad beaming grin, "is amazing."

"My sister," Shursta answered, "is a minx. What did you do, Nugget?"

"Nugget?" Laric repeated.

"Shursta!" Sharrar leaned over and snatched his plate away. "Just for that you don't get breakfast."

"Nugget?" Laric asked her delightedly. Sharrar took his plate as well. Hyrryai handed Shursta a roll.

"Friends," she admonished them. "We must not have dissension in the ranks. Not now that we've declared open war on my brothers."

Shursta looked at them all, alarmed. "You declared . . . *What did you do?*"

Sharrar clapped her hands and crowed, "We sewed them into their bedsheets!"

"You . . . "

"We did!" Laric assured him, rocking with laughter in his seat. "Dumwei, claiming his right as birthday boy, goaded his brothers into a drinking game. By midnight, all six of them were sprawled out and snoring like harvest hogs. So late last night . . . "

"This morning," Sharrar put in.

"This morning, Sharrar and Hyrryai and I . . . "

"*Hyrryai?*" Shursta looked at his mesh-mate. She would not lift her eyes to his, but the corners of her lips twitched as she tore her roll into bird-bite pieces.

" . . . Snuck into their chambers and sewed them in!"

Shursta hid his face in his hands. "Oh, by all the Drowned Cities in all the seas . . . "

Sharrar limped around the table to fling her arms about him. "Don't worry. No one will blame you. I made sure they'd know it was my idea."

He groaned again. "I'm afraid to ask."

"She signed their faces!" Laric threaded long fingers through his springy black hair. "I've not played pranks like this since I was a toddlekin. Or," he amended, "since my first-year wife left me for a man with more goats than brains."

Sharrar slid down beside him. "Laric, my friend—just *wait* till you hear my plans for the hoopball field!"

"Oh, the weeping gods . . . " Shursta covered his face again.

A knee nudged his knee. Hyrryai's flesh was warm beneath her linen trousers. He glanced at her between his fingers and she smiled.

"Courage, husband," she told him. "The best defense is offense. You never had brothers before, or you would know this. My brothers have been getting too sure of themselves. Three meshed already, their seeds gone for harvest, and they think they rule the world. Three of them recently come of age— brash, bold, considered prize studs of the market. Their heads are inflated like bladder balls."

Sharrar brandished her eating blade. "All it takes is a pinprick, my sweet ones!"

"Hush," Laric hissed. "Here come Plankin and Orssi."

The brothers had grim mouths, tousled hair, and murder in their bloodshot eyes. They had not bothered looking at themselves in the mirror that morning, for Sharrar's signature stood out bright and blue across their foreheads. Once they charged the breakfast table, however, they seemed uncertain upon whom they should fix their wrath. Sharrar had resumed her seat and was eating an innocent breakfast off three different plates. Laric kept trying to steal one of them back. Hyrryai's attention was wholly on the roll she decimated. Orssi glared at Shursta.

"Was it you, Sharkbait?" he demanded.

Shursta could still feel Hyrryai's knee pressed hard to his. His face flushed. His throat opened. He grinned at them both.

"Me, Shortsheets?" he asked. "Why, no. Of course not. I have minions to do that sort of thing for me."

He launched his breakfast roll into the air. It plonked Plankin right between the eyes. Unexpectedly, Plankin threw back his head, roaring out a laugh.

"Oh, hey," he said. "Breakfast! Thanks, brother."

Orssi, looking sly, made a martial leap and snatched the roll from Plankin's fingers. Yodeling victory, he took off running. With an indignant yelp, Plankin pelted after him. Hyrryai rolled her eyes. She reached across the table, took back the plate of oranges from Sharrar and popped a piece into Shursta's mouth before he could say another word. Her fingers brushed his lips, sticky with juice.

It did not surprise Shursta when, not one week later, Laric begged to have a word with him. "Privately," he said, "away from all these Blodestones. Come on, I'll take you to my favorite tavern. Very disreputable. No one of any note or name goes there. We won't be plagued."

Shursta agreed readily. He had not explored much of Droon beyond the family's holdings. Large as they were, they were starting to close in on him. Hyrryai's mother Dymorri had recently asked him whether a position as overseer of mines or of fields would better suit his taste. He had answered honestly that he knew nothing about either—and did the Blodestones have a fishing boat he might take out from time to time, to supply food for the family?

"Blodestones do not work the sea," she had replied, looking faintly amused.

Dymorri had high cheekbones, smooth rosy-bronze skin, and thick black eyebrows. Her hair was nearly white but for the single streak of black that started just off center of her hairline, and swept to the tip of a spiralling braid. Shursta would have been afraid of her, except that her eyes held the same sorrow permeating her daughter. He wondered if Kuista, the youngest Blodestone, had taken after her. Hyrryai had more the look of her grandmother, being taller and rangier, with a broader nose and wider mouth, black eyes instead of brown.

"Fishing's all I know," he'd told her.

"Hyrryai will teach you," she had said. "Think about it. There is no hurry. You have not been meshed a month."

True to his word, Laric propelled him around Droon, pointing out landmarks and places of interest. Shops, temples, old bits of wall, parks, famous houses, the seat of the Astrion Council. It was shaped like an eight-sided star, built of sparkling white quartz. Three hundred steps led up to the entrance, each step mosaiced in rainbow spirals of shell.

"Those shells came from the other Nine Islands," Laric told him. "When there were nine other islands."

"And you think there might be more?"

Laric cocked his ear for the hint of derision that usually flavored such questions. "I think," he answered slowly, "that there is more to this world than islands."

"Even if there isn't," Shursta sighed, "I wouldn't mind leaving this one. Even for a little while. Even if it meant nothing but stars and sea and a wooden boat forever."

"Exactly!" Laric clapped him on the back. "Ah, here we are. The Thirsty Seagull."

Laric Spectrox had not lied about the tavern. It was so old it had hunkered into the ground. The air was rank with fermentation and tobacco smoke. All the beams were blackened, all the tables scored with the graffitti of raffish nobodies whose names would never be sung, whose deeds would never be known, yet who had carved proof of their existence into the wood, as if to say, "Here, at least, I shall be recognized." Shursta fingered a stained, indelicate knife mark, feeling like his heart would break.

Taking a deep, appreciative breath, Laric pronounced, "Like coming home. Sit, sit. Let me buy you a drink. Beer?"

"All right," Shursta agreed, and sat, and waited. When Laric brought back the drinks, he sipped, and watched, and waited. The bulge in Laric's narrow throat bobbled. There was a sheen of sweat upon his brow. Shursta lowered his eyes, thinking Laric might find his task easier if he were not being watched. It seemed to help.

"Your sister," Laric began, "is . . . "

Shursta took a longer drink.

"Wonderful."

"Yes," Shursta agreed. He chanced to glance up. Laric was looking anywhere but at him, gesturing with his long hands.

"How is it that she wasn't snatched up by some clever fellow as soon as she came of age?"

"Well," Shursta pointed out, "she only recently did."

"I know, but . . . But in villages like Sif—small villages, I mean, well, even in Droon—surely some sparky critter had an eye on her these many years. Someone who grew up with her. Someone who thought, 'Soon as that Sarth girl casts her lure, I'll make damn sure I'm the fish for that hook! Take bait and line and pole and girl and dash for the far horizon . . . "

Shursta cleared his throat. "Hard to dash with a game leg."

Laric plunked down from the high altitude of his visions. "Pardon?"

"Hard to run off with a girl who can't walk without a cane." Shursta studied Laric, who in turn tried to read the careful deadpan of his face. "And then, what if her children are born crooked? You'd be polluting your line. Surely the Spectroxes are taunted enough without introducing little lame Sharrar Sarth into the mix. Aren't you afraid what your family will say?"

"*Damisel* Sharrar Sarth," Laric corrected him stiffly, emphasizing the honorific. He tried to govern his voice. "And . . . And any Spectrox who does not want to claim wit and brilliance and derring-do and that glorious bosom for kin can eat my . . . "

Shursta clinked his mug to Laric's. "Relax. Sharrar has already told me she is going to elope with you on your big wooden boat. Two days after she met you. She said she'd been prepared to befriend you, but had not thought to be brought low by your, how did she put it, incredible height, provocative fingers and . . . adorable teeth." He coughed. "She went on about your teeth at some length. Forgive me if I don't repeat all of it. I'm sure she's composed a poem about them by now. If you find a proposal drummed up in couplets and shoved under your door tonight, you'll have had time to prepare your soul."

The look on Laric's face was beyond the price of gemmajas. He reached his long arms across the table and pumped Shursta's hand with both of his, and Shursta could not help laughing.

"Now, my friend," he said. "Let *me* buy *you* a drink."

It was at the bar Shursta noticed the bleak man in the corner. He looked as if he'd been sitting there so long that dust had settled over him, that lichen had grown over him, that spiders had woven cobwebs over his weary face. The difference between his despair and Laric's elation struck Shursta with the force of a blow, and he asked, when he returned to Laric's side, who the man might be.

"Ah." Laric shook his head. "That's Myrar Yaspir, poor bastard."

"Poor bastard?" Shursta raised his eyebrows, inviting more. It was this same dark curiosity, he recognized, that had made him press Hyrryai for details about Kuista's death the first day they met. He was unused to considering himself a gossip. But then, he thought, he'd had no friends to gossip with in Sif.

"Well." Laric knocked back a mouthful. His gaze wandered up and to the right. Sharrar once told Shursta that you could always tell when someone was reaching for a memory, for they always looked up and to the right. He'd seen the expression on her face often as she memorized a story.

"All right. I guess it began when he meshed with Adularia Yaspir three years ago. Second mesh-rite for both. No children on either side. He courted her for nearly a year. You could see by his face on their meshing day that there was a man who had pursued the dream of a lifetime. That for him, this was not about the Yaspir name or industry or holdings, but about a great burning love that would have consumed him had he not won it for his own. Adularia—well. I think she wanted children. She liked him enough. You could see the pink in her cheeks, the glow in her eyes on her meshing day. And you thought—if any couple's in it past the one year mesh-mark, this is that couple. It's usually that way for second meshings. You know."

Shursta nodded.

"So the first year passes. No children. The second year passes. No children. Myrar starts coming here more often. Drinking hard. Talk around Droon was that Adularia wanted to leave him. He was arrested once for brawling. A second time, on more serious charges, for theft."

"Really?" Shursta watched from the corner of his eye, the man who sat so still flies landed on him.

"Not just any theft . . . Gems from the Blodestone mines."

Shursta loosed a low whistle. "Diamonds?"

"Not even!" Laric leaned in. "Semi-precious stones, uncut, unpolished. Not even cleaned yet. Just a handful of green chalcedonies, like the one you're wearing."

The breath left Shursta's body. He touched the stone hanging from his ear. He remembered suddenly how Kuista Blodestone's gemmaja had come up missing on her person, how that one small detail had so disturbed him that he had admonished his sister to hide her own upon her person, as if the red-speckled stone were some amulet of death. He opened his mouth. His throat clicked a few times before it started working.

"Why . . . why would he take such a thing?"

Shrugging, Laric said, "Don't know. They made him return them all, of course. He spent some time in the stocks. Had to beg his wife to take him back. Promised her the moon, I heard. Stopped drinking. But she said that if she was not pregnant by winter, she'd leave him, and that was that."

"What happened?"

"A few months later, she was pregnant. There was great rejoicing." Laric finished his drink. "Of course, none of us were paying much attention to the Yaspirs at that time, because we were all still grieving for Kuista."

"Kuista. Kuista Blodestone?"

Laric looked at Shursta, perturbed, as if to ask, *Who else but Kuista Blodestone?*

"Yes. We burned her pyre not a month before Adularia announced her pregnancy. Hyrryai was still bedridden. She didn't leave the darkness of her room for six months."

"And the child?" Shursta's mouth tasted like dried out fish scales.

"Stillborn. Delivered dead at nine months." Laric sighed. "Adularia has gone back to live with her sister. Sometimes Myrar shows up for work at the chandlery, sometimes not. Owner's his kin, so he's not been fired yet. But I think that the blood is thinning to water on one end, if you know what I mean."

"Yes," said Shursta, who was no longer listening. "I . . . Laric, please . . . Please excuse me."

Shursta had no memory of leaving the Thirsty Seagull, or of walking clear across Droon and leaving the city by the sea road gates. He saw nothing, heard nothing, the thoughts boiling in his head like a cauldron full of viscera. He felt sick. Gray. Late afternoon, evening, and the early hours of night he passed in that lonely cove where Kuista died. Where he had met Hyrryai. Long past the hour most people had retired, he trudged wearily back to the Blodestone house. Sharrar awaited him in the courtyard, sitting atop the breakfast table, bundled warmly in a shawl.

"You're back!"

When his sister made as if to go to him, Shursta noticed she was stiff from sitting. He waved her down, joined her on the tabletop. She clasped his cold hand, squeezing.

"Shursta, it's too dark to see your face. Thunder struck my chest when Laric told me how you left him. Are you all right? What died in you today?"

"Kuista Blodestone," he whispered.

Sharrar was silent. She was, he realized, waiting for him to explain. But he could not.

"Sharrar," he said wildly, "Wise Sharrar, if stones could speak, what would they say?"

"Nothing quickly," she quipped, her voice strained. Shursta knew her ears were pricked to any clue he might let fall. Almost, he saw a glow about her skull as her riddle-raveling brain stoked itself to triple intensity. However he tried, he could not force his tongue to speak in anything more clear than questions.

"What does a stone possess other than . . . its stoneness? If not for wealth . . . or rarity . . . or beauty—why would someone covet . . . a hunk of rock?"

"Oh!" Sharrar's laughter was too giddy, almost fevered, with relief. She knew this answer. "For its magic, of course!"

"Magic."

It was not a common word. Not taboo—like incest or infanticide or cannibalism—but not common. Magic had drowned, it was said, along with the Nine Cities.

"Ayup." Sharrar talked quickly, her hand clamped to his, as if words could staunch whatever she thought to be his running wound. "See, in the olden days before the wave that changed the world, there was magic everywhere. Magic fish. Magic birds. Magic rivers. Magic . . . magicians. Certain gems, saith the grayheads, were also magic. A rich household would name itself for a powerful gem, so as to endow its kinline with the gem's essence. So, for instance, of the lost lines, there is Adamassis, whose gem was diamond, said to call the lightning. A stormy household, as you can imagine—quite impetuous—weather workers. The Anabarrs had amber, the gem of health, the gem that holds the sun, said to wake even the dead. Dozens more like this. Much of the lore was lost to us when the Nine Islands drowned. Of the remaining kinlines, let me think . . . The Sarths have sard—like the red carnelian—that can reverse the effects of poison. Onyssix wears onyx, to ward off demons. The jasper of the Yaspirs averts the eyes of an enemy . . . "

"And the Blodestones?" Shursta withdrew his hand from her stranglehold only to grip the soft flesh of her upper arm. "The Blodestones wear green chalcedony . . . Why? What is this stone?"

"Fertility," Sharrar gasped. Shursta did not know if she were frightened or in pain. "The green chalcedony—the bloodstone—will bring life to a barren womb. If a man crushes it to powder and drinks it, he will stand to his lover for all hours of the night. He will flood her with the seed of springtime. Shursta . . . Why are you asking me this, Shursta? Shursta, please . . . "

He had already sprinted from the courtyard. Faintly and far behind him, he heard the cry, "Let me come with you!"

He did not stop.

The Thirsty Seagull was seedier by night than by day. Gadabouts and muckrakes, sailors, soldiers, fisherfolk, washing women, street sweepers, lamplighters and red lamplighters of all varieties patronized the tavern. There were no tables free, so Shursta made his way to the last barstool.

Shursta did not have to pretend to stumble or slur. His head ached and he saw only through a distortion, as if peering through a sheet of water. But words poured freely from his mouth. None of them true, or mostly not true. Lies like Sharrar could tell. Dark lies, coming from depths within him he had never yet till this night sounded.

"*Women!*" he announced in a bleared roar. "Pluck you, pluck you right up from your comfy home. Job you like. Job you know. People you know. Pluck you up and say, it's meshing time. Little mesh-mesh. Come to bed, dear. No, you stink of fish, Shursta. Wash your hands, Shursta. Oh, your breath is like a dead squid, Shursta. Don't do it open-mouthed, Shursta. Shursta, you snore, go sleep in the next room. I mean, who are these people? These *Blodestones*? Who do they think they are? In Sif—in Sif at least the women know how to use their hands. I mean, they *know* how to use their hands, you know? And all this talk, talk, talk . . . All this whining and complaining . . . All this saying I'm not good enough. What does she expect, a miracle? How can a man function, how can he *function* in these circumstances? How can he rise to the occasion, eh? Eh?"

Shursta nudged the nearest patron, who gave him a curled lip and turned her back on him. Sneering at her shoulderblades, Shursta muttered, "You're probably a Blodestone, eh? *All women are kin.* Think that's what a man's about, eh? Think that's all he is? A damned baby maker? Soon's you have your precious daughters, your bouncing boys, you forget all about us. Man's no good to you till he gets you pissful of those shrieking, wailing, mewling, shitting little shit machines? Eh? Well, what if he can't? What if he cannot—is he not still a man? *Is he not still a man?*"

By now the barkeep of the Thirsty Seagull was scowling black daggers at him. Someone shoved Shursta from behind. He spun around with fists balled up. Nobody was there.

"Eh," he spat. "Probably a Blodestone."

When he turned back to the bar, a hand slid a drink over to him. Shursta drank before looking to see who had placed it there.

Myrar Yaspir stared at him with avid eyes.

"Don't know you," Shursta mumbled. "Thanks for the nog. Raise my cup. Up. To you. Oh . . . It's empty." He slammed it down. "Barkeep, top her up. Spill her over. Fill her full. Come on, man. Don't be a Blodestone."

Amber liquid splashed over the glass's rim.

"You're the new Blodestone man," Myrar Yaspir whispered. "You're Damisel Hyrryai's new husband."

Shursta snarled. "Won't be her husband once my year's up. She'll be glad to see the back of me. Wretch. Horror. Harpy. Who needs her? Who wants her?" He began to blubber behind shaking hands. "Oh, but by all the gods below! How she gleams. How she catches the light. How will I live without her?"

A coin clinked down. Bottle touched tumbler. Myrar's whisper was like a naked palm brushing the sandpaper side of a shark.

"Are you having trouble, Blodestone man? Trouble in the meshing bed?"

"Ayup, trouble," Shursta agreed, not raising his snot-streaked face. "Trouble like an empty sausage casing. Trouble like . . . "

"Yes, trouble," Myrar cut him off. "Yet you sit here. You sit here drunk and stupid—you. You of all men. You, whose right as husband gives you access to that household. Don't you see, you stupid Blodestone man?" His hand shot out to grab Shursta's ear. The cartilage gave a twinge of protest, but Shursta set his teeth. When Myrar's hand came back, he cradled Shursta's gemmaja in his palm.

"Do you know what this is?"

Shursta burped. "Ayup. Green rock. Wife gave me. Wanna see my coral?" He fished for the cord beneath his shirt. "True Sarths wear carnelian, she says. Carnelian's the stone for Sarths. You ask me, coral's just as good. Hoity-toity rich folk."

"Not rock. This—is—not—*rock*," Myrar hissed. His fingers clenched and unclenched around the green chalcedony. By the dim light of the wall sconces, Shursta could barely make out the red speckles in the stone, like tiny drops of blood.

"This is your *child*. This is the love of your wife. This is life. *Life*, Blodestone man. Do you understand?" Myrar Yaspir scooted his stool closer. His breath was cold, like the inside of a tomb. "I was you once. Low. A cur who knew it was beaten. Beaten by life. By work. By women. By those haughty, high-nosed Blodestone bastards who own more than half this island and mean to marry into the other half, until there is nothing left for the rest of us. But last thing before he died, my grandad sat me down. Said he knew I was unhappy. Knew my . . . my Adularia wept at night for want of a child. He had a thing to tell me. A thing about stones."

Dull-eyed, Shursta blinked back at him.

"Stones," he repeated.

"Yes. Stones. Magic stones. So." Myrar Yaspir set the green chalcedony tenderly, even jealously, into Shursta's palm. "Take your little rock home with you, Blodestone man. Put it in a mortar—not a wooden one. A fine one, of marble. Take the best pestle to it. Grind it down. Grind it to powder. Drink it in a glass of wine—the Blodestone's finest. They have fine wine in that house. Drink it. Go to your wife. Don't listen to her voice. Her voice doesn't matter. When she sees how you come to her, her thighs will sing. Her legs will open to you. Make her eat her words. Pound her words back into her. Get her with that child. Who knows?" Myrar Yaspir sank back down, his eyes losing that feral light. "Who knows. It may gain you another year. What more can a man ask, whose wife no longer loves him? Just one more year. It's worth it."

All down his gullet, the amber drink burned. In another minute, Shursta knew, he would lose it again, vomiting all over himself. He swallowed hard. Then he bent his head to the man beside him, who had become bleak and still and silent once more, and asked, very softly:

"Was it worth the life of Kuista Blodestone? Myrar Yaspir, was it worth the death of a child?"

If cold rock could turn its head, if rock could turn the fissures of its eyes upon a living man, this rock was Myrar Yaspir.

"What did you say?"

"My wife is hunting for you."

Myrar Yaspir became flesh. Flinched. Began to shudder. Shursta did not loose him from his gaze.

"I give you three days, Domo Yaspir. Turn yourself in to the Astrion Council. Confess to the murder of Kuista Blodestone. If you do not speak by the third day, I will tell my wife what I know. And she will find you. Though you flee from coast to bay and back again, she will find you. And she will eat your heart by moonlight."

Glass shattered. A stool toppled. Myrar Yaspir fled the Thirsty Seagull, fast as his legs could carry him.

Shursta closed his eyes.

The next three days were the happiest days of Shursta's life, and he drank them in. It was as if he, alone of all men, had been given to know the exact hour of his death. He filled the hours between himself and death with sunlight.

For the first day, Sharrar watched him as the sister of a dying man watches her brother. But his smiles and his teasing—"Leave off, Nugget, or I'll teach Laric where you're ticklish!"—and the deep brilliance of peace in his eyes must have eased her, for on the second day, her spirits soared, and she was back to playing tricks on her mesh-brothers, and kissing Laric Spectrox around every corner and under every tree, and reciting stories and singing songs to the children of the house.

Hyrryai, who still prowled Droon every night, spent her days close to home. She invited Shursta to walk with her, along paths she knew blindfolded. He asked her to teach him about spinning fire and she said, "Let's start with juggling maybe," and taught him patterns with handfuls of fallen fruit.

Suppers with the Blodestones were loud and raucous. Every night turned into a competition. Some Shursta won (ring tossing out in the courtyard) and some he lost (matching drinks with Lochlin, now known to all—thanks to Sharrar—as Lunkhead), but he laughed more than he ever had in his life, and when he laughed, he felt Hyrryai watching him, and knew she smiled.

On evening of the third day, he evaded his brothers' invitation to play hoopball. Sharrar immediately volunteered—so long as she and Laric could count as one player. She would piggyback upon his shoulders, and he would be her legs. Plankin, Orssi and Dumwei were still vehemently arguing against this when Shursta approached his mesh-mate and set a purple hyacinth into her hands.

"Will you walk with me, wife?"

Her rich, rare skin flushed with the heat of roses. She took the hand he offered.

"I will, husband."

They strolled out into the scented night, oblivious to the hoots and calls of their kin. Their sandals made soft noises on the pavement. For many minutes, neither spoke. Hyrryai tucked the hyacinth into her hair.

An aimless by and by had passed when they came to a small park. Just a patch of grass, a bench, a fountain. As they had when they met, they sat on the ground with their backs to the bench. Hyrryai, for once, slumped silkily, neglecting to jolt upright every few minutes. When Shursta sank down to rest his head in her lap, her hand went to his hair. She stroked it from his face, traced designs on his forehead. He did not care that he forgot to breathe. He might never breathe again and die a happy man.

The moon was high, waxing gibbous. To Shursta's eyes, Hyrryai seemed chased in silver. He reached to catch the fingers tangled in his hair. He kissed her fingertips. Sat up to face her. Her smile was silver when she looked at him.

"The name of your sister's murderer is Myrar Yaspir," he said in a low voice. "I met him in a tavern at the edge of Droon. He had three day's grace to confess his crime to the Astrion Council. Let them have him, I thought, they who made him. But when I spoke to your grandmother before dinner, she said no one had yet come forward. I believe he decided to run. I am sorry."

The pulse in her throat beat an inaudible but profound tattoo through the night air.

To an unconcerned eye, nothing of Hyrryai would have seemed changed. Still she was silver in the moonlight. Still the purple flower glimmered against her wing-black hair. Only her breath was transformed. Inhalation and exhalation exactly matched. Perfect and total control. The pale light playing on her mouth did not curve gently upward. Her eyes stared straight ahead, unblinking sinkholes. The gleam in them was not of moonlight.

"You have known this for three days."

Shursta did not respond.

"You talked to him. You warned him."

Again, he said nothing. She answered anyway.

"He cannot run far enough."

"Hyrryai."

"*You—do—not—speak—to—me.*"

"Hyrryai—"

"No!"

Her hand flashed out, much as Myrar Yaspir's had. She took nothing from him but flesh. Fingernails raked his face. Shursta did not, at first, suffer any sting. What he did feel, way down at the bottom of his chest, was a deep snap as she broke the strand of pearl and teeth and stone she wore around her throat. Pieces of moonlight scattered. Fleet and silver as they, Hyrryai Blodestone bounded into the radiant darkness.

One by one—by glint, by ridge, by razor edge—Shursta picked up pieces from the tufted grass. What he could salvage, he placed in the pouch he had prepared. His rucksack he retrieved from the hollow of a tree where he had hidden it the night before. The night was young, but the road to Sif was long.

Despite having begged her in his goodbye letter to go on and live her life in joy, with Laric Spectrox and his dream of a distant horizon, far from a brother who could only bring her shame and sorrow, Sharrar came home to Sif. And when she did, she did not come alone.

She brought her new husband. She brought a ragged band of orphans, grayheads, widows, widowers. Joining her too were past-primers like Adularia Yaspir, face lined and eyes haunted. Even Oron Onyssix had joined them, itching for spaces ungoverned by crones, a place where he might breathe freely.

Sharrar also brought a boat.

It was a very large boat. Or rather, the frame of it. It was the biggest boat skeleton Shursta had ever seen. They wheeled it on slats all the way along the searoad from the outskirts of Droon where Laric had been building it. Shursta, who had thought he might never do so again, laughed.

"What is this, Nugget? Who are all these people?"

But he thought he knew.

"These," she told him, "are all our new kin. And this—" with a grand gesture to the unfinished monstrosity listing on its makeshift wagon, "is Grimgramal—the ship that sails the world!"

Shursta scrutinized it and said at last, "It doesn't look like much, your ship that sails the world."

Sharrar stuck her tongue out at him. "We have to *finish* it first, brother mine!"

"Ah."

"Everyone's helping. You'll help too."

Shursta stared at all the people milling about his property, pitching tents, lining up for the outhouse, exploring the dock, testing the sturdiness of his small fishing boat. "Will I?" he asked. "How?"

Laric came over to clap him on the shoulder. "However you can, my mesh-brother. Mend nets. Hem sails. Boil tar. Old man Alexo Alban is carving us a masthead. He says it's a gift from all the Halls of Ages on the Last Isle to Sharrar." Taking his mesh-mate's hand, he indicated the dispersed crowd. "She's the one who called them. She's been speaking the name Grimgramal to anyone who'll stand still to listen. And you know Sharrar—when she talks, no one can help but listen. Some sympathizers—a very few—like Alexo Alban, started demanding passage in exchange for labor. Though," his left shoulder lifted in a gesture eloquent of resignation, "most of the grayheads say they'll safe stay on dry land to see us off. Someone, they claim, must be left behind to tell the tale. And see?"

Laric dipped into his pocket, spilling out a palmful of frozen rainbows. Shursta reached to catch a falling star before it buried itself in the sand. A large, almost bluish, diamond winked between his fingers. Hastily, he returned it.

"Over the last few weeks, the grayheads have been coming to Sharrar. Some from far villages. Even a few crones of the Astrion Council—including Dymmori Blodestone. Each gave her a gem, and told her the lore behind it. Whatever is known, whatever has been surmised. Alexo Alban will embed them in the masthead like a crown. Nine Cities magic to protect us on our journey."

Shursta whistled through his teeth. "We're really going then?"

"Oh, yes," Sharrar said softly. "All of us. Before summer's end."

It was not to Rath Sea that Shursta looked then, but to the empty road that led away from Sif.

"*All* of us," Sharrar repeated. "You'll see."

Dumwei Blodestone arrived one afternoon, drenched from a late summer storm, beady-eyed with irritation and chilled to the bone.

"Is Sif the last village of the world? What a stupid place. At the end of the stupidest road. Mudholes the size of small islands. Swallow a horse, much less a man. Sharkbait, why do you let your roof leak? How can you expect to cross an ocean in a wooden boat when you can't even be bothered to fix a leaky roof? We'll all be drowned by the end of the week."

"We?" Sharrar asked brightly, slamming a bowl of chowder in front of him. "Are you planning on going somewhere, Dimwit?"

"Of course!" He glanced at her, astonished, and brandished a spoon in her face. "You don't really think I'm going to let you mutants have all the fun, do you? Orssi wanted to come too, but now he's got a girl. Mesh-mad, the pair of 'em."

His gaze flickered to the corner where Oron Onyssix sat carving fishhooks from antler and bone. Onyssix raised his high-arched eyebrows. Dumwei looked away.

With a great laugh, Laric broke a fresh loaf of bread in two and handed the larger portion to Dumwei.

"Poor Orssi. You'll just have to have enough adventure for the two of you."

Dumwei's chest expanded. "I intend to, Laric Spectrox!"

"Laric Sarth," he corrected.

"Oh, yes, that's right. Forgot. *Maybe* because you didn't *invite* me to your *meshing*."

"Sorry," the couple said in unison, sounding anything but.

"And speaking of impossible mesh-mates . . . " Dumwei turned to Shursta, who knelt on the floor, feeding the firepit. "My sister wants to see you, Shursta."

For a moment, none of the dozen or so people crammed in the room breathed. Dumwei did not notice. Or if he noticed, he did not care.

"Mumsa won't talk about her, you know. Well, she talks, but only to say things like, if her last living daughter wants to run off like a wild dog and file her teeth and declare herself *windwyddiam*, that's Hyrryai's decision. Maybe no one will care then, she says, when she declares herself a mother with six sons and no daughters. And then she cries. And granmumsa and Auntie Elbanni and Auntie Ralorra all cluck their tongues and huddle close, and it's all hugs and tears and clacking, and a man can't hear himself think."

Shursta, who had not risen from his knees, comprehended little of this. If he'd held a flaming brand just then instead of ordinary wood, he might not have heeded it.

Sharrar asked, carefully, "Have you seen Hyrryai then, Dumwei?"

"Oh, ayup, all the time. She ran off to live in a little sea cave, in the . . . *That* cove." Dumwei seemed to swallow the wrong way, though he had not started eating. Quickly, he ducked his head, inspecting his chowder as if for contaminants. When he raised his face again, his eyes were overbright. "You know . . . You know, Kuista was just two years younger than I. Hyrryai was like her second mumsa, maybe, but I was her best friend. Anyway. I hope Hyrryai does eat that killer's heart!"

In the corner of the room, Adularia Yaspir turned her face to the wall and closed her eyes.

Dumwei shrugged. "I hope she eats it and spits it out again for chum. A heart like Myrar Yaspir's wouldn't make anyone much of meal. As she's cast herself out of the kinline, Hyrryai has no roof or bed or board of her own.

And you can only eat so much fish. So I bring her food. It's not like they don't know back home. Granmumsa slips me other things, too, that Hyrryai might need. Last time I saw her . . . Yesterday? Day before?" He nodded at Shursta. "She asked for you."

Shursta sprang to his feet. "I'll go right now."

But Sharrar and Laric both grabbed fistfuls of Shursta's shirt and forced him down again.

"You'll wait till after the storm," said Laric.

"And you'll eat first," Sharrar put in.

"And perhaps," suggested Oron Onyssix from the corner, "you might wash your face. Dress in a clean change of clothes. Shave. What are they teaching young husbands these days?"

Dumwei snorted. "Think you can write that manual, Onyssix?"

"In my sleep," he replied, with the ghost of his reckless grin. Dumwei flushed past his ears, but he took his bowl of chowder and went to sit nearer him.

Obedient to his sister's narrowed eyes, Shursta went through the motions of eating. But as soon as her back was turned, he slipped out the front door.

It was full dark when Shursta finally squelched into the sea cave. He stood there a moment, dripping, startled at the glowing suddenness of shelter after three relentlessly rainy hours on the sea road. There was a hurricane lamp at the back of the cave, tucked into a small natural stone alcove. Its glass chimney was sooty, its wick on the spluttering end of low. What Shursta wanted most was to collapse. But a swift glance around the flickering hollow made it clear that amongst the neatly stacked storage crates, bedroll, the tiny folding camp table, the clay oven with its chimney near the cave mouth, the stockpile of weapons leaning in one corner, Hyrryai was not there.

He closed his eyes briefly. Wiping a wet sleeve over his wet face, Shursta contemplated stripping everything, wrapping himself in one of her blankets and waiting for her while he dried out. She hadn't meant to be gone long, he reasoned; she left the lamp burning. And there was a plate of food, half-eaten. Something had disturbed her. A strange sound, cutting through the wind and rain and surf. Or perhaps a face. Someone who, like he had done, glimpsed the light from her cave and sought shelter of a fellow wayfarer.

Already trembling from the cold, now Shursta's shivers grew violent, as if a hole had been bored into the bottom of his skull and was slowly filling his spine with ice water. Who might be ranging abroad on such a night? The sick or deranged, the elderly or the very young. The desperate, like himself. The outcasts, like Hyrrai. And the outlaws: lean, hungry, hunted. But why should they choose *this* cove, of all the crannies and caverns of the Last Isle?

Why this so particular haunted place, on such a howling night? Other than Hyrryai herself, Shursta could think of just one who'd have cause to come here. Who would be drawn here, inexorably, by ghosts or guilt or gloating.

His stomach turned to stone, his knees to mud. He put his hand on the damp wall to steady himself.

And what would Hyrryai have done, glancing up from her sad little supper to meet the shadowed, harrowed eyes of her sister's killer?

She would not have thought to grab her weapons. Or even her coat. Look, there it was, a well-oiled sealskin, draped over the camp stool. Her fork was on the floor there by the bedroll, but her dinner knife was missing.

Shursta bolted from the cave, into the rain.

The wind tore strips from the shroud of the sky. Moonlight splintered through, fanged like an anglerfish and as cold. Shurta slipped and slid around the first wall of boulders and began to clamber back up the stone steps to the sea road. He clutched at clumps of marram grass, which slicked through his fingers like seaweed. Wet sand and crumbled rock shifted beneath his feet. Gasping and drenched as he was, he clung to his claw-holds, knowing that if he fell he'd have to do it all over again. He'd almost attained the headland, had slapped first his left hand onto the blessedly flat surface, was following it by his right, meaning to beach himself from the cliff face onto the road in one great heave and lie there awhile, catching his breath, when a hand grasped his and hauled him up the rest of the way.

"Domo Blodestone!" gasped Myrar Yaspir. "You must help me. Your wife is hunting me."

The first time Shursta had seen Yaspir, he had looked like a man turned to stone and forgotten. The second time, his eyes had been livid as enraged wounds. Now he seemed scoured, nervous and alive, wet as Shursta. He wore an enormous rucksack and carried a walking stick which Shursta eyed speculatively. It had a smooth blunt end, well polished from age and handling.

"Is that how you killed Kuista Blodestone?" he blurted.

Myrar Yaspir followed his gaze. "This?" he asked, blankly. "No, it was a stone. I threw it into the sea, after." He grasped Shursta's collar and hefted. Myrar Yaspir was a ropy, long-limbed man whose bones seemed to poke right through his skin, but rather than attenuated, he seemed vigorously condensed, and his strength was enormous, almost electrical. Hauled to his feet, Shursta felt as though a piece of mortal-shaped lightning had smote down upon the Last Isle just to manhandle him. "Come," he commanded Shursta. "We must keep moving. She is circling us like a bone shark, closer, ever closer. Come, Domo Blodestone," he said again, blinking back rain from his burning eyes. "You must help me."

Shursta disengaged himself, though he felt little shocks go through him when his wrists knocked Myrar Yaspir's fists aside. "I already helped you, child-killer. I gave you three days to turn yourself into the Astrion Council. I am done with you."

Myrar Yaspir glanced at him, then shook his head. "You are not listening to me," he said with exasperated patience. "Your wife is hunting me. I will be safe nowhere on this island. Not here and not in Droon cowering in some straw cage built by those doddering bitches of the council." He bent his head close to Shursta's and whispered, "No, you must take me to Sif where you live. Word is you are sailing from this cursed place on a boat the size of a city. I will work for my passage. I work hard. I have worked all my life." He opened his hands as if to show the calluses there; as if, even empty, they had always been enough.

Shursta felt his voice go gentle, and could not prevent it, although he knew Myrar Yaspir would think him weakening.

"The Grimgrimal is the size, maybe, of a large house, and we who will sail on it are family. You, Domo Yaspir, are no one's family."

"My wife is on that boat!" Myrar flashed, his fist grasping the sodden cloth at Shursta's throat. His expression flickered from whetted volatility to bleak cobweb-clung despair, and after that, it seemed, he could express nothing because he no longer had a face. His was merely a sand-blasted and sun-bleached skull, dripping dark rain. The skull whispered, "My Adularia."

Shursta was afraid. He had only been so afraid once in his entire life, and that was last year, out on the open ocean, in that breathless half second before he jumped in after Gulak's young son, realizing even as he leapt that he would rather by far spool out the remainder of his days taunted and disliked and respected by none than dive into that particular death, where the boy floundered and the shark danced.

Now the words came with no stutter or click. "You have no wife."

The skull opened its mouth and screamed. It shrieked, raw and wordless, right into Shursta's face. Its fists closed again on the collar of Shursta's coat, twisted in a chokehold and jerked, lifting him off his feet as though he had been a small child. Shursta's legs dangled and his vision blackened and he struck out with his fists, but it was like pummeling a waterspout. Myrar was still screaming, but the sound soon floated off to a far away keening. Shursta, weightless between sky and sea, began to believe that Myrar had always been screaming, since the first time Shursta had beheld him sitting in the tavern, or maybe even before. Maybe he had been screaming since killing Kuista, the child he could not give his wife, and who, though a child, had all the esteem, joy of status, wealth and hope for the future that Myrar Yaspir, a man in his prime and a citizen of proud Droon, lacked.

Is it any wonder he screamed? Shursta thought. This was followed by another thought, further away: *I am dying.*

The moment he could breathe again was the moment his breath was knocked out of him. Myrar had released his chokehold on Shursta, but Shursta, barely conscious, had no time to find his feet before the ground leapt up to grapple him. He tried to groan, but all sound was sucked from the pit of his stomach into the sky. Rain splattered on his face. The wind ripped over everything except into his lungs.

By and by, he remembered how to breathe, and soon could do so without volunteering the effort. His mouth tasted coppery. His tongue was sore. Something had been bitten that probably should not have been. Shursta's hands closed over stones, trying to find one jagged enough to fend off further advances from a screaming skull-faced murderer. Where was his mesh-gift, the black knife Hyrryai had given him? Back in Sif, of course, in a box with his gemmaja, and the pressed petals of purple hyacinth that had fallen from her hair that night she left him. All his fingers found now were pebbles and blades of grass, and he could not seem to properly grip any of them. Shursta sat up.

Sometime between his falling and landing the awful screaming had stopped. There was only sobbing now: convulsive, curt, wretched, interrupted by bitter gasps for breath and short, sawtoothed cries of rage. Muffled, moist thumps punctuated each cry. Shursta had barely registered that it could not be Myrar Yaspir who wept—his tears had turned to dust long ago—when the thumps and sobs stopped. For a few minutes it was just rain and wind. Shursta blinked his eyes back into focus and took in the moon-battered, rain-silvered scene before him. His heart crashed in his chest like a fog-bell.

Hyrryai Blodestone crouched over the crumpled body of Myrar Yaspir. She grasped a large stone in her dominant hand. Myrar's bloody hair was tangled in her other. Her dinner knife was clamped between her teeth. As he watched, she let the head fall—another pulpy thump—tossed the dripping stone to one side and spat her knife into her hand. Her movements ragged and impatient, she sliced Myrar's shirt down the middle and laid her hand against his chest. She seemed startled by what she felt there—the last echoes of a heartbeat or the fact there was none, Shursta did not know.

"It's not worth," he said through chattering teeth, "the effort it would take to chew."

Hyrryai glanced at him, her face a shocky blank, eyes and nose and mouth streaming. She looked away again, then spat out a mouthful of excess saliva. The next second, she had keeled over and was vomiting over the side of a cliff. Shursta hurried to her side, tearing a strip from his sleeve as he did so, to gather her hair from her face and tie it back. His pockets were full of useless things. A coil of fishing line, a smooth white pebble, a pencil stub—ah! Bless Sharrar and her clever hands. A handkerchief. He pulled it out and wiped Hyrryai's face, taking care at the corners of her mouth.

Her lips were bloodied, as though she had already eaten Myrar Yaspir's heart. He realized this was because she had been careless of her teeth, newly filed into the needle points of the *windwyddiam*. Even a nervous gnawing of the lip might pierce the tender flesh there.

Blotting cautiously, he asked, "Did that hurt?"

The face Hyrryai lifted to Shursta was no longer hard and blank but so wide open that he feared for her, that whatever spirits of the night were prowling might seek to use her as a door. He moved his body more firmly between hers and Myrar Yaspir's. He wondered if this look of woeful wonder would ever be wiped from her eyes.

"Nothing hurts," she mumbled, turning away again. "I feel nothing."

"Then why are you crying?"

She shrugged, picking at the grass near her feet. Her agitated fingers brushed again a dark and jagged stone. It was as if she had accidently touched a rotten corpse. She jerked against Shursta, who flailed out his foot out to kick the stone over the cliff's edge. He wished he could kick Myrar Yaspir over and gone as well.

"Hyrryai—"

"D-Dumwei f-found you?" she asked at the same time.

"As you see."

"I c-called you to w-witness."

"Yes."

"I was going to make you, make you w-watch while I—" Hyrryai shook her head, baring her teeth as if to still their chattering. More slowly, she said, "It was going to be your punishment. Instead I came upon him as he was, as he was k-killing you."

And though his soul was sick, Shursta laughed. "Two at one blow, eh, Hyrryai?"

"Never," she growled at him, and took his face between her hands. "Never, never, *never*, Shursta Sarth, do you hear me? No one touches you. I will murder anyone who tries. I will eat their eyes, I will . . . "

He turned his face to kiss her blood-slicked hands. First one, then the other.

"Shh," he said. "Shh, Hyrryai. You saved my life. You saved me. It's over. It's over."

She slumped suddenly, pressing her face against his neck. Wrenched back, gasping. A small cut on her face bled a single thread of red. When next she spoke, her voice was wry.

"Your neck grew fangs, Shursta Sarth."

"Yes. Well. So."

Hyrryai fingered the strand of tooth and stone and pearl at his throat.

Shursta held his breath as her black eyes flickered up to meet his, holding them for a luminous moment.

"Thief," she breathed. "That's mine."

"Sorry." Shursta ducked his head, unclasped the necklace, and wound it down into her palm. Her fist snapped shut over it. "Destroy it again for all of me, Hyrryai."

Hyrryai leaned in to lay her forehead against his. Even with his eyes shut, Shursta felt her smile move against his mouth, very deliberately, very carefully.

"Never," she repeated. "I'd sooner destroy Droon."

They left Myrar Yaspir's body where it lie, for the plovers and the pipers and the gulls. From the sea cave they gathered what of Hyrryai's belongings she wanted with her when she sailed with the Grimgrimal into the unknown sky, and they knelt and kissed the place where Kuista Blodestone had fallen. These last things done, in silent exhaustion Shursta and Hyrryai climbed back up to the sea road.

Setting their faces for Sif, they turned their backs on Droon.

THEY SHALL SALT THE EARTH WITH SEEDS OF GLASS

ALAYA DAWN JOHNSON

It's noon, the middle of wheat harvest, and Tris is standing on the edge of the field while Bill and Harris and I drive three ancient combine threshers across the grain. It's dangerous to stand so close and Tris knows it. Tris knows better than to get in the way during harvest, too. Not a good idea if she wants to survive the winter. Fifteen days ago a cluster bomb dropped on the east field, so no combines there. No harvest. Just a feast for the crows.

Tris wrote the signs (with pictures for the ones who don't read) warning the kids to stay off the grass, stay out of the fields, don't pick up the bright-colored glass jewels. So I raise my hand, wave my straw hat in the sun—it's hot as hell out here, we could use a break, no problem—and the deafening noise of eighty-year-old engines forced unwillingly into service chokes, gasps, falls silent.

Bill stands and cups his hands over his mouth. "Something wrong with Meshach, Libby?"

I shake my head, realize he can't see, and holler, "The old man's doing fine. It's just hot. Give me ten?"

Harris, closer to me, takes a long drink from his bottle and climbs off Abednego. I don't mind his silence. This is the sort of sticky day that makes it hard to move, let alone bring in a harvest, and this sun is hot enough to burn darker skin than his.

It's enough to burn Tris, standing without a hat and wearing a skinny strappy dress of faded red that stands out against the wheat's dusty gold. I hop off Meshach, check to make sure he's not leaking oil, and head over to my sister. I'm a little worried. Tris wouldn't be here if it wasn't important. Another cluster bomb? But I haven't heard the whining drone of any reapers. The sky is clear. But even though I'm too far to read her expression, I can tell Tris is worried. That way she has of balancing on one leg, a red stork in a wheat marsh. I hurry as I get closer, though my overalls stick to the slick sweat on my thighs and I have to hitch them up like a skirt to move quickly.

"Is it Dad?" I ask, when I'm close.

She frowns and shakes her head. "Told me this morning he's going fishing again."

"And you let him?"

She shrugs. "What do you want me to do, take away his cane? He's old, Libs. A few toxic fish won't kill him any faster."

"They might," I grumble, but this is an old argument, one I'm not winning, and besides that's not why Tris is here.

"So what is it?"

She smiles, but it shakes at the edges. She's scared and I wonder if that makes her look old or just reminds me of our age. Dad is eighty, but I'm forty-two and we had a funeral for an eight-year-old last week. Every night since I was ten I've gone to sleep thinking I might not wake up the next morning. I don't know how you get to forty-two doing that.

Tris is thirty-eight, but she looks twenty-five—at least, when she isn't scanning the skies for reapers, or walking behind a tiny coffin in a funeral procession.

"Walk with me," she says, her voice low, as though Harris can hear us from under that magnolia tree twenty feet away. I sigh and roll my eyes and mutter under my breath, but she's my baby sister and she knows I'll follow her anywhere. We climb to the top of the hill, so I can see the muddy creek that irrigates the little postage stamp of our corn field, and the big hill just north of town, with its wood tower and reassuring white flag. Yolanda usually takes the morning shift, spending her hours watching the sky for that subtle disturbance, too smooth for a bird, too fast for a cloud. Reapers. If she rings the bell, some of us might get to cover in time.

Sometimes I don't like to look at the sky, so I sprawl belly-down on the ground, drink half of the warm water from my bottle and offer the rest to Tris. She finishes it and grimaces.

"Don't know how you stand it," she says. "Aren't you hot?"

"You won't complain when you're eating cornbread tonight."

"You made some?"

"Who does everything around here, bookworm?" I nudge her in the ribs and she laughs reluctantly and smiles at me with our smile. I remember learning to comb her hair after Mom got sick; the careful part I would make while she squirmed and hollered at me, the two hair balls I would twist and fasten to each side of her head. I would make the bottom of her hair immaculate: brushed and gelled and fastened into glossy, thick homogeneity. But on top it would sprout like a bunch of curly kale, straight up and out and olive-oil shiny. She would parade around the house in this flouncy slip she thought was a dress and pose for photos with her hand on her hip. I'm in a few of those pictures, usually in overalls or a smock. I look awkward and drab as an old sock next to her, but maybe it doesn't matter, because we have the same slightly bucked front teeth, the same fat cheeks, the same wide eyes going wider. We have a nice smile, Tris and I.

Tris doesn't wear afro-puffs any more. She keeps her hair in a bun and I keep mine short.

"Libs, oh Libs, things aren't so bad, are they?"

I look up at Tris, startled. She's sitting in the grass with her hands beneath her thighs and tears are dripping off the tip of her nose. I was lulled by her laugh—we don't often talk about the shit we can't control. Our lives, for instance.

I think about the field that we're going to leave for crows so no one gets blown up for touching one of a thousand beautiful multi-colored jewels. I think about funerals and Dad killing himself faster just so he can eat catfish with bellies full of white phosphorus.

"It's not that great, Tris."

"You think it's shit."

"No, not *shit*—"

"Close. You think it's close."

I sigh. "Some days. Tris. I have to get back to Meshach in a minute. What is going on?"

"I'm pregnant," she says.

I make myself meet her eyes, and see she's scared; almost as scared as I am.

"How do you know?"

"I suspected for a while. Yolanda finally got some test kits last night from a river trader."

Yolanda has done her best as the town midwife since she was drafted into service five years ago, when a glassman raid killed our last one. I'm surprised Tris managed to get a test at all.

"What are you going to do? Will you . . . " I can't even bring myself to say "keep it." But could Yolanda help her do anything else?

She reaches out, hugs me, buries her head in my shirt and sobs like a baby. Her muffled words sound like "Christ" and "Jesus" and "God," which ought to be funny since Tris is a capital-A atheist, but it isn't.

"No," she's saying, "Christ, no. I have to . . . someone has to . . . I need an abortion, Libby."

Relief like the first snow melt, like surviving another winter. Not someone else to worry about, to love, to feed.

But an abortion? There hasn't been a real doctor in this town since I was twelve.

• • •

Bill's mom used to be a registered nurse before the occupation, and she took care of everyone in town as best she could until glassman robots raided her house and called in reapers to bomb it five years ago. Bill left town after that. We never thought we'd see him again, but then two planting seasons ago, there he was with this green giant, a forty-year-old Deere combine—Shadrach, he called it, because it would make the third with our two older, smaller machines. He brought engine parts with him, too, and oil and enough seed for a poppy field. He had a bullet scar in his forearm and three strange, triangular burns on the back of his neck. You could see them because he'd been shaved bald and his hair was only starting to grow back, a patchy gray peach-fuzz.

He'd been in prison, that much was obvious. Whether the glassmen let him go or he escaped, he never said and we never asked. We harvested twice as much wheat from the field that season, and the money from the poppy paid for a new generator. If the bell on lookout hill rang more often than normal, if surveillance drones whirred through the grass and the water more than they used to, well, who was to say what the glassmen were doing? Killing us, that's all we knew, and Bill was one of our own.

So I ask Bill if his mother left anything behind that might help us—like a pill, or instructions for a procedure. He frowns.

"Aren't you a little old, Libby?" he says, and I tell him to fuck off. He puts a hand on my shoulder—conciliatory, regretful—and looks over to where Tris is trudging back home. "You saw what the reapers did to my Mom's house. I couldn't even find all of her *teeth*."

I'm not often on that side of town, but I can picture the ruin exactly. There's still a crater on Mill Street. I shuffle backward, contrite. "God, Bill. I'm sorry. I wasn't thinking."

He shrugs. "Sorry, Libs. Ask Yolanda, if you got to do something like that." I don't like the way he frowns at me; I can hear his judgment even when all he does is turn and climb back inside Shadrach.

"Fucking hot out here," I say, and walk back over to Meshach. I wish Bill wasn't so goddamn judgmental. I wish Tris hadn't messed up with whichever of her men provided the sperm donation. I wish we hadn't lost the east field to another cluster bomb.

But I can wish or I can drive, and the old man's engine coughs loud enough to drown even my thoughts.

Tris pukes right after dinner. That was some of my best cornbread, but I don't say anything. I just clean it up.

"How far along are you?" I ask. I feel like vomit entitles me to this much.

She pinches her lips together and I hope she isn't about to do it again. Instead, she stands up and walks out of the kitchen. I think that's her answer, but she returns a moment later with a box about the size of my hand. It's got a hole on one side and a dial like a gas gauge on the other. The gauge is marked with large glassman writing and regular letters in tiny print: "Fetal Progression," it reads, then on the far left "Not Pregnant," running through "Nine Months" on the far right. I can't imagine what the point of that last would be, but Tris's dial is still barely on the left hand side, settled neatly between three and four. A little late for morning sickness, but maybe it's terror as much as the baby that makes her queasy.

"There's a note on the side. It says 'All pregnant women will receive free rehabilitative healthcare in regional facilities.'" She says the last like she's spent a long day memorizing tiny print.

"Glassmen won't do abortions, Tris."

No one knows what they really look like. They only interact with us through their remote-controlled robots. Maybe they're made of glass themselves—they give us pregnancy kits, but won't bother with burn dressings. Dad says the glassmen are alien scientists studying our behavior, like a human would smash an anthill to see how they scatter. Reverend Beale always points to the pipeline a hundred miles west of us. They're just men stealing our resources, he says, like the white man stole the Africans', though even he can't say what those resources might be. It's a pipeline from nowhere, to nothing, as far as any of us know.

Tris leans against the exposed brick of our kitchen wall. "All fetuses are to be carried to full term," she whispers, and I turn the box over and see her words printed in plain English, in larger type than anything else on the box. Only one woman in our town ever took the glassmen up on their offer. I don't know how it went for her; she never came home.

"Three months!" I say, though I don't mean to.

Tris rubs her knuckles beneath her eyes, though she isn't crying. She looks fierce, daring me to ask her how the hell she waited this long. But I don't, because I know. Wishful thinking is a powerful curse, almost as bad as storytelling.

I don't go to church much these days, not after our old pastor died and Beale moved into town to take his place. Reverend Beale likes his fire and brimstone, week after week of too much punishment and too little brotherhood. I felt exhausted listening to him rant in that high collar, sweat pouring down his temples. But he's popular, and I wait on an old bench outside the red brick church for the congregation to let out. Main Street is quiet except for the faint echoes of the reverend's sonorous preaching. Mostly I hear the cicadas, the water lapping against a few old fishing boats and the long stretch of rotting pier. There used to be dozens of sailboats here, gleaming creations of white fiberglass and heavy canvas sails with names like "Bay Princess" and "Prospero's Dream." I know because Dad has pictures. Main Street was longer then, a stretch of brightly painted Tudors and Victorians with little shops and restaurants on the bottom floors and rooms above. A lot of those old buildings are boarded up now, and those that aren't look as patched-over and jury-rigged as our thresher combines. The church has held up the best of any of the town's buildings. Time has hardly worn its stately red brick and shingled steeples. It used to be Methodist, I think, but we don't have enough people to be overly concerned about denominations these days. I've heard of some towns where they make everyone go Baptist, or Lutheran, but we're lucky that no one's thought to do anything like that here. Though I'm sure Beale would try if he could get away with it. Maybe Tris was right to leave the whole thing behind. Now she sits the children while their parents go to church.

The sun tips past its zenith when the doors finally open and my neighbors walk out of the church in twos and threes. Beale shakes parishioners' hands as they leave, mopping his face with a handkerchief. His smile looks more like a grimace to me; three years in town and he still looks uncomfortable anywhere but behind a pulpit. Men like him think the glassmen are right to require "full gestation." Men like him think Tris is a damned sinner, just because she has a few men and won't settle down with one. He hates the glassmen as much as the rest of us, but his views help them just the same.

Bill comes out with Pam. The bones in her neck stand out like twigs, but she looks a hell of a lot better than the last time I saw her, at Georgia's funeral. Pam fainted when we laid her daughter in the earth, and Bill had to take her home before the ceremony ended. Pam is Bill's cousin, and Georgia was her only child—blown to bits after riding her bicycle over a hidden jewel in the fields outside town. To my surprise, Bill gives me a tired smile before walking Pam down the street.

Bill and I used to dig clams from the mud at low tide in the summers. We were in our twenties and my mother had just died of a cancer the glassmen could have cured if they gave a damn. Sometimes we would build fires of cedar and pine and whatever other tinder lay around and roast the clams right there by the water. We talked about anything in the world other than glassmen and dead friends while the moon arced above. We planned the cornfield eating those clams, and plotted all the ways we might get the threshers for the job. The cow dairy, the chicken coop, the extra garden plots—we schemed and dreamt of ways to help our town hurt a little less each winter. Bill had a girlfriend then, though she vanished not long after; we never did more than touch.

That was a long time ago, but I remember the taste of cedar ash and sea salt as I look at the back of him. I never once thought those moments would last forever, and yet here I am, regretful and old.

Yolanda is one of the last to leave, stately and elegant with her braided white hair and black church hat with netting. I catch up with her as she heads down the steps.

"Can we talk?" I ask.

Her shoulders slump a little when I ask, but she bids the reverend farewell and walks with me until we are out of earshot.

"Tris needs an abortion," I say.

Yolanda nods up and down like a sea bird, while she takes deep breaths. She became our midwife because she'd helped Bill's mother with some births, but I don't think she wants the job. There's just no one else.

"Libby, the glassmen don't like abortions."

"If the glassmen are paying us enough attention to notice, we have bigger problems."

"I don't have the proper equipment for a procedure. Even if I did, I couldn't."

"Don't tell me you agree with Beale."

She draws herself up and glares at me. "I don't know *how*, Libby! Do you want me to kill Tris to get rid of her baby? They say the midwife in Toddville can do them if it's early enough. How far along is she?"

I see the needle in my mind, far too close to the center line for comfort. "Three and a half months," I say.

She looks away, but she puts her arm around my shoulders. "I understand why she would, I do. But it's too late. We'll all help her."

Raise the child, she means. I know Yolanda is making sense, but I don't want to hear her. I don't want to think about Tris carrying a child she doesn't want to term. I don't want to think about that test kit needle pointing inexorably at *too fucking late*. So I thank Yolanda and head off in the other direction, down the cracked tarmac as familiar as a scar, to Pam's house. She lives in a small cottage Victorian with peeling gray paint that used to be blue. Sure enough, Bill sits in an old rocking chair on the porch, thumbing through a book. I loved to see him like that in our clam-digging days, just sitting and listening. I would dream of him after he disappeared.

"Libs?" he says. He leans forward.

"Help her, Bill. You've been outside, you know people. Help her find a doctor, someone who can do this after three months."

He sighs and the book thumps on the floor. "I'll see."

Three days later, Bill comes over after dinner.

"There's rumors of something closer to Annapolis," he says. "I couldn't find out more than that. None of my . . . I mean, I only know some dudes, Libby. And whoever runs this place only talks to women."

"Your mother didn't know?" Tris asks, braver than me.

Bill rubs the back of his head. "If she did, she sure didn't tell me."

"You've got to have more than that," she says. "Does this place even have a name? How near Annapolis? What do you want us to do, sail into the city and ask the nearest glassman which way to the abortion clinic?"

"What do I want you to do? Maybe I want you to count your goddamn blessings and not risk your life to murder a child. It's a *sin*, Tris, not like you'd care about that, but I'd've thought Libby would."

"God I know," I say, "but I've never had much use for sin. Now why don't you get your nose out of our business?"

"You invited me in, Libby."

"For *help*—"

He shakes his head. "If you could see what Pam's going through right now . . . "

Bill has dealt with as much grief as any of us. I can understand why he's moralizing in our kitchen, but that doesn't mean I have to tolerate it.

But Tris doesn't even give me time. She stands and shakes a wooden spatula under his nose. Bill's a big man, but he flinches. "So I should have this baby just so I can watch it get blown up later, is that it? Don't put Pam's grief on me, Bill. I'm sorrier than I can say about Georgia. I taught that girl to read! And I can't. I just can't."

Bill breathes ragged. His dark hands twist his muddy flannel shirt, his grip so tight his veins are stark against sun-baked skin. Tris is still holding that spatula.

Bill turns his head abruptly, stalks back to the kitchen door with a "Fuck," and he wipes his eyes. Tris leans against the sink.

"Esther," he says quietly, his back to us. "The name of a person, the name of a place, I don't know. But you ask for that, my buddy says you should find what you're after."

I follow him outside, barefoot and confused that I'd bother when he's so clearly had enough of us. I call his name, then start jogging and catch his elbow. He turns around.

"What, Libby?"

He's so angry. His hair didn't grow in very long or thick after he came back. He looks like someone mashed him up, stretched him out and then did a hasty job of putting him back together. Maybe I look like that, too.

"Thanks," I say. We don't touch.

"Don't die, Libs."

The air is thick with crickets chirping and fireflies glowing and the swampy, seaweed-and-salt air from the Chesapeake. He turns to walk away. I don't stop him.

We take Dad's boat. There's not enough gas left to visit Bishop's Head, the mouth of our estuary, let alone Annapolis. So we bring oars, along with enough supplies to keep the old dinghy low in the water.

"I hope we don't hit a storm," Tris says, squinting at the clear, indigo sky as though thunderheads might be hiding behind the stars.

"We're all right for now. Feel the air? Humidity's dropped at least 20 percent."

Tris has the right oar and I have the left. I don't want to use the gas unless we absolutely have to, and I'm hoping the low-tech approach will make us less noticeable to any patrolling glassmen. It's tough work, even in the relatively cool night air, and I check the stars to make sure we're heading in more or less the right direction. None of the towns on our estuary keep lights on at night. I only know when we pass Toddville because of the old lighthouse silhouetted against the stars. I lost sight of our home within five minutes of setting out, and God how a part of me wanted to turn the dinghy right around and go back. The rest of the world isn't safe. Home isn't either, but it's familiar.

Dad gave us a nautical chart of the Chesapeake Bay, with markers for towns long destroyed, lighthouses long abandoned, by people long dead. He marked our town and told us to get back safe. We promised him we would and we hugged like we might never see each other again.

"What if we hit a jewel?" Tris asks. In the dark, I can't tell if it's fear or exertion that aspirates her words. I've had that thought myself, but what can we do? The glassmen make sure their cluster bombs spread gifts everywhere.

"They don't detonate that well in water," I offer.

A shift in the dark; Tris rests her oar in the boat and stretches her arms. "Well enough to kill you slowly."

I'm not as tired, but I take the break. "We've got a gun. It ought to do the trick, if it comes to that."

"Promise?"

"To what? Mercy kill you?"

"Sure."

"Aren't you being a little melodramatic?"

"And we're just out here to do a little night fishing."

I laugh, though my belly aches like she's punched me. "Christ, Tris." I lean back in the boat, the canvas of our food sack rough and comforting on my slick skin, like Mom's gloves when she first taught me to plant seeds.

"Libs?"

"Yeah?"

"You really don't care who the father is?"

I snort. "If it were important, I'm sure you would have told me."

I look up at the sky: there's the Milky Way, the North Star, Orion's belt. I remember when I was six, before the occupation. There was so much light on the bay you could hardly see the moon.

"Reckon we'll get to Ohio, Jim?" Tris asks in a fake Southern drawl.

I grin. "Reckon we might. If'n we can figure out just how you got yerself pregnant, Huck."

Tris leans over the side of the boat, and a spray of brackish water hits my open mouth. I shriek and dump two handfuls on her head and she splutters and grabs me from behind so I can't do more than wiggle in her embrace.

"Promise," she says, breathing hard, still laughing.

The bay tastes like home to me, like everything I've ever loved. "Christ, Tris," I say, and I guess that's enough.

We round Bishop's Head at dawn. Tris is nearly asleep on her oar, though she hasn't complained. I'm worried about her, and it's dangerous to travel during the day until we can be sure the water is clear. We pull into Hopkins Cove, an Edenic horseshoe of brown sand and forest. It doesn't look like a human foot has touched this place since the invasion, which reassures me. Drones don't do much exploring. They care about people.

Tris falls asleep as soon as we pull the boat onto the sand. I wonder if I should feed her more—does she need extra for the baby? Then I wonder if that's irrational, since we're going all this way to kill it. But for now, at least, the fetus is part of her, which means we have to take it into consideration. I think about Bill with his big, dumb eyes and patchy bald head telling me that it's a *sin*, as though that has anything to do with your sister crying like her insides have been torn out.

I eat some cornbread and a peach, though I'm not hungry. I sit on the shore with my feet in the water and watch for other boats or drones or reapers overhead. I don't see anything but seagulls and ospreys and minnows that tickle my toes.

"Ain't nothing here, Libs," I say, in my mother's best imitation of *her* mother's voice. I never knew my grandmother, but Mom said she looked just like Tris, so I loved her on principle. She and Tris even share a name: Leatrice. I told Mom that I'd name my daughter Tamar, after her. I'd always sort of planned to, but when my monthlies stopped a year ago, I figured it was just as well. *Stupid Bill, and his stupid patchy hair,* I think.

I dream of giant combines made from black chrome and crystal, with headlights of wide, unblinking eyes. I take them to the fields, but something is wrong with the thresher. There's bonemeal dust on the wheat berries.

"Now, Libby," Bill says, but I can't hear the rest of what he's saying because the earth starts shaking and—

I scramble to my feet, kicking up sand with the dream still in my eyes. There's lights in the afternoon sky and this awful thunder, like a thousand lightning bolts are striking the earth at once.

"Oh, Christ," I say. A murder of reapers swarm to the north, and even with the sun in the sky their bombs light the ground beneath like hellfire. It's easier to see reapers from far away, because they paint their underbellies light blue to blend with the sky.

Tris stands beside me and grips my wrist. "That's not . . . it has to be Toddville, right? Or Cedar Creek? They're not far enough away for home, right?"

I don't say anything. I don't know. I can only look.

Bill's hair is patchy because the glassmen arrested him and they tortured him. Bill asked his outside contacts if they knew anything about a place to get an illegal abortion. Bill brought back a hundred thousand dollars' worth of farm equipment and scars from wounds that would have killed someone without access to a doctor. But what kind of prisoner has access to a real doctor? Why did the glassmen arrest him? What if his contacts are exactly the type of men the glassmen like to bomb with their reapers? What if Bill is?

But I know it isn't that simple. No one knows why the glassmen bomb us. No one *really* knows the reason for the whole damn mess, their reapers and their drones and their arcane rules you're shot for not following.

"Should we go back?"

She says it like she's declared war on a cardinal direction, like she really will get on that boat and walk into a reaper wasteland and salvage what's left of our lives and have that baby.

I squeeze her hand. "It's too close," I say. "Toddville, I think you're right. Let's get going, though. Probably not safe here."

She nods. She doesn't look me in the eye. We paddle through the choppy water until sun sets. And then, without saying anything, we ship the oars and I turn on the engine.

Three nights later, we see lights on the shore. It's a glassmen military installation. Dad marked it on the map, but still I'm surprised by its size, its brightness, the brazen way it sits on the coastline, as though daring to attract attention.

"I'd never thought a building could be so . . . "

"Angry?" Tris says.

"Violent."

"It's like a giant middle finger up the ass of the Chesapeake."

I laugh despite myself. "You're ridiculous."

We're whispering, though we're on the far side of the bay and the water is smooth and quiet. After that reaper drone attack, I'm remembering more than I like of my childhood terror of the glassmen. Dad and Mom had to talk to security drones a few times after the occupation, and I remember the oddly modulated voices, distinctly male, and the bright unblinking eyes behind the glass masks of their robot heads. I don't know anyone who has met a real glassman, instead of one of their remote robots. It's a retaliatory offense to harm a drone because the connection between the drone and the glassman on the other side of the world (or up in some space station) is so tight that sudden violence can cause brain damage. I wonder how they can square *potential brain damage* with *dead children*, but I guess I'm not a glassman.

So we row carefully, but fast as we can, hoping to distance our little fishing boat from the towering building complex. Its lights pulse so brightly they leave spots behind my eyes.

And then, above us, we hear the chopping whirr of blades cutting the air, the whine of unmanned machinery readying for deployment. I look up and shade my eyes: a reaper.

Tris drops her oar. It slides straight into the bay, but neither of us bother to catch it. If we don't get away now, a lost oar won't matter anyway. She lunges into our supply bag, brings out a bag of apples. The noise of the reaper is close, almost deafening. I can't hear what she yells at me before she jumps into the bay. I hesitate in the boat, afraid to leave our supplies and afraid to be blown to pieces by a reaper. I look back up and see a panel slide open on its bright blue belly. The panel reveals dark glass; behind it, a single, unblinking eye.

I jump into the water, but my foot catches on the remaining oar. The boat rocks behind me, but panic won't let me think—I tug and tug until the boat capsizes and suddenly ten pounds of supplies are falling on my head, dragging me deeper into the dark water. I try to kick out, but my leg is tangled with the drawstring of a canvas bag, and I can't make myself focus enough to get it loose. All I can think of is that big glass eye waiting to kill me. My chest burns and my ears fill to bursting with pressure. I'd always thought I would die in fire, but water isn't much better. I don't even know if Tris made it, or if the eye caught her, too.

I try to look up, but I'm too deep; it's too dark to even know which way that is. *God*, I think, *save her. Let her get back home.* It's rude to demand things of God, but I figure dying ought to excuse the presumption.

Something tickles my back. I gasp and the water flows in, drowning my lungs, flooding out what air I had left. But the thing in the water with me has a light on its head and strange, shiny legs and it's using them to get under my arms and drag me up until we reach the surface and I cough and retch and *breathe, thank you God.* The thing takes me to shore, where Tris is waiting to hug me and kiss my forehead like I'm the little sister.

"Jesus," she says, and I wonder if God really does take kindly to demands until I turn my head and understand: my savior is a drone.

"I will feed you," the glassman says. He looks like a spider with an oversized glassman head: eight chrome legs and two glass eyes. "The pregnant one should eat. Her daughter is growing."

I wonder if some glassman technology is translating his words into English. If in his language, whatever it is, *the pregnant one* is a kind of respectful address. Or maybe they taught him to speak to us that way.

I'm too busy appreciating the bounty of air in my lungs to notice the other thing he said.

"Daughter?" Tris says.

The glassman nods. "Yes. I have been equipped with a body-safe sonic scanning device. Your baby has not been harmed by your ordeal. I am here to help and reassure you."

Tris looks at me, carefully. I sit up. "You said something about food?"

"Yes!" It's hard to tell, his voice is so strange, but he sounds happy. As though rescuing two women threatened by one of his reaper fellows is the best piece of luck he's had all day. "I will be back," he says, and scuttles away, into the forest.

Tris hands me one of her rescued apples. "What the hell?" Her voice is low, but I'm afraid the glassman can hear us anyway.

"A trap?" I whisper, barely vocalizing into her left ear.

She shakes her head. "He seems awfully . . . "

"Eager?"

"Young."

The glassman comes back a minute later, walking on six legs and holding two boxes in the others. His robot must be a new model; the others I've seen look more human. "I have meals! A nearby convoy has provided them for you," he says, and places the boxes carefully in front of us. "The one with a red ribbon is for the pregnant one. It has nutrients."

Tris's hands shake as she opens it. The food doesn't look dangerous, though it resembles the strange pictures in Tris's old magazines more than the stuff I make at home. A perfectly rectangular steak, peas, corn mash. Mine is the same, except I have regular corn. We eat silently, while the glassman gives every impression of smiling upon us benevolently.

"Good news," he pipes, when I'm nearly done forcing the bland food down my raw throat. "I have been authorized to escort you both to a safe hospital facility."

"Hospital?" Tris asks, in a way that makes me sit up and put my arm around her.

"Yes," the glassman says. "To ensure the safe delivery of your daughter."

The next morning, the glassman takes us to an old highway a mile from the water's edge. A convoy waits for us, four armored tanks and two platform trucks. One of the platform beds is filled with mechanical supplies, including two dozen glass-and-chrome heads. The faces are blank, the heads unattached to any robot body, but the effect makes me nauseous. Tris digs her nails into my forearm. The other platform bed is mostly empty except for a few boxes and one man tied to the guardrails. He lies prone on the floor and doesn't move when we climb in after our glassman. At first I'm afraid that he's dead, but then he twitches and groans before falling silent again.

"Who is he?" Tris asks.

"Non-state actor," our glassman says, and pulls up the grate behind us.

"What?"

The convoy engines whirr to life—quiet compared to the three old men, but the noise shocks me after our days of silence on the bay.

The glassman swivels his head, his wide unblinking eyes fully focused on my sister. I'm afraid she's set him off and they'll tie us to the railings like that poor man. Instead, he clicks his two front legs together for no reason that I can see except maybe it gives him something to do.

"Terrorist," he says, quietly.

Tris looks at me and I widen my eyes: *don't you dare say another word*. She nods.

"The convoy will be moving now. You should sit for your safety."

He clacks away before we can respond. He hooks his hind legs through the side rail opposite us and settles down, looking like nothing so much as a contented cat.

The armored tanks get into formation around us and then we lurch forward, rattling over the broken road. Tris makes it for half an hour before she pukes over the side.

For two days, Tris and I barely speak. The other man in our truck wakes up about once every ten hours, just in time for one of the two-legged glassmen from the armored tanks to clomp over and give us all some food and water. The man gets less than we do, though none of it is very good. He eats in such perfect silence that I wonder if the glassmen have cut out his tongue. As soon as he finishes, one of the tank glassmen presses a glowing metal bar to the back of his neck. The mark it leaves is a perfect triangle, raw and red like a fresh burn. The prisoner doesn't struggle when the giant articulated metal hand grips his shoulders, he only stares, and soon after he slumps against the railing. I have lots of time to wonder about those marks; hour after slow hour with a rattling truck bruising my tailbone and regrets settling into my joints like dried tears. Sometimes Tris massages knots from my neck, and sometimes they come right back while I knead hers. I can't see any way to escape, so I try not to think about it. But there's no helping the sick, desperate knowledge that every hour we're closer to locking Tris in a hospital for six months so the glassmen can force her to have a baby.

During the third wake-up and feeding of the bound man, our glassman shakes out his legs and clacks over to the edge of the truck bed. The robots who drive the tanks are at least eight feet tall, with oversized arms and legs equipped with artillery rifles. They would be terrifying even if we weren't completely at their mercy. The two glassmen stare at each other, eerily silent and still.

The bound man, I'd guess Indian from his thick straight hair and dark skin, strains as far forward as he can. He nods at us.

"They're talking," he says. His words are slow and painstakingly formed. We crawl closer to hear him better. "In their real bodies."

I look back up, wondering how he knows. They're so still, but then glassmen are always uncanny.

Tris leans forward, so her lips are at my ear. "Their eyes," she whispers.

Glassman robot eyes never blink. But their pupils dilate and contract just like ours do. Only now both robots' eyes are pupil-blasted black despite the glaring noon sun. Talking in their real bodies? That must mean they've stopped paying us any attention.

"Could we leave?" I whisper. No one has tied us up. I think our glassman is under the impression he's doing us a favor.

Tris buries her face in the back of my short nappy hair and wraps her arms around me. I know it's a ploy, but it comforts me all the same. "The rest of the convoy."

Even as I nod, the two glassmen step away from each other, and our convoy is soon enough on its way. This time, though, the prisoner gets to pass his time awake and silent. No one tells us to move away from him.

"I have convinced the field soldier to allow me to watch the operative," our glassman says proudly.

"That's very nice," Tris says. She's hardly touched her food.

"I am glad you appreciate my efforts! It is my job to assess mission parameter achievables. Would you mind if I asked you questions?"

I frown at him and quickly look away. Tris, unfortunately, has decided she'd rather play with fire than her food.

"Of course," she says.

We spend the next few hours subjected to a tireless onslaught of questions. Things like, "How would you rate our society-building efforts in the Tidewater Region?" and "What issue would you most like to see addressed in the upcoming Societal Health Meeting?" and "Are you mostly satisfied or somewhat dissatisfied with the cleanliness of the estuary?"

"The fish are toxic," I say to this last question. My first honest answer. It seems to startle him. At least, that's how I interpret the way he clicks his front two legs together.

Tris pinches my arm, but I ignore her.

"Well," says the glassman. "That is potentially true. We have been monitoring the unusually high levels of radiation and heavy metal toxicity. But you can rest assured that we are addressing the problem and its potential harmful side-effects on Beneficial Societal Development."

"Like dying of mercury poisoning?" Tris pinches me again, but she smiles for the first time in days.

"I do not recommend it for the pregnant one! I have been serving you both nutritious foods well within the regulatory limits."

I have no idea what those regulatory limits might be, but I don't ask.

"In any case," he says. "Aside from that issue, the estuary is very clean."

"Thank you," Tris says, before I can respond.

"You're very welcome. We are here to help you."

"How far away is the hospital?" she asks.

I feel like a giant broom has swept the air from the convoy, like our glassman has tossed me back into the bay to drown. I knew Tris was desperate; I didn't realize how much.

"Oh," he says, and his pupils go very wide. I could kiss the prisoner for telling us what that means: no one's at home.

The man now leans toward us, noticing the same thing. "You pregnant?" he asks Tris.

She nods.

He whistles through a gap between his front teeth. "Some rotten luck," he says. "I never seen a baby leave one of their clinics. Fuck knows what they do to them."

"And the mothers?" I ask.

He doesn't answer, just lowers his eyes and looks sidelong at our dormant glassman. "Depends," he whispers, "on who they think you are."

That's all we have time for; the glassman's eyes contract again and his head tilts like a bird's. "There is a rehabilitative facility in the military installation to which we are bound. Twenty-three hours ETA."

"A prison?" Tris asks.

"A hospital," the glassman says firmly.

• • •

When we reach the pipeline, I know we're close. The truck bounces over fewer potholes and cracks; we even meet a convoy heading in the other direction. The pipeline is a perfect clear tube about sixteen feet high. It looks empty to me, a giant hollow tube that distorts the landscape on the other side like warped glass. It doesn't run near the bay, and no one from home knows enough to plot it on a map. Maybe this is the reason the glassmen are here. I wonder what could be so valuable in that hollow tube that Tris has to give birth in a cage, that little Georgia has to die, that a cluster bomb has to destroy half our wheat crop. What's so valuable that looks like nothing at all?

The man spends long hours staring out the railing of the truck, as though he's never seen anything more beautiful or more terrifying. Sometimes he talks to us, small nothings, pointing out a crane overhead or a derelict road with a speed limit sign—*55 miles per hour,* it says, *radar enforced.*

At first our glassman noses around these conversations, but he decides they're innocuous enough. He tells the man to "refrain from exerting a corrupting influence," and resumes his perch on the other side of the truck bed. The prisoner's name is Simon, he tells us, and he's on watch. For what, I wonder, but know well enough not to ask.

"What's in it?" I say instead, pointing to the towering pipeline.

"I heard it's a wormhole." He rests his chin on his hands, a gesture that draws careful, casual attention to the fact that his left hand has loosened the knots. He catches my eye for a blink and then looks away. My breath catches— Is he trying to escape? Do we dare?

"A wormhole? Like, in space?" Tris says, oblivious. Or maybe not. Looking at her, I realize she might just be a better actor.

I don't know what Tris means, but Simon nods. "A passage through space, that's what I heard."

"That is incorrect!"

The three of us snap our heads around, startled to see the glassman so close. His eyes whirr with excitement. "The Designated Area Project is not what you refer to as a wormhole, which are in fact impractical as transportation devices."

Simon shivers and looks down at his feet. My lips feel swollen with regret— what if he thinks we're corrupted? What if he notices Simon's left hand? But Tris raises her chin, stubborn and defiant at the worst possible time—I guess the threat of that glassman hospital is making her too crazy to feel anything as reasonable as fear.

"Then what is it?" she asks, so plainly that Simon's mouth opens, just a little.

Our glassman stutters forward on his delicate metallic legs. "I am not authorized to tell you," he says, clipped.

"Why not? It's the whole goddamned reason all your glassman reapers and drones and robots are swarming all over the place, isn't it? We don't even get to know what the hell it's all for?"

"Societal redevelopment is one of our highest mission priorities," he says, a little desperately.

I lean forward and grab Tris's hand as she takes a sharp, angry breath. "Honey," I say, "Tris, *please.*"

She pulls away from me, hard as a slap, but she stops talking. The glassman says nothing; just quietly urges us a few yards away from Simon. No more corruption on his watch.

Night falls, revealing artificial lights gleaming on the horizon. Our glassman doesn't sleep. Not even in his own place, I suppose, because whenever I check with a question his eyes stay the same and he answers without hesitation. Maybe they have drugs to keep themselves awake for a week at a time. Maybe he's not human. I don't ask—I'm still a little afraid he might shoot me for saying the wrong thing, and more afraid that he'll start talking about Ideal Societal Redevelopment.

At the first hint of dawn, Simon coughs and leans back against the railing, catching my eye. Tris is dozing on my shoulder, drool slowly soaking my shirt. Simon flexes his hands, now free. He can't speak, but our glassman isn't looking at him. He points to the floor of the truckbed, then lays himself out with his hands over his head. There's something urgent in his face. Something knowledgable. To the glassmen he's a terrorist, but what does that make him to us? I shake Tris awake.

"Libs?"

"Glassman," I say, "I have a question about societal redevelopment deliverables."

Tris sits straight up.

"I would be pleased to hear it!" the glassman says.

"I would like to know what you plan to do with my sister's baby."

"Oh," the glassman says. The movement of his pupils is hardly discernible in this low light, but I've been looking. I grab Tris by her shoulder and we scramble over to Simon.

"Duck!" he says. Tris goes down before I do, so only I can see the explosion light up the front of the convoy. Sparks and embers fly through the air like a starfall. The pipeline glows pink and purple and orange. Even the strafe of bullets seems beautiful until it blows out the tires of our truck. We crash and tumble. Tris holds onto me, because I've forgotten how to hold onto myself.

The glassmen are frozen. Some have tumbled from the overturned trucks, their glass and metal arms halfway to their guns. Their eyes don't move, not even when three men in muddy camouflage lob sticky black balls into the heart of the burning convoy.

Tris hauls me to my feet. Simon shouts something at one of the other men, who turns out to be a woman.

"What the hell was that?" I ask.

"EMP," Simon says. "Knocks them out for a minute or two. We have to haul ass."

The woman gives Simon a hard stare. "They're clean?"

"They were prisoners, too," he says.

The woman—light skinned, close-cropped hair—hoists an extra gun, unconvinced. Tris straightens up. "I'm pregnant," she says. "And ain't nothing going to convince me to stay here."

"Fair enough," the woman says, and hands Tris a gun. "We have ninety seconds. Just enough time to detonate."

Our glassman lies on his back, legs curled in the air. One of those sticky black balls has lodged a foot away from his blank glass face. It's a retaliatory offense to harm a drone. I remember what they say about brain damage when the glassmen are connected. Is he connected? Will this hurt him? I don't like the kid, but he's so young. Not unredeemable. He saved my life.

I don't know why I do it, but while Tris and the others are distracted, I use a broken piece of the guard rail to knock off the black ball. I watch it roll under the truck, yards away. I don't want to hurt him; I just want my sister and me safe and away.

"Libs!" It's Tris, looking too much like a terrorist with her big black gun. Dad taught us both to use them, but the difference between us is I wish that I didn't know how, and Tris is glad.

I run to catch up. A man idles a pickup ten yards down the road from the convoy.

"They're coming back on," he says.

"Detonating!" The woman's voice is a bird-call, a swoop from high to low. She presses a sequence of buttons on a remote and suddenly the light ahead is fiercer than the sun and it smells like gasoline and woodsmoke and tar. I've seen plenty enough bomb wreckage in my life; I feel like when it's *ours* it should look different. Better. It doesn't.

Tris pulls me into the back of the pickup and we're bouncing away before we can even shut the back door. We turn off the highway and drive down a long dirt road through the woods. I watch the back of the woman's head through the rear window. She has four triangular scars at the base of her neck, the same as Bill's.

Something breaks out of the underbrush on the side of the road. Something that moves unnaturally fast, even on the six legs he has left. Something that calls out, in that stupid, naive, inhuman voice:

"Stop the vehicle! Pregnant one, do not worry, I will—"

"Fuck!" Tris's terror cuts off the last of the speech. The car swerves, tossing me against the door. I must not have latched it properly, because next thing I know I'm tumbling to the dirt with a thud that jars my teeth. The glassman scrambles on top of me without any regard for the pricking pain of his long, metallic limbs.

"Kill that thing!" It's a man, I'm not sure who. I can't look, pinioned as I am.

"Pregnant one, step down from the terrorist vehicle and I will lead you to safety. There is a Reaper Support Flyer on its way."

He grips me between two metallic arms and hauls me up with surprising strength. The woman and Simon have guns trained on the glassman, but they hesitate—if they shoot him, they have to shoot me. Tris has her gun up as well, but she's shaking so hard she can't even get her finger on the trigger.

"Let go of me," I say to him. He presses his legs more firmly into my side.

"I will save the pregnant one," he repeats, as though to reassure both of us. He's young, but he's still a glassman. He knows enough to use me as a human shield.

Tris lowers the gun to her side. She slides from the truck bed and walks forward.

"Don't you dare, Tris!" I yell, but she just shakes her head. My sister, giving herself to a glassman? What would Dad say? I can't even free a hand to wipe my eyes. I hate this boy behind the glass face. I hate him because he's too young and ignorant to even understand what he's doing wrong. Evil is good to a glassman. Wrong is right. The pregnant one has to be saved.

I pray to God, then. I say, *God, please let her not be a fool. Please let her escape.*

And I guess God heard, because when she's just a couple of feet away she looks straight at me and smiles like she's about to cry. "I'm sorry, Libs," she whispers. "I love you. I just can't let him take me again."

"Pregnant one! Please drop your weapon and we will—"

And then she raises her gun and shoots.

My arm hurts. Goddamn it hurts, like there's some small, toothy animal burrowing inside. I groan and feel my sister's hands, cool on my forehead.

"They know the doctor," she says. "That Esther that Bill told us about, remember? She's a regular doctor, too, not just abortions. You'll be fine."

I squint up at her. The sun has moved since she shot me; I can hardly see her face for the light behind it. But even at the edges I can see her grief. Her tears drip on my hairline and down my forehead.

"I don't care," I say, with some effort. "I wanted you to do it."

"I was so afraid, Libs."

"I know."

"We'll get home now, won't we?"

"Sure," I say. *If it's there.*

The terrorists take us to a town fifty miles from Annapolis. Even though it's close to the city, the glassmen mostly leave it alone. It's far enough out from the pipeline, and there's not much here, otherwise: just a postage stamp of a barley field, thirty or so houses and one of those large, old, whitewashed barn-door churches. At night, the town is ghost empty.

Tris helps me down from the truck. Even that's an effort. My head feels half-filled with syrup. Simon and the others say their goodbyes and head out quickly. It's too dangerous for fighters to stay this close to the city. Depending on how much the glassmen know about Tris and me, it isn't safe for us either. But between a baby and a bullet, we don't have much choice.

Alone, now, we read the church's name above the door: *Esther Zion Congregation Church, Methodist.*

Tris and I look at each other. "Oh, Christ," she says. "Did Bill lie, Libby? Is he really so hung up on that sin bullshit that he sent me all the way out here, to a *church* . . . "

I lean against her and wonder how he ever survived to come back to us. It feels like a gift, now, with my life half bled out along the road behind. "Bill wouldn't lie, Tris. Maybe he got it wrong. But he wouldn't lie."

The pews are old but well-kept. The prayer books look like someone's been using them. The only person inside is a white lady, sweeping the altar.

"Simon and Sybil sent you," she says, not a question. Sybil—we never even asked the woman's name.

"My sister," we both say, and then, improbably, laugh.

A month later, Tris and I round Bishop's Head and face north. At the mouth of our estuary, we aren't close enough to see Toddville, let alone our home, but we can't see any drones either. The weather is chillier this time around, the water harder to navigate with the small boat. Tris looks healthy and happy; older and younger. No one will mistake her for twenty-five again, but there's nothing wrong with wisdom.

The doctor fixed up my arm and found us an old, leaky rowboat when it was clear we were determined to go back. Tris has had to do most of the work; her arms are starting to look like they belong to someone who doesn't spend all her time reading. I think about the harvest and hope the bombs didn't reap the grain before we could. If anyone could manage those fields without me, Bill can. We won't starve this winter, assuming reapers didn't destroy everything. Libby ships the oars and lets us float, staring at the deep gray sky and its reflection on the water that seems to stretch endlessly before us.

"Bill will have brought the harvest in just fine," I say.

"You love him, don't you?"

I think about his short, patchy hair. That giant green monster he brought back like a dowry. "He's good with the old engines. Better than me."

"I think he loves you. Maybe one of you could get around to doing something about it?"

"Maybe so."

Tris and I sit like that for a long time. The boat drifts toward shore, and neither of us stop it. A fish jumps in the water to my left; a heron circles overhead.

"Dad's probably out fishing," she says, maneuvering us around. "We might catch him on the way in."

"That'll be a surprise! Though he won't be happy about his boat."

"He might let it slide. Libby?"

"Yes?"

"I'm sorry—"

"You aren't sorry if you'd do it again," I say. "And I'm not sorry if I'd let you."

She holds my gaze. "Do you know how much I love you?"

We have the same smile, my sister and I. It's a nice smile, even when it's scared and a little sad.

A WINDOW OR A SMALL BOX

JEDEDIAH BERRY

They were on the run and forgetting how not to be. He wore his flowered shirt and she wore her straw hat so they could always spot each other in a crowd. The goons were a few steps behind them—had been since that day at the empty house by the sea—but they made friends where they needed friends, they bought bus tickets and street maps, and sometimes they stopped long enough for a movie or a beer, or for a quickie in a borrowed room. They were far from home, but they didn't know how far. They figured everything would turn out all right in the end.

"Everything will turn out all right in the end," she told him.

He was having a dark moment, crouched on the sidewalk with his hands on top of his head. At the bus stop on the corner, two boys wearing bulky backpacks exchanged a look.

"See," she said, "it's kind of like Los Angeles here."

Only this Los Angeles had too many doors: doors in the sidewalks, doors on every side of every house, little doors in the trees. Most doors didn't have anything behind them. They'd checked a few.

"Your aunt Meg probably thinks I kidnapped you," he said. "She's going to be so angry."

She crouched behind him, ignoring the looks from those kids, and put her arms around his middle. "My aunt Meg is always angry about something," she said.

They stayed like that for a while, she with her hair falling over his shoulders, he slowly unclenching. Then a bus pulled up to the curb, and the driver threw down a rope ladder. The two boys climbed aboard, and the babies in their backpacks woke and went wide-eyed at the ascent. Babies, fat and shining, grinning, everything new to them.

Because that was the other thing about this Los Angeles. Everyone here had babies.

"I need a drink," he said.

• • •

They'd seen a town where powdered wigs were strictly required. A town where the laws were made by observing how the alpacas grazed on a particular meadow. A town that was just a train station. They'd been in the country, and then in the mountains, and then in the desert. They learned to stop asking where they were, because people here didn't understand that question, mistook it for a joke. A big grin and "Why, you're right here!" was the typical reply.

What they wanted was to get home in time for the wedding—their wedding. They held hands as often as they could. They got used to not getting used to things. They knew that his name was Jim and that her name was Laura, and sometimes that was all they needed.

In the Set-It-Down Saloon, the bouncer bounced a baby on his knee. At every table, in every booth, at least one baby lolled. The bartender had a baby slung over his chest and a second laid out on a blanket next to the taps. "I'll tell you what you kids need," he said to Jim, and Jim thought he was going to say *a baby*, but what he said was "You need a sure thing. My cousin Louis, for example. This guy has a sure thing. Have you ever heard of muffins?"

"Muffins, yes, I've heard of muffins," said Jim.

"Louis is in the muffins business. It's going to be huge, you know? When people get a taste of these muffins, they're all going to want in on them. They're going to eat these things until they burst. Standing room only. There's a sure thing right there."

"I'll be right back," said Laura, and went off to find the restroom.

Jim took a long sip of his beer. "There are these goons," he said.

"Goons?"

"Thugs. Pinstripe suits, shiny black shoes. You can smell them when they get close. They smell like fried eggs."

"Fried eggs," the bartender said, wiping down the bar. "Never heard of fried eggs."

The baby on the bar—a boy baby—started peeing. The stream of urine splashed over the bar and over the baby's own legs. The bartender waited until it was done, then lifted the baby's legs, cleaned up underneath, and cleaned the baby, too, all with the same rag.

"A window or a small box," Jim said. "Does that mean anything to you?"

It was a fortune teller in Phoenix (except it wasn't *really* Phoenix) who'd said it to them. She lived in a little white house with a very green lawn and a sign out front with a picture of a crystal ball on it. She was out front, too, on a lawn chair, sunning herself in a two-piece. She was maybe nineteen. "You look lost," she'd said dreamily, and they *were* lost, and feeling a little desperate, so they followed her inside, and she'd gazed into her crystal ball and told them: "Your way home lies through a window. A window or a small box."

"I've got plenty of boxes out back," the bartender said. "Take all you need." The baby on the bar was crying now, so he swapped it for the one slung over his chest.

"I don't know if we're getting any closer," Jim said. And then, though he knew how this would probably go, he asked, "Hey, can you tell me where we are?"

"Now there's the first sensible question you've asked all night," the bartender said. "You're sitting at my bar, kid. It's called the Set-It-Down Saloon, and people come here to set things down, usually themselves. I've worked here for thirteen years, and sometimes I think it must be the absolute center of the universe." He looked around. "You smell something? I've never smelled anything like that. Like something frying in butter."

Jim rose from his stool and said, "Where's Laura?"

Laura had found too many doors at the back of the bar, none of them labeled *women* or *men*, *ladies* or *gents*. No helpful pictograms. So she'd picked a door at random and opened it on to darkness.

When she felt for the light switch someone grabbed her wrist, pulled her in, and closed the door. "Hi," someone said.

She reached for the doorknob, but the man in the dark got ahold of her other wrist and danced her deeper into the room. Then she was in a chair, and a lamp was on, and on the table next to the lamp was a half-eaten sandwich on a white plate. The man sat beside her. He was big in his big pinstripe suit, and he had big blond hair and a handsome smile.

"How'd you know which door I'd pick?" she asked.

"Didn't," he said. "But things usually go my way. Hungry?"

They were in a storage room, surrounded by open crates of promotional materials from breweries: neon signs, pint glasses, coasters, baby bibs.

"I'm not hungry," she said.

The man shrugged and took a bite of the sandwich. Cheese, it looked like. "So, you still with that guy?" he said. "What a loser."

"Guess how many," she said.

He stopped chewing. "How many what?"

"Tents. Guess how many tents we rented for the wedding."

He blinked his big blue eyes. "I don't want to guess."

"Three," she said. "One for the ceremony, one for the dinner, and one for the dancing."

"I don't want to talk about dancing," said the man, the man who was the leader of the goons, the goons who were out to get them, though he seemed to be alone this time. "I want to talk about love."

The room felt colder now.

"Do you love him?" the chief goon asked. "Do you really love that loser out there?"

"Guess how many guests," she said.

He threw his sandwich onto the plate. "I hate your questions. Your questions bring me to the very edge of doing something terrible."

"One hundred eighteen guests," she said. "Do you know how difficult it is to herd that many people? To make sure they all have a place to stay? To make sure they're seated at tables with people they don't hate?"

"Do you *love* him?" the chief goon asked again.

Laura thought of Jim on the sidewalk, thought of him weak and needy, and the only thing she felt was a hollow kind of anger. "I don't know if I love him," she said, and then she heard him outside, calling her name.

She ran for the door, but the chief goon moved faster, pinned her against the wall, and held her face in his big white hands, very gently. She screamed.

They were just two kids from upstate New York. Before, he'd been working for an agency that tracked fish populations. Seven hours each day, in a room he and his coworkers called "the dungeon," he sat at a window with a view on to a streambed, watching for flashes of silver in the murky light. He kept a counter in each hand, clicking one for shad, one for lampreys. Sometimes a lamprey would attach itself to the glass with its mouth and stay there for hours. Jim would try not to look at it, at its rings of teeth, at its flat yellow eyes.

"Weird as anything we've seen here," she'd said to him a few days after they'd crossed over (and this was how they referred to their arrival in this place, which they didn't remember, didn't understand).

"There were turtles sometimes," Jim said. "It always felt good to see turtles."

She'd been commuting into the city to work for a company that predicted trends in film, television, fashion. She'd earned a promotion and a measure of fame among her peers for her work on a report titled "The New Escapism," which proved to be about 90 percent accurate. The interns referred to her as "the seeress" and competed for the right to do her photocopying. Whenever someone asked her what she saw coming next, she usually said, "Me getting fired," and knew she sounded a little hopeful when she said it.

"I'll fire you if you want," he'd told her one night. They were alone on his parents' porch with a candle and bottles of beer.

"It would be kind of hot if you fired me," she said.

"You're fired, then. Completely, totally terminated. Don't even clean out your desk."

"Mm, nice," she said, sipping from her bottle.

"Don't stop by the water cooler. Don't try to take any interns with you. Your life is one big pink slip."

"Okay," she said, laughing. "That'll do, boss."

"Welcome to the real world," he said. "It's hell out here, and you're part of it now."

"Jim, that's enough," she said.

He was shaking and he didn't know why. He licked the tips of his thumb and index finger and pinched out the candle flame.

When Jim came through the door with a bottle in his fist, the chief goon let go of Laura and backed away. They all looked at one another for a moment, then Laura went to Jim. He smashed the bottle over the edge of a crate. The glass shattered and fell from his hand, useless.

The chief goon chuckled, and swept back his big blond hair. "People are placing bets, you know. On how long before I catch you. I give you another day or two, tops."

They ran. Out in the bar, everyone was crouched low at their tables and booths, leaning protectively over babies. A half dozen goons, rubbery in their pinstripe suits, slid like jellyfish from vents in the ceiling, through the windows, from under the jukebox. They shifted in their shiny black shoes, ankles wobbling as they solidified.

Laura grabbed her backpack from the bar and pulled Jim toward the door.

"Trouble at six o'clock!" the bartender cried, which was strange, Jim thought, because no one here told time that way, but apparently six o'clock still meant *right behind you*, because there was one of the goons, smiling and ready to pounce.

Jim swung at him. His punch connected, but Jim's fist sank into the still-gooey head. The goon's face bulged, looking like a balloon that's been squeezed on one side. His smile stretched and swelled.

Jim hollered and pulled back, but his hand was stuck fast, somewhere just below the goon's left eye. The goon was laughing now, and so were all the other goons. Jim's hand felt warm and tingly in there. It didn't feel good.

"Kid, I don't know what to tell you," the bartender said.

Laura swung her backpack at the goon's head. He was solid enough now that the impact meant something, and the goon's eyes fluttered shut. He fell against the bar, and Jim was free.

Free, but he only stared at the fallen goon, his face blank. Laura grabbed him by the arm, pulled him from the bar, pulled him down the sidewalk past the goons' black sedan, all the way to the closest monorail station, because this Los Angeles had a monorail. A train pulled in just as they passed through the turnstile. They hopped aboard, keeping low, and found two empty seats between a puppeteer and a woman with a basket of bananas on her head.

"At moments like this," Laura said to him, "I need you to work with me. And to move a little quicker, okay?"

Jim didn't look at her; he was staring at his right arm. Which ended, Laura now saw, just past the cuff of his flowered shirt—nothing where his hand should have been. The flesh was smooth and rounded, as though he'd never had a hand there.

Laura took his arm and held it between them, then held him close so he couldn't look at it.

The puppeteer, who had hissing snake heads on his fingertips, was watching. He leaned close and wagged the fingers of his right hand. "Can't take any chances," he said. "That's why I got these puppies insured."

They bought tickets for an afternoon show and sat in the back row. There were no movies in the city, only live theater. Jim stared at the spot where his hand used to be, ran the palm of his left hand over the stump. "Maybe this one will get more dexterous over time," he whispered.

At first he'd wondered how he was going to count shad and lampreys when he could hold only one clicker at a time. Then he wondered whether Laura would want to marry someone with one hand. There were things he did with that hand that she liked.

"This play is one of my favorites," she said, as though she'd seen it before. The play, as far as Jim could tell, was about stones that dreamed they were turtles.

"Could we trade seats?" he said.

"Why?" she said, then understood: he wanted to hold her hand, but he couldn't now unless she was on his left. She said, "Let's just watch the play, all right?" She kept her hands in her lap, under her straw hat.

He glanced toward the door, still expecting the goons to burst in. No sign of them, and not a trace of fried eggs, so he watched the play.

The stage, lit with blue and green lights, was covered with stones, most of them round and smooth. It reminded him of the bottom of the stream back home, the stream he'd come to think of as his stream. Offstage, someone played a zither. Turtle puppets with slowly moving limbs swung suspended in the light. From his perch on a bridge above, a curly-haired boy reached for them with an enormous net. When he caught a turtle, people in the audience clapped and bounced their babies on their knees.

"I don't get it," Jim said.

"They're happy because he caught a turtle," Laura said.

He went to get something to eat. The girl behind the lobby snack bar must have been from some other city: no baby, though she did have a chicken on the counter. She was teaching it to sort paperclips into little piles.

He didn't see any popcorn, but he asked anyway, and the girl set a packet the size of an old cassette tape on the counter. Jim opened it and looked inside. Not popcorn, exactly, but some kind of soft, white candy.

"Twenty cents," the girl said.

He fished two dimes out of his pocket, and she dropped them into the register without looking. This was something he and Laura had going for them: the currency here was similar enough that no one noticed the different set of faces on their coins and bills, and the exchange rate seemed to be in their favor. The few twenties they had with them when they crossed over were going a long way.

"I think that's for you," the girl said.

The lobby telephone was ringing in its booth.

"Why do you think it's for me?"

"It was for you last time it rang, and the time before that." The girl stroked her chicken with both hands, smoothing its feathers. "Please just answer it," she said.

Jim stuffed the not-popcorn in his pocket and went into the booth, closing the door behind him before he answered.

"I can't believe I got you on the line," someone said. It was a woman's voice, eastern European accent but not quite, and anyway did they even have an eastern Europe here?

"Who is this?"

"Who is which of us? You're Mr. Jim, aren't you?"

"Yes, I'm Jim, but who are you?"

"I know who I am, thank you. Oh, but you are doing that amazing thing you do. That funny way of speaking."

Jim could hear a scratching sound on the line. "Are you writing this down?" he asked.

"I'm writing it up," the woman said. "I'm a biographist, and I'm working on your biography. It's coming along nicely."

"I don't need a biographer," Jim said.

"Biogra*phist*," the woman said, laughing. "Listen, I want to meet you. For an interview? We could live together, maybe, just for a year or two. My publisher would be so pleased."

"No," Jim said. "Stop writing. Please, I don't want to be interviewed. Why would anyone want to publish my biography?"

"Haven't you been reading the papers? You are just wowing them, Mr. Jim. Wowing them with your . . . I don't know what to call it, exactly. But I want to figure it out, and turn it into something you can taste. Something you can slick back your hair with, you know?"

Jim hung up and stumbled out of the booth, suddenly nauseous. He went back to the snack bar and asked the girl if she had a copy of today's newspaper.

"The one with you on the cover?" she said. "Right here."

The photo showed him in profile, talking to someone at a bus station, holding out a map, asking for directions. He scanned the article—some of the words were different, but it was close enough to American English—and yes, he was apparently famous, and dozens of people he'd spoken to since they crossed over had been interviewed, and specialists of various kinds were giving opinions, opinions that didn't make much sense to him.

There was no mention of Laura, only references to a traveling companion. He was the one they were interested in.

He returned the newspaper, noticed that she had Purple Pow-Pow behind the counter and bought a bottle, then tucked that in his shirt pocket and went back into the theater. The boy with curly hair was center stage now. He stirred a cauldron of turtle soup and sang a kind of dirge.

Laura leaned forward in her seat. "This is getting really good."

"Yeah," he said, wondering: If he was famous here, why wasn't Laura famous? Probably because he was the one who talked too much, who got them into trouble, who bumbled through everything they were up against. And people here found that interesting.

"You get something to eat?" Laura asked.

He shook a few of the whatever-they-weres from the envelope into Laura's hand, then almost tried to pour some into his own right hand before he remembered. He tipped them straight into his mouth instead.

"Ugh, these are weird," Laura said. "Don't they have popcorn?"

"I kind of like them," Jim said.

She kept her eyes on the stage. The boy was still singing, stirring and singing, crying as he sang.

"Did you hear that?" Laura whispered.

Jim hadn't been paying attention to the words, but now he listened. "I want to go home," the boy sang. "I want to go home." And then, more quietly, "All I need is a window, a window or a small box."

After the show, Jim convinced the girl behind the snack bar to show them the way backstage. They found the young actor in his dressing room. He didn't want to talk about the play, didn't want to talk about the song he'd sung, or who'd written it. "I'm going to do bigger things," he said. He nodded at Jim and added, "He knows. He understands."

"Sure," Jim said, "you're obviously going places."

The boy smiled.

"Please," Laura said. "May I see the script?"

The boy rolled his eyes at Jim, knowingly, as though in some private understanding. Then he opened a trunk and brought out a stack of bound pages. "I think this is the one. I don't know. Maybe it's the last one I did. Or the one before that."

"*All the Swimming Things,*" Laura said, reading the title. "But who wrote it?"

"This conversation is so boring," the boy said. "Can't we talk about something else? Let's talk about *feelings.*"

He was still looking at Jim, and Laura noticed this time. She gave Jim a hard look.

Jim hunkered down and said, "So, thing is, we know this play's just pig and pepper to someone with your talents." Pig and pepper was a popular game here. At least, lots of people talked about it, though neither Jim nor Laura had seen it played. "But we really need to know who wrote this play. A lot of . . . a lot of feelings are riding on this. Ours, and some other people's. Our families, our friends. People with some pretty big feelings."

The boy nodded slowly. This was making an impression.

"So, what do you say?" Jim asked. "Can you help us out?"

The boy looked at his feet. "He's mean," he said. "Like, alpaca-spit mean."

"Who is?" Laura said.

"The man who wrote the play. He hurts people, and I don't like talking about him."

Laura knelt beside the boy and put one hand on his shoulder. "We won't tell him that we saw you," she said. "This can be our secret."

The boy looked at himself in his mirror, then looked at Laura. "He comes every few days, to drop off more pages. He gives us presents, presents that we hate. He makes us open them in front of him. He says we aren't good enough for his plays, that we should be happy just to know him. His name is Gray."

"Gray," Laura said. "Gray what?"

"Just Gray," the boy said.

The door opened and a tall man with a handlebar mustache ducked through, a marionette draped over his arms. Seeing it, the boy's face went pale. The man set the marionette in a chair.

"My contract," the boy said to Jim, as though he'd know what this meant. Jim rose from his seat. "You're all right?"

"I'm great," the boy said, though his voice was flat. The man with the handlebar mustache lifted him into his arms, and the boy went limp.

"Where are you taking him?" Laura said.

The man didn't look at her, didn't answer.

"Our secret, like you said," the boy told her.

She nodded, but the boy's eyes had closed, and the man carried him from the room, leaving them alone with the marionette. Jim was about to say something, but she shook her head to stop him, because she'd already seen it, seen the puppet's curly hair and brown eyes, its delicate fingers. It looked just like the boy.

"I want to go home," she said quietly. "I really just want to go home."

They'd been fighting about something, the day they crossed over, but now neither of them could remember what the fight was about. They couldn't remember how they'd crossed over, but they had their passports with them and their passports had been stamped. Were there customs officials? Inspections of some kind? Neither of them could say. The first thing they knew of this place was a roadside diner, and a menu they couldn't make sense of. Then a hot meal of something syrupy that came in three bowls, each a different color, each with a little plastic ship floating on top, then a panicked conversation in the parking lot, and apologies for the things they'd said that they couldn't remember.

"I do want to marry you," he'd told her, meaning it for the first time, maybe.

"I want to marry you too," she said. "Let's just get home in time, all right?"

The wedding was about two months off: plenty of time to find their way back. There were roadside hotels, and more diners, and drive-in movie theaters with big playgrounds under the screens. It was summer, and fireflies flashed in broad fields, and once they even managed to rent a car, but there was something in the contract they didn't understand, and an agent of the rental company came and took the car from them, shaking the wad of paper they'd signed and shouting about how hard his job was because of people like them.

They asked everyone they met which way to the border, but no one knew what they were talking about. They showed their passports, pointed at the stamps they'd been given, but got only shrugs and vacant looks in return. They asked, "Where are we?" until they learned not to bother asking.

On a bus, following a hint that a retired colonel in a seaside town might know about the country they'd come from, they decided to work on their wedding vows. "I don't want the usual nonsense about sickness and health," she said, tapping her pen against the notebook.

"You mean you'll leave me if I get sick?"

"Come on. What kind of marriage do we want, here? I thought you were looking for something a little off the beaten path."

"I don't know. Beaten paths are sounding good to me these days."

He saw the whiteness of her knuckles as she squeezed her pen. She needed this, needed something to hang on to, and he did too, maybe. So he said, "Okay, how about this? I promise, at least once a year, to learn a new craft and to craft something for you."

"Really?"

"Write it down."

She wrote it down and said, "Then I promise to bring you fresh flowers sometimes, especially on days for which there is no expectation of flowers."

"Thank you," he said. "I promise to do that thing you like when I—"

"You can't say that in front of my aunt Meg."

"Just put the first part, then. I promise to do that thing you like."

She wrote it down and said, "I promise to never make you feel bad about yourself on purpose, or to criticize you for making reasonable mistakes."

"And I, too," he said solemnly, "shall keep in mind that you are a fallible human being."

"But I won't have sex with other people," she said.

"Okay, ditto that one for me," he said.

And they were going to keep at it, but then the brass band at the back of the bus started rehearsing again, so they just held hands and watched the alpaca ranches roll by, until they came to the town by the sea, and to the colonel's enormous empty house, up there on the cliffs, and that was where the goons caught up with them, and they'd been running ever since.

They left the theater and found the nearest newsstand. *Newsstand* wasn't really the word for the thing. These roadside stalls, common to most every town they'd visited, were stocked with tools, small appliances, old photographs, and bits of junk neither of them could identify. But there were also books, maps, glossy magazines, and copies of the latest newspapers. They scoured the papers for mention of the play, for anything having to do with its author.

New merchandise was unloaded at a neighboring stand, and the other patrons swarmed away. A man in shiny green shorts came up to Laura and said, "Take these for a minute?" He dumped two babies into her arms and was gone before she could say anything.

"Unbelievable," Laura said, though it wasn't the first time this had happened. Because Laura and Jim didn't have babies of their own, people here thought it was fine to lend them theirs.

"Take one," she said to Jim.

He held up his handless right arm to protest, but she pushed the baby at him, and he bent to take it in his left.

Laura searched the magazines while Jim stood there.

"So, when did you first meet him?" he asked her.

"Meet who?"

"That asshole goon. There was something about the way you two looked at each other in the bar. Like it wasn't the first time you'd talked."

She kept turning pages as she spoke. "He came up to me in the first week, I think. You were—I don't know, in some store, looking for that soda you like."

"Purple Pow-Pow."

"He said he just wanted to talk. To explain some things."

"And did he?"

"No better than anyone else. He said they'd be keeping track of us. They're like border guards, I guess. And now he just kind of checks in with me sometimes."

"That's really great," Jim said, bouncing the baby against his side. "So as long as you guys are pals, do you think you could get us deported home or something? And while you're at it, maybe you could ask him for my hand back? Because I really liked having a right hand."

The proprietor of the place, who'd been dozing in a big rattan chair with three babies sprawled sleeping on top of him, opened his eyes a little.

"It's not like that," Laura said. "He doesn't want to help. It's more like he's waiting for me to slip up. Like he's looking for an excuse to—I don't know what. To do something really bad to us."

Jim tapped the stump of his arm against what looked like a toaster oven. "He already has done something really bad to us, Laura. But apparently you've got too big of a crush on this guy to worry about it."

He looked horrible to her, then, with his stump, with the baby on his hip starting to cry, and she felt horrible for thinking it. "I guess I'm pretty useless to you," she said.

"I guess you are," he said. He knocked over the thing that looked like a toaster oven, and trading cards of pig-and-pepper athletes spilled everywhere.

She said, "I've been counting, you know."

"Counting what?"

"It's tomorrow, or maybe the day after. The day we were supposed to get married." She shoved the other baby at him—now he had one on his left side and the other wobbling under his right arm. Both babies were red-faced and bawling as Laura ducked out of the stall and walked off.

Jim let her go, and he didn't watch her leave. He thought: I'm going to change out of this flowered shirt first chance I get.

He went over to the man in the rattan chair and said, "You know this guy, Gray? Gray. Turtle soup, singing. Come on, help me out here."

"Gray, sure, sure," the man said, standing up, shaking himself free of the babies. He took a utility knife out of his pocket and cut the twine from a bundle of thick books, then set them aside until he found the one he was looking for. The cover said simply *Gray* in big, blocky type.

Jim put the two babies in the rattan chair, and the other three immediately started crying, as though they'd caught it from the new arrivals. The proprietor looked flustered, but he handed the book to Jim.

It was heavy, the size of a big city phone book. Jim set it on the ground and flipped through pages of very small print, then found some pictures: a long-haired older man standing among alpacas, papier mâché alpacas on a stage, the same man kneeling by a stream, pointing with a stick at some turtles on a log.

"His biography," the proprietor said.

Jim flipped to the back of the book. "A Window or a Small Box" was the title of the last chapter.

"Twenty cents," the proprietor said. "But for you, my friend, who are so famous and so dashing, you can have that volume for free."

"Laura!" Jim shouted after her.

The man went back to the rattan chair and leaned over the babies, whose cries had turned to a chorus of shrieking. He cooed at them, but they only got louder.

"Laura!" Jim said again.

She'd already disappeared around the corner. Jim closed the book, tucked it under his arm, and ran in the direction she'd gone. He thought he spotted her straw hat, bouncing above the downtown lunch hour crowd, but it was just the basket on a melon salesman's head.

He shouted her name again, spinning in place. All around him, people went in and out of doors, and there were doors in everything, doors in the street, doors on second stories with ladders leading up to them, doors built into doors, doors in those doors.

"Laura!"

But she was gone, and he was lost, sweating as he wove through the crowd, the biography getting heavy under his arm.

"West or east?" he'd asked her one day. They were on a train that sped along the edge of a deep, river-hewn chasm. "I just want to know if we're going west or east."

"Sweetie," she'd told him, squeezing his hand, "I don't think they have west and east here."

That night, Jim sat in a sculpture garden in what he thought must be the center of the city. There were statues of cats, of moons, of arches shaped like horseshoes. It reminded him of something.

"That cereal," he said to the musician who was sharing his carafe of spiked Pow-Pow. "That breakfast cereal with all the little marshmallows in it!" But the musician just shook his head, and plucked a few notes on his zither while his two babies splashed in the fountain.

Jim used Gray's biography for a pillow, and in the morning it was all he had, because someone had stolen his knapsack and his shoes while he slept.

• • •

Laura hadn't gone more than a block from the newsstand before the goons got her.

She was so angry that she didn't even see the black sedan until it pulled up to the curb, didn't notice the smell of freshly cooked breakfast until the smell had engulfed her, until the swollen, gelatinous hands of her pursuers took her and dragged her into the car.

It was completely dark inside. The windows were no-way windows, tinted on both sides. But the engine roared, and the car veered and rattled, and somehow the driver was driving. The radio was on and tuned to something old-timey. The air was very cool, though Laura could feel the press of many bodies around her.

"You did the right thing, ditching that guy," came the voice of the chief goon from the front passenger seat. "It never would have worked out between you two."

"Take me back," she said.

"Remember that day?" said the chief goon. "The house by the sea, the second time I saw you? Stay, I wanted to tell you. Just stay with me."

She remembered: a cloudless afternoon, a dusty road out of town through tall grass, the ancient house on the high sea cliffs. The door was unlocked, and the retired colonel—the one they'd been told might know the way home— was dead or away or had never existed. She and Jim wandered countless bare rooms, dizzied by views of rock and wave and sky, until back in the entry hall they heard for the first time the sickening slosh of the goons' arrival. Only the handsome one, the one with thick blond hair and a big grin, the one who'd told her weeks before how it would go, walked in on solid feet. She thought maybe she could reason with him, but instead she'd said to Jim, "We have to run," and they ran, and kept running.

"Please," she said to the goon now. "Please just tell me where we're going."

"Going? Darling, we're already here. This is it."

"This is *what*?"

"This is what happens when we catch you. We drive around together, and you say interesting things for as long as you can."

The other goons were chuckling. There were more of them than could possibly fit inside that car: dozens, maybe. They could have filled a small theater.

"Keep it interesting, though. Because as soon as we get bored . . . "

More chuckling, and Laura's instinct was to fight—to kick and punch and claw her way out of there—but she'd heard the doors lock, and she knew what had happened to Jim when he tried to fight them. So she swallowed that back and said, "What do you want me to talk about?"

"Snacks," one of the goons said.

"Dinner," another said.

"Talk about the constellations," said a third.

"Zip it," said the chief goon. "I want to hear about the wedding plans. I always find your wedding plans so interesting."

"You hate it when I talk about my wedding plans," Laura said.

"You're right," the chief goon said. "That was a trap."

"I'm going to tell you a story," Laura said, and then goons were hushing other goons, and one of them switched off the radio, and for a moment all she could hear was the noise of the car's engine, which came as though from deep in the earth.

"The story is called 'A Window or a Small Box,' and it's about some stones at the bottom of a stream—"

"Boring," said one of the goons.

"Some stones," she said, "that dreamed they were turtles."

The same goon said, "Oooh," and Laura could hear the slopping sound of him as he settled back into his seat.

"They dreamed that they were turtles, and the turtles swam in the waters of the stream, up above the rocks that dreamed them . . . "

Jim wandered until he came to the bus station. He sat for a while, watching the drivers raise their rope ladders and motor away. Then he walked over to a food stall and watched sausages turn under the heat lamps. He was hungry but his money was gone. He said to the boy in the stall, "Hey, can I have one of those sausages and not pay you for it?"

The boy said, "Sure," and gave him one on a hard roll. Jim ate the sausage quickly, even though it was probably alpaca, and so far he'd managed to avoid eating alpaca.

He felt a little better after that. He stole a pen from a ticket booth window, then found a stack of leaflets advertising masks and baskets. The backs of the leaflets were blank. He made posters, drawing Laura's face with his left hand. The picture looked like something a five-year-old would make, all squiggly lines and smudges. But with some practice he got her eyes right, and the length of her hair.

Lost, he wrote at the top of each sheet, and then at the bottom, Please tell Jim if you see her.

A janitor saw what he was doing and gave him a little pot of glue. Jim put the posters up all over the bus station, then went outside and stuck them under windshield wipers. He pasted them to telephone poles, to construction site barriers, to windows, to doors. When he was hungry, he found an open-air market, ordered a bowl of noodle soup, and asked if he could have it for free. The chef just shrugged and said, "Sure, Jim, it's all yours."

He made more signs. He wrote, *Jim wants to marry this girl but he can't find her!* He plastered one neighborhood with them, took a bus to another neighborhood, plastered that one too. Sometimes people recognized him and cheered him on. A kid gave him a pair of nice blue sneakers with stars on them. They were too big, but he wore them anyway, letting them flop around as he walked.

By evening he was exhausted. He found a door in the base of an overpass, opened it, and went into the empty room on the other side. He curled up on the cement floor, said Laura's name aloud to himself, and slept.

" . . . the boy whose job it was to count the turtles sat on the shore all day, eating sandwiches and keeping a tally on his abacus. Sometimes the turtles floated by on logs, and he wasn't sure if he'd counted them or not, so he started painting white spots on their shells."

"Why did he have to count the turtles?"

"Because there are people who want to know how many turtles there are. The real problem, though, was that no one had counted dream turtles before. Should they be counted like regular turtles? And what if the stones woke up? What would happen to the turtles then? The boy knew he needed some good advice, so he went to the girl who could predict the future."

"Where did this story *come from*?"

"It's a collaboration between me and a writer named Gray. Have you heard of Gray?"

They chuckled, and their chuckling sounded a little dangerous, so she kept talking.

"Now, the girl who could predict the future was making a lot of money, but she was sad and she didn't know why. When the boy who counted turtles came to see her . . . "

Jim was awakened by a gentle knocking and the orange light of morning in his eyes. A woman stood in the doorway. She was short with short pale hair, and very pretty. "Mr. Jim?" she said. "Mr. Jim, I wonder if I could speak with you now?"

He knew her voice from the telephone. It was the biographer—no, the *biographist.*

"Um," he said, sitting up.

She took a notebook and pen from her vest. "Are you sleeping in here, Mr. Jim? I never thought of that before. Anyone could just walk right into one of these rooms and take up residence!"

"It wasn't locked."

The woman leaned against the doorway as she laughed, her knees buckling slightly. "Of course it wasn't!" she said. "Is this the real you, Mr. Jim? It is, it is. How can you keep it up?"

Jim realized that the biographist didn't have a baby. She wasn't from this city, and maybe not from this country. The thought dizzied him: other, stranger nations in this already too-strange place. "Listen," he said, "I think you've got the wrong idea about me. I'm not supposed to be famous. Back home, I'm pretty much just like everyone else."

She wrote that down. "It must be a *very* funny place."

Jim rubbed his cheeks. "You're right," he said. "It is a funny place."

She knelt beside him and looked him in the eyes. Her seriousness made him feel serious as she asked, "And tell me, are you interested in the work and life of the author Gray?"

She tapped the biography with her pen. A dozen times yesterday Jim had nearly left the book behind: hard enough hanging all those posters with one hand. But he'd kept it, and last night he'd used it as a pillow again.

He flipped through the biography as the biographist watched. "Yes," he said at last. "Yes, I am very interested in the life and work of the author Gray."

She was writing this down.

"I'll make a deal with you," Jim said.

"I have never made a deal before. How do we make it?"

"I say what I'm going to do for you, and also what I expect you to do for me, and then we negotiate."

She swayed back and forth a little, thinking. Then, "I am ready," she said.

"I'm going to take you on as my biographist."

"Really?"

"Yes, but listen. First you have to help me find Gray. That's the deal. What do you think?"

"We negotiate now?"

"Yes," he said.

"I accept!" she said, and hugged him. He put his arms around her and patted her back, twisting a little to keep them both from tumbling over.

"What's your name?" he asked.

"Is this part of the negotiations?"

"No, I'm just wondering what your name is."

"In that case," she said, and tapped his nose with her pen, "I am not telling."

She stood and walked out the door. He followed her. There was a bright yellow car parked beneath the overpass.

"Is this your car?" he asked.

"No, silly. It is Gray's car. He sent me to find you."

• • •

" . . . and just when the dream turtle soup was starting to get cold, the boy added more logs to the fire, and stirred the ladle in the cauldron. Turned out that a lot of people wanted to know what dream turtle soup tastes like, and a line had formed."

"What *does* dream turtle soup taste like?"

"It tastes like regular turtle soup, except fizzier, and it evaporates on your tongue. The boy ladled the soup into wooden bowls, and everyone had a little, and they all thought it was very good. But the girl who could predict the future arrived late, and there wasn't any left for her, and she told them about the bad things that were to come: the storm, and the battle, and the waking of the stones—"

"I hate this story," said the chief goon. "It's making me sad."

"It's not a happy story," Laura said, "and it doesn't turn out well." She took a breath to keep her voice steady, but when she tried to speak again her voice wasn't there at all. How long had she been in this car? How many hours, how many days? The silence, without her voice to break it, was terrible.

"Is that it, then?" the chief goon said.

"It," she said, trying to make it a question but failing.

Grumbles, now, from the dozens of goons in the audience. She had never heard annoyance sound so menacing.

"I want Jim," she said without thinking.

The grumbles got louder. She could feel the goons crowding close.

"Is that part of the story?" the chief goon said.

Even now, she thought, that monster in the front seat was enjoying this, enjoying his job. The goons loved getting angry, loved knowing that she would eventually disappoint them. Loved having the excuse they needed to snuff her out.

She choked back tears and said, "And the thing about this soup? Everyone who ate it was soon dreaming *they* were turtles, swimming in the stream and floating on logs in the sunlight . . . "

The goons settled in again, but as she told her story, she could tell they were no longer listening. She'd failed, somehow. The driver shifted gears, shifted direction. The car swayed, moving fast now, and Laura braced herself against the seat to keep upright, to keep herself from falling into one of those vile forms in the dark.

The biographist drove Jim into the hills, along winding roads choked nearly to the narrowness of a footpath by flowering bushes and vines. A gentle rain fell, but they kept the windows cracked. There were bottles of Purple Pow-Pow in a cooler in the back seat, and Jim helped himself. He had to hold the bottle between his legs while he twisted off the cap.

"Isn't it good?" the biographist asked him.

"Tastes like medicine, but it reminds me of home," Jim said.

An hour passed before they turned off the road and through an open wrought-iron gate. The biographist stopped the car there and let the engine idle. She gave Jim another serious look and said, "You don't have to do this."

"Do what?"

"Gray can be very mean to people. I heard he gave terrible, terrible presents to his own biographist. But you and me, Mr. Jim, we could keep on driving. Do you know how much coastline we have here? It just goes and goes."

Jim twirled the purple liquid at the bottom of his bottle. He could say yes, he thought, and his own old world would never know the difference. The two of them would drive, and he would talk, and she would write things down and laugh, and who knows?

But he was already shaking his head. "I have to talk to him. I have to find out if he knows where Laura is, and if anything here adds up to anything else."

She nodded, very solemn, and put the car back into gear. Neither of them spoke as they rode through more bushes and then out over a green meadow. The sun was clear of the clouds now, and the air was hot and damp. Beyond the fields, the broad valley was dotted here and there with houses and swimming pools.

But Jim didn't have time to take in the view, because the biographist was driving the car straight into something that looked a lot like a carnival.

"What is this?" he asked.

"Mr. Jim," she said sadly, "this is your wedding."

Before he and Laura crossed over, Jim had tried hard to love planning their wedding. He read wedding magazines, and pitched his ideas, even the ones he knew Laura's aunt wouldn't go for. "Everybody has doves," he said at dinner one night. "What would really liven things up is a falconry demonstration. And let's have a medieval feast. People can eat with their hands and drink tankards of ale."

He knew how far he could push things before Laura got upset, and he pushed things just that far, then stopped. The wedding he was talking about wasn't a wedding at all, but a spectacle meant to make people scratch their heads. A ceremony that didn't mean what it meant, because what it meant scared the hell out of him.

But nothing he'd come up with compared to what was underway here on this field in the hills.

Three great pavilions were festooned—*festooned* was the word—with streamers, blinking bulbs of glass, and giant glittery suns and moons. Beneath the tents and spilling out over the lawn were hundreds of revelers, people in suits and dresses but also in masks and wigs and corduroy clown costumes. People on stilts, or riding alpacas, or driving miniature cars with plastic eyes on the hoods and big furry wheels. Babies, painted bright colors and decorated with ribbon, rode laughing on shoulders or careened over the grass.

There were ice sculptures: birds, mountains, helicopters, treasure chests, symbols that might have been religious or might have been signs for money or mathematical functions, all melting into clear pools. Music came from one of the pavilions. It sounded like a brass band, heavy on percussion, piped through a Theremin. The noise made the car rattle.

The biographist must have brought him in through a back way, because more people were arriving by the minute, in cars and on motorcycles, sliding down ladders out of buses. She touched his hand. "We had only so much to go on. But the wedding, it sounds very important. So we wanted to build it proper."

Jim got out of the car. People saw him and cheered. They held up sheets of paper: the fliers he'd plastered all over town. *Jim wants to marry this girl!* Laura's poorly drawn face, hundreds of times over.

He ran through the crowd, and the biographist followed him. She had her notebook out again. "Mr. Jim, Mr. Jim," she said. "What are you feeling right now?"

Jim was thinking too much to think about what he was feeling. He was thinking about these tents. One was full of food (enormous aspics jiggling between piles of olive loaf and stacks of Pow-Pow), one was for dancing (laser lights bounced off euphoniums and shining steel drums), so maybe the third tent was for the ceremony. And maybe he'd find Laura there.

Streamers and flash bulbs popped as he strode over the lawn, his too-big sneakers flopping. People touched his arms, back, and neck, then whirled away screaming, as though they'd won a prize. A corduroy clown on stilts leaned back and bellowed, "No telling what'll happen, folks!"

Jim found the tent for the ceremony, the smallest of the three, heaped with pillows for people to sit on. In the center, a kind of altar: overlapping rugs, candles flickering on five-foot-tall holders, and suspended from the ceiling a great green sea turtle made of wire and fabric.

As soon as Jim entered the tent, the music stopped and the crowds hushed. A few people followed him inside and sat on pillows, set babies in their laps. Others peered in from just outside. Others, he saw, watched live feeds projected onto screens out in the field. The biographist kept close, and kept taking notes.

Standing at the altar was a man in loose-fitting brown clothes. Jim recognized the long hair, long nose, and wide eyes from the pictures in the biography. Gray opened his arms and said, "Jim, my boy. There you are. Such a long time I've been waiting for you."

In the darkness one of the goons said, "Ready?" and the dozens of others responded together, "Ready," and Laura heard a sound like a thousand bubbles popping. Her captors were going liquid.

The car stopped, doors opened. She closed her eyes against the light. The chief goon took her arm, and she grabbed her hat as he pulled her outside. His hand felt cool on her arm. "This isn't how I wanted things to go," he said. "I wanted a happy ending."

Damp grass brushed against her ankles as he led her forward. She put her hat on and pulled the brim low, squinting to see. She'd expected some nameless spot in the desert, buzzards overhead, a shovel to dig with, but here was a lush green place, full of people and noise and music. It looked as though a party was underway.

"What is this?"

"Dunno," the chief goon said. "It's Gray's thing. He said to bring you, but I figured if it worked out between you and me . . . " He threw his head back and set his jaw, making a show of not showing how hurt he was.

"Gray?" she said. "Gray the writer?"

The goon didn't answer, but led her across the field toward something so bright she couldn't look at it directly. An enormous mushroom, growing dome-like over the grass. No, it was a tent, and there were three of them. Three, just like she'd told the chief goon a few days ago at the Set-It-Down Saloon.

The goon must have seen the hopefulness on her face, because he said sharply, "Come on," and dragged her more roughly along. A dozen pinstripe suits slithered through the grass at their feet.

Gray. The wedding guests loved him. Loved him as he strutted over the rugs, telling Jim and Laura's story. They already knew how it went, but they loved hearing Gray tell it: the bus rides and train rides, evenings camped out in strange bars and diners, those jellyfish men close behind. The biographist, in a trance, listened and wrote everything down while the others swooned and held their breath.

Jim thought maybe he loved Gray, too. There was something familiar about him, like an uncle he'd forgotten he had. Or like all the mad scientists in all the movies that had mad scientists in them. Gray hugged Jim, and Jim hugged him back. Gray said, "Are you ready?"

"For what?" Jim said.

Gray turned to the crowd, arms wide. "For what, he wants to know!"

The people laughed and bounced their babies, and the babies laughed or cried or stared at other babies.

"Ready for your own marriage," said Gray, "so long in the making!" To Jim he added quietly, "And for the premiere of my greatest work to date. Congratulations, my boy. We're so pleased that you could be part of it."

He told the rest of the story. Told how Jim lost his hand—*gasp!*—told how the goons captured Laura—*groan!*—told how the goons had her still. "My footmen," Gray called them. Did they report to this man, then? Had they hunted Laura and him on Gray's behalf?

"I knew you'd come one day," Gray said. "But you got here on your own, didn't you? You found the clues I left."

Gray looked at him and waited. Everyone looked at him and waited. It was his turn to say something. He said, "It was in your play. *Everything That Swims.*"

"*All the Swimming Things,*" said Gray.

"And we'd heard it before. A fortuneteller told us how we'd get home. 'A window or a small box,' she said."

Gray clapped his hands together. "A window or a small box! That's the ticket!" And the guests laughed and cheered again.

Jim went close to Gray and grabbed his arm. He wanted to talk to him, not to everyone. "So you know what it means," he said.

Gray pulled his arm away. "Know what it means?" he bellowed. "No, I have no idea what it means!"

That got the guests going again, and while they laughed and applauded, Gray turned to Jim and spoke quietly and quickly. "A fortune teller said the same thing to me once. An old drunkard, lived down by the docks. He spread his cards over the top of a barrel and told me how to get home. 'A window or a small box,' he said. If it were a window *and* a small box, then maybe we'd have something. It might have to do with an arrangement of some kind: window, box, box, window. But which of the two is it? And which of the million windows and small boxes? For a while I thought it was a local turn of phrase, and I tried it out on everyone I met. Best I can tell, it doesn't mean anything at all. It's just something fortune tellers say to people like us."

"Like us?"

Gray frowned. The crowds were quiet now, trying to hear. It felt to Jim as though a thousand bodies leaned closer all at once.

"Don't you understand?" Gray said. "I'm not from around here, either. We're over the wrong rainbow, Jim. East of east of Eden. But it's ours, don't you see? I don't want to go home, and neither will you. They love us here. These people will gobble up anything, just anything. It pains me how easy it is. Watch."

Gray turned and raised his arms. "A wedding!" he said. "With the great turtle presiding over the ceremony!" The wire-and-fabric turtle suspended above the altar moved its head and legs, and the wedding guests roared.

Now Jim spotted a familiar face. The curly-haired boy from the theater walked up the aisle, carrying a plain hinged box in both hands. When he reached the altar, he stopped, knelt, and held the box up to Jim.

The guests hushed. The biographist stopped writing. She looked terrified.

"Ah!" said Gray. He clapped Jim on the back. "And now, my boy, it's time for your wedding present."

The chief goon dragged Laura through the crowds. People saw them coming and hopped out of the way; some danced and shrieked when they saw the goons in the grass. Laura glimpsed a screen in a field, and for a moment Jim's face appeared projected. She moved toward it, but the chief goon pulled her close.

"I know you'll only ever hurt me," he said to her as they walked. "And my wild, madcap heart can't bear it. I have to let you go, don't you see?"

But he didn't let her go, only pulled her more and more quickly toward the tents. The music had stopped, and the sun was going down. The chief goon said, "I wish I didn't feel like this. You've turned me into something I'm not, Laura. I never used to care. I never gave two bits about anyone!"

It's all right, she wanted to tell the goon, *everything is going to be all right*, but she didn't think that would help, and she didn't think it was true. Into the smallest of the three tents they went, and here was candlelight, and hundreds of people perched on pillows, and some kind of ceremony underway. A man in what looked like yoga clothes stood at the front of the crowd. And beside him was Jim, her own Jim.

She called his name, and the wedding guests turned and gazed at her. They shuffled to their feet and said, "Oooh!" as the chief goon led her down the aisle. Music struck up from the next tent over. It was a wedding. It was her wedding or something like it, and aside from the fact that Jim was here, it was all horribly, horribly wrong.

The other goons stood up, filling their shoes with themselves as they walked.

Jim, hearing Laura's voice, seeing her straw hat, pushed the box aside and went into the aisle. Gray took his arm and hissed, "Jim, you do want to open your present, don't you?"

What Jim wanted was to grab Laura and get the hell out of there. But the goons had her, and just seeing them made the stump of his arm tingle.

Gray pushed him toward the box. The old man was surprisingly strong.

How long had he been stuck in this place? Long enough to get used to being the most interesting thing around, Kal-El under a yellow sun. But this superman was jealous and spiteful, and when Jim and Laura's wedding began to eclipse him, he must have decided to claim it for himself.

Jim watched that big goon walk his bride grimly down the aisle. She stumbled, but he kept her marching. Would do worse, Jim thought, if he didn't stick to his role. So he put his hand on the box. It was warm to the touch.

The biographist, writing again, shook her head and said, "Oh, Mr. Jim," as though the whole thing was already written. And maybe it was. He found the catch and slid it aside.

He thought he heard Laura say, "No," but the box sprang open.

A small, spindly doll lay curled inside. Its wooden limbs were hinged, like those of a posable artists' mannequin. It wore blue jeans and a floral print shirt, and its face, Jim thought, looked a lot like his.

The doll stretched its arms and legs. Then, clacking and moving fast, it climbed out of the box and onto Jim's arm. It crawled up past his elbow, moving like a bug. Jim tried to fling it away, but the doll held tight. He screamed.

Laura screamed, too, and the wedding guests went silent. A few fainted, and babies began to cry. The music screeched to a stop. The goons grinned, all of them except their leader, who just looked sad about the whole thing.

"Now," Gray said, and stood at the back of the altar, smiling a benevolent priestly smile. Jim thought to charge him, to knock him over, but the thing on his arm seemed to know his thought, and it clambered up to his throat and squeezed.

Gray gestured with his left hand. The puppet didn't stop squeezing until Jim took his place there at his side. Even then it kept a strong grip.

The biographist wiped tears from her eyes as she scribbled notes. Gray gestured with his other hand, and the goon brought Laura forward. She stepped onto the rugs, but turned and took the goon's arm in both hands. "Please," she said to him. "Please help us."

The goon sighed and looked at Jim. "Look," he said, "I'm a free agent, but he's under contract now. Nothing I can do."

He sounded genuinely sorry. The other goons only smirked. She recognized the one from the Set-It-Down, the one that Jim had punched and that she had knocked out with her knapsack. She went to stand in front of him and his smirk fell away. He looked at the chief goon, as though for instructions, but Laura didn't give them the chance to talk it over.

She tore the goon's shirt open and plunged her hand into his chest. The goon's eyes widened, and his breath went out of him. The sound was echoed by the hundreds of wedding guests in the tent and beyond. Laura felt around in the gooey mess of the goon's innards, cool jelly between her fingers. She found what she was looking for and pulled, but the goon, showing his teeth, wouldn't release her.

Her hand began to tingle, and her fingers went numb. She looked at the chief goon. He seemed to understand what she was up to. He nodded at the other goon, and, frowning, the goon let her go.

In her hand was Jim's missing hand, perfectly preserved and dripping goo. The guests gasped at the sight, and Jim felt weak to see it there. His hand! They'd done so much together. He wanted to talk to it, wanted to hold it in his arms, his own baby.

But Laura didn't give it to him. She tossed it straight into the box the doll had crawled from, still open in the actor's hands. It landed with a thump and the boy looked at it.

The thing on Jim's throat perked up. It knew that the hand had something to do with Jim, and it was on to the scent. It crawled back down his arm, head turning as though to sniff the air.

Jim brought it closer to the box. The doll leapt down to investigate, and the boy snapped the lid shut.

A cheer rose up from the wedding guests. They laughed and bounced and held babies bouncing over their heads. Outside, people shouted and honked horns.

Gray went to the chief goon and grabbed him by the lapels. The guests were loving it, though, and the goons saw their new part in the show. They circled their former employer. He shouted at them to desist, to make room. But the chief goon gave a signal, and Gray vanished in a whirl of pinstripes.

Jim in Laura's arms, Laura in Jim's arms, the curly-haired boy clapping and hooting in his biggest role yet, and the food, and the dancing, and the biographist scribbling, scribbling, scribbling.

Later, there were fireworks, but Laura slept through them.

They got married. Not that night, but two weeks later, with just a few friends in attendance at the Set-It-Down Saloon. They were hoping for a cake, but no one knew what cake was, and when Laura explained the recipe to the chef, he laughed and said, "But alpacas don't lay eggs!"

Instead there were muffins, or something like muffins. The bartender's cousin brought them, and they were a hit, a sure thing. "Here's to a sure thing!" the bartender toasted.

They didn't dress up for the ceremony. He wore his flowered shirt, and she wore her straw hat, and the vows worked fine. For their honeymoon, they asked the goons to chase them for a while, and the goons obliged. They took buses and trains from town to town, and saw a lot of the country they hadn't seen before. They saw things that didn't make much sense to them, and some things that did. When they got back to the city that wasn't Los Angeles, Laura found one of the signs Jim had made glued to a telephone pole. They decided to stay.

For a while they lived in an apartment above the Set-It-Down Saloon, until one day the chief goon came by and offered them a gift: Gray's old house.

"Where is Gray?" Jim asked.

"Still in the car," the goon said. "He's churning out happy endings by the dozen."

"And when he runs out of them?"

The goon shrugged. "Maybe we'll go easy on him."

The house was at the edge of the field where Gray had tried to marry them. It was dark and low-slung, but Laura discovered a room in the back with a view of the broad valley below. "We'll take it," she said, though only Jim was there to hear her.

She began to write. She had some ideas for a play—for a few plays, it turned out. The plays did well, and one of the bigger productions made a real star of the boy with curly hair, who was free from his old contract. The biographist moved in, and when she was done with Jim's biography she started working on Laura's, and when Laura and Jim had children—a boy and a girl—she wrote their biographies, too.

Their children, Jim and Laura admitted to themselves, were a little strange to them. They went to school and were given babies to raise, and they were experts at pig and pepper, and they spoke to each other in a way that was different from how they spoke to their parents. But the children listened patiently to stories from the far-off land of upstate New York, like the one about the warrior who stalked the forests and was the last of his kind, and the one about the schoolteacher who saw a rider with no head, and the one about the man who fell asleep in the mountains and woke to find the world changed. Then they didn't want to hear those stories anymore, so Jim and Laura stopped telling them.

There were some hard times: Their son was often sick, and he did poorly at school. He ran away, got into some kind of trouble they didn't understand, trouble that plagued them for many years with documents and visits from officials. Later, the chief goon took him on as a kind of apprentice, and after a few years he went full-time, and they didn't see much of him after that.

Jim learned crafts. He learned to knit one-handed, and he learned how to brew Pow-Pow, and he learned spelunking, which wasn't a craft, exactly, but he took Laura with him into the caves. It was a popular thing to do here, and they made friends with fellow spelunkers, and got spelunking newsletters in the mail, and Laura wrote a play about spelunking that proved to be her biggest success.

She brought flowers from the garden sometimes, and presented them to him, and he put them in vases.

They got old, they got used to things, but sometimes they felt as lost as they had felt at that roadside diner all those years ago, and a panic would overcome them. Then he would say to her, "If only we could find a window or a small box," and Laura would laugh and they'd feel a little better.

They were sitting out back late one afternoon, watching the sun set over the mountains, and while they were talking they figured it out—*a window or a small box!*—of course, the answer was so obvious, how hadn't they thought of it before? But they didn't want to go back now, it was too late for that, and they stayed where they were.

"But where are we?" he asked, and she took his hand in both of hers and said, "Here. We're right here."

GAME OF CHANCE

CARRIE VAUGHN

—◆—

Once, they'd tried using sex to bring down a target. It had seemed a likely plan: Throw an affair in the man's path, guide events to a compromising situation, and momentum did the rest. That was the theory—a simple thing, not acting against the person directly, but slantwise. But it turned out it *was* too direct, almost an attack, touching on such vulnerable sensibilities. They'd lost Benton, who had nudged a certain woman into the path of a certain Republic Loyalist Party councilman and died because of it. He'd been so sure it would work.

Gerald had proposed trying this strategy again to discredit the RLP candidate in the next executive election. The man couldn't be allowed to take power if Gerald's own favored allies hoped to maintain any influence. But there was the problem of directness. His cohort considered ideas of how to subtly convince a man to ruin his life with sex. The problem remained: There were no truly subtle ways to accomplish this. They risked Benton's fate with no guaranteed outcome. Gathering before the chalkboard in their warehouse lair, mismatched chairs drawn together, they plotted.

Clare, sitting in back with Major, turned her head to whisper, "I like it better when we stop assassinations rather than instigate them."

"It's like chess," Major said. "Sometimes you protect a piece, sometimes you sacrifice one."

"It's a bit arrogant, isn't it, treating the world like our personal chess board?"

Major gave a lopsided smile. "Maybe, a bit."

"I think I have an idea," Clare said.

Gerald glanced their way and frowned.

Much more of this and he'd start accusing them of insubordination. She nudged Major and made a gesture with her hand: *Wait. We'll tell him later.* They sat back and waited, while Gerald held court and entertained opinions, from planting illegal pornography to obtaining compromising photographs. All of it too crass, too mundane. Not credible. Gerald sent them away with orders to "come up with something." Determined to brood, he turned his back as the others trailed to the corner of the warehouse that served as a parlor to scratch on blank pages and study books.

Clare and Major remained, seated, watching, until Gerald looked back at them and scowled.

"Clare has a different proposal," Major said, nodding for her to tell.

Clare ducked her gaze, shy, but knew she was right. "You can't use sex without acting on him, and that won't work. So don't act on him. Act on everything around him. A dozen tiny decisions a day can make a man fall."

Gerald was their leader because he could see the future. Well, almost. He could see paths, likely directions of events that fell one way instead of another. He used this knowledge and the talents of those he recruited to steer the course of history. Major liked the chess metaphor, but Gerald worked on the canvas of epic battles, of history itself. He scowled at Clare like she was speaking nonsense.

"Tiny decisions. Like whether he wears a red or blue tie? Like whether he forgets to brush his teeth? You mean to change the world by this?"

Major, who knew her so well, who knew her thoughts before she did, smiled his hunting smile. "How is the man's heart?"

"Yes. Exactly," she said.

"It'll take time," Major explained to a still frowning Gerald. "The actions will have to be lined up just so."

"All right," he said, because Major had proven himself. His voice held a weight that Clare's didn't. "But I want contingencies."

"Let the others make contingencies," Major said, and that made them all scowl.

Gerald left Clare and Major to work together, which was how she liked it best.

She'd never worked so hard on a plan. She searched for opportunities, studied all the ways they might encourage the target to harm himself. She found many ways, as it happened. The task left Clare drained, but happy, because it was working. Gerald would see. He'd be pleased. He'd start to listen to her, and she wouldn't need Major to speak for her.

"I don't mind speaking for you," Major said when she confided in him. "It's habit that makes him look right through you like he does. It's hard to get around that. He has to be the leader, the protector. He needs someone to be the weakest, and so doesn't see you. And the others only see what he sees."

"Why don't you?"

He shrugged. "I like to see things differently."

"Maybe there's a spell we could work to change him."

He smiled at that. The spells didn't work on them, because they were outside the whole system. Their spells put them outside. Gerald said they could change the world by living outside it like this. Clare kept thinking of it as gambling, and she never had liked games.

They worked: The target chose the greasiest, unhealthiest meals, always ate dessert, and took a coach everywhere—there always seemed to be one conveniently at hand. Some days, he forgot his medication, the little pills that kept his heart steady—the bottle was not in its place and he couldn't be bothered to look for it. Nothing to notice from day to day. But one night, in bed with his wife—no lurid affair necessary—their RLP candidate's weak heart gave out. A physician was summoned quickly enough, but to no avail. And that, Clare observed, was how one brought down a man with sex.

Gerald called it true. The man's death threw the election into chaos, and his beloved Populist Tradition Party was able to hold its seats in the Council.

Clare glowed with pride because her theory had worked. A dozen little changes, so indirect as to be unnoticeable. The perfect expression of their abilities.

But Gerald scowled. "It's not very impressive, in the main," he said and walked away.

"What's that supposed to mean?" Clare whispered.

"He's angry he didn't think of it himself," Major said.

"So it wasn't fireworks. I thought that was the point."

"I think you damaged his sensibilities," he said, and dropped a kind kiss on her forehead.

She had been a normal, everyday girl, though prone to daydreaming, according to her governess. She was brought up in proper drawing rooms, learning how to embroider, supervise servants, and orchestrate dinner parties. Often, though, she had to be reminded of her duties, of the fact that she would one day marry a fine gentleman, perhaps in the army or in government, and be the envy of society ladies everywhere. Otherwise she might sit in the large wingback armchair all day long, staring at the light coming in through the window, or at sparks in the fireplace, or at the tongue of flame dancing on the wick of the nearest lamp. "What can you possibly be thinking about?" her governess would ask. She'd learned to say, "Nothing." When she was young, she'd said things like, "I'm wondering, what if fire were alive? What if it traveled, and is all flame part of the same flame? Is a flame like a river, traveling and changing every moment?" This had alarmed the adults around her.

By the time she was eighteen, she'd learned to make herself presentable in fine gowns, and to arrange the curls of her hair to excite men's interest, and she'd already had three offers. She hadn't given any of them answer, but thought to accept the one her father most liked so at least somebody would be happy.

Then one day she'd stepped out of the house, parasol over her shoulder, intending a short walk to remind herself of her duty before that evening's dinner party, and there Gerald and Major had stood, at the foot of the stairs, two dashing figures from an adventure tale.

"What do you think about, when you look at the flame of a candle?" Gerald had asked.

She stared, parasol clutched in gloved hands, mind tumbling into an honest answer despite her learned poise. "I think of birds playing in sunlight. I wonder if the sun and the fire are the same. I think of how time slows down when you watch the hands of a clock move."

Major, the younger and handsomer of the pair, gave her a sly grin and offered his hand. "You're wasted here. Come with us."

At that moment she knew she'd never been in love before, because she lost her heart to Major. She set her parasol against the railing on the stairs, stepped forward, and took his hand. Gerald pulled the theatrical black cape he'd been wearing off his shoulders, turned it with a twist of his wrists, and swept it around himself, Major, and Clare. A second of cold followed, along with a feeling of drowning. Clare shut her eyes and covered her face. When Major murmured a word of comfort, she finally looked around her and saw the warehouse. Gerald introduced himself and the rest of his cohort, and explained that they were masters of the world, which they could manipulate however they liked. It seemed a very fine thing.

Thus she vanished from her old life as cleanly as if she had never existed. Part of her would always see Gerald and Major as her saviors.

Gerald's company, his band of unseen activists, waited in their warehouse headquarters until their next project, which would only happen when Gerald traced lines of influence to the next target. The next chess piece. Clare looked forward to the leisure time until she was in the middle of it, when she just wanted to go out and *do* something.

Maybe it was just that she'd realized a long time ago that she wasn't any good at the wild version of poker the others played to pass time. She sat the games out, tried to read a book, or daydreamed. Watched dust motes and candle flames.

The other four were the fighters. The competitive ones. She'd joined this company by accident.

Cards snicked as Major dealt them out. Clean-shaven, with short-cropped hair, he was dashing, military. He wore a dark blue uniform jacket without insignia; a white shirt, unbuttoned at the collar; boots that needed polishing, but that only showed how active he was. Always in the thick of it. Clare could watch him deal cards all day.

"Wait a minute. Are we on Tuesday rules or Wednesday?" Ildie asked.

Fred looked up from his hand, blinking in a moment of confusion. "Today's Thursday, isn't it?"

"Tuesday rules on Thursday. That's the fun of it," Marco said, voice flat, attention on the cards.

"I hate you all," Ildie said, scowling. They chuckled, because she always said that.

Ildie dressed like a man, in an oxford shirt, leather pants, and high boots. This sometimes still shocked Clare, who hadn't given up long skirts and braided hair when she'd left a proper parlor for this. Ildie had already been a rebel when she joined. At least Clare had learned not to tell Ildie how much nicer she'd look if she grew her hair out. Fred had sideburns, wore a loosened cravat, and out of all of them might be presentable in society with a little polish. Marco never would be. Stubble shadowed his face, and he always wore his duster to hide the pistols on his belt.

A pair of hurricane lamps on tables lit the scene. The warehouse was lived-in, the walls lined with shelves, which were piled with books, rolled up charts, atlases, sextants, hourglasses, a couple of dusty globes. They'd pushed together chairs and coffee tables for a parlor, and the far corner was curtained off into rooms with cots and washbasins. In the parlor, a freestanding chalkboard was covered with writing and charts, and more sheets of paper lay strewn on the floor, abandoned when the equations scrawled on them went wrong. When they went right, the sheets were pinned to the walls and shelves and became the next plan. At the moment, nothing was pinned up.

Clare considered: Was it a matter of tracing lines of influence to objects rather than personalities? Difficult, when influence was a matter of motivation, which was not possible with inanimate objects. So many times their tasks would have been easier if they could change someone's *mind*. But that was like bringing a sledgehammer down on delicate glasswork. So you changed the thing that would change someone's mind. How small a change could generate the greatest outcome? That was her challenge: Could removing a bottle of ink from a room change the world? She believed it could. If it was the right bottle of ink, the right room. Then perhaps a letter wouldn't be written, an order of execution wouldn't be signed.

But the risk—that was Gerald's argument. The risk of failure was too great. You might take a bolt from the wheel of a cannon, but if it was the wrong bolt, the wrong cannon . . . The variables became massive. Better to exert the most influence you could without being noticed. That didn't stop Clare from weaving her thought experiments. For want of a nail . . .

"I raise," Major said, and Clare looked up at the change in his voice. He had a plan; he was about to spring a trap. After the hundreds of games those four had played, couldn't they see it?

"You don't have anything." Marco looked at his hand, at the cards lying face up on the table, back again. Major gave him a "try me" look.

"He's bluffing." Ildie wore a thin smile, confident because Major had bluffed before. Just enough to keep them guessing. He did it on purpose, they very well knew, and he challenged them to outwit him. They thought they could—that was why they kept falling into his traps. But even Major had a tell, and Clare could see it if no one else could. Easy for her to say, though, sitting outside the game.

"Fine. Bet's raised. I see it," Fred countered.

Then they saw it coming, because that was part of Major's plan. Draw them in, spring the trap. He tapped a finger; the air popped, a tiny sound like an insect hitting a window, that was how small the spell was, but they all recognized the working of it, the way the world shifted just a bit, as one of them outside of it nudged a little. Major laid out his cards, which were all exactly the cards he needed, a perfect hand, against unlikely—but not impossible—odds.

Marco groaned, Ildie threw her cards, Fred laughed. "I should have known."

"Tuesday rules," Major said, spreading his hands in mock apology.

Major glanced at Clare, smiled. She smiled back. No, she didn't ever want to play this game against Major.

Marco gathered up the cards. "Again."

"Persistent," Major said.

"Have to be. Thursday rules this time. The way it's *meant* to be." They dealt the next hand.

Gerald came in from the curtained area that was his study, his wild eyes red and sleepless, a driven set to his jaw. They all knew what it meant.

"I have the next plot," he said.

Helping the cause sometimes meant working at cross-purposes with the real world. A PTP splinter group, frustrated and militant, had a plan, too, and Gerald wanted to stop it because it would do more harm than good.

Easier said than done, on such a scale. Clare preferred the games where they put a man's pills out of the way.

She and Major hunched in a doorway as the Council office building fell, brought down by cheap explosives. A wall of dust scoured the streets. People coated in the gray stuff wandered like ghosts. Clare and Major hardly noticed.

"We couldn't stop it," Clare murmured, speaking through a handkerchief.

Major stared at a playing card, a jack of diamonds. "We've done all we can."

"What? What did we do? We didn't stop it!" They were supposed to stop the explosion, stop the destruction. She had wanted so much to stop it, not for Gerald's sake, but for the sake of doing good.

Major looked hard at her. "Twenty-nine bureaucrats meant to be in that building overslept this morning. Eighteen stayed home sick. Another ten stayed home with hangovers from overindulging last night. Twenty-four more ran late because either their pets or children were sick. The horses of five coaches came up lame, preventing another fifteen from arriving. That's ninety-six people who weren't in that building. We did what we could." His glare held amazing conviction.

She said, "We're losing, aren't we? Gerald will never get what he wants."

So many of Gerald's plans had gone just like this. They counted victories in lives, like picking up spilled grains of rice. They were changing lives, but not the world.

"Come on," he ordered. "We've got a door."

He threw the card at the wall of the alley where they'd hidden. It stuck, glowed blue, and grew. Through the blue glare a gaping hole showed. Holding hands, they dove into it, and it collapsed behind them.

"Lame coach horses? Hangovers?" Gerald said, pacing back and forth along one of the bookshelves. "We're trying to save civilization."

"What is civilization but the people who live within it?" Clare said softly. It was how she said anything around Gerald.

"Ninety-six lives saved," Major said. "What did anyone else accomplish?" Silent gazes, filled with visions of destruction, looked back at him. The rest of them: Fred, Ildie, and Marco. Their jackets were ruffled, their faces weary, but they weren't covered with dust and ragged like Clare and Major were. They hadn't gotten that close.

Gerald paced. "In the end, what does it mean? For us?" The question was rhetorical because no answer would satisfy him. Though Clare thought, it means whatever we want it to mean.

Clare and Major never bothered hiding their attachment from the others. What could the company say to disapprove? Not even Gerald could stop them, though Ildie often looked at her askance, with a scowl, as if Clare had betrayed her. Major assured her that the other woman had never held a claim on him. Clare wondered if she might have fallen in love with any of the men— Fred, Benton, or even Marco—if any of them had stood by Gerald to recruit her instead of Major. But no, she felt her fate was to be with Major. She didn't feel small with him.

Hand in hand, careless, they'd leave the others and retreat to the closet in an unused corner of the warehouse's second floor, where they'd built a pallet just for them. A nest, Clare thought of it. Here, she had Major all to herself, and he seemed happy enough to be hers. She'd lay across his naked chest and he'd play with her hair. Bliss.

"Why did you follow Gerald when he came for you?" she asked after the disaster with the exploded building.

"He offered adventure."

"Not for the politics, then? Not because you believe in his party?"

"I imagine it's all one and the same in the long run."

The deep philosophy of this would have impressed her a few years ago. Now, it seemed like dodging the question. She propped herself on an elbow to study him. She was thinking out loud.

"Then why do you still follow him? You could find adventure without him, now that he's shown you the way."

He grinned sleepily and gathered her closer. "I'd wander aimlessly. His adventures are more interesting. It's a game."

"Oh."

"And why do you still follow him? Why did you take my hand the day we met?"

"You were more interesting than what I left behind."

"But I ask you the same question, now. I know you don't believe in his politics. So why do you still follow him?"

"I don't follow him. I follow you."

His expression turned serious, frowning almost. His hand moved from her hair to her cheek, tracing the line of her jaw as if she were fragile glass. "We're a silly pair, aren't we? No belief, no faith."

"Nothing wrong with that. Major—if neither of us is here for Gerald, we should leave. Let's go away from this, be our own cohort." Saying it felt like rebellion, even greater than the rebellion of leaving home in the first place.

His voice went soft, almost a whisper. "Could we really? How far would we get before we started missing this and came back?"

"I wouldn't miss the others," she said, jaw clenched.

"No, not them," he said. "But the game."

Gerald could fervently agitate for the opposite party, and Major would play the game with as much glee. She could understand and still not agree.

"You think we need Gerald, to do what we do?"

He shook his head, a questioning gesture rather than a denial. "I'm happy here. Aren't you?"

She could nod and not lie because here, at this small moment with him, she was happy.

One *could* change the world by nudging chances, Clare believed. Sometimes, she went off by herself to study chances the others wouldn't care about.

At a table in the corner of a café—the simple, homelike kind that students frequented, with worn armchairs, and chess boards and pieces stored in boxes under end tables with old lamps on them—Clare drew a pattern in a bit of tea that dripped from her saucer. Swirled the shape into two circles, forever linked. In front of the counter, a boy dropped a napkin. The girl behind him picked it up. Their hands brushed. He saw that she had a book of sonnets, which he never would have noticed if he hadn't dropped the napkin. She saw that he had a book of philosophy. They were students, maybe, or odd enthusiasts. One asked the other, are you a student? The answer didn't matter because the deed was done. In this world, in this moment, despite all the unhappiness, this small thing went right.

This whole thing started because Gerald saw patterns. She wondered later: Did he see the pattern, identify them because of it, and bring them together? Was that his talent? Or did he cause the pattern to happen? If not for Gerald, would she have gone on, free and ignorant, happily living her life with no knowledge of what she could do? Or was she always destined to follow this path, use this talent with or without the others? Might she have spent her time keeping kittens from running into busy streets or children from falling into rivers? And perhaps one of those children would grow up to be the leader Gerald sought, the one who would change the world.

All that had happened, all their work, and she still could not decide if she believed in destiny.

She wouldn't change how any of it had happened because of Major. The others marveled over Gerald's stern, Cossack determination. But she fell in love with Major, with his shining eyes.

"We have to do better, think harder, more creatively. Look how much we've done already, never forget how much we've done."

After almost a decade of this, only six of the original ten were left. The die-hards, as mad as Gerald. Even Major looked on him with that calculating light in his eyes. Did Gerald even realize that Major's passion was for tactics rather than outcome?

"Opportunities abound, if we have the courage to see them. The potential for good, great good, manifests everywhere. We must have the courage to see it."

Rallying the troops. Clare sighed. How many times had Gerald given variations of this speech in this dingy warehouse, hidden by spells and out of the world? They all sounded the same. She'd stopped being able to see the large patterns a long time ago and could only see the little things now. A dropped napkin in a café. She could only change the course of a few small lives.

"There's an assassination," said Gerald. "It will tip the balance into a hundred years of chaos. Do you see it?"

Fred smiled. "We can stop it. Maybe jam a rifle."

"A distraction, to throw off the assassin's aim."

"Or give him a hangover," Major said. "We've had great success with hangovers and oversleeping." He glanced at Clare with his starry smile. She beamed back. Fred rolled his eyes.

"Quaint," Gerald said, frowning.

The game was afoot. So many ways to change a pattern. Maybe Clare's problem was she saw them as people, not patterns. And maybe she was the one holding the rest back. Thinking too small. She wasn't part of *their* pattern anymore.

This rally was the largest Clare had ever seen. Her generation had grown up hearing grandparents' stories of protest and clashes (civil war, everyone knew, but the official history said clashes, which sounded temporary and isolated). While their parents grew up in a country that was tired and sedate, where they were content to consolidate their little lives and barricade themselves against the world, the children wondered what it must have been like to believe in idealism.

Gerald's target this time was the strongest candidate the PTP had ever put forward for Premier. The younger generation flocked to Jonathan Smith. People adored him—unless they supported the RLP. Rallies like this were the result. Great crowds of hope and belief, unafraid. And the crowds who opposed them.

Gerald said that Jonathan Smith was going to be assassinated. Here, today, at the rally, in front of thousands. All the portents pointed to this. But it would not result in martyrdom and change, because the assassin would be one of his own and people would think, *our parents were right*, and go home.

Clare and Major stood in the crowd like islands, unmoving, unfeeling, not able to be caught up in the exhilarating speech, the roaring response. She felt alien. These were her people, they were all human, but never had she felt so far removed. She might have felt god-like, if she believed in a god who took such close interest in creation as to move around it like this. God didn't have to, because there were people like Gerald and Major.

"It's nice to be saving someone," Clare said. "I've always liked that better."

"It only has to be a little thing," Major said. "Someone in the front row falls and breaks a bone. The commotion stalls the attack when Smith goes to help the victim. Because he's like that."

"We want to avoid having a victim at all, don't we?"

"Maybe it'll rain."

"We change coach horses, not the weather." But not so well that they couldn't keep an anarchist bomb from arriving at its destination. They weren't omnipotent. They weren't gods. If they were, they could control the weather.

She had tried sending a message about the government building behind Gerald's back. He would have called the action too direct, but she'd taken the risk. She'd called the police, the newspapers, everyone, with all the details they'd conjured. Her information went into official records, was filed for the appropriate authorities, all of which moved too slowly to be of any good. It wasn't too direct after all.

Inexorable. This path of history had the same feeling of being inexorable. Official channels here would welcome an assassination. The police would not believe her. They only had to save one life.

She wished for rain. The sky above was clear.

They walked among the crowd, and it was grand. She rested her hand in the crook of Major's elbow; he held it there. He wore a happy, silly smile on his face. They might have been in a park, strolling along a gentle river in a painting.

"There's change here," he said, gazing over the angry young crowd and their vitriolic signs.

She squeezed his arm and smiled back.

The ground they walked on was ancient cobblestone. This historic square had witnessed rallies like this for a thousand years. In such times of change, gallows had stood here, or hooded men with axes. How much blood had soaked between these cobbles?

That was where she nudged. From the edges of the crowd, they were able to move with the flow of people surging. They could linger at the edges with relative freedom of movement, so she spotted a bit of pavement before the steps climbing to the platform where the demagogue would speak. A toe caught on a broken cobblestone would delay him. Just for a second. Sometimes that was enough to change the pattern.

"Here," she said, squeezing Major's arm to anchor him. He nodded, pulled her to the wall of a townhouse, and waited.

While she focused on the platform, on the path that Jonathan Smith would take—on the victim—Major turned his attention to the crowd, looking for the barrel of a gun, the glint of sunlight off a spyglass, counter-stream movement in the enthusiastic surge. The assassin.

Someone else looking for suspicious movement in a crowd like this would find *them*, Clare thought. Though somehow no one ever did find them.

Sometimes, all they could do was wait. Sometimes, they waited and nothing happened. Sometimes they were too late or early, or one of the others had already nudged one thing or another.

"There," Major said, the same time that Clare gripped his arm and whispered, "There."

She was looking to the front where the iconic man, so different than the bodyguards around him, emerged and waved at the crowd. There, the cobblestone—she drew from her pocket a cube of sugar that had been soaked in amaretto, crumbled it, let the grains fall, then licked her fingers. The sweet, heady flavor stung her tongue.

Major lunged away from her. "No!"

The stone lifted, and the great Jonathan Smith tripped. A universal gasp went up.

Major wasn't looking to the front with everyone else. He was looking at a man in the crowd, twenty feet away, dissolute. A troublemaker. Hair ragged, shirt soiled, faded trousers, and a canvas jacket a size too large. Boots made for kicking. He held something in his right fist, in a white-knuckled grip.

This was it, the source, the gun—the locus, everything. This was where they learned if they nudged enough, and correctly. But the assassin didn't raise a straight arm to aim. He cocked back to throw. He didn't carry a gun, he held a grenade.

Gerald and the others had planned for a bullet. They hadn't planned for this.

Major put his shoulder to the man's chest and shoved. The would-be assassin stumbled, surprised, clutched the grenade to his chest—it wasn't active, he hadn't lit the fuse. Major stopped him. Stopped the explosive, stopped the assassin, and that was good. Except it wasn't, and he didn't.

Smith recovered from his near-fall. He mounted the platform. The bodyguard behind him drew his handgun, pointed at the back of Smith's head, and fired. The shot echoed and everyone saw it and spent a moment in frozen astonishment. Even the man with the grenade. Everyone but Major, who was on the ground, doubled over, shivering as if every nerve burned.

Clare fell on top of him, crying, clutching at him. His eyes rolled back, enough to look at her, enough for her to see the fear in them. If she could have held onto him, carried him with her, saved him, she would have. But he'd put himself back into the world. He'd acted, plunged back into a time and place he wasn't part of anymore, and now it tore him to pieces. The skin of his face cracked under her hands, and the blood and flesh underneath was black and crumbling to dust.

She couldn't sob hard enough to save him.

Clare was lost in chaos. Then Gerald was there with his cloak. So theatrical, Major always said. Gerald used the cloak like Major used the jack of diamonds. He swept it around the three of them, shoving them through a doorway.

But only Clare and Gerald emerged on the other side.

The first lesson they learned, that Major forgot for only a second, the wrong second: They could only build steps, not leap. They couldn't act directly, they couldn't be part of the history they made.

So Jonathan Smith died, and the military coup that followed ruined everything.

Five of them remained.

The problem was she could not imagine a world different from the burned-out husk that resulted from the war fought over the course of the next year. Gerald's plan might have worked, bringing forth a lush Eden where everyone drank nectar and played hopscotch with angelic children, and she still would have felt empty.

Gerald's goal had always been utopia. Clare no longer believed it was possible.

The others were very kind to her, in the way anyone was kind to a child they pitied. *Poor dear, but she should have known better.* Clare accepted the blanket Ildie put over her shoulders and the cup of hot tea Fred pressed into her hands.

"Be strong, Clare," Ildie said, and Clare thought, easy for her to say.

"What next, what next," Gerard paced the warehouse, head bent, snarling almost, his frown was so energetic.

"Corruption scandal?" Marco offered.

"Too direct."

"A single line of accounting, the wrong number in the right place, to discredit the regime," Ildie said.

Gerald stopped pacing. "Maybe."

Another meeting. As if nothing had happened. As if they could still go on.

"Major was the best of us," Clare murmured.

"We'll just have to be more careful," Ildie murmured back.

"He made a mistake. An elementary mistake," Gerald said, and never spoke of Major again.

The village a mile outside the city had once been greater, a way station and market town. Now, it was a skeleton. The war had crushed it, burned it, until only hovels remained, the scorched frames of buildings standing like trees in a forest. Brick walls had fallen and lay strewn, crumbling, decaying. Rough canvas stretched over alcoves provided shelter. Cooking fires burned under tripods and pots beaten out of other objects. What had been the cobbled town square still had the atmosphere of an open-air market, people shouting and milling, bartering fiercely, trading. The noise made a language all its own, and a dozen different scents mingled.

Despite the war and bombing, some of the people hadn't fled, but they hadn't tried to rebuild. Instead, they seemed to have crawled underground when the bombardment began, and when it ended they reemerged, continued their lives where they left off as best they could, with the materials they had at hand. Cockroaches, Clare thought, and shook the thought away.

At the end of the main street, where the twisted, naked foundations gave way and only shattered cobblestones remained, a group of men were digging a well into an old aquifer, part of the water system of the dying village. They were looking for water. Really, though, at this point they weren't digging, but observing the amount of dirt they'd already removed and arguing. They were about to give up and try again somewhere else. A whole day's work wasted, a day they could little afford when they had children to feed and material to scavenge.

Clare helped. Spit on her hands, put them on the dusty earth, then rubbed them together and drew patterns in the dust. Pressed her hands to the ground again. The aquifer that they had missed by just a few feet seeped into the ditch they'd dug. The well filled. The men cheered.

Wiping her hands on her skirt, Clare walked away. She was late for another meeting.

"What is the pattern?" Gerald asked. And no one answered. They were down to four.

Ildie had tried to cause a scandal by prompting a divorce between the RLP Premier and his popular wife. No matter how similar attempts had failed before. "This is different, it's not causing an affair, it's destroying one. I can do this," she had insisted, desperate to prove herself. But the targets couldn't be forced. She might as well have tried to cause an affair after all. Once again, too direct. Clare could have told her it wouldn't work. Clare recognized when people were in love. Even Republic Loyalists fell in love.

"What will change this path? We must make this better!"

She stared. "I just built a well."

Marco smirked. "What's the use of that?"

Fred tried to summon enthusiasm. They all missed Major even if she was the only one who admitted it. "It's on the army now, not the government. We remove the high command, destroy their headquarters perhaps—"

Marco said, "What, you think we can make earthquakes?"

"No, we create cracks in the foundation, then simply shift them—"

Clare shook her head. "I was never able to think so big. I wish—"

Fred sighed. "Clare, it's been two years, can you please—"

"It feels like yesterday," she said, and couldn't be sure that it *hadn't* been just yesterday, according to the clock her body kept. But she couldn't trust that instinct. She'd lost hours that felt like minutes, studying dust motes.

"Clare—" Gerald said, admonishing, a guru unhappy with a disciple. The thought made her smile, which he took badly, because she wasn't looking at him but at something the middle distance, unseen.

He shook his head, disappointment plain. The others stared at her with something like fascination or horror.

"You've been tired. Not up to this pressure," he explained kindly. "It's all right if you want to rest."

She didn't hear the rest of the planning. That was all right; she wasn't asked to take part.

She took a piece of charcoal from an abandoned campfire. This settlement was smaller than it had been. Twenty fires had once burned here, with iron pots and bubbling stews over them all.

Eight remained. Families ranged farther and farther to find food. Often young boys never came back. They were taken by the army. The well had gone bad. They collected rainwater in dirty tubs now.

And yet. Even here. She drew a pattern on a slab of broken wood. Watched a young man drop a brick of peat for the fire. Watched a young woman pick it up for him and look into his eyes. He smiled.

Now if only she knew the pattern that would ensure that they survived.

When they launched the next plan—collapse the army high command's headquarters, crippling the RLP and allowing the PTP to fill the vacuum, or so Gerald insisted—she had no part to play. She was not talented enough, Gerald didn't say, but she understood it. She could only play with detritus from a kitchen table. She could never think big enough for them. Major hadn't cared.

She did a little thing, though: scattered birdseed on a pool of soapy water, to send a tremor through the air and warn the pigeons, rats, and such that they ought to flee. And maybe that ruined the plan for the others. She'd nudged the pattern too far out of alignment for their pattern to work. The building didn't collapse, but the clock tower across the square from which Fred and Marco were watching did. As if they had planted explosives and been caught in the blast.

Too direct, of course.

• • •

She left. Escaped, rather, as she thought. She didn't want Gerald to find her. Didn't want to look him in the eye. She would either laugh at him or accuse him of killing Major and everyone else. Then she would strangle him, and since they were both equally out of history she just might be able to do it. It couldn't possibly be too direct, and the rest of the world couldn't possibly notice.

Very tempting, in those terms.

But she found her place, her niche, her purpose. Her little village on the edge of everything was starting to build itself into something bigger. She'd worried about it, but just last year the number of babies born exceeded the number of people who died of disease, age, and accident. A few more cook fires had been added. She watched, pleased.

But Gerald found her, eventually, because that was one of his talents: finding people who had the ability to move outside the world. She might as well have set out a lantern.

She didn't look up when he arrived. She was gathering mint leaves that she'd set out to dry, putting them in the tin box where she stored them. A spoonful of an earlier harvest was brewing in a cup of water over her little fire. Her small realm was tucked under the overhang formed by three walls that had fallen together. The witch's cave, she called it. It looked over the village so she could always watch her people.

Gerald stood at the edge of her cave for a long time, watching. He seemed deflated, his cloak worn, his skin pale. But his eyes still burned. With desperation this time, maybe, instead of ambition.

When he spoke, he sounded appalled. "Clare. What are you doing here? Why are you living in this . . . this pit?"

"Because it's my pit. Leave me alone, I'm working."

"Clare. Come away. Get out of there. Come with me."

She raised a brow at him. "No."

"You're not doing any good here."

She still did not give him more than a passing glance. The village below was full of the evening's activities: farmers returning from fields, groups bustling around cook fires. Someone was singing, another laughing, a third crying.

She pointed. "Maybe that little girl right there is the one who will grow up and turn this all around. Maybe I can keep her safe until she does."

He shook his head. "Not likely. You can't point to a random child and make such a claim. She'll be dead of influenza before she reaches maturity."

"It's the little things, you're always saying. But you don't think small enough," she said.

"Now what are you talking about?"

"Nails," she murmured.

"You have a talent," he said, desperately. "You see what other people overlook. Things other people take for granted. There are revolutions in little things. I understand that now. I didn't—"

"Why can't you let the revolutions take care of themselves?"

He stared at her, astonished. Might as well tell him to stop breathing. He didn't know how to do anything else. And no one had ever spoken to him like this.

"You can't go back," he said as if it was a threat. "You can't go back to being alive in the world."

"Does it look like I'm trying?" He couldn't answer, of course, because she only looked like she was making tea. "You're only here because there's no one left to help you. And you're *blind*."

Some days when she was in a very low mood she imagined Major here with her, and imagined that he'd be happy, even without the games.

"Clare. You shouldn't be alone. You can't leave me. Not after everything."

"I never did this for you. I never did this for history. There's no great sweep to any of this. Major saw a man with a weapon and acted on instinct. The grenade might have gone off and he'd have died just the same. It could have happened to anyone. I just wanted to help people. To try to make the world a little better. I like to think that if I weren't doing this I'd be working in a soup kitchen somewhere. In fact, maybe I'd have done more good if I'd worked in a soup kitchen."

"You can't do any good alone, Clare."

"I think you're the one who can't do any good alone," she said. She looked at him. "I have saved four hundred and thirty-two people who would have died because they did not have clean water. Because of me, forty-three people walked a different way home and didn't get mugged or pressed into the army. Thirty-eight kitchen fires *didn't* reach the cooking oil. Thirty-one fishermen did *not* drown when they fell overboard. I have helped two dozen people fall in love."

His chuckle was bitter. "You were never very ambitious."

"Ambitious enough," she said.

"I won't come for you again. I won't try to save you again."

"Thank you," she said.

She did not watch Gerald walk away and vanish in the swoop of his cloak.

Later, looking over the village, she reached for her tin box and drew out a sugar cube that had been soaked in brandy. Crumbling it and licking her fingers, she lifted a bit of earth, which made a small girl trip harmlessly four steps before she would have stumbled and fallen into a cook fire. Years later, after the girl had grown up to be the kind of revolutionary leader who saves the world, she would say she had a guardian angel.

LIVE ARCADE

ERIK AMUNDSEN

Murr must always be traveling to the right.

In the kid's language this is the same direction as reading and writing, the same direction in which he gnaws corn on a cob. Sometimes Murr has to travel left for a while. Sometimes there are towers or pits that call for up and down, but right always reasserts its dominance.

This is interaction, in one direction. The kid plays, the game responds.

The dapper little grayscale sprite chose his own name. The kid had eight characters and three chances in which to name Murr. These were FAGBALLS, URGAYLOL, and FFUCKYOU. Murr rejected these, announcing his own name with a smug little animation.

The kid dropped him down a pit.

Murr had no lives. The swampy-sunset sky behind the forked, slate-colored trees changed a little every time he got hurt, but there didn't seem to be a connection to Murr's condition. The backdrop had no stars, just a thin, diffuse crescent moon, some fireflies, also the dead.

They were skeleton men armed with torches and sickles. They slouched an endless path until Murr got close enough to trigger aggro animation: pulled up straight by invisible strings, they scooted toward him, dragging their bony toes and singing a thin, looping melody.

They didn't kill Murr when they caught him. They just grabbed hold and he shook them off, faster when the kid helped him.

Pits didn't kill Murr, either. He grabbed hold of something at the last second to pull himself out. Murr must always be traveling to the right.

He limped the first few steps, though.

After two more skeleton attacks and another trip down a pit a blue-black owl came down from the top of the screen with a hoot like the cycling of a jet engine, hollow and nasty. It caught Murr at the lip of the pit and threw him to the ground.

Murr flailed arms and legs, pushing at the beak, the claws. The wings flared; orange eyes at the tip of each primary feather. There was no prompt, no A no B, no X or Y.

Murr fought the monster bird off with hands and feet until it gave in and took back to the sky. It shrieked its frustration, and the kid realized he had been mashing the buttons with his palm.

Murr was truly limping, holding his middle with one hand. Was his palette a little lighter? The kid squinted, and a skeleton glomped Murr, singing its evil tune.

Murr threw it off in brutal animation and looked straight at the screen. Next to his head, in tiny, white letters:

you can give up if you want. i won't. i am going to rescue Sooney-Crow.

Play or don't play. Murr could not be killed, but the kid could make him suffer. He tried to see how much, because that's something you do. How many bad things Murr could endure, skeletons, owls, thorny vines and pits? If Murr had a limit, it was beyond the kid's.

The forums were useless and full of trolls. Someone blogged a walkthrough with a few screen shots that had nothing to do with the game the kid experienced. Characters named Bell, named Solace; different than Murr, but variations on the same theme, all moving to the right.

Creepypasta claimed the game was haunted. Really it was just the same shit they did with the old game where you kill the devil or that boring game with the blocks and the exploding bushes. The kid was glad that all he paid for the game was what amounted to the lint in the corner of the pocket of his Live Account.

Murr traveled to the right, in and out of grape arbors clustered with fireflies and black-golden grapes. Here there was one skinny tree with spider leg roots and eyes hung from its branches. It followed Murr, screen to screen, not attacking; it watched.

this thing will follow us all night. maybe we should wait.

The kid looked at the clock. It was later than he'd expected. It wasn't that he had an official bedtime, but Mom would not want to catch him up now. He went to bed.

When he came back to the game, the tree-monster was gone. The kid was kind of glad it was. He'd dreamed about it, watching. Sadly, the fetch quest a trio of creepy children had given him for the lantern he needed to get into the Dark Market was still here. The kid considered erasing the game and abandoning Murr for good.

Murr navigated to a meadow where a swallow with a red slash under her beak offered the needed whistle from her throat. Murr must bring her three flowers of the five kinds in the golden meadow in front of the bright black sky.

the devil will come if he likes the smell of your flowers, so be careful how you bring them

It was a sequence puzzle; the wrong sequence filled the first screen of the forest with the devil, a giant, cloaked hunchback with the face of a boar and fiery eyes. The devil knocked Murr to the ground with his orangey hoof-hand and took the flowers.

The kid cried out.

When Murr returned to the flower field, he stood over the black-blossomed hadesmantle and looked out of the screen for a moment.

these are Sooney-Crow's favorite flowers.

There was a building at the other end of the field.

i used to work here.

Inside, one of the light-blue-smocked potters (*this is Clee. we used to be friends*) working at a wheel offered to help Murr figure the flowers if he would throw a pot for her. Rhythm game.

do you want your old smock?

With it on, Murr and the potter looked very much like one another. When Murr tried to leave, a man came out of the office and forced Murr to sit at his old wheel and more rhythm. When it was done, Murr tried to leave again only to get caught by his boss and sent back to his wheel.

i don't want to go back to this life.

To get out, Murr gave the smock back to Clee. She might have laughed or cried; it was hard to tell. She held out a pot for Murr to reach into or not. Play or don't play.

Murr pulled a knife, like a chef's knife for a hand the size of the devil's burning hybrid appendage.

it's dangerous to come with me.

it's dangerous to go with you.

The *come* and *go*, the *me* and *you* flickered for a moment and an inventory screen opened full of empty slots, except the knife and a little pink heart. The knife was called "knife." The heart didn't have any name, any option to USE or DROP.

Murr left and slashed his way through the forest screens back to the meadow, two unconvincing animations, but a use for the B button; perhaps a way to give the devil a taste of his own medicine.

No such luck.

To get the rest of the flower puzzle, Murr had to go back to the potter's shed and threaten his boss with the knife.

The mother swallow made the medicine for her child at her nest in the red-sky forest. For the whistle, she told Murr he had to cut it out.

i don't have to, do i?

Not a question Murr was asking the swallow. The kid took Murr away from the nest and Mother Swallow's barred throat. He hunted through the forest, the levels back before. He went left, but found only skeletons. It was satisfying to knife them, but nothing new appeared.

No way forward without the whistle.

i don't have to, do i? No game had ever asked the kid not to play before. The kid couldn't tell Murr that, though. Play or don't play.

It wasn't a big deal. There was hardly any blood. Murr left the screen, but the screen remained for a moment and five little swallows fluttered down from the nest to stand by the remains of their mother. The music changed. It stayed changed for the rest of the level.

It was kind of late for a school night. The tree might be coming back.

The game had a mediocre rating. Half the reviews said it was genius and the other half said the people who liked it were wrong on the internet.

The kid drew a doodle of Murr in the margin of his Spanish notebook, the potter-boss dead at his feet. His friends asked if they could come over; the kid had a brother in college who moved in with some guys who had all the games the kid and his friends couldn't just get, so he left his copies at home. The kid told them his mom was wise to all that, and it shut them up for a while.

you should go to the river.

Murr traveled to the right, then down, as snow fell all around him. He descended crumbling construction frames, vermilion, realgar and verdigris, spots of smalt and India yellow, caput mortuum, ivory black. Murr pointed out each color as they passed.

The lantern was a better weapon than the knife, fierce orange arcs at the press of the attack button. The ubiquitous skeletons were now attired in great green overcoats, remnants of tattered uniforms.

Murr's coat had become chocolate brown and his hair more like walnut. His hands and face were a rich light brown. He had salmon-colored cheeks, big brown eyes. His hair grew out. The kid's notebook margin doodles followed suit.

Murr reached the bottom, but not the river. Instead, there was a billboard in that fake Cyrillic that looks Russian but reads in English. Well, it eventually read in English. The colors that Murr mentioned formed the puzzle for the billboard that the kid had to solve.

The kid was getting better at drawing Murr. The kid wasn't a very good note taker, but he had figured out the trick to tests, so the teachers let him get away with it, mostly. Murr started doing as much in his notebooks as on the downstairs TV.

His friends noticed, one asked him if that was his girlfriend in the notebook. The kid answered that with a gesture, but later he drew alternate Murr, distaff Murr (he picked up the term from the internet somewhere), with pigtails. When he was done, the kid turned the page, wrote some notes, left to right.

Realgar was an orange pigment made out of arsenic that they stopped using because it was toxic. Vermilion was made of mercury, verdigris from a toxic copper compound. Ivory black was burned ivory, India yellow came from the urine of cows fed mango leaves, which, from what the kid could dig up, was bad for them. Smalt was just a blue that was hard to make.

No help—no help ever—on the forums; you play or don't play, and the kid found out about the colors on his own, which made the puzzle fall into place. Next time registration came around, the kid decided to sign up for a period of art. The billboard resolved itself into lead white on vermilion:

MULTIPLAYER MODE UNLOCKED

There was no mention of a multiplayer mode anywhere on the forums but the darkest heart of the creepypasta grown around this game.

Dasha the Night Witch was down at the bottom of the structure. There were characters at the top that mentioned her, telegraphing a boss battle, but Dasha was a regular-sized girl-sprite in a uniform like those the skeletons wore and a pilot's leather cap. She stood next to an old plane.

i can't help you while my sisters are dead. remember us to someone and we'll live again and fly.

Skeletons filtered down the structure, took up the transparent appearance of female pilots and flew away in ghost planes.

A notion that the game was meant to be educational, like the programs they plunked a younger him down in front of like it was a *treat* annoyed the kid. He decided not to play, and stuck by that choice for about a week. Then he saw something in the library during a research period, when his Western Civ teacher had thrown the lot of them to the librarian to get topics for a paper.

In WW2, Russia employed women pilots in trainer planes to do nighttime bombing raids on the invading Germans. Night witches. So the kid had a paper topic, and when he got home, just out of curiosity, he checked the game with this new knowledge. If there was a puzzle, he couldn't find it. Instead, Dasha was waiting for Murr to climb into her plane with her.

No one online wrote about flying sections, about the series of harrowing runs along the treetops of a vast forest in the dark, setting Dasha up to bomb.

No owls with eyes on their feathers that boiled up from the trees in lieu of enemy planes.

Nobody warned him that *Luftwaffe* owls would attack his house and tear at his walls the moment he closed his eyes, leaving him only Murr's mustache-on-a-stick weapon to fight them from his dreams.

PLAY OR DON'T PLAY he shrieked at them.

Murr got a mustard yellow scarf that the kid thought looked ugly at first, but started to like around the time the paper was written and handed in. He drew a picture of Murr and Dasha holding hands. It made Murr look more like a guy.

Several people warned that the game would unlock portions and levels based on what you did IRL (whether that was something that the game could do through spooky powers or whether it was a clever electronic stage magician's illusion depended on the creepy to pasta ratio). Still, there was only one way for the kid to interact with the game.

Play or don't play. The choice you really have; it became apparent in all the other games. The kid wouldn't say he preferred the honesty, but Murr the former Potter continued moving right; Murr Shepard languished on his ship while vast synthetic monsters destroyed the earth.

The next time he had people over, well, the kid intended to load up the game they all came over to play, but instead he asked them, "Want to see something that isn't supposed to exist?"

Everyone got to choose characters, except for him. Dasha, the Flute Kids, the Devil, Mother Swallow, Clee Potter. . . . There was also a grayscale generic hero which had once been Murr, which gave those who chose him a chance to enter a name. It was a brawler, and aside from the characters' tendencies to help one another back onto the platforms after knocking them off, it wasn't bad.

None of the kids could believe the developers would keep quiet on this part of their game. It was fun. It passed the time. When they left, the kid didn't think one of them would not download the game. He wondered if their heroes would keep the names they gave them at his house.

After that, other heroes joined Murr when the kid played. There wasn't a way to hurt the others in singleplayer, but you could help them. Play or don't play; the names of the heroes appeared on the screen but not the account IDs.

Murr returned to the red-sky forest and defeated the devil to save a comrade who was making the same medicine for big-brother swallow's little brothers and sisters. While the other adventurer (Canon) was getting the right flowers, Murr overheard the children who had given him the lantern gloat about the third whistle they were getting, one for each.

i knew we shouldn't have. poor Mother Swallow.

The kid had a hard time looking at the screen. He looked at his hands on the controller, instead. When he looked up again, the kids were still in gloat animation.

There was only one way to answer back. Play or don't play. The kid pressed buttons.

Murr attacked. The children revealed themselves as bat-faced vampires with long, sinuous bodies that swayed like charmed cobras. That was the worst boss fight. The kid was sure that Murr was going to actually die in this, flattened to the ground or torn apart by their grabby vampire hands.

Canon's return might have saved Murr. The kid had figured Canon for a weaker character given where he was in the game, but he could jump high up to the vampire snake children's heads. Murr limped for the better part of the night after they won, and Canon never left his side. The kid drew him, too, fox-fur-colored scarf and winged boots.

The kid didn't come back to the game for days. He hung out with a couple of his friends down at the stream in one of the odd patches of forest where suburbia keeps all its secrets. They threw rocks into the water and talked about the creepy game the kid had gotten them to play. As they left, the kid thought he saw, through the leaf buds and catkins, a brown coat (caput mortuum, made of ground-up mummies) and a flash of yellow.

When he came back, the kid gave Canon Murr's lantern instead of letting him cut the whistle from Big-Brother Swallow's throat.

He didn't get anything for it. It didn't really make him mad. He had one of the red whistles from the vampire battle, but all it seemed to do was turn whatever music was playing into the music that played when he killed Mother Swallow.

i liked the river.

Murr got a book which turned out to be the strongest weapon yet, a fact that made the kid roll his eyes a little, but the history paper had come back an A, and those weren't really all that common outside of math class (always came easy) and gym (you can hardly fail badminton). The animations for it were cooler than the ones for the other weapons. Sometimes, when the kid left the controller idle, Murr would sit and start reading the book.

Reviews got pretty sparse on the game; it was a little long for the usual review cycle. The game ended sort of randomly, levels generating and regenerating until the final rescue of the princess (names varied, designation didn't) sort of unlocked itself. One lady blogging had been through almost a hundred levels with her armored, pigtailed avatar Solace. The kid was up over thirty, he was sure, but he hadn't really counted. Murr always traveled to the right.

Murr got stuck at a temple to Hermes that he needed to get into to get a blue orb that was going to unlock the gate to the base of a tower. It was a long game, the kid realized; he'd lost any real investment in the story or the recycled environments a while ago. At this point, he just wanted to see how it ended. To see how Murr ended. The guards turned him away.

no girls allowed

Murr went left. Came back right.

no girls allowed

Murr went left to the beginning of the level, past the respawning, ivory-colored bulls with dark red symbols on their flanks, fighting puzzles to open doors that closed again as Murr passed through them. Murr returned to the temple.

we need to find another way in.

The kid came back to the forums like an empty refrigerator; the only thing he found was that some protagonists seemed to develop more girly hairstyles as they developed—Solace and her pigtails. It was really rare; most posts about people's characters referred to them as "he" and the object of their quest as "she."

The kid couldn't find any conclusive proof that any of legions of right-traveling alternate Murrs were dudes. It wasn't like any of them were going to drop their pants. No pictures came up of facial hair, except for the fake moustache on a stick, a weapon that usually turned up around the middle levels. Murr used to pose with it when idle.

Murr's hair was longer than when the game started, but the kid's hair was longer than Murr's.

There were screen caps of the hero and the rescued embracing. Sooney-Crow's alternates were also a little ambiguous, sometimes, but most of them looked as much like girls as the graphics would permit.

There was fan art. There was fan art that made the kid clear the history on the browser and wish he could do the same for his head. The kid couldn't post the question on the forum, not with his own picture of Murr as an icon.

There was Murr holding the hands of Dasha the Night Witch in the kid's English notebook.

Meanwhile, in the memory of the console, Murr was standing outside the men-only temple telling the kid they needed to find another way to get the orb.

The kid wondered if Sooney-Crow was a boy. He wondered if she was a girl, if they both were; was that gross or cool or did it even matter? The embrace in the screencaps wasn't really sexy or anything, but that wasn't the way he'd seen it. It wasn't just the fan art talking. That's how it is. You go right, you beat the reptile, evade the ape, you get the girl, that's what she's there for, that's why you showed up.

The kid wondered if that was how things worked IRL, the invisible reptile, the unseen ape, apparent to some guys, but not him. The kid forced himself to imagine Murr a guy, but it always came back to the idle animation of Murr with the 'stache on a stick, dancing around, the devil's faux-16-bit twinkle in her eye.

There was no button on the controller to respond to this. Play or don't play. Jump and attack did not change this. Even not playing didn't change this. If Murr never made it to Sooney-Crow, it wouldn't change this.

Canon passed Murr and entered the tower, stopping for a moment and turning in place, which seemed to be the sign for I'll help you, before going inside.

what are you afraid of?

If Canon returned, the kid was not logged in to see him. Kids at school caught on to the game in waves, and for the most part, they dropped the game after a little while. The kid stopped playing games much at all, but summer was coming, so the constant battle with his mom to game instead of be OUT IN THE FRESH AIR turned out to be an easier one to lose than it had been in a while. He went to the river pretty often, but whether he came alone or with friends, no one was ever there.

The kid drew, a lot. He started coming to the art room as the year wound down and teachers were less inclined to care on his study periods. Blue smocks hung on hooks in the supply cage, but he never touched them.

He drew Murr, drew Murr saving Sooney-Crow (an actual crow, just giant), and flying off on her back. It might have been a cop-out, but it made more sense than taking the blue orb and going through the tower and whatever else happened after that.

Close to the end of the year, the kid left his sketchbook in the art room and remembered on the curb next to his bus. He ran back, heard the buses pull away.

The art room was dark but unlocked, and the weird last bell (the one that tells you that you missed the bus) rang. In the silence that followed the kid heard the sound of the pottery wheel, off to the right. He looked sidelong, just until a flash of blue smock came into view in front of the electric wheel.

"I thought you said you never wanted to go back to that life." The figure didn't answer, maybe didn't hear or didn't know to whom the kid was speaking. The kid didn't know to whom he was speaking, either.

"Murr?"

The girl at the wheel threw a puzzled look over her shoulder. He recognized her, she was a grade behind him, seemed an okay person. Maybe she looked a little like Murr might, IRL.

"Wait, you know about Murr?"

The kid shrugged.

"I'm Canon . . . I mean in the game. That's really weird. Do you play? Do you know who her player is?"

An illusionist's trick; clever, kind of cruel.

The kid nodded, which was easy, because he was kind of shaking. Play or don't play?

"I'm Murr." The kid said it at last. Canon smiled at him.

"He told me I would find out about her if I tried tracing her life. I guess . . . I have something for you? The blue orb from the temple they didn't let you . . . Murr . . . get. "

"No girls allowed."

Girl!Canon looked uncomfortable.

Boy!Murr shook his head. Then he started to chuckle. "How was it? The temple?"

"Nothing special."

Murr laughed. Murr's laugh got Canon laughing. "Stupid game."

"Yeah, I know. I was going to call my dad to pick me up. Do you need a ride? We can try to figure out how to meet in the game."

"My house isn't too far to walk."

Canon. Canon's player (Hazel) washed her hands and took off the smock.

"Do you mind if I walk with you, then? I don't feel right carrying around something in that game that says it's yours."

The kid thought about it for a second.

"Sure. I don't mind. You can call your dad to get you at my house or my mom can drop you off."

"Cool."

"Thanks for saving me from those vampires."

They went right, and out to the street.

SOCIAL SERVICES

MADELINE ASHBY

"But I want my own office," Lena said. "My own space to work from."

Social Services paused for a while to think. Lena knew that it was thinking, because the woman in the magic mirror kept animating her eyes this way and that behind cat-eye horn-rims. She did so in perfect meter, making her look like one of those old clocks where the cat wagged its tail and looked to and fro, to and fro, all day and all night, forever and ever. Lena had only ever seen those clocks in media, so she had no idea if they really ticked. But she imagined they ticked terribly. The real function of clocks, it seemed to her, was not to tell time but to mark its passage. Ticktickticktick. Byebyebyebye.

"I'm sorry, Lena, but your primary value to this organization lies in your location," Mrs. Dudley said. Lena had picked out her name when Social Services hired her. The name was Mrs. Dudley, after the teacher who rolled her eyes when Lena mispronounced "organism" as "orgasm" in fifth-grade health class. She'd made Social Services look like her, from the horn-rims to the puffy eyes to the shimmery coral lipstick melting into the wrinkles rivening her mouth. Now Mrs. Dudley was at her beck and call all the time and had to answer all the most inane questions, like what the weather was and if something looked infected or not.

"This organization has to remain nimble," Mrs. Dudley said. "We need people ready to work at the grassroots level. You're one of them. Aren't you?"

Now it was Lena's turn to think. She examined the bathroom. It had the best mirror, so it was where she did most of her communication with Social Services. The bathroom itself was tiny. Most of the time it was dirty. This had nothing to do with Lena and everything to do with her niece's baby, whose diapers currently clogged the wastebasket. There was supposed to be a special hamper just for them with a charcoal filter on it and an alert telling her niece when to empty it, but her niece didn't give a shit—literally. Lena had told her that ignoring the alert was a good way to get the company who made the hamper to ping Social Services—a lack of basic cleanliness was an easy way to signal neglect—but her niece just smiled and said: "That's why we have you around. To fix stuff like that."

"That is why you decided to come work for us, isn't it?" Mrs. Dudley asked.

Lena nodded her head a little too vigourously. "Yes," she said. "Yes, that's it exactly."

She had no idea what Social Services had just asked. Probably something about her commitment to her community or her empathy for others. Lena smiled her warm smile. It was one of a few she had catalogued especially for the purposes of work. She wore it to work like she wore her good leather gloves and her pretty pendant knife. Work outfit, work smile, work feelings. She reminded herself to look again for her gloves. They didn't have a sensor, so she had no idea how to find them.

"Here is your list for today," Mrs. Dudley said. The mirror showed her a list of addresses and tags. Not full case files, just tags and summaries compiled from the case files. Names, dates, bruises. Missed school, missed meals, missed court dates. "The car will be ready soon."

"Car?"

"The last appointment is quite far away." The appointment hove into view in the mirror. It showed a massive old McMansion in the suburbs. "Transit reviews claim that the way in is . . . unreliable," Mrs. Dudley said. "So we are sending you transport."

Lena watched her features start to manifest her doubts, but she reined them in before they could express much more. "But I . . . "

"The car drives itself, Lena. And you get it for the whole day. I'm sure that allays any of your possible anxieties, doesn't it?"

"Well, yes . . . "

"Good. The car has a Euler path all set up, so just go where it takes you and you'll be fine."

"Okay."

"And please do keep your chin up."

"Excuse me?"

"Your chin. Keep it up. When your chin is down, we can't see as well. You're our eyes and ears, Lena. Remember that."

She nodded. "I—"

A fist on the bathroom door interrupted her. Just like that, Mrs. Dudley vanished. That was Social Services security at work; the interface, such as it was, did not want to share information with anyone else in a space and so only recognized Lena's face. Her brother had tried to show it a picture of her, and then some video, but Lena had a special face that she made to log in, and the mirror politely told her brother to please leave.

"Open up!"

Lena opened the door. Her niece stood on the other side. She handed Lena the baby and beelined for the toilet. Yanking her pants down, she said: "Have you ever had to hold it in after an episiotomy?"

"No—"

"Well, you might someday, if you ever got a boyfriend, which you shouldn't, because they're fucking crap." The sound of her pissing echoed in the small room. "Someday I'm going to kill this fucking toilet." She reached behind herself, awkwardly, and slapped it. Her rings made scratching noises on its plastic side. "You were supposed to tell me I was knocked up."

Lena thought it was probably a bad time to tell her niece that her father, Lena's brother, was the one responsible for upgrading the toilet's firmware, and that he had instead chosen to attempt circumventing it so it would give them all its available features (temperature taking, diagnosis, warming, and so on) for no cost whatsoever. He didn't want the manufacturer knowing how much he used the bidet function, he said one night over dinner. That shit was private.

Her niece didn't bother washing her hands. She took the baby from Lena's arms and kissed it absently. "It's creepy to hear you talking to someone who isn't there," she said. Her eyes widened. Her eyeliner was a vivid pink today, with extra sparkles. Her makeup was always annoyingly perfect. She probably could have sold the motions of her hands to a robotics firm somewhere. "Don't you worry sometimes that you're, like . . . making it all up?"

Lena frowned. It wasn't like her niece to consider the existential. "Do you mean making it up as I go? Like life?"

"No no no no no. I mean, like, you're making up your job." She glanced quickly at the mirror, as though she feared it might be watching her. "Like maybe there's nobody in there at all."

Lena instantly allowed all of her professional affect to fall away, like cobwebs from an opened door. She turned her head to the old grey leather couch with its pillows and blankets neatly stacked, right where she'd left them that morning. She let her niece carry the full weight of her gaze. "Then where would the rent money come from?" she asked.

Her niece had the grace to look embarrassed. She hugged her baby a little tighter. "Sorry. It was just a joke." She blinked. "You know? Jokes?"

A little car rolled across Lena's field of vision. Its logo beeped at her. "My car is here," she said. "Try to leave some dinner for me."

"Is it true they make you all get the same haircut so they can hear better?"

Lena peered over the edges of her frames. Social Services didn't like it when she did that, but it was occasionally necessary. Jude, the adolescent standing before her, seemed genuinely curious and not sarcastic. That didn't make his question any less stupid.

"No," she said. "They don't make us wear a special haircut."

Jude shrugged. "You all just look like you've got the same haircut."

"Maybe you're just remembering the other times I've been here."

Jude smiled dopily around the straw hanging out of his mouth and slurped from the pouch attached to it. It likely contained makgeolli; that was the 22nd floor specialty. Her glasses told her he was mildly intoxicated; he wore a lab-on-a-chip under the skin of his left shoulder, in a spot that was notoriously difficult to scratch. The Spot was different for every user; triangulating it meant a gestural camera taking a full-body picture or extrapolating from an extant gaming profile. "Oh, yeah . . . Yeah, that's probably it."

"Why do you think I'm here, Jude?"

"Because the Fosters aren't."

The kid didn't miss a beat. The algorithm had first introduced them three years ago, when his foster parents took him in; he referred to them privately as "the Fosters." Three years in, "the Fosters" had given up. They collected their stipend just fine, but they left it to Lena to actually deal with Jude's problems.

His main problem these days was truancy; in a year he wouldn't have to go to school any longer unless he wanted to, and so he was experiencing an acute case of senioritis in his freshman year. If he chose to go on, though, it would score Lena some much-needed points on her own profile. There was little difference, really, between his marks and her own.

"Is there any particular reason you're not going to school these days?"

Jude shrugged and slurped on the pouch until it crinkled up and bubbled. He tossed the empty into the sink and leaned over to open the refrigerator. You didn't have to really move your feet in these rabbit hutch kitchens. He got another of the pouches out. "I just don't feel like it," he said.

"I didn't really much feel like going, either, when it was my turn, but I went."

Jude favoured her with a look that told her she had best shut her fucking mouth right fucking now. "School was different for you," he said simply. "You didn't have to wear a uniform."

"Well, that's true—"

"And your uniform didn't ping your teacher every time you got a fucking boner."

Lena blushed and then felt herself blushing, which only made it worse. She looked down. True, their school district was a little too keen on wearables, but Jude's were special. "You know why you have to wear those pants," she said.

"That was when I was thirteen!"

"Well, she was ten."

"I know she was ten. I fucking know that. There's no way I could possibly forget that, now." He crossed his arms and sighed deeply. "We didn't even do anything."

"That's not what you told your friends on 18."

He sucked his teeth. Lena had no idea if Jude had really done the things he said he did. The lab inside the little girl had logged enough dopamine to believe sexual activity had occurred, but it had no way of knowing if she'd helped herself along or if she'd had outside interference. The rape kit had the same opinion: penetration, not forced entry. When the relationship was discovered, the girl recanted everything and said that nothing had happened, and that it didn't matter anyway because even if something had happened, she really loved Jude. Jude did the same. Except he never said he loved her. This was probably the most honesty he had demonstrated during the entire episode.

"I know it's difficult," Lena said. "But completing your minimum course credits is part of your sentencing. It's part of why you get your record expunged when you turn eighteen. So you have to go." She reached into the sink and plucked out the pouch with her thumb and forefinger. It dangled there in her grasp, dripping sweet white fluid. "And you have to quit drinking, too."

"I know," he said. "It's stupid. I was just bored, and it was there."

"I understand. But you're hurting your chances of making it out of here. This kind of thing winds up on your transcript, you know. You can't get a job without a decent transcript."

Jude waved his hand. "The fabbers don't care about grades."

"Maybe not, but they care about you being able to show up on time. You know?"

He rolled his eyes. "Yeah. I know."

"So you'll go to school tomorrow?"

"Maybe. I need a new uniform first."

"Excuse me?"

"Well, it's really just the pants. I threw them out."

Lena blinked so that her glasses would listen to her. "Well, we have to find those pants."

The glasses showed her a magnifying glass zipping to and fro across the cramped, dirty apartment. It came back empty. "You really threw them out?" she asked, despite already knowing the answer. Maybe he'd given them to a friend. Or sold them. Maybe they could be brought back, somehow.

"I think they got all sliced up," Jude said, miming the action of scissors with his fingers. "I wore my gym clothes home yesterday, and I put my other stuff in my bag, and then under the viaduct, I gave them to this homeless dude. He found the sensors right away. Said he was gonna sell 'em."

She winced. "How do you know he's not wearing them?"

"They were too small."

It was beyond her power. She would have to arrange for a new uniform.

She'd probably have to take Jude to school tomorrow, too, just to smooth things over. He tended to start a new attendance streak if someone was actually bringing him there. The record said so, anyway. For a moment it snaked across her vision, undulating and irregular, and then she blinked and it was gone.

"I'll be here tomorrow at seven to take you to school," she said, and watched the appointment check itself into her schedule. "And don't even think about not being here, or not waking up, or getting your mom to send a note, or anything like that. I intend to show up, and if you don't do the same, Social Services will send someone else next time, and they won't be so understanding. Okay?"

Jude snorted. "Okay."

"I mean it. You have to show up. And you have to show up sober. I'll know if you're not, and so will your principal. He can suspend you for that, on sight."

"I know." Jude paused for a moment. He reached for the fresh pouch, and then seemed to think better of it. "I'm sorry, Lena."

"I know you're sorry. You can make it up to me by showing up tomorrow."

"I don't want them to send someone else. I didn't mean to get you in trouble. I was just mad, is all."

"You would have better impulse control if you quit drinking. You know that, right?"

"Yeah."

"So you know what we have to do next, right?"

He sighed. "Seriously?"

"Yes, seriously. I can't leave here without it."

They spent the next half hour cleaning out his stash. He even helped her bring it down to the car. "Are you sure this is it?" he asked, when it perked up at Lena's arrival.

"It's on loan," she said. "Some people lease their vehicles on a daily basis to Social Services, and the car drives itself back to them at the end of the day with a full charge."

"It's a piece of shit."

"Just put the box in the back, will you?"

Jude rolled his eyes as she popped the trunk. Technically, she shouldn't have allowed him to come down to the garage with her. It wasn't recommended. Her glasses had warned her about it as they neared the elevator. She made sure Jude carried the box full of pouches and pipes, though, so that he'd have to drop it if he wanted to try anything. Now she watched as he leaned over the trunk and set the box inside.

"Nice gloves." He reached in and brought something out: Lena's good leather gloves. They were real leather, not the fake stuff, with soft suede interiors and an elastic skirt that circled the wrist and kept out the cold air.

They were a pretty shade of purple. Distinctive. Recognizable. "Aren't these yours?" he asked.

"I . . ."

"I've seen you wearing them before." He frowned. "I thought you said this was someone else's car. On loan."

"It is . . ."

"So how did your gloves wind up in the trunk?"

Lena wished she could ask the glasses for help. But without sensors, the glasses and the gloves had no relationship. At least, nothing legitimate and quantifiable. They had only Lena to link them.

"I must have used this car before," she said. "That must be it. I must have forgotten them in here the last time and not used the trunk until then. And the owner left the gloves in the trunk, hoping that I'd find them."

"Why the trunk? Why not on the dash? How many times do you look in the trunk?"

Jude slammed the trunk shut. He held the gloves out. Lena took them gingerly between her thumb and forefinger. They felt like her gloves. A little chilled from riding around in the trunk, but still hers. How strange to think that they'd gone on their own little adventure without her. Hadn't the car's owner been the least bit tempted to take them? Or one of the other users? There were plenty of other women on the Social Services roster. Maybe they'd been worn out and then put back, just like the car. Maybe the last user was someone higher up on the chain, and they knew Lena would be taking this particular car out on this particular morning, and they put her gloves back where she would find them. That would explain how she'd never seen them until just now.

"Don't look so creeped out," Jude said. "They're just a pair of gloves, right?"

"Right," Lena said. "Thanks."

By the end of the day, Lena had to admit that the car did not look familiar in the least. That didn't mean it looked unfamiliar, either, just that it looked the same as all the other print jobs in the hands-free lane. The same flat mustard yellow, the same thick bumper that made the whole vehicle look like a little man with a mustache. It was entirely possible that she had used this car before. Perhaps even on the same day that she'd lost her gloves. She didn't remember losing them. That was the thing. She kept turning them in her hands, over and over, pulling them on and pulling them off, wiggling her fingers in their tips to feel if they were truly hers or not.

When had she last used a car for Social Services?

"February of last year," Mrs. Dudley said. "February fifteenth, to be exact."

Lena did not remember speaking the words aloud, either. But that hardly mattered. It was Social Services' job to understand problems before they became issues. That was how they'd first found Jude, after all. Surely the glasses had logged her examination of the gloves and the car and the system had put two and two together. It could do that. She was sure of it.

"You subvocalized it," Mrs. Dudley said.

Yes. That was it. People did that sometimes, didn't they? They muttered to themselves. It wasn't at all unusual.

"People do it all the time," Mrs. Dudley told her.

Lena forced herself to speak the next words out loud. "Did the owner of the car save the gloves for me?"

Mrs. Dudley paused. "That's one way of putting it."

"What do you mean?"

Outside, the highway seemed empty. So few people drove any longer. Once upon a time, four o'clock on a Friday afternoon in late October would have been replete with cars, and the cars would have been stuffed with mothers and fathers lead-footing their way into the suburbs, anxiously counting down the minutes until they earned a late fee at their daycare. Now the car whizzed along, straight and true, spotting its nearest fellow vehicle every ten minutes and pinging them cheerfully before zipping ahead.

It felt like driving into a village afflicted by plague.

"I think we need to bring you in for a memory exam, Lena," Mrs. Dudley said. "These lapses aren't normal for a woman in your demographic. You may have a blood clot."

"Oh," Lena said, perversely delighted by the thought.

"But first, you have to do this one last thing for us."

"Yes. The house in the suburbs."

"You must be very careful, Lena. Where you're going, there's no one else on the block. It's all been foreclosed. And it's going to be dark soon."

"I understand."

"The foreclosures mean that the local security forces have been diminished, too. Their budget is based on population density and property taxes, so there won't be anyone to come for you. Not right away, anyway. Everyone else lives closer to town."

"Except for the people in this house."

Another pause. "Yes. The ones who live there, live alone."

Jackson Hills was the name of the development. The hills themselves occupied unincorporated county land, the last free sliver of property in the whole area, and the crookedness of the rusting street signs seemed meant to tempt government interference. That was an old word for molestation, Lena remembered. You came across it in some of the oldest laws. Interference. As though the uncles she spent her days hearing about were nothing more than windmills getting in the way of a good signal.

Was it an uncle that was the trouble this time? The file was very scant. "Possible neglect," it read. The child in question wore old, ill-fitting clothes, a teacher said. His grades were starting to slip. His name was Theodore. People called him Teddy. His parents never came to Parent/Teacher Night. They attended no talent shows. But they were participatory parents online; their emails with Teddy's teachers were detailed and thoughtful, with perfect spelling and grammar.

"We intend to discuss Teddy's infractions with him as soon as possible," one read. "We understand that his hacking the school lunch system to obtain chicken fingers every day for a month is very serious, as well as nutritionally unwise."

Teddy had indeed hacked the school lunch system to order an excess of chicken fingers delivered to the school kitchen by supply truck. He did this by entering the kitchen while pretending to go on a bathroom break and carefully frying all the smart tags on all the boxes of frozen chicken fingers and fries with an acne zapper. With all the tags dead, the supplier instantly re-upped the entire order. The only truly dangerous part of the hack was the fact that he'd been in the walk-in freezer for a whole five minutes. Surveillance footage showed him ducking in with his coat zipped up all the way. The coat itself said that his body temperature had never dipped.

"I don't get any junk food at home," the boy said during his inevitable talk with the principal. "They don't deliver any."

The gate to Jackson Hills was still functional despite the absence of its residents. It slid open for Lena's car. As it did, a dervish of dead leaves whirled out and scattered away toward freedom. It felt like some sort of prisoner transfer. The exchange made, Lena drove past the gate.

The car drove her through the maze of empty houses as the dash lit up with advertisements for businesses that would probably never open. Burger joints. Day spas. Custom fabbers. In-house genome sequencing. All part of "town and country living at its finest." Some of the houses looked new; there were even stickers on the windows. As she rolled past, projections fluttered to life and showed laughing children running through sprinklers across the bare sod lawns, and men flipping steaks on grills, and women serving lemonade. It was the same family each time.

"WELCOME HOME," her dashboard read.

The house stood at the top of the topmost hill in Jackson Hills. Lena recognized it because the map said they were drawing closer, and because it was the only house on the cul-de-sac with any lights on. It was a big place, but not so different from the others, with fake Tudor styling and a sloping lawn whose sharpest incline was broken by terraced rock. Forget-me-nots grew between the stones. Moss sprang up through the seams in the tiled drive. There was no car, so Lena's slid in easily and shut itself off with a little sigh, like a child instantly falling asleep.

At the door, Lena took the time to remove her gloves (when had she put those on?) and adjust her hair. She rang the bell and waited. The lion in the doorknocker twinkled his eyes at her, and the door opened.

Teddy stood there, wearing a flannel pyjama and bathrobe set one size too small for his frame. "Hello, Lena," he said.

She blinked. "Hello, Teddy."

"It's nice to meet you. Please come in."

Inside, the house was dusty. Not dirty or even untidy, but dusty. Dust clung to the ceiling fans. Cobwebs stretched across the top of every shelf and under the span of every pendant light. The corners of each room had become hiding places for dust bunnies. But at Teddy's height, everything was clean.

"Where are your parents, Teddy?"

"Would you like some tea?" Teddy asked. "Earl Grey is your favorite, right?"

Earl Grey was her favorite. As she watched, Teddy padded over to the coffee table in the front room and poured tea from a real china service. It had little pink roses on it, and there was a sugar bowl with a lid and a creamer full of cream and even a tiny dish with whisper-thin slices of lemon. When he was finished pouring, Teddy added two sugars and a dash of cream to the cup. He handed her the cup on a saucer with both hands and then pressed something on his watch.

"It tells when it's done steeping," he said. "Would you like to sit down?"

Lena sat. The sofa shifted beneath her, almost as though she'd sat on a very large cat. A moment later it had moulded itself to her shape. "It's smart foam," Teddy said. "Please try some of your tea. I made it myself."

Lena sipped. "You've certainly done your homework, Teddy," she said. "You're not the only person to research me before my arrival, but you're the only one who's ever been this thorough."

"I wanted to make it nice for you."

It was an odd statement, but Lena let it pass. She took another sip. "This is a very lovely house, Teddy. Do you help your parents with the housework?"

He nodded emphatically. "Yes. Yes, I do."

"And are you happy living here?"

"Yes, I am."

"There don't seem to be many other kids to play with," Lena said. "Doesn't it get lonely?"

"I don't really get lonely," he said. "I have friends I play with online."

"But it can't be very safe to live here all alone."

His mouth twitched a little, as though he had just heard the distant sound of a small animal that he very much wanted to hunt. "I'm not alone," he said.

"Well, I meant the neighbours. Or rather, the lack of any."

His shoulders went back to their relaxed position. "I like it here," he said. "I like not having any neighbours. My parents didn't like it very much at first, but I liked it a lot."

Since he had left the door open, Lena decided to go through it. "So when are your parents coming?"

"They're here," he said. "They just can't come upstairs right now."

Lena frowned. "Are they not well?"

Teddy smiled. For a moment, he actually looked like a real eleven-year-old and not like a man who had shrunk down to size.

"They're busy," he said. "Besides, you're here to talk to me, right?"

"Well . . . Yes, that's true, but . . . " She blinked again, hard. It was tough to string words together for some reason. Maybe Mrs. Dudley was right. Maybe she did need her brain scanned. She felt as though the long drive in had somehow hypnotized her, and Teddy now seemed very far away.

"I hope that we can be friends, Lena," Teddy said. "I liked you the last time they sent you here."

Her mouth struggled to shape the words. "What? What are you talking about?"

"You wore those gloves last time," he said. "In February. You'd had a really lonely Valentine's Day the day before, and you were very sad. So I made you happy for a little while. I had some pills left over."

It was very hot in the room suddenly. "You've drugged me," Lena said.

Teddy beamed. "Gotcha!"

Lena tried to stand up. Her knees gave out and her forehead struck one corner of the coffee table. For a moment she thought the warmth trickling down her face was actually sweat. But it wasn't.

"Uh oh," Teddy said. "I'll get some wipes."

He bounded off for the kitchen. Lena focused on her knees. She could stand up if she just tried. She had her pendant knife. She could . . . what? Slash him? Threaten him? Threaten a child? She grasped the pendant in her hand. Pulled it off its cord. Unflipped the blade.

When Teddy came back with a cylinder of lemon-scented disinfectant wipes, she pounced. She was awkward and dizzy, but she was bigger than him, and she knocked him over easily. He saw the knife in her hand, gave a little shriek of delight, and bit her arm, hard. Then he shook his little head, like a dog with a chew toy. It hurt enough to make her lose her grip, and he recovered the knife. He held it facing downward, like scissors. He wiped his mouth with the back of his other hand.

"I knew I liked you, Lena," he said. "You're not like the others. You don't really like kids at all, do you? This is just your job. You'd rather be doing something else."

"That's . . . " Her vision wavered. "That's not true . . . "

"Yes, it is. And it's okay, because I don't like other kids, either. They're awful. They're mean and stupid and ugly and poor, and I don't want to see them ever again. I just want to stay home forever."

Lena heard herself laughing. It was a low, slow laugh. She couldn't remember the last time she had heard it.

"Why are you laughing?" Teddy asked.

"Because you're all the same," she said. "None of you want to go to school!" She laughed again. It was higher this time, and she felt the laugh itself begin to scrape the dusty expanse of the vaulted ceiling and the glittering chandelier that hung from it. She could feel the crystals trembling in response to her laughter. She had a pang for Jude, who would have absolutely loved whatever shit Teddy had dosed her with.

"I just need someone to create data," Teddy was saying. "I've tried to keep up the streams by myself, but I can't. There are too many sensors. I have to keep sleeping in their bed. I have to keep riding their bikes. Both of them. Do you even know how hard that is?"

Lena couldn't stop laughing. She lay on the floor now, watching her blood seep down into the fibres of the carpet. It was white, and it would stain badly. Maybe Teddy would want her to clean it up. That seemed to be her lot in life—cleaning up other people's messes. But as she watched, Teddy got down on his knees and began to scrub.

"It won't be that bad," he said. "I'll make it nice for you. All I need is someone to pretend to be my mom so I can do homeschool. I have all her chips still. I took them while she was still warm, and I kept them in agar jelly from my chemistry set." He winced. "I would have gotten Dad's, too, but he was too fat."

Teddy reached out his hand. "Do you think you can make it to the dining table?"

She let him help her up. "Social Services . . . "

"You can quit tomorrow," Teddy said. "Just tell them you can't do it anymore."

"But . . . My mirror . . . " Why was she entertaining any of this? Why was she helping him?

"I have a mirror," he said. "Your face is the login, right? You talked to my mirror the last time you were here. You just don't remember because you blacked out later."

She turned to him. "This is real?"

He smiled and squeezed her cold hand in his much warmer and smaller one. "Yes, Lena. It's all real. This is a real house with real deliveries and real media and a real live boy in it. It's not like a haunted house. It was, until you came. But it's your home now. Your own place, just for you and me."

"For . . ."

"Forever. For ever and ever and ever."

FOUND

ALEX DALLY MacFARLANE

Star Anise

Star anise was the contents of one drawer in my spice cabinet: was worth one good energy cell—or three not-so-good ones, or six bad ones, or eight that provided barely any power at all.

I had never traded for just one energy cell. None remained.

At this last asteroid, I had not traded for any. I had found its interior spaces open and airless, blast-marked, most of its equipment broken or gone, debris—shards of metal, rock, old synth materials, blackened bits of bone—still lodged in some deep crannies. In such a small asteroid, a sudden equipment failure could be unsurvivable. I knew this.

It shook me to see it true, after the changes and losses and accidents we had adapted to.

As I confirmed my trajectory and fired my small thrusters two times, once to get clear from the asteroid and once to push me to the next asteroid—just a bright dot in the distance, lost among the stars like another granule of salt—I couldn't stop myself thinking: *What if Aagot had lived there?*

Bay

I placed a bay leaf on my tongue.

I maneuvered my craft carefully into the landing crater: a process as natural, as easy as an asteroid's spin. Still, I sighed with relief when my craft hooked into place. It wouldn't survive a crash.

After triple-checking the integrity of my suit, I drifted out onto the asteroid's surface with my spice cabinet.

Cut into another part of the asteroid was a landing bay built for spacecraft far bigger than mine: craft that would have arrived to collect platinum and iron and enough liquid hydrogen to fuel their onward journeys. A story. A dream of the past. If I could land in the landing bay, I wouldn't have to go outside for the meters it took to reach the small airlock—outside, where the stars waited like teeth for my suit to fail—but its use required too much energy.

When the people from Cai Nu arrived, would they be welcomed into the asteroids' landing bays?

I winced. I wanted to think of something else.

I pressed the bay leaf to the roof of my mouth.

The people of this asteroid had barely opened their mouths before the words "Cai Nu" fell out. They gathered around me in the small communal room, wanting my words even more than my spices. "I have cardamom," I said. "We managed to get it growing again." And a few people sighed longingly, before one of them asked what people were saying privately, face-to-face—instead of on the inter-asteroid comms—about the impending arrival of the Cai Nu people. Almost everyone who lived in the asteroid was holding onto the poles running along the room's rock walls. I counted over twenty people. Though I recognized many of the faces, not one was Aagot's. "I don't know much more than what's on the comms," I said, reluctant to admit that I rarely listened to the messages my craft picked up between the asteroids. I knew that the Cai Nu people would arrive in less than a year. I knew that our lives in the asteroids would end.

The questions continued to come.

Eventually they realized that I could tell them nothing. Disappointed, a few people drifted away. Others spoke: explaining how many energy cells they could give me, asking what spices that was worth.

"What would you like?" I asked, touching the gray drawers of my cabinet. Etched into the iron were the names of the spices: star anise, cardamom pods, cloves, chilies, cinnamon bark, peppercorns, fennel seeds, coriander seeds, dried coriander leaves, dried sage leaves, juniper berries, lemongrass, dried makrut leaves, cumin seeds, dried mint leaves, dried bay leaves, sprigs of thyme and rosemary, flakes of galangal, flakes of turmeric. Flavor. Some people said that word like a plea at a shrine. Spices made our food—synthetic, completely nourishing, completely tasteless—alive, made it something we wanted to share with each other. Chewing a cardamom pod brought tears to people's eyes. A sage leaf provoked joyous laughter.

Nouf Kassem, who did most of this asteroid's trade, began to point to drawers. I opened them one by one, withdrawing pouches. The items of our trade hung in the air between us. When I had given ten bad energy cells' worth, Nouf didn't release the handle of her box.

"You trade as if you'll be able to reach all the asteroids before the Cai Nu people arrive," she said. "As if you've got a whole year. I hear that on Cai Nu the strips of cinnamon are as tall as the tallest woman, that they grow parsley and rose and sumac. I hear there are mounds of spices in powders. Are your family saving these spices for then?"

Silence surrounded us, sharp as space.

I wanted to say: *What makes you think everyone's leaving the asteroids?*

I wanted to say: *Why?*

I hadn't thought of trading all our stock, I hadn't thought of sending a message to my mothers asking whether I should make more generous offers. I hadn't—

"Just a few more pouches of cumin and mint," Nouf said.

I gave them to her.

In past visits, I had spent time with the people of the asteroid. I had invented stories with them. I had kissed a man called Ammar, laughed when he shrieked with joy at the bay leaf on my tongue—I had, years ago, chosen a spice per asteroid and placed that same spice on my tongue at every visit—and then I had kissed him again, shared the flavor between us. I had listened to the elders of the asteroid and played with the children and eaten turmeric-soaked food. How bright! How bitter!

How soon until these memories would not be renewed.

I slipped away, outside, into my craft and the space between the asteroids. The bay leaf's taste lingered. We would not.

Juniper Berries

The first story Aagot gave me, with juniper berries crushed on our tongues, was one created by Aagot as a child. I couldn't linger on that asteroid. I met Aagot there—one conversation on my trade visit, three hours of stories more precious than fuel cells.

Aagot told me of a child who needed a name: a new name, not the birth-name that lingered at their ears like the whine of a faulty air processor, as ill-fitting as "girl," as "boy."

I remembered Aagot's voice, saying: *When the spice trader comes, they bring flavors and news and new people from other asteroids. But there's one thing they don't bring: new names. There's no drawer in the spice trader's cabinet for that. For one child, this meant never finding one that fit.* But the spice trader in the story—like spice traders in many stories—took the child as an apprentice between the asteroids and there the child found their name: in the herb they most loved handling, crushing, coating their fingers with its scent. Thyme.

I remembered Aagot's voice, full of longing like a drawer of thyme.

I left.

Thyme

I finally realized, two years later, chewing thyme on an outlying asteroid where six people stubbornly survived, that I was like Thyme: ill-suited to "boy" or "girl."

• • •

Juniper Berries

When I returned to the juniper berry asteroid—when I realized how much I needed to speak to Aagot again—Aagot had left, bought passage a year after my visit on one of the rare other craft that still functioned. There were only nineteen asteroids—eighteen, now, with the disaster in the star anise asteroid—but I didn't visit every one annually, I didn't undertake every one of my family's trade journeys, I didn't see Aagot again.

I retold Aagot's story to myself between the asteroids.

Cinnamon

One of the earliest messages sent to us by the Cai Nu people had explained our abandonment: *Two hundred years ago we were too ambitious. We overextended ourselves. We should have focused on our settlements on Cai Nu, but we wanted the asteroids, we wanted the other habitable planets and moons of this solar system. So we established settlements in the Liu Yang asteroid family. Then, almost immediately, a health crisis struck and led to widespread social upheaval, in which much was lost, including knowledge of your continued survival. Now that we have recovered and grown our population, and rediscovered you, we can't leave you living in such poor conditions.*

Cumin

I approached the next asteroid on my trade journey. Plans traveled faster: communications sent between the asteroids. Questions. Debates. My name was mentioned often. "Lo Yiying can help bring people here." "What's the maximum amount of passengers and cargo that Lo Yiying's craft carries?" "Lo Yiying, how long until you reach Iskander? Can you collect us all?" "Aside from Lo Yiying, who can fly a craft to bring people to the Lo family's asteroid?"

I heard, for the first time, a firm date for the Cai Nu people's arrival: twenty-two weeks.

I would not have my spacecraft, I would not fly spices between the asteroids, I would not drift through the corridors of asteroids with my cabinet behind me and the taste of bay or cumin or thyme in my mouth.

Everyone would gather at my family's asteroid. A message was sent to the Cai Nu craft, telling them the asteroid's current co-ordinates so they could track it and adjust their approach accordingly. They confirmed its convenience for their current trajectory and fuel supplies.

My purpose changed: to reach the next asteroid—Iskander, cumin—and collect its inhabitants and turn, like a crooked stem, back to my family's asteroid. Sissel Haugli, who lived on the outermost asteroid at this end of the group, had already begun her journey towards the center, gathering the families I would not reach. Two people at other points in the asteroid group were also underway.

Trade was no longer important. My cabinet's drawers would remain unopened.

Still I journeyed, the next asteroid gradually growing from a mote to a seed—comm-conversations not once suggesting that anyone would remain behind after the Cai Nu people arrived, very few people discussing the difficulties we would face on Cai Nu—and then, the asteroid a spinning, dark rock, I concentrated on landing.

The landing bay door slowly opened. I carefully maneuvered my shuttle into the bay, where multiple lights shone: a brightness I rarely saw in any asteroid. The bay door closed. The unit on one wall restored air.

It was unusual, to arrive like this.

I instinctively went to my spice cabinet and picked up its harness.

I entered the asteroid without it, feeling not myself—though people greeted me, entering the landing bay in family-clusters, towing their possessions, saying "Lo Yiying!" and "Thank you for coming here!" as if I brought spices and news. "Do you think you'll be able to fit all of these boxes on your shuttle?" asked Inas Kassem, who had done most of the talking for this asteroid. "We've packed only important things: all of our fuel cells, the racks of moss so we can help keep your shuttle's air fresh. We've got food and water tanks. And some small things. Qurans, small shrine statues, old family journals, a few personal ornaments."

No one else came through the small door from the asteroid. Everyone hung in front of me, looking at me, at my shuttle, at the walls—the last part of their home they would see.

No Aagot.

"Shall we begin loading?" asked Inas.

"Yes."

I had crunched cumin seeds between my teeth before leaving my shuttle. The taste faded as we worked: arranging boxes in the cargo area of my shuttle, setting up the moss racks, deciding how people would sleep. Then we were ready. No one spoke as I closed my shuttle's door, as Inas showed me what signal to send to open the landing bay door. It creaked, in the moment before sound was lost. Beyond, the stars gleamed—and the ones that were not stars: asteroids, Cai Nu's planet, Cai Nu itself, smaller than a fragment of peppercorn. I didn't know what to say. Nor did anyone. So I began our journey.

Several people started to cry. Others talked, others remained silent, others sang: a braid of emotions in three languages, passed from mouth to mouth, lasting hours.

I cooked.

From the spice cabinet, secured beside my chair, I took cumin seeds and sprigs of thyme and peppercorns and cardamom pods and makrut leaves and lemongrass stalks and galangal. I cooked pot after pot, sometimes mixing spices, sometimes using just one, and passed carved chunks of the finished meal around the cargo area of my shuttle, where the people of the cumin asteroid had tethered themselves to the walls and their boxes.

On Cai Nu we would eat food we only knew from stories: rice, noodles, dumplings, bread, meat, vegetables, sweets. Spices wouldn't be the only flavors.

When people started discussing this, I retreated to my seat.

Two women followed. I knew Ma Wanlu, Inas' daughter. The other was introduced as her wife, Bilge Yılmaz, who wanted to see Cai Nu.

"It's nothing," I said. "A small dot."

"Our home," Bilge murmured, rapt at the sight: as if I'd offered her a handful of cumin seeds.

I looked away.

"What troubles you?" Ma Wanlu asked.

"We won't be able to go outside. We won't be able to work. We'll die in that place they're building for us, forgotten by our children, useless. Who will we be?"

Ma Wanlu frowned. "Well, what are we now?"

"We work—your family works on the fuel cells."

"Work!" Ma Wanlu almost choked on the word. "Work. Oh, we work. We desperately work to get a little more life from our dwindling resources."

"We are all trapped in our asteroids," Bilge said, "working every day to ensure our habitat is still intact, that our oxygen-exchange mosses aren't dying, that our fuel cells haven't stopped. When my cousin's pregnancy went wrong, what could we do? When my father got cancer, what could we do? Who will we be on Cai Nu? Not dying like this." Bilge's voice shook; she looked out of my craft, out at the stars and the bright dot of Cai Nu's planet. "And we try to move between asteroids, to keep from inbreeding, and people like my mother never see their parents and siblings and aunts and uncles and grandparents again, only hear them, just hundreds of thousands of kilometers away but it's as if they're on a rock around that star, or that one."

I thought of Aagot, lost among just eighteen asteroids.

"Here," Ma Wanlu said, "our children will die, gasping for air."

"When the Cai Nu people talk about never having to worry about energy supplies," Bilge said, "or medicine or food, I think of . . . I . . . "

Silence drifted between us like dust.

"I don't know if I want to go," I murmured: an admission I'd made only to my spice cabinet, to the stars.

Ma Wanlu and Bilge stared.

Finally Ma Wanlu said, "Your family's asteroid really must be better than all the others. I thought that was just a story." She maneuvered herself back into the cargo area. Bilge followed. I sat alone, staring at that small dot.

Cinnamon

I remembered the Cai Nu people's first message, sent in ten languages. I remembered shock and wonder. Questions. Possibilities. To know that there were people beyond the asteroids!

I had never believed those stories.

I had joined, as a child, in a ten-year Sending: a message flung towards the bright light we knew to be a planet and the smaller light of its moon. We had eaten cinnamon-flavored food and stayed awake for four hours, eight hours, long past the time when a reply could have come.

We live on the moon Cai Nu, the reply had come, six years after the most recent Sending. *We received your messages. Do you truly live in the asteroids?*

Somewhere on my latest trade journey, the possibilities had drifted away like carelessly handled cloves.

They had started with questions.

How many people live in each asteroid? How do you ensure a supply of fresh air and water? How do you celebrate New Year? What do you eat? What languages do you speak? Have you built shrines inside the asteroids? Mosques? Temples? What is your life expectancy? Your infant mortality rate? How has your bone density withstood little or no exposure to gravity? How has—

I had tried not to think about the questions, I had tried not to think about what I knew: that our ancestors' genes had been modified for low-gravity habitats, that it hadn't been enough, that the people of Cai Nu were far healthier than us.

That we wouldn't adapt well to the 0.8G of Cai Nu.

We have reviewed the information you've given us, one of their messages had said, just sixteen weeks ago. Team Leader Hu Leyi, whose voice we knew the best, had sent it: her speech carefully crafted to convey sorrow and hope. *We agree that you cannot survive in the asteroids much longer. We cannot, at this point, invest in improved infrastructure in the asteroids, which means that we must bring you to Cai Nu and from there decide how and where you will live.* Reassurances had followed. *When you reach Cai Nu, we will ensure that there are doctors who speak all of your languages. We will build a place where you can live comfortably while we find ways for you to adapt to life on Cai Nu. We will also find ways for you to use your current skills and gain new ones. We want your futures to be prosperous.*

Reactions had fallen from my craft's comm panel: loud, tearful, questioning, accepting.

And there were other conversations, a mass of them like a drawer of star anise and fennel seeds.

Team Leader Hu Leyi had asked, before their decision about our futures: *Our records indicate that an experiment in agricultural production was established in the asteroid XI-258. Is that experiment on-going?*

To that, Jidarat Chanprasert—the family head of one asteroid, where I placed a sliver of galangal on my tongue—had replied: *The Lo family inhabit an asteroid where spices are grown.*

How interesting! Several people here are very excited to hear this and would very much like to know more about what species have proved successful. Later, Team Leader Hu Leyi had talked of samples to be brought to Cai Nu.

Jidarat had replied: *Perhaps one of the Lo family would like to talk to Team Leader Hu Leyi about this.*

Later, I had heard Older Mother's voice take over, giving Team Leader Hu Leyi the full history of our fields, our production methods, our trade with the other asteroids. I imagined Older Mother walking among the fields inside our asteroid with Younger Mother at her side, talking as they worked.

Sometimes individuals—not heads of an asteroid's family, not important, knowledgeable people—got onto one of the comm units. One child asked: *How many classes are there at your schools?*

Team Leader Hu Leyi—or one of her colleagues—replied to every question. *There are many classes: mathematics, science, agriculture, history, literature, music, many different types of engineering, many languages.*

A day later, the girl said: *I want to make plants!*

A colleague replied: *We have a great interest in bioengineering at the moment, as we progress with the terraforming of the still-unnamed third planet in the system. It is a very exciting field.*

Can I do that?

Of course! We will provide an education for all of the children and any adults who want it. We want you to do work that fulfills you, whether it is in bioengineering or finance or poetic composition.

The Cai Nu person sounded delighted by the girl's interest, but the conversation did not turn to our adaptation. Perhaps it would be easier for children. Perhaps the Cai Nu people didn't know how much could be achieved with their technology.

In my comm's chiming I had heard excitement. I had heard joy: to listen to stories of millions of people, stories of great temples and mosques, stories of New Year celebrations that filled thousands of streets with food and color and people, and religious festivities and Landing, the anniversary of arriving on Cai Nu from a different star system, and birthdays in families of over a hundred relations—to listen to this was to marvel, to disbelieve, to hope.

Two days before my arrival at the cumin asteroid, Team Leader Hu Leyi had finally admitted what I had feared: *It will be very difficult for you. Your bodies have adapted to the absence of gravity. You will not be able to step from the landing craft onto the surface of our world, but we are building you a zero-gravity habitat, we are already researching the possibilities of technologically-assisted adaptation. However you are able to live here, we will strive to ensure comfort. You will never hunger, never lack medicine, never lack people to talk to. And your children will have every possibility laid out before them.*

I had replayed this message until I knew it as well as Aagot's story.

Thyme

I feared many things, but this was what stuck in me like a blockage in an air supply pipe, like a star anise's point in a throat: what if people didn't understand me. I imagined people like Thyme being so rare that they laughed. I imagined the people whose languages used gendered pronouns insisting that I choose male or female. I imagined every one of these one million people needing to be told that I was un-gendered, a different gender—if I didn't even know what to call myself, how could I expect to be taken seriously?—the way I had needed to tell everyone I knew in the asteroids when I was younger. I imagined giving up.

I told myself to stop being foolish. How could one million people have only two fixed genders?

But the only other person like me in all the asteroids was Aagot, who I couldn't find.

Fields

It was not quite the last time I would approach my family's asteroid: that pitted, dark peppercorn-shape, orbited by a moon only three kilometers in diameter, that landscape at the heart of my personal stories. Home. No, it was not quite the last time I would approach it, but I hurt enough to believe it was.

"Big Cousin!" my youngest cousin's voice came in over the comm. "We're opening the smaller landing bay for you. Bring everyone in!"

A hole slowly opened in the asteroid's side.

I wordlessly landed my craft, waited for the bay doors to close and the air to return, waited for the signal to unlock my craft's door. Unloading began. My family emerged from the corridors to help: to organize the storage of possessions, to lead people to places they could sleep and spend time until the Cai Nu people arrived.

I slipped away to the fields.

They filled four vast rooms: stacked shelves holding soil and spice-plants. I drifted above them, perpendicular to their ends, looking along each shelf at sage bushes, carefully stunted cinnamon trees, red-fruited chilies, long fennel stalks fronded with white flowers, clusters of bay and berry-heavy juniper and green-leafed plants hung with the star-seeds of anise. So many smells: green and sharp and sweet. Home-smells.

Many plants had been recently harvested: leaves thinned out—taken for drying—and seeds picked. Others soon would be. Our last harvest.

I went to a cluster of star anise plants.

The light gravity generator in the shelf pulled me to the soil. Clods between my toes. Glossy leaves against my legs. The weight of my body startled me, pulled me to my knees. I steadied myself. It was always uncomfortable, returning to the fields after a long journey. Soon—no. I sat. I placed an unripe seed—green, eight-pointed—on my tongue, I dug my fingers into the soil. My skin already smelled of the fields: green, earthy. Home.

Would I ever work in a field on Cai Nu? Would I ever adjust to that much gravity?

I wanted to think of nothing but star anise against my tongue, against my skin.

Younger Mother's voice cut through the air. "Oldest Child? Is that you?"

"Yes."

Boots clanged on metal: she climbed down from far above me, shelf to shelf, until she appeared at the end of mine and swung herself onto the soil with an ease I lacked. A bag of cinnamon hung from her shoulder. She walked towards me with bark-stained fingers and bare feet—and the way she walked, straight-backed and sturdy, reminded me suddenly of the pictures of the Cai Nu people.

"I didn't hear you working," I said.

"I was thinking about, well, a lot of things." She crouched at my side, smiling. "Why are you in here?"

"I wanted to sit in the fields, as we'll be abandoning them soon."

My voice was as brittle as a dried cardamom pod.

Younger Mother's smile faded.

I looked away, at the soil, at the star anise, as my mother quietly said, "It will be better. For everyone. Just—just imagine the fields there! Real fields, laid flat across the ground not stacked like this, like *shelves* because we don't have to room to do it any other way—and *sunshine!*"

"I see the sun regularly," I murmured.

Above our heads, the underside of the next shelf held UV lights that replicated the sun for the plants: a constellation of hundreds across the fields.

"I've read about rain and snow in a thousand poems," Younger Mother said, "but to see them! To feel them on my skin!"

We—I—wouldn't. I had grown up in the fields, gravity on my bones, but I had spent so much of the past ten years among the asteroids. I loved it: the cumin or clove or galangal on my tongue, the spice cabinet doors sliding open, the happiness I brought, the stories shared. But I doubted my body was much healthier than those of the people I traded with.

Would my field-working family adapt quickly? Would they work in real fields?

"And they will have new spices there," Younger Mother said, running her fingers over the star anise's leaves. "New flavors. New—so much."

New spices.

"It will be better."

"And difficult," I said. "No one seems to want to talk about that."

"What else can we do? You know this, you see the other asteroids and everything that's broken and old in them."

I remembered the star anise asteroid, broken open like a seed casing, all its contents—its people, who I had once known—spilled out.

"I need to get back to harvesting," Younger Mother said. "I know there won't be much need for all this on Cai Nu, but it would be a shame for it to go to waste."

"I'll eat it."

She smiled, then left me among the star anise plants, their seeds hanging around me like the view from an asteroid's surface. I couldn't imagine any other view.

I returned to my craft, to my journey—not a trade journey, any more.

Cinnamon, Turmeric, Rosemary, Cloves, Galangal, Sage

I started to forget to place spices on my tongue as I arrived at each asteroid, collecting its people—bringing them closer to the Cai Nu people's arrival. I started—slowly, reluctantly—to think of the ways life on Cai Nu would be better for them, for me.

Found

Everyone gathered. Everyone. Who had ever imagined such a sight? So many people holding onto the walls or drifting carefully, so many bags and boxes tethered with them, so many voices all at once—people who had never seen each other, only spoken over the comms, suddenly able to talk unending, to shyly smile and embrace and unhesitatingly kiss. A wonder. A hundred people, another hundred, another. A community, not stretched out like sparse flowers on an ill chili plant but here, together, one. Everyone.

I couldn't deny my excitement. I couldn't subdue my fear.

I looked and looked for Aagot.

Older Mother had set up comm units throughout the large loading bay, so that her voice could be heard everywhere in that vast space, among so many people. Periodically she said, "The Cai Nu craft is now two hours away!" and, "The Cai Nu craft is continuing its steady course, only an hour away!" until, suddenly, too soon, "The Cai Nu craft will enter the landing bay in ten minutes." I drifted through the loading bay. Around me, people drew in breath together, a long silence before new conversations streamed out like air into space.

Then—so soon—we heard the grinding as the landing bay doors opened for the first time in over a hundred years. We heard nothing, nothing, noise lost in vacuum—then a gentle set of metal-on-metal sounds. The Cai Nu craft landing. I drifted, unseeing. I only knew sounds. Arrival. The landing bay doors closing again. The first set of airlock doors between the two bays opening. I didn't breathe, I didn't speak—no one did. I reached a wall. I held.

The second set of airlock doors opened.

The people—five of them—wore dark blue suits and helmets with clear visors, but I was too far away to see their faces. Into our silence they slowly entered, using the handrails that spread across the wall like roots. They removed their helmets. They looked at us with cautious smiles. One said in Mandarin, "I am Team Leader Hu Leyi. It is a pleasure to finally be here and meeting you all."

Older Mother drifted forward, saying, "I am Lo Minyu. On behalf of everyone: welcome. You are very welcome here."

The other four Cai Nu people looked around the loading bay, as if trying to match faces to the voices they had heard over the comms.

"Are you all here?" Hu Leyi asked.

What did they think of us? What did they—

I saw, then, a long, thin braid of hair with a circular metal ornament fixed to its end.

I remembered: etched with a person crouched inside the shape of a bear.

"Aagot!" Then fear reached my tongue and I couldn't talk. Was this Aagot? Was this some other person, who did not know me, did not want to talk to me—

The person turned.

"Aagot," I managed.

A slight frown. "Ecralali, now."

Now. A name-change—a reason I hadn't been able to find Aagot Fossen, who no longer existed.

"Did we meet when I was younger?" Ecralali asked.

"Yes. Yes. I am Lo Yiying."

Quietly, Ecralali said, "I know you."

"Years ago, we talked about—" One or two people were interested in our conversation. I wanted privacy. I wanted no one to judge our words unimportant, irrelevant. Most of all, I wanted Ecralali to remember me. "We talked about Thyme and gender and—" I might as well have bared my skin in the space between the asteroids. "It was the most important conversation I've ever had."

Ecralali's face changed: astonishment and delight. Unless I interpreted wrongly, unless I imagined—

"I remember," Ecralali said, "I remember telling you about un-gendered Houyi—"

"I'd only ever known Houyi as a woman before then," I said, as full of wonder as if I was hearing the tale of Chang E and Houyi for the first time. "That's how my mothers always tell the story."

"—and the story of the stars, whose lives are not measured in gender."

"Thyme," I said, fennel-foliage soft, "who is like me."

"Yes."

Hu Leyi and her colleagues were still talking: moving among us, taking names, inventorying possessions, dividing us into groups.

"I know more stories now," Ecralali said.

"I—I would like to hear them."

"I know about Cai Nu—the founder, not the moon—I've read everything in our records, listened to every story. A lot of them tell that Cai Nu was fluidly gendered."

"The founder was . . . "

Ecralali's smile was as rich as a whole cabinet of spices.

I half-heard announcements. We would have a room for each family on the Cai Nu people's spacecraft, as well as several communal spaces, connected by a long corridor. I thought of stems. I thought of floating above the spices still growing on the shelves of my family's fields. They would shrivel and die and I would never again be Lo Yiying the spice trader. I would be far from my home. Then we would reach Cai Nu. Gleaming. Strange. Skied.

Storied.

"I want to know what stories are told there," Ecralali said.

"I would listen to every one."

It hadn't occurred to me—

I had needed to explain myself to my family, to people among the asteroids. Before that—to myself. That had taken almost twenty years. I had only found myself in the stories that fell from Ecralali's—once-Aagot's—mouth like star anise. To even imagine that I might be found in other stories—

I hadn't.

"My favorite stories," Ecralali said, "are those that say 'Cai Nu' is a chosen name."

One of Hu Leyi's colleagues reached us. As Ecralali said, "Ecralali Fos," and pointed to just one small bag, I thought of my own name: a gift from my mothers. Could I—No. I still wanted it. It had clung to me, all these years, like a grain of soil under a fingernail: a welcome reminder of my family on the long journeys between the asteroids. It fit me.

Below us, the first group passed through the airlock doors to the spacecraft.

"Lo Yiying," I said, and my voice was almost steady. "My possessions are with my family—Lo Minyu and Xu Weina are my mothers." I didn't think I needed to list the rest of my family—brother, cousins, aunts, uncles, a single grandfather. They all waited together, with the spice cabinet—full of the final harvest—between them.

The man made a note on the translucent screen that hovered in front of him, then moved on.

"I should go to my family," I said, though I couldn't imagine moving, couldn't imagine any of what would happen next.

"We have months of journeying ahead of us," Ecralali said. "Plenty of time for telling stories."

Thyme

The fourth story Ecralali gave me, with thyme on our tongues, was of Cai Nu: working on a team of scientists identifying planets and moons suitable for human settlement, finding the moon that would eventually bear their name, spending decades preparing the team for the long journey and the tireless tasks at the other end—then, being invited to join the team despite their advanced age.

Cai Nu lived a year on the moon before finally dying. They are remembered forever: their vision of people living on this moon, their hard work making it more than a story.

Their name, chosen in the same year that they first saw a promising moon in their data.

I pressed the thyme to the roof of my mouth.

I was not alone.

A BRIEF HISTORY OF THE TRANS-PACIFIC TUNNEL

KEN LIU

At the noodle shop, I wave the other waitress away, waiting for the American woman: skin pale and freckled as the Moon, swelling breasts that fill the bodice of her dress, long chestnut curls spilling past her shoulders, held back with a flowery bandanna. Her eyes, green like fresh tea leaves, radiate a bold and fearless smile that is rarely seen among Asians. And I like the wrinkles around them, fitting for a woman in her thirties.

"*Hai.*" She finally stops at my table, her lips pursed impatiently. "*Hoka no okyakusan ga imasu yo. Nani wo chuumon shimasu ka?*" Her Japanese is quite good, the pronunciation maybe even better than mine—though she is not using the honorific. It is still rare to see Americans here in the Japanese half of Midpoint City, but things are changing now, in the thirty-sixth year of the Shôwa Era (she, being an American, would think of it as 1961).

"A large bowl of *tonkotsu* ramen," I say, mostly in English. Then I realize how loud and rude I sound. Old Diggers like me always forget that not everyone is practically deaf. "Please," I add, a whisper.

Her eyes widen as she finally recognizes me. I've cut my hair and put on a clean shirt, and that's not how I looked the past few times I've come here. I haven't paid much attention to my appearance in a decade. There hasn't been any need to. Almost all my time is spent alone and at home. But the sight of her has quickened my pulse in a way I haven't felt in years, and I wanted to make an effort.

"Always the same thing," she says, and smiles.

I like hearing her English. It sounds more like her natural voice, not so high-pitched.

"You don't really like the noodles," she says, when she brings me my ramen. It isn't a question.

I laugh, but I don't deny it. The ramen in this place is terrible. If the owner were any good he wouldn't have left Japan to set up shop here at Midpoint City, where the tourists stopping for a break on their way through the Trans-Pacific Tunnel don't know any better. But I keep on coming, just to see her.

"You are not Japanese."

"No," I say. "I'm Formosan. Please call me Charlie." Back when I coordinated work with the American crew during the construction of Midpoint City, they called me Charlie because they couldn't pronounce my Hokkien name correctly. And I liked the way it sounded so I kept using it.

"Okay, Charlie. I'm Betty." She turns to leave.

"Wait," I say. I do not know from where I get this sudden burst of courage. It is the boldest thing I've done in a long time. "Can I see you when you are free?"

She considers this, biting her lip. "Come back in two hours."

From *The Novice Traveler's Guide to the Trans-Pacific Tunnel*, published by the TPT Transit Authority, 1963:

Welcome, traveler! This year marks the twenty-fifth anniversary of the completion of the Trans-Pacific Tunnel. We are excited to see that this is your first time through the Tunnel.

The Trans-Pacific Tunnel follows a Great Circle path just below the seafloor to connect Asia to North America, with three surface terminus stations in Shanghai, Tokyo, and Seattle. The Tunnel takes the shortest path between the cities, arcing north to follow the Pacific Rim mountain ranges. Although this course increased the construction cost of the Tunnel due to the need for earthquake-proofing, it also allows the Tunnel to tap into geothermal vents and hot spots along the way, which generate the electrical power needed for the Tunnel and its support infrastructure, such as the air-compression stations, oxygen generators, and sub-seafloor maintenance posts.

The Tunnel is in principle a larger—gigantic—version of the pneumatic tubes or capsule lines familiar to all of us for delivering interoffice mail in modern buildings. Two parallel concrete-enclosed steel transportation tubes, one each for westbound and eastbound traffic, 60 feet in diameter, are installed in the Tunnel. The transportation tubes are divided into numerous shorter self-sealing sections, each with multiple air-compression stations. The cylindrical capsules, containing passengers and goods, are propelled through the tubes by a partial vacuum pulling in front and by compressed air pushing from behind. The capsules ride on a monorail for reduced friction. Current maximum speed is about a hundred-and-twenty miles per hour, and a trip from Shanghai to Seattle takes a little more than two full days. Plans are under way to eventually increase maximum speed to two hundred MPH.

The Tunnel's combination of capacity, speed, and safety makes it superior to zeppelins, aeroplanes, and surface shipping for almost all trans-Pacific transportation needs. It is immune to storms, icebergs, and typhoons, and very cheap to operate, as it is powered by the boundless heat of the Earth itself. Today, it is the chief means by which passengers and manufactured goods flow between Asia and America. More than 30% of global container shipping each year goes through the Tunnel.

We hope you enjoy your travel along the Trans-Pacific Tunnel, and wish you a safe journey to your final destination.

I was born in the second year of the Taishô Era (1913), in a small village in Shinchiku Prefecture, in Formosa. My family were simple peasants who never participated in any of the uprisings against Japan. The way my father saw it, whether the Manchus on the mainland or the Japanese were in charge didn't much matter, since they all left us alone except when it came time for taxes. The lot of the Hoklo peasant was to toil and suffer in silence.

Politics was for those who had too much to eat. Besides, I always liked the Japanese workers from the lumber company, who would hand me candy during their lunch break. The Japanese colonist families we saw were polite, well-dressed, and very lettered. My father once said, "If I got to choose, in my next life I'd come back as a Japanese."

During my boyhood, a new prime minister in Japan announced a change in policy: natives in the colonies should be turned into good subjects of the Emperor. The Japanese governor-general set up village schools that everyone had to attend. The more clever boys could even expect to attend high schools formerly reserved for the Japanese, and then go on to study in Japan, where they would have bright futures.

I was not a good student, however, and never learned Japanese very well. I was content to know how to read a few characters and go back to the fields, the same as my father and his father before him.

All this changed in the year I turned seventeen (the fifth year of the Shôwa Era, or 1930), when a Japanese man in a Western suit came to our village, promising riches for the families of young men who knew how to work hard and didn't complain.

We stroll through Friendship Square, the heart of Midpoint City. A few pedestrians, both American and Japanese, stare and whisper as they see us walking together. But Betty does not care, and her carelessness is infectious.

Here, kilometers under the Pacific Ocean and the seafloor, it's late afternoon by the City's clock, and the arc lamps around us are turned up as bright as can be.

"I always feel like I'm at a night baseball game when I go through here,"

Betty says. "When my husband was alive, we went to many baseball games together as a family."

I nod. Betty usually keeps her reminiscences of her husband light. She mentioned once that he was a lawyer, and he had left their home in California to work in South Africa, where he died because some people didn't like who he was defending. "They called him a race traitor," she said. I didn't press for details.

Now that her children are old enough to be on their own, she's traveling the world for enlightenment and wisdom. Her capsule train to Japan had stopped at Midpoint Station for a standard one-hour break for passengers to get off and take some pictures, but she had wandered too far into the City and missed the train. She took it as a sign and stayed in the City, waiting to see what lessons the world had to teach her.

Only an American could lead such a life. Among Americans, there are many free spirits like hers.

We've been seeing each other for four weeks, usually on Betty's days off. We take walks around Midpoint City, and we talk. I prefer that we converse in English, mostly because I do not have to think much about how formal and polite to be.

As we pass by the bronze plaque in the middle of the Square, I point out to her my Japanese-style name on the plaque: Takumi Hayashi. The Japanese teacher in my village school had helped me pick the first name, and I had liked the characters: "open up, sea." The choice turned out to be prescient.

She is impressed. "That must have been something. You should tell me more about what it was like to work on the Tunnel."

There are not many of us old Diggers left now. The years of hard labor spent breathing hot and humid dust that stung our lungs had done invisible damage to our insides and joints. At forty-eight, I've said good-bye to all of my friends as they succumbed to illnesses. I am the last keeper of what we had done together.

When we finally blasted through the thin rock wall dividing our side from the American side and completed the Tunnel in the thirteenth year of the Shôwa Era (1938), I had the honor of being one of the shift supervisors invited to attend the ceremony. I explain to Betty that the blast-through spot is in the main tunnel due north of where we are standing, just beyond Midpoint Station.

We arrive at my apartment building, on the edge of the section of the City where most Formosans live. I invite her to come up. She accepts.

My apartment is a single room eight mats in size, but there is a window. Back when I bought it, it was considered a very luxurious place for Midpoint City, where space was and is at a premium. I mortgaged most of my pension on it, since I had no desire ever to move. Most men made do with coffin-like one-mat rooms. But to her American eyes, it probably seems very cramped and shabby. Americans like things to be open and big.

I make her tea. It is very relaxing to talk to her. She does not care that I am not Japanese, and assumes nothing about me. She takes out a joint, as is the custom for Americans, and we share it.

Outside the window, the arc lights have been dimmed. It's evening in Midpoint City. Betty does not get up and say that she has to leave. We stop talking. The air feels tense, but in a good way, expectant. I reach out for her hand, and she lets me. The touch is electric.

From *Splendid America*, AP ed., 1995:

In 1929, the fledging and weak Republic of China, in order to focus on the domestic Communist rebellion, appeased Japan by signing the Sino-Japanese Mutual Cooperation Treaty. The treaty formally ceded all Chinese territories in Manchuria to Japan, which averted the prospect of all-out war between China and Japan and halted Soviet ambitions in Manchuria. This was the capstone on Japan's 35-year drive for imperial expansion. Now, with Formosa, Korea, and Manchuria incorporated into the Empire and a collaborationist China within its orbit, Japan had access to vast reserves of natural resources, cheap labor, and a potential market of hundreds of millions for its manufactured goods.

Internationally, Japan announced that it would continue its rise as a Great Power henceforth by peaceful means. Western powers, however, led by Britain and the United States, were suspicious. They were especially alarmed by Japan's colonial ideology of a "Greater East Asia Co-Prosperity Sphere," which seemed to be a Japanese version of the Monroe Doctrine, and suggested a desire to drive European and American influence from Asia.

Before the Western powers could decide on a plan to contain and encircle Japan's "Peaceful Ascent," however, the Great Depression struck. The brilliant Emperor Hirohito seized the opportunity and suggested to President Herbert Hoover his vision of the Trans-Pacific Tunnel as the solution to the worldwide economic crisis.

The work was hard, and dangerous. Every day, men were injured and sometimes killed. It was also very hot. In the finished sections, they installed machines to cool the air. But in the most forward parts of the Tunnel, where the actual digging happened, we were exposed to the heat of the Earth, and we worked in nothing but our undershorts, sweating nonstop. The work crews were segregated by race—there were Koreans, Formosans, Okinawans, Filipinos, Chinese (separated again by topolect)—but after a while we all looked the same, covered in sweat and dust and mud, only little white circles of skin showing around our eyes.

It didn't take me long to get used to living underground, to the constant noise of dynamite, hydraulic drills, the bellows cycling cooling air, and the flickering faint yellow light of arc lamps. Even when you were sleeping, the next shift was already at it. Everyone grew hard of hearing after a while, and we stopped talking to each other. There was nothing to say anyway, just more digging.

But the pay was good, and I saved up and sent money home. However, visiting home was out of the question. By the time I started, the head of the tunnel was already halfway between Shanghai and Tokyo. They charged you a month's wages to ride the steam train carrying the excavated waste back to Shanghai and up to the surface. I couldn't afford such luxuries. As we made progress, the trip back only grew longer and more expensive.

It was best not to think too much about what we were doing, about the miles of water over our heads, and the fact that we were digging a tunnel through the Earth's crust to get to America. Some men did go crazy under those conditions, and had to be restrained before they could hurt themselves or others.

From *A Brief History of the Trans-Pacific Tunnel*, published by the TPT Transit Authority, 1960:

Osachi Hamaguchi, prime minister of Japan during the Great Depression, claimed that Emperor Hirohito was inspired by the American effort to build the Panama Canal to conceive of the Trans-Pacific Tunnel. "America has knit together two oceans," the Emperor supposedly said. "Now let us chain together two continents." President Hoover, trained as an engineer, enthusiastically promoted and backed the project as an antidote to the global economic contraction.

The Tunnel is, without a doubt, the greatest engineering project ever conceived by Man. Its sheer scale makes the Great Pyramids and the Great Wall of China seem like mere toys, and many critics at the time described it as hubristic lunacy, a modern Tower of Babel.

Although tubes and pressurized air have been used for passing around documents and small parcels since Victorian times, before the Tunnel, pneumatic tube transport of heavy goods and passengers had only been tried on a few intra-city subway demonstration programs. The extraordinary engineering demands of the Tunnel thus drove many technological advances, often beyond the core technologies involved, such as fast-tunneling directed explosives. As one illustration, thousands of young women with abacuses and notepads were employed as computers for engineering calculations at the start of the project, but by the end of the project electronic computers had taken their place.

In all, construction of the 5880-mile tunnel took ten years between 1929 and 1938. Some seven million men worked on it, with Japan and the United States providing the bulk of the workers. At its height, one in ten working men in the United States was employed in building the Tunnel. More than 13 billion cubic yards of material were excavated, almost fifty times the amount removed during the construction of the Panama Canal, and the fill was used to extend the shorelines of China, the Japanese home islands, and Puget Sound.

Afterward we lie still on the futon, our limbs entwined. In the darkness I can hear her heart beating, and the smell of sex and our sweat, unfamiliar in this apartment, is comforting.

She tells me about her son, who is still going to school in America. She says that he is traveling with his friends in the southern states of America, riding the buses together.

"Some of the friends are Negroes," she says.

I know some Negroes. They have their own section in the American half of the City, where they mostly keep to themselves. Some Japanese families hire the women to cook Western meals.

"I hope he's having a good time," I say.

My reaction surprises Betty. She turns to stare at me, and then laughs. "I forget that you cannot understand what this is about."

She sits up in bed. "In America, the Negroes and whites are separated: where they live, where they work, where they go to school."

I nod. That sounds familiar. Here in the Japanese half of the City, the races also keep to themselves. There are superior and inferior races. For example, there are many restaurants and clubs reserved only for the Japanese.

"The law says that whites and Negroes can ride the bus together, but the secret of America is that law is not followed by large swaths of the country. My son and his friends want to change that. They ride the buses together to make a statement, to make people pay attention to the secret. They ride in places where people do not want to see Negroes sitting in seats that belong only to whites. Things can become violent and dangerous when people get angry and form a mob."

This seems very foolish: to make statements that no one wants to hear, to speak when it is better to be quiet. What difference will a few boys riding a bus make?

"I don't know if it's going to make any difference, change anyone's mind. But it doesn't matter. It's good enough for me that he is speaking, that he is not silent. He's making the secret a little bit harder to keep, and that counts for something." Her voice is full of pride, and she is beautiful when she is proud.

I consider Betty's words. It is the obsession of Americans to speak, to express opinions on things that they are ignorant about. They believe in drawing attention to things that other people may prefer to keep quiet, to ignore and forget.

But I can't dismiss the image Betty has put into my head: a boy stands in darkness and silence. He speaks; his words float up like a bubble. It explodes, and the world is a little brighter, and a little less stiflingly silent.

I have read in the papers that back in Japan, they are debating about granting Formosans and Manchurians seats in the Imperial Diet. Britain is still fighting the native guerrillas in Africa and India, but may be forced soon to grant the colonies independence. The world is indeed changing.

"What's wrong?" Betty asks. She wipes the sweat from my forehead. She shifts to give me more of the flow from the air conditioner. I shiver. Outside, the great arc lights are still off, not yet dawn. "Another bad dream?"

We've been spending many of our nights together since that first time. Betty has upset my routine, but I don't mind at all. That was the routine of a man with one foot in the grave. Betty has made me feel alive after so many years under the ocean, alone in darkness and silence.

But being with Betty has also unblocked something within me, and memories are tumbling out.

If you really couldn't stand it, they provided comfort women from Korea for the men. But you had to pay a day's wages.

I tried it only once. We were both so dirty, and the girl stayed still like a dead fish. I never used the comfort women again.

A friend told me that some of the girls were not there willingly but had been sold to the Imperial Army, and maybe the one I had was like that. I didn't really feel sorry for her. I was too tired.

From *The Ignoramus's Guide to American History* , 1995:

So just when everyone was losing jobs and lining up for soup and bread, Japan came along and said, "Hey, America, let's build this big-ass tunnel and spend a whole lot of money and hire lots of workers and get the economy going again. Whaddya say?" And the idea basically worked, so everyone was like: "Doumo arigatou, Japan!"

Now, when you come up with a good idea like that, you get some chips you can cash in. So that's what Japan did the next year, in 1930. At the London Naval Conference, where the Big Bullies—oops, I meant "Great Powers"—figured out how many battleships and aircraft carriers each country got to build, Japan demanded to be allowed to build the same number of ships as the United States and Britain. And the US and Britain said fine.[1]

This concession to Japan turned out to be a big deal. Remember Hamaguchi, the Japanese prime minister, and the way he kept on talking about how Japan was going to "ascend peacefully" from then on? This had really annoyed the militarists and nationalists in Japan because they thought Hamaguchi was selling out the country. But when Hamaguchi came home with such an impressive diplomatic victory, he was hailed as a hero, and people began to believe that his "Peaceful Ascent" policy was going to make Japan strong. People thought maybe he really could get the Western powers to treat Japan as an equal without turning Japan into a giant army camp. The militarists and nationalists got less support after that.

At that fun party, the London Naval Conference, the Big Bullies also scrapped all those humiliating provisions of the Treaty of Versailles that made Germany toothless. Britain and Japan both had their own reasons for supporting this: they each thought Germany liked them better than the other, and would join up as an ally if a global brawl for Asian colonies broke out one day. Everyone was wary about the Soviets, too, and wanted to set up Germany as a guard dog of sorts for the polar bear.[2]

<u>Things to Think About in the Shower:</u>

1. Many economists describe the Tunnel as the first real Keynesian stimulus project, which shortened the Great Depression.

2. The Tunnel's biggest fan was probably President Hoover: he won an unprecedented four terms in office because of its success.

3. We now know that the Japanese military abused the rights of many of the workers during the Tunnel's construction, but it took decades for the facts to emerge. The Bibliography points to some more books on this subject.

4. The Tunnel ended up taking a lot of business away from surface shipping, and many Pacific ports went bust. The most famous example of this occurred in 1949, when Britain sold Hong Kong to Japan because it didn't think the harbor city was all that important anymore.

---

[1] The Washington Naval Treaty of 1922 had set the ratio of capital ships among the US, Britain, and Japan at 5:5:3. This was the ratio Japan got adjusted in 1930.

[2] Allowing Germany to re-arm also let the German government heave a big sigh of relief. The harsh Treaty of Versailles, especially those articles about neutering Germany, made a lot of Germans very angry and some of them joined a group of goose-stepping thugs called the German Nationalist Socialist Party, which scared everyone, including the government. After those provisions of the Treaty were scrapped, the thugs got no electoral support at the next election in 1930, and faded away. Heck, they are literally now a footnote of history, like this one.

5. The Great War (1914-1918) turned out to be the last global "hot war" of the 20th century (so far). Are we turning into wimps? Who wants to start a new world war?

After the main work on the Tunnel was completed in the thirteenth year of the Shôwa Era (1938), I returned home for the first and only time since I left, eight years earlier. I bought a window seat on the westbound capsule train from Midpoint Station, coach class. The ride was smooth and comfortable, the capsule quiet save for the low voices of my fellow passengers and a faint *whoosh* as we were pushed along by air. Young female attendants pushed carts of drinks and food up and down the aisles.

Some clever companies had bought advertising space along the inside of the tube and painted pictures at window height. As the capsule moved along, the pictures rushing by centimeters from the windows blurred together and became animated, like a silent film. My fellow passengers and I were mesmerized by the novel effect.

The elevator ride up to the surface in Shanghai filled me with trepidation, my ears popping with the changes in pressure. And then it was time to get on a boat bound for Formosa.

I hardly recognized my home. With the money I sent, my parents had built a new house and bought more land. My family was now rich, and my village a bustling town. I found it hard to speak to my siblings and my parents. I had been away so long that I did not understand much about their lives, and I could not explain to them how I felt. I did not realize how much I had been hardened and numbed by my experience, and there were things I had seen that I could not speak of. In some sense I felt that I had become like a turtle, with a shell around me that kept me from feeling anything.

My father had written to me to come home because it was long past time for me to find a wife. Since I had worked hard, stayed healthy, and kept my mouth shut—it also helped that as a Formosan I was considered superior to the other races except the Japanese and Koreans—I had been steadily promoted to crew chief and then to shift supervisor. I had money, and if I settled in my hometown, I would provide a good home.

But I could no longer imagine a life on the surface. It had been so long since I had seen the blinding light of the sun that I felt like a newborn when out in the open. Things were so quiet. Everyone was startled when I spoke because I was used to shouting. And the sky and tall buildings made me dizzy—I was so used to being underground, under the sea, in tight, confined spaces, that I had trouble breathing if I looked up.

I expressed my desire to stay underground and work in one of the station cities strung like pearls along the Tunnel. The faces of the fathers of all the girls tightened at this thought. I didn't blame them: who would want their daughter to spend the rest of her life underground, never seeing the light of day? The fathers whispered to each other that I was deranged.

I said good-bye to my family for the last time, and I did not feel I was home until I was back at Midpoint Station, the warmth and the noise of the heart of the Earth around me, a safe shell. When I saw the soldiers on the platform at the station, I knew that the world was finally back to normal. More work still had to be done to complete the side tunnels that would be expanded into Midpoint City.

"Soldiers," Betty says, "why were there soldiers at Midpoint City?"

I stand in darkness and silence. I cannot hear or see. Words churn in my throat, like a rising flood waiting to burst the dam. I have been holding my tongue for a long, long time.

"They were there to keep the reporters from snooping around," I say.

I tell Betty about my secret, the secret of my nightmares, something I've never spoken of all these years.

As the economy recovered, labor costs rose. There were fewer and fewer young men desperate enough to take jobs as Diggers in the Tunnel. Progress on the American side had slowed for a few years, and Japan was not doing much better. Even China seemed to run out of poor peasants who wanted this work.

Hideki Toujou, Army minister, came up with a solution. The Imperial Army's pacification of the Communist rebellions supported by the Soviet Union in Manchuria and China resulted in many prisoners. They could be put to work, for free.

The prisoners were brought into the Tunnel to take the place of regular work crews. As shift supervisor, I managed them with the aid of a squad of soldiers. The prisoners were a sorry sight, chained together, naked, thin like scarecrows. They did not look like dangerous and crafty Communist bandits. I wondered sometimes how there could be so many prisoners, since the news always said that the pacification of the Communists was going well and the Communists were not much of a threat.

They usually didn't last long. When a prisoner was discovered to have expired from the work, his body was released from the shackles and a soldier would shoot it a few times. We would then report the death as the result of an escape attempt.

To hide the involvement of the slave laborers, we kept visiting reporters away from work on the main Tunnel. They were used mainly on the side excavations, for station cities or power stations, in places that were not well surveyed and more dangerous.

One time, while making a side tunnel for a power station, my crew blasted through to a pocket of undetected slush and water, and the side tunnel began to flood. We had to seal the breach quickly before the flood got into the main Tunnel. I woke up the crew of the two other shifts, and sent a second chained crew into the side tunnel with sandbags to help with plugging up the break.

The corporal in charge of the squad of soldiers guarding the prisoners asked me, "What if they can't plug it?"

His meaning was obvious. We had to make sure that the water did not get into the main Tunnel, even if the repair crews we sent in failed. There was only one way to make sure, and as water was flowing back up the side tunnel, time was running out.

I directed the chained crew I'd kept behind as a reserve to begin placing dynamite around the side tunnel, behind the men we had sent in earlier. I did not much like this, but I told myself that these were hardened Communist terrorists, and they were probably sentenced to death already anyway.

The prisoners hesitated. They understood what we were trying to do, and they did not want to do it. Some worked slowly. Others just stood.

The corporal ordered one of the prisoners shot. This motivated the remaining ones to hurry.

I set off the charges. The side tunnel collapsed, and the pile of debris and falling rocks filled most of the entrance, but there was still some space at the top. I directed the remaining prisoners to climb up and seal the opening. Even I climbed up to help them.

The sound of the explosion told the prisoners we sent in earlier what was happening. The chained men lumbered back, sloshing through the rising water and the darkness, trying to get to us. The corporal ordered the soldiers to shoot a few of the men, but the rest kept on coming, dragging the dead bodies with their chains, begging us to let them through. They climbed up the pile of debris toward us.

The man at the front of the chain was only a few meters from us, and in the remaining cone of light cast by the small opening that was left I could see his face, contorted with fright.

"Please," he said. "Please let me through. I just stole some money. I don't deserve to die."

He spoke to me in Hokkien, my mother tongue. This shocked me. Was he a common criminal from back home in Formosa, and not a Chinese Communist from Manchuria?

He reached the opening and began to push away the rocks, to enlarge the opening and climb through. The corporal shouted at me to stop him. The water level was rising. Behind the man, the other chained prisoners were climbing to help him.

I lifted a heavy rock near me and smashed it down on the hands of the man grabbing onto the opening. He howled and fell back, dragging the other prisoners down with him. I heard the splash of water.

"Faster, faster!" I ordered the prisoners on our side of the collapsed tunnel. We sealed the opening, then retreated to set up more dynamite and blast down more rocks to solidify the seal.

When the work was finally done, the corporal ordered all of the remaining prisoners shot, and we buried their bodies under yet more blast debris.

There was a massive prisoner uprising. They attempted to sabotage the project, but failed and instead killed themselves.

This was the corporal's report of the incident, and I signed my name to it as well. Everyone understood that was the way to write up such reports.

I remember the face of the man begging me to stop very well. That was the face I saw in the dream last night.

The Square is deserted right before dawn. Overhead, neon advertising signs hang from the City's ceiling, a few hundred meters up. They take the place of long-forgotten constellations and the Moon.

Betty keeps an eye out for unlikely pedestrians while I swing the hammer against the chisel. Bronze is a hard material, but I have not lost the old skills I learned as a Digger. Soon the characters of my name are gone from the plaque, leaving behind a smooth rectangle.

I switch to a smaller chisel and begin to carve. The design is simple: three ovals interlinked, a chain. These are the links that bound two continents and three great cities together, and these are the shackles that bound men whose voices were forever silenced, whose names were forgotten. There is beauty and wonder here, and also horror and death.

With each strike of the hammer, I feel as though I am chipping away the shell around me, the numbness, the silence.

Make the secret a bit harder to keep. That counts for something.

"Hurry," Betty says.

My eyes are blurry. And suddenly the lights around the Square come on. It is morning under the Pacific Ocean.

ILSE, WHO SAW CLEARLY

E. LILY YU

Once, among the indigo mountains of Germany, there was a kingdom of blue-eyed men and women whose blood was tinged blue with cold. The citizens were skilled in clockwork, escapements, and piano manufacture, and the clocks and pianos of that country were famous throughout the world. Their children pulled on rabbit-fur gloves before they sat down to practice their etudes, for it was so cold the notes rang and clanged in the air. It was coldest of all in the town on the highest mountain, where there lived a girl called Ilse, who was neither beautiful nor ugly, neither good nor wicked. Yet she was not quite undistinguished, because she was in love.

One afternoon, when the air was glittering with the sounds of innumerable pianos, a stranger as stout as a barrel and swathed to his nosetip walked through the town, singing. Where he walked the pianos fell silent, and wheat-haired boys and girls cracked shutters into the bitter cold to peep at him. And what he sang was this:

> *Ice for sale, eyes for sale,*
> *If your complexion be dark or pale*
> *If your old eyes be sharp or frail,*
> *Come buy, come buy, bright ice for sale!*

Only his listeners could not tell whether he was selling ice or eyes, because he spoke in an odd accent and through a thick scarf.

He sang until he reached the square with its frozen marble fountain. The town had installed a clock face and a set of chimes in the ice, and now they were striking noon.

"Ice?" he said pleasantly to the crowd that had gathered. He unwound a few feet of his woolen cloak and took out a box. The hasp gave his mittens trouble, but finally it clicked open, and he raised the lid and held out the box for all to see. They craned their necks forward, and their startled breaths smoked the air.

The box was crammed with eyes.

There were blue eyes and green eyes and brown eyes, eyes red as lilies, golden as pollen; eyes like pickaxes and eyes like diamonds. Each eye had been carved and painted with enormous care, and the spaces between them were jammed with silk.

The stranger smiled at their astonishment. He unrolled a little more of his cloak and took out another box, and another, and then it was clear that he was really quite slender. He tugged his muffler past his mouth, revealing sunned skin and neat thin lips.

"The finest eyes," he said to the crowd. "Plucked from the lands along the Indian Ocean, where the peacock wears hundreds in his tail. Picked from the wine countries, where they grow as crisp as grapes. Young and good for years of seeing! Old but ground to perfect clarity, according to calculations by the wisest mathematicians in Alexandria!" His teeth flashed gold and silver as he talked.

He ran his fingers through the eyes, holding this one to the light, or that. "Is this not pretty?" he said. "Is this not splendid? Try, my good grandmother, try."

That old woman peered through eyes white with snow-glare at the gems in his hands. "I can't see them clearly," she admitted.

"Well, then!"

"Lucia," she said, touching her daughter's hand. "Find me a pair like I used to have."

"How much?" Lucia said.

"For you, the first, a pittance. An afterthought. Her old eyes and a gold ring."

"Done," the old woman said. Lucia, frowning, fingered two eyes as blue as shadows on snow.

The stranger extracted three slim silver knives with ivory handles from the lining of his cloak. With infinite care and exactitude, barely breathing, he slid the first knife beneath the old woman's eyelid, ran the second around the ball, and with the third cut the crimson embroidery that tied it in place. Twice he did this. Then, in one motion, he slid her old eyes out of their hollows and slipped in the new. Her old blind eyes froze at once in his hands, ringing when he flicked them with a fingernail. He dropped them into his pockets and tilted her chin toward him.

"I can count your teeth," the old woman said with wonder. "Your nose is thin. Your scarf is striped red and yellow."

"A wonder," someone said.

"A marvel of marvels."

"A magician."

"A miracle."

She pulled off her mitten and gave him the ring from her left hand. "He's been dead twenty years," she said to Lucia, who did not look happy. "I can see again. Clear as water. What a wonder."

Then, of course, the stranger had to replace the shortsighted schoolteacher's eyes, after which the old fellow cheerfully snapped his spectacles in two; the neglectful eyes of the town council; six clockmakers' strained eyes; crossed eyes; eyes bleared with snow light and sunlight; eyes that saw too clearly, or too deeply, or too much; eyes that wandered; eyes that were the wrong color.

When the sun was low and scarlet in the sky, the stranger announced that he would work no longer that day, for want of illumination. Half the town immediately offered him a bed and a roaring fire. But he passed that night and many more at the inn, where the fire was lower, colder, and less hospitable, and where, it was said unkindly, one's sleeping breath would freeze and fall like snow on the quilts. He ate cold soup and sliced meats in the farthest corner, answered all questions with a smile, and went to bed early.

After twelve days he bundled his boxes about him and left the town, his pockets sunken and swinging with gold. The townspeople watched as he goat-stepped down the steep trail until even their sharp new eyes could no longer distinguish him from the ice-bearded stones and the pines and the snow.

These new eyes, they found, were better than the old. The makers of escapements and wind-up toys found that they could do far more delicate work than before, and out of their workshops came pocket watches and pianos carved out of almond shells, marching soldiers made from bluebottles, wooden birds that flew and sang, mechanical chessboards that also played tippen, and other such wonders; and the fame of that town went out throughout the whole world.

Summer heard, in her house on the other side of the world, and came to see.

The first notice they had of her approach was a message in a blackbird's beak, then a couple red buds on the edges of twigs, and then she was there. Out of respect she had put on a few extra flowers this year. It was still cold—summer high in the mountains is like that—but the air was softer, the light gentler.

No one saw her courteous posies, however. A little before she arrived, their eyes had begun to blur, then blear, then melt. They saw each other crying and felt their own tears running down their faces, and for no reason at all except summer. Then they understood, and wept in earnest, but it was too late.

By summer's end everyone had cried out the new eyes. The workshops fell still and silent, and tools gathered tarnish on their benches. The hundreds of clocks around the town stopped, since no one could find their keys and keyholes to wind them up again. Only the pianos still rang out their frozen notes now and again, but the melodies were all in minor keys. The town was full of a cold, quiet grief.

Winter was coming, and they would have starved without Ilse, who hadn't sold her eyes. Her sweetheart had written atrocious poems to them, and although they were the same plain blue as anyone else's, she couldn't bear to part with them even for new eyes the colors of violets, blackberries, and marigolds. So she helped the town tend and bring in its meager harvests of beets and cabbage, and on Wednesdays she filled a sack with clocks and toys and went down the mountain to sell them at market, until there were none left. During the day her head swam with the pianos' lugubrious complaints, and at night she ached in every bone.

"Mother," she said, as they ate their bare breakfast together, "shouldn't someone go looking for the surgeon?"

"No one will find him."

"What will you do if you never find your eyes?"

"We'll manage. We have you to see for us."

"I'm going to look for him," she said.

"Absolutely not."

So Ilse packed up her summer clothes, a loaf of bread, two onions, and the fourteen silver coins her mother kept in a jar on the shelf, and the next day she set off down the mountain.

In all her sixteen years, she had never strayed beyond the market in the shadow of the mountain, where the town's clocks and pianos were sold. But now she passed town after town, few of which she knew, and bridges, and streams, and meadows stained with the dregs of summer, and now trees that did not stand as straight as soldiers but spread their shoulders broad and wide. She climbed up one of these as night fell, and tucked her head against her knees, and slept.

A soft noise, like paper or feathers, woke her in the middle of the night. Ilse opened her eyes in fear, expecting robbers and thieves, but saw nothing. Still she was full of dread. She thought of the silver she had stolen, and her sightless mother in a silent house, and her sweetheart, lonely and wondering. She thought of the long road ahead of her, with likely failure at its end, and shivered. For where could she begin to look?

"You are thinking too loud," someone said close to her ear. She nearly fell out of the tree. Next to her, an old crow shifted from foot to foot, cleared its throat, and spat.

"You can talk?"

"Only when people's thoughts are so noisy I can't sleep." It sighed. "What would it take to quiet down your brain?"

"I am looking for my townsmen's eyes."

"Eyes!" The crow whistled. "A treat, a delectable treat. I should follow you."

Ilse snatched sideways, swiping a bit of dark down between her fingers. The crow tumbled out of the tree with a screech.

"You'll do no such thing," she said.

"Peace, peace." A wing brushed her brow. "You'll find what you're looking for. You'll find your sight, and theirs. And you'll not like what you see when you see the world truly, too-quick girl with the odor of onions."

He flapped his way to a higher branch; she could hear him combing out his rumpled feathers. "I don't take kindly to being grabbed at, onion girl."

"Just let me find what I'm looking for," she said, and shut her eyes. Afterwards, but for the bit of down stuck to her clothes, she could not say whether she had dreamt it all.

On the third day, as she trudged down the road that went nowhere she knew, she met a flock of spotted goats with yellow bells about their necks, and then their shepherd, who was chewing a stalk of grass. He greeted her, and she asked with no great hope whether he'd heard of a peddler of eyes.

"Yes, miss," he said. "Walk a little farther, until you reach a village with sunflowers around it, and go down the street to the last house. My daughter is home, and she knows much more about your magician than I do."

Ilse thanked him and went on. The village ringed by sunflowers was smaller and muddier than her own, and the road ended at the smallest and muddiest house. The cat on the roof had only half his coat, as he had been a fierce warrior in his day, but he opened one eye and yawned at her. A young woman opened the door. Asked about the peddler, she smiled and winked her eyes one after the other. One of them was a shade greener than the other.

"I lost this one falling out of a window. My father and I waited four years before the good man came back. We had nothing to pay him with, at least nothing worth it, and I would have gladly taken a grandmother's cataract. But he said I was a lovely girl and picked out a greener eye than my first for me. A sweet soul."

"He left my village blind."

"You must be mistaken. He wouldn't do such a thing."

"He has three silver knives with ivory hafts, with ivy engraved in the ivory. His skin is dark and his nose is sharp."

"Well," the goatherd's daughter said. "Well. He does look like that. And he does have three knives. But I really don't think—"

"How can I find him?"

"Now, that's tricky. That will take a little explanation. But you're in no rush, are you? He doesn't travel quickly, and you don't look like you've eaten yet today." She hewed a generous piece of brown bread for Ilse and poured out a bowl of cream for her, as well as a bowl of milk for the cat.

"I still think you're wrong somewhere. Surely he wouldn't. So kind."

Ilse ate the bread and drank the cream so fast she left a crumb on her cheek and a pale spatter on her chin.

"Now," the goatherd's daughter said presently, "you'll be going to the city. If you unraveled today down the road, you'd find the city at the end of next week. There are three towers at the corners of the city, with three broad streets between them, and where the streets meet is a brick square. Ask in the square where your magician might be. Someone there will know more.

"But you're not taking the road in those clothes, are you?"

Ilse was suddenly aware of how heavy and hot her woolen summer smock and rabbit-fur cloak were, and how strongly they reeked of onions.

"Let me find you something lighter. You can leave those here, for when you return."

So Ilse exchanged her fur and wool for an armful of patched but comfortable linen, put a piece of bread and a slice of cheese in her pocket, and continued on her way. Now and then she passed a farm cart creaking on its way. Now and then, with a nod from the driver, she climbed into one of those carts and rested. She came upon a few crows pecking in the dust, but though she greeted them politely, they never answered.

The longer she traveled, the closer together grew the villages and fields. She was tired of the road and the yellow dust that lay in a film on her mouth, and she thought many times of her soft bed at home, and the color of her sweetheart's hair, and the air as pure as snow. Sometimes she considered turning around, but she never did. After wearing out her shoes by the thickness of seven days, she saw, black against the evening, three towers as formidable as teeth, and that was the city.

A soldier in fine scarlet-and-cream stood to attention at the gate, which was barred. He had a silver spear in his hand and silver mail beneath his tabard.

"It's past sunset," he said, frowning at her through his helmet. "No one enters or exits the city at night. Go home."

She said, "My home is in the mountains, but I've come looking for a magician, a doctor, who can take the eyes out of your head and put them in again. He took all the eyes out of our town."

"I've heard of such a doctor," said the soldier. "He mended my fourth cousin's weak eyes, years ago. But you can't mean him. He wouldn't do such a thing."

"Perhaps it was unintended."

"You'd do well to ask in the square tomorrow. Tomorrow, mind you. I cannot let you through." He held his spear a little straighter. "Unless you can show me something as bright as sunlight. That might fool me for a little while."

"I only have a little silver," she said, patting her pockets. But they were empty.

"Moonlight will do."

"No, I have nothing. I left my silver in my smock, and I left my smock at a goatherd's cottage, and that's a week's walking."

The soldier huffed into his moustache. "What a foolish girl you are." He took a key from his belt and opened a low door in the gate, just tall enough for her to slip through. "I have a little one your age, just as silly as you. You'd feed yourself to wolves if I kept you outside. Hurry up, won't you. And stay out of trouble."

"Thank you," Ilse said, and he shut and locked the door behind her.

Here and there the flame in a lamppost flickered and swayed. There were many more streets than she had expected, running every which way. Uncertain of what to do, she went back and forth, past dark windows and bolted doors; open doors with laughter, hectic music, and light spilling out of them; past rubbish in the gutters and pools of water shining in the dark. Shadows slid past her, silent and purposeful. She felt unseen eyes following her.

At last, lost and dispirited, she peered into a shop window and saw a vitrine lined with pocket watches and the pale faces of tall clock cases in the dimness beyond. Some of them looked familiar. She pressed her nose to the gold-lettered glass, wondering if she knew the hands that had made them. She wanted very much to touch them, but the door was locked.

There was nowhere else she could go. She sat down in the doorway and put her head in her hands and, unwillingly, fell asleep.

If strange hands riffled her pockets while she slept, they found nothing, and she did not know. When she woke, it was morning. An old man with a broom was standing over her, displeased.

"Well, get along now," he said. "Go on." He held the shop door open and swept a little dirt over her, then tried to sweep her off the step.

"Please, which way to the square?"

"Which way to the square?" The shopkeeper stared. "Are you mad?"

"I came into the city yesterday," she said.

"With no place to stay? You *are* mad."

"Won't you tell me?"

"Never let it be said I was uncharitable toward the insane," the shopkeeper said. He disappeared into the shop—a bell jangled inside—and just as she decided to leave, reappeared with a small stale cake.

"There you go," he said. "Down the lane, a left, a right, a right, a left, a right, two more lefts, and you're there." And he went back into the shop.

The square was broader than she expected, and busier, lively with stalls and carts and striped awnings, the glitter of gold and silver on tables, the odors of fruit and fish and spices, the squabble of bargainers and women shouting apples.

Weaving her way through the tables and crowds, dazzled and bewildered, she stopped beside a table set with magnificent glass apparatuses: telescopes, periscopes, beakers, loupes, spiral condensers, burning glasses, spectacles. Behind a towering stack of old books sat the glassblower, his nose in a book, a mole at the tip of his nose. She asked whether he knew the magician.

"Of course! Of course!" he snorted.

"Where can I find him?"

"Why, he's marrying our Queen next month! Only," he said, and winked, "no one knows that it's him, our peripatetic physician, our humble expeller-of-drusen, ablator-of-sties. Word is she's betrothed to a Solomonic magician from far away, the Indies, the Sahara, what have you. But she's had milk eyes from the day she was born, our poor Majesty, and only one fellow could have fixed those. The usual reward, of course, would have been half the kingdom, or ennoblement and emolument. But he's a handsome one, our doctor. And ambitious. Why are you looking for him? Did he steal your heart, too?"

She told him.

"Ha! What a mistake to make. It'll be easy to find him. He's caged in the royal palace; you can't miss it. Finest house in the city, and no one can have finer, for fear of beheading. Tallest house in the city, too, by law. She had all the weathervanes sawn off the churches, and would have chopped down the towers, too, except they persuaded her to build her house a little taller. You can see it from here."

It was indeed the finest house in the city, ringed by green gardens and ponds full of tame swans. Guards bright with old-fashioned weapons marched around its perimeter.

She crumbled a bit of her cake for the swans as she pondered what to do. Then she looked at the wet black legs of the swans.

It was not easy to tear one of her skirts to strips; she had to put her teeth to it. Every four inches she tied a loop, and when she had finished she spread it loosely and broke the rest of the cake over it. As the swans stabbed up the crumbs, she eased the knots shut around their scaly legs. Then she tugged. One of the swans hissed and bit her finger, but the rest, startled, took off in a white cloud. Clinging to their feet for dear life, she rose higher and higher in the air.

Once she was dizzyingly high above the city, she untied the swans one by one, until she held a single blustering cob by the feet. They sank together through the air, landing painfully on the tiles of the palace roof; and then she let him go, as well, and looked about her.

In one corner was a hunchbacked tower, patchy with lichen. To her left and right the castle walls plunged below the eaves. Ilse scrabbled across the slate tiles, kicking one loose—it skittered down the sloping roof and vanished over the edge—and losing a shoe. When she came to the open window she hauled herself up and into a rich bedroom.

A goat-slender man, studying himself in his mirror, whirled around at the noise. She thought she recognized the pointed nose and chin, the glittering eyes.

"Who are you?"

The room was hung with tapestries; the bed was spread with silks and velvets; even the magician's coat glittered thickly with jewels. She was suddenly, painfully aware of the patches on her clothes. But she thought of her sweetheart and mother, and she stood up straight and addressed him.

"Now!" the magician said, after she had finished her story. "I never meant to do that! I cut ice eyes for you because I thought they'd never melt."

"Will you give them their eyes back?"

"Impossible. Others needed them."

"What are you going to do?"

"I am going to marry the Queen in a month," he said. "It's about time I settled down. She's a lovely woman. Proud, though. She won't permit me to work as a petty physician. Must marry a man of leisure, you know. I can't even make you new eyes of rock crystal and glass. Who would restore them?"

"So you are leaving my town blind," Ilse said. "So you have taken away their eyes, their wedding rings, and their livelihoods, and you'll never return them. You are going to marry a Queen and live, as they say, happily ever after. What a marvelous magician you are!"

He hesitated. "That's putting it rather badly. I could teach you, I suppose. If you are intelligent enough. If you are nimble enough. It might take five years, or ten, depending on how quickly you learn." He glanced doubtfully at her clothes. "But afterward you could restore sight wherever you wished."

"Yes," Ilse said.

"But we must first ask the Queen."

They found the Queen reading Schiller with her feet propped on a leather ottoman, now and then weeping a decorous tear. She was not a cruel woman. She listened to Ilse's story and sighed, and afterwards gently reproached her betrothed. But their request displeased her.

"Am I to give you up, my love, for ten years so you can train the girl?"

"Hardly—"

"You may have his instruction," she said to Ilse, "for one year. I will postpone the wedding for that long, because it is unseemly for a King to teach surgery. But after one year we shall marry, and you will go home."

Grateful and dismayed, she kissed the Queen's white hand.

And so for a year she studied under the magician, by sunlight, moonlight, and candlelight, paging through abstruse medical texts and reproducing in wet, squiggling lines on blurry paper the elegant anatomical diagrams her teacher marked with a finger. Often she went without sleep and food in her haste to learn.

The magician taught her the structure and composition of the eye, its fine veining, innervation, and musculature; the operation of light and color; sixteen theories of sight from philosopher-doctors in various kingdoms; and common diseases and their remedies. All of this, he said, he had gathered from years of wandering in strange lands among strange people. And when she was exhausted with studying, he told her stories from his travels.

In the flicker of shadows on the wall, her eyes unfocused from much reading, she thought she could see the people he described: the woman who married a tiger, the parrots who kept state secrets, the ship that flew in the air. She fell asleep in her chair with his words still running in her ears, and he dropped a coat over her before he retired, and so they passed many nights.

By the end of the year she could switch the eyes of rabbits, cats, and sparrows without harming them, without even a drop of blood falling on the magician's knives.

"All that I can teach, you know," he told her one night. "Take my knives, and take this box. I have had time to fashion new eyes for you and yours. Glass and rock crystal, this time."

She fell on her knees and thanked him.

"But there is one more thing. I know no one as quick and capable as you, or as kind. If you will have me, I will marry you instead of the Queen."

"That is kind of you, but I have a sweetheart at home," Ilse said.

"He won't have waited for you."

"He has. I am certain."

"Very well," he said, annoyed. "Go home to him, then." He was not gracious enough to invite her to the wedding, or even to replace her tattered clothes. So with the box under her arm, and the three silver knives hung at her side, Ilse left the palace.

The soldier at the gate barred her path with his spear. He had a hard face and a rough red beard.

"What are you carrying, girl?"

"Eyes that the Queen's magician gave me."

"Gave you? You in those rags? Unlikely. An export fee of three gold crowns." He laughed at her. "Of course you can't pay. But you've a pretty face, and I'll overlook this for a kiss."

She turned to go.

"Or," he said thoughtfully, "I could have you arrested and imprisoned. For theft, probably."

And she saw that he meant it. So she kissed him on his bristly mouth, a sick twist in her stomach, feeling his hands slide up and down her sides, and then he laughed and waved her through.

The road seemed twice as long now. The days grew colder as she went, for it was autumn again, and her clothes were thin, and the road was rising toward the mountains. The crows in the trees croaked and chuckled as she passed.

After many days of weary walking, she saw with great relief the goatherd's village. The sunflowers were brown and rattled in the wind, but the cat still sat on the goatherd's roof, and it stretched and purred at her.

She rapped on the door. The goatherd's daughter opened it slightly. Faint lines were sketched into her forehead. Somewhere in the cottage, a child began to wail.

"What do you want?"

"I left a wool smock and a fur cloak with you. Last year, it was. And there were fourteen pieces of silver in the pocket."

"I don't know what you are talking about."

"You fed me and you gave me these clothes to wear. Don't you recognize them? Keep the clothes, if you like, but please give me my mother's silver."

"We feed paupers all the time. Of course I can't remember each one. But there's no food in the house today. There's no food in all the village." She shut the door.

Ilse had no choice but to continue. The higher she climbed, the colder it was, and she shivered when she lay down to sleep on the lichen-studded stones. But she kept herself warm remembering her sweetheart's smile and her mother waiting for her in darkness.

At last she heard the faint sound of pianos. Tired though she was, she quickened her pace. Soon she saw woodsmoke in the sky, then chimney pots, then houses.

It was as she remembered it. Only now the notes that rang in the cold air were cheerful, and the people walked as though they could see. Ilse went into her own house and found her mother slicing vegetables.

"Ilse?" the woman said uncertainly, lifting her face. Ilse caught it in both hands and kissed it.

"Mother, you'll never guess where I've been."

"Out into the world. But what are you wearing? Go put on something warm."

"Not yet. Hold still." And with practiced gentleness, Ilse set two blue eyes in her mother's face.

She visited her sweetheart's, then. She ran to him and embraced him and he said, "Ilse?"

"Yes, it's me, I'm home."

"Oh, Ilse—I'm happy you've come back." He paused. "This is Elsa—the goldsmith's daughter—I married her in the spring."

"How wonderful." She kissed him on the cheek. "I have something for both of you."

After a fortnight of careful work, all the town could see again. It turned out that they had fared well enough without their eyes. Ilse was well wished, well fed, blessed, and thanked, and made to tell her story again and again, until the smallest child could recite it. It was pleasant being home. She had missed the sound of ice-tuned pianos and the sweet mountain wind.

When Elsa the goldsmith's daughter gave birth, all agreed that the blue-eyed girl would be a matchless beauty and a legend in the kingdom. Her father wrote achingly terrible sonnets to those eyes.

Sometimes Ilse stood at the edge of town and looked over the world that fell away from her, farther than she could see. Sometimes she wondered how the magician and his Queen fared. More often, though, she thought of the strange lands he had told her about, where he had learned his strange arts: jewel-colored jungles, thick with flowers and snakes; or white sands running into a green sea; or dark pine forests alive with deer and wolves and red foxes. She would sit at the mountain's edge until her face was numb with cold, looking, wondering.

One day, no one could find her.

IT'S THE END OF THE WORLD AS WE KNOW IT, AND WE FEEL FINE

HARRY TURTLEDOVE

It's the future. Call it a few hundred years from now. Close enough. Maybe a little more, maybe a little less. Just how much matters less than you think. That's kinda the point, y'know?

What am I talking about? Hang on. You'll see.

Here's Willie. He's lying on the grass in his back yard, playing with his pet fox. The fox's name is Joe. If the fox had a last name, it would be Belyaev. But it doesn't, so don't worry about that. Willie has a last name, one he hardly remembers. You don't need to worry about that, either. Willie sure doesn't.

Willie sits up. He pulls a red, rubbery ball, just the right size, out of a pocket on his shorts. He tosses it into the air. Joe sits there watching, panting, making little excited yappy noises. Willie tosses the ball up again. Joe stares, his dark eyes shining.

Willie throws the ball halfway down the yard. It bounces a couple of times on the grass, then rolls almost to the flower bed at the far end. Joe's after it like a shot. He grabs it in his mouth and shakes his head from side to side as if he's killing it. One of his ears is floppy. It flaps as he shakes the ball.

Then, head high, bushy tail proud, Joe trots back to Willie and drops the ball in front of him. He can't yell *Do it again!*, but every line of his plump little body says it for him. Willie picks up the ball. He doesn't care about fox spit, or much of anything else. I mean, who does, these days?

Away goes the ball. Away goes Joe, fast as he can. Back he comes, ball in mouth. Drop. Wait.

This time, Willie gets cute. He makes the throwing motion, but he hangs on to the ball. Joe's faked out of his shoes, only he isn't wearing any (neither is Willie). The fox bounds across the lawn after . . . nothing. When he gets to about where the ball oughta be, he looks every which way at once, trying to figure out how the hell it went and disappeared on him.

Willie falls out laughing. It's the funniest thing that's happened to him since, well, the last funny thing that happened to him. Which wasn't very long ago, in case you want to know.

When Joe's just about to go, like, totally batshit, Willie calls, "Here it is, silly!" He throws the ball for real. Joe captures it and kills it extra good, as if to pay it back for fooling him. Then he brings it over to Willie. He's ready for more. You bet he is.

They kind of look alike, Willie and Joe. Yeah, and your Aunt Margaret looks like her basset hound, too, after twelve years together. Not like that, though. Like this.

We'll do Joe first. You think fox, you think sharp-nosed chicken thief and bunny cruncher. Joe isn't like that. Sure, his umpty-ump great-grandparents were, but so what? Your Aunt Margaret's basset hound's umpty-ump great-grandparents pulled down moose in the snowy forests right after the glaciers melted. Between them and him, there've been some changes made. And there've been some changes made from those chicken swipers to Joe.

He's plump. I already said that. Partly it's on account of Willie feeds him too much, but only partly. Plump is cute, and cute is what his breeders were after. His floppy ear is also cute. So is a tail that perks up when he sees people. He *likes* people. Since the days of his umpty-umps, liking people's been bred into him.

His fur is longer and thicker and fluffier than your wild woodsrunning fox's (yes, there still are wild woodsrunners, though not right around here). He has white patches all over, almost like a calico cat. His muzzle is maybe half as long as umpty-ump grandpa's, and quite a bit thicker. His teeth are scaled down, too. They don't have to work as hard as teeth did in the old days.

He's *cute*. I already said that before, too. I know. But he is. I mean, he's *really* cute.

And so is Willie. If you want to get mean about it, Willie looks kind of elfy-welfy. Being mean is *such* an old-time thing, though. He's got big eyes, a snub nose, and features that look as if you left 'em out in the sun a skosh—only a skosh, mind you—too long. Purely by coincidence, he has red hair, close to the color of Joe's. Not even slightly by coincidence, he has a couple of white streaks running through that red hair. Oh, yeah—he's on the plump side, too.

Cute. For sure. USDA prime cute, if you want to know the truth. Not that there's a USDA any more, but you get my drift.

Willie keeps throwing the ball. Joe keeps fetching it. Finally he just wears out, poor little guy. He brings the ball back one last time, drops it out of his mouth, and flops down on the grass, totally beat. He pants and pants, tongue hanging way, way out.

Willie pets him. Joe's tail thumps up and down. He rolls on his back and sticks all four legs in the air. Willie rubs his tummy. Joe wiggles like Jell-O. He doesn't just dig it. He digs it bigtime.

So does Willie. Willie digs everything he does bigtime. If you don't, why do it to begin with?

Here. Wait. I'll show you. Willie waves his hand. Out of nowhere, music starts to play. No, don't ask me how. It's the future. They can do stuff like that stuff here. Take a look at Willie. Is he digging it, or what?

Remember how once, just once, you scored the best dope in the world? Remember how you smoked till your mouth and your throat were all sandpaper and your lungs thought you'd gone down on a fireplace? Remember how you put on your headphones—took three tries, didn't it?—and cranked *Dark Side of the Moon* or "The Ride of the Valkyries" or whatever most got you off all the way up to *eleven*, man? Remember what it was like?

Of course you don't remember. You were wasted, you fool. But you sorta remember how awesome it was, right?

Okay. Willie's like that all the time, only more so. And everybody else in the future is like that, too. And those people don't need to pay big bucks to keep Mexican druglords in supermodels and swimming pools and RPGs, either. They don't need the dope. They're just like that. All the time. Naturally.

How? We're getting there. Trust me.

Belyaev! I just met a fox named Belyaev!

Old Belyaev had a farm, ee-eye-ee-eye-oh!

As a matter of fact, Dmitri Belyaev did. A fox farm. Outside of Novosibirsk, of all places. Even in the future that holds Willie and Joe, Novosibirsk is nowhere squared. Nowhere cubed, even. In the middle of what they called the twentieth century, Novosibirsk was nowhere cubed *and* behind the Iron Curtain.

Belyaev didn't care. Or if he did care, he couldn't do anything about it, which amounts to the same thing. He was trying to find out how people way back when turned wolves into dogs and the aurochs into Elsie the Borden cow and . . . well, and like that.

So he used foxes.

Foxes are—duh!—wild. Or they were when Belyaev started messing with them, anyhow. They don't like people. They're scared of people. A lot of evolution over a lot of years has made sure of that.

But some foxes don't like people less than others. Some foxes are less scared of people than others. Belyaev took the least unfriendly foxes he could find and bred them to one another. Then he did the same thing with the next generation. And the one after that. And the one after that, and the one . . .

Foxes have litters every year. It's a long-term experiment, yeah, but it's not like domesticating sequoias.

Or even people. We'll get there, too. We really will.

You can do stuff like that. Belyaev did it for science. Way back when, Ugh and Mrong and Gronk had no idea they were doing it. They'd never heard of science. They did it anyway. And it worked. If it didn't work, no Pluto. No Foghorn Leghorn. No Elsie, either, or Milky White if you're into musicals, or even Mr. Farnsworth, come to that.

It worked for Belyaev, too. It worked faster than he ever figured it would. By the fourth generation, he had foxes that wagged their tails when people came up. They whimpered for attention. They let people hold them. Hey, they *wanted* people to hold them.

They started looking different, too. Some of them had floppy ears. Some had white patches in their fur. Their tails curled up instead of hanging low. Every so often, some were born with shorter bones or fewer bones in their tails. They got shorter, blunter muzzles. They were turning, yes, cute.

How come? Well, changes in behavior, like, go with changes in biology. Hormones run growth and growth patterns. Hormones run aggression, too. Belyaev's tame foxes had lower stress-hormone levels in their blood. They had more serotonin—the big calmer—in their foxy brains. They were *mellow*, man.

Hormones run growth. And what runs hormones? Right the first time—genes.

Stay tuned. We'll be back.

Willie's taking Joe for a walk. Other people are out and about, too, walking their dogs and foxes and potbellied porkers and what have you. No, nobody's out walking her cat. This is the future, sure. I know. It's not Never-Never Land, though.

Joe says hi to other foxes about how you'd expect. He sniffs 'em here and there to see how they smell interesting and where they smell interesting. He's been fixed, so he doesn't try to hump the foxy female foxes he meets, but he gives 'em an olfactory once-over, all right. He doesn't remember why they smell so good, but he knows they do.

Dogs are a different story. Joe doesn't want much to do with dogs. Once upon a time, dogs were wolves. Something way down deep inside Joe remembers that, too. So does something deep inside the dogs. A lot of them, even ones no bigger than Joe is, think they're supposed to have him for a snack.

It doesn't happen. Willie doesn't let it happen. Neither do the other people. They joke about it, and smile, and laugh, and pat one another on the back or on the arm or on the head. They all kinda look like Willie's cousins. They're short-featured. They're smooth-featured. They're plumpish—not fat, but for sure plumpish. They have streaks and patches of white in their hair.

Dogs and foxes are nothing for them to get their bowels in an uproar about. It's the future. People don't sweat the small stuff. People don't hardly sweat the big stuff, either. What's the point? Ain't no point.

Well, ain't no point unless maybe you're Fritz. Fritz lives down the street from Willie. He's kind of funny-looking. People talk about it all the time, only not where he can hear them. His nose is a little too long and a little too sharp. His chin sticks out a little too much. He looks more like you and me than he's got any business doing, is what I'm saying.

He acts more like you and me than he's got any business doing, too. He's loud. He's brash. He's quarrelsome—he gets into fights, and this at a time and in a place where nobody, and I mean nobody, gets into fights. He has not one but two big, mean dogs. He only keeps them on the leash when he absolutely has to. Otherwise, he lets them run around loose and scare all the other pets in the neighborhood.

They scare the bejesus out of Joe. They would have done worse than that to him one time if he hadn't run like blazes back to his own house. They chased him as far as they could, baying and growling and making like the wolves their umpty-greats were way back when.

They're on the leash now, though. Fritz got into trouble not too long ago. He's walking soft right now. He's trying not to give the mostly automated Powers That Be any more excuse to come down on him. He may be funny-looking, Fritz, but he isn't dumb. He isn't bad, either, not really. He's just . . . different.

He's different the same way his dogs are different, only more so. It's no wonder he has dogs like that, is it? Like draws like, sure as hell.

But he's on his best behavior right now. Joe kinda sits behind Willie's heel, just in case, but Fritz doesn't let his dogs—their names are Otto and Ilse—make any mischief. He smiles at Willie. Even his smile seems odd. His teeth are too big and too sharp, and it looks as though he's got too many of them even if he doesn't.

"How's it goin', Willie?" he rumbles. His voice sounds deeper than it ought to, too.

"It's okay," Willie answers. When is it not okay? Well, it's not so real okay when he has to talk with Fritz, but he can see telling Fritz as much isn't the smartest thing he could do.

"Good. That's good." Fritz on his best behavior is almost harder to take than Fritz being Fritz. You can see the real him peeking out from behind the mask he puts on. He tries to act like everybody else, and the trying shows, and so does the acting.

But Willie is a friendly soul. Not many people these days aren't friendly souls. People like people. People are supposed to like people, and most of them can hardly help liking people most of the time. People are like that. They can't help being like that. So, in spite of seeing the mask, Willie goes, "What's up with you, Fritz?"

"Well, I'll tell you, man," Fritz says. "I've got this chance to bring in some serious cash, only I need me a little front money to help get things off the ground, know what I mean? How are you fixed these days?"

"I'm fine," Willie says, which is true enough. In this day and age, you really have to work at it not to be fine. Some people manage, of course. They may not work quite the same as they did way back when, but nobody's come up with a cure for human stupidity yet.

Take a look at Fritz, for instance. Although with Fritz, like I said before, it isn't exactly stupidity. Fritz just . . . doesn't quite belong where he's at. If he were selling you aluminum siding or something, chances are you'd like him fine. Which is a measure of your damnation, is what it is. And, considering that Fritz is where he's at, it's a measure of his damnation, too.

If he were selling you aluminum siding, you can bet it'd fade and blister in the hot sun. He'd promise you it was top grade, and he'd be long gone, promising other people other things, by the time you found out he was full of shit. The warranty he gave you wouldn't be worth the paper it was printed on, either. Surprise!

So he's sizing Willie up now. He's trying to look like he's being all friendly and everything, but he's sizing him up, all right. So much for best behavior. Sometimes you just can't help yourself, not if you're Fritz. "Listen, man," he says, "with your money and my know-how, we could do all right together, y'know?"

"Maybe," Willie says. He eyes Fritz the same way Joe eyes Otto and Ilse. Joe might like to be friends with them. Only he wonders whether he'll get eaten if he tries. Willie kinda wonders that about Fritz, too. But only kinda. Joe may worry about dogs, but he's fine with people. And so is Willie. People are fine with one another. Most people are, anyhow.

Hey, Fritz is fine with Willie—as long as Willie does what Fritz wants. "Why don't you come back to my place?" he says. "We can talk about it some more there." *I can talk you around there* are the words behind the words.

Willie doesn't hear the words behind the words. Willie is a trusting soul, like darn near everybody else in the future. He's not stupid, either, not exactly. But he's different from people in the old days. So is everybody else in the future. He smiles and goes, "Okey-doke."

Yeah, everybody in the future is different from the way people were back in the old days. Only some are less different than others. Fritz, for instance. He isn't nearly different enough. If he were, his answering smile couldn't have so much barracuda in it. "Come on, then," he says.

"Willie, *no*," a Voice says out of the air. Willie can stop Joe from misbehaving when he talks a certain way. The Voice stops him just like that. Then it goes on, "Fritz, you are sanctioned. Again. Go home. Now. By yourself, except for your dogs."

Fritz's heavy-featured face falls. "Aw, I didn't mean anything by it," he says. "Swear I didn't." He shouldn't be able to protest even that much, but he does.

"Bullshit." The Voice may be automated, but that doesn't mean it came to town on a turnip truck. "The sanction will go up because it's bullshit, too. Go home, I told you. With your dogs. Without Willie. Get moving right this minute, or I'll see what else I can tack on."

Fritz goes. All the other choices are worse. If looks could kill, Willie'd be lying there dead on the sidewalk. So would Joe. And so, especially, would the Voice. It isn't what you'd call corporeal, but Fritz doesn't care.

"I don't think he meant anything bad by it," Willie tells the Voice.

It doesn't sigh. It doesn't sound pleased, either. It's not designed that way. It just says, "I know you don't, Willie. That's why I'm here. Nothing's gonna harm you, not while I'm around. And I am."

Not quite *I am that I am*. Close enough for government work. Oh, wait. This is the future. No government, or not hardly, anyway. Willie and Joe go on with their walk. They're happy. Hey, what else are they gonna be?

Genes. It's all in the genes. Once upon a time, a comic with deciduous top cover complained, "They say going bald is in your genes. I *got* hair in my jeans. It's hair on my head I want!"

Usually, what they say is a crock of crap. Not this time. The difference between the hair apparent and the hair presumptive *is* in our genes.

So are lots of other things.

Dmitri Belyaev bred for tame foxes. A long, long time ago, Ugh bred for tame wolves, even though he might not have realized that was what he was doing. Belyaev—and Ugh—got other things, too. They got short tails and floppy ears and white patches of fur and short muzzles and the like. They got them . . . ? Let's hear it, people!

That's right! In the genes.

One of the places they particularly got them was in a DNA sequence near a gene labeled *WBSCR17*. This stretch of DNA shows a lot of differences between wolves and dogs, where most parts of the genome don't.

People have this *WBSCR17* gene, too. Back in the day, when something with it went wrong, the people it went wrong in were born with a genetic disease called Williams-Beuren syndrome. They looked kind of, well, elfy-welfy. The bridge of their nose was abridged, if you know what I mean. And they were the friendliest, most gregarious, most trusting people you ever saw in all your born days. They really, really got into music, too.

In a world where everybody wasn't just like that, they were friendly and gregarious and trusting to a fault. People with Williams-Beuren also had other troubles. Most of them were retarded, some a bit, some more than a bit. They were extra prone to heart disease.

But suppose changes in the human *WBSCR17* gene are a feature, not a bug. You don't need to suppose, of course, on account of that's where we're at. It's where we've been at since the old days turned into what we've got now, however long ago that was. I said it before and I'll say it again—since we are the way we are now, things like how long ago aren't really such a big deal.

After the last Big Fracas, everybody who was left could see that one more fracas and nobody would be left any more. Everybody could see that, if people stayed the way old-time people were, one more fracas was coming, too, sure as God made little green traffic lights.

Human nature doesn't change? Tell it to Belyaev's ghost. Tell it to his foxes, the most popular pets in the not-quite-new world. Change the genome and you change the fox—or the human. Change the human, and you change human nature.

Change *WBSCR17* the way they could after the last Big Fracas, make sure the change goes through the whole surviving population (not too hard, because it wasn't what you'd call big), and what you get is . . .

You get the upside of Williams-Beuren without the downside. No retardation. No heart disease. You get friendly, trusting, considerate, kindly people. All day, every day. They think as well as old-style humans, but not just like 'em. John Campbell would love them and hate them at the same time.

You get Willie, who's every bit as domesticated as Joe, and who likes it every bit as much. John Campbell's been dead one hell of a long time. That's kind of the point, too.

Fritz? Hey, things aren't perfect even in this best (or at least most peaceable) of all possible worlds. Mighty good, but not perfect. Dogs have been domesticated for upwards of fifteen thousand years. Once in a while, they still come out wolfish. Their genes get a funny roll of the dice, and we call 'em throwbacks. We call 'em trouble, too. If we can help it, they don't get to go swimming in the next gen's gene pool.

And neither will Fritz. The Voice and the other automated safety systems that watch out for things new-model people don't commonly worry about will make sure of that. Nothing cruel, mind you. Fritz can have as much fun as anybody else. But he's the end of his line. If you think that's sad, if his drives remind you of your own, you know what? That's also kind of the point.

• • •

Willie and Joe keep walking in the sun. Joe isn't sorry to see the last of Fritz's big old dogs, no sir. Willie is sorry Fritz got sanctioned. He can't imagine that happening to him. Hardly anybody these days can imagine stuff like that. Hardly anybody, but not quite nobody. That's how come the Voice is still around.

Here comes Keiko a little while on, heading his way. Keiko is just the cutest thing Willie's ever seen. Even if you don't look elfy-welfy yourself, you'd think Keiko was hot. Trust me. You would. If you do look like that . . . Willie smiles most of the time any which way. But he *smiles* now. Oh, yeah. So would you, pal.

Keiko's got a little fox on a leash, too. Daisy Mae is as cute a fox as Keiko is a girl. Joe's not supposed to appreciate Daisy Mae the way Willie appreciates Keiko. And he doesn't, not really. But he sorta-kinda whimpers, way down deep in his throat, as if he almost remembers he's forgotten something.

"Hey!" Willie says, and gives Keiko a hug. She squeezes him back. It feels *so* good. Let's hear it for gregariousness. Yeah!

"What's up with Fritz?" Keiko asks. People have ways of hearing about shit. It's the future. They don't even need smartphones to do it.

Willie was there. It was happening to him. But he doesn't know a whole lot more about it than Keiko does. What he does know, he doesn't hardly understand. If he did . . . Hell, if he did, he'd be Fritz. Bunches of people would be Fritz. And then we'd end up in the soup all over again.

So Willie shrugs a little. "I guess he was kinda on, you know, the selfish side of things." He looks down at his toes when the bad word comes out. I don't care if it's the future or not. There'll always be bad words. Being bad is one of the things words are for.

Keiko gasps a little. She knows about Fritz. If you live around there, you have to know about Fritz. That doesn't mean you enjoy thinking about him. Except for gossip's sake, of course. If gossip's not the flip side of gregariousness, what is it?

"Too bad," she says at last. "Oh, *too* bad!"

"Yeah, it is." Willie nods. "But what can you do?" He knows what he wants to do. You bet he does. "Feel like comin' back to my place? We can let the critters run around in the back yard while we fuck." That's not a bad word any more. It hasn't been for a long, long time.

"Sure!" Keiko says. They walk back hand in hand. Some of human nature's changed, uh-huh. Some, but not all. If *that* had changed, there wouldn't be any humans left to have natures any more. There almost weren't. But it's taken care of. It sure is. Look at Willie and Keiko if you don't believe me. Look at their frolicking foxes.

Poor Fritz.

KILLING CURSES: A CAUGHT-HEART QUEST

KRISTA HOEPPNER LEAHY

⸺◆⸺

A curse-killer shouldn't dream, but I do. I dream of a life where there is no drought, no mottling, and I never meet a Quixote. In that life, when I go home to Loblolly, I hold my own child, my dear wife beside me. In that life, I am not the last curse-killer left in the watersheds.

But all I know is this life, lit by its own blanched moonlight, and this life started the night my Momma died.

Momma always said death was the worst of the curses we couldn't kill, and the night she drowned I found that out.

One minute she was there—waist high in the night waters of Loblolly's dipping pool—the next she wasn't. All that long night, I dredged and re-dredged Loblolly's crescent-shaped dipping pool, searched the milky waters, sifted the pulverized pine cone sand, ripped out handful after handful of black wattle, bootlace, and spider grass, but found nothing. Not a finger-nail. Not a strand of silver hair. Not a curse-killing tooth.

I might have drowned myself, chasing her through the watersheds in my grief, but all night the dipping pool stayed closed to me—the milky water's *louche* opaque, the water itself violent in its stillness—no current tugging at my toes, as if Loblolly had been quarantined without warning, and with my momma's death the tide too had died.

Halfway through the night, fresh pain lanced my skin as my momma's metal teeth began to grow in on my lips—my too sudden inheritance. Interlocking pinwheeled sieves of iron and aluminum spiraled into the bones of my jaw—harsh welcome to the clenched, deadly business of being Loblolly's curse-killer.

At dawn, as the waters were switching from milk to ink, finally the tide returned to life, lapping my toes where I sat on the pinecone beach, beneath the towering loblollys which gave our watershed its name. Before I could dive in to travel the waterways, see if I could find where my momma'd died, the tide swept in a Quixote.

An armored knight of steely water, carrying a cirrus lance, with mad blue islands for eyes, he rode in on a horse of milky smoke, scented of coconuts and figs. He seemed to be followed by an oasis of palm trees.

"That was that, my child, but this is this."

"This is this?"

"So true. One fine, lost day, when I'd lost my faith to right wrongs, I sought counsel with your mother. Bless her and her beautiful teeth—she talked me out of killing my Quixote song. Rare for a curse-killer, plus she had those pretty teeth. So as a boon to her, I offered to right the wrong of her death. But she declined, noble soul, said I should fulfill my own quest. But to you, her only-born, I make the same offer, shall I undertake the quest to right the wrong of your death?"

Talking with a madman, in the wake of my mother's new absence, I had no idea how to respond.

"Don't you mean righting the wrong of *her* death?"

"No, no, no. She's dead. Gone. Too late. Death's one of the curses you can't kill, didn't she teach you that?"

I nodded, the metal of my new mouth stinging.

"But your death hasn't happened yet. If I undertake the quest in the present, I will return triumphant in the future, having righted a wrong not yet committed in the past."

I found myself nodding. Somehow he made a kind of sense. "And you can actually do this? Right the wrong of my death?"

"Well, truthfully, my fine young toothy friend, I don't know. Who am I to say whether or not this quest would be privileged to come in the near, far, or caught-heart party?"

"Caught-heart?"

"Caught-heart, always present, never here, the outlandish and unsatisfying, while always promising satisfaction never-failed-or-fulfilled-quest. Many wronged deaths I have sought to right remain caught-heart quests." His watery steed stamped, hooves roiling the water into steely, bloody fountains.

While he made no sense, something about this caught-heart quest eased my grief. If I couldn't right the wrong of my momma's death—that much at least I thought was true—if I had to live without her, going on a quest with this strange Quixote didn't sound half-bad.

"When do we leave?"

He threw his arms in the air, speckling his smoky white steed with water droplets. "No, no, no. You must remain here! I will undertake the quest alone, for how can I seek your death, to right its wrong, if you are not here, living your life? A gracious offer, my fine young toothy friend, but you must seek your life, while I seek your death. Understand?" He aimed his cloudy lance at my chest.

It had all been too much. A sob rose up, choking me. For a moment I could neither cry nor breathe, my mouth filling with fresh blood from my too-new teeth.

"Don't cry on my armor!" A fine mist spumed from his watery lips, and his smoky steed reared. "I will return when I have sought and fought your death! Troubadours will sing of my quest!" The sun rose over the loblollys, dispelling the smoke and shadows of the Quixote, and the coconut and fig scented promise of his oasis.

In that cold, lonely dawn, having just survived a visitation of a true Quixote or my own shock and grief—I didn't know and didn't know who could I ask— at last, when I finally realized I was all by myself, I wept.

So I lived my life, lonely as it was, best as I could.

In the years after my momma's death, the drought worsened, and on at least one other occasion the volatile, contracting waterways claimed lives. In the wake of those deaths I looked for the Quixote, but he never appeared again. Instead I found drought and desiccation, and slowly pieced together what must have happened to my momma.

Veldblau's waterfall—their entry point to the waterways, akin to our dipping pool—had been first and hardest hit by drought. When she'd opened a whirl to Veldblau that night, the parched waterfall had called her and her curse-killing mouth with such sudden force, the whole waterways system had seized. Gone into a kind of watershed wide quarantine, cutting off Veldblau to save the larger system.

Goodbye Veldblau. Goodbye momma. Hello loneliness.

Veldblau was gone, but there were other watersheds to tend, and as the only remaining curse-killer, plenty of curses to be killed—jealousy gone wrong, bad luck, a vex, a hex, klutziness, Casanova smile, Midas touch, colic cry—the list went on. I did not shirk my duty, nor the waterways and our dipping pool—where the ordinary folk saw in its beauty and danger reason to fear, I saw reason to live. Perhaps not much reason can be found in the promise of a mad Quixote, but reason enough to keep on living. A lonely reason, but loneliness was all I had, until, when I was eighteen, Midas came to live in Loblolly.

I'd just killed a combination curse on Tun Grier's vines.

I'd worried it was mottling—a beastly curse to kill, often necessitating quarantine, and dangerous precursor to drought. But luckily it was nothing more than a nasty combination of bad luck and a hex. By that time my metal mouth had grown thick with knowledge of those particular curses, and the simplest pinwheel form of my curse-killing sieve had sufficed.

Grier was Loblolly's Dionysus, and he'd rewarded me with a case of strawberry wine, two bottles of which I'd consumed as I sat by the dipping pool, in the shade of my momma's favorite loblolly pine. Sweet thick strawberry wine ran down my lips, and its stickiness seemed a welcome, happy thickness against my mouth's metal crunch.

Sitting under my momma's favorite loblolly pine, I was counting curses—how many I'd killed and how many I could not—when Midas walked out of the dipping pool. At first I thought the wine must have razzled my head, and I was seeing another Quixote walking out of the inky waves—but no, this man was not smoke and water, but flesh. A man who could have been my older brother, no less, with his lanky limbs, amber-freckled skin, and mop-top of silver hair. Course he lacked a metal mouth.

"Hello, stranger! What is this bee-yoo-tiful place?" he called, with a foolish grin that reminded me of the boy I'd once called myself.

I scrambled to my unsteady feet. "This here's Loblolly."

"Almost as bee-yoo-tiful as the Oasis."

"Kind of you to say. You from Tatouage then?"

The Oasis and its wild paradise could travel anywhere in the watersheds, but was most often found in the southern tip of Tatouage.

"That I am."

"Welcome. I'm the local curse-killer."

"Course you are, that mouth is more than wine-stained, any fool can see that. Quite an honor to meet you." He reached out his hand. "Call me Midas."

I flinched, fell back against the loblolly trunk. "If it's all the same to you, I'd rather not be turned to gold, Midas. I like my life."

Oh how he laughed. He picked up a pinecone, did something reminiscent of a pirouette, and tossed me the pinecone—which, in spite of myself, I caught. Its brown petaled scales were touched with golden hues, like any loblolly cone, but no hint of gold metal to be found.

"Don't worry. How'd I recognize that metal trap of a mouth if I hadn't been freed of my curse before now?"

"You . . . who killed your curse?"

"Oh, I don't know her name." He squinted up at the sun. "But she sure had some mighty crooked teeth."

"Where was this? Here?" The questions flew out.

"Naw, over in Tatouage. But she was from here all right."

"How do you know?"

"Loblolly's the only watershed had a curse-killer for at least a generation. I liked her, in spite of those crooked teeth. Liked her enough, I almost let her talk me out of having my curse killed." He scratched his chin, looked down at the open bottle.

I'd forgotten my manners. "Please, sit down." I plopped down in the needles, leaving the trunk open for Midas. "You care for some strawberry wine?"

"What a bee-yoo-ti-ful idea. Here, oasis fruit." With a face-shattering grin, he untied his knapsack, spilled out coconuts, apricots, plums, citrus-seeds, figs. He took a long pull from the bottle, settled in against the tree.

"What brings you to Loblolly?" I tossed a grapefruit citrus-seed in my mouth, the tart zest welcome after the wine.

"Drought's closed a lot of tributaries down, fewer folk coming to see the Oasis, or visit Tatouage. Thought I'd take a look for myself in the open waterways. Figure I'm old enough to want a wife, best go and find her—might die waiting if I wait for her to find me!" He laughed. "A toast. To finding wives!" He tipped the bottle back, drank deep, passed the wine to me.

I hesitated.

"Come on, curse-killer, no need to frown, you wouldn't be sitting all alone drinking this wine by yourself if you'd found a wife already, and sharing wine will share our luck."

"To finding wives." I sipped, passed the bottle back. I licked the sticky sweet off my lips, forcing myself to patience. "What did you mean, about Loblolly's curse-killer talking you out of killing your curse?"

He took another long pull, then sighed. "Before the killing, she told me I'd miss my curse. Said I'd miss the touch of gold, its kiss, every day of my life once I grew old enough to really know what missing meant. I didn't listen. All I knew was I didn't want to be a Midas anymore. My mother died in labor, and I'd never known my father. My aunt did all she could to raise me right, but she wasn't a Midas. I longed for human touch. So very, very much."

He popped two figs into his mouth.

"My aunt knew something about that, for she missed holding me, I know. Being held through golden silks and thin cottons is better than nothing, but it's not skin-to-skin. So I said I was sure, and the curse-killer with the crooked teeth killed my Midas curse." He tipped the wine back, and the red juice burbled in the bottle, gurgling out with a soft sigh.

"When she was done, the curse-killer had tears in her eyes. Said when I missed the gold, I should look for it elsewhere. Then she said if I ever changed my mind, to come find her, she'd give me a resurrection. I've never forgotten her advice, or the tears in her eyes."

I'd had too much wine, or not enough, for one of my teeth ached sharp and bright, filling my mouth with *gold, burnished beyond, sunlight, fire, hue of a fresh cut peach, dark stars you see when you close your eyes at night* . . . I swallowed, bit down. The taste disappeared, but I knew what it meant, surprising as it was. "She was my momma. Your curse-killer."

"Figured as much."

My turn to tip the bottle back. A resurrection made for a trickier curse-killing, and I wondered why my momma'd bothered. Something in his story didn't make sense. "But, you call yourself Midas now."

"Well. Your momma was right. Once I was old enough to understand what missing meant, I changed my name back. Helps to find gold. Look. Ta-da!" He tossed me another golden-hued pinecone. He smiled, a wide-open foolish grin, and even though his eyes smiled wide with his grin, they also shone bright and wet. "Took me a while to figure out 'resurrection' was just a fancy way of helping me remember who I'd been."

"Midas." I squinted in the strawberry-tinged sunlight. "The resurrection's more than a way to remember who you were—it's dangerous, but I wear my momma's mouth, and I think I could resurrect your curse for you, if you wanted."

For a moment his eyes pooled wide, but then he smiled, "Naw. I have my heart set on finding a wife. Holding my own baby. Living skin-to-skin. Maybe years from now, if I can't find a wife, I'll take you up on your offer. What's your name anyway?"

"My friends call me Petech."

"Petech. If we're going to be friends, seek wives and the like, I have to ask you a question."

"Okay."

"Don't you ever smile?"

And even though I was a curse-killer, even though I still wore my momma's metal mouth, and wanted to make her proud, in the warmth of newfound friendship, tasting of strawberry wine, on that sunny afternoon, I confess I smiled.

Oh then how I lived. Thank the curses for those years of laughter and friendship and looking for wives—half the fun the looking, and half the fun the friendship, and loneliness only something to remember, not something to bear. The drought receded, and while we heard of a case of mottling here and there, those were joyous years of peace and water.

Year after year, I killed curses and he sought a woman's kiss sweeter than the kiss of gold. We celebrated our successes and mourned our failures with feasts of oasis fruit and Tun Grier's strawberry wine—until the year Grier died, and his vines died with him.

We sent him to his peace in the waterways, as befit any watershed-born, and though I lingered to see if a Quixote would come to pay his respects, none did.

But I was glad I'd lingered, for late in the night a wonder of a walking-tree came to pay her respects to our Dionysus.

We met, and once met, never parted. My beloved Purla.

That was that, I thought, remembering the Quixote's words, *but this is this.* As I fell heart-first into her verdant eyes, I felt like I might be embarking on a caught-heart quest of my own.

And thank the curses, she and Midas got along bee-yoo-ti-fully. Everything was simple and sweet as fresh syrup, until the night honey gathered over Purla's branches as our baby girl Melisande struggled to be born. Oh how the curse of love plays roulette.

Hours passed in a riot of foliage and fruit—pine, magnolia, honeycombed maple, cottonwood, cherryfern, golden aspen, sour plum, coconut palm, giant redwood—just a few of the varieties that emerged from my beloved Purla's limbs through the long hours of labor. As I held her trunk tight through every contraction, every new orchard burst, my skin was transformed too by sap and loam, wood and leaf, bud and bloom. Except for my metal mouth, which resisted the leafing upheaval, my skin reeled with every forest seeded since the world began. Never have I loved my wife so much.

A final long groan of wood splitting, and then out of Purla's birthknot, into my hands, slipped a sappy, beautiful mess of a perfectly formed baby girl. Except for the sap, the miniature twigs of her fingers, tightly curled leaves instead of wisps of hair, she looked ordinary enough. Ten toes, two legs, two arms, two eyes, two ears—perhaps a slight lignin feel to her almond-shaded skin. All in all, a better curse than I'd feared. But she was awfully quiet. Too quiet.

I pinched her, hard, to make sure she was breathing.

"Petech!" My wife slapped my hand away with a maple branch as Melisande began to wail.

"I had to be sure, Purla. Sure she was alive and real. She's supposed to cry."

"Well, now she's crying." Purla rocked Melisande in her lower willow boughs, comforting her with a cherry blossom bud. Melisande suckled greedily at the bud and its sweet sap.

"Now she's not." I reached to take the cherry blossom bud away.

Purla uprooted herself, moved away from me. "Enough crying. She's my daughter too."

"Mother's son, father's daughter. You may be a walking tree, but she's bound to me, to be a curse-killer. A curse-killer must know the curse in order to learn how to kill it."

"She's a baby. She doesn't need to know how to kill anything." Thick sap was running from her birthknot, and I worried at her being uprooted from the ground's sustenance this shortly after giving birth.

"Purla, please. To make another curse-killer is the whole reason we wed."

"The *whole* reason? Petech?"

"That's not what I meant."

"What did you mean?" The bark on her sapling boughs roughened.

"Purla, you know how I feel about you. Never felt like a curse, falling in love with you. But you know as well as I do the need for a new curse-killer presses against all the watersheds, not just ours."

"What I know is that our child is bound to me as well as you, and that life will make her cry soon enough. To make her cry is cruel. What she needs now is love."

What could I say? I only had the truth to offer her. The only truth I knew then. "The sooner she cries, the sooner she'll learn to kill the pain herself. To not prepare her for what she has to face, in the name of *love*, now that would be *cruel*."

Purla's exposed roots trembled, and a cascade of maple, oak, and aspen leaves fell from her eyes. Something of her mother's distress must have scared Melisande, for she cried again, a full-lunged colic cry. The sound killed me and made me proud, all at the same time. I reached for them both, to comfort and hold them, as I'd held them all through the long hours of labor. But Purla wheeled away, sending a spray of wet earth into my everyday eyes and metal mouth. The shock stopped me before the pain. Choking on mud, blinded by grit, I stumbled after my crying child and wife.

By the time I cleared my eyes, and could breathe again, they were gone. I uprooted every ordinary tree in the orchard that day and night, searched all Loblolly watershed. Everyone I asked shook their heads no—in fear or denial or plain ordinary ignorance, I couldn't tell—when I asked them if they'd seen my wife or child. The only one who might have known was Midas, but that night, he was nowhere to be found.

Three months later, Midas went nowhere again. He and I were supposed to have one of our oasis feasts by the dipping pool—we'd promised each other we'd eat and drink until we didn't care about our missing wives. I didn't know which of us to feel sorrier for—me, having so recently lost a wife, or him, never having found one.

But when the sun rose high above the inky waves and he still hadn't shown, I worried. He'd been bothering me for several months about trying a resurrection—or "killing-curse-reverse" as he liked to say—but I'd been putting him off, out of fear and my own concerns. Perhaps he'd been more desperate than I realized. When the sun began to sink, I went to search for my friend. He'd been headed for Tatouage and the Oasis, so that's where I started.

Tatouage's entry point to the waterways was an open-air aqueduct, running through a canopy of tattooed redwoods. No sign of drought, thank the curses. But at the top of the disembarkment redwood, the scent of burnt anise dizzied me, and I nearly slipped. Mottling, here? I inhaled through my mouth, gripped the carved handholds, and let my fear focus how I put one foot below the other.

The anise reek increased as I descended, troubling my breathing, but finally I reached the ground, only to find an unconscious Midas passed out beneath the laddered redwood, surrounded by spilled oasis fruit.

Across his neck splayed the characteristic green-grey web of wormwood mottling. I knelt by him, pushing aside the hard coconuts and citrus-seeds, turned him on his back, grateful to hear him groan and find his face mottle-free. Not too late, I could still save him. But what of Tatouage? Fear iced my metal mouth, as I examined the grove.

Mottling laced several of the tattooed redwoods. Were the mottling to reach the tops of the trees, the aqueduct would be vulnerable, and through the aqueduct, all of the watersheds. As soon as I saved Midas, Tatouage would have to be quarantined.

I spiraled the metal sleeve of my mouth open, teeth interlocking and extending into the pinwheel form of my individual curse-killing sieve. Placing Midas' thumbs in the sharp corners of the metal pinwheel, I put my knee on his chest, gripped his arms to have better control, and then bit down.

Far off I heard Midas scream, but I was caught in the killing, sinking into its bloody immediacy as the mottling filled my mouth—*anise languor, strangling, trade your death for eternal green, growing dreams*—an old tooth ached with *gold, burnished beyond sunlight, fire, hue of a fresh cut peach . . .* and for a moment I was distracted, remembering my momma's mouth had killed curses for Midas before—but then the mottling gushed again and my killing sieve snapped shut, sifting the curse from Midas' blood. One heartbeat, two.

His bleeding, but intact, thumbs dropped from my mouth, as the sharp pinwheels of my sieve sped up, spinning faster and faster as I killed the curse. My momma's metal mouth whipped though *anise, almond, grey webs, mushroom longing, smoke, parasitic clawing, regret*—even an odd trace of honey. Finally, the killing puree frothed, the world whirled, and I fell backwards.

"Petech, are you okay?" Midas knelt now, while I was the one prone.

I swallowed—nothing left but my own tasteless spit. The purification killing was complete. "Small puree, but potent."

I sat, picked up one of the nearby citrus-seeds. "What a costly feast. I'm sorry, my friend, but I must quarantine Tatouage, close off its waterway."

"But—" he bowed his head, his silver bangs hiding his expression.

"But what?"

"I promised not to tell, but Purla and Melisande are rooted in the Oasis."

Some decisions only take a breath to make.

"Burn the grove, Midas." It might not save Tatouage, but it would keep the waterways safe until I returned. "I'll be back as soon as I can. Can you find fire?"

"Fire's just another word for gold." Some spirit of his usual joy flared up in the words, made me think everything was going to be all right. He smiled his bee-yoo-ti-ful grin. "My name's not Midas for nothing."

I ran towards the Oasis.

As if nothing had ever been wrong anywhere, anytime, ever, the Oasis shimmered its garden of tiered pleasures—fresh blue water, neck-high wheat and millet fields, lush fig, plum, and apricot trees, all perpetually shaded by towering palms. No visible sign of mottling, thankfully. And while the palm trees and fields of grain swayed their dance of green and gold, they didn't shimmer with milky smoke. I hoped it would stay that way—easier to find my wife and child if the Oasis didn't move.

I plunged into the fields, following the river—if they were here, they'd be rooted near water.

Thwack, scratch. The boughs of cherryfern and fig scratched my face and limbs, snagging my tunic, closing me out. The risk of quarantine was fresh in my mind, so, after asking politely, and being denied, I extended a few metal teeth and bit the sapling bough of what I hoped was an ordinary cherryfern. Its creaking cry brought tears to my eyes. The orchard of trees thickened, circled me, boughs menacing. The Oasis still smelled of paradise—sweet apricot, fig, coconut, and through it all the clean burble of fresh water—but smoke rose from the trees in front of me. If ever I was to find my wife and child, the time was now.

I fell to my knees. "Purla! Please! Don't leave! Please, I only want to talk!"

The smoke subsided, falling to a low mist on the ground.

The Oasis orchard parted, and through it walked my once wife.

She walked as a willow, aspen barked, with cherryfern boughs trailing behind her in a thick red and green train—her oh so human mouth and eyes peering out. Such evergreen eyes, amidst the wooden beauty of sap and sun, break a man's heart.

"What do you want?"

"Tatouage is going to be quarantined. Come with me back to Loblolly where I know you'll be safe."

"Why quarantined?"

"Wormwood mottling, in the redwood grove that hosts the aqueduct. I can't risk all the watersheds, even if it means losing Tatouage."

"Thank you for your concern, but we'll stay in the Oasis."

"But if Tatouage is quarantined, you'll be trapped."

"The Oasis is never trapped, have you forgotten? We walk wherever we choose." As if to remind me of this, smoke curled around her lower boughs. "Besides, the Oasis is our home now. More so than any of the watersheds. Leave us alone."

With great dignity, she turned and walked away, as if having dismissed some rude stranger, not her once-husband. The shame of it drove me to my feet, and I grabbed a handful of her cherryfern train. Through the lifting canopy of her retreating train, peeked a pair of bright eyes, blinking beneath a crown of silverlaced leaves.

"Melisande?" I reached out.

"No! Don't—" Purla whirled, but too late—Melisande had already crept free from her mother's train, and was exploring my pale, freckled arms with the stiff twigs of her darker, barked limbs.

Reunited with Melisande, joy rose in my throat, and I thought I might blossom into a walking tree myself. But something was very wrong. Melisande was too small, far too small. And quiet—too quiet—grey webbing covered her mouth. "Purla, what's happened to her mouth?"

"Mother's son, father's daughter. She's growing a curse-killer's mouth."

"No, Purla." Ice curled around my heart as I felt the rigid strictures of what I feared were not my daughter's bark. My heartbeat slowed, as if by force of will I could reverse time. "A curse-killer's mouth is red not grey, and comes only after rites. This is something else."

"What?"

I chipped off one of the outer husks of my metal teeth—a harmless red triangle glinting in the sun—and gave it to Melisande. She was as entranced as I'd been when my mother'd done the same for me. I covered the whorls of Melisande's ears so she wouldn't hear what I was about to say. "Mottle. Melisande's caught the mottling. Purla, we . . . "

I couldn't finish the thought. Of everything I expected to have to deal with—not being able to find Purla, her refusing to talk to me, even both of them being dead—I wasn't prepared for this.

I cradled Melisande in my arms, savoring the smell of pine and almonds from her silverlaced leaves. No sign of mottling on Purla, or in the Oasis Orchard, but everywhere on my little girl, from the muzzle of her mouth to the twiggy tips of her toes, a mottling web so dense, I'd at first mistaken it as the bark of her skin.

"How long?" Too long, I knew already, but I had to ask.

"It's only been visible the last two weeks, but I think it started before. She's never made a sound since we left Loblolly. Could it have started as long ago as that?"

"I don't know." But I was afraid. Holding my only precious child, cradling her as if she were still that slippery, perfect newborn, I knelt. I was scared to try, and yet I knew I must. I extended my killing sieve.

"Petech, don't—"

"Purla, by all the curses, I promise I won't hurt her. But I have to assess the mottling." I placed the tip of the smallest twig of her arm in my mouth, and very, very gently, bit down. Nothing, no taste, no mottling siren cry, just tacky resistance and then, a snap.

My heart shattered into its own mottled web with the sound of that snap. Melisande was the mottling and the mottling was Melisande—there was no separate curse to kill.

"Petech!" Purla swept her lower boughs towards me, trying to knock me back, but I pivoted away.

"Purla, I won't hurt her! Now let me think." With every ounce of my heart and mind, I thought.

Was the mottling due to her not learning to kill her own pain, like the curse-killer she was supposed to be? Or was it an inevitable outgrowth of my and Purla's match? Or of our fighting at her birth? More to the moment, could I kill her curse without killing her? How quickly her little twigs crumbled. Could I risk trying? Could I risk not?

All the questions circled around, as if the tempest in my mind could somehow change the choice: How could I choose between killing my own child and letting her kill the watersheds?

Damn the curses. Damn them all. My eyes stung and I told myself it was the damn smoke from the Oasis. Damn smoke. Damn milky smoke. Where had I seen smoke like this before?

Maybe there was a way to beat this horrible spin, and these stupid, damnable facts. I took a deep breath. "Purla, is there a Quixote in the Oasis?"

Her aspen leaves shimmered, milky smoke curled up around her trunk. "What are you talking about, Petech? Quixotes are extinct. There hasn't been one seen for generations."

"Then he and I must both be lost on a caught-heart quest." Harsh laughter scraped my throat as I heard my momma's voice telling me to count my curses and wipe that foolish grin off my face. My laughter flared into a forest fire threatening to burn me down where I knelt, holding my wooden daughter, trapped in her own mottling curse.

"Stop laughing, Petech. Do you smell something burning?"

Not my laughter. The redwood grove. Midas. The echo of an idea trying to surface deep within my mind.

Some choices only take a breath to make.

"Come Purla, we haven't much time."

We ran, Purla's leaves streaming behind us, maple, aspen, oak—a trail of foliage reminding me of the day Melisande was born. Melisande's bright green gaze never left my face—the only sign of life in her mottling-strangled face.

The redwood grove was ablaze.

"Hurry!" Midas was halfway up the laddered redwood. I pushed Purla up a nearby tattooed giant; her exposed roots wrapped themselves tightly around the trunk. She climbed to safety above the flames, but I knew she wouldn't leave without Melisande.

I had only one idea, strange and perhaps impossible, but my momma's mouth itched and I hoped it knew something I didn't know.

"Midas, I need you to come down."

Thank the curses, he didn't question me, but hurried down.

"There isn't much time. Take her." I thrust Melisande into his arms before he could object. Curses forgive me, I knew I shouldn't ask, but with the fire blazing all around, my wife crying, my daughter's life at stake—I didn't know what else to do.

"You still want that resurrection?"

"Killing-curse-reverse. About time. But don't you think you'd better hurry?" He grinned his unmistakable grin, waved his arms at the approaching fire.

"This may hurt. Close your eyes, and give me your free hand."

He closed his eyes.

I extended my killing sieve. I placed his thumb in one corner, one of Melisande's small boughs in the other. I bit down. With both in my mouth, his recently mottled blood, her nearly bloodless wooden flesh, I twisted open the old tooth that ached of Midas touch—a trickle filled my mouth—*gold burnished beyond sunlight fire hue of a fresh cut peach dark stars you see when you close your eyes at night*—and as my mouth filled, I counted the curses we can't kill, the ones I've survived—*birth, breath, touch, sight, sound, smell, taste, love, thought, death*—and with every breath I willed them to my daughter, so that she might have the chance to survive them too, win the long shot of being alive.

What a froth.

I never expected dying to take so long. But after the blended resurrection, the shared transfusion, the dual killing-curse-reverse, what will you, I lingered on in the blaze, my own limbs shining golden and I wondered if somehow I too had become a Midas, until the fire crackled, and dark smoke rose before my eyes. So thoroughly had I learned to kill pain that, moments from death, burning alive, all I felt was numbness.

"Quest complete!" An old impossible voice cried, as milky smoke curled down from the aqueduct. A steely cataract gushed down the redwoods, followed by drifting clouds of coconut and figs, as my Quixote and his watery steed splashed down, his cirrus lance sweeping across the blazing grove, dousing the flames.

He'd come—if he'd come at all—too late for me. My jaws still worked and words still formed, but I didn't know how. "Purla said you were extinct."

"Extant indeed. As you see, at your service, caught-heart quest complete. Triumphantly I return; the wrong of your death righted, my debt discharged, and now, with your permission, I'll be off to travel the waters, right wrongs not yet wrung."

Talking to a wet madman, who kept dripping on my skull, was actually rather peaceful. "May I join you in your quest now that I'm dead?"

"No, no, no. Not dead. Right the wrong of your death, that's what we agreed. If we right the righting, we'll feel wrong. Besides, other quests await." He galloped off on the roiling river of his steed, his oasis following.

I would miss him. He always made so little sense.

His watery departure quenched the last of the fires that had sprung up around the redwood grove. Seemed impossible that he could be the master of that much water. Where had all that water come from?

Another echo rang through my too-slow mind.

Damnable drought.

Clear as curses, my momma'd died from that drought.

If I weren't dead, I'd have to hunt him down.

I looked down at what had to be my corpse. The fire had incinerated my tunic, no surprise, but how odd to see my amber-freckled limbs free of burns. My mouth itched. I shouldn't be alive, but it seemed I was. Clear as curses, no matter what else, I owed the Quixote my life. Course, even so, once I'd recovered, I'd hunt him down.

Around me, smoke sputtered and steam rose from an ashy landscape, burnt and black but for a duo shining in the twilight. Midas and Melisande both, shining golden bright—bright as fire embraced, survived—honeyed into a bearable curse.

The resurrection had worked. Midas shone in his former glory as he cradled my daughter Melisande—her mottling transformed into a beautiful, but harmless, gold filigree, a shade darker than the rest of her golden skin. My gorgeous daughter. Alive. But what a cost. At least Midas would get to hold her skin-to-skin.

"Petech?" The welcome surprise of my wife's voice brought new tears to my eyes. I had not yet dared to think if the Quixote had been in time to save her as well.

Purla was gingerly making her way down the charred disembarkment redwood, her branches singed, only a few leaves and fruit having survived the fire, but thank the curses, alive.

"Purla! I thought the fire had you, for sure!" Midas stepped clear of the redwood's trunk, making space for Purla to enter the grove. Two perfect footprints of golden grass showed where he had weathered the fire, and warned how perfectly his curse had returned.

"The aqueduct broke. Saved us all, thank the waters," said Purla, reaching for Melisande.

"No, Purla!" I forced myself to my feet, staggered towards them. "Don't touch her! She's a Midas now."

"What?"

"He's right, Purla. You should keep clear for now. Not for long though, right, Petech? You can kill her Midas curse, just like your momma killed mine." He danced a quick soft-shoe, turning a patch of ash gold. "Happy for my resurrection, but this little one has another fate, I'm sure."

"No, Midas." I spoke slowly, for all our sakes. "Melisande will have to remain a Midas, or else the mottling will be released again—its strangling curse, killing everything she touches, until it finally kills her. This was the only way I could save her and the watersheds."

"I never caught the mottling." Purla's bare branches snapped close to my face.

"Yes, but you're her mother, and so immune. The rest of the watersheds are not so lucky," I said.

"Well, fine then. I'll become a Midas too." She reached out.

"No, Purla!" I staggered between them.

"If you touch her, you won't become a Midas." Midas was the one who spoke, a trail of gold ash marking his retreat to the edge of the burnt grove. "You'll turn to gold."

"Fine then, I'll be a golden walking tree."

"You'd walk no longer."

"But . . . I don't understand."

I picked a golden blade of grass from Midas' footprints, and snapped it in two. "Gold is dead."

"Why its kiss is so exquisite," said Midas.

"I'm so sorry, Purla. Sorrier than I'll ever be able to tell you. But not much is immune from the Midas touch besides the waterways and its water. It was the only way, Purla." I meant it as an apology, but even to my ears it sounded like a defense. "We can . . . we can hold her through silks, right, Midas?"

"That's right, or cotton, burlap, leaves—really anything, once she turns stuff gold, it's safe for you to touch. Soon as we get home, we'll get her swaddled close, then you can hold her. The gold protects you from each other."

"Protects us from . . . *each other*?" Chunks of Purla's bark buckled.

"It'll be okay, Purla. Watch." I picked another blade of glass, ran the gold along one of Melisande's golden feet.

Melisande laughed.

A strong, joyous laugh that made me—well, I wouldn't call it happy, but I couldn't call it sad.

"You wanna try, Purla?" I offered her the golden blade of grass.

"No, I—I . . . " Purla's evergreen eyes clouded, shriveled leaves falling from her eyes. "You should never have come to Tatouage. You should have left us alone!" She whirled, her limbs and roots trembling, burnt bits of bark and fruit cascading as she fled the grove.

Melisande whimpered.

I started after Purla, but Melisande's whimper turned into a howl, stopping me.

"Petech. Petech, what should I do?" Midas held my bawling daughter on his shoulder, patting her back, trying to calm her down.

Damn how love played roulette. I loved them all—my golden friend, my newly minted daughter, my fled wife, but mixed up in all that love was so much loss. How to go on?

"Petech?" Midas asked.

Melisande screeched louder.

"Try putting your pinky in her mouth."

He reached around her, nuzzling his pinky into her little golden lips, but Melisande was having none of it. I thought her awful howls would surely call Purla back, but as Melisande howled and the sun slipped out of sight, no one joined us in the grove.

I knelt on the ground, picked up the remains of a burnt fruit fallen from Purla's boughs, and bit through the blackened skin. A plum or peach, I couldn't tell, but some juice left. Didn't know if its taste or comfort would survive the Midas touch, but we had to try something.

"Give her this." I tossed Midas the fruit.

The fruit turned golden the instant it hit his palm, and I thought, *well, that was that.* But he squeezed the fruit above her wailing, open mouth, and golden juice oozed out from its now golden flesh and, thank the curses, Melisande quieted.

Her soft suckling filled the grove, and after a moment, Midas spoke. "Never thought I'd be lucky enough to feel gold's kiss skin-to-skin. Your daughter, she's, she's . . . "

An old tooth itched *salt copper fury misspent . . . pricking regret*—jealousy gone wrong. Not surprising, really, seeing my dear friend hold Melisande, knowing I would never again be able to touch my daughter skin to skin.

But at least she was alive, I reminded myself. And so long as I didn't succumb to the first curse I'd learned to kill, Melisande would have her own chance to count the curses, sneak the peach, win the long shot of being alive.

This is this.

My curse-killing sieve whirled, *grievance dried sweat blood ill will . . .* and three times I pureed that curse, making sure I sifted out every little bitter drop of jealousy gone wrong, before I spoke. Oh it hurt worse than any curse I'd ever learned to kill, but I was strong enough, thank the curses. "I think you mean she's bee-yoo-ti-ful."

Midas almost smiled. "But motherless."

"Not for long. Once Purla realizes Melisande doesn't have to be a curse-killer, she'll think some good came out of this whole thing, and come back." I had to hope.

"What now, Petech?"

Unsure what to say, I whirled and unwhirled the metal sleeve of my curse-killing mouth. Hints of coconut and fig lingered amidst the smoke. I needed to hunt the Quixote down—cut short his quest and its consequences.

But first, there was my daughter to think about.

"We go home. Do the best we can." I smiled at him and Melisande and, thank the curses, none of my teeth ached.

My hands caked with wet ash as I climbed the scorched ladder to Tatouage's aqueduct. Beneath the sooty bark, fresh sap ran, but not a whiff of anise—the mottling had been routed. The grove would come back. Above, the golden light of the rising moon and soft gurgle of the waterways beckoned me home to Loblolly.

One day I'll tell Melisande about what happened tonight—who sacrificed what for her golden life, how the watersheds were threatened, and how many curses her grandmomma and I killed. Or maybe I won't.

Maybe instead, I'll spin her a story of being watershed born, and how in every life, no matter where we wander, the moon drenches us in peach-hued beauty—fresh cut and familiar—lighting our way home.

FIREBRAND

PETER WATTS

It had taken a while, but the voters were finally getting used to the idea of spontaneous human combustion.

It wasn't, after all, as if it were really anything *new*. Anecdotal reports of people bursting into flame dated back to the Middle Ages at least. And if it seemed to be happening a bit more often in recent years, it was doubtless because—as the pundits pointed out—the new administration's policy of scrupulous and transparent record-keeping was simply more efficient at detecting those events when they occurred.

Here for example was Ryan Fletcher, igniting in front of his whole family while watching an after-dinner episode of *Death Row Death Match* on his recliner. According to eyewitness reports he had lit up the single Benson-and-Hedges Gold he permitted himself each day, brought it to his lips, and breathed a sudden surprising jet of fire into the room—"just like a dragon!", as eight-year-old Sheldon Fletcher had put it to the police not twenty minutes later. He must have belched. There was no explicit mention of that in the report, but it was the only way that oxygen could have backwashed into Fletcher's GI tract where an estimated two-and-a-half liters of dodecane was sloshing around with the usual mix of bile, methane, and prefecal lumps.

The resulting explosion had occurred in two stages. The first had blown open the stomach and exposed the anaerobic environs of the intestine to oxygen, catalyzing a secondary detonation that left cauterized bits of Ryan Fletcher stuck to the mirror at the end of the hall, five meters away.

Fletcher had had no professional connection with the biofuel industry. He had, however—according to the GPS log recovered from his Subaru—passed downwind of a GreenHex facility two weeks earlier, during the time when a gasket had failed on one of their bioreactors. Fortunately, no one would ever make that connection.

Instead, Dora Skilette decided, people would then blame the Poles.

• • •

According to media reports, the Polish alcohol-industrial complex had experienced an unexpected renaissance of late. It was impossible to regulate. The EU had tried, with their ever-widening definitions of "toxic waste." Exorbitant licensing fees made it all but impossible to purchase the product even in the restaurants and hotels of Poland itself—and yet it persisted, wound inextricably through the very DNA of the culture. Meaderies plied a hundred types of hooch on rickety tables in town squares; unmarked crates crossed national boundaries in search of more-forgiving environmental standards; homemade stills bubbled and dripped in every basement. Alcohol even played a prominent role in Polish justice; a traditional form of capital punishment back in Medieval times had involved forcing wine down the condemned's throat through a tube until his guts exploded. (Some whispered that the practice persisted even now, in the remote woodlands of Lubelskie.)

Over the past couple of years the *win* and the *wódka kawa* had been making inroads into North America, and its devastating effects were showing up in the most graphic PSAs the Bureau could muster. It hooked those you'd least expect, real family-values types who'd never touch a chemical that didn't come from a pharmacy or a tobacconist. Then one day you'd find their feet, still clad in socks and shoes like a couple of smoldering galoshes on the living room carpet. Maybe a bit of carbonized tibia poking through those cauterized stumps. After the funeral you'd go downstairs to pack up their tools for Goodwill and there you'd find it, back behind the water heater where no one would ever think to look: the box with the bottles inside, still half full of that mysterious pink liquid, viscous as machine oil. The labels with the funny accents over the Cs and the strange little slashes through the Ls and all those words ending in *ski*. And you would curse the vile Poles and their vile killer moonshine, and you would rage at the injustice of bad things happening to good people, and words like *plasmid* and *lateral transfer* would never even cross your mind.

Dora had a screensaver that marched around her desk during the lulls between case files, a quote from a Prussian King back in the seventeen hundreds: "Fortunate are those who have never tasted Polish wine." That quote had inspired her to win Energy & Infrastructure's very first James Hoar Award for Analytical Innovation, two years earlier. *Fortunate indeed*, she reflected, and filled out the Fletchers' home address for the folks in the van with the nondescript Florist's logo on the side.

The next file was straightforward—Mei-Li Badura, a hiker who'd exploded in an outhouse up at Garibaldi. Toilet-related incidents, unsurprisingly, outnumbered all other sponcoms combined; they even had their own acronym on the SR1 (*defdet*—although despite repeated memos from the Deputy Minister, *Great Bowls of Fire* continued to serve as an informal synonym even though it didn't fit into the character field). Too many people stocked their bathrooms with scented candles these days, though Dora suspected that brute-force natural selection might reduce that imbalance over time.

Evidently Badura had lit a match.

Dora implicated a leaky can of starter fluid in the hiker's backback (not even that far from the truth, she reflected) and moved on to Greta and Roger Young of Steveston, whose charred bodies had been found side-by-side in their own bed. Neither had smoked.

Dora drummed her fingers on the desktop; smart paint flickered uncertain staccatos at her fingertips. After a moment she ran a search on next-of-kin: Five children. Twice as many grand.

HEL yes, Dora thought.

She'd always had a fondness for the Human Extinction League. They actually existed, for one thing—or they *had* at least, even if in reality they'd been strictly nonviolent and their *real* motto had been lame. *HEL-Yes* was far punchier, and made a much better match with the crude spray-painted stick-figure families—hand-in-hand, with Xs for eyes—that had begun appearing down the alleyways of urban centers. Not that those granola-eaters would show her much gratitude even if they knew, but it was thanks to Dora's (admittedly unsolicited) makeover that they'd ever even made it onto the public radar. It was how she'd scored her second Hoar.

Greta and Roger Young, devout Catholics with a whole flock of sprogs, would have been perfect targets for those Human-extinction radicals. She plugged in the numbers.

The desk beeped irritably back at her: Rejected - Quota Exception. She cursed and called up details. Gayle Vincent had already invoked the League this month.

She had to admit it made sense. You couldn't go back to the same well too often: people would stop talking about sponcoms and start talking about why the gummint wasn't doing something about all the murderous enviroradicals. Still, Dora felt a certain possessiveness about the HEL. She V2T'd Gayle's line: "Thanks for hogging the League again. Get your own terrorists, why don't you?"

Sorry Dory, Gayle came back. Buy you coffee, call it even?

"Maybe. *If* you throw in a muffin."

An amber star ignited in the upper-left corner of Dora's visual field; she'd programmed her specs for news alerts relating to the biofuel industry. She back-burnered this one for the moment; it would still be there when she'd figured out what to do about the Youngs. So would the little green star that popped up a moment later: a news item that tied specifically to GreenHex. Same story, probably.

The purple star (Dept of Energy & Infrastructure) appeared perhaps thirty seconds after that, along with a sudden awareness of ambient *change*: the usual background burble suddenly extinguished, some dense moist mass oozing invisibly into the building, and settling down, and making Dora's ears pop.

She leaned back from her cubby and looked down the row: everyone was frozen to googlespecs and desktops. No one was saying a word.

V2T from Gayle, crawling across her personal eyespace: HOLY FUCK ARE YOU GETTING THIS?

A crimson nova, laser-bright. The Minister of E&I himself. Crown jewel of a bright little constellation grown suddenly ominous in Dora's zodiac.

She tuned in.

MACRONET BREAKING NEWS,

the pixels screamed, and

The Doomsday Smoothie?

but the image between those headlines showed nothing but a little green helix twisted into a loop: a donut of DNA that Dora recognized instantly.

"—plug-and-play toolkits that gengineers use to confer special powers," the voiceover continued, already in progress. "Unlike normal genes, plasmids are not simply passed from generation to generation; these portable instruction-sets jump between species in a process called *lateral transfer*, letting different kinds of bacteria— or even bacteria and higher life-forms, such as yeast or algae—acquire traits from one another. Custom plasmids turn ordinary microorganisms into little factories that churn out vast quantities of food, drugs—or, in the case of the Biofuel Industry, gasoline."

The view zoomed back: one animated plasmid dwindled and disappeared into a swarm of many, dissolved in turn into the vague chlorophyllous soup within a mass of filamentous corkscrews.

"GreenHex inserts their patented *Firebrand* plasmid into an algae closely related to these *Spirulina*, the main ingredient of the popular Shamrock Smoothie—"

Distinct filaments receded into a goop of green slime; green slime congealed with new-found minty freshness, topped with chocolate sprinkles—

"—recently rebranded to great success after decades languishing as a niche product in health-food stores."

—contained in a paper cup gripped in a hand attached to an arm against a background of beige tiles and suddenly, magically, Macronet's animation had segued into archival securicam footage looking down into a coffee shop somewhere in the real world. The dissolve had been seamless; Dora would have whistled in appreciation if not for sudden heavy knot of dread slowly tearing a hole in her diaphragm.

She knew where this was going. On some level, she realized, she'd been expecting it for years.

"And while we may never know exactly what happened on the afternoon of the 25th in this Burnaby Starbucks, we do know one thing."

A sweet old lady in a lemon dumbweave blouse turned from the counter and tottered endearingly towards an empty table, her frail hand clutching a venti paper cup.

"We know that Stacey Herlihey was very fond of her Shamrock Smoothies."

MacroNet's image-recognition filters ensured that the sight of Stacey Herlihey's explosive and unexpected immolation was sufficiently blurred to avoid any violation of community standards.

The screams came through just fine, though.

There was more, of course. Prof. Piotr Dembowski of the University of Maryland, talking about how difficult it had been to crack the GRM. Someone else from Simon Fraser, reporting that something *like* Firebrand ("it's always hard to tell when dealing with encrypted genes") was showing up in some microbe—*Bacteroides thetasomethingorother*—that lived exclusively in the human gut ("Small mercies, actually. If it was viable in, say, *E. coli*, everything from puppies to pigeons would be pooping fire and brimstone by now, heh heh.") The obligatory *hastily-called press conference* at which a GreenHex spokesman insisted that the allegations were absurd ("It was designed for the warm, wet, methane-rich conditions of our anaerobic reactors, *not* the human digestive system"), and that even if Firebrand *had* gotten out it couldn't possibly have persisted in the wild for anywhere near the year-and-a-half since Greenhex had phased out their lagoon operations and gone 100% closed-loop. Which was briefly reassuring, until some biomedical statistician from the University of fucking Buzzkill went on record about the myth of the perfect failsafe, and how any industry that scaled up fast enough to replace fossil fuels in less than two decades would probably be dealing with a couple dozen accidents a day even if it *hadn't* built its entire operation on a product that self-replicated.

Ms. Disembodied Voiceover returned long enough to announce that GreenHex intended to pursue legal action against both Prof. Dembowski and the University of Maryland for copyright infringement. Dora's great-great-grandboss, the Deputy Minister of Energy and Infrastructure herself, assured the people of this great nation that any stories of government collusion with the biofuel industry in "covering up hundreds of deaths a year" were completely absurd, in fact almost treasonous, as an internal investigation would doubtless prove once and for all.

But by that time Dora Skilette was already calling up her resumé, and the voices still nattering in her head spoke from the far end of a deep, dark well.

The breathalyzer at Second Cup was gimped. She tried three times and got nothing but a click and a buzz; the door remained stubbornly locked. It wasn't until a maraschino-haired woman in a chromatherm jacket rapped and pointed from the other side of the glass that Dora noticed the out-of-service notice, taped just below a buzzboard hawking Pfizer antiplasmidics.

Please use other entrance.

The redhead rapped again, spread her hands in a theatrical shrug: *Well?*

"Gayle?" Dora said uncertainly, and then "Gayle!"

Well, duh, Gayle mimed, although it *had* been a year.

"So, wow," Dora said, clutching a regular Mocha Minx after the obligatory *been-too-long* hug. "You've certainly changed."

Gayle touched her hair as she sat back down— "This is nothing"—with a look that said *You certainly haven't.*

Dora set down her drink, spilling a little on some gap-toothed shark swimming towards whatever camera the table was tuned to (*Sydney C-bed*, according to the logo). "So where are you now?" Obviously not government.

"You wouldn't believe me." Gayle nodded toward the main entrance, past which a fortysomething in googlespecs was trying to get the breathalyzer to work. "Oh, look. Door got another one."

Dora rolled her eyes. "I swear I don't know why we have to use those fucking things."

"It's the law, for starters." Gayle's blazer rippled with pastel heatprints as she nibbled her Danish. Dora found it vaguely distracting.

"They never even work half the time."

"They went from CAD to retail in under a year. We're lucky *any* of 'em work."

Dora mopped the shark's face with her napkin. "Even when they do, when was the last time you saw them actually catch anyone? It's like spending millions of dollars on shark patrols. In Utah."

"Fireside Theater. People want to feel safe."

"People *are* safe." Except for the occasional exploding grandma, of course. Now that Dora thought of it, Stacey Herlihey had gone up in a place very much like this.

"Think of the boost all those useless gizmos give the economy, though." Gayle grabbed Dora's soiled napkin, wadded it up and tossed it in a perfect arc at the receptacle by the wall: *Score.* "Not to mention the boom in fire extinguishers. My brother got a job with Amarex right after the news broke, and he just bought his second house. More than makes up for a few unemployed purveyors of backyard BBQs, hmmm?"

And even those markets were coming back, Dora had read. It turned out people were surprisingly willing to move on, just so long as it was someone else's grandma who bought it. And it always was. Statistically, anyway.

"I gotta say I'm surprised at how it turned out," she admitted.

"What, that people would choose a couple thousand sponcoms over millions of deaths from cancer and heat stroke and killer smog? That they'd rather deal with a few charred corpses than annual oil slicks stretching all the way to the horizon?"

"That's not how it works and you know it. You could've posted *hours* of video showing people dying quietly of black lung. Everyone would've totally forgotten about it the moment they saw thirty seconds of Grandma Stacey bursting into flames." She sipped her Minx and shook her head, disgusted at the memory. "Those were the worst fucking optics in history."

Gayle shrugged. "You wanna talk about bad optics, try traffic accidents. You don't just go up in flames in a car wreck; you could get torn limb-from-limb in the bargain, or splatted on the pavement like a rotten pumpkin. And *those* images are everywhere too, if you take about five seconds to look—" her hands hovered threateningly over the table, poised to surf.

Dora waved her off. "Take your word for it. Thanks."

Gayle withdrew. On the table between them a school of fishy blue silhouettes, too distant for detail, milled where the shark had been. "My point," Gayle continued, "is: pictures gruesome enough to make granny flambé look like Kittens On Parade and a death rate *five times* higher than the worst-case sponcom scenario. Optics *and* hard numbers. Yet people haven't stopped driving. Driving more than ever, in fact."

"Well, of course. They're paying thirty cents a liter instead of a buck-seventy . . ."

"Bingo." Gayle raised a knowing eyebrow. "*Plus ca change.*"

Dora stared into her Minx. "Things *do* change," she said softly.

"Breathalyzers that don't work. Brand new plasmid pills, even if Johnson & Johnson *does* have to threaten lawsuits against anyone who so much as whispers about drug-resistance. Oh, and let's not forget the TSA; now they've got one more reason to ram their fists up your ass during check-in, because now *everyone* can be a suicide bomber." Gayle extended a finger, drew a line across a sprinkle of spilled sugar. "Some things change. Others, not so much." She gave Dora an appraising look. "What about you, Dory?"

Dora blinked. "Me?"

"What are you up to these days?"

"Oh." Dora shrugged. "Not much. Temping as a fire inspector out in Langley." One of the few gigs for which a history with E&I was actually an advantage. It was amazing how much practical knowledge you picked up over two years of inventing alibis for suspicious house fires. "You?"

Gayle stood. "Let's walk. I got a craving."

• • •

Gayle pulled out a pack of Rothmans when they hit the street, but didn't light up; she just eyed the little box in her hand and said "This could be a felony before long, you know that? Someone introduced a private member's bill."

"I didn't even know you smoked," Dora said.

"Didn't used to. Mom died of cancer."

"So what changed?"

Gayle made a sound: half grunt, half laugh. "Me."

"You and a lot of others." Smoking, paradoxically, had only risen in popularity since the news had broken. It was a kind of safe-sign among strangers: anyone who could light up without *lighting up* was someone you could at least risk standing next to at the bus stop.

They walked. A public buzzboard across the street flickered with images of some battered desert city smouldering beneath a black and oily sky. "Look at those guys," Gayle remarked. "*They've* been setting themselves on fire for a thousand years and more."

Dora squinted. The crawl said *Tehran* but these days it could've been anywhere east of the Med.

"Nice change, though, isn't it?" Gayle asked.

"What?"

"That we finally don't have to give a shit."

Dora stopped and turned to face the other woman. "When did you get so cynical?"

Gayle half-smiled. "When did you *stop*? I mean, was it my imagination, or did you and I spend a couple of years writing cover stories about spontaneous human combustion?"

"I guess we did. Seems a long time ago." Dora shrugged, granting the point. "You never did tell me what *you* were up to these days."

"Working for GreenHex." And then, at the sight of Dora's raised eyebrows, "I *said* you wouldn't believe me."

"There is no GreenHex. Not any more."

"Names change. GreenHex goes on. There was GreenHex before it was GreenHex, there is GreenHex after."

"What's that, some kind of corporate benediction?"

"You know how these things work."

"It mutated."

Gayle chuckled. "Pretty much has to, doesn't it? Genetic engineering's what we *do*."

"So what do you do there?"

"Engineering, kid. Just like everyone else."

"When did *you* get a degree in genetics?"

"Not genetic. Although genes *are* just—words, I guess. Information. And engineers are just editors. And the one thing both of us crawled out of E&I with was first-class editing skills. They even gave you an award for it, as I recall."

Two, actually. "Not the same thing. Those guys are rewriting *life*."

"You're making my point. People care more about packaging than contents. It's all just information, but you get— *emotional*—about the kind that happens to be wrapped up in genes. So any business built on optimizing one kind of info is naturally going to value folks who know how to optimize the other. Some of our most life-changing products would never get to market otherwise." She finally seemed to notice the cigarette pack in her hand, extracted one. "They're hiring, you know."

"Really," Dora said.

"I could put in a word."

"Thanks, I—thanks. That means a lot to me."

"Don't mention it."

"I don't know, though. GreenHex by any other name, and all. And if you'll remember, our last *editing* gig didn't turn out so well for either of us."

"Things change, Dory. Gotta change with them. That's what life does." She raised cupped hands against the breeze, lit up, dragged. Wisps of gray smoke trailed back out of her mouth as Dora stared in disbelief.

"It adapts."

She left her card behind. And the memory of that cigarette, flaring to life by the light of the clear blue flame that danced from the tip of her tongue.

THE MEMORY BOOK

MAUREEN McHUGH

Laura Anne presented herself at the door of her new employer on Monday morning, while London was still awash in mist. From the bottom of the steps, her younger brother Peter, who had escorted her, waited until the maid opened the door and said, "Oh. I shall fetch Mrs. Finch." He lifted one hand in a kind of half-wave—he was really a tiresome boy—and then skipped off.

Mrs. Finch was a short, buxom woman, with her hair pulled severely back. Her Monday morning washing dress, Laura Anne noted, was plain and damp in places. And unflattering. Not because the cut was so obviously from a few years before, since that was to be expected, but because even when new it would likely not to have been flattering. Mama was not nearly so favored by nature in her figure as Mrs. Finch and yet she was ever so much smarter. Laura Anne knew that even in her mourning (black Bombazine from Black Peter Robinson's on Regent Street and cut in the latest Continental manner which served admirably to accentuate her tiny waist) she far outshone dowdy Mrs. Finch. Mrs. Finch flicked her eye up and down Laura Anne and apparently knew so as well.

The dining room, where Laura Anne had been engaged to be the Finches' governess was as she remembered it. Mrs. Finch sat at a cunning little desk and Laura Anne stood demurely. "You are very young, and without a character," Mrs. Finch said. Laura Anne did not feel this was quite fair. She had a character, that is, a character reference, from her pastor, but of course she could not have one from a former employer because she had never been employed, and would not now if it were not for the death of her dear Papa. "But given your circumstance, we felt it a Christian service to give you this opportunity," Mrs. Finch continued.

Mrs. Finch had the children called for introductions. The nurse brought them down, dressed in their best. Henry, five, looked sleepy. Elizabeth, seven, hid her face in the nurse's skirts and would not look at Laura Anne. The nurse, a tall, awkward woman with a hatchet of a chin and narrow eyes, had obviously been crying. Now that the children were old enough for a governess, she would be leaving. "Nurse will show you the arrangements," Mrs. Finch said.

From down the stairs, Laura Anne caught the whiff of boiling laundry. At least as governess she would be spared the ordeal of laundry day.

The second floor had three bedrooms. The nurse, the children, and Laura Anne trooped past the bedrooms on the floor and then climbed the narrow stairs to the third floor. At the top of the house were the nursery and the nurse's room, the latter stripped bare now, only a lone carpet valise sitting in the middle of the floor. The nursery was whitewashed, and had a high fireguard in front of the fire, bars on the windows, and a table in the center, covered in a bright red and white oil cloth so it could be washed down. On one wall was an eye of God, watching them all. They no sooner got to the nursery then the nurse dropped to her knees and hugged both children. The little girl, Elizabeth, immediately began to cry, a high, keening, "eh-ehh-ehh," that put Laura Anne's teeth on edge. William was set off by his sister and sobbed, too. Elizabeth was going to need correction, Laura Anne thought.

Laura Anne didn't quite know what to do with herself, faced with this extraordinary performance. The nurse sobbed out something about how the children liked their tea, and some other generalities about their preferences. By the by, she kissed them both, called them her ducklings, her angels, her own dear loves. Then she stood up and said, "This is your new governess, Miss Huntley. Be lambs and be good for her and remember your prayers." She went to her room and got her valise.

Elizabeth let out a high screech and ran after her, throwing herself against the woman's skirts in a most theatrical manner. William, of course, copied. There was more sobbing.

The maid came up the stairs, the front of her dress soaked. "Miss Huntley," she said.

"Yes?" Laura Anne said.

"The mistress sent me up special to say that the carrying on up here won't do and to get the little 'uns under control." The maid delivered this without rancor and turned and clumped down the stairs again.

The nurse heard and soothed the children, quieting them. She sat them at the table, and got them scrap pieces of paper and crayons. "William is a right proper artist," she told Laura Anne mournfully.

"I'm a right proper artist, too, aren't I?" Elizabeth said.

"You've got a nice eye, and that's an ornament on a young lady," the nurse said.

She had a common way of speaking that Elizabeth adopted easily; proof, Laura Ann reflected that it was good that she was leaving. After more sighs, the nurse and her valise clumped down the stairs.

Laura Anne sat down and watched the children color for awhile. William was drawing a house, she thought. Or a square face. It was very difficult to determine. Elizabeth explained she was drawing an angel. Laura Anne was grateful that Elizabeth had told her because she was not sure she would have known otherwise.

Elizabeth handed her drawing to Laura Anne who pronounced it "very nice."

"What do we do now?" Elizabeth asked.

Laura Anne had no idea.

By the time Peter met Laura Anne to walk her home, she had a horrible headache. She had determined that the thing to do was to teach the children the capitals of Europe but William had proven impossible. Elizabeth was not much better, but at least she managed Paris and Madrid. Then Laura Anne had read to them from the Bible while they fidgeted and William whined. Finally, she had taken them for a walk which wore her out much more than it wore them out. She was certain she had a natural way with children, but these children were heathenish little creatures who had obviously been spoiled by that awful nurse.

She waited for Peter to ask how her day had been. Peter walked along the other side of the sidewalk, now and again giving her a sidelong glance.

"How was school today?" she asked, to prompt him to ask about her day, but he just said, "Fine," and sulked along like usual.

At home she went to her room and got down her regular scrapbooks, not the special one, just the ones anyone could see. Everyone knew she was quite mad about scrapbooks. She dug around until she found a scrap sheet of butterfly fairies, little sweet cherub faces with wings like stained glass. She cut out a fairy—it didn't look like Elizabeth at all, the hair was the wrong color, black and curly, and centered it on the page. Underneath she wrote, "My first day of teaching." She needed a quote, and Tennyson was always good. She found a quote about Knowledge in the book of quotations, and copied it out:

> Who loves not Knowledge? Who shall rail
> Against her beauty? May she mix
> With men and prosper! Who shall fix
> Her pillars? Let her work prevail."

Her sister, Jane, was twelve and the youngest, and shared a room with her and of course it was at this moment that Jane chose to come in and sit on her bed. "We're having a cold joint tonight."

Laura Anne said without looking up, "We always have a cold dinner on

Monday." Because it was laundry day of course, and their mother and Sarah, the maid, were too busy to cook.

"What are the people like?" Jane asked.

"What people?" Laura Anne said. She got out her paste pot and carefully applied paste to the back of the butterfly fairy.

"The people you work for? Are they above our station? Are they rich?"

"Of course they are above our station. They have a governess."

Jane sighed. "Is their house beautiful? Do they have a coach-and-four?"

"No," Laura Anne said. "They are a bit vulgar, I think. And they don't have a coach-and-four. They have a terrace house, like us."

"Like our house?"

"Bigger. Five bedrooms. Jane, go downstairs and help our mother. I'm busy."

"You're just doing your scrapbook."

Without looking up, Laura Anne said, "You know what will happen if you don't do as I say."

Jane got still a moment, and then got up and quietly went out. It was not good to cross Laura Anne. Laura Anne listened until she was sure Jane had gone downstairs and then she pulled out her own, her special scrapbook, her memory book. She stroked the deeply embossed, rich red leather cover. It was her favorite scrapbook and she kept it hidden so no one could ever look at it. It fell open to a page she had done a few months ago. It was a tracing of a photograph of her father on tracing paper—she had stolen the photograph from her parents' room. It had been taken years ago, long before she'd been born, but it was the only photograph of him they had had, at least until he had taken sick and died. (Then her mother had had a photographer in to take a photograph of him, deceased, but seated in the drawing room, one hand on a book, looking a little stiff and with one side of his face still droopy but if one didn't think about it, it could almost be as if he had fallen asleep there.)

Laura Anne had traced it very carefully and drawn many curlicues around it, and as she was quite good at curlicues she fancied it had turned out very well, perhaps her best drawing ever. She remembered how angry she was when she drew it and how her anger had come out in the ink, careful curlicues of anger, all around him. Then she had stuck a sewing needle, over, under, over, through the head of the drawing.

Now she did not like to think about it.

She flipped to a new page now and chose a butterfly fairy that had fair hair and blue eyes like Elizabeth. She pasted it down and put an old piece of flannel over it in case the pages stuck together although she was very careful with her paste and that almost never happened. Then she closed the scrapbook, her red memory book, and was about to hide it back up in the top of the wardrobe, making a note as she did so that Jane was getting tall enough she might see it. Laura Anne thought she would have to find a new hiding place soon. Then she had a bolt of inspiration and took it down and opened it up. She inked out the little butterfly fairy's eyes so that they were two black pits. She admired the effect for a moment. Underneath it she wrote "Elizabeth Finch" and the date. Then she closed it and hid it.

Mrs. Finch had a brother who was four years younger than she, although he was still an ancient twenty-two. Laura Anne met him coming down from the nursery one evening as he arrived for dinner. He was handing his umbrella and hat to the maid. The Finches appeared to entertain unfashionably early, serving dinner at five as if they were someone's grandparents. At Laura Anne's, when Papa was alive they had never eaten before six, and when they entertained, it was usually seven o'clock when dinner was served. Now, it was true, things were at sixes and sevens. Mama had let things slip terribly since Papa died, and often took to her bed, leaving the house in a state of total disarray.

"Good afternoon, Miss Huntley," Mrs. Finch said. "This is my brother, Anson Risewell. Anson, Miss Huntley is the new governess."

Anson Risewell nodded graciously, and murmured his pleasure.

Mrs. Finch asked, "How does William do?"

Laura Anne lied. "I think he is taking to geography most admirably, ma'am."

"And how is Elizabeth this day?"

Laura Anne looked serious and troubled. "It is difficult, of course. She loses so many days to her headaches that it is often one step forward and two steps back."

"We have recently started her on Dr. J Collis Browne's Chlorodyne when she has an attack," Mrs. Finch explained to her brother. "There has been a tremendous improvement."

Laura Anne thought so, as well. When dosed, little Elizabeth was placid, her pupils so large they turned her blue eyes dark. It was not the result that Laura Anne had anticipated, but the butterfly fairy image had not really looked very much like Elizabeth.

Anson Risewell pursed his lips. "A difficult trial for you, Louise," he said to his sister. He had very fair hair and very dark brown eyes. It was, Laura Anne thought, a striking combination. And he had a wonderful, ticklish looking blond moustache, a very dashing thing. His sister was cut from the same cloth, but what looked fleshy and common on her gave him an athletic robustness that Laura Anne found quite attractive.

As Laura Anne was collecting her rainwear, she overheard Anson Risewell say, "So things are working out?"

"Certainly until William goes to school," Mrs. Finch said.

"Of course," Anson Risewell replied.

Mrs. Finch sighed, "I can't be expected to take care of them without a nurse, what do I know about children?"

Laura Anne rather agreed.

"But when William goes to school, I think I will teach Elizabeth myself."

Anson Risewell nodded. "Excellent," he said. "Miss Huntley seems quite charming but," and here he leaned a little closer to Mrs. Finch to say quietly, "She seems very young."

Laura Anne was furious, and her brother Peter was late, which left her standing on the street waiting. He rounded the corner, running and panting. She slapped him. "How dare you keep me standing here like some common woman," she snapped.

Startled, he burst into tears. "But the omnibus kept stopping and stopping! I ran the whole last six blocks!"

"Just because father said you were the favorite, don't think it was true," Laura Anne hissed at him.

He blanched and was silent all the way home.

She began to watch for Anson Risewell. He did not come over often, of course. A gentleman like himself certainly had much more interesting things to do than eat dinner with his dull sister and her dull husband (a drab little man who Laura Anne rarely saw, although she sometimes heard him come upstairs and vanish into his study on the second floor.)

Near the end of the summer, the air thickened and the Finches decided the only escape was a holiday to Brighton. It was decided that this would be good for Elizabeth, as well. They booked three rooms at the Royal Albion Hotel—not as exclusive as the Grand Hotel, but on the King's Road overlooking the promenade and very respectable. Laura Anne was to accompany them and share a room with the two children. Anson would meet them there as well.

The preparations for a week away were immense. William was over-excited, prone to running around the nursery screeching, and Elizabeth developed a headache so severe she could keep no food down, nor could she swallow Dr. J Collis Browne's Chlorodyne. Laura Anne cleaned up after her, since the maid was overwhelmed with airing and sorting and packing. It was a perfectly dreadful week, and not even the season. The Finches never seemed to quite manage to do things the right way. Laura Anne had quickly realized that she had been hired as a sort of pretension, and that they were not people of means sufficient to hire a governess. Which was why all the business about her not having a character and them hiring her out of Christian charity was claptrap. They had hired her because her inexperience made her cheap. And now they were going to Brighton when the only people there would day trippers and desperate sorts.

But Laura Anne had never been to Brighton. And it would be a chance to see more of Anson.

The train trip was a horror. Elizabeth was still sick and William would not settle and be quiet, no matter what Laura Anne did. Mr. Finch sat in the corner, parked behind his newspapers and invisible. Mrs. Finch said, "Miss Huntley, please control William!" several times. It was all Laura Anne could do to keep from bursting out that he was a horrid and spoiled child when she got him and whose fault was that?

But when Mrs. Finch rebuked Laura Anne the third time, Anson Risewell said, "Oh Louise, you know how boys are."

Mrs. Finch said sharply, "I certainly do not."

"I was just as difficult," Anson Risewell said. "William, come here." Anson lifted the boy on his lap and pointed out the window. "You see, we're outside of London now. You've never been outside of London, have you?"

The boy stared out the window, thoughtful. "Where are we?" he asked. "Are we in Madrid?"

Everyone laughed.

"What makes you think that?" Anson asked.

"Madrid is the capital of Spain," William said, as if this explained everything.

"Yes," Anson said. "Very smart! Did Miss Huntley teach you that?"

To Laura Anne's astonishment, William went on to list a half dozen European capitals, Athens, Greece; Rome, Italy; Vienna and Budapest, Austria-Hungary; Berne, Switzerland; and triumphantly, London. He was an obstinate little thing usually, unable to remember anything she taught him. But now Anson beamed at her. "Capital, little man!" he said, but she knew it was really a compliment to her and her heart lifted.

They made the transit from the train station to the hotel in a flurry of luggage and porters.

The air smelled of sea and everything was so clean after the soot and fog of London. Even Elizabeth seemed revived although she said that the sun hurt her eyes. The hotel rooms were clean, bright and airy, and as it was not the season, they had been able to get them overlooking the ocean. The ocean was entrancing. Anson declared they should go down to the promenade immediately.

"We are all in need of a rest after the journey," Mrs. Finch said.

To Laura Anne's surprise, Mr. Finch said, "Louise, we have come all this way, it seems foolish not to take a turn on the promenade."

Elizabeth began to cry. "My head hurts," she whimpered.

Laura Anne could feel Anson's eyes upon her and the child. She felt a rush of fury. Now she would be forced to sit in this room with two children while everyone else enjoyed Brighton. But she smiled and sat down and gathered Elizabeth to her, pretending to be unaware of the observers to her performance. "It's all right," she said. "You and I will stay here and you can rest your little head and breathe the clean air. I'm sure that by the end of the week you'll be right as rain."

Elizabeth was startled into immobility by Laura Anne's unaccustomed embrace. Really, it was the wrong way to treat the child, giving in to her whims. But men were stupid about childrearing.

Anson said, "I have a wonderful idea, Lizzie dear. Why don't we get you a push chair? That way you won't have to do a thing and I will push your carriage up and down the promenade and you can be a princess."

Elizabeth wavered.

Mrs. Finch looked worried. "She's really over stimulated, Anson."

"Nonsense," Anson said. "Nothing will be better for her than good sea air. Put color in her cheeks." He was looking a little irritable.

So they all trooped down. Anson procured a big wheeled wicker chair and deposited Elizabeth in it and started down the promenade. The sea crashed and there were seagulls everywhere, just like in pictures. But pictures did not give a sense of how the ocean just went on and on until it disappeared. In pictures there was something cozy about the ocean. Laura Anne felt uneasy. Resolutely she set her eyes on all the promenaders, dressed in summer linens. She felt a little shabby in her mourning Bombazine, but as she was still in second mourning, all she had been able to do was add linen cuffs and collar to her two dresses.

She had really liked the theatricality of mourning, but seeing all the women in jaunty dresses this day she was sick of it. She wanted a nice hat. She wanted to be noticed. No one noticed girls in mourning.

The Promenade was crowded. There was a Minstrel band including a Negro with a banjo and checkered pants. Men and women thronged the beach, many of the women carrying black umbrellas against the sun. Boys stood on the rocky beach or waded in the water, their shoes and socks discarded, their pants rolled up exposing their white legs. There was a man with a monkey that capered and turned somersaults. Elizabeth clapped.

There was a man in a bowler and coat standing next to a cart with a sign that said *Beach Photographs While You Wait, 6d.*

"Mr. Risewell," Laura Anne said, "you must get your photograph."

Every one turned to her, startled.

"It would mean so much to the children," she said. "They so adore you and to have a little memento of this occasion."

For a moment she thought she had been too bold, even for Anson. But a man's vanity could always be counted on and even as the Finches frowned, he laughed. "Lizzie? Would you like my photograph?"

Elizabeth nodded solemnly.

Mrs. Finch said, "Oh Anson, don't be foolish."

"It's a lovely sentiment," said the photographer, a short, common looking fellow with sideburns that stood away from his face.

Once Anson had decided there was nothing to be done. The photographer prepared the plate, asking them how long they had been at Brighton. William was intensely curious, whispering to Laura Anne, "What is he doing?"

"Making a tintype of Mr. Risewell," Laura Anne said.

After a moment, William whispered, "What is he doing now?" The man was sliding the plate into the camera. "It's all part of making the tintype," Laura Anne said.

There were tintypes on display and William gazed at them. "Can I have a tintype?"

"You will have one of your uncle, to keep. But you must share it with your sister."

"No," William whined. "I mean one of me."

"They're six pence." She frowned at him. "Now be quiet."

Anson posed and the photographer whisked the cap off the lens. Everything hung still, expectant, and then the photographer covered the lens. "There you go," he said, "and if you'll just wait a minute's time, we'll have this ready for you."

But it was more than just a minute as the man busied himself at the cart, the tintype hidden as he swished it around in some liquid.

"What's he doing now?" William whispered.

Mrs. Finch glared.

Laura Anne told herself it didn't matter.

The tintype was finally produced. It was fine, if a bit dark. Even Mrs. Finch had to admire it. Anson held it out. "I don't know, Miss Huntley. Maybe I should keep the thing."

"I want to see it, please!" William said.

Anson laughed. "So you shall." He handed it to William.

"May I see it?" Elizabeth asked.

"Certainly, Princess," Anson said. "Just let your brother have his turn."

The tintype had caught his expression very well, Laura Anne thought. It would do nicely.

The week in Brighton was a mixed success. Elizabeth was terribly sick for the first three days, but then the sea air seemed to work its improvements upon her, for which Laura Anne was grateful since she had spent those three days in the hotel room with the little girl while the rest enjoyed the pleasures of the promenade and the piers.

Near the end of the trip, the unthinkable happened.

Their little party was gathered in the lobby, deciding on tea when Anson spied newcomers and happily hailed them. They were an older couple, genial and well dressed. The woman wore a dark red dress with a bustle, much in contrast to Mrs. Finch's old fashioned crinoline skirt. But it was the daughter accompanying them that drew all eyes. She wore a dress of emerald green and white shot silk, artfully trimmed in black velvet ribbon. Mrs. Finch murmured, "Surely that is from Worth."

Anson strode across the lobby to meet them and brought them back. Once close, the girl was a mild-faced thing, not quite so pretty as her elaborate couture, Laura Anne thought. "Mr. and Mrs. Gower, Annabelle, may I present my sister, Louise Finch, and her husband George Finch." He beamed, "I believe I am able to announce that I have offered Annabelle a proposal of marriage, which she has been so kind as to accept."

Laura Anne felt the shock to her nerves, vibrating through her. For a moment everything in the lobby drew far away and she saw dancing specks of white. It was so impossibly warm, and she heard nothing of what was around her. But then her vision cleared. Anson was beaming at the girl and everyone else was looking on, except William who had started off across the lobby towards one of the potted palms. He was unhealthily fascinated with them.

Laura Anne caught up with him, scolded him in a whisper, and brought him back. "So we shall meet you for dinner then," Mrs. Gower said. "At eight."

"I do so look forward to it," Mrs. Finch said.

"Until then," Anson said to Annabelle.

The Finches strolled out to the promenade. "Are they connected to the Leveson-Gowers?" Mrs. Finch asked.

"Yes, I believe Mr. Gower is a distant cousin of the Duke of Sutherland," Anson said lightly, as though this were a bit of trivia.

"What does father say?" Mrs. Finch breathed.

Anson laughed. "He said they'll do, even if they are Scots."

Everyone laughed, even William, who had no idea what he was laughing at. Only Elizabeth and Laura Anne did not laugh.

They came home on Saturday because Mrs. Finch preferred service at her own church, and thought perhaps it was not quite right to travel on Sunday. Mrs. Finch was very punctilious in her relationship with Our Lord. Mr. Finch, to Laura Anne's surprise, did not go to church. She did not quite understand Mr. Finch, who seemed to be such a milquetoast but who on closer examination was prone to unexpected actions and statements. But of course, this was the first time she had ever spent even the smallest amount of time in his presence.

She was so delighted to be home she could have cried. She was exhausted from dealing with Elizabeth and William, and still quite disturbed by all that had happened in Brighton. Jane came running down the hall when she got in. "You're home!" Jane said. "What was it like?"

"It was very nice and very healthy and I brought you a post card," Laura Anne said. She dug out the post card—tucked next it was the tintype of Anson, which she left in her bag. The postcard was a scene of the Promenade and the beach, with the West Pier off in the distance. Jane tucked her skirts behind and sat down on the stairs to admire the card.

From the drawing room, Laura Anne's mother called her.

Mother looked sallow and tired. She was seated at her desk with her writing slope. Her hair was not carefully done and her dress was stained. She so did not take care of herself these days. She had been so tiresome since Papa had died. It was all very well to mourn, but there were standards, and even Mrs. Finch, who had none of Mother's old style, looked better.

Propped on the writing slope was Laura Anne's own, her special memory book.

She was speechless.

"The maid found it," her mother said. "I am only grateful that Jane did not."

"You should not meddle with that," Laura Anne finally managed.

Her mother opened the book, paged through it, the images of family flickering past, Papa with the needle through his head, Elizabeth as a butterfly fairy with blackened eyes. She paged back to the image of Papa.

"Why him?" she asked. When Laura Ann didn't answer. "Why not me? He always doted on you. He didn't see—" She sighed. "It would have been so much better if it had been me. As it was, you might as well have stuck that needle through my heart."

She closed the book and handed it to Laura Anne. She looked down at the desk, lost in thought. It was as if she had forgotten Laura Anne was there.

Why had she stuck the needle in Papa instead of her mother? She didn't like to think about these things, it made her thoughts skitterish and disturbed. But she and her Mother had not always gotten along. Papa had understood that Laura Anne needed special things, had snuck her toast with marmalade when most people thought it was wicked to give it to children. Papa had teased and cajoled and called her pet names.

Peter had recited his poem from school and Papa had said, "My favorite boy! There is nothing closer to a father's heart than his son."

Laura Anne had said without thinking, "But I'm your favorite!"

"Laura Anne," her father replied, "don't be foolish."

He meant it.

"Because you never betrayed me," Laura Anne whispered.

Her mother's head jerked up and they met each other, eye to eye. Her mother's eyes were wild, red-rimmed. "You were such a angel when you were a baby," she said. Her voice ground with despair.

Everything felt hollow for a moment and Laura Anne thought she would cry. She wanted to throw herself on her mother and cry and cry. But her mother would not comfort her. Fury surged through Laura Anne, red and then white, burning out the tears. She could feel the colors chasing her face. Her mother was watching her.

"If something happened to me," her mother said evenly, "I should not care for myself, but I would feel saddest I think for you, for it would be on you that would fall the burden of this house, and of raising Peter and Jane. There is not so much money, and if you did not work, we would have to let the maid go. It is," she said deliberately, "perhaps the one thing that keeps me going on, that your dear Papa loved his children so and I must take care of them as best I can."

Laura Anne fled upstairs and flung herself across her bed, her memory book clutched to her.

She had to escape this house. She could not stay here. And she did not want to be a governess all her life. With a character from Mrs. Finch she could get a good position in a more prosperous house but she would always be invisible. No one had introduced her to the Gowers. She had been taken to Brighton as a servant, and Mrs. Finch was already tiring of her, she could tell.

She had a plan, it was a good thing. The poor little Miss Gower would never know what had happened.

At the door to the bedroom, Jane said, "Laura Anne—"

"Get out," Laura Anne hissed.

Jane looked her and fled.

Laura Anne took out the tintype of Anson Risewell. She dug out scraps of cloth, black wool, and made a little coat for him to wear and a top hat. She made buttons out of little knots of thread, quite cunning. Then she dug out a square of red cotton and folded it and cut out a heart. She opened the heart and carefully wrote "Laura Anne" on the heart. She was buzzing, buzzing the way she had the night she drew the tracing of her father, and the tintype was even better, she knew. She felt powerful. She glued the heart to Anson's chest and then covered it in the coat, so that the tintype was "dressed." She added the top hat.

She pasted it in the memory book. It was very stiff and she would have to be careful. She would have to hide the memory book again, this time where no one would find it. She would. She would think about that in a moment.

But first, she surveyed the result.

Anson Risewell at the beach, wearing a coat and hat glued on, and underneath it, the barely visible lump of the heart. Underneath the tintype she wrote, "Mine."

Anson was rather drunk, although it was just after three in the afternoon. He turned when Laura Anne came into the drawing room and his face registered delight, a flicker of something, perhaps dismay, and then again the flood of delight. "Sweetheart," he said.

It was almost two years from the day she had pasted the tintype in her memory book. The day she had decided she had to get out of her house. Breaking off an engagement takes a little time, and then there is the new engagement period and the picking out of a house—a bigger house than the Finches'. (How was Laura Anne to have known that Louisa, her dear sister-in-law, had married down. For love.) There were the furnishings to pick out.

The house had turned out very well, Laura Anne thought. This room in particular, with its red trimmed in black. And she had her own Morning Room.

Anson had not turned out as she expected. "We are going out tonight," she reminded him.

He looked chagrined. "A little spirits, it's nothing."

She let him see her displeasure.

Again, his face was a curious mixture, dismay, and then a crack of something smothered breaking out, disgust and maybe even a bit of fear? But it all disappeared again under his embarrassment.

Still, she could barely look at him now. Such a disappointment he had turned out to be. She had thought he would be fun, he had been so buff and hardy in the first days of their engagement. Now he looked as if he was going to fat.

"Oh," she said, "photos have come." They were *carte de visite* photographs, pages of eight the size of visiting cards. There was a page of Anson in the coat and hat he had worn on their wedding day, and a page of her in her wedding dress and veil. Eight little Ansons, eight little Laura Annes. Except the Laura Anne page was missing one. She had already cut it out.

Anson glanced at them. "Very nice, sweet."

"I like photographs," she said. "Remember when I asked you to have the tintype taken for Elizabeth and William?"

He frowned.

"At Brighton," she prompted.

"Oh yes," he said, although she was fairly certain that he did not. "What became of that?"

"The children lost it, I do not doubt," she said. "Louise lets her children run like heathens."

Anson did not like it when she criticized his sister, but he did not like to disagree with her, either. He busied himself topping off his glass of claret.

She was growing very tired of Anson. She had not expected to be so lonely when she was married. But there had been a lot of fuss and discomfort when Anson had broken off the engagement with Miss Gower. And very many people had preferred to blame her. Mostly, Anson was not good company. But he drank quite a bit these days and things happened to people who drank. They fell down stairs, or stepped in front of carriages.

She had taken care of her loneliness.

Just now, she had pasted a wedding picture of herself in the memory book. She had covered her wedding dress with an actual piece of watered silk cut from the hem of the actual dress. Underneath it, on the belly, was pasted a picture of a tiny baby.

An angelic tiny baby. Not like Louise Finch's children at all. Hers. Her very own.

THE DEAD
SEA-BOTTOM SCROLLS

HOWARD WALDROP

(A Re-creation of Oud's Journey by **Slimshang** *from Tharsis to Solis Lacus,
by George Weeton, Fourth Mars Settlement Wave, 1981)*

So I am standing here on a cold morning, beside the best approximation of
a *slimshang* of which Terran science is capable—polycarbonates and (Earth)
man-made fabrics instead of the original hardened plant fibers and outer
coverings of animals long extinct. It looks fast, probably faster than any
native-made *slimshang*, but it will have to do.

One thing it's missing is the series of gears, cogs, plates, and knobs with
which a sort of music was made as it rolled. Martians spoke of "coming at full
melody"—since the reproduction was mechanical, like a music box, the faster
the *slimshang* went, the louder and more rackety the tune.

Instead, I have a tape deck with me, on which I have chosen to put an
endless loop of the early-1960s tune "The Martian Hop."

It's appropriate and fitting.

What I am doing is to set out in the recreated *slimshang* to follow the route
(if not the incidents and feelings) of Oud's famous journey from Tharsis to
Solis Lacus.

It's the most famous Martian travelogue we have (for many, and varying,
reasons).

Oud was the first thinking commentator on the changes Mars was
undergoing in his (long) lifetime. Others had noted the transformation, but
not the underlying processes. And Oud's personal experiences added much
to the classic stature of his tale.

So on this cold morning at Settlement #6 (vying, like many, for the AAS to
officially rechristen it Lowell City), I shook hands with the three people who
had come outside the temporary bubble dome to see me off.

We stood exchanging small talk for a few minutes, then Oud's words came to me: "A Being has to do what a Being has to do."

So I climbed into my high-tech *slimshang*, up-sailed, waved to the others (who were already heading back for the haven of air they could breathe), and set my course west, playing "The Martian Hop" as I jumped some scattered pinkish dunes.

Think of Oud as a Martian Windwagon Smith.

He set out from Tharsis (on the old volcanic shield) toward Solis Lacus (the site of some till-then-inexact place of cultural revelation), and recorded what would have been to other Martians a pleasant (as we understand it) few days' jaunt in the equivalent of a hot-rod windwagon (which most *slimshangs* were, and Oud's definitely was; I'm assuming that his approached mine in elegance, if not materials).

That Oud started in winter was unusual. The weather was colder and the winds less predictable then, given to frequent planet-girdling dust storms. Winter and spring trips were not unknown, but most were taken in mid-Martian summer, when temperatures sometimes rose to the low forties Fahrenheit.

This tradition was left over from an earlier Mars (along with cultural patterns and the development of the *slimshang*). No one thought to do it any other way.

The Martians were nothing if not a tradition-bound species. But there's a lot to be said for customs that get you through ten or fifteen million years (the jury is still out).

I'm sure, in the future, someone will read my retracing of Oud's journey and point out the know-it-allness of earlier humans jumping in with inexact knowledge and pronouncements of age off by factors of three or four, and will comment on them in footnotes.[1]

From Oud: "Weather fine (for the time of year). Not much debris, sands fairly smooth and sessile. Skirted two or three eroded gulleys. Smooth running till dark. Saw one other being all day, walking, near an above-ground single habitation. Pulled slimshang over at dark and buttoned up for the night. Very comfortable."[2]

He should have seen the place today. I had to dodge erratic rocks the size of railroad freight cars, and the two or three eroded gulleys now look like the Channeled Scablands of the northwest United States.

Oud lived, we think, at the start of the Great Bombardment (see later), before the largest of the geologic upheavals, the rise of the shield volcanoes

---

[1] Well put. Weeton's guess was fairly accurate, one of the few times early colonists and philologists were. Other places, he's less reliable.

[2] Elenkua N'Kuba, ed. *Weeton's Oud Narrative*: A facsimile reproduction. Elsevier, the Hague: 2231.

and the great asteroid impacts that released untold amounts of suddenly-boiling permafrost and loosed water vapor and pyroclastic flows that changed the even-then everchanging face of Mars.

After the now-eroded features of my first day's route, I was slowing myself where necessary to cover exactly the same distances as Oud: only once in the whole trip had Oud's *slimshang*, which must really have been something, made better time than mine through (in his day) worse terrain. Give or take a boulder the size of an Airstream trailer, the ground was a gradual slope off the Tharsis plateau.

I settled in for the night, calling in my position to Mars Central, watched the sunset (which comes fast in these parts), and saw one of the hurtling moons of Mars hurtle by. Then, like Oud, millennia before, went to sleep.

Day 2:

Oud, on his original route, commented that, in former days, *slimshangs* had made part of this day's journey by "otherwise"—i.e., water. He dismissed how easy such an old journey must have been—on land, water for most of the day, then back to land.

Oud (and I) had to make our way around more dried channels. In Oud's time, some still contained surface ice, as opposed to the open-water lakes they must have been in Oud's ancestors' times. Now not even ice remains, sublimated into the air. Just old worn watercourses, which made today's trip a tough mother. I thought once I might have damaged a wheel (I have spares, but changing one out is not easy), but had only picked up a small, persistent rock.

Oud was one of the first to notice that the air was getting thinner. Others had seen the effects, but had attributed it to other causes. The loss of water was one. *Slimshang* sails had once been small affairs. By Oud's time, they were twice as large—my reproduction is 7/10 sail and sometimes that's not enough.

It was also on this second day that Oud saw an asteroid hit in the distance.

From Oud: "A sudden plume of dust and steam on the horizon that rose a *cretop* (five miles) high. Much scattering of debris. Had to trim the *slimshang* close-to to avoid falling boulders, and navigate carefully around many more. The cloud hung in the air till sundown, and probably after."

My present course shows some remnants of Oud's event and later ones, including a string of frosted craters off to my right. There are also a couple of shield craters or later volcanic (still active) cones that followed on that cataclysm.

The navigating was even dicier than Oud's had been.

Some idea of the upheavals of Oud's time may be gained by his referral (in an earlier narrative) to what is now Olympus Mons as "the new hill."

So on went Oud on his winter journey, unconcerned by small things like the sky falling and mountains building on the horizon line.

It's only an accident of sound that Oud's name is the same as the English one for a Turkish mandolin. (I believe there is an album called *The Kings of the Oud on Oud*, put out by Picwick Records, supposedly music inspired by Oud's journey, done by a bunch of studio musicians, rumored to have included Lou Reed and Glen Campbell, among others. I have never heard it: people who have said that it was "pretty uninspired by anything.")

The third day of both our journeys was fairly downhill, uneventful, and of no great consequence. Night was the same. Oud did not even mention it.

The fourth day, I had some trouble with the rigging of the *slimshang*. Oud had troubles of a differing kind.

His narrative is deceptive. After complaining about the low quality of the foodstuffs he could find for his breakfast (he had noticed the decline in traditional plant life from his ancestors' time earlier in the narrative), and speculating about his probably paltry lunch ("slim mossings" is the phrase he used), a few hours into the day comes the line, "If I didn't know better, and this wasn't winter season, I would think I was undergoing *grexagging*."

Well. I wasn't undergoing *grexagging* (no human ever had), but I was having the devil's own time getting over a series of long gullies without my sail luffing. I resorted to the last ignominy of *slimshanging*: I got out and pushed.

Eventually, I gained height and wind simultaneously, and made off at a fast clip, Solis Lacusward.

I had left Oud in his travels sure that he was not undergoing *grexagging*. After some more navigational and observational entries, his next sentence may take the reader by surprise.

"Bud has the tiller now. Since he knows almost everything I know, but is only just learning to use his pseudopodia, I let him learn by experience what a glorious thing a *slimshang* is, but also how ungainly it can become in seconds."

Bud? asks the reader. Bud? Who is this? Where did he come from?

Oud cannot resist his little joke:

"I watch him clumsily take us around boulders and over dunes. I see how his movements and coordination become smoother and more assured as time—and miles—pass. He reminds me of myself when younger."

Of course he did. Oud had undergone *grexagging* (meiosis). Bud was a younger Oud.

This is the only time in Martian literature that a narrator has *grexagged* in the course of an ongoing narrative. *Grexagging* usually took place in one's domicile, attended by nest-brothers, and was celebrated with ritual exchanges of foodstuffs, chattel, and good wishes. *Grexagging* usually occurred in the spring or summer season, foretold by mood swings, dietary changes, and agoraphobia.

It had happened to Oud in the winter, with no presaging except the *slimshang* wanderlust. He must have attributed his body's stirrings to that, sublimating the others.

Scientist to the end, he described his changes: "I have less weight than in 393rd year. To think I *grexagged* at such an advanced age, with no forewarnings, and in the winter season, is as surprising to me as anyone.

"It is said that Flimo of the (Syrtis Major) nest had an off-bud at 419 years, but that it was unviable, and was ritually eaten at the Festival of Foregiving, and the nest stayed away for the customary year before being allowed to attend the next All-Nest Convention.

"Bud looks viable to me—in the last few hours, his handling of the *slimshang* has grown as assured as that of someone who'd been doing it for a century or so.

"We run now at full jangle across the flat of the former sea-bottom that stretches toward (Solis Lacus). It does a Being good to watch his bud-descendant proud and confident at the tiller of his *slimshang.*"

It's still debated (especially by us first wave of humans on Mars) what event it was that took place at the cultural shrine toward which Oud and Bud made their way.

Before Oud, the literature was conflicting and rather non-informative. (On Earth, when anthropologists can't find instant meaning in any cultural artifact, they say "This obviously had deep religious significance.")

What had happened in the dim Martian past? we asked, before Oud's manuscript was unearthed. Was there some Fatima or Lourdes-type event? Was it a recurring event and ritual, a Martian Eleusinian Mystery? Rather than either, it appeared to have been a singular event, so important that its effects lasted for several million years. Whatever it was, it must have been a doozy. No Being ever really talked about it before Oud. It seemed to be part of them, a piece of general knowledge, perhaps as known to Bud a few hours after his off-budding as to Oud after his 394 years.

So onward they went toward Solis Lacus; so onward I followed them (some three hundred thousand to four hundred thousand years later), me happy in the long-gone companions of the journey: Oud proud of his new off-spring; Bud probably hooting from the sheer joy of being alive and at the tiller of a fine slimshang, on a dying planet that was losing its oxygen, its water, and its heat.

"As with all nest-fathers," says Oud, "I instructed Bud on how to more efficiently rid himself of his waste products on waking in the morning, and how to use his haze-eyes to better see distant objects. He only took a few minutes to learn those skills that would last him a lifetime."

Now Oud the scientist takes over the narrative:

"I notice that for the past two days we have had only dry snow (carbon dioxide frost), with only a few patches of real snow here and there. Not like in our ancestors's time, when dry snow was the rarity."

His (and their, and my) next day of the trip would bring us to our goal—changed though it was since their time.

On old maps of Mars, Solis Lacus (The Lake of the Sun) was a bright circular feature in the midst of a darker area, thought at the time to be an irrigated, heavily vegetated patch, with the stark circularity of Solis Lacus in its midst.

We now know that the dark part was heavy volcanic dust and ash; the bright roundness a raised area swept by winds and kept clear.

In Oud's time, it was a long fold of the edge of the old bottom of a remnant sea, like prehistoric Lake Bonneville on Earth. As they rolled toward it, Oud said "Ancestors described the wonder and majesty of (Old Bitter Sea) with its rolled margin of amaranth and turquoise gleaming in the sunset after a long day's *slimshanging*. Now it's an almost featureless rise of the landscape, hardly worth a second two-looks."

Oud reefed his sail as they slid out onto the brightness of the middle of Solis Lacus.

Bud said, "It is quiet here, Father."

"Indeed," said Oud, "for here is where it started."

"Were you born here, Father?

Oud looked around.

"We were all born here," said Oud. He pointed to the raised lump in the cold distance. "That is where the Life-Rock fell from the sky. From where we, and all living things, come. In the ancestors' days, we returned each year for the Festival of Wow, to appreciate that, and to think and wonder on its happening. It must have been something, then, all the nests gathered, all hooting and racket, such music as they had."

"Are you sad, Father?" asked Bud.

"Sadness is for those who have personally lost something," said Oud. "How can I be sad? I have made a fine journey in a good *slimshang*, in the low season. I have arrived at the place of our First-Birth. And I have a new bud-son who will live to see other wonders on this elder twilight world. How could I be sad?"

"Thank you for bringing me here," said Bud.

"No," said Oud, "thank you."

• • •

Weeton here again. We leave Bud and Oud in a sort of valetudinarian idyll (I like to think), staring into the setting sun with Solis Lacus around them, and Thyle I and II far away.

Meanwhile, I'm out here on this empty rise where the edge of a sea once rolled, trying to find what is dragging on my retro-*slimshang*. The sun is setting here, probably adding to my anthropomorphization of those two Martians now dead four hundred thousand years.

After exploring the Life-Rock for a day ("If you've seen one rock, you've seen them all"—Oud), his narrative ends two days into the return journey back to Tharsis.

Oud, as far as we can find so far, never wrote another word.

Bud, except for his appearance in Oud's narrative, is unknown to history or Martian literature.

I hope, so far as I'm able, that they lived satisfying, productive Martian lives.

We'll never know. While Mars and the Martians were dying, we were still looking up, grunting, out of the caves, at the pretty red dot in the sky.

A FINE SHOW ON THE ABYSSAL PLAIN

KARIN TIDBECK

On a beach by the sea stands a gutted stone tower. A man is climbing up the remains of a staircase that spirals up the tower's interior. Vivi sits on the roof, oblivious, counting coins that have spilled from her breast pocket: one fiver, three ones, one golden ten. She's only wearing a worn pair of pajamas, and the damp breeze from the sea is making her shiver. She has no memory of how she arrived, but is vaguely aware of the sound of footsteps.

Eventually the footsteps arrive at the top, and stop. The man who has appeared on the roof is dressed in khakis and worn boots. Dark locks tumble down the left side of his face, which is beautiful in that ruddy way that belongs to adolescence.

Vivi looks up, startled. "Who are you?"

"I should ask you the same." The man's barely winded. "You're trespassing. We've claimed this place."

"I don't understand," says Vivi. "Who are you? And who are 'we'?"

"Exploratory actors, of course." He makes a mock bow. "We're the Documentary Theatre Troupe. And you, as I said, are trespassing on our territory. I must ask you to come with me."

Vivi follows him down the stairs, down the beach, and into a lush forest where the Documentary Theatre Troupe have made camp and eagerly greet their new audience.

The play is called *The Tragedy of King Vallonius*. Contrary to the title's promise, the story is about a girl named Rosella, famed for her beauty and especially her lovely head of hair, so striking that she must wear a headscarf outside lest she attract unwanted attention. One day Rosella forgets to put her scarf on and goes for a walk with her head uncovered. A pedestrian passing by on the other side of the street sees her bright red hair and runs into a lamppost. The shopping bag he was carrying spills its contents in the street: vegetables, a bottle of milk, and a packet of soft butter. A man riding by on his bicycle slips in the patch of butter and falls over, cracking his head open on the stones. And this is where the Tragedy of King Vallonius comes in. The man on the bicycle was in fact the beloved monarch who liked to disguise himself as a commoner to see how his subjects were faring. Now that the king is dead, the country is plunged into a war with its neighboring nation. Rosella, in terror, shaves her head and never leaves her home again.

When the play is done, the troupe lines up and bows for applause. They look bewildered when Vivi doesn't clap her hands.

"What did we do wrong?" says the Pedestrian.

"Nothing," says Vivi. "I just don't like it. Maybe the setting is wrong."

"How about winter?" says Rosella, pulling off her skin-coloured rubber cap, letting her luxurious hair spill out.

Vivi wrinkles her nose. "I don't like winter. And I don't like Rosella. Also this would never happen in real life."

"It would," says the dead king from the floor, twirling his thick grey moustache. "This is based on real events. King Vallonius I died just this way, and that is how the kingdom of Pavalona fell to the Fedrans. We only enact stories that are true."

"Absolutely, one hundred percent true," Rosella agrees.

"There was never a king named Vallonius," says Vivi.

"Of course there was," replies the Pedestrian. "But not in your world."

Apprentice hates playing Vivi, the sniveling girl from a boring dayworld that "encounters" strangeness and through that strangeness tells the story of a "documentary theatre troupe." There are too many meta levels, too much self-referencing. Why would you set up a play about setting up a play? And the casting is always the same. Apprentice never gets to play the actor who does Rosella, or King Vallonius, or the Pedestrian; she has to be boring old Vivi, and Vivi's grey tedium is sinking into her bones.

"You have to feel her to play her," says Director, the third time she interrupts the play to correct Vivi. "Let her emotions bleed into yours."

"She doesn't have any," Apprentice replies. "She's a protagonist. She's an empty vessel waiting to be filled by the audience."

"That," Director replies, "is what you read in some book. Now go back to your seat, be Vivi, watch the play. Do whatever Vivi would do."

"She'd do exactly what I'm doing," says Apprentice. "She'd be yawning and not liking it."

"But only in the beginning," says Director, "and you know it. She'll become dazzled and intrigued by the strangeness of it all."

"All right, all right. But I want to play someone else after this."

"We'll see," says Director, and steps onto the stage, slipping back into the actor who plays Rosella.

Apprentice returns to her seat and to Vivi. It's such a tedious, washed-out mind.

Vivi claps, mesmerized. The actors take her up onto the stage and put a red wig on her, almost as red as the one the other actress wears.

"You are now Rosella," the old Rosella intones, "and this is what happened inside the Pedestrian's head."

The Pedestrian steps forward and touches Vivi's—no, Rosella's—breast. Rosella is less experienced than Vivi; Vivi frowns at her terror of this other man grasping at her body, but she must play along. Rosella's fear and disgust bleeds into her, mingling with the unbearable excitement that comes from weeks of no sex, no touching. Vivi wants it. Rosella does not. Rosella screams, a short, high-pitched yelp as the Pedestrian starts tearing at her clothes. It is what he must do, as the Pedestrian, and Rosella must squeal and weep and eventually succumb to the desire his rough hands awaken in her, because deep down every woman hides a dream of being ravished by strange men.

King Vallonius, still dead in a pool of his own blood and brains, leers from the cobblestones. They chant in unison as Rosella passes through the stages of fear, terror, despair, surrender, and ecstasy. She rises up, naked and bleeding, a complete woman. The others clap their hands and cheer.

Vivi takes her wig off and thanks the Pedestrian, who is now just the actor shyly hunched over his own naked form.

"Now that was a good play," says Vivi. "Well done! I feel refreshed." She puts her pajamas back on.

"Excellent," says the King, and sits up. "Let us have lunch and then push our stage out of Pavalona and to another place."

"The Arctic?" asks the Pedestrian hopefully.

"I was rather hoping the Cyclades," says Rosella.

"You think too small." The King rips off his moustache. "But do let's have lunch first."

Everyone laughs. The Pedestrian claps his hands, and they all fall silent. As one, they turn outward, take each others' hands, and make a slow bow. The trees respond with a compact silence.

"You have been watching *Vivi and the Documentary Theatre Troupe!*" Rosella bellows at the trees. "I present to you, in order of appearance: Apprentice, as Vivi!"

Apprentice takes a step forward and curtseys, pinching her pajama legs as if they were a skirt.

"Journeyman, as The Mysterious Guide and the Pedestrian!"

Journeyman—who, unlike the actor in the play, is unbothered by his nudity—makes an elegant court bow.

"The Eccentric Owner and the King, played by our beloved Nestor!"

Nestor hops forward, grace belying his aged face.

"And finally," Rosella steps forward, "Nameless Actress and Rosella, played by myself. I am Director, and I hope you have enjoyed our show this evening, whoever you are and wherever you may be."

They bow again. The trees whisper.

Apprentice goes to bed with a stomachache. Vivi's character clings to her like grime. All Vivi wants is another rough fuck from that Pedestrian. She's such a nasty cluster of control fantasies and boredom.

"Is anyone even watching?" Apprentice asks as they lie in their sleeping bags.

"Of course," says Nestor. He scratches his upper lip with a dry noise. The King's moustache gives him a rash.

"How do you know that?"

"Oh, I hear them sometimes, rustling their confectionery bags."

Apprentice peers out into the darkness, the trees, the pinprick stars between their branches.

The next day, they are at the bottom of the sea. Director has decided on a straightforward play: *The Prince and the Abyssal Queen*. Journeyman is the Prince of Yr, and Director the Queen of the Abyssal Plain; Apprentice is The Sly Fish and Nestor the God of the Abyss.

The play begins as the fish has lured the fair Prince into an enchanted boat, which dives down into the ocean depths, the Sly Fish gleefully pulling it along on a string. The Prince is distraught, of course: He's been abducted, he's afraid of water and the dark. Three little anglerfish keep pace with the boat, lighting it with their lanterns. One of the smaller anglerfish tries to attach itself to the biggest one. It must be mating season.

The Prince reaches the bottom, treads onto the Abyssal Plain, and becomes the Queen's consort. He's snared by her spells and stays there for a year before the spell is broken. He begs the Sly Fish to help him flee to the surface; the fish agrees, in exchange for the Prince's promise of the first living thing he loves. In a very striking scene, the Queen appeals to the God of the Abyss for aid, and he grants her the Harp of the Deep. The Queen sits on her throne, playing her harp to lure the Prince back.

Of course, there are twists. Quickly rising to the surface, the Prince's ears are so damaged by the pressure changes that he is rendered deaf. He returns to the kingdom of Yr, where he enters into an arranged and unhappy marriage, but has a son he loves dearly. Over the years, he forgets about his promise to the Sly Fish, and one day brings his family to the beach. When the boy takes his first steps into the ocean, the Sly Fish pulls him under. But as soon as the boy's head comes under the surface, the Harp of the Deep claims him; it's in his blood to return to the Abyssal Plain. Thus the Sly Fish loses as it always must, and the Queen receives something but not what she asked for, and the Prince of Yr pays for his idiocy in blood.

They make camp under the boat, which is much more roomy when turned upside down. Two of the anglerfish have disappeared off to somewhere, leaving the third one to float alone under the ceiling. Director and Journeyman embrace in the fore, both moved to tears by the story's unbearably sad conclusion. Nestor is sound asleep at the aft, chin reduced to a rashy mess from the ocean god's beard. Apprentice lies in the middle, still in her fish costume, listlessly flopping her ventral fins. The Sly Fish's dreams of love, just a little love, insist on crowding her thoughts. It's the loneliest creature in the ocean. She eventually falls asleep, lulled by the sound of blood rushing in her ears and the rhythmic rasp of the anglerfish's lantern scraping the hull.

Apprentice wakes with flailing arms. Her hand hits something soft, and Nestor mutters irritably in his sleep. Disturbed by the motion, silt tickles her arms. It's crept up on her while she slept. In the pale light of the anglerfish's lantern, everyone else seems to be asleep. Apprentice is wide awake. She gently catches the anglerfish in her hand and crawls out from under the upended boat.

The water outside is crushingly cold, pressing down with the weight of the world. Outside of the tiny sphere of light the weakly struggling anglerfish gives off, darkness is absolute. Apprentice slowly steps out onto the abyssal plain, back bent under kilometers of sea. She can just about see her own feet shuffling through the silt, sometimes disturbing the odd object: a Roman coin, a blackened silver fork. Blind and transparent fish appear in the gloom. Some of them follow, the wanderers between the depths, those who still have eyes; they flash arcane patterns at her in fluorescent blue and green. In the utter silence, Apprentice thinks she hears the sound of flutes far away, a discordant piping.

Eventually something winks in the distance, like a star, or another swinging lantern. Apprentice strides toward it.

It's a bathyscaphe, round like a fruit, with a porthole out of which spills a warm yellow light. The winking light comes from a small headlight at the top. There's a face in the porthole that doesn't belong to anyone in the company.

It's a stranger. A woman. She motions for Apprentice to walk around to the other side of the bathyscaphe, to where a little airlock protrudes from the sphere. Apprentice turns the wheel, stops inside, closes the door and watches the water drain out. The inner door opens, releasing a puff of warm air.

The woman is in her fifties. She's dressed in dungarees and a knitted sweater, one of those sweaters with a pattern that stops at the waist, because the rest is for tucking inside the dungarees. She's barefoot. Apprentice wonders if the pattern belongs to a particular family.

"Hello," says the woman and peers at Apprentice. Her eyes are a little glassy and unfocused.

"Hello," says Apprentice.

They look at each other in silence.

"You're dressed like a fish," the woman remarks.

"I play the Sly Fish." Apprentice flaps a ventral fin.

The woman nods slowly. "All right. I'm Ada." She extends a hand.

Apprentice shakes it. "Apprentice. Are you the audience?"

"Apprentice what?"

"Just Apprentice."

"I see. And what are you doing here? It's the bottom of the ocean." Ada tilts her head. "I expect you're a hallucination. I must be suffocating already."

"You're very pink," says Apprentice. "People who suffocate are blue. Anyway I'm here with the troupe. Are you the audience?"

"Troupe?"

"Yes, the troupe! We're here!"

Ada shakes her head. "What do you do exactly?"

"We . . . " Apprentice falters. "It's we who play the stories."

"Never heard of you."

"So you're not here to watch?"

"I wasn't supposed to be here in the first place." She extends a hand to caress a cluster of tubes running down the inside of the wall. "This is the *Laika*. I thought it was a fitting name. Small, round, and lonely, you know?" Ada chuckles to herself. "Anyway, I was taking her for a test drive. Checking the systems and such. We were going into the Mariana Trench, eventually. Not the Challenger Deep, mind. Not yet. Anyway, I knew there was a risk. Should have known better than to christen her *Laika*. I'm Laika, really."

"Uh," says Apprentice. "Who's Laika?"

"She was a dog that . . . oh, never mind. The point is, the cable snapped and so did the oxygen line." Ada pauses. "Actually I'm not sure. I think maybe something chewed on it. It's gone, anyway. I'm done for."

"Oh," says Apprentice absently. She swallows at the knot that's suddenly formed in her throat.

"I'm just waiting for the oxygen to run out." Ada sighs. "Didn't expect to meet anyone down here, though. Nothing like you. So I'm probably hallucinating already. I should be grateful, I suppose."

Wet warmth spills down Apprentice's face.

"Oh, come on," says Ada. "You don't have to feel sorry for me."

Apprentice wipes her face with her fin, her stupid fish fin. "I . . . " The word drowns in a sob. She tries again. "I thought you were here to watch." She pulls snot back into her nose. "I keep telling Nestor, what if there's no one who's watching, and he says of course they are, but I was always unsure, and now that you were here I thought . . . but you're not. You're just here to die."

Ada's expression goes from surprise to faint disgust to a sad smile. She pats Apprentice on the shoulder.

"You know, I'd love to watch a play."

Apprentice returns to the boat, waking the rest of the troupe up with her shouts: "We have an audience! We have an audience! A real one!"

"We always have an audience," mumbles Nestor.

"Not like this. I promise."

They walk the boat over to Ada's bathyscaphe, and there's Ada in the window, smiling and waving. Under the cover of the boat, Director slips into the Queen's regalia, Nestor fastens his beard and Journeyman combs his long hair.

In variation number two of *The Prince and the Abyssal Queen*, the Prince regrets his return to the surface. Deafened from his journey upward, he can hear nothing but the whisper of the ocean, which fills him with longing. The daylight is too bright, the air too dry, the servants too clumsy. One moonlit night, he wades out into the sea where the Sly Fish comes to fetch him.

"Where is my present?" says the Sly Fish in the silent language spoken on the ocean floor. "You must keep your part of our agreement."

"You will have it soon," says the Prince.

Of course he has no present for the Fish; he has not yet fallen in love, but he is trying to buy time, so that the Fish will at least deliver him to the Abyssal Plain.

The moment his feet touch the silt, the Queen appears.

"I miss the sea," says the Prince, "but I will not be your slave. I will stay here as your courtier."

"Very well," says the Queen. "I have treated you unfairly. As compensation, you may stay in my court for a year."

As the Prince takes the Queen's pale hand and looks into her transparent eyes, he finally realizes the truth. "I love you," he says. "You need no spell but your own self."

The Sly Fish collapses in horror. Of all the living things the Prince loved first, it had to be the Queen. And as the Queen created the Sly Fish out of her own flesh, it would be like promising the Fish to itself, which is impossible. The bargain is null and void, and the Fish once again thwarted. Apprentice lives out the Sly Fish's misery in an exquisite dance.

Ada watches through her porthole the whole time. As the ensemble take their bows, she claps her hands soundlessly. She is beginning to look a little tired, but nods with a smile when Director mimes her an offer of another variation.

When the God of the Abyss has deus ex machinaed, and the Sly Fish's devilish attempt at toppling the Queen has been averted, and the Queen and the Prince live happily ever after, Ada has slumped forward with her forehead against the glass. Her broken eyes stare blindly into the ocean gloom. The Company takes one last bow.

"We had a spectator," says Apprentice.

"We always have spectators," says Nestor. "But this time we had a spectator *up close*."

"Can we do it again?" says Journeyman.

Director nods.

They perform all the varieties of the Abyssal Plain stories, including some where the Sly Fish also gets to live happily ever after, until they have no more and Journeyman is so suffused with the Prince's feelings he cannot speak his lines and Director must hold him while he cries. By then most of the anglerfish have left.

"I think it's time to move on," states Director.

They bring the bathyscaphe, Apprentice tugging it along on a string. Ada is such a good and appreciative audience, and they have many more plays for her to enjoy. Transporting the bathyscape on land will be a problem for later.

OUT IN THE DARK

LINDA NAGATA

—◆—

After three years out in the dark among the rocks, Kiel Chaladur docked his prospecting boat, the *Gold Witch*, at Sato Station. It had been a successful voyage. He'd found, sold, and sent in-system a comet remnant dense with volatiles. The money he'd taken for it had made his fortune and that of his two-person crew—but wealth wasn't the only prize Kiel Chaladur brought back with him. Against all odds, he'd found a wife out there, born and grown among the rocks.

Shay Antigo stepped through the port gate at Sato Station as an unknown citizen. She was met by the local watch officer of the Commonwealth Police, who confirmed her status and shepherded her through the process of establishing a legal existence. As I read the brief, it struck me as an engaging story—and almost certainly untrue.

Three days after the initial report was filed, I was assigned to investigate.

"Name?" the brisk voice of a Dull Intelligence asked, prodding me into wakefulness within the close embrace of a cold-sleep pod.

I drew a deep breath into lungs that had never been used before. "Zeke Choy," I answered. And then, anticipating its next question, "Field officer, Commonwealth Police."

I'd entered cold sleep in the inner system, ghosting to Sato Station as an electronic persona, completing in eleven minutes a journey that would have consumed years if I'd traveled in physical form. The arrival of my ghost had wakened a stored husk—a precisely grown replica of the body I'd left behind. By Commonwealth law, a citizen was limited to one physical incarnation at a time. It was part of the definition of being human, and no exceptions were allowed, not even for an on-duty cop. So that version of me that I'd left behind eleven minutes ago would remain locked down in cold sleep until I'd finished my investigation at Sato Station.

When the DI was satisfied that I fully occupied my new platform, it opened the cold-sleep pod. I got up, glancing at my projection in the image panel. I stood taller than most men, strong and lean and with a stern gaze. It was a physical appearance considered ideal for instilling order and compelling respect. I'd been less imposing when I'd entered the academy, but judicious engineering during my months of training had given me the size and bearing of a cop.

A locker linked to my identity popped open. Inside was a uniform and a collection of glossy gel ribbons in different colors, each ten centimeters long and containing a different chemical armament. They were the standard weapons of a field officer. I laid the ribbons against the skin of my forearms and they adhered immediately, syncing to my atrium—a neural organ used by all residents of the Commonwealth to link mind and machine. Of course, Daoud Pana, the watch officer I'd come to investigate, would be similarly armed, but if it came to an overt confrontation, I had an authorization level that would shut down every one of his police-issue weapons.

A DI popped into my atrium with a map of Sato Station. Around the wheel, the location of each one of 308 current residents was marked, some as stationary points, others on the move, all of them tracked by their implanted ID chips, marking them as citizens of the Commonwealth. Neither Shay Antigo nor Kiel Chaladur was among them. The brief I'd scanned when the case came in had told me they'd already left through the station's data gate, their ghosts bound for Mars. Chaladur's other two crew had taken off to destinations of their own, all of them authorizing that the husks they left behind be dissolved, indicating that none of them intended to return.

Officer Pana's position was highlighted. He was the only officer-in-residence at Sato Station, and presently he was outside the station itself, doing a walk-through inspection of a recently arrived ship. He didn't know yet that he was suspected of colluding to manufacture a new identity for Shay Antigo, and that an investigation had been launched against him. And he didn't know I was here. The alert that would normally have gone out when anyone arrived in the cold-sleep mausoleum had been suppressed.

I pulled on the uniform: knee-length shorts and a black pullover with long sleeves designed to hide the gel ribbons. I was not a police officer by choice. I'd been drafted into the service, where it became my duty to enforce the Commonwealth's conservative definition of what it meant to be human: a singular physical existence and no invented quirks—only natural, human physiology, except that aging had been ruled a defect and had been cured, and we were all allowed an atrium.

In my primary duty I was the watch officer at Nahiku, a small celestial city in the inner system, but every cop takes on special duties too. Mine was to investigate other officers. Commonwealth law is strict, punishment is severe, and the unfortunate reality is that cops hold the power of life and death over the citizens of their watch. Some cops are judicious, but others take advantage of their power. It was far more likely that Daoud Pana was a corrupt cop who'd fabricated this case for some kind of payoff, than that Shay Antigo was truly unknown.

Using my atrium, I linked into the station's surveillance network to get a first look at my quarry. Pana had set a flock of inspection bees buzzing through the levels of the newly arrived ship, each one of the tiny devices sending back datastreams as they used their camera eyes to search every visible space, and their molecular sensors to taste the air and assay the surfaces.

I commandeered an inspection bee that was hovering close to Pana, turning it around so that its gaze fell on him: a man as tall as me—cop height, we called it—with a broad face and wide nose. No smile at all as he questioned the crew. Brusque and imposing in his black uniform. I watched him for several minutes, and found him neither overly friendly nor overly strict. If he was looking for a bribe or a kickback, I couldn't see it. Maybe he only did favors for those who took care to make arrangements in advance.

The mausoleum was in a warehouse district, so at first I saw only small transport robots in the main corridor, but as I rounded the wheel I encountered people. They looked at me in idle curiosity, until they realized I was not the cop they'd grown used to seeing. Then their expressions shifted—sometimes to curiosity, but often to shock, and even fear, because the appearance of a strange cop at a remote station like this one could only mean trouble.

I was still watching Pana within my atrium, and I found it easy to mark the precise moment someone pinged him with the news that I was there. His jaw tightened. His lips drew back. He looked up, looked around, until he spotted the surveillance bee that I controlled.

"On my way," he growled in an undertone. Then he barked at the cargo ship's three-person crew. "Do *not* attempt to disembark. You have not been cleared and you will not be allowed to pass through the station gate."

He waved off their objections, and, leaving his flock of bees to continue the job, he left through the ship's lock. The station gate knew him, and he was allowed back into the wheel with only a cursory surface scan.

Pana worked out of an office with a small reception room in front, and interrogation and lab space in the back—a standard layout for watch officers. I let myself in, did a quick walk-through of all the rooms, checked the storage lockers, and then took a seat on a couch in one of the interrogation rooms to wait for his arrival. A DI had put together a summary of the surveillance recorded on the day the unknown citizen, Shay Antigo, had come in. I used the time to review it.

After Kiel Chaladur's prospecting boat had docked at the station, Daoud Pana had gone onboard to do a walk-through inspection just like he'd done today with the cargo ship. Inside the *Gold Witch*, he'd been met by Chaladur, a small man with sharp features and not much flesh beneath his charcoal skin, whose thin shoulders were a little hunched even in Sato's low-gee. The video identified Shay Antigo as the woman standing beside him. They both wore their hair close-shaven, but that was the limit of the resemblance. Shay stood taller by a few centimeters, with a wide, pretty face, and demure features. My DI confirmed the anxiety I sensed in her gaze as she eyed Officer Pana.

In the video, an alert spoke, notifying Pana that she lacked an ID chip. He drew back. His hand rose slightly, and I knew the gel ribbons he carried under his sleeve were gliding down his forearm to his palm, where they would be ready for use.

But no resistance was offered—not by Shay Antigo, or Kiel Chaladur, or his two-person crew. Shay submitted to every scan and test that procedure required, and in the end Pana certified her as a previously unknown citizen, granting her a Commonwealth ID chip, and a new existence without the burden of a past.

Daoud Pana was scowling when he strode into the interrogation room. He didn't bother with introductions. "It's the unknown, isn't it?" he demanded. "I knew trouble was coming when I filed that report."

"You filed it anyway."

"It was my job to file it. I conducted the required investigation and I drew the only conclusion I could. She was legit. No record of her in the system. I didn't write her a free pass."

Every celestial city operated under its own charter, but in matters of molecular science, biology, and machine intelligence, Commonwealth law applied, and it was merciless. For most violations, those found guilty-with-intent faced death as a penalty. Their only recourse was to disappear and become someone else.

Cops had been bribed before.

I studied Pana. My DI had flagged no lie in his words, but some people learned to fool the DIs.

Pana's lip curled. "You've done this before? Investigated another cop?"

"I've been called out a couple of times."

"Yeah? And were they experienced cops that you investigated? Or were they new?" He shook his head. "You don't have to answer. Only the new-issues are dumb enough to think they can pad their accounts and no one the wiser."

It was true that most cops who leaned toward corruption were exposed in their first years, but I saw it as a Darwinian process. Those who didn't get caught early were the smart ones, and the longer they survived, the smarter they got, and the smarter they got, the more they tried to get away with. People believe all the time in the magic of their own success.

I guess I believed in magic too. "Tell me about her," I said, confident that I could discern his thoughts and intentions by watching his face, hearing his voice, even though I knew moods could be quirked, and voice rhythms could be steadied with tranks.

He scowled and shook his head again, making it clear I was wasting his time. "It's all in the report. Everything. You've watched it, haven't you? The detainment vid?"

"Tell me anyway."

Pana understood that the best way to get rid of me was to cooperate, so, sitting on the couch opposite mine, he started talking, his deep voice flat and fluid, as if he was reading the words.

"I meet every ship that comes in. It's not strictly required—I could just send the bees to inspect the cargo—but it's my policy. We're spread thin out here. Indies working out in the rocks, they'll try out illegal biomods, figuring it's long odds on getting caught—but eventually everyone comes in. If they know I'm going to be down at the gates every time, they might think a little harder before they push the wall."

I hated to admit that this made sense to me. People get in trouble when they think no one's looking. But did the threat of a cop waiting at the station gate really balance out the temptation that grew in the dark, in those years when you were out in the rocks, alone with your thoughts, and free to run any experiment your tools allowed? Pana must have seen a lot of mods over the years, but his arrest record was thin. Sometimes that's a sign of a good watch officer—someone who knows how to make a mess quietly disappear before it's ever official. I'd done it myself. People who understand their jeopardy willingly cooperate, and life goes on.

Pana leaned back in his chair and scowled again. It seemed to be his default expression. "So, this prospecting boat came in. The *Gold Witch*. There'd been chatter about it. They hit big. Found a snowball. Auctioned it for a nice gain. That was over a year ago."

"It took them that long to come in?"

He nodded. "They were way out in the dark. God knows what goes on out there."

"What did go on?"

He shrugged. "No one patrols the Belt. There's no way to really know, but everyone's heard stories. Sometimes these prospectors let the dark inside their heads, and they decide they don't want to come back. They find a rock far away from everything, and they tunnel it, set up housekeeping, declare themselves beyond the bounds of the Commonwealth."

The legality of independent holdings was heavily debated, but the cold fact was that the Commonwealth police could establish jurisdiction simply by force of arms. It was only ever a matter of time.

"And Shay Antigo? She came from an indie holding?"

Doubt shadowed his face. I caught it before my DI did.

"That was her story. I couldn't refute it. The DI picked up a low level of deception, nothing clear cut. I think she'd been in a station, but not one with a police presence."

"So she wasn't scanned."

"That's my guess. I couldn't ask for a full history without cause."

"Being an unknown citizen isn't sufficient cause?"

"Didn't seem like it at the time." His eyes narrowed, and he leaned forward. "You think she's a fake because she doesn't look like a freak, because she could hold a human conversation, because she knew what a cop was, and what it meant to get through a station gate."

I nodded. "She grew up in the dark."

He shrugged. "She has an atrium. You know how indies get by out there? They live through their atriums. They spend all their downtime in virtual worlds, a lot of 'em based on real places. It's the damnedest thing. They interact with machine personas, learn the accent and habits of some city they've never seen, and you'd swear they were birthright citizens. Indies can masquerade as anyone they want to be."

A DI brought a report into my atrium. I'd sent it hunting through Pana's background. He'd saved up a good-sized nest egg. He had family, but none that were close. He'd been married twice, both had ended when the contract expired. He held citizenship in two celestial cities and one Earth nation. Nothing in his record was suspicious . . . but he would have known to keep his record clean.

He was studying me, no doubt using the same interpretive DI that I was using to assess his mood. "You won't find anything," he told me in a satisfied tone. "Because there's nothing to find."

I took a walk around the ring of the station. Eight ships were docked to the gates, one of them the *Gold Witch*. Kiel Chaladur had ordered it cleaned and refurbished immediately on his return. It had been on the market a little more than forty hours when it sold to an experienced prospector. I found her supervising the loading of food and supplies for what looked to be a long expedition. Pana must have warned her I was on my way, because she didn't look surprised when I came through the station gate—a small, gray-eyed woman, soft and plump, with a smile sincere enough to hide mass murder behind it.

Most people don't smile when a Commonwealth cop comes to ask them questions.

"Do you want to inspect us?" she asked me without preamble.

The cleaning crew had been through. We both knew there would be nothing to find. "Did you know Kiel Chaladur?" I asked her.

Her eyes were fixed on me with eerie intensity. Despite her smile, my DI picked up hostility, but I didn't think it was directed at me. "I knew him. I crewed with him twice, way back. He had no luck then, so I moved on."

"He had luck this last trip."

"You never know when it'll hit."

"What do you know about Shay Antigo?"

She crossed her arms and her smile disappeared. "It's hard to believe sometimes, what goes on out there."

"What do you mean?"

"Just what I said. Some stories are hard to believe."

"You've been prospecting a long time, haven't you?"

"Nineteen years. Six expeditions. Maybe this time I'll finally hit gold."

"You must have seen a lot out there."

Her smile flashed, fierce and bitter. "I wouldn't say that. The Belt's a big place. But it's mostly empty space, and you know what? There's nothing much to see out there. There aren't any mysteries. Just a few rocks and a whole lot of silence."

"No mysteries? No unknowns?"

"Not that I've ever seen."

Pana's report included a copy of the *Gold Witch's* log file, which had a few entries from the start of the voyage, but nothing more. As an owner-operator, Chaladur wasn't required to keep a log and I guessed that if he'd kept a record at all, it was locked up safe inside his head. I knew that he'd set out with three souls aboard and returned with four, and that there was no data gate on the *Gold Witch,* and no crèche in which a fresh husk could be grown. So Shay could not have been regenerated. She had come from somewhere: either an independent holding as she'd claimed, or from another boat.

I sent a DI to look for any discrepancies in ship crews: a list of the dead and the missing, all those who had never come back. I set another DI to assembling a map of radio chatter recorded over the years, to see if a pattern could be recovered suggesting a habitation in the sector where Kiel had found his strike.

Then I went over the DNA evidence collected by Pana. He'd run a standard assessment of Shay's profile and had found no matches in the Commonwealth central library. I decided to look deeper.

I ordered the sample pulled from storage and subjected it to a more detailed profiling. The new report turned up a fair amount of radiation damage— nothing that couldn't be repaired, but highly indicative of time spent in the rocks. More suspect were the splices: well-known segments of artificial DNA with no actual function. They'd been devised as copyright marks, but they'd been adapted for use as placeholders that could throw off a basic DNA match. It was possible Shay had inherited the splices, but a smart amateur with the proper molecular toolkit could easily achieve the result.

The two reports I'd requested earlier had come back while I was working. The radio map failed to show any consistent point source of chatter in the sector Chaladur had been prospecting, but the list of the dead was more interesting. It was longer than I expected: a hundred ninety-seven who'd had to be restored from backups. Most had died of injuries or air loss, with a few suicides in the mix. Nearly all the bodies had been recovered and the organics recycled.

A single exception caught my eye. Thirty-two years ago a prospecting boat had disappeared with its crew of three. No one had ever reported sighting the ghost ship. No word had ever come of its crew.

The radiation damage in Shay's DNA sample had indicated a long time spent in the rocks.

I sent a DI hunting information on the missing crew—and in seconds it returned an initial report: only one of them had been female, her name was Mika Brennan, and the last time the local database had been synced with the Commonwealth central library, the version of her that had been restored from backup was living with her family in one of the oldest celestial cities, Eden-2. I compared her video ID with that of Shay Antigo and found marked differences. Mika's face was more slender, her features sharper than Shay's, her eyes green not gray . . . but people changed their features all the time.

I wanted to hear what the surviving Mika Brennan knew about her long-ago disappearance. So I generated a ghost within my atrium and, leaving my physical presence behind to continue searching the historical records, I passed through the station's data gate.

There is no awareness during the journey between data gates and none in the receiving platform. It's like stepping through a door, from one world to another. In my next moment of awareness I existed in a virtual reality within Mika Brennan's atrium, one that perfectly reflected the hard reality around her.

Most people get nervous when a cop comes to talk to them. Mika Brennan only seemed perplexed. "Officer Zeke Choy?" she asked, her head cocked to one side. "The request said you had questions? About my death?"

We were in a park in Eden-2. Not far away, two young girls were climbing boldly through a jungle tree. They shared Mika's lean features, her thick, dark hair, and the deep, clove-brown color of her skin. "Mommy, watch!" one of them shouted.

My ghost existed within Mika's atrium. I was written onto her reality, so that from her perspective, I was as solid and real as the two kids—but from the kids' perspective I did not exist. At best, I was a phantom that only Mommy could see.

"I'm talking," she called back to them. "We'll play in a minute." Then she cocked an eyebrow at me. "At least I hope you don't plan to detain me?"

"I'd like to hear the story of what happened to you out there. It might have some bearing on a current case."

"I went out there more than once, you know."

That surprised me, but then I hadn't bothered to pull a complete dossier.

She nodded. "I don't remember what happened that first time, of course. That branch of my existence ended. I presume there was an accident. After a couple of years with no word from me, no word of my ship, my parents sought permission to restore me from a backup made before I left." Her gaze followed the progress of the girls as they clambered around the jungle tree. "It shook me up, knowing I'd died out there. But that other me, she'd sent a lot of video journals to my parents. I watched them, and I came to understand that I'd loved it out there in the raw, cold dark. We went places where no one had ever been, where no one was ever meant to be." She grinned. "And anyway, she'd left me with a lot of debt. So I went out again, and twelve years ago, I got lucky. We found a rock loaded with rare metals. Everything I owed to anybody was paid off, with wealth to spare, so I came home." She nodded at the two kids. "And started the next phase of my life."

I asked her if she knew anything about indies living in holdings out in the rocks, raising families there. She snorted. "Fables. People like to tell stories, but that's all they are. I remember one time, a couple, a man and a woman, were marooned on a rock. They did some excavating. Lived there a few months, while their ship self-repaired. And then they got the fuck out of there as soon as they could." She looked up at me, with an open, honest gaze that I admired. "No one lives out there. Not that I ever saw, or heard, and I was out there more than twenty years."

I asked her if she'd ever go out again, and she laughed, bright-eyed and buoyant. "Maybe. We have forever, don't we? To do anything we want?" She turned again to the kids. "Not any time soon, though."

"So you didn't leave a husk out there?"

"No. You understand . . . the years in micro-gee, the constant radiation. Even with ongoing repairs, the integrity of the husk is doubtful. If I ever go back, I'll start fresh. I can afford a new husk. So I had my old one dissolved and the matter sold off. There's nothing of me out there anymore."

Back at Sato Station, I started to pull Mika's DNA record from her latest scan, but I hesitated. There were implications to what I might find. Mika could be drawn into this case, even if she had no immediate involvement . . . but I needed to know what had happened, before I could know what to do—and I didn't have to include everything I found in my final report. So I went ahead with it, comparing DNA samples from Mika and Shay. And I found what I expected: outside the spliced segments, and with some exceptions for radiation damage and repairs, they were a match. Somehow, the Mika who'd disappeared thirty-two years ago had finally made it back from the dark.

How had it happened? And had Officer Daoud Pana known the truth? Had Kiel Chaladur given him a cut of the profits for certifying Shay as an unknown citizen? Or had Pana been played?

I'd been so sure of this case when I started, but I wasn't sure anymore.

I got up from the couch where I'd been working. Pana was in his office, talking to a ghost I couldn't see, but he turned his attention to me when I looked in the doorway. "I'm leaving."

"Did you find anything?" he asked in a cold voice. "Should I start preparing a defense?"

"I'll let you know."

It was time for me to go to Mars.

On Sato Station I returned my husk to cold storage, and a moment later in my perspective, I opened the eyes of another husk, this one in the mausoleum in Confluencia, the largest city on Mars.

Confluencia was a good place for someone with a questionable identity to disappear. The city snaked for hundreds of miles through Mariner Valley and the Martians weren't big on security, so no gates existed between the city's districts. A person could live a hundred years in Confluencia and never be scanned.

I wondered about her, this unknown, Shay Antigo, who was once Mika Brennan. What had she done out in the dark? How had she lost herself for so many years? And why had she finally chosen to come back . . . as someone else?

The Martian husk was heavier than the one I usually used, adapted to a higher gravity, but it didn't take long to master my balance, and within minutes I was dressed and armed and heading out into the city.

In most parts of the Commonwealth, locating a citizen is a simple matter of having a city's network of listening posts search for the ping of an ID chip, but the Martians of Confluencia liked their privacy, and the only listening posts were on the walls of government buildings. So I did the next best thing: I followed the money, requesting real time account activity for both Shay Antigo and Kiel Chaladur.

In a city as vast as Confluencia, it's impossible to go anywhere without constantly paying for transportation, and given that my quarry was newly flush with money and fresh from the austerity of the Belt, I expected to see frequent transactions mapping a bright electronic trail.

To my surprise, it took more than an hour for the first transaction to occur, but a location was attached to it, a mall, a few kilometers down the valley.

By the time I reached the mall, a second transaction put their location at a designer clothing store—and minutes later, I saw them. Kiel Chaladur looked taller and more robust than he had stepping off the *Gold Witch* at Sato Station, while Shay Antigo looked much the same, her hair still close-cropped and her soft features suggesting nothing of Mika Brennan's bold face.

I didn't need to talk to them right away. I was close enough to register the ping of their ID chips, and that made them easy to follow. So I tracked them through two more stores, then waited while they had a drink. Anything said or done in public was likely to be recorded, either by a security device or a passerby, and then all chance of discretion was gone. So I bided my time, and after an hour my patience was rewarded when Shay and Kiel disappeared through the lobby doors of a luxury hotel.

I gave them a minute to get onto the elevator before I followed. The hotel yielded their room number, and before long a chime was announcing my presence at their door.

No one answered, not for three minutes or more. I imagined the frantic, whispered conversation that must be going on inside as they considered why a Commonwealth police officer stood on their threshold. The door finally slid back to reveal Shay, gazing up at me with a sorrowful look.

Asking no questions, she stepped aside—a gesture I took as an invitation to enter. Kiel stood on the balcony, a glass-encased ledge that overlooked the canyon as it wended south. His arms were crossed over his chest and from the look on his face, I knew that if there was no glass barrier there, he would enjoy throwing me over the precipice.

The door whispered in its tracks, and as it closed my atrium informed me I was signal-dead, cut-off from the network. I froze in shock—though I should have expected it. This was a luxury hotel, offering the best, including electronic privacy, and Shay and Kiel were fugitives.

I sent a gel ribbon gliding down my arm, wondering what else they were willing to do to protect themselves.

Shay circled around me, keeping her eyes fixed on me as she gave me a wide berth. "What was I supposed to do?" she asked me in a desperate voice.

"What *did* you do?" I wondered.

"I came in from the dark. That's all."

"So it is you? Mika Brennan. How much did Officer Pana make you pay for your new identity?"

My DI confirmed the confusion I saw on her face. "It wasn't like that—"

"And her name is Shay Antigo," Kiel interrupted, stepping in from the balcony.

"Kiel, please. You need to stay out of it."

He didn't listen, no more than I would have in the same situation. "She *is* Shay Antigo. An unknown from the rocks. The cop at Sato confirmed it and we didn't pay him a damned thing."

"It's true," Shay said. "There was no record of me in the system, because I came to life out there in the rocks."

The DI studied her, and to my surprise it did not suggest she was lying— but then, time changes the way we define ourselves. "You came to life after Mika Brennan died?" I asked her.

"The prospector? I heard that story. It was a long time ago."

"She never went home."

"That's not what I heard. I heard her family restored her from backup. I heard she made it home."

Kiel added, "I heard that too. I heard she made a fortune, and set up a life for herself."

"A good life," Shay added, tears glinting in her eyes. "A life I wish I'd had."

"What happened out there?" I asked her.

She turned and, crossing the room, she sank slowly onto a sofa.

"There was an accident."

Mika Brennan had been one of a crew of three, on a prospecting boat running on marginal resources. They'd found a comet remnant and knew their fortunes were made. Engines were fixed to the ice, but there were fault lines that they didn't detect, and when the engines fired, a massive chunk of ice sheared away and struck the ship.

"We lost all power," Shay said. "The reactor was damaged. It was only a matter of time before the radiation killed us. But we figured if we could get back to the main ice fragment, eventually another prospector would come along and we'd be found."

So they wrestled cold sleep pods and a bivouac tent to the hopper bay. Mika jumped first, taking her pod with her. And because she was the lightest, she took the bivouac tent too. Her hopper was fully fueled, and she made it.

Her companions didn't. They overshot the ice, and had no fuel left to turn around.

The three of them talked, until the distance was too great for the suit radios. Then Mika bolted her cold sleep pod to the ice. She set up the bivouac tent around it, inflating it with the last of her air reserve. Then she stripped off her suit, and before the cold could kill her, she climbed into the pod.

"I thought it'd be a year or two before I was picked up. But it was thirty-one years until Kiel and his crew found me, and by then I didn't exist anymore. I mean, the Mika Brennan of thirty-two years ago, *she* no longer existed in the Commonwealth. It was too late for me to go home."

"Shay's harmed no one," Kiel said gruffly. "She's done no wrong."

I wished that was true. "She lied about her name."

Shay wasn't going to give in easily. "It wasn't a lie! That name didn't belong to me anymore—and you know what would have happened if I tried to take back my life."

I didn't answer right away. Instead, I walked out to the balcony, thinking about the choice she'd had to make. She could have claimed her true name. It was her right. She could have seized back the life of Mika Brennan, but she'd chosen not to.

I felt a shy touch against my arm and looked down, surprised to see that Shay had followed me. "She's the version of me that my parents know. She's the one my brothers and sisters love. She's the mother of my children. For thirty years we've grown apart, and it's too late now to ever put us back together."

Shay was right, of course. A ghost can join its memories to its progenitor, but only for a while. As they grow apart, it becomes impossible to meld one mind with another. But in the Commonwealth, individuals are allowed only one physical copy of themselves.

"If I took back my name," Shay said, "I'd take her life away. Do you think my family would even want me if I could do a thing like that?"

"You know it doesn't work that way," I told her.

We all want to see shades of meaning in what we do, but Commonwealth law is absolute. It's concerned with limits, not justice.

"You were first," I said. "She was second. Under the law, that makes her an illegal copy."

"No, she was approved. There was a legal certification."

"Based on the assumption of your death, but you're not dead. She's the backup, so you have precedence. You knew it. That's why you decided to disappear."

Shay stared out at the sprawl of gleaming towers and the canyon's seemingly infinite walls. Kiel came to stand on her other side. He took her hand.

"What was I supposed to do?" she asked me—that same question she'd met me with when I first came in the door. Only this time, there was steel in her voice, the stern conviction of a woman who'd survived out in the dark, alone. "I gave Mika my life. I didn't ask for it back. I just wanted my own."

"And Officer Pana gave it to you."

"He's a good cop," Kiel said. "With a reputation for playing fair. Not like the jackboot cops of the inner system."

I wasn't going to argue. Pana had done a better job than me. Sometimes, being a good cop means knowing when to stop asking questions.

I'd been so determined to prove that Pana had been paid off, I'd followed this case too far. If I reported what I knew, the life of Mika Brennan, resident of Eden-2, would be forfeit as an illegal copy of a living person. And when she was gone, Shay would be tried and convicted of counterfeiting her identity, and she would be executed for it. Hardly a just reward for what she'd been through, and what she'd given up.

I drew a breath and let it out slowly. "The radiation out there in the dark," I said. "It damages the DNA. The repair programs . . . sometimes it seems like they're copying patterns from the wrong DNA source."

"Like a cousin or something?" Kiel asked tentatively. "Even a sibling?"

"Like that," I agreed.

Daoud Pana had known the truth, I didn't doubt it, and he'd chosen to let Shay through the station gate because it was the right thing to do. Now I'd entered into his conspiracy.

I turned and walked back across the hotel room. The door opened at my touch. I felt my connection restored. Looking back at Shay and Kiel, I saw they were still standing together on the balcony. "Thank you for answering my questions," I said. "Assessments such as this one help us maintain the integrity of our officers. My report will state that, based on the evidence, Daoud Pana followed procedure and made the right call. This case is closed."

I took a step into the hall before I thought to turn back. "And welcome to the Commonwealth, Shay Antigo. I think you'll like it here."

"Better than the rocks," she allowed, in whispery relief.

I nodded and went on my way.

In my mind I started composing my report. I would have liked to open it with the truth: that strange things happen out in the dark.

But I don't want anyone else to get curious and start digging into this story . . . not until the law is changed—and that will happen. It must.

ON THE ORIGIN OF SONG

NAIM KABIR

Note: Doyen-Générale, enclosed is the full catalogue of documents pertaining to the individual known as Ciallah Daroun, as per your request. I only ask that you keep the card registries intact, so that they may again be archived in a timely manner.

—*Commissaire de l'Académie, Aveline Duvachelle*

• • •

Envelope 32-R (Reichstagg's Report):
Stamped with Gold wax and Phoenix of the Sunrook solarium.
1117th turn, 4th moon.

Chercheur-Commandant Dupont,
    The Sunrook Conservatory had received reports of a large stranger harassing citizens for three weeks. This giant was dressed in grey-black rags, with his face covered in the way of highwaymen. He was estimated to stand at a height of twenty-one hands, with a wide frame, though other physical features were obscured by rough cloth. His voice was not of this world, and was, as one report mentioned, like two fists of shale scraped against one another.

    The individual was first confronted by Conservatory marshals outside the solarium, at which time Lecteur-Marèchale Ericcson charged him with the illegal hunting of solarium sunbirds. I commanded the stranger to identify himself, and he gave the name "Chala Darune," then remarked that he was not a hunter but a naturalist. He cited the sixth and tenth Academy commandments before requesting that he be allowed to continue on his way. The marshals and I issued a warning but complied.

    Later the Cartographer Brecker sent word of the individual Darune and further aberrant behavior. After observing the Cartographer's griffins, Darune had asked to buy inks and vellum, paying with foreign iron ingots. Subsequently, without any use of Song, the stranger Darune swallowed the inks and stamped his foot upon the vellum. According to the esteemed

Cartographer's testimony, writing had filled the vellum in the colour of the imbibed inks, all while the stranger remained silent.

Though these actions were not illegal, they were deemed deviant, and so Lecteur-Marèchale Davisson, Chanteur-Marèchale Redwyn, and I set off in pursuit. Darune left the city of Sunrook by dusk and disappeared beyond the Shore into the Desert. However, he left deep footprints in which we observed rich printed text. The marshals and I immediately made plaster casts rubbed with charcoal and copied in triplicate, all of which have been delivered to you with this letter.

Salut,

Connaisseur-Captaine Reichstagg

• • •

Charcoal scratching,
Package 32-R (Reichstagg's Plaster-Casts):
Original plaster in Le Conservatoire de l'Académie.

Note: Observe how the letters are formed in such a way that it appears to have been printed from a Press. The font has not yet been identified.

—*Commissaire-Aspirant de l'Académie, Jean Lamarck*

though I have seen the phoenixes from my home on the mesa, they are quite something else when observed from close by. They seem to be wholly domesticated here in Sunrook, though this Mountain is their native, wild ground. I saw one hunt a small desert mouse outside of my home-tent on the mesa, though here in the city they are fed by the solarium's keepers. It appears they are used for the delivery of messages. The ever-present constantly shifting lights in the night sky, I surmise, are correspondence flown between all the solariums of the world.

This phoenician Song seems to be composed of augmented chords in the high-to-mid octaves, and is associated with their sun-bright light. Jaanbab Al-Marack would have us believe that these traits are passed on in the blood, but I find it curious that the other wildlife on this Mountain is possessed of the same traits.

The gryffones, both captive and wild, also Sing with augmented and major chords, though they are lower in octave, and they too spit hot, bright light. The peoples of Sunrook mirror these sounds with flutes and Woodwinds, and much of their Music is focused upon production of warmth and illumination. Even during nighttime, the Songs of the population keep the Mountain lit as if it were high noon. Behavior seems to be shared among the people and their Singing beasts, as well: all seem haughty and highbrowed, and lend themselves easily towards arrogance.

I inquired as to whether much intermating occurs between the Men and Beasts of the region and was immediately reported to the Conservatory authorities for speaking deviant words and causing a disturbance. As it was taken as an insult, I believe it can be fairly inferred that no such mating occurs, and that these Musical traits are not passed in blood lineage.

My hypothesis remains that an environmental factor inspires the abilities of Song, perhaps in the weather or geography. I am convinced that it must relate to <u>sound</u>: it cannot be sheer coincidence that the mesa of Benihajr is dry and in the still and silent doldrums, and that my people cannot Sing.

• • •

Testimony Thirty-Three:
Spoken by Seer Halldën.
Stamped in Court, with Ash wax and the Dragon of Gjallihöll.
Transcribed by Chasseur-Ècrivain Aimée.
1117th turn, 7th moon.

O, he came past the Cave-Gates in black robes and stood like a stormy mountain, but he told us he was a scholar. Though he didn't have the look of you Academy men. Too humble. Too hushed. And you letters-men never feel the need to cover your face—but he did.

He paid Hunter Gudrun with gold bars he called dinars—and that was enough to buy old-fashioned Gjallihöll trust—and even though the stranger wasn't man enough to show his head, he did give us his name: Çal Darwun. That was enough to convince the hunter band to take him down past the Chamber-Gates and Smoke-Gates on their expedition to bring back a Dragon's tooth.

When offered a lyre or horn, he held it like a leg of ham to be inspected and handed it back, saying he needed no such weapons. Though he did want the hunters to demonstrate its use, which they did, proudly Singing smoking fireballs and arrows of earth into the cave walls. During camp he would scribe some words with those feet hidden under his robes, using some strange Song that none of the hunters had heard of but assumed was some smart scholar-Music that could even be played silently. Whatever the Song was, he could write a page a second and make copies quicker than lightning. Most of the men couldn't read, but he gave them some calfskin pages as a gift, which of course they took graciously.

It was four days until we reached the Hindrunlands, where the salamanders stop lighting the tunnels with their tails and where the shadow dances with the light. That's where the Dragons live. But Çal told us that he'd continue on into the dark, if we wanted to join. We laughed, of course. Höllmen don't go into the dark—that's a place fit only for the skuggaver, crawling blind and praying to their slinking shadow gods. We would not go, we came for

Dragons, not to visit the stinking Skuggstað. Skugg-sty, more like. He offered more dinars, but we wouldn't step a foot where the salamanders won't light the way.

That's when the big gaurrin pulled out a jar of salamanders and tickled them on their heads, shining light in twenty different directions. He'd been taming them while we were busy scouting tunnels for ash piles and claw sharps, the mad fool. Somehow, his hands never burned, and he never shouted when he poked their flaring little bellies.

But no. We had come for Dragons, not shadows. We would not go. So he disappeared into the dark alone. Half the men were mauled by a big brute Drake after the next sleep, and we ran back home. Some of the men blamed the stranger Darwun, said he was a bad Song and a bad omen; even went as far as to ask help from the Academy's nearest Conservatory. The big man came up from the tunnels after some of the hunters had already sent a sunbird from the solarium, with more of that inked-up calfskin written so evenly with his feet. Me and a couple of the others who meant him no ill took the gifts and thanked him.

It was only 'till after he left that I could read the words, and then I realized.

You know, most Höllmen don't read, but I'm a Seer. I fill our Libraries with our Records, and I know 'em all, too. We don't let anyone take our Memories, even you schoolboys who stooped so low as to come into our caves to take 'em. They just get better hid.

In Gjallihöll, our books still remember the Slave-Men even when *we* don't. Our books still know the man-mountains your stinking Academy sent to the Desert Table, and I know who this Darwun is. Should've known it the first time he talked in that cracklin' brimstone voice.

The question is, what'll you do to help me forget?

Note: Unfortunately, I could not conduct further interviews. Seer Halldën tragically succumbed to a lethal heart tremor a few days past. His family was generous enough to donate some of his belongings to the Academy, including several books and documents.

—Chasseur-Ècrivain Aimée

• • •

Halldën's vellum;
Printed by Ciallah Daroun.

in the magma vents located deeper down. I am familiar with desert monitors, but based on the bones I've glimpsed in the Gjallihöll long-halls, Dragons are of a completely different family. The legs are oriented underneath the body instead of splayed to the sides, and thus they walk in a manner closer to four-legged birds than to lizards.

However, there is nothing avian about their Song. It is a strong major chord that evokes an explosive flame, a kind of roaring trumpet that clearly inspired the Gjallihöll hunting horns. A similar mood is produced by the Salamanders I have used to light my path through the darkness and down into Skuggstað. Though they employ a different methodology: they pluck membranes on their skin to produce the Music. I believe the lyres and lutes endemic to the magma-city are inspired by this finger-plucked Songstyle, and all the sounds employed suggest power and confidence. Fitting, for a place as industrial as Gjallihöll.

As of yet, my voice is still unable to carry any of the chords or melodies I have learned of; nor are my hands delicate enough to handle any instrumentation. Al-Marack would say this is due to my inherent disability: a child of the Benihajr makes no Music. They may build material objects and more Benihajrin, but not Song.

But I am closer to gathering evidence for my hypothesis that Song is inspired in animals and Men by their environment. I have noted that the volcanic activity that surrounds the Höllmen produces, mostly, the same major chords (of all octaves) observed in the local wildlife.

The same is the case in the deep ice caverns of the Skuggstað. A phenomenon similar to Benihajr freeze-trays occurs in these caverns: deep ground water is heated to a boil in the upper rock strata by magma, and the thin water layer below is cooled and frozen by the quick evaporation. When this ice slips through the porous limestone of the Skuggstað, it appears as if it is snowing underground. The cool air causes a chill wind to stream through the stalactites, producing a very gloomy minor chord.

This is the same chord hummed and chanted by the skuggaveri peoples who reside here, as well as the whitebats and centipedes. Their Song seems to be able to sap vitality in the same way Sunrook Songs may restore it; for when I approached their village for the first time, their cantos drained the life from my Salamander lantern and left me in weary darkness.

Their language was similar enough to Gjallish that I could understand them, and I gathered that their existence was one of scavenging and worship. I asked them why they chant so much and so often, and they replied that it is in tribute to the Music that has always blessed the Skuggstað.

Every moment of their day rests in somber prayer. To whom or what, I cannot say, though I did notice a curious phenomenon: the chants of the skuggaver are able to freeze water. This suggests that the snow from the ceiling may be produced on the power of their Song alone, and not by my theorized evaporative cooling. The implication, then, is that the gloomy minor chord echoing through these halls may have been here long before there was any wind, or any deep village.

The source of this sound, I've not yet deduced.

• • •

**Official Statement of Resignation,
Emissary-Chevalier Donall,
Dispatched by Runner from the Exile's Plateau.
Delivered 1117th turn, 7th moon.**

Doyen-Générale Lenoir,

I cannot in good conscience continue my tenure with the Academy.

We have imposed an immoral exile upon the Benihajrin for far too long. It is not permissible to punish an entire race of thinking creatures solely because they appear to defy one hundred years' research. It would not be permissible even had we collected one *thousand* years of research.

The Plateau-Men are an honorable folk, with much industriousness, kindness, and genius. I have seen burn-engines rivaling those that bear the höllmark, created from scarce iron pulled from the mesa. I have seen reagents not unlike linren medicines made from the lizards and shrubbery, and I've borne witness to their vast and rich Living Libraries. The lifetime of a Plateau-Man always goes recorded; for instead of some limbs, most have fashioned movable presses that work and create without the slightest use of Song.

They have advanced much since the days they were created. The old accounts describe dumb husks that followed Sung commands, but now they speak and write as well as any man in Voix Royaume. It is time to accept that the *Histoire Naturelle* is incomplete or incorrect: the Song of life is not reserved just for Man and Beast. It was not bestowed by a favoring Cosmic Composer. It *can* take form in sand. It can manifest upon the Silent Mesa. It can fill rock Plateau-Men with souls and much wisdom.

They are languishing in isolation, and the doldrums here doom them to perpetual quietude. Many are more frightened of Academy retribution than they are tired of the silence and loneliness, but there is one who is ready to defy you.

I have had no qualms helping him slip past the Banished Gates, and once he has seen the whole of the world, I will have no qualms welcoming him back to his people.

—*Emissary-Chevalier Donall*

**Formal Complaints for the 2nd week, 9th moon, 1117th turn.
Stamped in Verdant wax with the Mill of Port Falsa's solarium,
Compiled and sent by sunbird by Connaisseur-Captaine Marethari.**

Dawnday

Daly O'Shea: Today some more bhaidinmenn sailors came into my bar and caused a disturbance, damaging the property in an amount summed to more than 200 keys. It was again the Captain Oisin Niall and his first mate,

Conor Darragh. I am calling upon the Falsa Conservatory marshals for their immediate arrest or fine.

Actions taken: Visit to the City Inn, issuing of debt papers to the Captain of *Oileand's Oar*, Oisin Niall.

Mornday

Merrill O'Donnel: Bhaidinmenn have played violin and cello all night, bringing seawater and wind into the coastside tenements and flooding several rooms. I couldn't see any of their faces, but they sounded like the seamen under the command of Captain Niall.

Conor Darragh: I've heard that some lily-livered cathairmenn have been filing complaints about us, so I'd like to complain a little, too. One, I'd like to complain about these cathairs being gutless bastards who've settled on foreign coasts instead of keeping on the search for the homeland. Two, I'd like to complain that they seem to have replaced their bollocks with windmills and waterwheels. Three, I'd like to complain that they use the Menn Songs of the high seas for their bleeding farms and bakeries. Last, but most definitely not least, I'd like to complain that they're all twats.

Actions taken: Attempted confiscation of bhaidin instruments, resulting in a small skirmish and stand off. Captain Oisin Niall has agreed to pay further damages as well as 100 extra silver keys in exchange for the right to keep all Musical tools, citing that they are necessary for sailing and thus the men's livelihoods. The marshals accepted and the matter was closed.

Noonday

Cashel McBride: The fugitive of the Academy is being harbored by the bhaidinmenn on the docks. I and several other witnesses had seen him without his mask as he tried to board a ship out of the bay. The sailors would not allow us to collect him and our bounty, and hid him on their ship.

Captain Oison Niall: The unruly citizens of Falsa have attempted to illegally board my ship this morning, looking after some stone-armored giant they believe is on my boat. Three sons of the McConnels and one from the McBrides were caught trying to force open a porthole after midnight.

Conor Darragh: The cathairmenn are a bunch of bell-ends.

Actions taken: Reminder delivered to both cathair houses and bhaidin boats that the complaint filing system is not to be abused.

Duskday

Kayla McKinley: *Oileand's Oar* is housing the criminal posted on Academy bounty, and they won't release him. He's a wanted criminal, marshals. I don't want him so close to my children.

Douglas O'Brien: Oisin Niall is protecting that stone-knight giant from the Plateau. The academy-men have done told us he's some kind of dangerous monster, but the bhaidin are keeping him in their hold!

Conan McOrrin: I heard the bhaidin arguing yesterday morning with a giant stranger, and they made him show his face and tell them his name. He was clearly the rock-armored beast from the herald's speeches, the one from the Desert Table. But after, they let him stay in the belly of their ship! I call for the immediate arrest of the captain of *Oileand's Oar,* and any crew that are directly involved.

Conor Darragh: Yep, still twats.

Captain Oisin Niall: The cathairmenn will no doubt be coming to the Falsa Conservatory with more complaints about me and my ship, so I want to make a few things clear.

One: No, I don't think that the citizens of Falsa are a bunch of coward-bred, artless swine that have given up on the search for Oileand and deserve to be scraped and stabbed upon the reefs; Two: I don't want to wreck all the cathair farms and take their windmakers and seasingers before they can ever use them again for their safe and landlocked mills; Three: I'm not harboring Ciallah Daroun upon my ship and most certainly am not shielding him from prying Academy pig-dog jailors; and Four: *Oileand's Oar* will definitely *not* set out across the Dividing Sea at eventide.

· · ·

Poems From Across the Dividing Sea.
Delivered by Blue Bird of Paradise to Voix Royaume,
Stamped in Marine wax and Anchor of Port Hearn,
Attached to sunbird by Connaisseur-Captaine Jamaira.
1118th turn, 2nd moon.

1. Mottled green and rippled light
2. shine through the leaves of Lùguo
3. tonight, the giant
4. trees and cascade falls
5. make a man feel small when he
6. comes to the port across the Dividing Sea.

7. The poet's breath fights the Forever Storm,
8. that rages and threatens to blow away
9. this page and its brothers
10. the fast wind it smothers and covers
11. his hands with flown leaves so his works
12. are slathered with lemon and lime.

13. Pink blossoms fly too and then comes

14. the rain, so he builds a red fire to

15. Heat up the words

16. that have frozen shivering in his throat

17. and by the light of that warmth, he leans

18. to see the truth hidden here

19. in the wind-whipped air.

Note: The meter and structure of the verse suggests that this letter was a cipher from an embedded agent across the Dividing Sea. The actual message lies in every third line.

—Commissaire-Aspirant de l'Académie, Triame Puissant

• • •

Copy of hidden text, from Poems Across the Dividing Sea.
Written in Lemonbleed ink, Uncovered by the heat of a flame,
Copied by Commissaire-Aspirant Triame Puissant.
1118th turn, 2nd moon.

The Benihajr fugitive came to the Linren port by way of a bhaidinmenn ship, and stayed for a period of weeks. He has now set off for the floodplain village of Shobdtho but has left several copied texts among the natives. Some are even in the local Linwen language. By my best estimation . . . this Ciallah Daroun is no threat. Your messages made me expect a violent revolutionary, but by all accounts he is just a researcher, like the Academy's best. I suggest that you hold off on your invasion of the Exile Plateau—the escapee seems largely innocent. Here is a sample of his writing:

Time aboard the bhaidinmenn ship *Oileand's Oar* has been educational, for the sailors themselves agree that the power of their Song comes from their surroundings: the Sea. The waves in calm and stormy conditions produce sustained chords, and the seamen add to the rhythms with cello and violin. The wind and waves shaped by this concerted Music propel the ship at remarkable speeds. This constant velocity is what allows the bhaidin to be such successful trawler fishermen and continue to search for their lost home island in such a systematic manner.

I would have enjoyed visiting Oileand, but the bhaidin say that it disappeared while the fleet had left to do battle with the armies of Voix Royaume in the 1000th turn, as though some maelstrom had swallowed it up overnight. More likely, some of the civilians on the island used the Sea Song to move it while it came under a flanking invasion by the Royaume Navy.

After three moons of us combing the oceans, an attack by roving Sea Serpents caused damage that could only be repaired in dry-dock. The creatures were unlike anything I've ever seen: slick skin that shone in the sun, and an attack with such coordination that I'm almost certain they could speak to each other. There were no visible heads, though the bellies of the beasts were covered in sucking discs, and sometimes hook teeth. They damaged the keel of the boat and punctured the starboard side, forcing us to begin an immediate tacking course towards the Linren port city of Lùguo.

The trees here are unlike any I have ever witnessed. Some resemble giant 300-hand willows with leaves dangling down to the ground, studded in pink blossoms and swaying in the constant wind. There are many that are simple wooden spires that spike into the sky, but closer inspection makes it evident that these are man-carved constructions that make up the bulk of the vertical Lùguo city.

The locals have learned to use Music to stitch skin and bind flesh, using sustained chords of the latter octaves. Exploration of the surrounding forest revealed the presence of a colossal waterfall that they call Ryuzu, which produces the same chords at a constant rate as the water thrums against the bottom rocks. Determined carp can be seen leaping in pools alongside the tributary cascades, splashing a rhythm to accompany the Music. Some of the local monks lead meditations among the boulders and add the power of their throats.

The same chords are apparent in the Mushigong tree-spider population, as they halt the dragonflies and giant wasps in the air with their sustained Song while on the otherwise silent hunt. A satellite village called Tiánzhong also uses the chords, but in a version much bassier and lower than that in Lùguo. Their Musics appear to condense water vapor and cause storming and lightning. According to the Tiánren who live in this cloud village, the Forever Storm in the northeast rainforest is caused by a giant black and white bear they call the Dai-de-Shiong, constantly Singing brontide beats into the earth with padded paws and clicking claws.

Though amazing, the peoples of this forest tell me far more spectacular creatures inhabit the border of the jungle and the floodplains. I hear tell of blazing jungle cats and perfectly beautiful Birds of Paradise, and wise elders of the Shobdtho village. At noon I will gather

• • •

General Request regarding Ciallah Daroun.
Drafted by Doyen-Générale Lenoir for the Esteemed Board,
Stamped in Murex wax and the Book of the Academy.
1118th turn, 4th moon.

I understand there is some talk that the Golem from the mesa is no danger, and I would like further your education. The *Histoire Naturelle* is quite clear in this matter:

"Hypothesis speaks of a heartbeat's Song and the soul's ringing Music that flows through the veins of all men and the beasts and the trees, though hard Theory from these hundred turns show the clear lack in the sand, rock, and earth; and so our Conclusion must focus on building *histoire naturelle* of the moving and breathing and all the combined Musics of the beauty we call Life."

—Observations 1:11

We have built our entire natural history upon the breathing and dying, and would have continued at peace if not for the invention of the Stone Slaves. They produce the illusion that dead rock and ash can be as ensouled as a man and cause our libraries to crumble as the foundations are jerked from beneath.

Their very existence causes a questioning of the Academy's teachings and thus our *authority*. If the public realizes even once that this Ciallah Daroun is not just some giant in stone armor or black cloaks, but a seemingly thinking and feeling thing made from earth, where will we be?

The hunt for him must continue, and we must go forward in sending Orchestral Marches to invade and clear the Plateau. Without Music they will be an easy target and we will suffer minimal casualties.

By the power vested in me by the Convergence of Scholars, I ask as Doyen-Générale for full control of our Military Symphonies and the right to march North past the Shore into the Desert. It is a course as clear as physics and as simple as astronomy:

"For the path to the solution follows the star of Parsimony: it is the quick and easy, the simplest of all the choices that are set before you; and with this guide in the mind and eye, you may walk forward with palms raised and faith that the laws of nature will ease your way."

—Recommendations 2:15

Salut,
Doyen-Générale Lenoir

• • •

Dialogue With A Boulder.
Written on Jungle Broadleaf,
Discovered during Royaume-Shobdho Exchange.
Found in the 1213th turn, 7th moon,
Estimated to be written in 1118th turn, 5th moon.

The elder stretches out, and the honor guards shift to allow entry to the guest. The elder begins to speak in characteristic slow, creaking lilt.

Elder: You have been waiting to speak with us for several weeks, now.

Visitor strides to the center of our Orchard, just beyond the reach of our limbs.

Visitor: I have. I am a traveler, learning as much as I can about the world.

The elder considers this weightily.

Elder: We are of a kind, then. Though we cannot travel, we would always like to learn.

The others shift eagerly as if buffeted by the wind, leaning in to listen to the words.

Visitor: What would you like to know?

Elder: What is your name? What is your nature? Where do you hail from? What is it like? Why are you here?

The guest reels his head, overwhelmed, but begins speaking calmly.

Visitor: My name is Ciallah Daroun. I am a scholar and a traveler from the mesa of the Benihajr, a dry silent place far across the Dividing Sea, at the center of a distant continent. I have come here to study. Animals and peoples, I wish to learn of them both.

The silence hangs heavy for some minutes.

Elder: Animals and peoples? Ah, but we are neither!

Visitor: Perhaps not animals, but you are surely peoples. You think. You speak. You are like me in many ways—I have even learned that you maintain libraries like that of my homeland, recording all that you speak and hear!

Visitor brandishes columns of steel and rock in the place of legs, showing the typed letters that shine there. A wooden groan escapes from the Orchard as we all shift to see.

Elder: Yes, our lives are writ upon our leaves, as yours are pressed upon your pages.

The elder's branches curve and his bark softens, as he observes the strange guest.

Elder: Thank you, for this learning experience. What is it you wish to ask?

Visitor pauses.

Visitor: I want to know how you Sing.

The Orchard regards this silently.

Visitor: The venomous Jholbagh and fiery Rabikhan, you keep them at bay simply by Singing. The floods that threaten to kill this forest, you dam them solely with Music! But you are like me. Where I am made of rock, you are wood. I believed that Song may be inspired by the symphonies of nature, but I've been away from my quiet home for more than a turn, and I am still silent! I have been beginning to think that it's true, that my people are stone and that stone cannot Sing, that they'll forever be cursed to wallow in dusty tents while the worlds of men rose ever-upwards, but then I saw *you*. How do you do it? How can a tree make Music?

The wind rustles our leaves as the visitor breathes heavily.

Elder: You have already lost hope?

The guest sinks to his knees.

Elder: Yet you have no reason to. We can feel it inside of you.

Our roots grow tender and lick the vibrations from the soil.

Visitor: What do you feel?

The Orchard sighs a happy, knowing sigh.

Elder: The beating Song that pulses with the slow confident rhythm of a mountain range. The Music that streams from your soul.

The bark creaks as the elder mulls hard truths.

Elder: It will take hard-fought struggle and strife to truly set it loose—and much sacrifice. The first Singer amongst the Trees lost his heart of Oak to a lightning storm, and the first man to Sing in the southern reaches swam to the top of an enormous waterfall. But perhaps your trials are nearly done?

We shake consoling leaves upon the boulder guest's shoulders.

Elder: Reach deep inside, Scholar Daroun, and brace yourself. You'll find your Song, somewhere.

Note: Are you sure you want to read this, Doyen-Générale? It may be distressing to see your grandfather's death recorded in such a clinical fashion. No one truly has a heart of stone, sir. Think on it.

—*Commissaire de l'Académie, Aveline Duvachelle*

• • •

Coroner's Report 55-D.
Signed by Docteur Depardieux, Senior Investigator.
Stamped in Black wax and Knife of l'Hôpital,
Sent by crow from the field.
1119th turn, 1st moon.

On the morning of Duskday on the Second Week, the Hospital had received word from the Palace chambermaids that an investigation would likely be required in the second-last chamber-room on the northwest side of the building. A short time afterwards, the death of the patient had been reported to the Hospital and to the Conservatory of the Academy.

Location: Chamber-room marked '3,' northwest corner of the Voix Palace.

Witness Statements: Palace residents Elizabeth Curvoire and Lilian Verve had first seen a team of five strange men dragging a large black sack into the room. They commented that muffled moans had been heard emerging from the bag, before it was taken behind the door. They had also heard speech while outside the chamber and deduced that some sort of violent interrogation had been occurring inside. Mademoiselle Curvoire testifies that a discordant Song was heard as well as a series of terrible screams. Lilian Verve paraphrases the interrogation thusly:

Q: Why have you left once more? This was no mere stroll past the Banished Gates.

A: I have seen too much of the world to stay locked away.

Q: Would you like to suffer more of this minuet, instead?

A: I have suffered dragon's flames, shadows, sea monsters, and a host of things in the rainforest that would make your skin crawl and your blood curdle. Your torture is nothing.

Q: What were you doing, hunting in the Royal Forest?

A: I needed more stretched hides.

Q: Why?

A: That my people might be free, even if I will never be able to hear it.

It was at this point that there was only more screaming, and both ladies sent a crow to bid me to the Palace.

Scene Description: Guest bathroom number 3 of the Voix Palace. Decedent is lying supine, with head pointing north. A series of chamber pots have been emptied over his head, and their shattered remains lie in piles to the left and right of the body. White scratch marks in the hardwood follow the body from the room's entrance to the location of death.

Body Exam: Body is positioned as described above, with several pots' worth of human waste emptied atop his head and chest. Body shows signs of late rigor mortis, as the limbs and torso are stiff to the touch. Body is cool throughout, and initial measurements show it is already at ambient temperature. Erratic etchings in the hardwood floor at the place of death suggest severe seizures, and when correlated with Mademoiselle Verve's testimony, indicate use of a Minuet of Pain. Patient is wearing rough-woven black cloth, much weathered and very well used. Most of the robes appear grey due to wear and sun bleaching of the dye. An incision was made with 2⊠ scalpel to completely remove the cloak, and it was revealed that the body is not quite human. Its segments consist of several boulder-like pieces hewn into the shape of a man, though they now appear cracked and broken by repeated trauma. Some iron is incorporated with the stone body in the lower segments and implanted with a series of sliding block type-letters arranged in various formats. Face is frozen in the expression of a pained shout.

Evidence: In haste, the offending interrogators had left behind a single desert flute, carved only to hold discordant notes.

Notification: Academy Conservatory immediately contacted after conclusion of the report. Investigation handed over to Chanteur-Marèchale Corvais.

• • •

Gold-level Resource Request,
Sent by Runner from the Banished Gates,
1119th turn, 1st moon.

PUSH AHEAD WITH ORCHESTRAL MARCH.
DRUM BEATS HEARD FROM ATOP THE DESERT TABLE.
EARTHQUAKES WRACKING THE DOLDRUMS.
WHOLE MESA BEATING LIKE A DRUM.

STONE MEN ON THE WARPATH.

• • •

Note: Doyen-Générale, the history of the war can be found in the Military Records outside the Academy campus. I'd ask why you bothered to comb our archives when you can simply leaf through the Living Libraries, but I suppose I already know your answer. As you say: we must always see things from another point of view. It is a lesson I've learned well, and for that I am grateful.

As thanks, perhaps you will accept an old, dusty gift from an old, dusty curator. A hand-drum of Naturalist Daroun's personal make, in the central glass gallery of the Conservatoire. As far as I can recall, it is the very first.

—*Commissaire de l'Académie, Aveline Duvachelle*

CALL GIRL

TANG FEI

Translated by Ken Liu

1

Morning climbs in through the window as shadow recedes from Tang Xiaoyi's body like a green tide imbued with the fragrance of trees. Where the tidewater used to be, now there is just Xiaoyi's slender body, naked under the thin sunlight.

She opens her eyes, gets up, dresses, brushes her teeth, wipes away the foam at the corner of her mouth with a towel. Staring at the mirror, all serious, her face eventually breaks into a fifteen-year-old's smile. Above her, a section of the rose-colored wallpaper applied to the ceiling droops down. This is the fourth place where this has happened.

My house is full of blooming flowers, Xiaoyi thinks.

"There must be another leak in the pipes," her mother says. "There's a large water stain growing on the wall."

They sit down together to have a lavish breakfast: soy milk, eggs, pan-fried *baozi*, porridge. Xiaoyi eats without speaking.

When she's ready to leave the apartment, she takes out a stack of money from her backpack and leaves it on the table. Her mother pretends not to see as she turns to do the dishes. She has turned up the faucet so that the sound of the gushing water is louder than Xiaoyi's footsteps.

Xiaoyi walks past her mother and the money on the table and closes the door. She can no longer hear the water. It's so quiet she doesn't hear anything at all.

Her knees shake.

She reaches up for the silver pendant hanging from her neck, a dog whistle.

2

The school is on the other side of the city, and Xiaoyi has to transfer buses three times to get there.

Li Bingbing once asked Xiaoyi whether she wanted to get a ride with her in Bingbing's father's car. *Being chauffeured around in a BMW is very comfortable.*

But Xiaoyi had said no because she didn't think it was a big deal to ride the bus. School was so boring anyway; it was like riding another bus. *Since she had to ride the bus, as it were, what did it matter where she got on?* Of course, Xiaoyi didn't say *that* to Bingbing. As a general rule, she doesn't like talking, unless it's to *them.*

They would never appear at the school, which makes school even more boring. Xiaoyi sits in the last row, next to the window. All day long, she sits and broods. Whether it's during class or recess, no one bothers her.

She has no friends. No one talks to her. No one sees her. The girls like to form cliques: those with bigger boobs in one clique, those with smaller boobs in another. Once in a while a busty girl might be friends with a flat-chested girl, but that never lasts.

Xiaoyi is different from all of them. She doesn't wear a bra. Never. Many found this odd. Then, the girls found out about *them.* So, wherever Xiaoyi went, there would be a sudden circle of silence. But as soon as she had left the area—but not so far that she couldn't hear them—the buzz of conversation would start again: "Look, that's Tang Xiaoyi!"

Yes, that's Tang Xiaoyi. No one knows what to do with her. If it weren't for Bingbing, who sometimes got obsessive, Xiaoyi would have a completely peaceful life.

"Hey, you know that Li Jian and Ding Meng are together now?" says Bingbing.

It's the end of Geography, the last morning class. Bingbing sits down next to her and starts babbling. Once in a while, she pauses in her monologue and takes a drag from her cigarette. When she's finally done with the cigarette, she can't hold back any longer.

"Xiaoyi, you know that lots of people are talking about you behind your back. Is it true? Are they all really old and really rich? Are they richer than my dad? How much do they pay you each time?"

Xiaoyi rests her chin on a palm and stares out the window. The lunch queue outside the cafeteria grows longer and longer, all the way to the wutong tree at the school gate.

Just then a nondescript little car stops at the gate. The car door opens, but no one gets out. He's waiting, waiting for Xiaoyi.

Xiaoyi stands up slowly and strides out of the classroom, her steps lightly echoing against the ground, her hair waving over her shoulder, as though a breeze is blowing in her face.

There's no sound around her. Sunlight slices across her shoulders like a knife blade.

• • •

3

"I did as you said and switched to a different car. Can you tell me why? It's . . . unusual."

The middle-aged man turns to gaze at Xiaoyi. This is the first time they've met. The two are squeezed tightly into the backseat of the little Daihatsu Charade: the schoolgirl in her dark blue, short skirt, the man in his elegant *hanfu*. Once in a while, in a moment of carelessness, their knees bump into each other and separate immediately.

In the driver's seat is the chauffeur, his uniform neatly pressed, silver epaulettes on his shoulders, brand-new white gloves on his hands.

"You brought a chauffeur." Xiaoyi frowns.

"I haven't driven in a long time."

Xiaoyi turns her eyes to the flow of traffic outside the window—which is not flowing at all. It's Friday, and the traffic jam started at noon. It doesn't really matter. They're not in any hurry. The man takes out a handkerchief to wipe the sweat from his brow. The Charade's air conditioning isn't working—unpleasant for those used to Cadillacs.

"Where to?" he asks.

"Nowhere."

"Okay. Just so long as you're happy."

They are always so good tempered, treating her like a pet, adoration mixed with contempt. Before they really start, they're all the same.

Xiaoyi turns to give the middle-aged man a careful look. His eyes are dark, strange but friendly. They seize her and don't let go.

"What do you want me to do?" she asks.

"Like you do with the others."

"So you haven't thought through what you want, yourself."

The man laughs. "I just can't be sure that you can satisfy me."

"You're greedy." Xiaoyi winks. Her eyelashes are long and dark, fanning seductively.

The man's Adam's apple moves up and down. The way Xiaoyi's shirt clings to her body tells him that she's not wearing a bra.

"Let's start now," Xiaoyi says.

"In the car?"

Xiaoyi reaches out and closes the man's eyelids. Her hands are ice cold.

4

The man opens his eyes and looks around. Nothing has changed. The Charade is still the Charade. The road is still as congested as a constipated colon.

But the chauffeur is gone.

He's an experienced man. He knows when he must remain calm.

"They're right about you. I guess I finally found the right one."

"You can straighten out your legs. There's lots of legroom."

The man does as she suggests. He sees his own legs slowly passing through the front seat, as easily as passing through a shadow. He relaxes and leans back. Much more comfortable. He has paid the fee and he should enjoy it; this is part of the transaction.

For a long time now, private clubs, custom services, and other forms of high-class entertainment haven't been able to satisfy him. He's been looking for special experiences, like this girl. The web site described her this way: *I sell stories. Special. Expensive. No substitutes. You must come in a beat-up car. You must bring enough money. No matter what happens, you may never come see me again.*

His right index finger trembles. Everything is set. He sits, expectant. He begins to believe that she can offer him what she claims.

"I'm ready," he says.

Xiaoyi nods. Without him noticing it, she's now sitting across from him, in an armchair located where the driver's seat ought to be.

"I'm going to ask you again: what do you want?"

"I have everything."

Xiaoyi says nothing as she stares at the man. Suddenly, she takes off her shoes and tucks her feet under her on the armchair. She curls her whole body into a ball and sinks into the soft white leather.

"When you've thought it through, tell me. I'm on the clock, by the way."

This is a difficult client, she thinks. *He's going to wear me out.* Xiaoyi decides to close her eyes and conserve her strength.

"Why don't you tell me something special, something I don't have or haven't experienced?"

"A story," Xiaoyi says.

"That's right."

Xiaoyi opens her eyes, but keeps her body in the same position.

"They tell me that you're really good, unique. But you're expensive. All those who had used your services, they say that you . . . " The man seems not to notice that his voice is too excited.

The noise of other cars honking interrupts his speech. The sounds seem to come from far away. He begins to feel that something is wrong. The air feels thin; the sunlight seems harsh; a susurration fills his ears. He has trouble telling the density of things. This is another world.

The man stands and walks around the confines of the shadowy outline of the little Charade. But the walk takes him ten minutes to complete. He's never even dared to think that the passage of time can change.

When the man sits down again, Xiaoyi says, "I'll tell you a gentle story."

"I've heard such stories. They're liquid. Sticky, wet, filled with the smell of tears and mucus. I don't like them."

"Stories are not liquid." Xiaoyi glares at him.

Before the man can argue with her, something tumbles from above and falls into his lap. It's warm, furry, and squirms around: a pure white puppy! Round, dark eyes. Wet nose. Oh, it's sticking out its pink tongue and licking the man's finger.

"Stories are like dogs," Xiaoyi explains. "When called, they appear."

"How did you do this?" the man asks, carefully cradling the puppy and watching it suck on his finger.

"With this." She shakes the pendant hanging from her neck.

"A dog whistle?"

"Only I can work it. When stories hear my call, they come, and then people take them away." Xiaoyi leans up. "So, do you want this one?"

The man looks at the puppy. "I'd like to see some others."

5

"How about this one? Do you like it?" Xiaoyi asks.

The man shakes his head.

Xiaoyi glances around the car. It's filled with dogs she's called here. They sit quietly, their faces expectant. More than twenty pairs of eyes stare at her innocently.

The Rottweiler that she just summoned pushes against her hand with his wet nose. Xiaoyi absentmindedly strokes his ears. She's tired and cold. The cold feeling is close to her skin, like a soaked-through shirt.

"Do you need to take a break?" the man asks. But his eyes say *Keep going! Faster! Faster! I want my story!*

Xiaoyi stands up and grabs the man's hand.

Wind against their faces. An unfamiliar smell.

The sky spins. An ancient, somber prayer song echoes around them.

The herdsmen have lit a bonfire of cypress leaves. Goshawks gather from all around and land with puffs of dust around them.

The old priest-shaman sings with a trembling voice. He sharpens his knife and hook until they glisten. The living bow their backs as the dead lie with their naked chests exposed. The goshawks flap their wings and take off, circle in the air, cry out.

In the far distance, at the limit of vision, bright flags flap in the wind.

They're standing under a big sky, on a limitless prairie, bathed in bright, harsh sunlight.

The man blanches. "What the . . . ?"

"To simplify somewhat, this story is too big. Moving us is simpler than having him move." Xiaoyi moves to the side.

The man now sees the hound. Though, strictly speaking, it's not a "hound" at all.

It's gigantic. Its mouth is wide and its nose broad. Its teeth are as sharp as knives. It crouches, not moving, only its thick fur waving with the wind. Ancient blood thousands of years old courses through its veins. It is the embodiment of the cruel and strict law of nature. It is a sacred beast.

"Do you like him? He's very expensive."

"You're saying that I can bring him with me?"

"Yes, if you're willing to spend that much."

"A very high price to pay, and not just in money?"

Xiaoyi's throat tightens. She nods.

The man looks at the massive hound, which still isn't moving but seems to arrogantly take in everything before him. In the end, the man shakes his head.

"Any others?"

"You are sure you want to keep looking?"

The man doesn't say anything. He doesn't need to.

Saaaaa-saaaa. The sound of the wind comes from Xiaoyi's chest: thin, dry, lingering, like sand passing through an hourglass.

6

Everywhere they look, it's the same. The world is one substance. Bright light sparkles from the deep blue.

They're at the bottom of the sea. The water pushes and pulls noiselessly.

Xiaoyi's hair and skirt drift alongside the kelp.

The man opens his mouth. No bubbles. There is no need to breathe at the bottom of the sea.

"This is my last story."

The man's eyes quickly grow used to the ocean. He looks around but cannot see any dogs. "Where is it?"

"The dog is only a shape, to make them easier to call and to be accepted. But here, you see them in their native state. No, that's not exactly right either. Fundamental nature consists of zeros and ones, part of the ultimate database. This sea is an illusion, a projection of that fundamental nature. The sea of data is too big to be compressed into the shape of a dog. Of course, you may still call it a dog. From the perspective of the story, nothing is impossible."

Xiaoyi pauses and takes a drink of seawater. It's salty, and makes her even thirstier. "This place has existed for a long time, and it's too strong. My computing power is insufficient to alter it, to call it. I can only . . . be called *by* it."

"You've brought others here before?"

"Most people are easier to satisfy."

"What happened to those you did bring here?"

Xiaoyi smiles without answering.

The man can feel the transparent currents—1100110111—pass by him. They'll flow to the countless trenches and caves at the bottom of the sea and leave this place behind. Some day, this ancient source will dry up, too. But not now. As far as the man is concerned, it is eternity.

He takes a step forward. The sea trembles; the sky trembles; everything in the sky and in the sea trembles. If, someday, a bird dives toward the surface of the sea, then he will feel the excitement and joy of that dive through the seawater, as well.

"You like this?"

"Yes."

"It's even more expensive than you think."

"I know."

"What I mean is that I don't have any way for you to bring it with you."

The man is silent. Far to the north, a part of the sea roils with dark, surging currents. He can no longer think it over.

"Then I won't leave."

Xiaoyi bites her lips. After a long silence, she opens her mouth, and lets out a word soundlessly.

A school of orange lyretails swims between them, obscuring their faces from each other.

When they can see each other again, both are smiling.

7

Six p.m. Rush hour. A tidal wave of humanity emerges from the subway stations, fills the shops, the roads, the overpasses.

Xiaoyi gets out of the Charade. This is the world of the present. Dusk burns brightly and gently. Pedestrians part around her.

Behind her is her shadow, stretched very long. Together, they walk slowly, with great effort.

Xiaoyi lifts her hand to find the dog whistle hanging around her neck, touches it.

They exist. They've always existed.

She's not alone at all.

She does not cry.

PARANORMAL ROMANCE

CHRISTOPHER BARZAK

—◆—

This is a story about a witch. Not the kind you're thinking of either. She didn't have a long nose with a wart on it. She didn't have green skin or long black hair. She didn't wear a pointed hat or a cape, and she didn't have a cat, a spider, a rat, or any of those animals that are usually hanging around witches. She didn't live in a ramshackle house, a gingerbread house, a Victorian house, or a cave. And she didn't have any sisters. This witch wasn't the kind you read about in fairytales and in plays by Shakespeare. This witch lived in a red brick bungalow that had been turned into an upstairs/downstairs apartment house on an old industrial street that had lost all of its industry in Cleveland, Ohio. The apartment house had two other people living in it: a young gay couple who were terribly in love with one another. The couple had a dog, an incredibly happy-faced Eskimo they'd named Snowman, but the witch never spoke to it, even though she could. She didn't like dogs, but she did like the gay couple. She tried not to hold their pet against them.

The witch—her name was Sheila—specialized in love magic. She didn't like curses. Curses were all about hate and—occasionally—vengeance, and Sheila had long ago decided that she'd spend her time productively, rather than wasting energy on dealing with perceived injustices located in her—or someone else's—past. Years ago, when she was in college, she had dabbled in curses, but they were mainly favors the girls in her dorm asked of her, usually after a boyfriend dumped them, cheated on them, used them as a means for money and mobility, or some other power or shame thing. A curse always sounded nice to them. Fast and dirty justice. Sheila sometimes helped them, but soon she grew tired of the knocks on her door in the middle of the night, grew annoyed after opening the door to find a teary-eyed girl just back from a frat party with blood boiling so hard that the skin on her face seemed to roil. Eventually Sheila started closing the door on their tear-stained faces, and after a while the girls stopped bothering her for curses. Instead, they started coming to her for love charms.

The gay couple who lived in the downstairs rooms of the apartment house were named Trent and Gary. They'd been together for nearly two years, but had only lived together for the past ten months. Their love was still fresh. Sheila could smell it whenever she stopped in to visit them on weekends, when Trent and Gary could be found on the back deck, barbequing and drinking glasses of red wine. They could make ordinary things like cooking out feel magical because of the sheer completeness they exuded, like a fine sparking mist, when they were near each other. That was pure early love, in Sheila's assessment, and she sipped at it from the edges.

Trent was the manager of a small software company and Gary worked at an environmental nonprofit. They'd met in college ten years ago, but had circled around each other at the time. They'd shared a Venn diagram of friends, but naturally some of them didn't like each other. Their mutual friends spent a lot of time telling Trent about how much they hated Gary's friends, or telling Gary about how much they hated Trent's. Because of this, for years Trent and Gary had kept a safe distance from each other, assuming that they would also hate each other. Which was probably a good thing, they said now, nodding in accord on the back deck of the red brick bungalow, where Trent turned shish kabobs on the grill and Gary poured Sheila another glass of wine.

"Why was it probably a good thing you assumed you'd hate each other?" Sheila asked.

"Because," Gary said as he spilled wine into Sheila's glass, "we were so young and stupid back then."

"Also kind of bitchy," Trent added over his shoulder.

"We would have hurt each other," said Gary, "before we knew what we had to lose."

Sheila blushed at this open display of emotion and Gary laughed. "Look at you!" he said, pointing a finger and turning to look over his shoulder at Trent. "Trent," he said, "Look. We've embarrassed Sheila."

Trent laughed, too, and Sheila rolled her eyes. "I'm not embarrassed, you jerks," she said. "I know what love is. People pay me to help them find it or make it. It's just that, with you two—I don't know—there's something special about your love."

Trent turned a kabob with his tongs and said, "Maybe it's because we didn't need you to make it happen."

It was quite possible that Trent's theory had some kind of truth to it, but whatever the reason, Sheila didn't care. She just wanted to sit with them and drink wine and watch the lightning bugs blink in the backyard on a midsummer evening in Cleveland.

It was a good night. The shish kabobs were spiced with dill and lemon. The wine was a middlebrow Syrah. Trent and Gary always provided good thirtysomethings conversation. Listening to the two of them, Sheila felt like she understood much of what she would have gleaned from reading a newspaper or an intelligent magazine. For the past three months, she'd simply begun to rely on them to relay the goings-on of the world to her, and to supply her with these evenings where, for a small moment in time, she could feel normal.

In the center of the deck several scraps of wood burned in a fire pit, throwing shadows and orange light over their faces as smoke climbed into the darkening sky. Trent swirled his glass of wine before taking the last sip, then stood and slid the back door open so he could go inside to retrieve a fresh bottle.

"That sounds terrible," Sheila was saying as Trent left. Gary had been complaining about natural gas companies coming into Ohio to frack for gas deposits beneath the shale, and how his nonprofit was about to hold a forum on the dangers of the process. But before Sheila could say another word, her cell phone rang. "One second," she said, holding up a finger as she looked at the screen. "It's my mom. I've got to take this."

Sheila pressed the answer button. "Hey, Mom," she said. "What's up?"

"Where are you?" her mother asked, blunt as a bludgeoning weapon as usual.

"I'm having a glass of wine with the boys," Sheila said. Right then, Trent returned, twisting the cork out of the new bottle as he attempted to slide the back door shut with his foot. Sheila furrowed her brows and shook her head at him. "Is there something you need, Mom?" she asked.

Before her mother could answer, though, and before Trent could slide the door shut, the dog Sheila disliked in the way that she disliked all dogs—without any particular hatred for the individual, just the species—darted out the open door and raced past Sheila's legs, down the deck steps, into the bushes at the bottom of the backyard.

"Hey!" Gary said, rising from his chair, nearly spilling his wine. He looked out at the dog, a white furry thing with an impossibly red tongue hanging out of its permanently smiling face, and then placed his glass on the deck railing before heading down the stairs. "Snowman!" he called. "Get back here!"

"Oh, Christ," Trent said, one foot still held against the sliding door he hadn't shut in time. "That dog is going to be the death of me."

"What's going on over there?" Sheila's mother asked. Her voice was loud and drawn out, as if she were speaking to someone hard of hearing.

"Dog escaped," said Sheila. "Hold on a second, Mom."

Sheila held the phone against her chest and said, "Guys, I've got to go. Gary, I hope your forum goes well. Snowman, stop being so bad!" Then she edged through the door Trent still held open, crossed through their kitchen and living room to the front foyer they shared, and took the steps up to her second floor apartment.

"Sorry about that," she said when she sat down at her kitchen table.

"Why do you continue living there, Sheila?" her mother said. Sheila could hear steam hissing off her mother's voice, flat as an iron. "Why," her mother said, "do you continue to live with this illusion of having a full life, my daughter?"

"Ma," Sheila said. "What are you talking about now?"

"*The boys,*" said her mother. "You're always with *the boys.* But those boys like each other, Sheila, not you. You should find other boys. Boys who like girls. When are you going to grow up, make your own life? Don't you want children?"

"I have a life," said Sheila, evenly, as she might speak to a demanding child. "And I don't want children." She could have also told her mother that she was open to girls who liked girls, and had even had a fling or two that had never developed into anything substantial; looking around the kitchen, however, Sheila realized she'd unfortunately forgotten to bring her wine with her, which she would have needed to have that conversation.

"Well, you should want something," her mother said. "I'm worried about you. You don't know how much I worry about you."

Sheila knew how much her mother worried about her. Her mother had been telling her how much she worried about her for years now. Probably from before Sheila was even conceived, her mother was worrying about her. But it was when Sheila turned fifteen that she'd started to make sure Sheila knew just how much. Sheila was now thirty-seven, and the verbal reminders of worry that had started when she'd begun dating had never stopped, even after she took a break from it. So far, it had been a six-year break.

Sheila didn't miss dating, really. Besides, being alone—being a single woman—was the one witchlike quality she possessed, and it was probably the best of the stereotypical witch features to have if she had to have one.

"Ma," Sheila said.

But before she could tell her mother that she didn't have time to play games, her mother said, "I've met someone."

Sheila blinked. "You've met someone?" she said. Was her mother now, at the age of fifty-eight, going to surprise Sheila and find love with someone after being divorced for the past eighteen years?

"Yes," her mother said. "A man. I'd like you to meet him."

"Ma," Sheila said. "I'm speechless. Of course I'll meet him. If he's someone important to you, I'd love to meet him."

"Thank you, lovey," her mother said, and Sheila knew that she'd made her mother happy. "I think you'll like him."

"I'm sure I'll like him, Mom, but I'm just happy if you like him." What Sheila didn't say was how, at that moment, it felt like a huge weight was being lifted from her.

"Well, no," her mother said. "You have to like him, too. As much as I'm glad you trust my judgment in men, it's you who will be going on the date with him."

"*Ma*," Sheila said, and the weight resumed its old position across her shoulders.

Her mother made a guttural noise, though, a sound that meant she was not going to listen to anything Sheila said after the guttural noise reached completion.

"He'll pick you up at seven o'clock tomorrow. Be ready to go to dinner. Don't bring up witch stuff. No talking shop on a date. His name is Lyle."

"Lyle?" Sheila said, as if the name seemed completely made-up—a fantasy novel sort of name, one of those books with a cover that features castle spires and portentous red moons covered in strands of cloud. One of those novels where people are called things like Roland, Aristial, Leandor, Jandari, or . . . Lyle.

"Lyle," said her mother. Then the phone went dead. Sheila looked down at it for a while as if it were a gun that had accidentally gone off, leaving a bullet lodged in her stomach.

The bullet sat in Sheila's stomach and festered for the rest of that night, and the feeling was not unfamiliar. Sheila's mother had a habit of mugging her with unwanted surprises. Furniture that didn't go with Sheila's décor. Clothes that didn't fit her. Blind dates with men named Lyle.

Her mother was a mugger. Always had been. So why was she still surprised whenever it happened, as if this were a sudden, unexpected event? By the next morning, Sheila had come up with several jokes about her mother the mugger that she would tell to the two clients who had appointments with her that afternoon.

"Mugger fucker," Sheila mumbled as she brushed her hair in the bathroom mirror. "Mugger Goose. Holy Mugger of God. Mugger may I?"

Her first client was a regular named Mary, who was forty-three, had three children, and was married to a husband she'd fallen out of love with four years ago. Mary came every other month for a reboot of the spell that helped her love her husband a little longer. She'd tried counseling, she'd tried herbal remedies, she'd even tried Zumba (both individually and with several girlfriends as a group), but nothing seemed to work, and in desperation she'd found Sheila through a friend of a friend of a former client who Sheila had helped rekindle a relationship gone sour years ago, back when Sheila had first started to make her living by witching instead of working at the drugstore that had hired her while she was in college.

The knock came at exactly ten in the morning. Mary was never late and never early. Her sessions always lasted for exactly thirty minutes. Sheila was willing to go beyond that, but Mary said she felt that Sheila's power faded a little more with every second past the thirty-minute mark. She still paid Sheila three hundred dollars for each session, and walked away a happy—or at least a happ*ier*—woman. She'd go home and, for five to six weeks, she'd love her husband. Sheila couldn't work a permanent fix for Mary, because Mary had fallen so out of love with her husband that no spell could sustain it forever. Their relationship was an old, used-up car in constant need of repairs. Sheila was the mechanic.

When Sheila opened the door, Mary pushed in, already complaining loudly about her husband, Ted. Sheila had never met him, though she did have a lock of his hair in an envelope that stayed in her living room curio cabinet. Except on appointment days with Mary; on those days, Sheila would bring the hair out for the renewal ritual.

"I don't know if I want the spell again," Mary said. She hadn't even looked at Sheila yet. She just sat down heavily on the living room couch and sighed. "I don't know if I want to fix things any longer."

"What else would you do?" Sheila asked, closing the door before coming over to sit in the chair across from Mary. "Divorce? Start over? You know you could do that, right?"

Mary clutched a small black beaded purse in her lap. She was a beautiful woman, long limbed, peach-skinned, with dark hair that fell to the small of her back like a curtain. She exercised, ate healthy, and didn't drink too much alcohol—even when alcohol sounded like a good idea. She wore upper middle class clothes that weren't particularly major designer labels but weren't from a mall store, either.

"I don't know," Mary said, pushing a piece of her layered black hair away from her face. Sheila noticed that Mary had gotten a nose piercing in the time between their last appointment and this one. A tiny diamond stud glinted in the sunlight coming through the living room windows. "The children . . . " said Mary. Sheila nodded, and stood, then went to her curio cabinet and took out the envelope with the hank of Ted's hair in it.

Sheila opened the envelope and placed the lock of hair on the coffee table between them. It was a thick brown curl that Mary had cut from Ted's mop one night while he was asleep. When Mary had come to Sheila for help four years ago, Sheila had said, "I'll need you to bring me something of his. Something you love about him. Otherwise, I'll have nothing to work with." Mary had said she didn't love him anymore, so how could she bring Sheila anything? "Surely you must love *something* about him," Sheila said, and Mary had nodded, her mouth a firm line, and said that, yes, she did love Ted's hair. It was beautiful. Thick and curly. She loved to run her fingers through it, even after she'd stopped loving Ted.

Now Mary looked down at the lock of curled hair as if it were a dead mouse Sheila had set out in front of her. "You know the drill," Sheila said, and together the two pinched an end of the hair and lifted it into the air above the coffee table.

Sheila closed her eyes and tried to feel Mary's love come through the coil of hair. Like an electrical current, a slight hum flowed through it, but it was weaker than ever and Sheila worried that she wouldn't be able to help Mary once this slight affection for Ted's hair eventually disappeared. She took the lingering love in through her fingers anyway, whipped it like cream, semi-consciously chanting an incantation—or more like noises that helped her focus on the energy in the feeling than anything of significance—and after she'd turned Mary's weak affection into a fluffy meringue-like substance, Sheila pushed it back through the hair, slowly but surely, until Mary was filled with a large, aerated love.

When Sheila opened her eyes, she noticed Mary's face had lifted a little. The firm line of her mouth had softened and curled up at the edges, as if she wanted to smile but was perhaps just a little shy. "Thank you, Sheila," said Mary, blinking sweetly on the couch. This was when Sheila went soft, too. Whenever a client like Mary, hardened by a deficiency of love, took on a shade of her former self—a youthful self who loved and was loved, who trusted in love to see her through—Sheila had to fight to hold back tears. Not because seeing the return of love made her happy—no, the pressure behind her eyes was more a force of sadness, because the person in front of her was under an illusion, and no illusion, thought Sheila, was pleasant. They were more like the narcotics those with chronic pain took to ease their days. This returned love would only be brief and temporary.

At the door, Mary took out three hundred-dollar bills. "Worth every penny," she said, folding them into Sheila's palm, meeting Sheila's eyes and holding her stare.

When Sheila closed the door behind her, she turned and looked at the face of her cell phone. Thirty minutes had passed. On the dot.

Her next client was new: a good-looking young man who was a bit too earnest for only being a twenty-three-year-old recent college graduate. His name was Ben, and he had just acquired a decent job with an advertising company. He'd gotten a mortgage, purchased a house, and was ready to fill it with someone else and him together, the kids, the dogs, the cats: the works. Sheila could see all of this as he sat in front of her and told her that he wanted to find love. That was simple, really. No need to drum up love where love already fizzed and popped. He just needed someone to really see him. Someone who wanted the same things. He wasn't the completely bland sort of guy that no one would notice, but he wasn't emitting a strong signal either. Sheila did a quick invocation that would enhance Ben's desire so that it would beam like a lighthouse toward ships looking for harbor.

She charged him a hundred dollars and told him that if he didn't get engaged within a year, she'd give him his money back. Ben thanked her, and after she saw him out of the house, it was time for Sheila to sit in her living room and stare at the television, where the vague outline of her body was reflected in the blank screen.

Lyle would be coming to pick her up in several hours. *Lyle, Lyle.* She said his name a few times, but it was no good. She still couldn't believe a man named Lyle was coming for her.

Sheila had tried to make the thing that made her different the most normal aspect of her life. Hence her business: Paranormal Romance. She had business cards and left them on the bulletin boards of grocery store entryways, in the fishbowls full of cards that sat on the register counters of some restaurants, and on the bars of every lowdown drink-your-blues-away kind of joint in the city of Cleveland, where people sometimes, while crying into a beer, would notice the card propped against the napkin holder in front of them and think about Sheila possibly being the solution to their loneliness, as the cards declared.

She had made herself as non-paranormal as possible, while at the same time living completely out in the open about being a witch, probably because of what her father had once told her, years ago, when she was just a little girl and even Sheila hadn't known she had magic in her fingertips. "If I had to be some creepy weirdo like the vampires and werewolves or whatever the hell else is out there these days," her father had said while watching a news report about the increasing appearance of paranormal creatures, "then I suppose a witch would be the way to go."

The way to go. That's what he'd said. As though there was a choice about being cursed or born with magic flowing through you. Vampire, werewolf. *Whatever the hell else.* The memory stuck with Sheila because of the way her father had talked as if it were one of those "If you had to" games.

If you had to lose a sense, which one?

If you had to live on a deserted island with only one book, which one?

It was only later, after Sheila felt magic welling up in her as a teenager, that she realized how upset he was when she accidentally revealed her abilities—a tactless spell she'd cast to bring him and her mother closer. Unfortunately, her father had noticed Sheila's fingers weaving through the air as she attempted to surreptitiously cast the spell while her parents were watching television one evening. Her mother stuck by Sheila, but he filed for divorce and disappeared from their lives altogether.

Thus her business, *Paranormal Romance*, was born. She would make it work for her, Sheila decided in her late twenties. She would use this magic in a way that someone with good legs, flexibility, and balance might become a dancer or a yoga instructor.

This desire for normality also explained why Sheila wanted to kill her mother after she opened the door that evening to find a man dressed in a black leather jacket, tight blue jeans, a black v-neck shirt, and work boots, sporting a scraggly goatee, whose first words were, "Wow, you don't look like a witch. That's interesting."

"Probably the least interesting thing about me," said Sheila. She tried to restrain herself, but couldn't refrain from arching her eyebrows as a cat might raise its back.

"I'm Lyle. Nice to meet you," the somewhat ruggedly good-looking Lyle said.

"Charmed," Sheila said, trying to sound like she meant it.

"No," said Lyle, "that's what you're supposed to do to me, right?" He winked. Sheila's smile felt frail, as if it might begin to splinter.

"How do you know I'm a witch," Sheila asked, "when my mother specifically told me not to bring it up?"

"Don't know why she told you that," said Lyle. "First thing she mentioned to me was that's what you are."

"Great," said Sheila. "And I know nothing about you to make it even, and here we are, standing in my doorway like we're new neighbors instead of going somewhere."

Lyle nodded his head in the direction of the staircase and said, "I got us a reservation at a great steakhouse downtown."

Sheila smiled. It was a lip-only smile—no teeth—but she followed Lyle down the steps of her apartment to the front porch, where she found Gary dragging Snowman up the steps by his collar. The dog had its ridiculous grin plastered on as usual, but started to yap in the direction of Lyle as soon as he noticed him. Gary himself was grimacing with frustration. "What's the matter?" Sheila asked.

"This guy," said Gary. "When he ran off last night, he really ran off. Someone on the neighborhood Facebook group messaged me to say she had him penned in her backyard. Three blocks from here. You're a bad dog, Snowman. A bad dog, you hear?"

Snowman was barking like crazy now, twisting around Gary's legs. He looked up at Lyle and for the first time in Sheila's experience, the dog did not look like it was smiling, but was baring its teeth.

"Woof!" said Lyle, and Snowman began to whimper.

"Well, it's a good thing she was able to corral him," Sheila said, even as she attempted to telepathically communicate with Gary: *Did this guy just* woof? "I've never gotten along with dogs, so he'd have probably run away from me if I were the one to find him."

"Oh, really?" Lyle raised his brows, as if Sheila had suddenly taken off a mask and revealed herself to be an alien with tentacles wriggling, Medusa-like, out of her head. "You don't like dogs?"

"And dogs," Sheila said, "don't like me."

"I can't believe that," said Lyle, shaking his head and wincing.

Sheila shrugged and said, "That's just the way things are, I guess."

"Who *are* you again?" Gary asked, looking at Lyle with narrowed eyes, as if he'd put Lyle under a microscope.

Sheila apologized for not introducing them. "This is my date," she said, trying to signal to Gary that it was also the last date by rolling her eyes as she turned away from Lyle.

"A *date*?" Gary said, clapping one hand over his mouth as he said it. "Sheila is going on a *date*?"

"That's right," said Lyle. He nodded curtly. "And we should probably get started. Come on," he said, pointing toward his car parked against the curb. Sheila inwardly groaned when she saw that it was one of those muscle cars macho guys collect, like they're still little boys with Matchbox vehicles. "Let's go get some grub," Lyle said, patting his stomach.

"*Grub*?" Gary whispered as Lyle and Sheila went past him, and Sheila could only look over her shoulder with a *Help Me!* look painfully stretched across her face.

The steakhouse Lyle took her to was one of those places where people crack peanuts open, dislodge the nut, and discard the shells on the floor. The lighting was dim, but the room was permeated with the glow from a variety of neon beer signs that hung on every wall like a collection in an art gallery. Lyle said it was his favorite place to dine.

He said it like that too, Sheila could already hear herself saying later as she recounted the evening to Trent and Gary. *He said, "It's my favorite place to dine." Can you believe it? What was my mother thinking?*

"Oh, really," Sheila said. The server had just brought her a vodka martini with a slice of lemon dangling over the rim. Sheila looked up at her briefly to say thank you, and noticed immediately that the server—a young woman with long mahogany hair and caramel-colored skin—was a witch. The employee tag on the server's shirt said her name was Corrine; she winked as Sheila grasped after her words. "Thank you," Sheila managed to say without making the moment of recognition awkward. She took a sip, licked her lips, then turned back to Lyle as the server walked away, and said, "What were you saying?"

" 'This is my favorite place to dine,' I said. I come here a couple of times a week," said Lyle. "Best steaks in town."

Sheila said, "I don't eat meat."

To which Lyle's face dropped like a hot air balloon that had lost all of its hot air. "Your mother didn't tell me that," said Lyle.

"No," said Sheila, "but for some reason she *did* tell you that I'm a witch, even after she forbade me from speaking of it. Clearly the woman can't be trusted."

"Clearly," Lyle agreed, which actually scored him a tiny little point for the first time that evening. There it was in Sheila's mind's eye, a little scoreboard. *Lyle: 1. Sheila: Anxious.*

He apologized profusely, in a rough-around-the-edges way that seemed to be who he was down to his core. He wasn't really Sheila's type, not that Sheila had a specific type, but he wasn't the sort of guy she'd ever gone out on a date with before, either. Her mother would have known that too. Sheila's mother had always wanted to know what was going on, back when Sheila actually dated. When Myspace and Facebook came around, and her mother began commenting on photos Sheila had posted from some of her date nights with statements like, "He's a hottie!" and "Now that's a keeper!" Sheila had had to block her mother. And only weeks later she discovered that on her mother's own social networking walls, her mother was publicly bemoaning the fact that her daughter had blocked her.

But really, her mother would have known that Lyle wasn't her sort of guy. "So what gives?" she finally asked, after Lyle had finished a tall beer and she'd gotten close to the bottom of her martini. "How do you know my mother? Why would she think we'd make a good pair?"

"I'm her butcher."

Sheila almost spat out the vodka swirling in her mouth, but managed to swallow before saying, "Her butcher? Really? I didn't know my mother *had* a butcher."

"She comes to the West Side Market every Saturday," said Lyle. "I work at Doreen's Meats. Your mother always buys her meat for the week there. As for why would she think we'd make a good pair? I don't know." Lyle shrugged and held his palms up in the air. "I guess maybe she thought we'd get along because of what we have in common."

Sheila snorted, then raised her hand to signal Corrine back over. "I'd like another martini," she said, and smiled in the way some people do when they need to smother an uncivil reaction: lips firmly held together. She turned back to Lyle, who was cracking another peanut shell between his thick, hairy fingers, and said, "So what do we have in common, besides my mother?"

"I'm a werewolf," said Lyle. Then he flicked the peanut off his thumb and snatched it out of the air, midflight, in his mouth.

Sheila watched as Lyle crunched the peanut, and noticed only after he'd swallowed and smiled across the table at her that he had a particularly large set of canines. "You're kidding," said Sheila. "Ha ha, very funny. You might as well start telling witch jokes at this point."

"Not kidding," said Lyle. Corrine stopped at their table, halting the conversation as she placed another tall beer in front of Lyle, another martini in front of Sheila, and asked what they'd like to order.

"I think we're just here to drink tonight," said Lyle, not taking his eyes off Sheila.

Sheila nodded vigorously at Corrine, though, agreeing. And after she left, Sheila said, "Well, this is a new achievement for my mother. Set her daughter up with a werewolf."

"What? You don't like werewolves?" Lyle asked. One corner of his mouth lifted into a 1970s drug dealer grin.

Sheila blinked a lot for a while, took another sip of her martini, then shrugged. "It's not something I've ever thought about, you know," she said. "I mean, werewolves aren't generally on my radar. I get a lot of people who come around with minor psychic powers, and they're attracted to me because they can sense I'm something out of the ordinary but can't quite place *what* exactly, and of course I know a decent amount of witches—we can spot each other on the street without knowing one another, really—but werewolves are generally outside of my experience. Especially my dating experience."

"From what I understand, your dating experience has been pretty non-existent in general."

Sheila decided it was time to take yet another drink. After swallowing a large gulp of vodka, she said, "My mother has a big mouth for someone who hasn't gotten back in the saddle since my father left her nearly two decades ago. And you can tell her I said that next time she comes in to stock up on meat."

Lyle laughed. It was a full, throaty laugh that made heads turn in the steakhouse. When he realized this, he reined himself in, but Sheila could see that the laugh—the sheer volume of it when he'd let himself go—was beyond ordinary. It bordered on the wild. She could imagine him as a wolf in that moment, howling at a blood red moon.

"So what is it? Once a month you get hairy and run around the city killing people?" Sheila asked.

Lyle leaned back on his side of the booth and said, "Are you serious?"

"Well, I don't know," said Sheila. "I hear it's quite difficult to control blood-lust in times like that."

"I make arrangements for those times," said Lyle.

"Arrangements, huh," said Sheila. "What sort of arrangements?"

"I rent an underground garage, have it filled with plenty of raw steaks, and get locked in for the night."

"That's responsible of you," said Sheila.

"What about you?" Lyle asked. "Any inclinations to doing evil? Casting hexes?"

"No bloodlust for witches," said Sheila, "and I gave up the vicious cycle of curse drama in college. Not worth it. That shit comes back on you sevenfold."

Lyle snickered. He ran his thumb and forefinger over his scraggly goatee, then took another drink of beer. "Looks like we're a pair," he said, "just like your mother imagined."

"Why?" Sheila asked. "Because you put yourself in a werewolf kennel on full moon nights and I don't dabble in wreaking havoc in other people's lives?"

Lyle nodded, his lips rising into a grin that revealed his pointy, slightly yellowed canines.

"I hardly think that constitutes being a pair," said Sheila. "We certainly have that in common, but it's a bit like saying we should start dating because we're both single and living in Cleveland."

"Why *are* you so single?" Lyle asked. His nostrils flared several times.

Oh my God, he is totally sniffing me! "I need to use the ladies' room," she said.

In the restroom, Sheila leaned against the counter and stared at herself in the mirror. She was wearing a short black dress and had hung her favorite opal earrings on her earlobes. They glowed in the strange orange neon beer-sign light of the restroom. She shouldn't have answered when he knocked. She should have kept things in order. Weekend BBQs with Trent and Gary, even with the obnoxious Snowman running between their legs and wanting to jump on her and lick her. Working a few hours a day with clients, helping them to love or be loved, to find love. Evening runs in the park. Grocery shopping on Wednesdays. That's what she wanted, not a werewolf butcher/lover her mother had found in the West Side Market.

The last time Sheila dated someone had been slightly less than underwhelming. He'd been an utterly normal man named Paul who worked at the Federal Reserve Bank of Cleveland downtown, and he talked endlessly of bank capitalization and exchange-traded funds. Sheila had tried to love him, but it was as if all the bank talk was more powerful than any spell she might cast on herself, and so she'd had to add Paul to her long list of previous candidates for love.

There had been Jim, a guy who owned a car dealership in Lakewood, but he always came off as a salesman, and Sheila wasn't the consumer type. There had been Alexis, a law student at Case Western, but despite her girlish good looks and intelligence, Alexis had worried about Sheila's under-the-table Paranormal Romance business—concerned that she was possibly defrauding the government of taxable income. There had been Mark, the CPA (say no more). There had been Lola, the karaoke DJ (say no more). And there had been a string of potentials before that, too, once Sheila began sorting through the memories of her twenties, a long line of cute young men and women whose faces faded a little more each day. She had tried—she had tried so hard— hoping one of them would take the weight of her existence and toss it into the air like a beach ball. The love line went back and back and back, so far back, but none of those boys or girls had been able to do this. None of them.

Except Trent and Gary, of course. Not that they were romance for Sheila. But they did love her. They cared about her. They didn't make her feel like she had to be anyone but who she wanted to be, even if who Sheila wanted to be wasn't entirely who Sheila was.

Sheila washed her hands under the faucet and dried them with the air dryer, appreciating the whir of the fan drowning out the voice in her head. She would walk out on Lyle, she decided. She'd go home and call her mother and tell her, "Never again," then hang up on her. She would sit in front of the blank television screen, watching her shadowy reflection held within it, and maybe she would let herself cry, just a little bit, for being a love witch who couldn't make love happen for herself.

"Are you okay?" a voice said over the whir of the hand dryer. Sheila blinked and turned. Behind her, Corrine the server was coming out of a stall. She came to stand beside Sheila at the sinks and quickly washed her hands.

"You're a witch," Sheila said stupidly, and realized at that moment that two martinis were too many for her.

Corrine laughed, but nodded and said, "Yes. I am. So are you." Corrine reached for the paper towel to dry her hands, since Sheila was spellbound in front of the electric dryer. "What kind?" she asked Sheila as she wiped her hands.

"Love," said Sheila.

"Love?" said Corrine, raising her thin eyebrows. "That's pretty fancy."

"It's okay," said Sheila.

"Just okay?" said Corrine. "I don't know. Sounds nice to be able to do something like that with it. Me? I can't do much but weird things."

"What do you mean?" Sheila asked.

"You know," said Corrine. "Odds and ends. Nothing so defined as love. Bad end of the magic stick, maybe. I can smell fear on people, or danger. And I can open doors. But that's about it."

"Open doors?" said Sheila.

"Yeah," said Corrine. "Doors. I guess it does make a kind of sense when I think about it long enough. I smell danger coming, I can get out of just about anywhere if I want to. Open a door. Any old door. It might look like it leads into a broom closet or an office, but I can make it open onto other places I've been, or have at least seen in a picture."

"Wow," said Sheila. "You should totally be a cat burglar."

Corrine laughed. Sheila laughed with her. "Sorry," she said. "I don't know why I said that."

"It's okay," Corrine said. "It was funny. I think you said it because it was funny."

"I guess I better get back out there," said Sheila.

"Date?" said Corrine.

"Blind date," Sheila answered. "Bad date. Last date."

Corrine frowned in sympathy. "I knew it wasn't going well."

"How?" Sheila asked.

"I could smell it on you. Not quite fear, but anxiety and frustration. I figured that's why you asked for the second martini. That guy comes in a lot. He seems okay, but yeah, I couldn't imagine why you were here with him."

Sheila looked down at her hands, which were twitching a little, as if her fingers had minds of their own. They were twitching in Corrine's direction, like they wanted to go to her. Sheila laughed. Her poor fingers. All of that love magic stored up inside them and nowhere to go.

"You need help?" Corrine asked suddenly. She had just taken off her name badge and was now fluffing her hair in the mirror.

"Help?" said Sheila.

Corrine looked over and said, "If you want out, we can just go. You don't even have to say goodbye to him. My shift's over. A friend of mine will be closing out your table. We can leave by the bathroom door."

Sheila laughed. Her fingers twitched again. She took one hand and clamped it over the other.

"What are you afraid of?" Corrine asked. Her eyes had started to narrow. "I'm getting a sense that you're afraid of me now."

"You?" Sheila said. "No, no, not you."

"Well, you're giving off the vibe," said Corrine. She dropped her name badge into her purse and took out a tube of lipstick, applied some to her lips so that they were a shade of dark ruby. When she was done, she slipped the tube into her purse and turned to Sheila. "What's wrong with your hands?" she asked.

Sheila was still fidgeting. "I think," she said. "I think they like you."

Corrine threw her head back and laughed. "Like?" she said, grinning. "That's sweet of them. You can tell your hands I like them too."

Sheila said, "I'm so sorry. This is embarrassing. I'm usually not such a weirdo." For a moment, Sheila heard her father's voice come through—*Creepy weirdoes. Whatever the hell else is out there*—and she shivered.

"You're not weird," said Corrine. "Just flustered. It happens."

It happens. Sheila blinked and blinked again. Actually, it didn't happen. Not for her. Her fingers only twitched like this when she was working magic for other people. Anytime she had tried to work magic for herself, they were still and cold, as if she had bad circulation. "No," Sheila said. "It doesn't usually happen. Not for me. This is strange."

"Listen," said Corrine. "You seem interesting. I'm off shift and you have a bad blind date happening. I'm about to leave by that door and go somewhere I know that has good music and way better food than this place. And it's friendly to people like you and me. What do you say?"

Sheila thought of her plans for the rest of the evening in a blinding flash.

Awkward moment before she ditched Lyle.

Awkward and angry moment on the phone while she told her mother off.

The vague reflection of her body held in the screen of the television as she allowed herself to cry a little.

Then she looked up at Corrine, who was pulling on a zippered hoody, and said, "I say yes."

"Yes?" Corrine said, smiling.

"Yes," said Sheila. "Yes, let's go there, wherever it is you're going."

Corrine held her hand out, and Sheila looked down at her own hands again, clamped together as if in prayer, holding each other back from the world. "You can let one of them go," Corrine said, grinning. "Otherwise, I can't take you with me."

Sheila laughed nervously and nodded. She released her hands from one another and cautiously put one into the palm of Corrine's hand, where it settled in smoothly and turned warm in an instant. "This way," Corrine said, and put her other hand on the bathroom doorknob, twisted, then opened it.

For a moment, Sheila could see nothing but a bright light fill the space of the doorway—no Lyle or the sounds of rock and roll music spilled in from the dining area—and she worried that she'd made a mistake, not being able to see where she was going with this woman who was a complete stranger. Then Corrine looked back at her and said, "Don't be afraid," and Sheila heard the sound of jazz music suddenly float toward her, a soft saxophone, a piano melody, though the doorway was still filled with white light she couldn't see through.

"I'm not," said Sheila suddenly, and was surprised to realize that she truly wasn't.

Corrine winked at her the way she had done at the table, as if they shared a secret, which, of course, they did. Then she tugged on Sheila's hand and they stepped through the white light into somewhere different.

TOWN'S END

YUKIMI OGAWA

At the counter of a marriage agency at the end of the town, I felt my lip twitch in spite of myself. "Pardon me, ma'am?"

"I need a male," the woman in front of me repeated. "I badly need to bear a child."

I looked down at the PC and tapped the corner of my mouth, hoping it would stop twitching. It didn't help. "Well, I see you're a very straightforward person. But perhaps that sort of statement could wait until you are closer to the man."

"But why?"

"It'd scare the man."

"Really? I didn't know."

The woman looked nervous and tucked a strand of hair behind her ear, behind the string that was holding her mask in place. The mask looked old-fashioned, made of cotton not unwoven cloth. "Do you have a cold? Or is that for an allergy?" I asked.

She shook her head, her thick, long black hair almost unmoving.

Below this old-fashioned hair style and mask, she wore a long, one-piece dress that was almost stark-white, which didn't help her pale skin. I wondered if I would have to advise her on what to wear. "I think that would scare them, too. Never taking a mask off for some secret reason."

"Oh, really? Oh my . . . "

This woman, Saeko Kimura, claimed to be from a faraway region, which she had said was why she wouldn't give me the name of the high school she'd graduated from. She gave me no information that would tell me about her life, not even her age, but she looked to be about the same age as I, mid-thirties or so. She was the first client since I started working here *four* months ago. I had come back from the city to this small town last year after I had split up with my boyfriend, and for a half year I couldn't find a job. When I finally found the position at this marriage agency at the end of my hometown, I had no other choice but to take it.

The firm stood adjacent to a house the boss had said he lived in but never seemed to be using. I had never seen the boss, except for the one time when I saw a shadow of a tall, lean figure reflected on the screen door of the house a few weeks back. Our communication had been solely through emails. Not even phone calls.

"But me taking off the mask would scare them away, too," Kimura was saying. Wrinkles formed between her downward-slanting brows, giving her the atmosphere of an unlucky woman. "I really need a man's seed."

For five years in the city I worked as a receptionist at an English language school, where I had to deal with countless, groundless complaints and had developed a Noh-mask on my face devoid of any real expression. But even that was nothing to fight against this. "You just want to sleep with someone?"

"Yes," the answer came quick. "Without a condom."

I actually chuckled. "In that case you shouldn't be here. This is where people who want to find a husband or wife come. You should sign up for an SNS that is famous for that sort of community."

"What's an SNS?"

"You know condom and don't know SNS?"

"I've seen couples using a condom and discarding the thing in the woods."

"Huh. You have a mobile, right?"

"No."

"No?" I asked, incredulous. "What about a PC?"

"No way."

I considered this. It would be easier if I just told her to find a mobile and Google for a service that suited her purposes. But she was my first client here, and after four months of having nothing to do but cleaning this very small firm, it was just nice to have someone to talk to.

"I have to ask my boss first," I said, "but I could let you use this PC and teach you how to use these SNS sites. For, perhaps—one third of the fee you'd usually have to pay here. If my boss says yes, would you like that?"

Kimura's eyes shone brightly. She nodded so eagerly that I feared her head might drop off her neck.

The boss said yes via email. I phoned Kimura on the fixed line (she had warned me that it would take a long time before she could answer, and asked me not to give up), and she said she'd come back next day. And she did. We chose a service that seemed to be favored by older people, sent out a few messages which wouldn't give away too much of her but weren't lies, either. A message came back. I let her use my firm as the meeting point. I told her to tell the guy that she took pills. What pills, don't mention.

A few days later Kimura came trotting up to the firm and hugged me over the counter. "Thank you," she said and I could even feel her smile behind my shoulder. "He even liked my mask and gave me a thing that would cover my entire face to wear when I was naked!"

"O-okay, good. But you don't know if you got the seed you needed yet," I said, patting her back a few times.

"Oh, I know I have. We always know."

"Who we?"

"My kin."

"Uh-huh."

When she finally pulled back she was frowning. "What?" I asked.

"You don't ask too many questions, do you? I know I've been a little . . . queer."

That made me smile. "Not my business, you're a grown woman."

"Well, thank you. You've been great."

"Glad I helped."

She had already paid, but as her personal thank-you she gave me an envelope. It contained a few partially used prepaid cards. They amounted to about thirty thousand yen. "This is too much." I shook my head and tried to give them back to her.

Kimura shook her own head and closed my fingers around the cards. "They were all we could gather. This has been a very important step for us, and it's not enough to show our gratitude, but cash doesn't come in very handy, you know?"

"Mmm?" A ridiculous sound came out through my lips. I understood nothing of what she had just said.

Kimura smiled and squeezed my hand. "Thank you," she said again and left.

I emailed my boss about what had just happened, stupidly including everything about the prepaid cards. His reply was only one word: "Good."

And what had I just done? A few days later I had twin brothers across my counter. "We heard a lot about you," the one on my left said. "That you helped them."

"I helped Kimura-san, yes. But you look a lot younger." I had already given up my Noh-mask.

"We have a lady that we protect," the left one said. "We need someone to come for her." The one on my right said nothing.

"Where to?"

"The shrine in the woods."

I very vaguely remembered the place. "The one with the sun-goddess?"

"That's the place."

"And she 'needs the seed'?"

"Yep."

I wasn't sure if I wanted to laugh or scream. "Can you at least bring her to some hotel? It's not easy to bring in a stranger into your own place, you know."

The twins looked at each other and then back at me. "She's too weak."

"She's too weak but can have sex?"

"Within her own place it's okay."

"You mean she's the priestess?"

The left one glanced at his brother. His brother shrugged, saying nothing. "Something like that," the speaking one said. For the first time he didn't meet my eyes.

" . . . You're not going to do any harm to the guy, are you?"

"No! Did Sae do anything to hurt the man?"

I considered this. And also the fact that I hadn't heard anything really bad happening around here, anyway. "Well. Okay, then. But we have to make up some excuse for luring the guy into this shrine of yours."

"Do you have any suggestions?" The left one looked relieved and nervous at the same time.

I looked into my PC screen, thinking hard. "Perhaps you could just say your lady is a priestess."

"Huh?"

"Some people get more aroused by abnormal situations," I said. "In this case, you tell him your lady is a priestess locked up in a shrine. When the guy goes in she tells him she shouldn't be doing it there because it's a holy place, and the concept itself makes him want to do it there more and he wants to tear her robes away from her . . . "

The twins blushed. "Ah, well, it sounds—okay. Could you make an ad calling for that?" His speech faltered from time to time, and his not-speaking brother was even looking down at his feet.

I grinned. "Yeah, no problem. Tell the plan to your lady and come back tomorrow. I'll have her profile and message ready."

"Okay, thanks."

After they left I realized I hadn't asked for my boss's permission. I emailed him, to which he replied with "OK."

The twins came back the next day, saying they had even prepared a nice set of robes for the occasion. I let out a laugh and started searching for an appropriate service.

"What does she look like?"

"Beautiful," the left one said and blushed. "Slender. A bit sharp-featured, but beautiful."

" 'Cool beauty'?"

"Yeah."

I frowned. "You really okay with her sleeping with another guy?"

"What do you mean?"

"You don't want to do that yourself?"

The twins both went deep, deep red in the face. "Oh, no. We aren't her kin. We can't."

"Oh."

I wanted to ask what "kin" meant in their context, and Kimura's. But somehow it didn't seem a very wise thing to ask. I shrugged it off and Googled a few services.

A few days later we got a message from a guy who seemed to be really thrilled about the idea of making it in the tiny shrine building. I let them use the firm's phone number in case the guy couldn't find the place. But it turned out it wasn't necessary.

The next day after their meeting the twins came hopping into the office. "She was really, really pleased. The man seemed pleased, too."

"Did you watch them?"

"N-no! Oh, no!"

I laughed.

The boys hesitated a few moments before handing me a tiny, purple crepe sachet. Inside it I found a small piece of wood with a strange character written on it; it didn't mean anything to me.

"It's a token," the speaker-boy said, his expression grave. "It would protect you no matter what. You won't even have to worry about earthquakes again."

"I've heard something very similar from a woman who tried to sell me a 'spiritual' painting."

I meant it to be a joke but the boys didn't even smile. "It's really powerful and I've never seen her give it to one of your kind. Don't show it off, okay? There are some clans who would be really jealous."

I closed my fingers tight around the sachet. "Okay. Thanks."

They smiled and nodded. "Thanks to *you*. We won't forget. There are some things that won't fade."

I cocked my head, not fully understanding, but the next moment they had turned their heels and were out of the door.

Perhaps I should have asked them what they meant. Kimura and the boys. Because more, some of them acting queerer than the previous clients, followed. A woman came, paler even than Kimura, and she brought a very fine kimono and said she wanted to pay with it. It was made of some fabric I had never seen or felt, and the boss said okay so I accepted it. Another woman, dressed all in black, asked me to teach her how to get to a mountain at the far end of Tokyo. For this I couldn't let her pay and so she touched my forehead and said, "May the good wind always be at your back."

Then one day a girl came, obviously too young for all this, so I just gave her a chocolate from my drawer.

The girl ate the chocolate and smiled widely. "What can I give you for this?"

"You don't have to. Just eat it up and leave, and never even think of doing this until you're five years older."

"But I'm of age, according to our kin's standard. I'm ready to have children."

Kin again. "Well, why don't you have them with a boy of your own kin, then?"

She licked her fingers and frowned. "They said you wouldn't ask questions."

"You don't have to answer it if you won't make me find your mate."

The girl giggled. "I like you, I think," she said. "I almost never liked a human."

"Oh, I'm honored."

The girl suddenly sobered. "You should come with me. I'll show you how I'm old enough."

"How will you show me?"

"Oh, I'll show you. But not here."

The girl stared at me. Her brown eyes had a strange quality I couldn't name. It felt as though they were boring into my brain through my eyes. I tried to look away but somehow failed.

I shook my head. "I can't leave this place. I work here."

"But after?"

"I need to do some grocery shopping."

The girl smiled. "Sooner or later I'll come. You'll come."

She left. I sensed a waft of strange odor under the chocolate, so I stood and opened the windows. But it lingered for a long time.

I emailed my mysterious boss about the girl. As usual the message contained only one word: "Don't." I wondered if he meant don't give a chocolate to a stranger, don't open the windows, or don't bother letting in a young girl in the first place.

Or don't go after the girl.

The next day I had off. I spent the day sluggishly, doing some laundry and browsing through the Internet. When at dusk I thought of cooking dinner, I realized I had run out of soy sauce. Which was weird. I had thought I had at least one meal's worth left in the bottle. How had I been mistaken?

I sighed and got into my car. Perhaps my aunt in the next town had a stock bottle. I didn't want to go into a shop because I had been dressed lightly and had no makeup, and my hair was a mess.

I started the engine. By that time dusk had turned into night. After a few minutes I was running on a narrow road which cut through corn fields. There were no street lights along the path, and it was just so dark . . .

Then I felt something collide with my bumper.

I hit the brake. I didn't see anyone running across the path, so it must have been a cat or something. Something very small. But it was the first time I ever hit anything. My hands started trembling. With the engine on and the lights gleaming, I stepped out of my car to check.

The bumper showed no sign of collision. I looked around. It was just so dark. The headlights lit the path in front of the car, but that was all that was visible.

At the corner of my eye something moved.

I spun around and squinted into darkness. Something was trying to go into the corn field. And it whined. I gasped.

"It's you, isn't it?" I said. I didn't remember asking for her name. "You . . . I gave you a chocolate . . . "

The girl whined again and went through the high corn plants. "Wait! Are you hurt?" I said and went after her.

Don't.

Something pulsed. Not my heartbeat. I felt for the breast pocket of my polo shirt.

The token the twins had given me.

But the girl whined once more. Her movement sounded as if she was limping.

I hurried after her.

Rows after rows of corn plants. I'd lost count, but at the back of my head I knew it was summing up to too many. Ripe corns. Young ones. All weaving a strange pattern, the one which invaded your brain just before you fell asleep. I ran. My breaths sang a rhythm that was nonsense. And why was I running?

At the end of the corn field was a stream.

Fireflies danced everywhere. When their lights touched the long-faded hydrangeas the flowers sprung to life, their blues, purples, and pinks so vivid in this dim place. I looked up and saw the Milky Way. The stream reflected the stars, becoming the Milky Way itself, only on the ground.

On the other side, a man stood, hands in his pockets. He smiled.

"Why?" I heard myself say. "Why are you here?"

"I came for you."

"You're lying."

He shook his head, smiling sadly. "I've been wrong. I shouldn't have gone to her. I shouldn't have let you go. I'm sorry. You're the one I love."

"You—you're lying . . . Aren't you?"

My ex-boyfriend pulled his hands out of his pockets and jumped across the Milky Way to stand in front of me. He took my hands. "I'm sorry. Will you forgive me?"

Another pulse, not my heartbeat.

"But . . ."

Don't.

"Please," he said and kissed me.

And why did it feel the same way as it always had? We had never kissed under the Milky Way, or beside it. It made no sense; I felt my desire, the one that I had pushed away so deep within me, coming back to the surface. Or perhaps it was the way I had wanted it to feel, not the way I really remembered. It didn't matter. The world spun, leaving us motionless at its center. I felt his tongue seek mine. Soon my legs would cease to support me. His hand slowly extended downwards . . .

"I said *don't!*"

I gasped and pushed him away from me. It wasn't his voice; we'd been kissing. The lady's token pulsed again, the strongest I had felt, and then swashed through the space with its hot, white light. My ex-boyfriend—someone who looked like him—stumbled and splashed into the stream.

And the space dissolved into nothing—

Just before my consciousness faltered, I felt someone else's arms under me.

I opened my eyes and found Kimura looking down at me. She smiled and I felt a hand squeeze mine. "She's awake," she said.

At her word there was a commotion around me. More faces appeared into my sight. The twins, the woman with the kimono, and other former clients.

I was lying on a thin futon, and though I couldn't see very much of my surroundings, from the way the ceiling looked I was probably in the main building of a shrine. I looked to the twins. "Your place?"

They nodded. A face stuck out from my head's side, upside down. A very beautiful face. "Hello, human."

I grinned. "Hi, goddess." With an effort I sat up; Kimura helped me. "So what's all this about?" I asked her.

Kimura sighed and looked down. Then she looked up again and said, "We don't mean any harm to you, okay?"

"If you did you'd already have done it, right?"

She nodded, and unhooked her mask from behind her ears. Under the mask was a huge mouth, from ear to ear, and I almost choked at the sight.

The twins sprung up, did loops in the air and came back onto the floor as two guardian dogs of a shrine; one of them had a mouth that was forever closed, that was why this one wouldn't speak. The woman with the kimono spun around on the spot, and when she stopped she was a beautiful crane.

Others followed. The woman in black smiled and showed me her magnificent wings. A snow-woman blew some diamond dust. I shook my head, grinning helplessly. "But why did you want to have sex with humans?"

Kimura put her mask back on, probably just for my sake. "We are running short in number. Soon our kinds will extinguish. To stop that, we decided, we needed to mate and have children, but we couldn't find enough male ones of our kind. We decided mating with humans would do, for the time being. Our genes are dominant, you know."

No, I didn't. "I see," I said anyway.

"I'm sorry, I shouldn't have spread the word so widely. I didn't imagine the tanuki would try to do the same."

"Tanuki? You mean . . . raccoon dogs that metamorphose to deceive humans?"

"Right. The ones you just met."

I nodded. So it wasn't him. Of course, my ex-boyfriend had dumped me and went to a prettier, richer woman. "They were trying to make me pregnant?"

"We just can't believe it." One of the guardian-dogs frowned with his already ancient-and-wrinkled brows. "We animal-shaped ones know we cannot mate with human-shaped ones. And borrowing a few seeds from a man and taking the earth from a woman are really different things."

Other creatures around me murmured agreement.

I sat straight facing the lady of the shrine. "Thank you, I think your token helped me."

The lady nodded. "Yes. But you have to say thanks to the man who brought you here, too."

"Who brought me here?"

"Well, who was it?"

The lady looked around. No one answered. Kimura shook her head and said, "We didn't know him. He was probably a human."

I felt a pang of hope. "Was he about my age? Tanned and big?"

She shook her head. "He didn't look like it at all. Lean, tall, and pale. Did he wear glasses?"

Some said yes, some said no to this. I felt my hope shrink to nothing. So it wasn't my ex-boyfriend.

Then we heard a car. It stopped in front of the shrine and the engine died. The twins volunteered to go check. When they came back they both cocked their heads. "Someone left the car at the foot of the gate, and placed this on my pedestal," the twin said and pushed a pair of keys bound by a chain.

"It's my keys."

"The driver was already gone."

I took the keys and turned them around on my palm. It was slightly warm. And I remembered the voice, "I said *don't!*"

I smiled at Kimura and others. "I'm going home now. I promise not to go after a tanuki again."

The lady nodded gravely. "If you get into trouble you come here, okay?" she said. "At least the twins are always at the gate."

"Thanks. And you all tell me when your babies are due, okay?"

Kimura looked amazed at that. "I'd thought you would never want anything to do with us again."

I grinned. "Who wouldn't want to see her client being happy because of the service she had offered?"

On the way home I dropped by at the firm and emailed my boss. I said, "Thank you."

A few minutes later a message came back.

"You're welcome," it said.

THE DISCOVERED COUNTRY

IAN R. MacLEOD

The trees of Farside are incredible. Fireash and oak. Greenbloom and maple. Shot through with every color of autumn as late afternoon sunlight blazes over the Seven Mountains' white peaks. He'd never seen such beauty as this when he was alive.

The virtual Bentley takes the bridge over the next gorge at a tirescream, then speeds on through crimson and gold. Another few miles, and he's following the coastal road beside the Westering Ocean. The sands are burnished, the rocks silver-threaded. Every new vista a fabulous creation. Then ahead, just as purple glower sweeps in from his rear-view over those dragon-haunted mountains, come the silhouette lights of a vast castle, high up on a ridge. It's the only habitation he's seen in hours.

This has to be it.

Northover lets the rise of the hill pull at the Bentley's impetus as its headlights sweep the driveway trees. Another turn, another glimpse of a headland, and there's Elsinore again, rising dark and sheer.

He tries to refuse the offer to carry his luggage made by the neat little creature that emerges into the lamp lit courtyard to greet him with clipboard, sharp shoes, and lemony smile. He's encountered many chimeras by now. The shop assistants, the street cleaners, the crew on the steamer ferry that brought him here. All substantially humanoid, and invariably polite, although amended as necessary to perform their tasks, and far stranger to his mind than the truly dead.

He follows a stairway up through rough-hewn stone. The thing's name is Kasaya. Ah, now. The east wing. I think you'll find what we have here more than adequate. If not . . . Well, you *must* promise to let me know. And this is called the Willow Room. And *do* enjoy your stay. . . .

Northover wanders. Northover touches. Northover breathes. The interior of this large high-ceilinged suite with its crackling applewood fire and narrow, deep-set windows is done out in an elegantly understated arts-and-craftsy style. Among her many attributes, Thea Lorentz always did have excellent taste.

What's struck him most about Farside since he jerked into new existence on the bed in the cabin of that ship bound for New Erin is how unremittingly *real* everything seems. But the slick feel of this patterned silk bed throw . . . the spiky roughness of the teasels in the flower display . . . he's given up telling himself that everything he's experiencing is just some clever construct. The thing about it, the thing that makes it all so impossibly overwhelming, is that *he's* here as well. Dead, but alive. The evidence of his corpse doubtless already incinerated, but his consciousness—the singularity of his existence, what philosophers once called "the conscious I," and theologians the soul, along with his memories and personality, the whole sense of self that had once inhabited pale jelly in his skull—transferred.

The bathroom is no surprise to him now. The dead do so many things the living do, so why not piss and shit as well? He strips and stands in the shower's warm blaze. He soaps, rinses. Reminds himself of what he must do, and say. He'd been warned that he'd soon become attracted to the blatant glories of this world, along with the new, young man's body he now inhabits. Better just to accept it rather than fight. All that matters is that he holds to the core of his resolve.

He towels himself dry. He pulls his watch back on—seemingly a Rolex, but a steel model, neatly unostentatious—and winds it carefully. He dresses. Hangs up his clothes in a walnut paneled wardrobe that smells faintly of mothballs, and hears a knock at the doors just as he slides his case beneath the bed.

"Yes? Come in. . . . "

When he turns, he's expecting another chimera servant. But it's Thea Lorentz.

This, too, is something they'd tried to prepare him for. But encountering her after so long is much less of a shock than he's been expecting. Thea's image is as ubiquitous as that of Marilyn Munroe or the Virgin Mary back on Lifeside, and she really hasn't changed. She's dressed in a loose-fitting shirt. Loafers and slacks. Hair tied-back. No obvious evidence of any make-up. But the crisp white shirt with its rolled up cuffs shows her dark brown skin to perfection, and one loose strand of her tied back hair plays teasingly at her sculpted neck. A tangle of silver bracelets slide on her wrist as she steps forward to embrace him. Her breasts are unbound and she still smells warmly of the patchouli she always used to favor. Everything about her feels exactly the same. But why not? After all, she was already perfect when she was alive.

"Well . . . !" That warm blaze is still in her eyes, as well. "It really *is* you."

"I know I'm springing a huge surprise. Just turning up from out of nowhere like this."

"I can take these kind of surprises any day! And I hear it's only been—what?—less than a week since you transferred. Everything must feel so very strange to you still."

It went without saying that his and Thea's existences had headed off in different directions back on Lifeside. She, of course, had already been well on her way toward some or other kind of immortality when they'd lost touch. And he . . . well, it was just one of those stupid lucky breaks. A short, ironic keyboard riff he'd written to help promote some old online performance thing—no, no, it was nothing she'd been involved in—had ended up being picked up many years later as the standard message-send fail signal on the global net. Yeah, that was the one. Of course, Thea knew it. Everyone, once they thought about it for a moment, did.

"You know, Jon," she says, her voice more measured now, "you're the one person I thought would never choose to make this decision. None of us can pretend that being Farside isn't a position of immense privilege, when most of the living can't afford food, shelter, good health. You always were a man of principle, and I sometimes thought you'd just fallen to . . . well, the same place that most performers fall, I suppose, which is no particular place at all. I even considered trying to find you and get in touch, offer . . . " She gestures around her. "Well, this. But you wouldn't have taken it, would you? Not on those terms."

He shakes his head. In so many ways she still has him right. He detested—no, he quietly reminds himself—*detests* everything about this vast vampiric sham of a world that sucks life, hope, and power from the living. But she hadn't come to him, either, had she? Hadn't offered what she now so casually calls *this*. For all her fame, for all her good works, for all the aid funds she sponsors and the good causes she promotes, Thea Lorentz and the rest of the dead have made no effort to extend their constituency beyond the very rich, and almost certainly never will. After all, why should they? Would the gods invite the merely mortal to join them on Mount Olympus?

She smiles and steps close to him again. Weights both his hands in her own. "Most people I know, Jon—most of those I have to meet and talk to and deal with, and even those I have to call friends—they all think that I'm Thea Lorentz. Both Farside and Lifeside, it's long been the same. But only you and a very few others really know who I am. You can't imagine how precious and important it is to have you here. . . . "

He stands gazing at the door after she's left. Willing everything to dissolve, fade, crash, melt. But nothing changes. He's still dead. He's still standing here in this Farside room. Can still even breathe the faint patchouli of Thea's scent. He finishes dressing—a tie, a jacket, the same supple leather shoes he arrived in—and heads out into the corridor.

Elsinore really is *big*—and resolutely, heavily, emphatically, the ancient building it wishes to be. Cold gusts pass along its corridors. Heavy doors groan and creak. Of course, the delights of Farside are near-infinite. He's passed through forests of mist and silver. Seen the vast, miles-wide back of some great island of a seabeast drift past when he was still out at sea. The dead can grow wings, sprout gills, spread roots into the soil and raise their arms and become trees. All these things are not only possible, but visibly, virtually, achievably real. But he thinks they still hanker after life, and all the things of life the living, for all their disadvantages, possess.

He passes many fine-looking paintings as he descends the stairs. They have a Pre-Raphaelite feel, and from the little he knows of art, seem finely executed, but he doesn't recognize any of them. Have these been created by virtual hands, in some virtual workshop, or have they simply sprung into existence? And what would happen if he took that sword that also hangs on display, and slashed it through a canvas? Would it be gone forever? Almost certainly not. One thing he knows for sure about the Farside's vast database is that it's endlessly backed up, scattered, diffused and re-collated across many secure and heavily armed vaults back in what's left of the world of the living. There are very few guaranteed ways of destroying any of it, least of all by the dead.

Further down, there are holo-images, all done in stylish black and white. Somehow, even in a castle, they don't even look out of place. Thea, as always, looks like she's stepped out of a fashion shoot. The dying jungle suits her. As does this war zone, and this flooded hospital, and this burnt-out shanty town. The kids, and it is mostly kids, who surround her with their pot bellies and missing limbs, somehow manage to absorb a little of her glamour. On these famous trips of hers back to view the suffering living, she makes an incredibly beautiful ghost.

Two big fires burn in Elsinore's great hall, and there's a long table for dinner, and the heads of many real and mythic creatures loom upon the walls. Basilisk, boar, unicorn . . . hardly noticing the chimera servant who rakes his chair out for him, Northover sits down. Thea's space at the top of the table is still empty.

In this Valhalla where the lucky, eternal dead feast forever, what strikes Northover most strongly is the sight of Sam Bartleby sitting beside Thea's vacant chair. Not that he doesn't know that the man has been part of what's termed *Thea Lorentz's inner circle* for more than a decade. But, even when they were all still alive and working together on *Bard on Wheels*, he'd never been able to understand why she put up with the man. Of course, Bartleby made his fortune with those ridiculous action virtuals, but the producers deepened his voice so much, and enhanced his body so ridiculously, that it was a wonder, Northover thought, they bothered to use the actor at all. Now, though, he's chosen to bulk himself out and cut his hair in a Roman fringe. He senses Northover's gaze, and raises his glass, and gives an ironic nod. He still has the self-regarding manner of someone who thinks himself far better looking, not to mention cleverer, than he actually is.

Few of the dead, though, choose to be beautiful. Most elect for the look that expresses themselves at what they thought of as the most fruitful and self-expressive period of their lives. Among people this wealthy, this often equates to late middle age. The fat, the bald, the matronly, and the downright ugly rub shoulders, secure in the knowledge that they can become young and beautiful again whenever they wish.

"So? What are you here for?"

The woman beside him already seems flushed from the wine, and has a homely face and a dimpled smile, although she sports pointed teeth, elfin ears, and her eyes are cattish slots.

"For?"

"Name's Wilhelmina Howard. People just call me Will...." She offers him a claw-nailed hand to shake. "Made my money doing windfarm recycling in the non-federal states. All that lovely superconductor and copper we need right here to keep our power supplies as they should be. Not that we ever had much of a presence in England, which I'm guessing is where you were from...?"

He gives a guarded nod.

"But isn't it just so *great* to be here at Elsinore? *Such* a privilege. Thea's everything people say she is, isn't she, and then a whole lot more as well? *Such* compassion, and all the marvelous things she's done! Still, I know she's invited me here because she wants to get hold of some of my money. Give back a little of what we've taken an' all. Not that I won't give. That's for sure. Those poor souls back on Lifeside. We really have to do something, don't we, all of us...?"

"To be honest, I'm here because I used to work with Thea. Back when we were both alive."

"So, does that make you an *actor?*" Wilhelmina's looking at him more closely now. Her slot pupils have widened. "Should I *recognize* you? Were you in any of the famous—"

"No, no." As if in defeat, he holds up a hand. Another chance to roll out his story. More a musician, a keyboard player, although there wasn't much he hadn't turned his hand to over the years. Master of many trades, and what have you—at least, until that message fail signal came along.

"So, pretty much a lucky break," murmurs this ex-take-no-shit businesswoman who died and became a fat elf, "rather than any kind of lifetime endeavor . . . ?"

Then Thea enters the hall, and she's changed into something more purposefully elegant—a light grey dress that shows her fine breasts and shoulders without seeming immodest—and her hair is differently done, and Northover understands all the more why most of the dead make no attempt to be beautiful. After all, how could they, when Thea Lorentz does it so unassailably well? She stands waiting for a moment as if expectant silence hasn't already fallen, then says a few phrases about how pleased she is to have so many charming and interesting guests. Applause follows. Just as she used to do for many an encore, Thea nods and smiles and looks genuinely touched.

The rest of the evening at Elsinore passes in a blur of amazing food and superb wine, all served with the kind of discreet inevitability that Northover has decided only chimeras are capable of. Just like Wilhelmina, everyone wants to know who he's with, or for, or from. The story about that jingle works perfectly; many even claim to have heard of him and his success. Their curiosity only increases when he explains his and Thea's friendship. After all, he could be the route of special access to her famously compassionate ear.

There're about twenty guests here at Elsinore tonight, all told, if you don't count the several hundred chimeras, which of course no one does. Most of the dead, if you look at them closely enough, have adorned themselves with small eccentricities; a forked tongue here, an extra finger there, a crimson badger-stripe of hair. Some are new to each other, but the interactions flow on easy rails. Genuine fame itself is rare here—after all, entertainment has long been a cheapened currency—but there's a relaxed feeling-out between strangers in the knowledge that some shared acquaintance or interest will soon be reached. Wealth always was an exclusive club, and it's even more exclusive here.

Much of the talk is of new Lifeside investment. Viral re-programming of food crops, all kinds of nano-engineering, weather, flood, and even birth control—although the last strikes Northover as odd considering how rapidly the human population is decreasing—and every other kind of plan imaginable to make the Earth a place worth living in again is discussed. Many of these schemes, he soon realizes, would be mutually incompatible, and potentially incredibly destructive, and all are about making money.

Cigars are lit after the cheeses and sorbets. Rare, exquisite whiskeys are poured. Just like everyone else, he can't help but keep glancing at Thea. She still has that way of seeming part of the crowd yet somehow apart from—or above—it. She always had been a master of managing social occasions, even those rowdy parties they'd hosted back in the day. A few words, a calming hand and smile, and even the most annoying drunk would agree that it was time they took a taxi. For all her gifts as a performer, her true moments of transcendent success were at the lunches, the less-than-chance-encounters, the launch parties. Even her put-downs or betrayals left you feeling grateful.

Everything Farside is so spectacularly different, yet so little about her has changed. The one thing he does notice, though, is her habit of toying with those silver bangles she's still wearing on her left wrist. Then, at what feels like precisely the right moment, and thus fractionally before anyone expects, she stands up and taps her wineglass to say a few more words. From anyone else's lips, they would sound like vague expressions of pointless hope. But, coming from her, it's hard not to be stirred.

Then, with a bow, a nod, and what Northover was almost sure is a small conspiratorial blink in his direction—which somehow seems to acknowledge the inherent falsity of what she has just done, but also the absolute need for it—she's gone from the hall, and the air suddenly seems stale. He stands up and grabs at the tilt of his chair before a chimera servant can get to it. He feels extraordinarily tired, and more than a little drunk.

In search of some air, he follows a stairway that winds up and up. He steps out high on the battlements. He hears feminine chuckles. Around a corner, shadows tussle. He catches the starlit glimpse of a bared breast, and turns the other way. It's near-freezing up out on these battlements. Clouds cut ragged by a blazing sickle moon. Northover leans over and touches the winding crown of his Rolex watch and studies the distant lace of waves. Then, glancing back, he thinks he sees another figure behind him. Not the lovers, certainly. This shape bulks far larger, and is alone. Yet the dim outlines of the battlement gleam though it. A malfunction? A premonition? A genuine ghost? But then, as Northover moves, the figure moves with him, and he realizes that he's seeing nothing but his own shadow thrown by the moon.

He dreams that night that he's alive again, but no longer the young and hopeful man he once was. He's mad old Northy. Living, if you call it living, so high up in the commune tower that no one else bothers him much, and with nothing but an old piano he's somehow managed to restore for company. Back in his old body, as well, with its old aches, fatigues, and irritations. But for once, it isn't raining, and frail sparks of sunlight cling to shattered glass in the ruined rooms, and the whole flooded, once-great city of London is almost beautiful, far below.

Then, looking back, he sees a figure standing at the far end of the corridor that leads through rubble to the core stairs. They come up sometimes, do the kids. They taunt him and try to steal his last few precious things. Northy swears and lumbers forward, grabbing an old broom. But the kid doesn't curse or throw things. Neither does he turn and run, although it looks as if he's come up here alone.

"You're Northy, aren't you?" the boy called Haru says, his voice an adolescent squawk.

He awakes with a start to new light, good health, comforting warmth. A sense, just as he opens his eyes and knowledge of who and what he is returns, that the door to his room has just clicked shut. He'd closed the curtains here in the Willow Room in Elsinore, as well, and now they're open. And the fire grate has been cleared, the applewood logs restocked. He reaches quickly for his Rolex, and begins to relax as he slips it on. The servants, the chimeras, will have been trained, programmed, to perform their work near-invisibly, and silently.

He showers again. He meets the gaze of his own eyes in the mirror as he shaves. Whatever view there might be from his windows is hidden in a mist so thick that the world beyond could be the blank screen of some old computer from his youth. The route to breakfast is signaled by conversation and a stream of guests. The hall is smaller than the one they were in last night, but still large enough. A big fire crackles in a soot-stained hearth, but steam rises from the food as cold air wafts in through the open doors.

Dogs are barking in the main courtyard. Horses are being led out. Elsinore's battlements and towers hover like ghosts in the blanketing fog. People are milling, many wearing thick gauntlets, leather helmets, and what look like padded vests and kilts. The horses are big, beautifully groomed, but convincingly skittish in the way that Northover surmises expensively pedigreed beasts are. Or were. Curious, he goes over to one as a chimera stable boy fusses with its saddle and reins.

The very essence of equine haughtiness, the creature tosses its head and does that lip-blubber thing horses do. Everything about this creature is impressive. The flare of its nostrils. The deep, clean, horsy smell. Even, when he looks down and under, the impressive, seemingly part-swollen heft of its horsey cock.

"Pretty spectacular, isn't he?"

Northover finds that Sam Bartleby is standing beside him. Dressed as if for battle, and holding a silver goblet of something steaming and red. Even his voice is bigger and deeper than it was. The weird thing is, he seems more like Sam Bartleby than the living Sam Bartleby ever did. Even in those stupid action virtuals.

"His name's Aleph—means alpha, of course, or the first. You may have heard of him. He won, yes, didn't you . . . ?" By now, Bartleby's murmuring into the beast's neck. "The last ever Grand Steeplechase de Paris."

Slowly, Northover nods. The process of transfer is incredibly expensive, but there's no reason in principle why creatures other than humans can't join Farside's exclusive club. The dead are bound to want the most prestigious and expensive toys. So, why not the trapped, transferred consciousness of a multi-million dollar racehorse?

"You don't ride, do you?" Bartleby, still fondling Aleph—who, Northover notices, is now displaying an even more impressive erection—asks.

"It wasn't something I ever got around to."

"But you've got plenty of time now, and there are few things better than a day out hunting in the forest. I suggest you start with one of the lesser, easier, mounts over there, and work your way up to a real beast like this. Perhaps that pretty roan? Even then, though, you'll have to put up with a fair few falls. Although, if you really want to cheat and bend the rules, and know the right people, there are shortcuts. . . . "

"As you say, there's plenty of time."

"So," Bartleby slides up into the saddle with what even Northover has to admit is impressive grace. "Why are you here? Oh, I don't mean getting *here* with that stupid jingle. You always were a lucky sod. I mean, at Elsinore. I suppose you want something from Thea. That's why most people come. Whether or not they've got some kind of past with her."

"Isn't friendship enough?"

Bartleby is now looking down at Northover in a manner even more condescending than the horse. "You should know better than most, Jon, that friendship's just another currency." He pauses as he's handed a long spear, its tip a clear, icy substance that could be diamond. "I should warn you that whatever it is you want, you're unlikely to get it. At least, not in the way you expect. A favor for some cherished project, maybe?" His lips curl. "But that's not *it* with you, is it? We know each other too well, Jon, and you really haven't changed. Not one jot. What you really want is Thea, isn't it? Want her wrapped up and whole, even though we both know that's impossible. Thea being Thea just as she always was. And, believe me, I'd do anything to defend her. Anything to stop her being hurt. . . . "

With a final derisory snort and a spark of cobbles, Bartleby and Aleph clatter off.

The rooms, halls, and corridors of Elsinore are filled with chatter and bustle. Impromptu meetings. Accidental collisions and confusions that have surely been long planned. Kisses and business cards are exchanged. Deals are brokered. Promises offered. The spread of the desert that has now consumed most of north Africa could be turned around by new cloud-seeding technologies, yet untold fortunes have been spent providing virtual coffee, or varieties of herb tea if preferred for Farside instead.

No sign of Thea, though. In a way she's more obvious Lifeside, where you can buy as much Thea Lorentz merchandise as even the most fervent fanatic could possibly want. Figurines. Candles. Wallscreens. T-shirts. Some of it, apparently, she even endorses. Although always, of course, in a good cause. Apart from those bothersome kids, it was the main reason Northover spent so much of his last years high up and out of reach of the rest of the commune. He hated being reminded of the way people wasted what little hope and money they had on stupid illusions. Her presence here at Elsinore is palpable, though. Her name is the ghost at the edge of every conversation. Yes, but Thea . . . Thea . . . and Thea . . . Thea . . . Always, always, everything is about Thea Lorentz.

He realizes this place she's elected to call Elsinore isn't any kind of home at all—but he supposes castles have always fulfilled a political function, at least when they weren't under siege. People came from near-impossible distances to plead their cause, and, just as here, probably ended up being fobbed off. Of course, Thea's chimera servants mingle amid the many guests. Northover notices Kasaya many times. A smile here. A mincing gesture there.

He calls after him the next time he sees him bustling down a corridor.

"Yes, Mister Northover . . . ?" Clipboard at the ready, Kasaya spins round on his toes.

"I was just wondering, seeing as you seem to be about so much, if there happen to be more than one of you here at Elsinore?"

"That isn't necessary. It's really just about good organization and hard work."

"So . . . " Was that *really* slight irritation he detected, followed by a small flash of pride? " . . . you can't be in several places at once?"

"That's simply isn't required. Although Elsinore does have many shortcuts."

"You mean, hidden passageways? Like a real castle?"

Kasaya, who clearly has more important things than this to see to, manages a smile. "I think that that would be a good analogy."

"But you just said think. You *do* think?"

"Yes." He's raised his clipboard almost like a shield now. "I believe I do."

"How long have you been here?"

"Oh . . . " He blinks in seeming recollection. "Many years."

"And before that?"

"Before that, I wasn't here." Hugging his clipboard more tightly than ever, Kasaya glances longingly down the corridor. "Perhaps there's something you need? I could summon someone. . . . "

"No, I'm fine. I was just curious about what it must be like to be you, Kasaya. I mean, are you always on duty? Do your kind *sleep?* Do you change out of those clothes and wash your hair and—"

"I'm sorry, sir," the chimera intervenes, now distantly firm. "I really can't discuss these matters when I'm on duty. If I may . . . ?"

Then he's off without a backward glance. Deserts may fail to bloom if the correct kind of finger food isn't served at precisely the right moment. Children blinded by onchocerciasis might not get the implants that will allow them to see grainy shapes for lack of a decent meeting room. And, after all, Kasaya is responding in the way that any servant would—at least, if a guest accosted them and started asking inappropriately personal questions when they were at work. Northover can't help but feel sorry for these creatures, who clearly seem to have at least the illusion of consciousness. To be trapped forever in crowd scenes at the edges of the lives of the truly dead . . .

Northover comes to another door set in a kind of side-turn that he almost walks past. Is this where the chimera servants go? Down this way, Elsinore certainly seems less grand. Bright sea air rattles the arrowslit glass. The walls are raw stone, and stained with white tidemarks of damp. This, he imagines some virtual guide pronouncing, is by far the oldest part of the castle. It certainly feels that way.

He lifts a hessian curtain and steps into a dark, cool space. A single barred, high skylight fans down on what could almost have been a dungeon. Or a monastic cell. Some warped old bookcases and other odd bits of furniture, all cheaply practical, populate a roughly paved floor. In one corner, some kind of divan or bed. In another, a wicker chair. The change of light is so pronounced that it's a moment before he sees that someone is sitting there. A further beat before he realizes it's Thea Lorentz, and that she's seated before a mirror, and her fingers are turning those bangles on her left wrist. Frail as frost, the silver circles tink and click. Otherwise, she's motionless. She barely seems to breathe.

Not a mirror at all, Northover realizes as he shifts quietly around her, but some kind of tunnel or gateway. Through it, he sees a street. It's raining, the sky is reddish with windblown earth, and the puddles seem bright as blood. Lean-to shacks, their gutters sluicing, line something too irregular to be called a street. A dead power pylon leans in the mid-distance. A woman stumbles into view, drenched and wading up to the knee. She's holding something wrapped in rags with a wary possessiveness that suggests it's either a baby or food. This could be the suburbs of London, New York, or Sydney. That doesn't matter. What does matter is how she falls to her knees at what she sees floating before her in the rain. Thea . . . ! She almost drops whatever she carrying as her fingers claw upward and her ruined mouth shapes the name. She's weeping, and Thea's weeping as well—two silver trails that follow the perfect contours of her face. Then, the scene fades in another shudder of rain, and Thea Lorentz is looking out at him from the reformed surface of a mirror with the same soft sorrow that poor, ruined woman must have seen in her gaze.

"Jon."

"This, er . . . " he gestures.

She stands up. She's wearing a long tweed skirt, rumpled boots, a loose turtleneck woolen top. "Oh, it's probably everything people say it is. The truth is that, once you're Farside, it's too easy to forget what Lifeside is really like. People make all the right noises—I'm sure you've heard them already. But that isn't the same thing."

"Going there—being seen as some virtual projection in random places like that—aren't you just perpetuating the myth?"

She nods slowly. "But is that really such a terrible thing? And that cat-eyed woman you sat next to yesterday at dinner. What's her name, Wilhelmina? Kasaya's already committed her to invest in new sewerage processing works and food aid, all of which will be targeted on that particular area of Barcelona. I know she's a tedious creature—you only have to look at her to see that—but what's the choice? You can stand back, and do nothing, or step in, and use whatever you have to try to make things slightly better."

"Is that what you really think?"

"Yes. I believe I do. But how about *you*, Jon? What do you think?"

"You know me," he says. "More than capable of thinking several things at once. And believing, or not believing, all of them."

"Doubting Thomas," she says, taking another step forward so he can smell patchouli.

"Or Hamlet."

"Here of all places, why not?"

For a while, they stand there in silence.

"This whole castle is designed to be incredibly protective of me," she says eventually. "It admits very few people this far. Only the best and oldest of friends. And Bartleby insists I wear these as an extra precaution, even though they can sometimes be distracting. . . . " She raises her braceletted wrist. "As you've probably already gathered, he's pretty protective of me, too."

"We've spoken. It wasn't exactly the happiest reunion."

She smiles. "The way you both are, it would have been strange if it was. But look, you've come all this incredible way. Why don't we go out somewhere?"

"You must have work to do. Projects—I don't know—that you need to approve. People to meet."

"The thing about being in Elsinore is that things generally go more smoothly when Thea Lorentz isn't in the way. You saw what it was like last night at dinner. Every time I open my mouth people expect to hear some new universal truth. I ask them practical questions and their mouths drop. Important deals fall apart when people get distracted because Thea's in the room. That's why Kasaya's so useful. He does all that's necessary—joins up the dots and bangs the odd head. And people scarcely even notice him."

"I don't think he likes it much when they do."

"*More* questions, Jon?" She raises an eyebrow. "But everything here on Farside must still seem so strange to you, when there's so much to explore. . . ."

Down stairways. Along corridors. Through storerooms. Perhaps these are the secret routes Kasaya hinted at, winding through the castle like Escher tunnels in whispers of sea-wet stone. Then they are down in a great, electric-lit cavern of a garage. His Bentley is here, along with lines of other fine and vintage machines long crumbled to rust back on Lifeside. Maseratis. Morgans. Lamborghinis. Other things that look like Dan Dare spaceships or Fabergé submarines. The cold air reeks of new gas, clean oil, polished metal. In a far corner and wildly out of place, squatting above a small black pool, is an old VW Beetle.

"Well," she says. "What do you think?"

He smiles as he walks around it. The dents and scratches are old friends. "It's perfect."

"Well, it was never *that*. But we had some fun with it, didn't we?"

"How does this work? I mean, creating it? Did you have some old pictures of it? Did you manage to access—"

"Jon." She dangles a key from her hand. "Do you want to go out for a drive, or what?"

"The steering even *pulls* the same way. It's amazing. . . . "

Out on roads that climb and camber, giving glimpses through the slowly thinning mist of flanks of forest, deep drops. Headlights on, although it makes little difference and there doesn't seem to be any other traffic. She twiddles the radio. Finds a station that must have stopped transmitting more than fifty years ago. Van Morrison, Springsteen, and Dylan. So very, very out of date—but still good—even back then. And even now, with his brown-eyed girl beside him again. It's the same useless deejay, the same pointless advertisements. As the road climbs higher, the signal fades to a bubbling hiss.

"Take that turn up there. You see, the track right there in the trees . . . ?"

The road now scarcely a road. The Beetle a jumble of metallic jolts and yelps. He has to laugh, and Thea laughs as well, the way they're being bounced around. A tunnel through the trees, and then some kind of clearing, where he stops the engine and squawks the handbrake, and everything falls still.

"Do you remember?"

He climbs out slowly, as if fearing a sudden movement might cause it all to dissolve. "Of course I do. . . . "

Thea, though, strides ahead. Climbs the sagging cabin steps.

"This is . . . "

"I know," she agrees, testing the door. Which—just as it had always been—is unlocked.

This, he thinks as he stumbles forward, is what it really means to be dead. Forget the gills and wings and the fine wines and the spectacular food and the incredible scenery. What this is, what it means . . .

Is *this*.

The same cabin. It could be the same day. Thea, she'd called after him as he walked down the street away from an old actors' pub off what was still called Covent Garden after celebrating—although that wasn't the word—the end of *Bard on Wheels* with a farewell pint and spliff. Farewell and fuck off as far as Northover was concerned, Sam Bartleby and his stupid sword fights especially. Shakespeare and most other kinds of real performance being well and truly dead, and everyone heading for well-deserved obscurity. The sole exception being Thea Lorentz, who could sing and act and do most things better than all the rest of them combined, and had an air of being destined for higher things that didn't seem like arrogant bullshit even if it probably was. Out of his class, really, both professionally and personally. But she'd called to him, and he'd wandered back, for where else was he heading? She'd said she had a kind of proposal, and why didn't they go out for a while out in her old VW? All the bridges over the Thames hadn't yet been down then, and they'd driven past the burnt-out cars and abandoned shops until they came to this stretch of woodland where the trees were still alive, and they'd ended up exactly here. In this clearing, inside this cabin.

There's an old woodburner stove that Northover sets about lighting, and a few tins along the cobwebbed shelves, which he inspects, then settles on a can of soup, which he nearly cuts his thumb struggling to open, and sets to warm on the top of the fire as it begins to send out amber shadows. He goes to the window, clears a space in the dust, pretending to check if he turned the VW's lights off, but in reality trying to grab a little thinking time. He didn't, doesn't, know Thea Lorentz that well at this or any point. But he knows her well enough to understand that her spontaneous suggestions are nothing if not measured.

"Is this how it was, do you think?" she asks, shrugging off her coat and coming to stand behind him. Again, that smell of patchouli. She slides her arms around his waist. Nestles her chin against his shoulder. "I wanted you to be what I called producer and musical director for my Emily Dickinson thing. And you agreed."

"Not before I'd asked if you meant roadie and general dogsbody."

He feels her chuckle. "That as well. . . . "

"What else was I going to do, anyway?" Dimly, in the gaining glow of the fire, he can see her and his face in reflection.

"And how about now?"

"I suppose it's much the same."

He turns. It's he who clasps her face, draws her mouth to his. Another thing about Thea is that, even when you know it's always really her, it somehow seems to be you.

Their teeth clash. It's been a long time. This is the first time ever. She draws back, breathless, pulls off that loose-fitting jumper she's wearing. He helps her with the shift beneath, traces, remembers, discovers or rediscovers, the shape and weight of her breasts. Thumbs her hardening nipples. Then, she pulls away his shirt, undoes his belt buckle. Difficult here to be graceful, even if you're Thea Lorentz, struggle-hopping with zips, shoes, and panties. Even harder for Northover with one sock off and the other caught on something or other, not to mention his young man's erection, as he throws a dusty blanket over the creaky divan. But laughter helps. Laughter always did. That, and Thea's knowing smile as she takes hold of him for a moment in her cool fingers. Then, Christ, she lets go of him again. A final pause, and he almost thinks this isn't going to work, but all she's doing is pulling off those silver bracelets, and then, before he can realize what else it is she wants, she's snapping off the bangle of his Rolex as well and pulling him down, and now there's nothing else to be done, for they really are naked.

Northover, he's drowning in memory. Greedy at first, hard to hold back, especially with the things she does, but then trying to be slow, trying to be gentle. Or, at least, a gentleman. He remembers, anyway—or is it now happening?—that time she took his head between her hands and raised it to her gaze. *You don't have to be so careful,* she murmurs. Or murmured. *I'm flesh and blood, Jon. Just like you. . . .*

He lies back. Collapsed. Drenched. Exhausted. Sated. He turns from the cobwebbed ceiling and sees that the Rolex lies cast on the gritty floor. Softly ticking. Just within reach. But already, Thea is stirring. She scratches, stretches. Bracelet hoops glitter as they slip back over her knuckles. He stands up. Pads over to a stained sink. There's a trickle of water. What might pass for a towel. Dead or living, it seems, the lineaments of love remain the same.

"You never were much of a one for falling asleep after," Thea comments, straightening her sleeves as she dresses.

"Not much of a man, then."

"Some might say that. . . . " She laughs as she fluffs her hair. "But we had something, didn't we, Jon? We really did. So why not again?"

There it is. Just when he thinks the past's finally over and done with. Not Emily Dickinson this time, or not only that project, but a kind of greatest hits. Stuff they did together with *Bard on Wheels,* although this time it'll be just them, a two-hander, a proper double act, and, yes Jon, absolutely guaranteed no Sam fucking Bartleby. Other things as well. A few songs, sketches. Bits and bobs. Fun, of course. But wasn't the best kind of fun always the stuff you took seriously? And why not start here and see how it goes? Why not tonight, back at Elsinore?

As ever, what can he say but yes?

Thea drives. He supposes she did before, although he can't really remember how they got back to London. The mist has cleared. She, the sea, the mountains, all look magnificent. That Emily Dickinson thing, the one they did before, was a huge commercial and critical success. Even if people did call it a one-woman show, when he'd written half the script and all the music. To have those looks, and yet be able to hold the stage and sing and act so expressively! Not to mention, although the critics generally did, that starlike ability to assume a role, yet still be Thea Lorentz. Audrey Hepburn got a mention. So did Grace Kelly. A fashion icon, too, then. But Thea could carry a tune better than either. Even for the brief time they were actually living together in that flat in Pimlico, Northover sometimes found himself simply looking—staring, really—at Thea. Especially when she was sleeping. She just seemed so angelic. Who are you really, he'd wondered. Where are you from? Why are you here, and with me of all people?

He never did work out the full chain of events that brought her to join *Bard on Wheels.* Of course, she'd popped up in other troupes and performances— the evidence was still to be found on blocky online postings and all those commemorative hagiographies, but remembrances were shaky and it was hard to work out the exact chain of where and when. A free spirit, certainly. A natural talent. Not the sort who'd ever needed instructing. She claimed that she'd lost both her parents to the Hn3i epidemic, and had grown up in one of those giant orphanages they set up at Heathrow. As to where she got that poise, or the studied assurance she always displayed, all the many claims, speculations, myths, and stories that eventually emerged—and which she never made any real attempt to quash—drowned out whatever had been the truth.

They didn't finish the full tour. Already, the offers were pouring in. He followed her once to pre-earthquake, pre-nuke Los Angeles, but by then people weren't sure what his role exactly was in the growing snowball of Thea Lorentz's fame, and neither was he. Flunky, most likely. Not that she was unfaithful. At least, not to his knowledge. She probably never had the time. Pretty clear to everyone, though, that Thea Lorentz was moving on and up. And that he wasn't. Without her, although he tried getting other people involved, the Emily Dickinson poem arrangements sounded like the journeyman pieces they probably were. Without her, he even began to wonder about the current whereabouts of his other old sparring partners in *Bard on Wheels*.

It was out in old LA, at a meal at the Four Seasons, that he'd met, encountered, experienced—whatever the word for it was—his first dead person. They were still pretty rare back then, and this one had made its arrival on the roof of the hotel by veetol just to show that it could, when it really should have just popped into existence in the newly installed reality fields at their table like Aladdin's genie. The thing had jittered and buzzed, and its voice seemed over-amplified. Of course, it couldn't eat, but it pretended to consume a virtual plate of quail in puff pastry with foie gras in a truffle sauce, which it pretended to enjoy with virtual relish. You couldn't fault the thing's business sense, but Northover took the whole experience as another expression of the world's growing sickness.

Soon, it was the Barbican and the Sydney Opera House for Thea (and how sad it was that so many of these great venues were situated next to the rising shorelines) and odd jobs or no jobs at all for him. The flat in Pimlico went, and so, somewhere, did hope. The world of entertainment was careening, lemming-like, toward the cliffs of pure virtuality, with just a few bright stars such as Thea to give it the illusion of humanity. Crappy fantasy-dramas or rubbish docu-musicals that she could sail through and do her Thea Lorentz thing, giving them an undeserved illusion of class. At least, and unlike that idiot buffoon Bartleby, Northover could see why she was in such demand. When he thought of what Thea Lorentz had become, with her fame and her wealth and her well-publicized visits to disaster areas and her audiences with the Pope and the Dalai Lama, he didn't exactly feel surprised or bitter. After all, she was only doing whatever it was that she'd always done.

Like all truly beautiful women, at least those who take care of themselves, she didn't age in the way that the rest of the world did. If anything, the slight sharpening of those famous cheekbones and the small care lines that drew around her eyes and mouth made her seem even more breath-takingly elegant. Everyone knew that she would mature slowly and gracefully and that she would make—just like the saints with whom she was now most often compared—a beautiful, and probably incorruptible, corpse. So, when news broke that she'd contracted a strain of new-variant septicemic plague when she was on a fact-finding trip in Manhattan, the world fell into mourning as it hadn't done since . . . well, there was no comparison, although JFK and Martin Luther King got a mention, along with Gandhi and Jesus Christ and Joan of Arc and Marylyn Monroe and that lost Mars mission and Kate and Diana.

Transfer—a process of assisted death and personality uploading—was becoming a popular option. At least, amongst the few who could afford it. The idea that the blessed Thea might refuse to do this thing, and deprive a grieving world of the chance to know that somehow, somewhere, she was still there, and on their side, and sorrowing as they sorrowed, was unthinkable. By now well ensconced high up in his commune with his broom and his reputation as an angry hermit, left with nothing but his memories and that wrecked piano he was trying to get into tune, even Northover couldn't help but follow this ongoing spectacle. Still, he felt strangely detached. He'd long fallen out of love with Thea, and now fell out of admiring her as well. All that will-she won't-she crap that she was doubtless engineering even as she lay there on her deathbed! All she was doing was just exactly what she'd always done, and twisting the whole fucking world around her fucking little finger. But then maybe, just possibly, he was getting the tiniest little bit bitter. . . .

Back at Elsinore, Kasaya has already been at work. Lights, a low stage, decent mikes and P.A. system, along with a spectacular grand piano, have all been installed at the far end of the great hall where they sat for yesterday's dinner. The long tables have been removed, the chairs re-arranged. Or replaced. It really does look like a bijou theatre. The piano's a Steinway. If asked, Northover might have gone for a Bechstein. The action, to his mind, and with the little chance he's even had to ever play such machines, being a tad more responsive. But you can't have everything, he supposes. Not even here.

The space is cool, half-dark. The light from the windows is settling. Bartleby and his troupe of merry men have just returned from their day of tally-ho slaughter with a giant boar hung on ropes. Tonight, by sizzling flamelight out in the yard, the dining will be alfresco. And after that . . . well, word has already got out that Thea and this newly arrived guy at Elsinore are planning some kind of reunion performance. No wonder the air in this empty hall feels expectant.

He sits down. Wondrous and mysterious as Thea Lorentz's smile, the keys—which are surely real ivory—gleam back at him. He plays a soft e-minor chord. The sound shivers out. Beautiful. Although that's mostly the piano. Never a real musician, Northy. Nor much of a real actor, either. Never a real anything. Not that much of a stagehand, even. Just got lucky for a while with a troupe of traveling players. Then, as luck tends to do, it ran out on you. But still. He hasn't sat at one of these things since he died, yet it couldn't feel more natural. As the sound fades, and the gathering night washes in, he can hear the hastening tick of his Rolex.

The door at the far end bangs. He thinks it's most likely Kasaya. But it's Thea. Barefoot now. Her feet slip on the polished floor. Dark slacks, an old, knotted shirt. Hair tied back. She looks the business. She's carrying loose sheaves of stuff—notes, bits of script and sheet music—almost all of which he recognizes as she slings them down across the gleaming lid of the piano.

"Well," she says, "shall we do this thing?"

Back in his room, he stands for a long time in the steam heat of the shower. Finds he's soaping and scrubbing himself until his skin feels raw and his head is dizzy. He'd always wondered about those guys from al-Qaeda and Hezbollah and the Taliban and New Orthodoxy. Why they felt such a need to shave and cleanse the bodies they would soon be destroying. Now, though, he understands perfectly. The world is ruined and time is out of joint, but this isn't just a thing you do out of conviction. The moment has to be right, as well.

Killing the dead isn't easy. In fact, it's near impossible. But not quite. The dead's great strength is the sheer overpowering sense of reality they bring to the sick fantasy they call Farside. Everything must work. Everything has to be what it is, right down to the minutest detail. Everything must be what it seems to be. But this is also their greatest weakness. Of course, they told Northy when they took off his blindfold as he sat chained to a chair that was bolted to the concrete floor in that deserted shopping mall, we can try to destroy them by trying to tear everything in Farside apart. We can fly planes into their reactors, introduce viruses into their processing suites, flood their precious data vaults with seawater. But there's always a backup. There's always another power source. We can never wreck enough of Farside to have even a marginal effect upon the whole. But the dead themselves are different. Break down the singularity of their existence for even an instant, and you destroy it forever. The dead become truly dead.

Seeing as it didn't exist as a real object, they had to show him the Rolex he'd be wearing through a set of VR gloves and goggles. Heavy-seeming, of course, and ridiculously over-engineered, but then designer watches had been that way for decades. This is what you must put on along with your newly assumed identity when you return to consciousness in a cabin on board a steamer ferry bound for New Erin. In many ways, the watch is what it appears to be. It ticks. It tells the time. You'll even need to remember to wind it up. But carefully. Pull the crown out and turn it backward—no, no, not now, not even here, you mustn't—and it will initiate a massive databurst. The Farside equivalent of an explosion of about half a pound of semtex, atomizing anything within a three-meter radius—yourself, of course, included, which is something we've already discussed—and causing damage, depending on conditions, in a much wider sphere. Basically, though, you need to be within touching distance of Thea Lorentz to be sure, to be certain. But that alone isn't enough. She'll be wearing some kind of protection that will download her to a safe backup even in the instant of time it takes the blast to expand. We don't know what that protection will be, although we believe she changes it regularly. But, whatever it is, it must be removed.

A blare of lights. A quieting of the murmuring audience as Northover steps out. Stands center stage. Reaches in his pocket. Starts tossing a coin. Which, when Thea emerges, he drops. The slight sound, along with her presence, rings out. One thing to rehearse, but this is something else. He'd forgotten, he really had, how Thea raises her game when you're out here with her, and it's up to you to try to keep up.

A clever idea that went back to *Bard on Wheels,* to re-reflect *Hamlet* through some of the scenes of Stoppard's *Rozencrantz and Guildenstern Are Dead,* where two minor characters bicker and debate as the whole famous tragedy grinds on in the background. Northover doubts if this dumb, rich, dead audience get many of the references, but that really doesn't matter when the thing flows as well as it does. Along with the jokes and witty wordplay, all the stuff about death, and life in a box being better than no life at all, gains a new resonance when it's performed here on Farside. The audience are laughing fit to bust by the end of the sequence, but you can tell in the falls of silence that come between that they know something deeper and darker is really going on.

It's the same when he turns to the piano, and Thea sings a few of Shakespeare's jollier songs. For, as she says as she stands there alone in the spotlight and her face glows and those bangles slide upon her arms, "The man that hath no music in himself, the motions of his spirit are dull as night." She even endows his arrangement of "Under the Greenwood Tree," which he always thought too saccharine, with a bittersweet air.

This, Northover thinks, as they move on to the Emily Dickinson section—which, of course, is mostly about death—is why I have to do this thing. Not because Thea's fake or because she doesn't believe in what she's doing. Not because she isn't Thea Lorentz any longer and has been turned inside out by the dead apologists into some parasitic ghost. Not because what she does here at Elsinore is a sham. I must do this because she is, and always was, the treacherous dream of some higher vision of humanity, and people will only ever wake up and begin to shake off their shackles when they realize that living is really about forgetting such illusions, and looking around them, and picking up a fucking broom and clearing up the mess of the world themselves. The dead take our power, certainly—both physically and figuratively. The reactors that drive the Farside engines use resources and technologies the living can barely afford. Their clever systems subvert and subsume our own. They take our money, too. Masses and masses of it. Who'd have thought that an entirely virtual economy could do so much better than one that's supposedly real? But what they really take from us, and the illusion that Thea Lorentz will continue to foster as long as she continues to exist, is hope.

Because I did not stop for death . . . Not knowing when the dawn will come, I open every door. . . . It all rings so true. You could cut the air with a knife. You could pull down the walls of the world. Poor Emily Dickinson, stuck in that homestead with her dying mother and that sparse yet volcanic talent that no one even knew about. Then, and just when the audience are probably expecting something lighter to finish off, it's back to Hamlet, and sad, mad Ophelia's songs—which are scattered about the play just as she is; a wandering, hopeless, hopeful ghost—although Northover has gathered them together as a poignant posy in what he reckons is some of his best work. Thea knows it as well. Her instincts for these things are more honed than his ever were. After all, she's a trouper. A legend. She's Thea Lorentz. She holds and holds the audience as new silence falls. Then, just as she did in rehearsal, she slides the bangles off her arm, and places them atop the piano, where they lie bright as rain circles in a puddle.

"Keep this low and slow and quiet," she murmurs, just loud enough for everyone in the hall to hear as she steps back to the main mike. He lays his hands on the keys. Waits, just as they always did, for the absolute stilling of the last cough, mutter, and shuffle. Plays the chords that rise and mingle with her perfect, perfect voice. The lights shine down on them from out of sheer blackness, and it's goodnight, sweet ladies, and rosemary for remembrance, which bewept along the primrose path to the grave where I did go. . . .

As the last chord dies, the audience erupts. Thea Lorentz nods, bows, smiles as the applause washes over her in great, sonorous, adoring waves. It's just the way it always was. The spotlight loves her, and Northover sits at the piano for what feels like a very long time. Forgotten. Ignored. It would seem churlish for him not to clap as well. So he does. But Thea knows the timing of these things better than anyone, and the crowd loves it all the more when, the bangles looped where she left them on the piano, she beckons him over. He stands up. Crosses the little stage to join her in the spotlight. Her bare left arm slips easily around his waist as he bows. This could be Carnegie Hall. This could be the Bolshoi. The manacling weight of the Rolex drags at his wrist. Thea smells of patchouli and of Thea, and the play's the thing, and there could not, never could be, a better moment.

There's even Sam Bartleby, grinning but pissed-off right there on the front row and well within range of the blast.

They bow again, *thankyouthankyouthankyou*, and by now Thea's holding him surprisingly tightly, and it's difficult for him to reach casually around to the Rolex, even though he knows it must be done. Conscience doth make cowards of us all, but the time for doubt is gone, and he's just about to pull and turn the crown of his watch when Thea murmurs something toward his ear which, in all this continuing racket, is surely intended only for him.

"What?" he shouts back.

Her hand cups his ear more closely. Her breath, her entire seemingly living body, leans into him. Surely one of those bon mots that performers share with each other in times of triumph such as this. Just something else that the crowds love to see.

"Why don't you do it now?" Thea Lorentz says to Jon Northover. "What's stopping you . . . ?"

He's standing out on the moonlit battlements. He doesn't know how much time has passed, but his body is coated in sweat and his hands are trembling and his ears still seem to be ringing and his head hurts. Performance comedown to end all performance come-downs, and surely it's only a matter of minutes before Sam Bartleby, or perhaps Kasaya, or whatever kind of amazing Farside device it is that really works the security here at Elsinore, comes to get him. Perhaps not even that. Maybe he'll just vanish. Would that be so terrible? But then, they have cellars here at Elsinore. Dungeons, even. Put to the question. Matters of concern and interest. Things they need to know. He wonders how much full-on pain a young, fit body such as the one he now inhabits is capable of bearing. . . . He fingers the Rolex, and studies the drop, but somehow he can't bring himself to do it.

When someone does come, it's Thea Lorentz. Stepping out from the shadows into the spotlight glare of the moon. He sees that she's still not wearing those bangles, but she keeps further back from him now, and he knows it's already too late.

"What made you realize?"

She shrugs. Shivers. Pulls down her sleeves. "Wasn't it one of the first things I said to you? That you were too principled to ever come here?"

"That was what I used to think as well."

"Then what made you change your mind?"

Her eyes look sadder than ever. More compassionate. He wants to bury his face in her hair. After all, Thea could always get more out of him than anyone. So he tells her about mad old Northy, with that wrecked piano he'd found in what had once been a rooftop bar up in his eyrie above the commune, which he'd spent his time restoring because what else was there to do? Last working piano in London, or England, most likely. Or the whole fucking world come to that. Not that it was ever that much of a great shakes. Nothing like here. Cheaply built in Mexico of all places. But then this kid called Haru comes up, and he says he's curious about music, and he asks Northy to show him his machine for playing it, and Northy trusts the kid, which feels like a huge risk. Even that first time he sits Haru down at it, though, he knows he's something special. He just has that air.

"And you know, Thea . . . " Northover finds he's actually laughing. "You know what the biggest joke is? Haru didn't even *realize*. He could read music quicker than I can read words, and play like Chopin and Chick Corea, and to him it was all just this lark of a thing he sometimes did with this mad old git up on the fortieth floor. . . .

"But he was growing older. Kids still do, you know, back on Lifeside. And one day he's not there, and when he does next turn up, there's this girl downstairs who's apparently the most amazing thing in the history of everything, and I shout at him and tell him just how fucking brilliant he really is. I probably even used the phrase *God-given talent*, whatever the hell that's supposed to mean. But anyway . . . "

"Yes?"

Northover sighs. This is the hard bit, even though he's played it over a million times in his head. "They become a couple, and she soon gets pregnant, and she has a healthy baby, even though they seem ridiculously young. A kind of miracle. They're so proud they even take the kid up to show me, and he plongs his little hands on my piano, and I wonder if he'll come up one day to see old Northy, too. Given a few years, and assuming old Northy's still alive, that is, which is less than likely. But that isn't how it happens. The baby gets sick. It's winter and there's an epidemic of some new variant of the nano flu. Not to say there isn't a cure. But the cure needs money—I mean, you know what these retrovirals cost better than anyone, Thea—which they simply don't have. And this is why I should have kept my big old mouth shut, because Haru must have remembered what I yelled at him about his rare, exceptional musical ability. And he decides his baby's only just starting on his life, and he's had a good innings of eighteen or so years. And if there's something he can do, some sacrifice he can make for his kid . . . So that's what he does. . . . "

"You're saying?"

"Oh, come on, Thea! I know it's not legal, either Lifeside or here. But we both know it goes on. Everything has its price, especially talent. And the dead have more than enough vanity and time, if not the application, to fancy themselves as brilliant musicians, just the same way they might want to ride an expensive thoroughbred, or fuck like Casanova, or paint like Picasso. So

Haru sold himself, or the little bit that someone here wanted, and the baby survived and he didn't. It's not that unusual a story, Thea, in the great scheme of things. But it's different, when it happens to someone you know, and you feel you're to blame."

"I'm sorry," she says.

"Do you think that's enough?"

"Nothing's ever enough. But do you really believe that whatever arm of the resistance you made contact with actually wanted me, Thea Lorentz, fully dead? What about the reprisals? What about the global outpouring of grief? What about all the inevitable, endless let's-do-this-for-Thea bullshit? Don't you think it would suit the interests of Farside itself far better to remove this awkward woman who makes unfashionable causes fashionable and brings attention to unwanted truths? Wouldn't *they* prefer to extinguish Thea Lorentz and turn her into a pure symbol they can manipulate and market however they wish? Wouldn't that make far better sense than whatever it was you thought you were doing?"

The sea heaves. The whole night heaves with it.

"If you want to kill me, Jon, you can do so now. But I don't think you will. You can't, can you? That's where the true weakness of whoever conceived you and this plan lies. You *had* to be what you are, or were, to get this close to me. You had to have free will, or at least the illusion of it. . . . "

"What the hell are you saying?"

"I'm sorry. You might think you're Jon Northover—in fact, I'm sure you do—but you're not. You're not him really."

"That's—"

"No. Hear me out. You and I both know in our hearts that the real Jon Northover wouldn't be here on Farside. He'd have seen through the things I've just explained to you, even if he had ever contemplated actively joining the resistance. But that isn't it, either. Not really. I loved you, Jon Northover. Loved *him*. It's gone, of course, but I've treasured the memories. Turned them and polished them, I suppose. Made them into something realer and clearer than ever existed. This afternoon, for instance. It was all too perfect. You haven't changed, Jon. You haven't changed at all. People, real people, either dead or living, they shift and they alter like ghosts in a reflection, but you haven't. You stepped out of my past, and there you were, and I'm so, so, sorry to have to tell you these things, for I fully believe that you're a conscious entity that feels pain and doubt just like all the rest of us. But the real Jon Northover is most likely long dead. He's probably lying in some mass grave. He's just another lost statistic. He's gone beyond all recovery, Jon, and I mourn for him deeply. All you are is something that's been put together from my stolen memories. You're too, too perfect."

"You're just saying that. You don't know."

"But I do. That's the difference between us. One day, perhaps, chimeras such as you will share the same rights as the dead, not to mention the living. But that's one campaign too far even for Thea Lorentz—at least, while she still has some control over her own consciousness. But I think you know, or at least you *think* you do, how to tune a piano. Do you know what inharmonicity is?"

"Of course I do, Thea. It was me who told you about it. If the tone of a piano's going to sound right, you can't tune all the individual strings to exactly the correct pitch. You have to balance them out slightly to the sharp or the flat. Essentially, you tune a piano ever so marginally out of tune, because of the way the strings vibrate and react. Which is imperfectly . . . Which is . . . I mean . . . which is . . . "

He trails off. A flag flaps. The clouds hang ragged. Cold moonlight pours down like silver sleet. Thea's face, when he brings himself to look at it, seems more beautiful than ever.

The trees of Farside are magnificent. Fireash and oak. Greenbloom and maple. Shot through with every color of autumn as dawn blazes toward the white peaks of the Seven Mountains. He's never seen such beauty as this. The tide's further in today. Its salt smell, as he winds down the window and breathes it in, is somehow incredibly poignant. Then the road sweeps up from the coast. Away from the Westering Ocean. As the virtual Bentley takes a bridge over a gorge at a tirescream, it dissolves in a roaring pulse of flame.

A few machine parts twist jaggedly upward, but they settle as the wind bears away the sound and the smoke. Soon, there's only the sigh of the trees, and the hiss of a nearby waterfall. Then there's nothing at all.

THE WILDFIRES OF ANTARCTICA

ALAN DeNIRO

I loaned *Roxy: Shark * Flower* to the Antarctica Institute for the Arts because I wanted a better life for her; at the same time, it soon became apparent that the same problems that vexed me in regards to her behavior would trouble the museum. Although she was out of my hands I still carried a concern about her well-being, as well as an aesthetic sense of pride, and an interest in whether her time in the museum would appreciate her value.

Was it punitive on my part? I suppose it was. But she was the one who threw everything away. Roxy once had everything she ever wanted: protection from thieves, food.

There are many others like her in the museum—though no two alike; that indeed could be a journeyman's definition of art—and I was assured there would be opportunities for supervised interactions with other *objets d'art* with her same level of genetic provenance. And no expense would be spared in her preservation. Her display case contained the ambient full-spectrum lights that she needed for the chrysanthemums and poppies and amaranths to grow along the seams of her arms. Roxy would not be able to harm herself or others with her serrated molars, since they were capped; when they shed, the cap would grow with the new tooth. (The museum and I agreed to a fifty/fifty split on residuals for the aftermarket sale for the teeth no longer in her mouth, for the scrimshaw of majestic oaks the artist had encoded there.) A daily spore spritz and dry would keep her hair—coarse on her crown and spine, ultra-fine on her arms and legs—from losing its luminous sheen.

And of course the museum gave me the opportunity to watch her every hour of the day. The surveillance bees would always be with her. I was a busy man, but I rarely left the villa, so I often checked on Roxy throughout my day. It soothed my soul.

Here is Roxy sleeping, curled up in a ball in the corner of her case, the bees bobbing around her head.

Here is Roxy eating a block of nutrience, then another.

Here is Roxy in the greenhouse yard—named *The Van Gogh Arboretum*—with a soothing panorama of the Dutch countryside circa 1900 all around her. The museum, of course, is in West Antarctica, and the Dutch countryside is underwater, but Roxy has no way to know of these affairs. She hangs from her tail from one of the oak trees (a predisposition on her part that the artist cleverly integrated into her DNA) and swings gently, watching everything. There are only five or six other pieces of the collection allowed in the greenhouse at the same time. I certainly have interest in seeing what else is being accomplished in the field, and by whom. Two particular pieces catch my eye: Mareanxerias' *The Epoxy Disaster of Late Model Capitalism* (a hairless golden bear cub with horse quarters) and *Paint! Paint! Paint!* (a taxidermied wolf head attached to a cherry-colored, wheel-less motorcycle chassis and eight spidery legs) by the sublime master Ya Li.

Epoxy and Paint always stand next to each other, and rarely exercise or relax. Their legs twitch. At first I think it is a glitch but after a museum guard attempts to separate the two, I realize that they are communicating to each other. The two shuffle apart before the guard can reach them but slowly gravitate back together after his departure. This occurs over the course of several days during their hour-long stays in the Van Gogh Arboretum.

Roxy begins to find this curious. She has never been willing to make the first move with anything, but one time she presses her body against the glass of the panorama, close to Epoxy and Paint. As if trying to capture the false sunlight in her body. (She does not photosynthesize.) Eventually Epoxy and Paint look over at her in unison, and soon the two in conversation-by-tapping become three, though I have no way to know how Roxy has picked up on such a vernacular, since she was never taught such things in my villa.

Still, this is worrisome. I alert my concierge at the museum and soon enough several guards come into the Arboretum to put a stop to this extraneous socialization. They are heavily armed with non-lethal coercive wands. Roxy sees them approach and her nostrils flare. I try to connect to my concierge again to warn the museum staff but before that can happen, Roxy wraps her tail around one of the guards' necks and snaps it.

Roxy tries to dash away, but nano-netting swoops down from the ceiling.

Even Epoxy and Paint seem scandalized. They try to disentangle themselves from the melee, but are caught in the netting as well.

Roxy's access to the Arboretum is revoked, and a guard is in sight of her display case at all times. I should feel horrified and disappointed, but I am not. Because I know that Roxy's errant behavior is deep-seated and incapable of being cured. I once tried instilling discipline into Roxy by telling her which rooms she could and couldn't enter in the villa. The kitchen: only when it was time for her to eat. The foyer: only when guests were present for a reception and she was beckoned to remain motionless there. The study: never, under any circumstances. The library: never. My wife's rooms: never.

But she never listened.

The next day I send an invitation to Roxy's artist for a light afternoon lunch at the villa and a leisurely suborbital artillery firing. He agrees. I can tell he is reluctant.

Artists are a necessary evil in my world.

John Priestly—such an old-fashioned name—flies in from New Yellowknife. His skin has a bluish sheen to it, and I can't tell whether that is a side effect from his latest anti-aging treatments or preparation for using his own body as a genetic canvas yet again. Perhaps they are the same thing.

On the rooftop overlooking the burning hills, we sit down for lunch and I ask him about a possible restoration job of Roxy. One, would this be feasible with a minimum of cost overruns, and two, would this decrease her resale value at auction?

He sips his tea and stares at me for a long time. "*Roxy: Shark * Flower*," he says at last, "is far more perfect than you can ever imagine. I wouldn't dream of altering her, not a single strand of code."

I smile and recount her aberrant behavior, perhaps laying the blame for her disposition at his feet. After all, I have always believed the artist has a certain moral responsibility for the very act of creation.

John leans forward and pierces a grape with his fingernail. He draws the grape to his mouth, as if he is a poison-tester. "Each piece of art is unique, and has a different effect upon each person who encounters the work. Would you have asked Goya to make *Saturn Devouring His Own Son* a little less violent? Perhaps, you know, 'tone it down'?"

I tell him, this time without a smile, that I paid 500 million for Roxy, and that he's no Goya.

He laughs. "No, no I am not. No one is, anymore. Not even Ya Li."

I stare at him, and tell him that maintaining his artistic integrity is all well and good, but that Roxy is slowly becoming a menace, if she is not one already.

"And how do you not know that this, too, is part of what makes her beautiful?" He shakes his head, and speaks to himself, as if I had suddenly disappeared, and he was left alone in a stranger's house. "I once thought like you did. I worked so hard on my craft, and to make sure that people like you remained pleased. But now . . . no." He is sure of his rightness, and I find this frightening.

I stand up, and he follows suit, and shuffles to his helicopter without a farewell. It turns out that we will not be shooting satellite armaments into the ruins of Buenos Aires—not together, at least. I discount his outburst as mere petulance. He loves his helicopters and studio-fortress and fame too much. He will never change.

After a week of constant confinement, Roxy appears to have calmed, though her behavior is a bit erratic. She paces, she sleeps, she makes tiny trilling noises from the back of her throat. She tips her head back and laughs. I have never seen her laugh before. A troupe of teenagers from New Dubai traipse through the museum halls, disinterested in any of the work, soldiering on as if polar explorers from another century. As they walk past Roxy—the tour guide wisely decides not to dwell on her—she splays herself on the glass of her case and bares her teeth, her double line of fangs.

All of her teeth are uncapped.

Several of them begin shrieking, placing calls to their parents and nannies to rescue the teenagers. The tour guide fumbles with the emergency response interface attached to her arm. A sleeping gas fills the case and fogs it. Roxy struggles and lashes out, longer than I thought would have been possible, until at last she slumbers. She is taken to the Department of Restoration.

The next morning I decide that I need to buy some new art to clear my head. A fresh start for my collection.

As I make preparations to fly to Cape Adare—my favorite gallery spot—I wonder how Roxy will respond to restoration. John Priestly would have been the ideal candidate for the task, of course, but that is out of the question. The museum has the best team on the continent. So they say. I hear that Epoxy and Paint are in restoration as well. The atmosphere has been growing more chaotic in the Arboretum, even with Roxy's absence: more scuffles with guards, more cunning attempts at communication with other pieces of art.

In a way I am already beginning to say goodbye to Roxy, as a squandered investment to write off. It will hurt, but not as much as these constant tantrums on her part. Art, above everything else, is a sign of one's station in life, and it is difficult to properly display one's station if there is not decorum.

I am about to put on my favorite art-buying suit and go up to the helipad, but I get the ping from the museum.

Roxy has escaped.

My body trembles. I desperately want to harangue the museum concierge, but instead I hang up and retreat to my study. I turn on the camera view of Roxy and breathe a sigh of relief: the surveillance bees are still active.

I see cacophony. An alarm has gone off and Roxy is running, alongside a galloping Paint and Epoxy, past display case after display case. Many are opened and empty. A museum guard stands in front of them, sparks flying off his gloves. Paint leaps forward in an arc and punctures the guard's heart with one of his legs. Roxy fumbles through the guard's red uniform, and rips the interface patch off his arm, and puts it between her teeth.

They keep running. Roxy thinks she is going to make it. She thinks she's going to be safe—though she's still terrified, even I can sense that. More guards behind them—they hesitate. Those three works of art are worth more than a thousand of the guards' lifetime salaries combined. In that second, Epoxy puts a hand on Roxy's shoulder, and pushes her in another direction, away from the oncoming crush. She runs into a colder, narrower tunnel, and affords herself only one look back. The look is anguished. The halogens affixed in the ceiling grow dimmer, and then it's almost dark, and she stops.

The bees have kept up, and they start to luminesce. She scowls at them. The link is still there. I can't imagine what I would do without that lifeline. She puts her hands on her knees and catches her breath in the near-dark. It must be a service tunnel she is in, for museum employees.

She hears screams and shouts, and considers going back. But she takes a few steps, and there is dim light ahead. She begins walking forward again, her hand on the wall, which is jagged and powdery. The air's ventilation is thin here. The tunnel curves left, then right. She is determined, which is clear from the look on her face, in her hunched shoulders and tense tail.

When the light grows bright enough to see by, she takes her hand off the wall and starts running again to the end of the tunnel. There must be lag; the bees struggle to keep up and I see the back of her ragged shirt as she runs.

The end of the tunnel is a rock wall with a door with a porthole set into it.

She presses her face against the window. She sees a hangar on the other side. A huge space, as large as my villa, with a ceiling that can't be seen. About a dozen large-scale art installations are in the hangar—massive, bulbous. The airlock to the arid outdoors is closed. The largest installations float, and *The Leviathan* is the largest of them all—three blue whales conjoined at the head and attached to a hovercraft, looking like the floating petals of a gargantuan poppy flower. On their sides are embedded the complete works of Jackson Pollock. The artist, a native to the continent named Tin Hester, was funded by the Antarctic Arts Research Council to buy the paintings on the cheap, since Pollock really hasn't been in favor for quite some time.

It is magnificent.

About a dozen people in gray suits work in the hangar—jetting near the larger installations and hovering like dragonflies to tweak a propulsion unit or diagnose an adhesion rivet.

Roxy crosses her arms and tries to decide what to do next. They will find her; she is sure of that.

No—I see it in her eyes. She is trying to figure out *how* to do what she already plans to do.

This is the moment that should be flagged, sent higher up the food chain, when a predator is neither contained with other predators nor immediately threatened.

Roxy says something, but I can't understand it. She bangs on the window, and then takes the guard's interface out of her mouth. She presses a few buttons on it and casts it aside. Then she retrieves something else from her mouth, from underneath her long tongue. She slaps a small patch of yellow goo on the window and she takes a few steps back. I'm told that they've finally made a connection with her again. They are coming for her.

She covers her face. The door blows open. Metal shards nick her, but she manages to sidestep most of them. There's a yellowish fog in the corridor; the goo keeps emitting smoke. Behind her, guards call for her. She calls back, but again I can't understand what she's saying.

She darts into the hangar, choking but staggering forward. I can't see her because of the mist. The guards plunge through the broken doorway as well, but they are not prepared for the mist, and they halt and begin coughing.

I cannot see Roxy in the hangar at all, but in another minute, the hangar door heaves open, letting in the bright, unyielding Antarctic sunlight, and the dry, bitter air.

The art installations' cables have snapped; whether it's because of the mist, I cannot say. I am shaking. They slowly float out of the hangar: a hot air balloon attached to a large black heron, a hybrid of a dragon and a biplane. *The Leviathan* is the last to leave, as the whales' bodies rotate slowly. Roxy is still nowhere to be seen.

That's when my bees start to die. The view of the hangar gets fainter and scratchier, and then there is only the blank screen the color of black pearl.

I feel feverish. I stand up and check on my wife, who is resting in the study. I see—if for only an instant—Roxy's face in hers. That is why it is important to understand art before you buy it, to know how to see what is in front of you. But after my wife entered her coma, I became not only a connoisseur, but a patron. Commissioning Roxy with my wife's DNA was not theoretically legal, even in Antarctica. But I would not be deterred.

I stroke my wife's gray locks of hair. She doesn't stir. I feel the air from her breathing apparatus. When Roxy broke into the study—what did she know? How could she have known of my wife? She must have stared at my wife's face and seen something of herself there, some unblemished vision, without the animal splicings, without the flowers blossoming inside her arms.

That's when she tried to unplug my wife. I found her just in time. She shrieked at me in babble—of course it was incomprehensible—and darted past me. I called the local militia and explained the situation as I struggled to keep up with her roaming through the villa. I should have known that Roxy was veering toward my wife's old suites. She managed to break in and lock the main door behind her. When the militia finally entered the locked-off rooms by cutting a hole in the ceiling, Roxy was dressed in my wife's favorite peacock gown and had torn all her favorite paintings off the walls—Degas, Twombly, Hals—and stacked them in a pile. My wife had always been old-fashioned; she cared little for contemporary art.

Roxy was also wielding, with her tail, a broadsword from my wife's extensive medieval armor collection. The first fool who dropped through the ceiling was beheaded with surprising force. Blood gushed everywhere, but Roxy was careful to put herself in front of the paintings, so that they wouldn't get spoiled. It took a dozen militia soldiers to stun and subdue Roxy.

That was when I decided she needed to be loaned out. I immediately sold all of the paintings that she had torn off the wall. I could not bear to have them within my villa.

Roxy would have ruined everything with my wife. Yet I am upset that she is gone, and likely dead, because she didn't give me the chance to ruin her.

I exit the study and put on my suit and then go outside. There is a smog advisory around Ross Bay. Along the shore, the hills of bell heather and the crabgrass burn, only a few kilometers from the villa. No one is going to stop them from burning. There's no point. The weeds will grow again and burn again. The air has a pink tinge; I actually think it's beautiful.

If *The Leviathan* were to come to me, I would not see it descend, until it was almost too late. What would my wife have thought of those Jackson Pollocks? Surely she would have been riveted by the sight?

I go back inside. I try to put the incident behind me. Cashing the insurance settlement helps. Many of the works from the museum are recovered—albeit damaged—but not Roxy. I decide that I want to go shopping in earnest this time, for a work of art that, by active contemplation of it, will help ease my unease. I put out feelers for a few weeks to the best galleries.

I cross John Priestly off my list, naturally.

After a week, when I am ready to visit my favorite galleries in person to bargain for a sale, I receive a package, about half my height. It doesn't list a sender. I am often the recipient of enticements from galleries. After the courier leaves, I take it to my study—it is not heavy at all—and press my hands against the black box. The sides flop open.

Inside the package is a sculpture of me. Though only a meter tall, it is like me in every aspect. Its skin gleams white as mine gleams. Its eyes are opalesque like mine. Its hands are at its sides. I am filled with both flattery and fear; flattery at the daring attempt at hyperrealism, and fear from the blank, unnerving stare from my miniature twin.

It is staring at me. Its head has moved imperceptibly, but it now looks in my eyes. I am transfixed, despite my best efforts. I immediately desire to know who the artist is, and what the genetic provenance is. As I take a step toward it, the sculpture turns its head to one side. It's like a glitch, or as if the sculpture is thinking or listening to an inner voice.

Then the *objet d'art* puts both hands against its ears, squeezes tightly, and rips its own head off.

The sculpture holds its head over its body. Yellow mist spews from its neck. I manage to look at my wife, before the mist overtakes us.

KORMAK THE LUCKY

ELEANOR ARNASON

There was a man named Kormak. He was a native of Ireland, but when he was ten or twelve, Norwegians came to his part of the country and captured him, along with many other people. They were packed into a ship and carried north, along with all the silver the Norwegians could find, most of it from churches: reliquaries and crosses, which they broke into bits so it could be traded or spent.

The Norwegians planned to take their cargo to one of the great market towns, Kaupang in Norway or Hedeby in Denmark. There the Irish folk would be sold as slaves.

The ship left Ireland late and got caught in an autumn storm that blew it off course. Instead of reaching Norway, it made land in Iceland, sailing into the harbor at Reykjavik in bad condition. The Norwegians decided it would be too dangerous to continue the journey through the stormy weather. Instead, they found Icelanders who were willing to host them for the winter. The Irish were sold. They brought less than they would have in Kaupang or Hedeby, but the Norwegians did not have to house and feed them through the winter.

In this manner, Kormak came to Iceland and became a slave. He was a sturdy boy, sharp-witted and clever with his hands. But he was also lazy and curious and easily distracted. This did not make him a good worker. As a result, he was sold and traded from one farmstead to another, going first east, then north and west, finally back south to Borgarfjord. It took eight years for Kormak to make this journey around Iceland. In this time, he became a tall young man with broad shoulders and rust-red hair. His eyes were green. He had a beard, though it was thin and patchy, and he kept it short when possible. A long scar ran down the side of his face, the result of a beating. It pulled at the corner of his mouth, so it appeared that he always had a one-sided, mocking smile.

The next-to-last man who owned him was a farmer named Helgi, who did not like his work habits better than any of Kormak's previous owners. "It's past my ability to get a good day's work out of you," Helgi said, "so I am selling you to the Marsh Men at Borg, and I can tell you for certain, you'll be sorry."

"Why?" asked Kormak.

"The master of the house at Borg is named Egil. He's an old man now, but he used to be a famous Viking. He's larger than most human people, ugly as a troll, and still strong, though his sight is mostly gone. The people at Borg are all afraid of him and so are the neighbors, including me."

"Why?" asked Kormak a second time.

"Egil is bad-tempered, avaricious, self-willed, and knows at least some magic, though mostly he has used brute force to get his way. He's also the finest poet in Iceland."

This didn't sound good to Kormak. "You said he's old and mostly blind. How can he rule the household?"

"His son Thorstein does most of the managing. He's an even-tempered man and a good neighbor. He will cross his father if it's a serious matter, but most of the time he leaves the old man alone. If you make Egil angry, he will kill you, in spite of his blindness and age."

Several days later, Thorstein Egilsson came down the fjord to claim Kormak. He was middle-aged, fair-haired, and handsome with keen blue eyes. He rode a dun horse with black mane and tail and carried a silver-mounted riding whip. A second horse, a worn-out mare, followed the first. *My mount*, Kormak thought.

Thorstein paid for Kormak, then told him to mount the mare, which had a bridle but no saddle. Kormak obeyed.

They rode north. The season was spring, and the fields around them were green. Wild swans nested among the grazing sheep.

After a while, Thorstein said, "Helgi says you are strong, which looks true to me, and intelligent, but also lazy. You have been a slave for many years. You should have learned better habits. I warn you that I expect work from you."

"Yes," replied Kormak.

"I know you can't help your smile," Thorstein added, "but I want no sarcasm from you. There are enough difficult people at my homestead already."

They continued riding up the valley. After a while, Thorstein said, "I have one more thing to tell you: stay away from my father."

"Why?" asked Kormak, though he was almost certain he knew the answer to this question.

"He used to be a great Viking. Now he's old and blind, and it makes him angry. I plan to use you in the outbuildings away from the hall. It isn't likely you'll meet him. If you do and he asks you to do anything, obey and then get away from him as quickly as you can."

"Very well," said Kormak.

They came over a rise, and he saw the farm at Borg. There was a large long hall, numerous outbuildings, and a home field fenced with stone and wood. Horses and cattle grazed there. Farther out were open fields that spread across the valley's floor, dotted with sheep. A river edged with marshy ground ran past the farm buildings. Everything looked prosperous and well made. It was a better place than any farm he'd known before.

They rode down together, and Thorstein led the way to an outbuilding. A large man stood in front of it. He was middle-aged with ragged black hair and a thick black beard.

"This is Svart," Thorstein said. "You'll work for him, and he will make sure you do your work."

Svart grunted.

That must be agreement, Kormk thought.

Thorstein and Kormak dismounted, and Svart took the reins of Thorstein's horse. "Come," he said to Kormak.

They unsaddled Thorstein's mount and rubbed the two animals down, then led them to the marshy river to drink. Kormak's feet sank deep into the mucky ground.

Svart said, "Thorstein is a good farmer and a good householder, but he's firm. Do exactly as he tells you. No back talk and no hiding from work."

"Yes," said Kormak, thinking this might be a difficult place.

They let the horses free in the home field to graze, and Svart began to tell Kormak about the labor he would do.

So began Kormak's stay among the Marsh Men. The family got its nickname from their land, which was marshy in many places. Channels had been cut in the turf to draw water out and carry it to the river. This helped the fields. Nothing could make the riverbanks anything but mucky.

Svart was a slave, but he was good with animals and knew ironsmithing. This made him valuable. He was left alone to do his work, which was caring for the farm's horses. Kormak's job was to help him and obey his commands. If he was slow, Svart hit him, either with his hand or a riding whip. Nonetheless, at day's end they would rest together. Svart would talk about the family at Borg, as well as his travels with Thorstein to other farmsteads and to the great assembly, the Althing, at Thingvellir. The Marsh Men were a strong and respected family. When Thorstein traveled, he wore an embroidered shirt and a cloak fastened with a gold brooch. His horse was always handsome. Retainers traveled with him, and Svart came along to care for the animals.

"Everything in his life is well regulated, except for his father," Svart said.

Kormak said nothing, but he thought that the old man could hardly cause much harm. Eighty years old and blind!

He had no reason to visit the long hall, but he'd seen the members of the family at a distance. For the most part, they were handsome people who wore fine clothing even when they were home. The old man was unlike the rest: tall and gaunt and ugly, his head bald and his beard streaked white and gray. Thick eyebrows hid his sightless eyes. He felt his way around the farmstead with a staff or guided by one of his daughters.

Svart went on talking. He had spent most of his life at Borg and remembered Egil's father Skallagrim, another big, dark, ugly man with an uncertain temper. Strange as it appeared to Kormak, Svart was proud of the family and interested in what they did. The servants who worked in the long hall told him stories about Thorstein and the rest of the Marsh Men. He repeated these to Kormak.

"Thorstein rarely crosses his father, but he did so recently. The old man has two chests of silver, which he got from the English king Athelstein. Athelstein gave him the silver as compensation for Egil's brother, who died fighting for the king. The money should have gone to Skallagrim, who was still alive then. It was Skallagrim who'd lost a good son, who could have defended him from enemies and supported him in old age. 'Bare is the back with no brother behind him,' and even worse is a back unprotected by sons. But Egil kept the chests, because he is avaricious.

"Now that he's old and enjoys little, Egil decided to play a game with the silver. He planned to take it to the Althing, to the Law Rock, which is the most sacred place in Iceland. When he got there, he planned to open the chests and scatter the silver as widely as he could. Of course men would struggle to get it. Egil hoped they would draw weapons and break the Thing Peace; and he hoped that he would be able to hear them fight.

"The old man has always settled problems through violence or magic. But Thorstein is a different person, and he said the old man couldn't break the Thing Peace. 'The land is built on law,' as the saying goes. 'Without law it becomes a wilderness.' Thorstein would not let anyone in his household make a wilderness of Iceland. So now the old man is sulking, because he couldn't do the harm he wanted to."

Let him sulk , thought Kormak. *What kind of man would plan this kind of harm* ? Though it was pleasant to think about the prosperous farmers of Iceland fighting over bits of silver.

Svart told this story one day in summer, when the sun rarely left the sky. Then came fall, when the days shortened and the sheep were gathered in, then winter, dark and long. Kormak tended the horses in their barn. In all this time, nothing important happened, either good or bad, though he did become a better worker. He learned that he liked horses and the skills that Svart taught him. He even learned some smithing during the dark winter days.

Spring came again. The sky filled with light, which spilled down over everything, and the wild birds returned to nest. Falcons stole the nestlings, swooping down from the brilliant sky. The farmworkers watched for eagles, which could take a lamb.

One day Egil came to their building, feeling his way with his staff. Close up, he was uglier than at a distance. His nose was wide and flat; his eyes, barely visible under bristling eyebrows, were covered with gray film; his teeth were yellow and broken. *A monster* , Kormak thought.

"Svart?" he called in a harsh voice. "Saddle three horses. I want to ride into the mountains with you and the Irish slave."

Svart looked surprised, then said, "Yes."

They had both been told to obey Egil's commands, but Kormak felt uneasy. Thorstein was away visiting neighbors. They could not go to him. The people left on the farm would not oppose Egil.

What could they do, except what they did?

They saddled the horses with the old man standing near, leaning on his staff and listening. The one picked for Egil was an even-tempered gelding, entirely black except for his mane, which had red hairs mixed with the black. It reminded Kormak of rusty iron. Svart picked another gelding for himself, brown with a light mane and tail. Kormak got a mare that was spotted white and blue-gray. They were all good horses, but Egil's was the best.

When they were done, Svart helped the old man into the saddle, and the two of them mounted.

"To the long hall first," the old man said.

They obeyed and stopped by a side wall. Two bags lay on the ground. "Get them," Egil said.

Kormak dismounted and put a hand on the first. It was so heavy he needed both hands to lift it. Inside the leather was something with edges, a box or chest.

It might have been magic, or maybe the old man had some sight left. He appeared to know what Kormak was doing and said, "Give one bag to Svart and take the other yourself."

Kormak obeyed, heaving one bag up to Svart and then heaving the other onto his mare, which moved a little and nickered softly. He knew what she was saying. *Don't do this* .

What choice did he have? He mounted and settled the bag in front of him. Egil carried nothing except his long staff and the sword at his side.

"Go up along the river," the old man said.

They rode, Svart first, leading Egil's horse. Kormak came last. How had the old man been able to move the bags by himself? Had someone helped him, or was he that strong?

A trail ran along the river. They followed it, going up over rising land. Around them the spring fields were full of sheep and lambs. Svart kept talking, telling Egil what they were passing. At last, the old man told them to turn off the trail. Their horses climbed over stones, among bushes and a few trees, small and bent by the wind. The land had been forested when the settlers came, or so Kormak had been told. But the trees had been cut for firewood, and sheep had eaten the saplings that tried to rise. Now the country was grass and bare rock and—in the mountains—snow and ice.

They came finally to the edge of a narrow, deep ravine. A waterfall rushed down into it, and a stream tumbled along the bottom, foaming white in the shadow.

"Dismount and help me to dismount," Egil said, his harsh voice angry. This was a man who had needed little help in his life. He had served one king and quarreled with another, driving Eirik Bloodaxe out of Norway through magic. He'd fought berserkers and saved his own life by composing a praise poem for Eirik, when Norway's former king held him captive in York. Now a slave had to give him assistance when he climbed down off a horse.

Kormak knew all this from Svart. He dismounted, lifted the bag to the ground, and watched as Svart helped Egil down.

"There are chests inside the bags," Egil said. "Take them out and empty them into the waterfall."

Svart moved first, pulling a chest from his bag and opening it. "It's full of silver," he said to Egil.

"I know that, fool!" Egil said. "This is the money Thorstein would not let me spend at the Althing. He's not going to inherit it when I die. Toss it into the ravine!"

Svart took the chest to the ravine's edge and turned it over. Bright silver spilled out, shining briefly in the sunlight before it fell into the ravine's shadow.

"Now you," Egil said and turned his head toward Kormak. The eyes under his heavy brows were as white as two moons.

Kormak pulled the chest from his bag and carried it to the ravine's edge. Pulling the top up, he spilled the silver—coins and bracelets and broken pieces—into the river below him. As he did so, he heard a cry and glanced around. Svart was down. Egil stood above him with a sword. Blood dripped from the blade. Kormak tossed his chest into the river and turned to face the old man, who came at him, swinging his bloody sword. How could he see?

The blade, swinging wildly from side to side, almost touched Kormak. He twisted away, losing his balance, and fell into the ravine, shouting with surprise.

He fell a short distance only, landing on a narrow ledge and scrambling onto his knees. His back hurt, as well as a shoulder and an elbow. But he didn't pay attention to the pain. Instead he looked up. The old man was directly above him, looking down with his blind eyes. "I heard you cry out, Kormak. Did you fall in the river? Or are you hiding? If so, I will find you, either with my staff or magic. I want no one to tell Thorstein what I did with the silver."

Kormak said nothing. After a moment, the old man vanished. Shortly after, Svart's body tumbled off the ravine edge, falling past Kormak. An outflung hand hit Kormak as the body passed. He almost cried out a second time, but did not. Instead, he crouched against the cliff wall, pressing his lips together. Below him, Svart vanished into the river's foam. Cold spray from the waterfall came down on Kormak like fine rain, making the ledge slippery.

The old man reappeared at the ravine's edge. "I can bring stones and roll them down on you. If you haven't joined Svart in the river, you will then."

The old man was trying to trick him into making a noise. Kormak kept his lips pressed together.

Egil knelt clumsily at the cliff rim and pushed his staff down along the stone wall, swinging it from side to side. Kormak lay on his back, making himself as flat as possible. The staff's tip swung above him, almost touching. Kormak sucked his belly in and tried not to breathe.

"Well, then," the old man said finally. "It will have to be stones. I wish you had been more cooperative. Look at Svart. He gave me no trouble at all."

The old man stood stiffly. Once again he vanished. Kormak sat up and looked around for an escape. But the cliff wall was sheer. He could see only one way off the ledge: jumping into the turbulent, dangerous river below him. He stood, thinking he would have to risk this.

As he stood, a door opened in the cliff wall a short distance from him, at one end of the ledge. A man looked out. He was tall and even handsomer than Thorstein Egilsson, with long, silver-blond hair that flowed over his shoulders and a neatly trimmed silver-blond mustache. His shirt was bright red; his pants were dark green; and his belt had a gold buckle. The man smiled and beckoned.

This seemed a better choice than the river. Kormak walked to the door. The man beckoned a second time. Kormak stepped inside, and the man closed the door. They were in a corridor made of stone and lit by lanterns. It extended into the distance, empty except for the two of them.

"Welcome to the land of the elves," the man said. "I am Alfhjalm, a retainer of the local lord."

Kormak gave his name and thanked the elf for saving him from Egil.

"We keep track of the Marsh Men, because they have always been troublesome neighbors," Alfhjalm said. "As a rule, we don't cross them, since we don't want to attract attention. But we have a grudge against Egil, and now that he is old and weak, we are willing to disrupt his plans."

"Will he die out there?" Kormak asked, hoping that Egil would. The old man had killed Svart, who trusted him.

"We don't want Thorstein coming here to bother us, as he certainly will if he can't find his father. He has no magic powers, but he is a persistent man. Some of my companions have gone to lead the horses away, making enough noise that Egil will be able to follow. In this way, they will lure him out of the mountains and close to home. Then they'll help him catch the horses, so he can ride home with dignity. If they do their job well, he will never know that elves were involved. We like to remain hidden and unknown. As for you—come with me."

They walked along the corridor, which went on and on. After a while, Kormak noticed that the lamps cast a strange light, pale and steady, not at all like the light of burning wood or oil. He stopped and looked into a lamp. Inside was a pile of clear stones with sharp edges. The light came from them.

"They are sun stones," the elf said. "If we set them in sunlight, they take the sunlight in and then pour it out like water from a jug, until they are empty and go dark. Then our slaves replace the stones with fresh ones, full of light."

"You have slaves?" Kormak asked.

"We are like Icelanders, except more clever, fortunate, healthy, and prosperous. The Icelanders have slaves, and so do we."

This made Kormak uneasy. But he kept walking beside the elf, who was taller than he was and had a sword at his side.

At last they came to an open space. Light shone from above, though it was dimmer than the spring light in Borgarfjord. Looking up, Kormak saw a dark roof, dotted with many brilliant points of light.

"Are those stars?" he asked.

"No," said the elf. "They are sun stones, like the ones in our lamps. If the stones are solitary, they gradually fade. But we can connect them, laying them one after another through channels in the rock. Then each pours light on the next and renews it. In this way they bring sunlight from the high mountains into our home. They never dim in the summer, but in winter it can be dark here."

Below the roof were high, black cliffs ringing a flat valley dotted with groves of trees. Animals grazed in green fields. In the middle of all this was a long hall, larger than the one at Borg. The roof shone as if covered with gold.

"That is my lord's hall," Alfhjalm said. "Come and meet him."

They walked down a slope into the valley. The fields around them were full of thick, lush grass. The animals grazing—sheep and cattle and horses—all looked healthy and well fed. Many had young, which meant it was spring in Elfland as well as in Iceland.

He had never seen handsomer horses. They were larger than Icelandic horses and every color: tan, red-brown, dark-brown, black, blue-gray, and white, with black or blond manes. As he and the elf walked past, the horses lifted their heads, regarding them with calm, curious, dark eyes.

At last they came to a road paved with pieces of stone. "Our kin in the south learned how to do this from the Romans," Alfhjalm told him. "You can say what you want about the Romans—they know how to build roads."

Kormak barely knew who the Romans were. But he was glad to be walking on a smooth pavement rather than a twisting trail.

The road led to the long hall. When they were close, Kormak saw the roof was covered with shields. Some shone silver, others gold.

"They are bronze, covered with gold or silver leaf," Alfhjalm said. "It would be difficult to make the roof solid gold. We elves are more prosperous than Icelanders and have more precious metal, but our wealth is not unending. And if needed, we can pull the shields down and use them in war."

They entered the long hall. A fire burned low in a pit that ran the hall's length. At the end were two high seats made of carved wood. One was empty. The other contained a handsome old man. Firelight flickered over him, making his white hair and beard shine. He wore a crown, a simple band of gold, and a gold-hilted sword lay across his knees.

"This is Alfrad," Alfhjalm said. "Our lord."

They walked the length of the hall and bowed to the old man.

"Welcome," he said in a deep, impressive voice. "Tell me why you came here."

Kormak told the story of his journey with Egil and Svart and how the old man had killed Svart and tried to kill him, all to hide two chests of silver that he didn't want his son to inherit.

"They are a difficult family," the elf lord said finally. "Not good neighbors. I will send men to recover the silver from the river. There is no reason to leave it in the water. You will be our guest until I decide what to do with you."

They bowed again and left the long hall. Once outside, Kormak gave a sigh of relief. He was not used to speaking with lords, especially elf lords. Alfhjalm took him to another building, where food lay on a table: bread and meat and ale. Kormak learned later that this often happened in Elfland. If something was needed—a meal, a tool, an article of clothing—it would be found close by, though he never saw servants bringing whatever it was. Maybe this was magic, or maybe the elves had servants who could not be seen: the Hidden Folk's hidden folk.

They sat down and ate. Kormak found he was hungry. "There are two high seats," he said to Alfhjalm, after he was full.

"The other belongs to Alfrad's wife Bevin. She is an Irish fey who grew weary of the north and went home to Ireland, though she left a daughter here, who is named Svanhild. She is the loveliest maiden in Elfland and also the richest. I am courting her, along with many other men, but she is not interested in any of us."

"What is your quarrel with the family at Borg?" Kormak asked next. He was always curious. It was one of the qualities that made him a difficult slave.

"Manyfold," Alfhjalm replied. "We came to Iceland before humans did, leaving Norway because it became too crowded with people. There was no one here in those days except a few Irish monks. We frightened them, and they kept to small islands off the coast, while we had all of Iceland for our own. The country was empty, except for birds and foxes. There were forests of birch and aspen, which the humans have cut down, and broad fields where we could pasture our animals, black mountains with caps of white snow, and the brilliant sky of summer. As lovely as Norway had been, this seemed lovelier.

"But then the settlers came. They were violent, greedy folk. We are less numerous than the elves of Norway, and we did not have the strength to oppose the settlers. We withdrew into the mountains to avoid them, becoming the Hidden Folk. When we traveled, it was at night, when no one could see us. That was our first quarrel with the Marsh Men. Egil's grandfather Kveldulf would grow sleepy late in the day and sit hunched in a corner of their hall. Then his spirit would go out in the form of a huge wolf, roaming through Borgarfjord. There are no wolves in Iceland, as you must know, only foxes and a few white bears that float into the northern fjords on sheets of ice."

Of course Kormak knew this. He had even seen the skin of a white bear, when he was a slave in the north. It had been yellow rather than white and not nearly as soft as a fox's pelt.

"The foxes are too small to bother us, and we don't have a problem with bears in this part of Iceland. But it was an ugly surprise when Kveldulf appeared in wolf form, and it made our night journeys unpleasant. He was a frightening sight. We elves do not like to be afraid."

No one does, thought Kormak.

"We thought of killing his wolf form, but it was possible that Kveldulf would be unharmed and wake up, knowing about us. Life was easier when we had Iceland—and Borgarfjord—to ourselves." Alfhjalm lifted a pitcher and poured more ale. "He died of old age finally, and the wolf was not seen again. Then his son Skallagrim inherited the farm at Borg. He was another man like Egil, big and strong and ugly, almost a giant; and he was an ironsmith, which sounds better than a wolf. But we elves are not entirely comfortable with iron. Though we can use it and even work it, we prefer other metals. We are able to cast spells over copper, tin, silver, and gold, making the metal stronger, sharper, brighter, luckier, and better to use. Iron resists our magic. If we make an iron blade, it cuts less well than a blade of bronze. If we make an iron pot, it cooks food badly. Iron tools turn in our hands. Everything becomes less useful and lucky.

"Skallagrim made us uneasy, since he had great skill with iron, and we suspected his skill was magical. He never did us any harm. Nonetheless, we avoided him and watched him for signs of danger. In the end, he died in bed like his father, and Egil became the farmer at Borg. He is the worst of the three: a Viking, a poet, and a magician. There is no question about his magical power, though it appears diminished now.

"He knows a spell that can compel land spirits, such as we are. He cast it on our kin in Norway, so they could not rest until they drove King Eirik Bloodaxe from the country. If he could do this to Norwegian elves, he can do it to us. It's a difficult spell that requires killing a mare and cutting off its head, then setting the head on a pole carved with runes. We are not sure he can still do it, but we are always careful around him."

"Why did you help me?" Kormak asked.

"I wanted to know what Egil was doing. He was killing men on our doorstep. Who could say what that meant? And he had a mare with him. It was possible that he intended to cast a spell on us. I am willing to cross him, if I can do it without him knowing. We have lived in fear of the Marsh Men for a long time, and it's been angering. Now this seems to be ending. Egil will die soon. Thorstein is a good farmer, but not at all magical. He will cause us no more trouble than any other human."

"What will happen to me?" Kormak asked.

"I think Alfrad will make you a slave. Do you have any special abilities?"

"I have worked with horses," Kormak said. He did not add that he'd learned some ironsmithing from Svart.

"We have fine horses, as you have seen, and we take good care of them. You have a useful skill."

This was his fate, Kormak thought, to go from owner to owner, a slave to farmers in Iceland, then a slave to Icelandic elves. It was a discouraging idea. At least he was alive, unlike Svart, and he was away from the horrible old man. If it was his fate to labor for the elves, he would not trust them. Svart had trusted the Marsh Men and been killed.

He slept in an outbuilding. The next day the elf lord announced that he would be a slave and sent him to work with the elf horses. They were intelligent, well-mannered animals, and Kormak enjoyed them.

All the slaves in Elfland were human. The elves did not own one another. But when humans came into their land, they enslaved them. There is always dirty work to be done everywhere, in Midgard and Alfheim and Jotunheim and Asgard. Even magical beings had work they did not want to do, either with their hands or magic. The slaves were a miserable group, badly dressed, dirty, and sullen.

Kormak was sure he remembered stories about humans who went into Elfland and had fine lives, sleeping with elf ladies, hunting with elf lords, till they woke and realized a hundred years had passed. Instead he mucked out stables and groomed horses. Well, life was never like stories. In time, he began to help an elf smith, who forged gear for horses out of bronze. The smith had some iron, which he never used. "An evil metal," he told Kormak. But he kept the ingots tucked in a corner of his smithy, and Kormak remembered where the iron was.

So the days passed. There was no winter in Elfland, though the sky grew dark when winter came to the land outside. Still, it was warm. He never had to follow animals through the snow. One period of darkness came and went, then another, then a third. He had been in Elfland three years. Egil must be dead by now. Should he try to escape? Was it possible?

Elves came to get horses and ride them inside or outside Elfland. Some were tall and handsome men. Others were beautiful women. One was the lord's daughter, Svanhild. Her favorite mount was a dun mare with white mane and tail. No horse was lovelier, and no rider was more beautiful. Svanhild was blue-eyed with blond hair as white as her horse's mane. Her dress was usually blue, a deep and pure color; and her cloak was scarlet. Gold bracelets shone on her arms. Of course Kormak was interested in her, but he was not crazy. He kept his ideas to himself and helped the elf girl on and off her horse.

One day she came by herself. The elf smith was gone from the forge, and Kormak worked alone. "I know you have been watching me," she said. "I think you want to have sex with me. I also know you are Irish, like my mother."

"I am Irish," said Kormak. "I am also a slave, and I take my pleasure with other slaves, not with noble women."

"That may be," Svanhild replied. "I want to go to my mother's country. My father is narrow-minded and avaricious. Look at what he did with the treasure you and your companion brought to the river. You don't have it. My father does, and he has not shared. Instead, you are a slave, though you brought him wealth."

"Yes," said Kormak.

"The men here want to marry me because I am my father's heir. I have no interest in any of them. In my mother's country, I might be free."

"Or maybe not," Kormak replied. "I have not found freedom anywhere."

"I am willing to try," Svanhild replied. "Will you come with me and help me?"

"Why should I?"

"Once we reach the land of the fey, I will set you free. You will be in Ireland then, which is your native country."

He would be taking a risk, but maybe it was time to do so. He did not want to spend the rest of his life as a slave in Elfland. Kormak answered, "Yes."

The woman smiled, and her smile was an arrow going into Kormak's heart.

She left, and he had a thought. While the elf smith was gone, he shod two horses with iron. One was Svanhild's favorite horse, the dun mare with white mane and tail. The other was an iron-gray gelding with black mane and tail. The iron shoes made the horses uneasy. They sidled and danced. But they endured the iron.

Three days later, Svanhild returned. She rode a red mare and wore a chain-mail shirt. Two full bags were fastened to her saddle.

"Is this the animal you want to take?" Kormak asked, disturbed. He was relying on the iron shoes.

"No. I needed it to carry my bags, but my dun mare is sturdier and better tempered."

Kormak unsaddled the animal and moved the saddle to the dun mare. As he did so, he noticed that the bags were heavy. "I hope you have directions."

"I have a map, which my mother left me."

"Good." Kormak's horse was the iron-gray gelding, a strong animal, intelligent and calm. He did not want trouble on this journey. Fire was fine for war and stallion fights. But what he needed now was sturdy endurance.

They mounted. Svanhild led, and Kormak followed. *This is hardly wise*, he told himself. He was risking his life for a girl who had no interest in him and for the hope of freedom. But he was tired of Elfland and Iceland.

They rode up a slope in the brief, dim daylight of winter, then entered a tunnel. The horses' hooves rang on stone. The air smelled of dust. There were only a few of the sun-stone lamps here, possibly because the tunnel led down. Who would want to go away from sunlight and open air? A tunnel like this one must be little traveled.

Each lamp shone like a star in the distance. When they reached one, they rode through a brief region of brightness, then back into darkness, with the next lamp shining dimly in front of them.

On and on they went, until they reached a place with no more lamps. Svanhild reined her horse and opened a saddlebag. Out came a lamp made of bronze and glass and full of brightly shining sun stones. She gave it to Kormak to hold, then took out a bronze stick and unfolded it, till it became a long pole with a hook at one end. "Put the lamp on the hook," she told Kormak, "then hold it up, so it casts light over us."

Kormak did as he was told.

They went on, riding slowly, lit by the lamp that Kormak held.

At length they came to a spring that spurted out of the tunnel wall and flowed across the stone until it reached another hole and vanished. They dismounted and watered the horses, then drank themselves.

"How long is the journey?" Kormak asked.

"Twenty-five days by horse," the girl replied.

"Is it all like this?" Kormak asked, waving around at the tunnel.

"I think so."

"The horses will need to eat, and so will we."

"There are folk down here, dark elves mostly. They are kin to us, though they prefer darkness to light. We used to live in the sunlight, as I think you know, but they have always lived underground. This is their tunnel."

"Do they have hay?" Kormak asked.

"I think so."

They mounted and rode on.

There was no way to tell time in the darkness, but they continued until Kormak and the horses were tired. He was about to say they would have to stop when a light appeared ahead of them. It wasn't a sun-stone lamp, he realized as they came nearer. The light was too yellow and uncertain. It came from a lantern fixed to the tunnel's stone wall. A man stood under it, leaning on a spear. The still air smelled of hot oil.

He was as tall as one of the elf warriors, but broader through the shoulders and chest. His hair and beard were black. His skin was dark, and his eyes—glinting below heavy brows—were like two pieces of obsidian. He wore a mail shirt that shone like silver and a helmet inlaid with gold.

"What do we have here?" he asked in a deep voice.

"I am Svanhild, the daughter of Alfrad, a lord of the light elves and kin to you. This human is my slave. We are going to my mother's country in Ireland. I ask your help in getting there."

"I can't make that decision, as you ought to know. But I'll send you to those who can decide." He put two fingers in his mouth and whistled sharply. A dog emerged from the darkness, iron-gray and wolfish. When it reached the elf warrior, it stopped. Its back was level with the warrior's belt, and every part of the animal was thick and powerful. A man could ride it, Kormak thought, if he pulled his feet up, and the dog was willing.

It opened its mouth, revealing knife-sharp, gray teeth and a gray tongue that lolled out.

It was made from iron, Kormak realized, though it moved as easily as a real dog. The dog regarded Kormak and the girl with eyes that glowed like two red coals.

"A marvel, isn't he?" the dark elf said. "Made of iron and magic. We can't do this kind of work any longer, but our ancestor Volund could. He made the dog after he fled the court of King Nidhad of Nerike, where he had been a prisoner. He took his revenge on Nidhad by killing the king's two sons and making goblets of their skulls and a brooch of their teeth. He gave the goblets to the king and the brooch to the king's wife, who was the boys' mother. In addition, because he was someone who did nothing by halves, he raped Bodvild, the king's lovely and innocent daughter. Then he flew away on iron wings. He couldn't walk because the king had cut his hamstrings, wanting to keep Volund as a smith.

"Once he was safe, he forged the dog, working on crutches. He wanted a servant who was intelligent and trusty, but not any kind of man. By then he was tired of men, even of himself."

"What happened to the girl?" Svanhild asked.

"She bore two children, products of the rape, which happened while she was in a drunken sleep, so she didn't know it had happened until she began to grow in size. Her father kept the boy but put the girl out on a hillside to die. The child lived, but that's a story too long for me to tell." The dark elf looked down at the iron dog. "Take them to the Thing for All Trades."

The dog replied with a bark.

"Follow him," the dark elf ordered.

They did, riding into a side tunnel dimly lit by a few oil lamps.

"What do you know about these people?" Kormak asked.

"They are ironsmiths who use no magic. They say iron is sufficient and better than any other metal, though we think it's obdurate and uncooperative. I had not realized that Volund could enchant iron. He was a prince of the dark elves and famous for his skill as a smith. These days the dark elves have no princes, nor any lords. No one could equal Volund, they say. Instead, they form assemblies, where every elf has an equal voice."

"Like the Althing in Iceland," Kormak said. "Though rich and powerful men have more say there, and slaves have no say."

After a pause, Svanhild said, "The dark elves do not distinguish between rich and poor or between men and women. All work, and all join the assembly for their trade."

"Why are they so different from you?" Kormak asked.

"Iron," Svanhild replied. "And lack of magic! All beauty and nobility come from magic."

Kormak was not sure of this. There was little magic in Iceland, except for a few witches and men like Egil. But the black mountains and green fields seemed lovely to him, also the rushing rivers and the waves that beat against the country's coast. He could praise the flight of a falcon across the summer sky or the smooth gait of a running horse. At times, he was at the edge of speaking poetry. But the words did not come; he was left with the memory of what he'd seen.

The tunnel opened into a cave. No sun stones shone from the cave's roof. Instead, the floor was dotted with lights. Some looked to be lamps or torches. Others—brighter—might be forge fires. Hammers rang out, louder and more regular than any he'd heard before.

The dog kept going. They followed it down a slope. There was a track, lit by the lantern Kormak held: two ruts in the stony ground. It led into a little town. The low houses were built of stone. Lantern light shone through open doors and windows. Torches flared, fastened on exterior walls. Here and there, Kormak saw people: tall and powerful and dark. A woman swept her doorway. A man wielded a pick, pulling cobbles out of the street.

Now they rode next to a stream, rushing between stone banks. Rapids threw up mist that floated in the air. Kormak felt it gratefully.

Ahead was a hall, torches blazing along its front. Two elven warriors stood before the door, armed with swords and metal shields.

Kormak and Svanhild reined their horses. "We were sent here by the guard in the tunnel," Svanhild said in her clear, pure voice. "I am Svanhild, the daughter of Alfrad, your kinswoman from the north."

"We know Alfgeir sent you, because the dog Elding is with you," a guard replied.

"What do you want?"

"Passage to my mother's country in the south."

"Who is your mother?"

"Bevin of the White Arms."

"Irish fey," said the second guard. "We know them, though we don't much like them. Still, it's up to the thing-chiefs to decide your fate." He turned and pushed through the hall's metal door.

They waited for a while, staying on their horses. Finally, the guard came back out. "Go in."

Svanhild and Kormak dismounted.

The first guard said, "I'll water your horses while you're gone. They are fine animals, better than any we have, though they look weary and thirsty."

"Not too much water," Kormak warned.

"We know iron better than animals. Nonetheless, we have some horses, and I have cared for them. I know what to do."

They walked inside, the iron dog pacing next to them. The hall was as large as Alfrad's. Stone pillars held up the roof, and stone benches ran along the two side walls, unoccupied at present. A long fire pit ran down the middle, full of ash. Here and there red light shone from the ash, and a thin trail of smoke rose, but most of the light came from torches burning around the high seats at the hall's far end. There were six. Three held old men with broad, white beards; and three held old women with long, white braids. The dog barked. Kormak and Svanhild walked forward and bowed to the thing-chiefs.

"Who are you?" an old woman asked, leaning forward. She was bone-thin, with skin the gray hue of a twilight sky. Her eyes were dark and keen.

"Svanhild, the daughter of Alfrad. My father is an elf lord and your kin, as he has often told me. This man is my slave."

He was tired of this introduction, Kormak thought, but said nothing.

"Why have you come?" an old man asked. He was darker than the woman, though his skin had the same faint tint of blue. His eyes were as pale as ice.

"I seek help in reaching my mother's country in Ireland."

"Why should we help?" another woman asked, this one fat and black. Her blue eyes looked like stars to Kormak. No woman this old should have eyes so bright.

The dog opened its mouth and spoke in a harsh voice that Kormak could barely understand.

> "Hat-hidden, Odin
> tests human hosting.
> Hard the fate
> of those who fail."

"Nonsense," another old man, as gray as granite, put in. "We are not human, and both of these people have two eyes."

"And no ravens," the third old man said. He was the palest of the chiefs. "They are not Odin."

The third woman, twilight-colored like the first woman, said, "The All-Father judges all, not just humans; and the dog reminds us that he requires hospitality."

The black woman leaned forward. "But in honor of our ancestor Volund, we need to ask for fair payment for what we do—in gold or silver, stories, music, or revenge."

"I can pay," Svanhild replied. "We came here with two horses. One is a gelding, but the other is a fine mare, able to improve your breed. I will give you the horses in return for our passage."

"That seems fair," the black woman said. "Two good horses for a ride in one of our lightning carts. They will be going to Ireland and Wales even if there are no passengers."

"Why?" asked Kormak, the man who asked questions.

"Why do they go?" the palest man answered, stroking his silky beard. "They go to Ireland to deliver jewels and fine smithing to the fey there. No iron, of course. The fey hate iron. They go to Wales for coal. We mine it from below and send it to our forges in the north."

"Are you willing to give us passage?" Svanhild asked.

One by one, the elf chiefs nodded.

"Come with me," a voice said next to Kormak. It was Alfgeir, the guard from the tunnel. He must have followed them, Kormak thought, and slipped into the hall while they waited outside. He wore a cloak now, as if he planned to travel. "I know the woman's name, but who are you?"

Kormak introduced himself as the elf warrior led them from the hall. The two guards were still there, watering the horses in the stream.

"These are ours now," Alfgeir said. "It was clever of you to shoe them with iron. Svanhild's kin could not track them with magic."

"I thought that might be true," said Kormak, "but I did not know for certain."

Svanhild gestured at her mare, and Kormak took off the saddlebags, staggering a little under their weight. What had the elf maid packed? He lifted the bags over one shoulder and followed Alfgeir and Svanhild. She had the lantern. It lit their way to the edge of town.

A low platform stood there. Torches on poles cast a wavering light. They climbed onto the platform. Kormak walked to the far side and looked down, seeing ground covered with gravel. Planks of wood lay in the gravel. Two long, narrow pieces of iron lay across the wood. It looked like a fence lying down.

"Where do you get the wood?" he asked.

"From Ireland," said Alfgeir. "They have mighty forests of oak and pine and birch."

"What's it for?"

"You will see."

After a while he heard a noise he didn't recognize. He looked toward it and saw a lantern moving in the darkness. The noise grew louder. The light grew larger and brighter. Kormak stepped away from the platform's edge.

The thing, whatever it was, lurched and rattled toward him. He stepped farther back as the thing slowed and came to a stop. It was a metal cart with a tall metal tube rising from its roof. Smoke billowed from the tube. Fire burned within the cart, and two figures moved there, lit by the red glare. He couldn't make out what they were doing.

Behind the cart was a second cart, full of pieces of shiny, black rock. Beyond this were more carts, some with roofs and others open. The elf warrior pointed at one of the roofed carts. "Get in."

They did and found it contained metal benches, set along the walls like benches in a long hall. Kormak put the saddlebags down. The dog settled next to them, its gray tongue hanging out between sharp, gray teeth, and the three of them sat on the metal benches. The cart jerked and then the entire thing, whatever it was, moved forward. They left the platform behind and went into darkness, except for the dog's red eyes and the lantern that Svanhild held.

For a long time they rattled on. Either the cavern was huge or they were going from one cave to another. Sometimes the region around them was completely dark. Sometimes there were clusters of lights that must have been stone towns or great, flaring forges with gigantic hammers that rose and fell. The hammers were far too large to be held by men or elves. Nonetheless, they moved. Kormak saw no sign of trolls.

Svanhild's lantern cast enough light so he could see both of his companions. The elf warrior sprawled on a bench, looking comfortable. Svanhild sat stiffly, her face expressionless. *Afraid* , thought Kormak, as was he. The iron dog panted gently.

At last, the line of carts slowed and stopped.

"This can't be Ireland," Svanhild said, looking around at the darkness.

The elf warrior laughed. "We are still a long distance from your mother's country. But we are about to enter the tunnel that goes under the ocean. We can't use fire devices there. Out here, in the caves, their smoke rises and spreads. But the tunnel is low and narrow. The devices' smoke would fill it, and we'd choke. Workers used to die in the tunnel, before we invented a new kind of device."

There were noises outside their cart, movement and some light, but Kormak could not see enough to understand what was happening.

"We are changing devices," the elf warrior said. "Before, our power came from burning coal. Now it will come from a fluid that we call lightning, since it shares qualities with Thor's lightning, though it is quieter and better behaved. Our smiths have taught it to run in copper wires. We fasten these to the roof of the tunnel. A rod brings the fluid into our new device, and it moves without fire or smoke."

"Another wonder," Svanhild said in a calm tone.

The warrior said, "Much can be achieved without magic. We do not trick or compel materials to behave against their nature. Instead, we learn what each material can do."

The activity outside stopped and the carts moved forward again. The smoke that had whirled around them was gone, and there was less noise, though the carts still clanked and rattled.

"The lands of the elves are full of wonders," Svanhild said. "But they do not equal my mother's country."

"Wait and see," Alfgeir said.

"How can you raise horses in this darkness?" Kormak asked.

"We pasture them outside in high valleys or on unsettled islands. It's been more difficult since humans settled Iceland and Greenland. In the end, we may give them up and rely on devices. But not yet."

"Why don't you use sun stones?" Svanhild asked all at once.

"Surely you realize they are magic. They would fade quickly here—we use too much iron."

Kormak looked at the lantern Svanhild held. Yes, it was dimmer than before.

"This journey is boring," Svanhild said.

"Then I will entertain you by telling you more of the story of Volund, our ancestor," Alfgeir said.

"Very well," said Svanhild.

"King Nidhad went to Volund's forge and said, 'Where are my children?'

" 'I will tell you,' Volund replied, 'but first you must make me a promise. If a child of mine ever enters your court, you must do him no harm.'

"This seemed like a simple request. Odin encourages us to be hospitable, as you have found out; and as far as Nidhad knew, Volund had no children.

"So he promised. Of course, he was a fool. Volund told him that the two boys were dead. Their skulls were the king's gold and ivory drinking cups. Their teeth were the queen's gold and ivory brooch.

"Nidhad drew his sword, intending to slay Volund, but not yet. 'What about Bodvild, my lovely and innocent daughter?'

" 'She lies drunk. She came to my forge, looking for fine jewelry. Instead, I gave her ale and raped her when she was not able to resist.'

"Nidhad raised his sword. In reply, Volund raised his arms, on which were magical iron wings. Before the king could reach him, he'd brought the wings down, lifting himself into air. 'Remember your promise, King,' he called and flew away.

"That was the last Nidhad saw of Volund. As for his daughter, she grew big and bigger and gave birth to twins: a boy and a girl. Nidhad considered his promise. He had said he would not harm a child, but here were two. Did his promise cover both? It seemed reasonable to keep the boy and put the girl on a hillside.

"The boy was named Vidga. Bodvild nursed him and raised him. His grandfather the king treated him harshly, remembering the two fine boys he had lost. Why should Volund have a son, when he had none? As soon as the boy was able, he left home. He became a famous hero, a soldier for the great King Thidrik of Bern. In the end he died, as heroes do.

"As for the girl, a farm wife found her crying on the hillside. She was a woman who had no children and even a girl seemed worth saving. She gathered the baby up and carried her home, where she fed her with a piece of cloth soaked in milk. Sucking on this, the baby grew strong.

"She was raised to be a farm wife, though her father was an elf prince and her mother was the daughter of a king.

"The farm wife named the girl Alda, which means 'wave.' She took after her mother as far as appearances went, being blond and fair-skinned with eyes like blue stars. But she had her father's skill with materials, though—in her case—it came out as spinning and weaving. The thread she spun was like gossamer. The cloth she wove was like silk, though it was made of wool taken from sturdy Swedish sheep.

"When she worked spinning or weaving, Alda sang:

> " *'What is my fate?*
> *Where is my husband?*
> *Who will I be*
> *In ten years or more?'*

"One day a fey, wandering far from his native soil, heard her song and followed the sound of her voice. It's rare to find fey in Scandinavia. For the most part, they keep to their Irish mounds. But this man, who was named Hogshead, came to Alda's house. There she sat, outside in the sunlight, spinning thread that shone like gold.

"Of course, the fey had to have her. Of course, she could not resist a handsome man, dressed in fine clothes and wearing gold rings on his wrists and fingers.

"Without a word to the people who had raised her, she left her spindle and the house. Together, they followed the hidden ways that go from Europe to the Atlantic islands. When they reached Ireland and entered the fey's home mound, he changed. His body remained as it had been, but his head turned into the head of huge, hairy, ugly boar with jutting tusks and little, hard eyes.

"Alda was her father's daughter. She did not scream, as most human women would, and her expression did not change, but she took a step back.

"The fey made a grunting sound that might have been a laugh. Then he bowed deeply. As he straightened, his head changed, and he was once again a handsome man. 'You don't like my true appearance?'

" 'No,' said Alda.

" 'Well, then, I suppose we have no future. I like to be comfortable at home and look the way I am. Nonetheless, you must meet our queen.'

"He led her to the mound's queen, who was—and is—your mother, though this was long before she married Alfrad. Hogshead told the queen about Alda's spinning and weaving.

" 'Show me,' the queen said.

"A spindle and loom were brought, along with wool. Alda spun the wool into yarn and wove it into a fine, thin cloth.

" 'You must make my clothes!' the queen exclaimed. 'But not out of wool. We'll find you silk, and I'll be the envy of all the fey in Ireland!'

"There Alda remains in the mound. She has learned to spin and weave silk, and she makes the queen the finest clothing in Ireland."

"That's it?" Kormak asked.

"So far."

"That isn't much of an ending. She should have escaped from the fey or died. That's the way most stories end—with a victory or death. Why didn't Volund rescue her?"

"We can't find him to ask him. Maybe the dog knows where he is."

The iron dog lifted its head, but said nothing.

"He always cared more for his craft than for any person, except—possibly— his Valkyrie wife, who left him. It's said that he always frowned deeply and grew grim when he heard 'yo-to-ho.' "

After that, Kormak grew sleepy and lay down, waking now and then to the rattle of the cart over its metal trail. The lantern had grown dimmer, and the cart was mostly dark. Sometimes he saw the red glare of the dog's eyes.

At length, he woke completely and sat up. Svanhild and the elf warrior sat together near the lantern, sharing bread and wine in its glow. Kormak joined them. There were mushrooms, which Alfgeir laid between two pieces of bread and ate. Kormak followed suit. The mushrooms were delicious, thick and meaty and juicy. The bread was a little dry. He drank enough wine to feel it, then sat by a window and looked out. The lantern on the foremost cart lit the tunnel's stone walls and the metal track ahead of it. Now and then, a second light flashed above the cart, brilliant and white.

"That is the lightning," Alfgeir said.

So it went. Kormak dozed and slept. They ate a second time. The sun-stone lantern had grown dimmer.

"Tell me about my mother's land," Svanhild said.

"Didn't she tell you about it?" the elf warrior asked.

"Only that it was far more pleasant than my father's country. She left when I was young."

"We live in stone," Alfgeir said, "as do you. But the fey live below earthen mounds. Their underground country does not look like a cave, as do our homes, but rather like open land, though the sky is sunless and moonless. Magic lights it. There is no winter. The trees bear flowers and fruit at the same time. The streams are full of cold, fresh water. The ground is covered with soft, green grass like a carpet.

"When the fey hunt—and they do; it's their favorite occupation—they bring down fat deer. When they angle, they bring up succulent fish. Everything about their land is lovely and rich.

"They love music and dancing and good-looking people like Volund's daughter Alda. They keep them as servants and lovers."

They would not love him, Kormak thought, with the scar across his face. Well, he had no desire to live among the fey. He remembered them dimly from stories he'd heard as a child. They were more dangerous than the northern elves, who mostly kept to themselves and did not bother their neighbors.

The iron dog growled and spoke:

> "Brightness is not best.
> Honor is better.
> Loveliness leads nowhere
> If the heart is hard."

"That may be," Alfgeir said, "but you do not know for certain, Elding. You have never been in their country, nor spent time with any of them." He looked to Kormak and Svanhild. "When we get close to the land of the fey, the carts will stop and you will have to walk. The fey do not tolerate iron in their country. The dog cannot come. Nor can I. I will not give up my iron."

Kormak went back to sleep and woke again. The sun-stone lantern was so dim that his companions were barely visible, though he could still find the dog by the glare of its eyes.

They finished off the rest of the food and wine in silence. Then Kormak sat in darkness, listening to the cart rattle on and on. He slept again and woke and found the carts were motionless. A pale light, like the dawn through mist, shone outside. He could see a platform and a tunnel leading up.

Svanhild lay on the bench opposite him, sleeping and snoring softly, like a cat purring.

"We are here," Alfgeir said. "She won't wake soon, so we have time to talk."

"How do you know she won't wake?" Kormak asked.

"She drank the rest of the wine. That by itself should have put her deeply asleep, but I added a spell."

"You said that dark elves do no magic."

Alfgeir grinned, showing square, white teeth. "No elf is entirely trustworthy, though we are far more reliable than the fey. For the most part, I have told you the truth. Iron makes magic difficult, and dark elves rarely perform it. We always prefer iron. But we're a long way from our country here and close to the country of the fey. Magic is easier here. I have something I want you to do."

"What?" asked Kormak.

"Go into the country of the fey with Svanhild."

"Why should I do this?"

"Look around you. There is nothing here except stone, and it's a long walk back to the country of the dark elves. Dangerous, too. You might be hit by one of our trains. You could go in the other direction, of course, and end in the coal mines of Wales. If you do as I ask, I will be grateful."

"What is your gratitude worth to me?"

"Enough silver to establish yourself among the humans of Ireland. You will be free, and you will be an elf friend."

"That sounds good," Kormak said. "What do you want me to do?"

Alfgeir pulled a bag from somewhere in his clothing and took a gold bracelet from it. "Look for Alda in the fey court. Get her alone and give her this. Tell her to wear it on her arm, but keep it hidden under her sleeve. If the fey see it, they will steal it from her."

"Yes," Kormak said and took the bracelet.

"The second time you see her, give her this." Alfgeir pulled out a gold and ivory brooch. "Tell her to pin it to her undergarment, so it will be hidden from the fey. Make sure that she knows to pin it over her heart."

"Do you think she will do this?" Kormak asked.

"She is the child of her mother and the grandchild of Nidhad's queen. Both women loved gold." The elf warrior took a final object from his bag. It was a golden dog, small enough to be held in a woman's hand. The eyes were garnet. A golden tongue hung out between tiny, sharp ivory teeth.

"The third time, you won't have seek her out. She will come to you. Give her this, and see what happens."

"Very well," Kormak said. He put the three objects in their bag and hid the bag in his clothing.

"Now," said Alfgeir. He touched the sleeping woman, and she woke. "Go into the tunnel. It will lead you to the country of the fey."

Svanhild climbed out of the iron cart. Kormak followed, carrying Svanhild's bags, which had not become any easier to carry. They walked along the platform and into the tunnel. Light filled it. There was no point of origin— the air itself seemed to glow—and he could see only a short distance. The glowing whiteness closed in like a mist. The tunnel slanted up and twisted like a snake, rising and turning. They began to climb.

This went on for a long time, till he was weary from carrying Svanhild's saddlebags. If the dark elf had been telling the truth, he would come out of this with freedom and silver. That was worth some effort. Did he trust the elf? Not entirely. But what choice did he have? He had learned one thing when the northerners came to his village and burned it and took slaves: he did not control his fate.

At last they came to a door made of polished wood and covered with carvings of interlaced animals. There was a bronze ring set in the door. Svanhild took hold of it and knocked.

The door opened, revealing a handsome man dressed in green. His hair was red and curly. His face was clean-shaven and his skin was fair. He wore a heavy, twisted, golden torque around his neck. "Well?" he asked.

"I am Svanhild, the daughter of Bevin of the White Arms. I've come to find my mother."

"She's here, though I don't know if she will want to see you. Nonetheless, come in."

They did. As Kormak passed through the doorway, the stone groaned loudly. The man looked suddenly wary. "What are you?"

"He's human and my slave," Svanhild said. "Don't you have human slaves?"

"Why should we? We are served by magical beings. Humans are for making music and love. Since he belongs to you, I will let him in."

Beyond the door was a wide, green country. A meadow lay before them, where noble-looking people played a bowling game with golden balls. On the far side, the land rose into wooded hills. Many of the trees were flowering. A sweet scent filled the air. The sky above was misty white.

"I will escort you to the queen," the man said.

"Do you have a name?" Kormak asked.

"My name is Secret," the fey replied. "And you?"

"Kormak."

"Are you Irish?"

"Yes."

"Our favorite humans!"

They circled the meadow to avoid the bowlers. A wooden bridge led over a crystal-clear river. Looking down, Kormak saw silver trout floating above the river's pebbled floor. Apple trees with fragrant white blossoms leaned over the water, dropping petals. He saw red fruit among the blooms. A miraculous land!

The next thing he knew, they were climbing a hill. On top was a grove of oak trees, their branches thick with acorns. The ground was carpeted with acorns, and a huge boar was feeding on them. Its lean body was covered with long, black, bristling hair, and yellow tusks sprouted from its mouth.

Svanhild paused. "Is this safe?"

"That's Hogshead," the fey answered. "He'll do no harm."

The boar lifted its head, then reared up till it was standing on its hind legs. Kormak had never seen any kind of pig do this. A moment later, a man dressed in scarlet stood where the boar had been.

"How are the acorns?" their fey asked.

The man grunted happily, and they walked on, leaving him standing under the oak trees.

Well, that was strange , Kormak thought. He glanced at Svanhild. Usually she had a calm, determined expression, but now she looked drunk or dazed, her eyes wide open and her lips parted. Was this Alfgeir's magic? Or was she so in love with her mother's land?

They descended the hill to another meadow. A silver tent stood in the middle. The fabric shone like water and moved like water in the gentle wind.

"This is her bower," their fey said.

One side was open. Inside sat richly dressed ladies, listening to a harper play. Some had human heads and faces. Others had the heads of deer with large ears and large, dark eyes. One had the long neck and sharp, narrow beak of a crane, though her shoulders—white and sloping—were those of a woman, and she had a woman's graceful arms and hands.

In the middle sat the queen, who looked human, more fair than any woman Kormak had ever seen. She held up a hand to silence the harper, then beckoned.

They approached.

"Who are you?" the queen asked.

"I am Svanhild, the daughter of Alfrad and Bevin of the White Arms. This man is human and a slave."

"If that is so, you are my daughter. If you wish, you can stay a while. But the human is ugly, scarred, and worn with labor. Send him away. Maybe someone in my land will find him interesting, but I don't want to look at him."

Svanhild glanced at Kormak. "Do as the queen says. Put down my saddle-bags and go."

Kormak did as he was told. The harper began playing. The music was sweeter than any he had heard before, and he would have liked to stay. But the queen had a cold face. What had the iron dog called it? Loveliness with a hard heart.

Their fey walked with him from the tent.

"What will I do?" Kormak asked.

"There are humans here who no longer interest us. Former lovers. Former harpers and pipers. They live in our forests. When we have finished banquets— we usually eat out of doors, so we can enjoy the scented air and the birds that fly from tree to tree—they come and eat whatever food remains. Sometimes we hunt them for amusement."

This was worse than living in Elfland. It might even be worse than Iceland.

"Do you know of a banquet that might be over?" Kormak asked. "I'm hungry."

The fey pointed. Kormak walked through the lush, green grass to a grove of apple trees. He pulled an apple from among the blossoms and ate as he walked. In the middle of the grove was a long table made of wooden boards. Dishes covered it, full of the remains of a feast: roast pork, white bread, wine, a half-eaten salmon. Ragged humans fed there, using their hands. He joined in. Everything was delicious, though cold.

"Do you know the human woman Alda?" he asked when he was full.

The man next to him stopped chewing on a ham bone and said, "There's a cave in that far hill." He used the ham bone to point. "She's there, always weaving. She won't pay any attention to you. She's under an enchantment, as I used to be, when the noble lady Weasel loved me. I wish I still were. I was happy then. Now I am not."

Kormak went on. Maybe he should have refused this task. But that would have left him in the stone tunnel, with no alternative except to walk back to the land of dark elves.

There was a trail, no more than an animal track, which wound through forest and meadow. He followed it to the hill. As the man had said, there was a cave. Lamps shone inside. Kormak entered. A woman sat at a loom, weaving. She was young with long, blond hair. For a human, she was lovely, though not as lovely as the fey with human heads.

He greeted her. She kept weaving, paying him no attention.

What could he do? He took out the gold bracelet and held it between her and the loom. She paused. "What is this?"

"A gift for you. Take it and wear it, but be sure to keep it under your sleeve—the fey will steal it if they see it."

"This is true." She took the bracelet and pushed it onto her arm, under the sleeve. Then she looked at Kormak. Her blue eyes were dim, as if hidden behind a fine veil. "Who are you?"

"An emissary from someone who wants to give you gifts. I know no more than that."

"Are there more?" the woman asked.

"Yes, but not today."

"I could tell the fey about you."

"And lose the gifts. You know the fey share little."

The woman nodded. "I have been here a long time, weaving and weaving. They have never given me gold, though they have plenty." Then she returned to weaving.

Kormak left her and went up into the forest on the hill. He found a clearing in a pine grove, where the air was sweet with the scent of the needles. One huge tree had a hollow at its base. He used that as a bed.

In the middle of the night, he woke. A splendid stag stood in front of him, rimmed with light.

"What are you?" Kormak asked.

"I used to be human. Now I am prey. Can you hide me?"

Kormak scrambled up and looked at his hollow, then at the stag. "You are too big."

"Then I will have to run," the stag replied, and ran.

As it left his little clearing, dogs appeared, baying loudly. After them came fey on horseback with bows and spears. Kormak crouched down. They did not appear to see him. Instead, they raced through the clearing and were gone.

The stag had no chance. The light that rimmed him made him a clear target. He would die. Kormak wrapped his arms around his knees and shook. Finally, he went back to sleep. In the morning, he remembered the stag dimly. Had it been a dream?

The day was misty, as if the silver-white sky had descended and hung now among the hilltops. Trees were shadowy. The air felt damp. Kormak wandered down into meadows, looking for another banquet. He found nothing. In the end, he picked apples from among the apple blossoms and ate them to break his fast. In spite of the mist, the land looked more beautiful than on the previous day. Flowers shone like jewels in the grass. The birds sang more sweetly than any birds he'd ever heard, even as a child in Ireland. The birds in Iceland had not been singers. Instead, they had quacked, honked, whistled, and screamed.

He reached Alda's cave and entered. She sat at her loom, her hands unmoving. "I dreamed of my foster parents last night and the farm where I grew up. How could I have forgotten?"

"I know nothing about that," Kormak replied. "But here is your second gift." He held out the gold and ivory brooch. "Pin it to your undergarment, over your heart, and make sure the fey do not see it."

Alda did as he said. "I feel restless today, unwilling to weave."

"Do you have to?"

"The queen will be angry if I don't."

"Does she come here often?"

"No."

He sat down, leaning against the cave wall, and they talked. He told her about his life in Iceland and among the light elves, though he didn't tell her about Alfgeir or the dark elves.

She talked about her foster family. It was hard to talk about the fey, she said. Events in their country were difficult to remember. "My dream last night is clearer to me than my days here."

At last, he rose. "I will come again."

"Yes," said Alda.

He walked out. The mist had lifted, and the land lay bright under the white sky. Kormak's heart rose. He spent the rest of the day wandering. Deer grazed in meadows. A sow with piglets drank from a crystal stream. Once a cavalcade of fey rode by. He stepped into the shadow of trees and watched them, admiring their embroidered garments, gold torques, and gold crowns.

The white sky slowly darkened. At length he found the remains of a banquet. Torches on poles blazed around it, and ragged humans fed at the board. He joined them, gathering bread, roasted fowl and wine.

He ate until a fey appeared. It was short and looked like a badger, covered with gray fur, with white stripes on its head. Unlike any animal Kormak had seen before, it wore pants and shoes. The pants were bright blue and the shoes red. The badger's beady eyes were intelligent, and it could speak. "Away! Away, you miserable vermin! Eat acorns in the forest! Eat worms in the meadows! Don't eat the food of your betters!"

Kormak ran. No one followed him. After wandering awhile, he found the hollow where he'd slept the night before. He settled down and slept. In the morning, he woke in a kind of daze. His promises to Alfgeir and Alda were no longer important. Why should he visit the weaver in the cave? Why should he deliver the golden dog? It seemed more reasonable to wander in the woods and meadows, watching the fey from a distance, admiring their beauty.

That day—or another—he found a well and leaned over the stone wall that rimmed it. Below was water. A salmon rose to the surface and said, "Well, you are a sad case."

"What do you mean?" Kormak asked, not surprised that the fish could talk.

"You were given a task, but you have not completed it. Instead, you have let the country of the fey enchant you."

"It's better than Iceland or Elfland," Kormak said.

"There is more than one kind of slavery," the salmon replied and dove.

He left the well, dismissing the salmon's words.

He had no idea how many days passed after that. The sky darkened and then grew light, but there was never sun or moon to keep time. He remembered meals, though not well, and tumbling in a pine-needle bed with a woman, not a fey, but a ragged human. They were both drunk. After, she told him of the days when she had been the lover of a noble fey. Everything had been magical then: the fey's loving, the wine, the gowns she wore, the music and dancing.

The woman left in the morning. He had a terrible hangover and slept most of the day. More time passed. He had more food, but no more sex. One morning he woke and saw Alda standing by his hollow. "You didn't come back," she said.

"I forgot," he said after a moment.

"That can happen here. It's dangerous. Always try to remember. You said you had one more gift for me."

He dug in the earth of his sleeping hollow till he found the bag Alfgeir had given him.

"I have dreamed of my childhood every night," Alda said. "of my foster parents and our neighbors. Ordinary things, though sometimes—not often—I have dreamed of a man working in a forge, leaning on crutches, his legs withered. His shoulders are wide and strong, his hammer blows powerful. I don't know who he is."

Volund, thought Kormak. But how could she dream of a man she had never met?

Alda continued, "This country seems dim now. I no longer find it attractive, and weaving has become tiresome. I want to return to the land outside. I suspect you may know the way, so I came to find you."

Kormak scrambled to his feet. He pulled out the gold dog with garnet eyes, the last of Alfgeir's gifts, and Alda took it. As soon as it was in her hand, the gold shell split in two. Inside was a dog made of black metal. Alda cried out and dropped the tiny thing. As soon as it was on the ground, it began to grow larger and larger, until it was the size of an Icelandic horse.

"Mount me," it growled. "I will carry you from this place."

"Will you do this?" Kormak asked Alda.

"Yes."

"You as well, Kormak," the dog growled.

He hesitated.

"The fey will punish you when they find Alda gone," the dog growled.

They mounted the iron dog, Kormak first, Alda behind him, her arms around his waist.

The moment they were on the dog, the sky darkened.

"The fey know I'm here," the dog said. "Though there is little they can do, except send apparitions. Their magic cannot harm me, nor you as long you ride me. Hold tight! And ignore what you see!"

Frozen rain began to fall, hitting them like stones. The dog ran. Monsters emerged from the gray sleet: animals like wolves, but much larger. They kept pace with the dog, snarling and snapping. Then the ground, covered with hail, began to move. Other monsters rose from it, long and sinuous and white. Kormak had no idea what they were. Their mouths were full of sharp teeth, and liquid dripped from their narrow tongues. Was it poison? The dog kept running, leaping from monster to monster, never slipping on the wet, scaly backs. Like the wolves, the worms snapped. But they could not reach the dog or its riders.

The storm ended suddenly. They ran among flowering trees. Lovely men and women paced next to them now, riding on handsome horses. "Don't leave, dear Alda. Whatever you want, we'll give you."

Alda's arms tightened around Kormak's waist.

"And you, Kormak? What do you want? Gold? A fey lover? Music, rare food, dancing? In the land outside, you will be a slave again. Here you can be a noble lord."

The air around them filled with harping. Dancers appeared among the flowering trees.

"Run faster!" Alda cried.

The dog entered a tunnel. Flying things pursued them: giant dragonflies and little birds with teeth. They darted around the dog, almost touching. The wings of the dragonflies whirred loudly. The little birds cried, "Return! Return!"

"Don't bat at them," the dog warned. "If you touch them, you will lose the safety I give you!"

Holes appeared in the tunnel floor. The dog leaped these easily, undistracted by the birds and dragonflies. Looking down as the dog passed over, Kormak saw deep pits. Some held water, where huge fish swam. Others held fire.

The tunnel ended in a door. The dog paused and lifted a foreleg, striking the wood. It split.

They passed through and were outside, in the green land of Ireland. Hills rolled around them, covered with forest. The sun shone down. A man stood waiting.

It was Alfgeir, of course. He looked older and more formidable than he had before, and his legs were encased in iron rods, with hinges at the knees. The rods were inlaid with silver patterns that glinted in the Irish sunlight.

"Don't get off the dog till you hear what I have to say," he told them. "Kormak, you've been in the realm of the elves and fey for thirty years. When you step down and touch the ground, you will be more than fifty. Consider whether you want to do this. Alda, you have been among the fey for many centuries. You are part-elf, and we age more slowly than humans. Still, you will be much older if you touch the ground."

"What alternative do we have?" Kormak asked.

"I can tell the dog to carry you into the country of the elves. You will remain your present ages there."

"I am tired of magic," Alda said. "I will risk age in order to live in sunlight." She slid down from the dog, standing on the green turf of Ireland. As soon as she did this, she changed, becoming an upright, handsome old woman with silver hair. Her blue eyes shone brightly, no longer veiled. Although her face was lined, it was still lovely.

"And you, Kormak?" Alfgeir asked.

He sat awhile on the iron dog, looking over the hills of Ireland. Thirty years! Well, he had experienced a lot in that time: the light elves, the dark elves, the fey. He could not say the time was wasted. Like Alda, he was tired of enchantments; and Alda—old though she might be—looked better to him than the fey or their human slaves. Lack of aging made the fey indolent and selfish, while their human slaves became greedy and envious. The Icelanders had been better. They knew about old age and death. The best of them—the heroes—faced it fighting, like Egil.

It surprised him that he thought of Egil with approval. The old monster! The killer! How angry he must have been at his son and his dying body! That was no excuse for killing Svart. He would do better, Kormak thought. He could not excel Egil in fighting, but he could excel him in growing old.

"I will risk age as well." He swung down off the dog. As he touched the ground, he felt his body thicken. He was heavier than before, though still strong. A gray beard bristled over his chest. He brushed his hand across it. Hairs prickled against his palm. Age, or his stay in the country of the elves, had made it thicker and more manly.

"Well, then," Alfgeir said. "I ought to tell you my true name. I am Volund, Alda's father. I could not enter the country of the fey to rescue her. The doors leading into the land of the fey have wards against anything that is foreign and might be dangerous: humans, iron, unfamiliar magic, and magicians who are not fey. My leg braces are iron and magic, and they cannot be made otherwise. In addition, I am a great magician. The fey doors would have roared like dragons if I had tried to enter. The fey let you in, because you seemed harmless.

"I gave you three magical gifts to give Alda. The first two would wake her and break the magical bonds that held her, because they contain what the fey hate most: death and history. As much as possible, they try to live beyond time and change. Memory fails in their country. Although they love to hunt, they do not like to touch blood or death. Their human servants strike the killing blow and butcher the animals.

"But, as Odin said:

> " 'Cattle die. Kinsmen die.
> You yourself will die.
> I know one thing that does not die.
> The fame of the dead.'

"That is what's real for humans: blood and death and history; and that is what I gave to Alda with my first two gifts.

"Bodvild asked me to make the bracelet when she came to my forge. Foolish child! Later, when she lay drunk on the smithy floor, I raped her, breaking her maidenhead, and took back the bracelet. She was your mother, Alda."

"A cruel gift," Alda said.

"The brooch was made for your grandmother, the wife of King Nidhad. He took me prisoner and made me lame. In return, I killed his sons, your two uncles, and made their skulls into drinking cups. Their teeth became the ivory in the brooch. I recovered it before I flew from Nidhad's court, but left the cups for Nidhad to enjoy."

Alda's hands went up to her breast, touching the brooch under her dress. "Another cruel gift."

"Yes," Volund said. "But remember the third gift. The dog could not enter the land of the fey any more than I could. But hidden in its golden shell and carried by you, Kormak, it could slip in. When the shell broke, it could carry you away."

"Why did it take you so long?" asked Kormak, always curious. "Alda was a prisoner for centuries. Did you not care for her at all?"

"How could he?" Alda asked. "I come from blood and death."

Volund smiled, showing strong, square, white teeth. "I am comfortable with blood and death, as my history ought to tell you; and kin matter to me. I knew your brother, Alda, and made him a sword that he used until he died. A famous warrior! But not as lucky as he might have been.

"It took me a long time to learn that Alda was still alive and then discover where she had gone. Then—hardest of all—I had to find someone who could enter the land of the fey unsuspected. You could, Kormak. A human and a slave. No one would fear you or suspect you, since you came with Svanhild."

"What will happen to her?" Kormak asked.

"She is as hard-hearted as her mother—you must have noticed that. She will be fine among the fey. Her father may try to recover her, but I doubt that she will go back.

"I promised you silver," Volund added. He bent down and lifted up two bags. "This is the silver that Egil hid in the waterfall. Svanhild stole it from her father, so she would have a gift to give her mother. I took it from her while she was sleeping on the train. The treasure you carried into the land of the fey is gravel, enchanted to look like silver. When you entered, did the doorway groan?"

"Yes," said Kormak.

"That was because you are human, and also because you carried magic— the gravel and the three gifts. Since you were not turned away, the guard must have thought the door was groaning for only one reason."

"Yes."

Volund grinned again, showing his strong, white teeth. "The spell on the gravel will wear off, but this is real. You are a rich man now." He held the bags out.

Kormak took them. They were as heavy as ever. "This is what I carried all the way from the country of the light elves?"

"Yes."

"Won't the fey be angry with me?" Kormak asked.

"Yes. I suggest you go into the part of Ireland that the Norwegians and Danes have settled. You know their language. The fey have little power there."

Volund gestured down the grassy slope behind him. At the bottom, three horses grazed. "I will accompany you for a while. I would like to know my daughter. And the iron dog will make sure that no one bothers us."

They rode together into the part of Ireland the Norwegians held. The iron dog made sure they had no more adventures. Kormak bought a farm, and Alda stayed with him, as did Volund for a while. Kormak had more questions to ask him. How had Volund known to be in the tunnel, when Kormak and Svanhild came riding? Was it an accident that Svanhild and Kormak were traveling together, or was that part of Volund's plan? How far back did the elf prince's planning go? To the elf who opened the door in the cliff and beckoned Kormak in?

But Volund had grown silent and refused to answer these questions, except to say two things. "I plan deeply and slowly, as the story of Nidhad tells you. The king thought I was reconciled to life in the smithy, and he thought I was safe. I was not."

In addition, he said, "Not everything is planned."

He spent most of his time with Alda, sitting by her loom and watching her weave, his withered legs stretched out in front of him, encased in iron. His hands, folded in front of him, were thick and strong. His face was worn. Though elves aged slowly, he was obviously not young.

Of all the people Kormak had met—Egil, the lord of the light elves, the chiefs of the dark elves, the queen of the fey—Volund was the most formidable.

Sometimes he talked about the swords he had made. All were famous. More often, he listened to Alda speak about her childhood. She never spoke about her long stay in the land of the fey.

In the end, Volund returned to the lands of magic. Before he left, he said to Alda, "If you ever want to visit Elfland, send the iron dog to find me. He will always know where I am."

The dog growled. Volund touched it, and it suddenly looked like an ordinary wolfhound. "Stay here, Elding."

The dog said:

"Decent behavior
outshines silver.
Kindness is better
than gold or fame.

"Glad am I
to be a farm dog,
guarding the farmer,
guarding the sheep."

"I don't intend to raise sheep," Kormak said, scratching the dog behind its ears.

"Nonetheless, I will guard you and Alda," the dog growled.

Volund rode away.

"A hard man to understand," Alda said. "I'm glad he's gone."

"I wish he had answered more of my questions," Kormak replied.

Kormak raised horses and sold them at a good price. Alda wove. Her cloth became well known among the Norwegian and Danish settlers. Noble women, whose husbands had grown rich through raiding, bought it. They had no children, but the wars in Ireland produced many orphans, and they found several to foster. Kormak lived thirty years more, aging slowly and remaining strong. Alda did not age at all.

At last, Kormak grew sick and took to his bed. "What will you do?" he asked Alda.

"Go to Elfland," she replied. "The dog will know the way. Our foster children can have the farm and the silver that remains. I still have the gold bracelet and the gold and ivory brooch, though I have never worn either. I want to return them to Volund."

"Have you ever regretted staying here?" Kormak asked.

"I have liked it better than the country of the fey," Alda replied. "As for Elfland, I will find out how I like it."

Alda sat beside Kormak until he died. After he was buried, she picked out a horse. "The farm is yours," she told her foster children. "I am taking this horse and the dog."

The children—grown men and women—begged her to stay.

"I want to see my father and the lands of my kin," she replied. "The dog will guard me."

And she rode away.

BIOGRAPHIES

James Patrick Kelly has won the Hugo, Nebula and Locus awards; his fiction has been translated into twenty-two languages. He writes a column on the internet for *Asimov's Science Fiction Magazine* and is on the faculty of the Stonecoast Creative Writing MFA Program at the University of Southern Maine.

Angélica Gorodischer was born in Buenos Aires and has lived most of her life in Rosario, Argentina. She is the author of thirty-three books in several genres. Oral narrative techniques are a strong influence in her work, most notably in *Kalpa Imperial*, which—in the English-speaking world—is considered a major work of modern fantasy narrative. She has received many awards including, most recently, the World Fantasy Lifetime Achievement Award.

Amalia Gladhart is the translator of two novels by Ecuadorian novelist Alicia Yánez Cossío. Her chapbook *Detours* won the Burnside Review Fiction Chapbook Contest. Her poetry and short fiction have appeared in *Iowa Review*, *Bellingham Review*, *Stone Canoe*, and elsewhere. She is Professor of Spanish at the University of Oregon.

Tom Purdom lives in downtown Philadelphia where he spends his days writing science fiction, reviewing classical music for an online publication called *The Broad Street Review*, and pursuing the pleasures of urban life. He started reading science fiction in 1950, when it was just emerging from the pulp ghetto, and sold his first story in 1957, just before he turned twenty-one. In the last twenty-five years, he has produced a string of novelettes and short stories that have mostly appeared in *Asimov's*. Fantastic Press recently published a collection of his *Asimov's* stories, *Lovers and Fighters, Starships and Dragons*.

Theodora Goss' publications include the short story collection *In the Forest of Forgetting* (2006); *Interfictions* (2007), a short story anthology coedited with Delia Sherman; *Voices from Fairyland* (2008), a poetry anthology with critical essays and a selection of her own poems; and *The Thorn and the*

Blossom (2012), a novella in a two-sided accordion format. Her work has been translated into nine languages, including French, Japanese, and Turkish. She has been a finalist for the Nebula, Crawford, Locus, and Mythopoeic Awards, and on the Tiptree Award Honor List. Her short story "Singing of Mount Abora" (2007) won the World Fantasy Award.

Yoon Ha Lee lives in Louisiana with her family and has not yet been eaten by gators. Her works have appeared in *Clarkesworld, Lightspeed, Tor.com, The Magazine of Fantasy and Science Fiction*, and other venues. She used to make her own paper dolls.

Maria Dahvana Headley is the author of the novel *Queen of Kings*, and the memoir *The Year of Yes*. Her Nebula-nominated short fiction has recently appeared in *Lightspeed, Nightmare, Apex, The Journal of Unlikely Entomology, Subterranean* & *Glitter & Mayhem,* and Jurassic London's *The Lowest Heaven* and *The Book of the Dead*. With Neil Gaiman, she is the *New York Times*-bestselling co-editor of the anthology *Unnatural Creatures*. She lives in Brooklyn in an apartment shared with a seven-foot-long stuffed crocodile.

Robert Reed is the author of numerous SF works and a few hard-to-categorize ventures. His latest novel is a trilogy in one volume: *The Memory of Sky,* published by Prime Books, is set in Reed's best known creation, the universe of Marrow and the Great Ship. In 2007, Reed won a Hugo for his novella, "A Billion Eves." He lives in Lincoln, Nebraska with his wife and daughter.

Benjanun Sriduangkaew enjoys writing love letters to cities real and speculative. Her work can be found in *Clarkesworld Magazine, Beneath Ceaseless Skies, The Dark,* and Jonathan Strahan's *The Best Science Fiction and Fantasy of the Year.*

After a brief and inglorious career in the legal profession, **K.J. Parker** took to writing full time and has to date produced three trilogies, five standalone novels, five novellas (two of which won the World Fantasy Award) and a gaggle of short stories. When not writing, Parker works on a tiny smallholding in the West of England and makes things out of wood and metal. K.J. Parker isn't K.J. Parker's real name; but even if you knew K.J. Parker's real name, it wouldn't mean anything to you.

Lavie Tidhar is the World Fantasy Award winning author of *Osama*. He has also won a British Fantasy Award and a BSFA Award. His latest novel is *The Violent Century* and, forthcoming, *The Drummer*.

• • •

E. Lily Yu was the 2012 recipient of the John W. Campbell Award for Best New Writer and a 2012 Hugo, Nebula, and World Fantasy Award nominee. Her stories have recently appeared in *McSweeney's*, *Clarkesworld*, *Boston Review*, and *Apex*.

C.S.E. Cooney lives and writes in a well-appointed Rhode Island garret, right across the street from a Victorian Strolling Park. She is the author of *How To Flirt in Faerieland and Other Wild Rhymes* and *Jack o' the Hills*. With her fellow artists in the Banjo Apocalypse Crinoline Troubadours, she appears at conventions and other venues, dramatizing excerpts from her fiction, singing songs, and performing such story-poems as "The Sea King's Second Bride," for which she won the Rhysling Award in 2011. Her website can be found at csecooney.com.

Alaya Dawn Johnson is the author of five novels for adults and young adults. Her most recent, *The Summer Prince*, was longlisted for the National Book Award for Young People's Literature. Her short stories have appeared in many magazines and anthologies, including *Asimov's*, *Interzone*, *Subterranean*, *Zombies vs. Unicorns* and *Welcome to Bordertown*.

Jedediah Berry is the author of a novel, *The Manual of Detection*, winner of the Crawford Award and the Dashiell Hammett Prize. The book was adapted for broadcast by BBC Radio and has been widely translated. His short stories have appeared or are forthcoming in *Conjunctions*, *Unstuck*, *Massachusetts Review*, and *Ninth Letter*, online at *Tor.com* and *Interfictions*, and in anthologies including *Best American Fantasy*, *Gigantic Worlds*, and *Best Bizarro Fiction of the Decade*. He serves as roaming editor for Small Beer Press.

Carrie Vaughn is the author of the *New York Times* bestselling series of novels about a werewolf named Kitty. She's also written a handful of stand-alone fantasy novels and upwards of seventy short stories. She's a graduate of the Odyssey Fantasy Writing Workshop, and in 2011 she was nominated for a Hugo Award for best short story. She's had the usual round of day jobs, but has been writing full-time since 2007. An Air Force brat, she survived her nomadic childhood and managed to put down roots in Boulder, Colorado, where she lives with a fluffy attack dog and too many hobbies. Visit her at carrievaughn.com.

Erik Amundsen is always Chaotic Evil.

Madeline Ashby is a science fiction writer and futurist living in Toronto. She is the author of the Machine Dynasty series from Angry Robot Books, and her short fiction has appeared in *Escape Pod*, *Flurb*, *Nature*, and elsewhere. As a futurist, she had worked with Institute for the Future, Intel Labs, SciFutures, and InteraXon to develop narrative prototypes about technologies in development. You can find her at madelineashby.com, or on Twitter @ madelineashby.

Alex Dally MacFarlane is a writer, editor and historian. When not researching narrative maps in the legendary traditions of Alexander III of Macedon, she writes stories, found in *Clarkesworld Magazine*, *Strange Horizons*, *Beneath Ceaseless Skies*, *Heiresses of Russ 2013: The Year's Best Lesbian Speculative Fiction* and other anthologies. Poetry can be found in *Stone Telling*, *The Moment of Change* and *Here, We Cross*. She is the editor of *Aliens: Recent Encounters* (2013) and *The Mammoth Book of SF Stories by Women* (forthcoming in late 2014).

Ken Liu (kenliu.name) is an author and translator of speculative fiction, as well as a lawyer and programmer. His fiction has appeared in *F&SF*, *Asimov's*, *Analog*, *Clarkesworld*, *Lightspeed*, and *Strange Horizons*, among other places. He has won a Nebula, two Hugos, a World Fantasy Award, and a Science Fiction & Fantasy Translation Award, and been nominated for the Sturgeon and the Locus Awards. He lives with his family near Boston, Massachusetts. Ken's debut novel, *The Chrysanthemum and the Dandelion*, the first in a fantasy series, will be published by Simon & Schuster's new genre fiction imprint in 2015.

Harry Turtledove writes science fiction (including a lot of alternate history), fantasy, and, when he can get away with it, historical fiction. His novels include *The Guns of the South*, *Ruled Britannia*, *In the Presence of Mine Enemies*, and *Every Inch a King*. He is an escaped Byzantine historian, and lives in Los Angeles with his wife, fellow writer Laura Frankos. They have three daughters, one granddaughter, and the required writers' cat.

Krista Hoeppner Leahy is a writer and actor. Her work has appeared in *ASIM*, *Raritan*, *Shimmer*, *Tin House*, *The Way of the Wizard*, *Writers of the Future*, and elsewhere. She attended the Odyssey Writing Workshop in 2007 and lives in Brooklyn with her husband and two children.

Peter Watts—author of *Blindsight*, the so-called Rifters Trilogy, and an obscure video-game tie-in—is an ex-marine-biologist and convicted felon who seems especially popular among people who don't know him. At least, his awards generally hail from overseas except for a Hugo (won thanks to fan outrage over an altercation with Homeland Security) and a Jackson (won thanks to fan sympathy over nearly dying from flesh-eating disease). *Blindsight* is a core text for university courses ranging from Philosophy to Neuropsychology, despite an unhealthy focus on space vampires. The sequel, *Echopraxia*, is probably out by now.

Maureen McHugh's first novel, *China Mountain Zhang* (Tor) won the Tiptree Award. Her most recent collection, *After the Apocalypse* (Small Beer Press) was one of *Publishers Weekly's* 10 Best Books of 2011. She was born in Ohio and has lived in New York City, Sijiazhuang, China, Austin, Texas and Los Angeles, California.

Karin Tidbeck is the award-winning author of *Jagannath* and *Amatka*. She lives in Malmö, Sweden, where she works as a creative writing teacher, translator and consultant of all things fictional and interactive. She writes in Swedish and English and has published short stories and poetry in Swedish since 2002 and English since 2010. Her short fiction has appeared in publications like *Weird Tales*, *Tor.com*, *Lightspeed Magazine* and numerous anthologies including *The Time-Travelers Almanac*, *Steampunk Revolution* and *Aliens: Recent Encounters*.

Linda Nagata is the recipient of the Locus Award for best first novel (*The Bohr Maker*) and the Nebula award for best novella ("Goddesses"). Her 2013 story "Nahiku West"—a prequel to "Out In The Dark"—was a finalist for the Theodore Sturgeon Memorial Award. Her newest novel is *The Red: Trials*, a sequel to the near-future thriller *The Red: First Light*. Linda has spent most of her life in Hawaii, where she's been a writer, a mom, a programmer of database-driven websites, and lately an independent publisher. Find her online at: MythicIsland.com

Naim Kabir is a current student at the University of Pennsylvania. The goal is to do some good research over the years and eventually end up on the ISS. You know, where all science suddenly becomes space science. When he's not studying or writing, he's drawing badly. You can check out the art to go along with his stories on KabirCreates.com.

Tang Fei is a speculative fiction writer whose work has been featured (under various pen names) in magazines in China such as *Science Fiction World, Jiuzhou Fantasy, Fantasy Old and New*. She has written fantasy, science fiction, fairy tales, and wuxia (martial arts fantasy), but prefers to write in a way that straddles or stretches genre boundaries. She is also a genre critic, and her critical essays have been published in *The Economic Observer*. She lives in Beijing (though she tries to escape it as often as she can), and considers herself a foodie with a particular appreciation for dark chocolate, blue cheese, and good wine.

Christopher Barzak is the author of the Crawford Fantasy Award winning novel, *One for Sorrow*, which has been made into the Sundance feature film "Jamie Marks is Dead." His second novel, *The Love We Share Without Knowing*, was a finalist for the Nebula and Tiptree Awards. He is also the author of two collections: *Birds and Birthdays*, a collection of surrealist fantasy stories, and *Before and Afterlives*, a collection of supernatural fantasies. He grew up in rural Ohio, has lived in a southern California beach town, the capital of Michigan, and has taught English outside of Tokyo, Japan, where he lived for two years. His next novel, *Wonders of the Invisible World*, will be published by Knopf in 2015. Currently he teaches fiction writing in the Northeast Ohio MFA program at Youngstown State University.

Yukimi Ogawa lives in a small town in Tokyo, where she writes in English but never speaks the language. She still wonders why it works that way. Her fiction has appeared in such places as *Strange Horizons* and *Clockwork Phoenix 4*.

Ian R. MacLeod grew up in the West Midlands, studied law, and worked for many years at honing his writing skills under his desk in the Civil Service before moving on to house-husbandry and education. His stories and novels at the more adventurous edges of the fantastic genres have won numerous awards and been translated into many languages. He now lives with his wife in the riverside town of Bewdley.

Alan DeNiro is the author of the novel *Total Oblivion, More or Less* (Spectra) and the short story collection *Tyrannia* (Small Beer Press), which came out last year. His short fiction has appeared in *Asimov's, Interfictions, One Story*, and elsewhere, and has been shortlisted for the O. Henry Award. He lives outside St. Paul, Minnesota.

Eleanor Arnason published her first story in 1973. Since then, she has published five novels and forty works of shorter fiction. Her novel *A Woman of the Iron People* won the Tiptree and Mythopoeic Society Awards. Her story "Dapple" won the Spectrum Award. She lives in the Twin Cities Metro Area and is currently finishing a sequel to her novel *Ring of Swords*. "Kormak the Lucky" is one of series of short stories based on Icelandic medieval literature and Icelandic folklore. "Kormak" draws on the Egils saga Skallagrimssonar and an Eddic poem about the famous smith Volund.

RECOMMENDED READING

Joe Abercrombie, "Some Desperado" (**Dangerous Women**)
Mike Allen, "Still Life with Skull" (**Solaris Rising 2**)
Nina Allen, "Spin" (**Spin**)
Charlie Jane Anders, "Complicated and Stupid" (*Strange Horizons*, 8/5/13)
Charlie Jane Anders, "The Master Conjurer" (*Lightspeed*, 10/13)
Neal Asher, "Memories of Earth" (*Asimov's*, 10-11/13)
Peter M. Ball, "On the Arrival of the Paddle-Steamer on the Docks of V—"
    (*Eclipse Online*, 2/13)
Stephen Baxter, "StarCall" (**Starship Century**)
Gregory Benford, "Backscatter" (*Tor.com*)
M. Bennardo, "The Herons of Mer de l'Ouest" (*Lightspeed*, 2/13)
M. Bennardo "Water Finds Its Level" (*Lightspeed*, 5/13)
Gregory Norman Bossert, "Bloom" (*Asimov's*, 12/13)
Gregory Norman Bossert, "Lost Wax" (*Asimov's*, 8/13)
Damien Broderick, "Do Unto Others" (*Cosmos*, 1-2/13)
Damien Broderick, "Quicken" (**Beyond The Doors Of Death**)
Rae Carson and C. C. Finlay, "The Great Zeppelin Heist of Oz"
    (**Oz Reimagined**)
Ted Chiang, "The Truth of Fact, the Truth of Feeling"
    (*Subterranean*, Fall 2013)
Jacob Clifton, "This is Why We Jump" (*Clarkesworld*, 7/13)
C.S.E. Cooney, "Life on the Sun" (*Black Gate*, 2/10/13)
F. Brett Cox, "The Amnesia Helmet" (*Eclipse Online*, 1/13)
Benjamin Crowell, "A Hole in the Ether" (*Asimov's*, 9/13)
Indrapramit Dis, "Karina Who Kissed Spacetime"
    (*Apex Magazine*, 6/13)
Aliette de Bodard, "The Waiting Stars" (**The Other Half of the Sky**)
Paul Di Filippo, "Redskins of the Badlands" (*Analog*, 11/13)
Haris A. Durrani, "Tethered" (*Analog*, 7-8/13)
Greg Egan, "Zero for Conduct" (**Twelve Tomorrows**)
Kate Elliott, "Leaf and Branch and Tree and Vine" (**Fearsome Journeys**)

Gemma Files, "Two Captains" (*Beneath Ceaseless Skies* #125-126, 7/13)

Jeffrey Ford, "The Fairy Enterprise" (**Queen Victoria's Book of Spells**)

Jeffrey Ford, "The Pittsburgh Technology"
      (**The Mad Scientist's Guide to World Domination**)

Eugie Foster, "Whatever Skin You Wear" (**Solaris Rising 2**)

Gregory Frost, "No Others are Genuine" (**Asimov's**, 10-11/13)

Greer Gilman, **Cry Murder! In a Small Voice** (Small Beer Press)

Theodora Goss, "Estella Saves the Village" (**Queen Victoria's Book of Spells**)

Lev Grossman, "The Girl in the Mirror" (**Dangerous Women**)

Daniel Hatch, "The Chorus Line" (*Analog*, 12/13)

Maria Dhavana Headley, "The Psammophile" (*Unlikely Stories 7*, 11/13)

Thomas Olde Heuvelt, "The Ink Readers of Doi Saket" (*Tor.com*, 4/13)

M.K. Hobson, "Baba Makosh" (*F&SF*, 11-12/13)

Kat Howard, "Painted Birds and Shivered Bones" (*Subterranean*, Spring 2013)

Matthew Hughes, "And Then Some" (*Asimov's*, 2/13)

Matthew Hughes, "The Ugly Duckling" (**Old Mars**)

Alex Irvine, "Watching the Cow" (*F&SF*, 1-2/13)

Alexander Jablokov, "Feral Moon" (*Asimov's*, 3/13)

K.J. Kabza, "The Color of Sand" (*F&SF*, 7-8/13)

Vylar Kaftan, "The Weight of the Sunrise" (*Asimov's*, 2/13)

James Patrick Kelly, "The Promise of Space" (*Clarkesworld*, 9/13)

Sylvia Kelso, **Spring in Geneva** (Aqueduct Press)

Nancy Kress, "Pathways" (**Twelve Tomorrows**)

Matthew Kressel, "The Sounds of Old Earth" (*Lightspeed*, 1/13)

Marc Laidlaw, "Bemused" (*F&SF*, 9-10/13)

Margo Lanagan, **We Three Kids** (PS Publishing)

Yoon Ha Lee, "The Coin of Heart's Desire"
      (**Once Upon a Time: New Fairy Tales**)

Yoon Ha Lee, "Iseul's Lexicon" (**Conservation of Shadows**)

Yoon Ha Lee, "The Knight of Chains, the Deuce of Stars"
      (*Lightspeed*, 08/13)

David D. Levine, "The Wreck of the *Mars Adventure*" (**Old Mars**)

Heather Lindsley, "The Angel of Death Has a Business Plan"
      (**The Mad Scientist's Guide to World Domination**)

Marissa Lingen, "Armistice Day" (*Beneath Ceaseless Skies*, 3/21/13)

Ken Liu, "Ghost Days" (*Lightspeed*, 10/13)

Ken Liu, "The Litigation Master and the Monkey King"
      (*Lightspeed*, 08/13)

Scott Lynch, "The Effigy Engine: A Tale of the Red Hats" (**Fearsome Journeys**)

Alex Dally MacFarlane, "Unwritten in Green" (**Futuredaze**)

Ian R. MacLeod, "Entangled" (*Asimov's*, 12/13)

Kate MacLeod, "Din Ba Din" (*Strange Horizons*, 08/13)

Paul McAuley, "Transitional Forms" (**Twelve Tomorrows**)

Ian McDonald, "The Queen of the Night's Aria" (**Old Mars**)

Ian McDonald, "The Revolution Will Not Be Refrigerated"
    (**Twelve Tomorrows**)

Ian McHugh, "The Canal Barge Magician's Number Nine Daughter"
    (**Clockwork Phoenix 4**)

Will McIntosh, "Over There" (*Asimov's*, 1/13)

Sean McMullen, "The Firewall and the Door" (*Analog*, 3/13)

Sean McMullen, "Technarion" (*Interzone* #248, 9-10/13)

Sam J. Miller, "The Beasts We Want to Be" (*Electric Velocipede*, Winter/13)

Eugene Mirabelli, "The Shore at the End of the World" (*F&SF*, 9-10/13)

Ramez Naam, "Water" (**An Aura of Familiarity:**
    Visions from the Coming Age of Networked Matter)

Alec Nevala-Lee, "The Whale God" (*Analog*, 09/13)

Val Nolan, "The Irish Astronaut" (*Electric Velocipede* #26, Spring 2013)

G. David Nordley, "The Fountain" (*Asimov's*, 6/13) (RH-Yes)

An Owomoyela, "In Metal, In Bone" (*Eclipse Online*, 3/13)

Suzanne Palmer, "Hotel" (*Asimov's*, 1/13)

K.J. Parker, "The Sun and I" (*Subterranean*, Summer 2013)

Richard Parks, "Cherry Blossoms on the River of Souls"
    (*Beneath Ceaseless Skies* #131, 10/13)

Rachel Pollack, "The Queen of Eyes" (*F&SF*, 9-10/13)

Tim Pratt, "Revels in the Land of Ice" (**Glitter and Mayhem**)

Robert Reed, "Among Us" (*F&SF*, 1-2/13)

Robert Reed, "Mystic Falls" (*Clarkesworld*)

Robert Reed, "Precious Mental" (*Asimov's*, 6/13)

Christopher Rowe, "Jack of Coins" (*Tor.com*, 05/13)

Sofia Samatar, "Selkies Stories are for Losers" (*Strange Horizons*, 01/13)

Jason Sanford, "Monday's Monk" (*Asimov's*, 3/13)

Georghe Sasarman, "Sah-Hara" (**Squaring the Circle**)

Kenneth Schneyer, "Selected Program Notes from the Retrospective
    Exhibition of Theresa Rosenberg Latimer" (**Clockwork Phoenix 4**)

Priya Sharma, "Rag and Bone" (*Tor.com*, 4/10/13)

John Shirley, "The Kindest Man in Stormland" (*Interzone*, 10-12/13)

Vandana Singh, "Cry of the Kharchal" (*Clarkesworld*, 08/13)

Vandana Singh, "Sailing the Antarsa" (The **Other Half of the Sky**)

Angela Slatter, "Flight" (**Once Upon a Time: New Fairy Tales**)

Zadie Smith, "Meet the President" (*The New Yorker*, 08/12/13 & 08/19/13)

Neal Stephenson, "Atmosphaera Incognita" (**Starship Century**)

Sathya Stone, "Jinki and the Paradox" (*Strange Horizons*, 6/3/13)

Michael Swanwick, "The She-Wolf's Hidden Grin" (**Shadows of the New Sun**)
Rachel Swirsky, "What Lies at the Edge of a Petal is Love" (*The Dark*, 10/13)
Rachel Swirsky, "If You Were a Dinosaur, My Love" (*Apex*, 03/13)
Karin Tidbeck, "Sing" (*Tor.com*, 04/13)
Lavie Tidhar, "The Book Seller" (*Interzone* #244, 1-2/13)
A.B. Treadwell, "Bakemono, or, The Thing That Changes"
          (*Beneath Ceaseless Skies*, 3/13)
Tori Truslow, "Boat in Shadows, Crossing"
          (*Beneath Ceaseless Skies* #112-113, 1/13)
Lisa Tuttle, "The Dream Detective" (*Lightspeed*, 3/13)
Genevieve Valentine, "86, 87, 88, 89" (*Clarkesworld*, 3/13)
Genevieve Valentine, "Abyssus Abyssum Invocat"
          (*Lightspeed*, 2/13)
Carrie Vaughn, "The Art of Homecoming" (*Asimov's*, 7/13)
Carrie Vaughn, "The Best We Can" (*Tor.com*, 7/17/13)
Desmond Warzel, "The Blue Celeb" (*F&SF*, 1-2/13)
Rick Wilbur, "At Palomar" (*Asimov's*, 7/13)
Liz Williams, "The Lighthouse" (**Solaris Rising 2**)
Liz Williams, "Out of Scarlight" (**Old Mars**)
Sean Williams, "Face Value" (*Lightspeed*, 8/13)
A.C. Wise, "The Last Survivor of the Great Sexbot Revolution"
          (*Clarkesworld*, 3/13)
Gene Wolfe, "The Sea of Memory" (**Shadows of the New Sun**)
Patricia C. Wrede, "Mad Hamlet's Mother" (*Apex Magazine*, 2/13)
E. Lily Yu, "The Pilgrim and the Angel" (*McSweeney's* 45)

PUBLICATION HISTORY

ABOUT THE EDITOR

Rich Horton is an Associate Technical Fellow in Software for a major aerospace corporation. He is also a columnist for *Locus* and for *Black Gate*. He edits a series of Best of the Year anthologies for Prime Books, and also for Prime Books he has co-edited *Robots: The Recent A.I.* and *War & Space: Recent Combat*.

SF/FANTASY YEARS
The year's best
science fiction &

08/12/19